A Spellster

TO POISON
A PRINCE

ALDREA ALIEN

Thardrandian Publications

For information contact:
http://www.aldreaalien.com

Cover design by Leonardo Borazio
https://dleoblack.deviantart.com

Map Design by renflowergrapx
https://www.fiverr.com/renflowergrapx

ISBN: 978-0-9922645-8-1
First Edition: July 2021

10 9 8 7 6 5 4 3 2 1

Dedicated to my
critique partners, my editor
and beta readers.

THE **KNOWN**

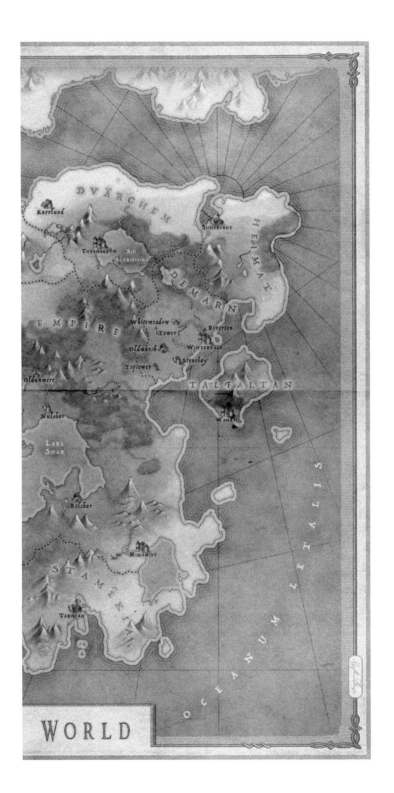

WORLD

Prologue

*M*arriage *changes a man.*

Darshan had heard those words from the lips of so many that he had forgotten who first spoke them to him. *Probably Grandfather.* The man had been catty enough to utter such statements, usually addressed to his own son. The phrase was often uttered to Darshan in the hopes of having him take that heinous leap towards courting this or that noblewoman.

He never would've considered they were actually right. Even the thought of admitting such rather brought upon the urge to scoff at his younger self. How arrogant he had been to believe he'd understood the world.

What he wished he *had* done back then was ask a simple question to those platitude-spewing faces. *How so?* Maybe then he might've had an answer as to why his sleep, which had once resembled that of the dead, was now disturbed at the slightest jostle of his husband.

Like right now.

Groaning, Darshan rolled over. Every morning, ever since they had left Hamish's homeland, he awoke to the same hurried attempt of the man dressing. He had hoped it would've improved the further they travelled from the Tirglasian border.

It hadn't.

Sitting up, Darshan groped for his glasses even as he squinted into the darkness. *Gods, it's not even dawn.* The moon sat high in the gossamer clouds, barely a crescent. The lack of light hampered his attempts to distinguish Hamish's figure creeping across the floor. Even his glasses didn't do much to help.

His ears picked up the gentle rustle of clothes being gathered from wherever they had flung them during last night's frenzied stripping as they made for the bed. As it had earlier, his husband's panting dominated the otherwise silent inn room, albeit far less pleasing than the pleasure-drenched gasps that had serenaded him a few hours ago.

Darshan extended his hand and summoned a small globe of light to balance on his palm, increasing the orb's brightness until the walls were bathed in its glow. It threw stark shadows across everything, warping their lines.

Including that of his husband.

"Hamish?" Darshan whispered. With that broad-shouldered back turned to him, there was no actual way to tell if the man wasn't getting dressed in his sleep. He might not have been during the last umpteen times he had woken Darshan this way, but there was always a first.

The bulk of his husband straightened at the address. The shadow he threw engulfed half the far wall. He whirled about, his sapphiric eyes wide and glistening with fear. His ragged panting lessened but didn't fade completely. It could've been the stark lighting, but the brown shade of his skin seemed a touch on the grey side.

"Another nightmare?" Darshan kept his voice light. Hard to do when the foreign words sat so thickly on his tongue, but his husband responded to his native Tirglasian language far better when in this state.

There had been so many nightmares over the weeks. Ghostly mockeries of the oppressive life Hamish had been forced to live for so many years. How Darshan wished he could pluck them free and gift the man some measure of rest.

"Aye." His husband's admission came on the wings of a blustering, teary sigh.

"The bear again?" Darshan dreaded those nightmares the most. Even speaking the word conjured the image of his husband lying broken and bleeding in the beast's jaws.

Hamish shook his head, the coils of unbound fiery orange-red hair swaying at the motion. Deceptively, they tumbled just to the middle of the man's back, but were long enough to reach his backside when pulled straight. "Worse. Me mum..." Giving a tear-rattling sniff, he turned his back on Darshan. "You— She— I dreamt she had... had—"

The soft, sibilant hiss of a hush that escaped Darshan's lips was out before he could think. He slid across the mattress, slowly so as not to startle the man, and sat on the edge. "Come here, *mea lux.*" He patted the blankets, ignoring the slight grittiness that coated his fingers.

Hamish responded woodenly, settling on the bed with a rather hefty thud.

Darshan's fingers brushed the man's light undershirt, the thin fabric already damp with sweat despite being recently donned. He shuffled behind Hamish to wrap his arms around the broad shoulders. "It is all right," he mumbled into his husband's neck. This close, the rapid beat of Hamish's heart was palpable through Darshan's chest. "You are safe. This is real. *I* am real and very much alive. We are far from her influence."

The body in his grasp shuddered. "Dar..."

"Hush." He wrapped his legs around Hamish's waist, holding tight lest the hairy beast of a man decided he knew better. "Just be still for a bit. Let your body calm down."

The muscles under his arms stiffened. "But—"

"I said, hush." He burrowed his face into the man's neck, seeking the damp skin to smother it in little kisses. His lips brushed the puckered scars adorning this side. The puncture marks of bear fangs. "I am not going anywhere. And no one is coming to spirit you away. I promise."

Hamish took a deep breath and sighed. "I'm sorry," he mumbled.

Darshan pressed his lips together, trying not to let his irritation show. It wasn't Hamish's fault that waking in a room other than his own quarters set off a once very real fear of being dragged away by his mother's guards to be imprisoned like a wayward child. "There is nothing to be sorry for, *mea lux.*"

There had to be a way to rid Hamish of this lingering terror. They would find it. Together.

"I didnae mean to wake you."

"I'm a light sleeper," he purred in his own tongue. It wasn't entirely a lie. Even if it hadn't been true his whole life, it was now. *Thank the gods for small mercies.* Who knew where Hamish would wind up before common sense got the best of him if Darshan never woke to calm him? "Sleep is overrated anyway." His gaze drifted to the window. Still no sign of dawn. "Would you prefer an early start?" It would give them a great deal of time on the road. "We could reach Nulshar's gates by midday." Perhaps they could even book passage on a lakeship and be across the Shar before anyone in the city, like his half-sister's cronies, noticed their arrival.

This bit of news was greeted by silence.

" 'Mish?"

Again, Hamish sighed. This time, it was weary. "I dinnae understand why you're so eager to reach Minamist. You cannae expect me to believe your father will be pleased about you marrying me."

No. Not pleased would be an understatement. His father, ruler of all Udynea and Mighty Hammer of the South, would be furious. Not only for Darshan's impertinence to marry a man when there was no sign of an heir forthcoming, but also for the distinct lack of announcement or even an alliance with Tirglas. Nor would there be until another took the Tirglasian throne as Hamish's mother had been on the brink of threatening war before disowning her son.

Darshan patted his husband's chest. "Let me worry about that." It was going to take a fair bit of talking to convince his father that an endless supply of assassins couldn't fix what would no doubt be seen as Darshan's blatant disregard of his duties. Hopefully, he could placate his father with his plans for an heir. It was what everyone had always wanted from him, after all. "Instead, let us focus on getting you back into bed."

"I'll nae be able to sleep," Hamish mumbled. Nevertheless, he followed Darshan's guiding hands and slipped beneath the covers.

"Just lie there." Darshan fussed with the blankets, ensuring Hamish was tucked in before snuggling against him. Lying at Hamish's back, he was suddenly confronted by just how much of a climb his husband was to a rather less gigantic form such as himself. Hamish's body had been moulded from years of archery and it definitely showed in the definition of his shoulders and back. "This looked rather different in my head."

Chuckling, Hamish rolled over. "I'm nae one for lying on me side anyway. Come here." He wriggled his arm beneath Darshan's head before curling it around a shoulder.

A small, contented sigh slipped from Darshan's lips. His husband might not have any great strength when it came to magic, but the warm press of his embrace definitely made up for it.

He smoothed back his husband's hair, not an easy task as the coils failed to heed all but Hamish's ministrations. Very much unlike Darshan's own brown curls that actually did go where they were told.

"You know, I fell for you the first time I saw you," Darshan murmured in his own tongue, attempting to fill the air and get the man's mind off his nightmare.

He thought back to the day they had first met, barely a few months ago. Before his arrival at Tirglas, he had despaired taking up the task of ambassador—and not only because of the dreadful journey across the rocky seas. Tirglas was a land where the locals were suspicious of both him and his magic. The only relief to the idea of being surrounded by people had been in the hope that the trade negotiations would've been swift.

Then he had clapped eyes on Hamish and had forgotten *all* about his duties.

The deep rumble of his husband's laughter vibrated through the bed. "Even with the bloody mess I'd been in?" Hamish had arrived late. Too much so to properly greet what he had expected would be a Udynean countess. Consequently, he had entered the castle courtyard

4

still splattered with pig's blood from hunting down a rogue boar for a neighbouring farmer.

"Even standing there like a vengeful god." Darshan caressed Hamish's jawline, mindful of his rings so they didn't snag in the man's thick beard. "As soon as I looked into your eyes." *Like gems.* He used to find the comparison ridiculous, but it was true. *The bluest aquamarine.* One look was all it had taken to dazzle him. "And I knew, I had found my light."

Their bodies bounced further as another huff of laughter snorted out Hamish's nose. "Fortunate that I like men then, isnae it?"

He grinned. "Oh, I'm sure I could have persuaded you otherwise."

Scoffing, Hamish rolled his eyes. "Even if I'd been married? With children?"

Darshan's throat tightened. That would've been Hamish's fate a long time ago had the man been at all inclined towards any woman. "It wouldn't have been the first time I slept with a married man," he mumbled. *Or betrothed ones.* Being the *vris Mhanek* and heir to the empire, quite a few men in the Crystal Court were more than eager to offer up their bodies in the hope of garnering his favour.

"*Really?*"

Darshan sat up, leaning on his outstretched arm. "You think that wouldn't have happened? I am quite the whore." Even though he never gave a single soul his word, never mind anything of substance, that he chose to indulge in whatever took his fancy had rather been a bone of contention for his father.

Still, overstepping those boundaries had seen him sent to Tirglas as an ambassador. Where he had landed right into Hamish's arms and thrown a wasp's nest into the man's world.

"Nae anymore." Hamish rolled over, pinning Darshan beneath him. "I've made an honest man out of you, remember?"

Darshan chuckled to himself. "That you have." Him? *Married?* His father was barely going to believe it. "I guess I shall have to leave a slew of broken-hearted men in our wake."

"There'll nae be too many of them, I hope."

"A stubborn few." There were always those who believed they could get a little extra if they just pushed hard enough. He caressed Hamish's side, curling over the bulk to rub deep circles beneath the shoulder blade. "Or maybe they'll understand once they see you."

A soft moan gusted from Hamish's lips. He dropped his shoulder, the act gifting Darshan a better angle to keep massaging to the accompaniment of Hamish's sighs. One sapphiric eye cracked open to peer at Darshan. "Have I ever told you how glad I am you didnae listen to me about competing for me hand?"

Many times. Darshan didn't think he would ever tire of hearing it, for it meant Hamish had no regrets about confronting his mother, Queen Fiona, or the disownment and exile she had lashed back with. "I never would have left you there, *mea lux*." The mere thought of walking away and allowing Hamish's mother to subject him to a life of matrimony with a woman the man didn't want...

He couldn't think of it any further.

He wound his limbs around Hamish, pulling him closer and not caring how his chest objected to the suddenness of his husband's weight landing on him. Hamish moulded to him so well that it was hard to picture him being anywhere else.

"Do you ever think that...?" Hamish mumbled into Darshan's shoulder. "That maybe I... succumbed to me injuries and this is actually me afterlife?"

Darshan pushed his husband back far enough to see the man's face. "If you had, then that would have to mean I perished alongside you." They didn't often talk about that fateful morning, for it brought on too many painful memories. He ran his hands up his husband's neck, seeking the scars adorning either side. The remnants of wounds that had nearly taken Hamish's life.

The memory of the attack flashed through his mind. Of Hamish dying soundlessly beneath the bear, too far gone to scream. Of how the beast still tore into him. How the stench of burning fur and flesh filled the air as Darshan retaliated to the attack.

Then there was only the red pulse of his husband's blood flowing onto the forest floor and the searing torture of Darshan draining the life from the surrounding land, straddling the line between acceptable and forbidden magic, all to bring Hamish back from the brink.

Saving his husband's life had been no small feat. But he would do it all again if necessary.

"If this is what comes after," Darshan murmured, trying to keep his voice light. "Then your Goddess is terrible to make you travel months on the road, especially in this weather." After the fine weather that had greeted their arrival to Udynea, only the light showers proceeding the dry season had dominated the skies. "One of our gods would've immediately had you sitting in the lap of luxury."

"Or all this travelling is a penance for seeking to take me own life." Smiling mirthlessly, Hamish patted Darshan's flank, the gentle slap of his palm on bare flesh rather loud. "Come on, let go of me."

Darshan relented, unwinding himself from the man. "Quite right, we should be on our way." Home awaited, after all, even if it would take some weeks to reach the imperial capital.

And finally face his father's disapproval.

Chapter 1

"Come on," Darshan groaned, flopping his head back against the armrest of his chaise lounge. An age must've passed since he had first reclined here and, still, Hamish had yet to emerge from the blasted walk-in wardrobe. How difficult could it be for the man to pull on a few clothes and fasten some toggles?

If it had been the same fiddly buttons that adorned Darshan's outfit, he would've understood the delay, but he had expressly demanded ease from the tailors when it came to his husband's clothes.

He took another swig of wine, savouring the fruity flavour. Holding up the wineglass allowed the sunlight to glitter through the wine—the rays a splay of prismatic colour thanks to the stained-glass doors at his back.

Those same rainbow-hued beams also warmed the room, which made keeping the balcony doors closed more troublesome the longer they lingered. As it was, the doors were closed not only to ward off any chill and contain the bustle out in the courtyard below, but to also give Darshan some reprieve from the endless whispers rustling on the wind. He would need to speak with a hedgewitch about the latter once they arrived at Minamist; there was generally one wandering the palace grounds.

Swallowing his mouthful of wine, Darshan returned to verbalising his complaints in the hopes that it would hasten his husband along. "It cannot be that much of a disaster."

"Soon," Hamish promised.

Darshan tapped a finger against the stem of his wine glass. Each clink of his ring gave off a different musical note, the variations added by him slowly lowering the level of the pale wine. "I want to see."

What he actually wanted was to be free of this accursed city. If there was a place in all of the Udynea Empire that Darshan could hate more than the lakeside city of Nulshar, he hadn't found it. As the slave capital of the empire, its main export was people and pain.

The city knew it was largely reviled. The city didn't care. The Udynea Empire ran on the backs of its slaves. They had to come from somewhere. As much as he hated that thought, reversing centuries of indoctrination would take more than his lifetime and he could do nothing with the laws until taking his father's place on the throne.

But this city was also the home of Onella; the eldest of his half-sisters. And his biggest annoyance.

To top it off, his homicidal sibling had invited them to her estate this evening under the guise of a soirée. She had even seen that it was held in honour of his approaching birthday. And since he was in the city, social convention kept him from declining the invitation. At least, it would be bad form to refuse without illness or injury, either of which would need to be life-threatening to bypass his magic's innate healing abilities. And he wasn't prepared to have Hamish fake anything either.

He could just see it now if he tried, all the vicious rumours she would spread about Hamish's influence on their vris Mhanek in Darshan's absence. He couldn't allow any of Onella's rumours to take hold, for Hamish's sake.

Huffing, he once more unrolled the scroll bearing the now-broken seal of a vlossina. Being the only one of the Mhanek's daughters who resided in this dismal city, she hardly needed to use it or the signature on the bottom of the letter. To have both marking the parchment hinted at uncertainty in her status. As she should be.

The invite was curt and as two-faced as its inscriber. And for her to explicitly talk about him bringing Hamish? Dying to meet him.

There was no mention of his husband by name, although she had to know it. What do you have planned? Darshan was certain this soirée was more a case of her wanting his husband in a convenient position to ascertain Hamish's weaknesses, if not see the man dead. Quite a few means to that end.

How he hated throwing Hamish into the deep end with this blasted soirée, but if they managed his half-sister well enough, then there was little else the Crystal Court could throw at them that they wouldn't be able to handle together.

Darshan tapped a forefinger on the edge of the parchment and absently scratched at the chain around his neck. The act disturbed the heart-shaped ruby pendant; Hamish's favour, gifted after Darshan had made it through the second trial for his husband's hand. He hadn't removed it once since then.

He would need to keep a close eye on Hamish during their stay. That could be irksome and possibly signal an opening to those who wanted their vris Mhanek dead. Perhaps he could play off the whole newly-wedded bliss angle.

It was largely true. They'd only been married for a little over two months.

In and out. That was all he had required from this leg of their journey. The plan to arrange a lakeship passage for them and their horses across the Shar should've been a simple one. They could've easily taken their leave of this city before nightfall. And they would have, had there not been that blasted messenger waiting for him at the docks.

I should've kept the damn thing quiet. But Hamish had asked and they had promised to keep nothing from each other.

They had argued about it whilst standing on the dockside for a solid half-hour with Darshan insistent on keeping to their plan whilst Hamish queried the consequences of ignoring an invite to a soirée hosted specifically for the vris Mhanek.

You cannae let her have any quarter, nae even to protect me. Hamish's reminder echoed through his mind.

Darshan was used to having his words thrown back at him. He just hadn't expected it from his husband. He'd been far more preoccupied with wondering if Onella had known they would reach the docks at that time. It seemed more likely that her messenger had sat around for days waiting for their arrival. According to his own network, those under his half-sister's employ were a useless sort.

Yet, she knew he was married. That alone smacked of her relying on siphoning the dregs from their father's imperial network of eyes and ears. If she still had access to them, then she was still in their father's favour and surely wouldn't jeopardise that position by going back on her promise to refrain from endangering Darshan's life.

He was confident the protection from her machinations would stand as long as their father still lived, just as he had been forbidden to permanently remove her. Their spouses and any children were likewise exempt from a lethal strike, not that Darshan had any desire to drag his nephew into their little spat.

All this, Hamish knew. And he still agreed that attending would be better than just slipping out of the city.

"Do hurry it along, mea lux," Darshan muttered. Catching his sour expression in the floor-to-ceiling mirror that made up one wall of the royal dressing suite, he rubbed a thumb and forefinger across his moustache in an attempt to soothe his impatience. His fingers idly followed the itchy path of slightly shorter hairs he was growing down either side of his mouth, before finally stroking his goatee. "We'll barely have time to make it as it is." Fashionably late was one thing, tardy was unacceptable.

"Unknot whatever bunch you've got your smalls in, will you?" his husband growled in his native Tirglasian. "I'm coming out. Just dinnae you snicker, you hear? This whole bloody outfit was your decision."

Darshan flicked his attention from his reflection to Hamish, pushing his glasses back up his nose to garner the clearest view as his husband finally exited the wardrobe to examine himself in the mirror.

They had spent two months travelling across the Udynea Empire. During that time, the finery Darshan preferred had been pushed aside for practicality and warmth. But whilst they'd been in agreement that their travel attires were hardly appropriate for a soirée, Darshan had been greeted with his usual array of choices awaiting his perusal within his wardrobe. Hamish had only the clothes on his back.

Until now.

Darshan had spent a good half hour explicitly stating what his husband's newly commissioned outfit would require. Complementing his husband's glorious eyes—the perfect shade of aquamarine blue that so did remind him of the sea near Minamist—had been a must. But not too much. His husband not only detested the colour, but all hues thereof. It was a miracle in itself that Hamish had accepted Darshan's original, and rather impromptu, gift of a silver ring with a gem that matched his eyes precisely.

Darshan's throat tightened as his gaze slunk down the vision that was Hamish decked in silken threads the dusty white of hazy summer clouds. He'd been careful in specifying the cut was close in style to his husband's overcoat, but he hadn't counted on Hamish's broad shoulders filling out the thigh-length sherwani enough to give him an intimidating silhouette. His height only adding to the effect.

The trousers were far more distracting. Tirglasian weather asked for a certain modesty in fashion that lighter fabrics couldn't maintain without excessive, and unflattering, undergarments helping with the retaining of body heat. Darshan had grown accustomed to seeing Hamish in loose woollen fabric, not this snug slide of silk. What a shame that had been for, as glorious as his husband was in his shapeless attire, the new trousers framed his backside splendidly. He almost regretted that the sherwani would hide most of it from view. Almost.

He had to be the luckiest man alive for the gods to bless him with a husband that could've easily remained only real in his dreams. His light. His beacon.

"I feel like a right tit," Hamish mumbled, shaking Darshan from his reverie.

"Well, I think you look positively ravishing." Darshan lurched to his feet, the wine glass dangling indulgently in his fingers. "But what would I know?" He tilted his head, drinking the vision in even as he downed the last of his wine. "And it seems I was right about the colour."

"I sparkle. A man should nae twinkle like a bauble."

Darshan looked down at his own formal attire. The metallic thread and small gemstones glittered upon the golden silk. "Shouldn't I?"

Hamish gave an exasperated huff. "I didnae mean you. You're the vris Mhanek, you're meant to stand out. You're used to it. I've spent me whole life trying to blend in."

In more ways than one. And the attempt to hide his true self had almost cost him his life. "I'm afraid there's little chance of you avoiding drawing attention regardless of what you wore." Even without arriving on Darshan's arm, Hamish's height would have him standing literally head and shoulders above much of the court.

Setting the wineglass aside, Darshan extended a forefinger as he rotated the digit in a languid circle. "How about you give us a twirl, mea lux. Let me see the rest."

Grinning, Hamish obeyed. He ran his hands along the front, fiddling with the silver toggles until the last of them were closed. The toggles continued to glint in the sunlight as he twisted this way and that. It was fine work, especially done on such short notice. Whilst the sherwani was absent of the copious amounts of embroidery and gems that often adorned Darshan's outfits, the tailors had made an attempt on the edges in crystalline thread that carried only a faint hint of blueness. If there had been the time, Darshan would've insisted on a few gems to accentuate the embroidery.

Darshan strode closer, his steps measured even as he openly admired his husband. The man's boots didn't exactly match the rest, but it couldn't be helped beyond Hamish going barefoot and that would've given everyone the wrong impression. Only two types of people went without footwear: slaves and the impoverished.

Hamish fidgeted and tugged at the inner seam of his trousers. "I think they cut these a wee bit tight."

"Nonsense." Darshan had ensured the tailor understood that the cut needed to be a little looser than the current trend. "You're merely used to having a glorified sail around your backside." Still, the outfit was missing a little something. "Zahaan," he called over his shoulder, summoning the elven man who he knew would be waiting just outside the door to the suite.

Zahaan entered swiftly enough, not bothering with a bow in favour of eyeing the room as though a threat might've snuck by his keen gaze. It was a habit Darshan had long since become accustomed to. But his stiffness, as well as the way he eyed Hamish, was new.

"Could you fetch me my slate grey shawl?"

"At once, vris Mhanek." Zahaan paused in crossing the room to the wardrobe only to look Hamish over with a more critical eye. The act shifted the slim chain around his neck, crafted from magic-suppressing infitialis and emblazoned with the symbol of the vris Mhanek. It gleamed a dull purple in the sunlight as Zahaan turned on his heel. "For yourself? Or your husband?"

Darshan spread his arms wide, shaking out the shawl already wound around his shoulders. The fabric on himself was dyed a fiery orange-red that neatly complemented the shade of Hamish's hair, whereas the gold thread in the trimming matched the pale gold of Darshan's formal attire. "Clearly, not for myself, Zah."

"One never knows with you," Zahaan muttered before clearing his throat. As the sole son of Nanny Daama—who still oversaw the collective group of slaves Darshan and his twin, Anjali, had been gifted over the years—the elf was just as free with his tongue as his mother. "I would recommend the light blue."

"No," Darshan insisted at the same time his husband verbalised a similar sentiment.

Zahaan halted. The twitch of one brow was the only emotion upon his face. "The gold, then? Or possibly the silver."

"I shall differ to your judgement on whichever." Not taking his gaze off Hamish, Darshan waved the man on.

"Are you sure you're willing to accept his suggestion without a thought?" his husband asked as Zahaan vanished into the wardrobe.

"When it comes to colours? Yes. Elves see the world a little more vividly than us humans. And I trust Zah to refrain from embarrassing either of us." The man had grown up around both Darshan and Anjali, often learning the same subjects. He was the closest Darshan had to a brother. Older, too. By about three months.

Officially, Zahaan was here as Darshan's emissary in a major trade hub. But Daama had trained her son well in espionage and Darshan utilised that talent in having Zahaan as his spymaster. Having all manner of news reached Darshan's ears before it should had proved beneficial multiple times over the years.

That it also made for an interesting show when others interacted with the man was somewhat of a bonus. Many didn't expect an elf to be so well-read, despite several holding high ranks amongst the palace staff.

Darshan ran a hand up Hamish's chest, still admiring the sight whilst mumbling to himself. "A bit more embroidery would have this looking immensely better, but that can't be helped. Maybe I can have it done once we reach Rolshar." He stroked along the overcoat's collar in whispering glides, smoothing out the wrinkles and adjusting the toggles.

Hamish remained still, seemingly captivated by the movements.

Satisfied that no one would disturb them for a few moments, Darshan curled his fingers into the cool fabric. The topmost toggle popped open with a quick flick of his magic. Then the next.

The outfit parted like it was made for him alone to remove.

"Gods," Darshan growled in Tirglasian. His hand slid beneath the opening to splay across Hamish's chest. The warmth of his husband's skin soaked through the thin undershirt, blatantly teasing him. "I almost cannot wait to strip these from you tonight." He tipped his head to one side, grinning wickedly as he fingered the sherwani. "Or maybe have you wear only this whilst you ride me."

What a vision that would be. The pale silk glowing against Hamish's brown skin as they both ground and thrust towards climax.

"Dar!" his name slipped out his husband's lips on a wisp of a gasp. Hamish's cheeks darkened, even as he jerked out of Darshan's grip. Was he scandalised by the idea? They'd done similar a great many times throughout their journey from Tirglas to here. "I ken your passion feeds off your magic—and that the stronger the magic, the more it affects a spellster, and yadda-yadda—but do show a little decorum."

Darshan had spent his weeks as an ambassador in Tirglas keeping his desires on a tight rein. It hadn't been terribly difficult, what with the trials for Hamish's hand and the man's attempt at taking his own life. Even without those two points hanging over everything like a shroud, discretion had been advised on account of the land not being entirely forgiving about the activities of men like themselves. Not that Hamish would've considered Darshan as being at all restrained.

But they were in Udynea now. People would still care Darshan paraded about with a man on his arm, but only because it wasn't them.

"Well, forgive me for finding my husband sexually attractive," Darshan replied, the words a little sharper than the jesting tone he had meant. "Clearly, I should have found myself some utterly loathsome creature instead of a veritable god."

Despite the acerbic note, Hamish's lips still skewed into a poorly hidden smile. "Maybe you should have," he mumbled into his beard, his attention dropping to the toggles. He fastened each one almost as swiftly as they had come undone. "I'm naewhere near as insatiable as you."

Doubtful. Darshan bit his lip to keep the word from leaving his mouth. After his husband had weathered thirteen years of forced abstinence, anything Darshan offered would've seemed excessive. But this was a far cry from Darshan's own hedonistic past that had seen him sent to Tirglas as a punitive measure.

Hamish glanced up as he finished fussing with the last toggle. "And I thought we agreed you wouldnae talk that way in public?"

Darshan spread his hands wide, gesturing to the entirety of the dressing room. Yes, he had most certainly agreed to spare Hamish his blushing in the presence of those who would use his husband's easily flustered personality against him. However... "This is hardly public."

The area might not have a bed or any other furniture to denote it as a place of intimate activities, but it was still part of his personal suite. They were free to be themselves within the confines of these walls and not have to worry about any act or word being used as fodder for those who meant the crown harm.

"We're nae alone." His gaze darted towards the wardrobe doorway, no doubt in search of Zahaan. "He might hear you."

Darshan chuckled. "I've no doubt that he can." Elves had an exceptional range of hearing that far surpassed humans and dwarves. But his spymaster had walked in on worse things. He also had enough sense to keep himself scarce. "But it is of no consequence. No one here can understand your language except for us. Naturally, that shall change in due course, but I plan to utilise this rare opportunity."

"By whispering indecent things to me in the presence of others?"

"I assure you, my people are used to showing the utmost discretion."

Hamish's brows lowered. The twist of his mouth, almost hidden in his beard, suggested disbelief. And a touch of distaste.

Darshan didn't blame him. Not when he knew his husband had spent a lifetime of having every little misdeed be known to the one person he should've been able to trust implicitly.

Zahaan cleared his throat. "The shawl, vris Mhanek?"

"Ah." Darshan returned to his native language as he turned to Zahaan. He relinquished the swath of pearlescent cloth from the elf's grasp. The shawl was heavy with silver embroidery and one Darshan loathed. Hopefully, it would look somewhat less heinous draped over Hamish than it did upon himself. "See to it that my husband's measurements are sent to the imperial estate in Rolshar. I wish to commission attire suitable for the theatre. Something in slate, I would think."

Zahaan bowed. "At once, vris Mhanek." He hastened out the door.

"Does it nae get tiresome always having people refer to your title?" Hamish asked whilst Darshan fussed with the shawl.

"Should it? I don't see how it's any different to all the times you're called your highness." It wasn't entirely comparable. Tirglas seemed to have a slightly more lax approach between their citizens and the nobility.

Hamish wrinkled his nose.

"There," Darshan finally declared, stepping back. He had tucked the shawl into Hamish's belt at the front, then arranged the light grey silk over his husband's shoulders to drape delicately in the crook of his arm. It was the same position Darshan wore his own shawl.

Hamish mimicked Darshan's stance, placing one hand at his waist where his fingers curled near the shawl as it travelled upwards.

Darshan caught a glimpse of them in the mirror. Whilst his own pose radiated the power and grace years of schooling had hammered into him, there was a lingering stiffness and uncertainty in Hamish's posture. It'll do. Perhaps the same confidence would come in time.

"Are you sure I cannae wear me own clothes?" Hamish asked.

"These are yours," Darshan replied, once again stressing that point. Everything might've been thrown together at the last minute, but that didn't make the attire any less of a gift.

"I mean the ones I came here in."

"Wear travel garb to a soirée? Or the theatre?" He grimaced. Claiming they were pressed for time could've worked, had Darshan not immediately sent for tailors after getting the invitation. No doubt, a full report of what Hamish wore would've reached noble ears by now.

Hamish sighed. "Forget I asked, me heart."

"Forgotten." Darshan waved his hand, brushing the thought aside. It might take Hamish time to adjust to certain views held within the Crystal Court, but his husband was sharp. He would grasp the important things swiftly enough.

"But we dinnae have to go to the theatre."

"Mea lux..." Darshan rubbed at his temple. "My original goal was to see you in Minamist before your debut at court. But if I have to entertain certain social standings by attending my dear half-sister's soirée, I might as well enjoy our time alone. That includes a stop at one of Rolshar's prestigious theatres."

"And I need a new outfit for that? This isnae good enough?" He indicated the sherwani, the shawl slipping off his shoulder.

A gasping laugh briefly left Darshan's lips before he pressed a hand to them, although the act did little to still the mirth quivering in his guts. "You simply cannot wear the same thing to two events like that. What if someone saw?" Had Hamish been travelling on his own, or at least without a guide well-versed in such matters, then the gaffe likely would've been excused. Not without ridicule, but swept aside as another mistake from the uncultured. Darshan couldn't allow that.

"Will they nae think I'm being frugal with me husband's money?"

"Trust me, with the investments I've made, a few new outfits will hardly leave me destitute." Darshan clasped his husband's hands, squeezing the fingers tight. "And, I promise, you'll love the theatre." Certainly more than either of them were about to enjoy the upcoming night.

Hamish rocked his head from side to side. His hair, the fiery orange-red coils gathered into its customary tail, bobbed like a pennant in the breeze. "I admit, I am a wee bit curious."

"Now come." Tugging Hamish along with him, Darshan marched for the dressing room entrance. "We should have just enough time for a small meal before the carriage is ready."

"I thought you were in a hurry to leave. Will your sister nae feed us?"

"She certainly will try. And no doubt it shall be in copious amounts." Onella loved to flaunt the size of her husband's estate and the food it produced. Darshan expected no change in that respect tonight. "But I shall need you to eat beforehand." Whilst he had been away from the court for far too many months, certain practices would've undoubtedly remained the same.

"And the reason we'll nae be eating there is— What?" Hamish grumbled as they strode down the corridors leading to the dining room. "Will the food be poisoned?" A wisp of jesting slithered along the words, not quite masking his concern.

"That is always a possibility, but hopefully, my dear half-sister won't stoop to something so crass." He shook his head. Just how aware was Onella on the topic of Hamish's lack of magical abilities? Especially when it came to anything beyond the act of precisely placing an arrow where the man aimed.

They would need to remain vigilant.

"The matter is somewhat more complicated," Darshan continued on in Tirglasian. Whilst he trusted his own slaves and servants, a great deal of them awaited his return to the imperial capital of Minamist. Unlike their time in Tirglas, they hadn't the luxury of casually chatting in the corridors. Not if they didn't want other ears to hear them. "Most within the court like to use gatherings such as this as yardsticks upon which to measure the competition."

"All right." Hamish lengthened his stride for a few steps until he walked beside Darshan, where his husband's longer legs enabled him to affect a sauntering air. "I'm nae seeing a connection to this and the grub being out of bounds, but carry on."

"The current trend is towards benevolence, or rather, the veneer of it. Mostly towards slaves." If only the court had kept within the spirit of the act, rather than how their gestures looked to others. He was certain a few of the upper nobility abused their rank by purchasing already healthy people to parade about before shipping them off.

His husband's brows lowered in thought. "Wouldnae that be a good thing?"

It should've been. It had been, at first. Now? It was something of a sport. "In some circles," he muttered. "But keeping slaves well-fed is not something that should need to be touted." There shouldn't even be slaves in his opinion, but trying to convince the senate otherwise could bring about a coup. He couldn't risk that. "But a lot of those in the court love crowing about their supposed good deeds. And in some of the most ridiculous fashions."

"Like at the soirée?" The last word fell clumsily from his husband's lips. Not exactly one they had practised on their journeys.

Darshan inclined his head as he gestured for Hamish to enter through the doors at their right.

The dining hall had but one long table. The dark wooden frame and its chairs dominated the otherwise sparse room, the gilding accents glittering in the afternoon sun. Two places had been set at the far end, necessitating that they walk the length of the room, but it also meant Darshan wouldn't have his back to the main door. With his father still ensconced upon his throne in Minamist, Darshan was free to sit at the head of the table.

The westward wall was largely an array of glass doors that opened out onto a lavish rooftop garden. Despite the heat, every single door was shut. Again, at Darshan's insistence.

He was pleased to find the servants had also removed the potted bushes that generally adorned the eastward wall. He didn't think he could stomach eating a bite whilst the cries of bound roots hummed in his head. At least the flowers on the table were dead enough to not scream, unlike the freshly cut ones that had greeted him in his bedchamber.

Already, he could see himself gaining a fresh reputation for having a strangely sudden distaste for the once pleasing floral arrangements. It was either that or allow the constant noise to drive him to distraction.

Hamish settled into the other chair, his head sitting just above the high back. "So, what will I be expecting once we get to your sister's estate?"

Darshan sniffed. Technically, it was her husband's estate, but few made that distinction. "Well, after the usual fanfare and mingling, there is—" Darshan fell silent despite still using Tirglasian to speak, as the door creaked open to allow a pair of elven men bearing covered platters to enter.

A third servant, a human woman, hurried in not long after and had joined the other two by the time they reached Darshan and Hamish. She carried a bottle of wine and a frothy tankard. Beer, as requested.

The men gracefully lowered the platters onto the table, removing the crystalline cloches as the woman hastened to set the tankard before Hamish and uncork the bottle. The aroma of mint and rosemary drifted up with the steam. Whatever the head cook's objections were to Darshan's request, it seemed they had tackled the task with their usual energy.

The roast lamb wasn't exactly a Udynean staple, certainly not amongst the nobility, and Zahaan had wrinkled his nose at the very idea of Darshan requesting the preparation of what the man had called peasant food. But, embarrassingly, Darshan had grown fond of it during his time abroad.

Darshan raised his goblet, allowing the woman to fill it with deep red wine. He took a sip, spitting it straight back out as a rancid odour hit his senses. "This." He set the goblet down and pushed it across the table. "Has spoiled."

"It can't have," she insisted. "It... I—"

He raised a querying brow at her.

Gasping, the woman fell to her knees. "I humbly beg your forgiveness, vris Mhanek." She clasped her hands, raising them above her head in supplication. "Of course, you would know better than I."

Darshan's stomach rolled at the sight. After the obstinate indifference shown to him by the servants at Castle Mullhind, he had forgotten the servile nature of his own people. It would only get worse as they ventured further south.

He gestured for her to stand. "These things happen." At least, according to the man currently running Darshan's vineyard. "Merely fetch another bottle, preferably of another vintage." On the edge of his vision, the sight slightly warped by his glasses' lens, he spied Hamish sniffing his tankard. "How is your drink?"

His husband's nose wrinkled. "This doesnae even smell good enough for pig's swill." Still, he took a sip. "Tastes all right." He grinned and winked at Darshan. "A bit on the weak side, though. I could almost mistake it for dirty water."

Darshan barely lifted his gaze from Hamish, indicating the woman hasten to fulfil his request with the wave of a hand. "Could that possibly be because your brewers actually do put iron bars into that dreadfully dark ale you like so much, mea lux?"

"Puts hairs on your chest."

"That would explain a lot." Beneath the silk and fine linen of Hamish's attire, he bore more than enough hair to keep several bodies warm.

Hamish's eyes crinkled as he continued to drink. His sapphiric gaze drifted slightly and Darshan became all too aware of how the men still stood patiently to attention at his elbow.

"You may leave us," he curtly commanded. Even if these men were in service to the empire, that didn't absolve them from also being handsomely paid for any snippets of conversation they may garner.

Bowing, the men swiftly made themselves scarce.

Darshan waited until the door finally clicked shut. "As I was saying, we will be expected to mingle with whichever members of the court are in attendance." A great deal of the lower nobility typically crowded Onella's functions, hanging on her every word in an effort to garner favour. He didn't expect this to be any different.

Hamish grunted around a chunk of lamb. They were both familiar with that part of court proceedings. Albeit, the Tirglasian court was a little more lax in interacting with their princes.

"Then there shall be dancing." That had always been Darshan's favourite part. And, this time, he'd be able to do so with Hamish. Whilst they had already danced together during his stay in Tirglas, they had only been able to do so in secret. "I cannot be entirely certain of the music, but it shall certainly be somewhat less vigorous than you are used to." He picked up his fork and speared a heavily spiced yam.

"Does that mean there will be nae convincing you to dance a few steps of the Thrashing of the Reeds?"

Darshan laughed around his mouthful, recollecting how utterly lost he had been in most of the Tirglasian dances. "Was that the one that had that dreadful wailing instrument? Do you want me falling on my face in front of everyone?" Admittedly, the steps hadn't been too much trouble when it was just the two of them, rather than the customary four, but most Udynean court music was far too light for any sort of high-intensity dancing.

"So, I guess dinner happens after the dancing?"

Darshan inclined his head. "That's when you cannot eat. Even though they'll set several courses of huge trays, brimming with all the delicacies you could want, before you."

They both ate a few more mouthfuls in silence.

"Nae even a morsel?" Hamish mumbled into his drink.

"Well, the food isn't really for eating." Not by them.

"It's nae for—?" Hamish slammed down his tankard, slopping beer onto the tabletop. "What's the point of food you cannae eat?"

"It's a test to see how much you will leave for your slaves."

Giving a lip-rippling sigh, his husband leant back in the chair. "But I dinnae own any and all yours are in Minamist." He glanced at the door, likely recalling his introduction to Zahaan. "Well, most of them. Are you nae bringing him along? That elven man is one of your slaves, right?"

"Technically, yes." He hadn't missed the thinly veiled disapproval in his husband's voice. He had tried to explain how he often forgot about such details, just as he needed the occasional reminder that his Nanny Daama still belonged to his twin and himself. They'd grown up together. Daama had raised him. And Zahaan? "He is here under a different capacity, not as my valet."

Hamish's brow lifted, but he said nothing further.

Darshan popped another forkful into his mouth, chewing slowly as he tried to ignore his husband's silent prodding. His resolve didn't last long. "Not having any of our own slaves there hardly exempts us from people's prying eyes." He could bring Zahaan along rather than have the man attend to his usual duties, but offering up his full platter to Onella's slaves in order to tweak her nose was an opportunity Darshan couldn't resist.

"What about Onella? How much trouble should I be worried about her stirring?"

"She'll scheme," he replied with a shrug. "She always does, but we're married. That should keep her from trying to harm you." Onella was the main reason he had insisted on the ceremony before they left Tirglas.

"Should?"

"Her promise not to kill me whilst our father lives extends to my spouse," he reminded Hamish. There was a risk that his half-sister wouldn't believe they were actually wed, but Darshan was prepared for that. "She wants her son on the throne more than anything." With her no doubt pulling the strings, seeing that the boy was around the same age as Hamish's nephews. "Harming you would guarantee that never happened."

"But it'll also nae happen even if she doesnae try to kill me," Hamish pointed out.

That was true and it could make her desperate. "We could just not go." That was his preference.

"You've already said. But you cannae hide me from the court, or her, forever."

Darshan sighed. He couldn't. But he would've felt vastly better about a confrontation if they were in the palace, where the Nulled Ones could keep a close eye on her movements. "Just follow my lead. We shall get through this night and be on our way to Rolshar tomorrow. For now?" He scooped up a small forkful of sliced beans. "Eat."

Chapter 2

Hamish had expected some sort of fanfare. That was generally what happened on the rare occasions his mother visited other clan's castles. Twilight had greeted them as their carriage rattled into the front courtyard—brimming with short hedges and bushes blooming in yellow and orange. They had climbed the marble staircase to enter the mansion with little fuss beyond the bustle and fluster of servants.

But it was just the two of them, watched over by a dozen or so sets of eyes as they crossed the antechamber to a door that stood twice his height. The natural wood grain would've been a marvellous sight just shining in its various shades of honey brown. It had clearly been altered beyond its original design and the massive tree, carved from a blackish-red wood he couldn't identify, took up much of the door's surface.

"Gods," Darshan moaned. His husband also surveyed the door, albeit with a far more critical gleam lighting his hazel eyes. "Could she be any more obvious about her intentions?" He sniffed, his cheek twitching as he gave a slight sneer. "Just look at this clunky monstrosity."

"Why a tree?" The sparkle of colour drew Hamish's gaze upward to where several large gemstones of green and red glittered in the candlelight. Was it meant to be someone's attempt at leaves and fruit? They hadn't done anywhere near as good a job there as with the tree.

His husband exhaled in a long, blustery sigh. "My bet would be on Onella mimicking the entrance to the imperial palace's throne room. Poorly, I may add." He flapped his hand, dismissing the sight. Darshan hadn't remained still since entering Nulshar. When his hands weren't fluttering in some dramatic gesture as he talked, he would stroke his tiny beard. The once stylised wings of his waxed moustache had long gone, the tips merging with a small circle-shaped beard that only encompassed his mouth and chin. "This design was clearly done by someone who has never set foot in Minamist, never mind the palace grounds. I would be ashamed to have this adorning my doors."

Hamish cleared his throat and glanced around. When they had approached the building, the mansion obviously had two equally enormous wings and there were at least three doors leading off this room on either side. He didn't think an attack was imminent—not that he could hope to put up much of defence against spellsters—but that didn't mean he could rule out any sort of altercation. Not when Onella was the half-sister who had no compunction with shooting an arrow into her brother.

Mindful of that any number of people could be listening, Hamish bent closer and whispered in his native tongue, "You look a little uneasy."

His husband's eyes widened, the expression amplified by the kohl ringing them. Muddied by the thick lens of his glasses, the irises looked brown. But Hamish had seen them close up enough times to know the earthy brown centres were ringed by a deep forest green. Whilst Darshan often remarked that Hamish's eyes reminded him of jewels and the crystalline blue ocean near Minamist, Hamish only ever saw the world in his husband's eyes.

Darshan opened his mouth, a clear protest on his tongue, before biting his lip. "Well." He offered up a sheepish smile. "It just occurred to me that, given my half-sister's penchant of surrounding herself with those of the lower nobility, there is likely to be a number of men here who have... seen me in some form of undress, if you catch my meaning."

"And?" Hamish might've spent thirteen years prior to meeting his husband in a sort of self-enforced celibacy, but he couldn't have been labelled as ignorant when it came to intimacy between men. "It's nae as if you havenae told me your ship has docked at a lot of ports." His husband's hedonistic attitude to court life had been the sole reason the *Mhanek* sent his heir to Tirglas on an ambassadorial mission, even after the appointed countess was assassinated.

His husband's lips twisted sourly. "Nevertheless, I hardly think you expected to be faced with a mob of them during your debut at court. And I believe a number of them will be most put out that I have found a... permanent place to moor, so to speak."

"You dinnae think they'd want to see their *vris Mhanek* happy?" He was willing to believe a few of the noble houses would vastly prefer to have the throne under their own power and see Darshan's entire family slaughtered, but he doubted everyone felt that way. The *Mhanek* wouldn't be able to maintain power if his whole court was against his rule.

"When it means their chances of convincing me to grant them favours goes from zero to never?" His face creased in disbelief. "Do be careful."

"I do ken me way around a court." Hamish craned his neck up, taking in the full view of the door that stood between them and the party-goers already mingling in the mansion's central hall. Try as he might to maintain a casual air about his stance, he couldn't halt the fidgeting of his feet. "I ken you dinnae want to be here, but if we just left, it wouldnae be quietly." Not when their presence had certainly been marked by the servants—and no doubt revealed to the lady of the house.

Darshan grunted. "True, I would prefer not to have more rumours chase us across the land before I have spoken with my father, but... I am the *vris Mhanek*. I can shirk what is proper if I feel like it."

If anyone was able to dismiss social convention, it would be the bloody crowned prince. "But it's nae that simple."

Sighing, his husband offered up a weary smile. "I can wish."

The door swung inwards as they neared, bisecting the image of the tree and allowing golden light to spill into the foyer. Darshan strode through the doorway with barely a pause, leaving Hamish to follow.

The whole room shone with a golden light. Hamish halted beside his husband at the top of the stairs, blinking to see anything beyond the glow. He caught flashes of colour when he squinted, but little else.

An elven man also shared the landing, there to announce attendees as they entered. He bowed, his tanned face gaining a sickly shade. "His imperial highness," he announced to the crowd, his booming voice neatly cutting the chatter below. "Darshan *vris Mhanek*, and..." With his face gaining colour at double the speed he had lost it, the man's eyes darted from Darshan to Hamish. The elf wet his lips, clearly torn between assuming and enquiring. "His husband...?" The tight note of a question lingered in that last word.

Darshan tipped his head slightly. "Prince Hamish of the Mathan Clan from Tirglas," he supplied, to the man's visible relief.

The title wasn't one Hamish had been wholly comfortable using, given his mother's disownment. Until Darshan pointed out that marrying the imperial heir also came with a similar title for his spouse. Although, in those cases, it had meant another princess in the ranks. Udynea hadn't a formal title for their *vris Mhanek* marrying a man.

Bowing low, the elf repeated Darshan's words in a far less hesitant manner than he had done with the rest.

Hamish's eyes had adjusted to the bright light by the time they were to descend the stairs. He laid a hand on Darshan's proffered arm, steadfastly ignoring the heat flaring in his cheeks. It had taken some time for him to stop blushing whenever Darshan introduced him, but this was different. Such gestures had a certain hierarchy that had been absent in their travels. But then, much of the journey from his homeland had taken them through small villages and towns. All places where those of the Crystal Court were unlikely to be found.

And now? They mingled at the foot of the stairs like sharks waiting for them to enter the water.

Gold candle stands and chandeliers rimmed the room, gleaming against marble columns and gilded wood reliefs. The main source of the light was a great magical globe hanging in the centre of the ceiling like a miniature moon come to roost.

Beside him, Darshan softly cleared his throat. "Do try to look a little less wide-eyed," he murmured in Tirglasian. "I would prefer not to give my half-sister any further fodder with which to grease the gossip wheel."

"It's like being inside the sun," Hamish breathed. Somewhere, there was a spellster, likely one of Onella's slaves, who was hard at work keeping that globe aloft and shining bright. Despite Hamish's magic never being capable of reaching the same heights as that of his husband's, or even the majority of those within this room, Darshan had still given him enough schooling to know how things like those light globes were made.

Knowing the power behind it made the act no less impressive. *He* couldn't do it.

One side of Darshan's mouth twitched upwards, an act he swiftly attempted to cover even as he escorted Hamish down the stairs. "Just you wait until you see the palace ballroom in full formal arrangement," he insisted, seamlessly switching back into his native tongue as they reached the halfway point of the staircase. "The ceiling is black marble—intricately carved by the empire's best—and, come nightfall, it glows with all the constellations. It would put this gaudy show to shame."

"Come now, *vris Mhanek*," said a man waiting at the bottom step, his voice almost as deep as the waist-height bow he offered them once they reached the base of the stairs. Grinning, he gestured to the whole room with a languid wave of his hand. The movement upset his gauzy shawl, which was an almost peachy shade of orange and pinned to his shoulder rather than artfully draped. "You do my estate a disservice. Not every mansion can hope to attain the same decorative heights as the imperial palace."

Darshan halted before the man. The wrinkles around his eyes

deepened as if he beamed, but there was little other evidence that his husband was happy to see the man. "Come to greet us before your wife steals the attention as always?" His gaze darted about the room like a starling before his attention turned to Hamish. "Allow me to introduce Count Aagney, the lord of the household and my half-sister's husband."

"You humble me, *uris Mhanek*," Aagney said, giving another bow. "Most are so fixated on the latter that they tend to forget the former."

Hamish clasped the man's shoulder. "Well met, brother." He hadn't expected to meet members of his new family so soon, but he hadn't forgotten his manners.

A flicker of confusion crossed the man's face. His gaze swung to Darshan, seeking clarification. Or perhaps forgiveness, judging by the hunching of his shoulders and the swiftness of how he wormed away from Hamish's touch. "I would not dare be so familiar with his highness' personage."

"Are you nae married to me husband's kin?"

Hamish waited as the man seemed to consider the words. Even though his ability to speak Udynean had grown to a point where he stumbled on just a few phrases, his accent gave them a harsher quality. At least, according to Darshan. It took people longer to understand him but, after a lifetime of casually conversing with foreign dignitaries, Hamish was used to that.

At Aagney's answering nod, Hamish swung to query Darshan. "Is it nae custom for those of marriage to consider their spouse's family as part of their own?"

"Not with such closeness, no."

"It is that way in Tirglas?" Aagney asked, smiling. "What a charming custom."

Hamish peered at the man. He'd been travelling through imperial lands for a few months now, and the accents were definitely starting to shift the further south they went, but he couldn't quite be sure if Aagney was being sincere or not.

Darshan nudged the count, garnering the man's attention. "You must tell me what tasteless demon has possessed 'Nell this time." His sweeping gesture encompassed the golden-lit room. "I almost mistook myself for being transported to that ghastly Stamekian palace."

"I see the *uris Mhanek* is as tactful as ever," the man chuckled.

"Although I must say, it *is* an improvement on the blue and white motif. This just scours the eyes rather than trying to convince one to expel the guts."

Aagney grinned into his wineglass. "Don't let 'Nell hear you. You've already caused quite a stir in the court as is."

"Oh?" Darshan's brows lifted to their height. "Without me being here? She must be livid. Tell me, how ever did I manage that?" His grin turned feral. "And do you think I can do it again?"

Aagney twirled the stem of his wineglass, swirling the liquid. "Everyone has been fretting that they might miss the usual annual night of drunken debauchery in the celebration of your birth. Onella tells me that the *Mhanek* won't even acknowledge it whilst you're still travelling some backwater road on your way home. But here you are."

"You didnae tell me your birthday was near," Hamish muttered in Tirglasian. Clearly, they shared a commonality to his homeland in celebrating the occasion—although Tirglasian custom was a mild affair, certainly no drunken debauchery. So why hadn't his husband divulged it was near?

Confusion tweaked Aagney's brow. His gaze flicked between them, perhaps hoping for an explanation, but said nothing on the change in language.

"Did I not?" Darshan replied in the same tongue. He grunted, a flush of redness tingeing his olive-brown cheeks. "Well, there were other concerns pulling my focus at the time. It was hardly important."

"When?" Hamish pressed, his frustration lending an acidic sharpness to the word. Darshan couldn't have forgotten.

There was a hint of unease on the count's face, the expression growing more pronounced the longer they spoke. Hamish would've changed back into a language the man understood, if only to ease Aagney.

"It is near the beginning of the next month, actually," Darshan replied, seemingly content to leave his brother-by-marriage in the dark. "The third, to be specific."

Hamish nodded. If they weren't terribly delayed, they would still be on the way to Minamist. *Nae doubt travelling from one inn to another.* And hardly in a position to celebrate in the mass festivities that Aagney described.

"You trying to catch up to me, now?" Hamish needled. He had passed his thirty-seventh year during the midwinter just gone. Meanwhile, his husband had some years to go before reaching such a mark, even with it being the better part of three weeks until the date celebrating his thirty-fourth year arrived.

"That is a race I shall fail for some time," Darshan murmured. "And one I do not relish the thought of winning."

Music drifted above the muted chatter of the surrounding crowd. Hamish picked out the airy notes of flutes, accompanied by the delicate strumming of a lap harp. The tune seemed familiar, the same as what was played in all the coffee houses they had stopped at along the way south.

Aagney perked up at the sound. "Would the *vris Mhanek...*" A flicker of panic widened his eyes as they landed on Hamish. "And your highness, of course," he hastened to add. "Would either of you be interested in watching the dancers? 'Nell bought the finest money can buy."

Hamish tried to keep his expression neutral. Ever since entering Udynean lands, he could never be sure that such a phrase didn't mean purchased slaves rather than paying for the person's time and skills.

The count tilted his head to one side, eyeing Hamish. "Has his highness seen veil dancers before?"

Hamish fidgeted a little under the man's scrutiny. He had witnessed a few barely clothed dancers during his travels, typically as entertainment in coffee houses or in some of the more luxurious inns. "I—"

"Actually," Darshan said before Hamish could fully answer the count. "I think I would vastly prefer to dance rather than watch." He held out his hand in invitation to Hamish. "Care to join me, *mea lux?*"

Aagney's eyes narrowed at the address. Whilst Darshan spoke the last two words in Ancient Domian, a language of a people long since eradicated by the Udynean Empire, it was also one that the higher nobility spoke from birth.

Hamish thoroughly believed that the expression was one used freely as a term of endearment, but he had begun to wonder. Not on the meaning itself, as he was confident Darshan wouldn't lie about the translation. *Me light.* But on how deeply the affections behind the words were considered to run. Udynean lore put a lot of stock into Araasi, their Queenly Goddess of Fire and Hearth, and the Flame Eternal who was her once mortal lover. Announcing someone was their light was akin to professing one's heart. It didn't matter if the words were uttered in Tirglasian, Udynean or Ancient Domian, they still meant the same thing.

Hamish clasped his husband's hand, the multitude of rings Darshan wore biting into his skin. "We can do that here?" He had properly danced once with his husband during their time in Tirglas, but that had been tucked away in the shadowy embrace of a small mezzanine as his brother guarded the only entrance. Otherwise, he wouldn't have dared. "Nae one will object?"

Darshan scoffed. "You're my husband. And it's a ballroom. It's made specifically for people to dance in. Of course they won't mind."

"Never!" Aagney gasped, seemingly aghast at the thought of denying Udynea's *vris Mhanek* anything. "I shall command the musicians to play something appropriate at once."

"No need," Darshan said before the count could take more than a single step. "This melody is fine." He marched down the room, heading for a pair of doors that sat halfway open. More of the golden light leaked through the gap. The music grew louder, not quite drowning out the gasps of people scuttling back from Darshan's passage.

The crowd watched them, shuffling into little groups to whisper behind upraised glasses or fancy laced fans. The latter item had come with the Udyneans during their invasion of the north-eastern lands over two thousand years ago.

There was a language amongst those fluttering pieces of wood and fabric. Darshan had tried to teach him—although his husband knew it intimately, Darshan had confessed to hardly ever using the signals—but Hamish had only managed to pick out the obvious gestures. Some held them closed near their face or laid it firmly within their other hand, whilst others snapped their fans open and shut with a birdlike quickness or brushed another's shoulder with the closed tip.

None gave any signal that looked like a command. Not even to their servants. It seemed they were mostly curious. He hoped it stayed that way.

Group by group, the people followed Darshan's march into the ballroom, drawn like nails to a loadstone.

The ballroom was circular and, judging by the height of the domed ceiling, this looked to take up two of the mansion's three stories. The golden glow came from above where the light of five great chandeliers bounced off the marble. Massive pillars supported a balcony that wound around the upper floor. A few people were already up there, engaged in the entertainment.

A small group of men, dressed in gauzy trousers and waving ribbons of the same fabric, danced in the middle of the room. More of the ribbons adorned the surrounding polished marble floor—set with a floral design Hamish couldn't quite make out. The men gyrated and ground against each other. Some paused to pose lewdly for the crowd above whilst flexing their stomachs before continuing.

Hamish's face grew increasingly hotter the closer they got to the group. He had seen that style of clothing during their travels—when they'd lodged at an inn that, if he had understood Darshan right, hadn't been far from a house of ill repute. But the people back then hadn't actually danced.

The men halted upon realising their *vris Mhanek*, who had barely paused at the sight, was currently striding in their direction. They exchanged worried and confused glances amongst themselves before slithering onto the floor, their arms stretched out flat before them.

The musicians, sitting in the shadows of a balcony, also faltered. Other seats had been arranged between the pillars, slowly claimed by those in the crowd.

"Don't mind us," Darshan said to the men before swinging around to clasp Hamish's waist. "I trust you remember the dance I taught you back in Oldunmere?" he asked of Hamish.

"Vaguely." They had spent much of their travel hopping from one inn to the other where their nights often turned to a quiet drink in the taverns before burrowing beneath blankets to sleep until dawn for a repeat of the same. Oldunmere had been the first time Darshan had lingered in any of the small towns they came upon. And Hamish's first chance since their arrival in Udynean territory to soak in the atmosphere. "But when you said there'd be dancing, I didnae think you meant us."

"It wouldn't be, typically." He jerked his head to one side, indicating the group of men dressed in gauzy trousers. "They're supposed to be the night's entertainment. But why not dance? Now that we can do so together." He raised his hand, signalling for the musicians to play.

A few reedy notes drifted up, followed by a shriek of strings and a murmur of hushed voices as the musicians spoke amongst themselves.

"We've danced before," Hamish pointed out. There had been a number of opportunities on the road, although the pace Darshan had insisted they travel at meant they'd been too knackered to actually indulge in much of it. Beyond a few instructional steps in Oldunmere, their last actual dance had been in Castle Mullhind. "Back in Tirglas."

"But that dance wasn't in public."

Nae. He wouldn't have dared risk being found out back home. It had been in the dark, way up on a balcony where even the superior vision of elves would fail to spy them. He had been so afraid back then, terrified that his mother would swoop in to snatch this last chance of happiness from his grasp.

She had already tried by calling for the union contest—a competition for his hand by every eligible noble in Tirglas—but Darshan had thwarted her there. He had competed in secret, his identity known to but a few, and claimed Hamish's hand right out from under everyone's nose.

A few light trills of a flute pierced the air. It seemed the musicians had made up their minds on just what to play.

"I dinnae remember any of the steps," he admitted. The music was nothing like the heady beats of home. He knew what to do with that sort of rhythm. And if someone got hurt? The ensuing brawl merely added a little more excitement to the dance.

"Just follow my lead. I promise, I shall stick to something

familiar." With that, Darshan took the first few steps forward.

Chuckling, Hamish trailed along. "It seems like I've been doing naething but following since we left Tirglas." The change between the two lands hadn't been a gradual one, such as what would've happened had they trodden the borders between his homeland and Udynea, but a sudden jump from a southern port in Tirglas to the nearest imperial port on the western shore. Their first month of travel had been quite the shock.

"You will adapt, *mea lux*."

He already had in quite a number of ways. "I just need time, right?" And lessons. He dreaded those. Whilst Darshan had taught him a smattering of topics, any proper education would also come with books. Despite Hamish's attempts, Udynean wasn't the easiest script to decipher. He had trouble with written words at the best of times, especially with the way they tended to shift on him.

They twirled across the floor. The dance Darshan had chosen didn't quite match the tempo, being a four-step when the beats were clearly for a three, but the dance was one Hamish knew and it meant he didn't need to focus on their every movement.

It also left him free to take in the room and the crowd, of how the majority still chattered behind fans or into their drinks. "Everyone's staring at us."

"Of course they are," his husband murmured. "They have never seen me this happy." Grimacing, he added, "Not without a moderate application of alcohol and sex." Darshan beamed up at him as he stepped to one side and guided them in a small circle. "That is entirely your doing. My heart swells having you, my flame eternal, at my side that I can't contain such joy."

More heat flooded Hamish's face, slinking its way down his neck. "Cannae you stop that?"

"Stop what, *mea lux*?" Although his eyes were wide in a wonderful display of innocence, the faint curve of his lips hinted at another barely restrained grin.

"You bloody ken exactly what," he hissed, pulling Darshan closer even though the dance steps called for the lead to twirl their partner. "You're purposely saying things that'll make me blush. Stop it."

"Absolutely not. It's adorable."

The music's lulling rhythm slowly increased in volume. Darshan shifted their steps to match as they spun around the ballroom, grimacing as he seemed to catch the change. "Forgive me, I—"

"It's all right. I think I can match it." They had practised it, and he was sure he remembered most of the steps even if Tirglas had nothing remotely similar to the soft, flowing movements the dance required. He just had to be careful not to tread on his husband's toes when it came time for him to step forward.

They had travelled about halfway around the ballroom before others started to join in. Hamish took in the swirls of coloured silk and the glitter of jewels, gold and silver. "I see why you prefer to dress in ivory."

Darshan silently raised a brow at him in query.

"All this colour, the sparkle." He freed a hand from Darshan's shoulder to encompass the room and its many dancers. "The simplicity of ivory and gold makes you stand out."

His husband scrunched his hook of a nose, but a certain puppy-like glee danced in his eyes and skewed his lips. "I wear the colour because it looks good on me. The rest is merely a pleasing side effect."

Hamish silently appraised the golden outfit Darshan currently wore. It was a show of his status. Only those with a direct blood kinship to the *Mhanek* would dare to don such colours. "This also looks good on you."

"It looks better on the floor." Darshan waggled his brows as if Hamish hadn't caught the suggestiveness behind the words.

"Dar!" Hamish gasped.

His husband chuckled. "That I look good in this is more good luck and flattering lighting than anything. I've seen some simply dreadful portraits where the colour wasn't at all flattering on them." The corners of his eyes creased. "But thank you." His gaze drifted off into the crowd. "In all honesty, I wish you had a better debut at court than this. It's so substandard in comparison to the soirée I was planning on holding in your honour once we got to Minamist."

"What's stopping you from doing it anyway?" Hamish didn't care about having lavish festivities thrown just for him, but if it aligned with his current social standing and made his husband happy...

"Two welcoming parties?" Darshan laughed. "My, my. Even *I'm* not that greedy."

Hamish bent his head close and, cheekily taking the lead for a few beats of their dance, subtly dipped his husband. "I'm pretty sure all this is supposed to be more in *your* honour than mine. For your upcoming birthday?"

Darshan rolled his eyes and straightened himself, pushing Hamish back with a burst of strength that could only have been him bolstering his muscles with magic. "I apologise for not telling you sooner, *mea lux*. I've spent so many years having everyone know that it simply slipped my mind how you wouldn't be one of them. But do you really think that pandering to me was entirely my half-sister's goal tonight?"

Probably nae. Onella had mentioned wanting to meet Hamish, so she was aware of him. But if she was so eager then, where was she hiding now? He had thought she would be the first to greet them, not her husband. Was she waiting until the evening meal to introduce herself? Or after?

He glanced at the balcony as Darshan's leading steps swung them around in a lazy circle. Some of the crowd watched on, conversing and drinking as they'd done when Darshan had first led them into the ballroom. None of them seemed any more intent from one couple to the other. His gaze drifted to the chairs set up between the pillars. That was mostly populated by grey-haired nobles, with a few younger ones chatted animatedly away.

"Maybe I will take up your suggestion on a welcoming soirée once we're home," Darshan said. "It would be fun to see the court scamper about trying to adapt to a few of your delightful customs."

"Such as?" Why was he even trying to search for Onella in the crowd? He wouldn't recognise the woman, even though she and Darshan shared more than a father. The *Mhanek* had turned to his wife's sister during his first year of grief over the death of Darshan's mother, making Onella also Darshan's cousin.

Sharing such close bloodlines didn't mean much. Whilst he hadn't truly paid much attention to the distinction himself, Hamish's own younger sister looked quite different to the rest of them. Her parentage had even been briefly questioned when her magic first flared to life, but their mother had quelled it almost as swiftly. Right before sending her off to the cloister and renouncing all claims of having two daughters.

"One of your dances?" Darshan suggested, brightening. "We could do one now."

"The music's too slow." Even the slowest Tirglasian dance sped along at a pace that would leave this beat far behind.

"That can be fixed easily enough." They twirled around the dance floor, aiming for the musicians planted atop a short dais. "May I make a request?" Darshan asked the woman who seemed to be directing the musicians with a small golden pointer.

The woman turned, her head cocked. "Our mistress has instructed us to—" Her eyes widened and she fell to her knees. "My *vris Mhanek!* Of course! Anything you desire."

The flicker of a grimace twitched across Darshan's face before the expression vanished beneath that perfect emotionless mask he was so adept at applying. "Play something with a little *oomph.*"

The woman's head lifted, her brow furrowed. "As you command, *vris Mhanek.*" She turned her back on them to converse amongst the musicians.

"Whatever they choose to play," Darshan said, tucking Hamish's hand into the crook of his arm and leading the way into the middle of the dance floor. "I want you to take the lead."

He glanced around them, taking in how the other dancers milled about and shared confused looks between themselves. "I dinnae ken any Udynean dances except the one you taught me."

"I meant a Tirglasian one."

"What if it doesnae match their rhythm?"

"Then make something up. No one will be any the wiser. And if I fumble?" He shrugged. "That's on me."

The boom of tiny drums rumbled through the ballroom. Lap harps chimed in with deep thrums he hadn't thought possible from something so small. The flautists attempted to deepen the melody, their red faces turning purple. The blast of a trumpet resounded out of nowhere and Hamish turned back to confirm it had indeed come from the musicians.

The sound was like nothing Hamish had ever heard. Yet, as the clash of two metal discs came together and the drummer's pounding grew more confident, a beat became apparent. It swelled his chest and stirred his blood. *A little oomph?* This was almost a battle march.

He took hold of Darshan's hand, clasping it as if greeting an old friend, and stepped back until both of them held their arms out at the full length. "You promise you'll be able to keep up?"

Darshan's answering grin was feral. A wild, gambling glee sparkled to life in his eyes. "Just try and stop me."

He knew no dance that suited this raw melody. His feet fell instinctively, following the beat as he stalked a circle with Darshan mimicking him at every step. Unlike with the flowing movements of the dance they'd previously enjoyed, his new trousers tugged distractingly around his thighs. At least they hadn't been cut to fit as tightly as Darshan preferred his clothes, leaving Hamish with enough room to perform a kick to his own backside at every fourth step.

The other dancers had stopped entirely to watch.

He kept to simple movements, making sure Darshan was able to follow with each change as they swung from holding both hands to one. But the disappointment radiating off his husband was almost strong enough to glow. Whatever Darshan had been expecting, this clearly wasn't it.

He wants fast? Already, they were moving twice the speed of their previous dance. But he could increase that easily enough. As well as change the steps to something a little more complicated.

Releasing his hold on his husband's hand, he spun away for three beats. Memory had him clapping once to the metallic clash of discs, then sliding back to Darshan. He clasped the man's hands and slung both of them into a sidestep before pulling his husband closer and whirling them about.

Darshan stumbled, momentum taking his husband on a wider arc than Hamish had planned. Hamish tightened his hold, pulling them closer in the hopes of keeping Darshan upright. They spun as the act upset his own balance. Darshan tipped back, his descent barely halted by the death grip he maintained on Hamish's sleeves.

The music stuttered to a halt.

Chapter 3

Hamish froze, not quite sure whether he should try to incorporate his husband's blundering steps into a completed dance move or return Darshan to his feet as gracefully as he was able.

Darshan threw his head back, laughing as he took in their audience. "Quite the display we gave them, don't you think?" He relaxed into Hamish's grasp, grinning up at him. "I had no idea you could dance like that." One brow arched as he comically peered at Hamish. "What other secrets are you keeping, hmm?"

"Secrets?" he echoed, tipping Darshan back onto his feet. "I dinnae think I have any." He had left all his reasons for secrecy back in Tirglas, alongside the lie of a life he'd been forced into.

Although Darshan's eyes creased with humour at Hamish's answer, his attention seemed drawn to the far side of the room. "You'll be all right mingling on your own, won't you?"

Hamish scoffed. "This isnae me first time at a party." Granted, the ones thrown in Castle Mullhind had less of an uneasy air about them. They had a lot more feasting, dancing and general revelry, too.

"The drinks should be safe," his husband added in Tirglasian. "They prefer to keep the stronger stuff until after the main meal. But do not eat anything."

"Poison?" He couldn't see it likely in amongst all these people. Servants walked the rim of the ballroom with trays of food or glasses and jugs. With such a haphazard serving method, it would be all too easy to poison the wrong person.

Darshan's lips flattened into a thin line. "Possibly. I cannot be entirely sure of my half-sister's intentions until I have spoken with her. And she..." His gaze slid across the room. "Still has yet to show her face it would seem, but I shall not be long." Giving Hamish's bicep a hearty pat, he whisked off into the crowd.

Hamish tracked his husband's passage across the room to where a woman dressed in the traditional apron skirt of the dwarves watched the festivities. *A hedgewitch?* Hadn't Darshan muttered something about speaking with the dwarves once they reached Minamist? Fortuitous for them to meet one during their travels. Maybe the conversation would alleviate whatever concern gnawed at his husband.

The musicians began another melody, similar to the wispy notes of their first dance. Hamish left the middle of the ballroom to circle the outer edge, looking for a quiet spot to watch as others continued to dance. The swirls of colour and flowing movements as they circled the room were almost hypnotic. There appeared to be a pattern formed by the couples, one he couldn't quite make out no matter how much he strained to increase his height.

His gaze lifted to the balcony. More people stood at the railing. The sight from above would definitely enable him to see everything.

He glanced about, failing to spy a way within the ballroom to access the upper level. Did he dare venture beyond earshot of Darshan to seek out a stairway? Getting lost in a strange place wouldn't be ideal without the added possibility of that same place being the home of someone who could potentially be after his demise.

Shaking his head, he continued his search for a quiet spot and settled for leaning against one of the pillars. A good view of the dancing just wasn't worth the risk of death. Maybe they could leave the lower level once Darshan had spoken with the hedgewitch. It would likely give them a better view to spy Darshan's sister once she showed her face.

The dancers had barely done more than a quarter rotation of the room when someone behind Hamish whistled low and loud.

He turned to find a woman standing there. She wore a flowing gown of golden silk and sheer lace, all practically dripping jewels. Even never having met her before, the relation to his husband was undeniable. They'd the same proud, hook-like nose, same hazel eyes— although hers weren't hidden behind glasses—even the same dark brown hair. Her olive-brown skin was a touch lighter, but the flawless matte sheen suggested powder played a small part there.

Onella. His husband's murderous half-sister.

"Well, now," she murmured, her voice breathy. She fanned herself, her gaze running over him like a barn cat eyeing up a mouse. "It seems that my brother hasn't changed an iota in always wanting to be the centre of attention. Although, *you* look like you could've usurped my soirée without his help."

Hamish squirmed, shuffling his feet on the spot. He hadn't

considered the idea of meeting any of Darshan's relatives without the man at his side. *I should've gone with him.* Standing like a lump whilst his husband chatted to the hedgewitch, or even politely conversing as he was introduced to a dearth of new faces, didn't seem that bad. And if Darshan was in good standing with the hedgewitch, then he might've been able to fob off any other conversations by keeping to the dwarf's side.

"You would be Onella, then?" he managed, realising how brainless he sounded once the words reached his ears. Who else could be talking about his husband in such a fashion? Still, his mouth refused to fall back into silence. "Darshan's sister?" After the tales Darshan had spun about his eldest half-sister, Hamish hadn't expected the woman to swan about without an entourage.

Shock had her long lashes fluttering, even as she snapped her fan shut and laid it upon her silk-enrobed bosom. "*Half*-sister."

Of course. He recalled Darshan mentioning how his eldest half-sister could be prickly about her parentage.

"I am guessing my brother has spoken of me, then?" One thin brow arched as her lips twitched with amusement. "All bad things, I assume."

He inclined his head. Although he had done his best to reserve judgement until after he had met his sisters-in-law, it was harder when he knew how the woman had made it her personal goal to see Darshan's time on the throne was short. Or non-existent.

"Still, I believe proper introductions are in order." She extended her hand whilst fanning her face with the other. "Onella *vlos Mhanek.*"

Hamish had spent quite a few hours being schooled on the various titles through the Crystal Court during their weeks of travelling. Whilst *vlos* was respectable—identifying them as the first princess in a long line of about a dozen—Onella wasn't the name his husband accredited to the rank. Did it mean Darshan's twin sister was dead? Or was Onella testing him?

Heeding his husband's instructions upon meeting the man's siblings, Hamish clasped the woman's hand in both of his. He offered up a small bow over them, noting how her face pinched at his actions. "Well met, sister. I am Prince Hamish Mathan of Tirglas."

Onella's lashes lowered, veiling the hint of mischief gleaming just beneath. "I am surprised to see you here. My brother doesn't typically bring his current flings to dally at my soirées."

Hamish ran his tongue along his teeth. If that little jibe was the best she could do, then perhaps Darshan's evaluation of her being a threat was clouded by memory and kinship. "I'm nae his *fling*," he softly corrected her. "I'm his husband." The ceremony uniting them might've been modest and the vows wholly Tirglasian in nature, but he doubted Onella was party to such information. Nor was she likely to be aware of how a Tirglasian marriage lasted for only two years unless a child was born within that timeframe.

To her, their marriage likely had the sniff of permanence. Binding until death.

"So I have heard." Her lips pursed. If she knew her brother was married, then she had to be aware that Hamish outranked her. By a wide margin.

"Did you think it mere rumour?"

"Not precisely." She snatched up a full wine glass from a passing servant and sipped at the amber liquid whilst fluttering her half-open fan close to her chin. "But it's quite the feat to manage from my hedonistic big brother. He doesn't tend to gift favours lightly."

Hamish ground his teeth. Although Darshan *had* used that very word to describe himself—back when their intimate entanglements involved a grand total of two nights—it had seemed more as a self-deprecating warning for Hamish not to emotionally invest himself than the truth. Even after entering Udynea, he had yet to see any actual displays of hedonism from his husband.

But to hear that same evaluation of Darshan's character from the man's half-sister...

She's just trying to get a rise out of you. Clearly, she'd been watching them dance. *From a vantage point Dar couldnae see.* Which meant she had specifically waited for Darshan to depart Hamish's side before making her presence known. All in an effort to upset her brother.

Hamish wished he could say her attempts to aggravate him weren't working.

Onella peered at him over her glass and grinned. Her eyes glittered with the malicious glee of a starved ship rat. "Whatever his reasons, I'm sure my brother's..." She paused, making a display of searching for the right word. "...exuberance at the festivals shall be missed by quite a few."

Grunting, Hamish folded his arms. She was going to play it that way, was she? Well, he knew the game rightly enough from his teenage years. "Nae doubt the priests will be overjoyed at keeping their statues intact for more than a year."

Her eyes widened. The fan paused for a heartbeat before redoubling its efforts.

He leant forward, towering over her until she took a step back. "Did you think he wouldnae have told me everything that you might've been able to use as ammunition?" he hissed. "Your petty little games willnae have me running that easily."

Onella hummed, her lips twisting into a pout before she hid the expression behind her fan. "I suppose he wouldn't have wanted you caught *that* unawares. However..." Her brow arched in an almost perfect imitation of her brother. She lowered her fan, revealing a wide grin. "Him admitting his true nature to you doesn't negate the fact you must be quite big to keep my brother's attention, never mind him wanting you all to himself."

Heat seeped into his cheeks. She couldn't possibly mean what his thoughts had first settled on. "You can see how tall I am." He was head and shoulders above the majority of the people he had come across in Udynea—he even sat a full foot taller than his husband. And the locals seemed to be shrinking the further south they ventured.

"*Tall?*" She pressed the rim of her glass to her lips, giggling before taking a sip. "So my brother's fancy this year is innocence. I see why he's so fond of you." Letting the fan drop to dangle from her wrist on a small golden chain, Onella extended her hand as if she planned to lay it upon his chest. Her fingers halted a hairsbreadth from him, much to his relief. "I must admit, I thought my sources were kidding when they said you were a giant. But you *are* quite lofty, aren't you?"

"So I've been told," he managed, taking a slow step back. Of all the things he had learnt about Udynea, especially as they'd travelled further south, the rarity of tall people had been an unexpected one. The average Tirglasian height pushed six feet, and his family had been no exception. "I'm nae the tallest in me family, you ken?" That honour went to his father, who neared seven feet. Hamish's brother was the next tallest after that.

"You're being modest, surely." Even with the light and motherly tone to her voice, that poorly concealed smirk still graced her lips. "They say your people breed for tall and strong."

The statement was half right. A strong and hardy bloodline was the general reason for marriage, and thus children, in Tirglas. Harsh winters demanded a certain toughness. The tallness was more of a bi-product. It was akin to how the spellsters in Udynea mingled their bloodlines to create those with stronger magic and occasionally wound up with Nulled Ones, those who couldn't be affected by direct magic.

"They who?" he asked. This far south, he had met no one who could place his homeland.

"Everybody." Onella swung her arms wide. The jewels in her wing-like sleeves glittered in the candlelight. "But your height wasn't quite what I was enquiring about." She stepped closer. "Since you seem the shy sort, why don't I just find out for myself?"

Hamish took another step back, his breath catching in his throat.

She wasn't really planning on feeling him up, was she? Darshan had said she sought to undo anything he attempted, but Hamish had thought it an exaggeration. "You're really nae me type."

She rolled her eyes, her head tipping to one side. "Now, how would you know that without even making an attempt?"

His third step from the woman had the column greeting his backside, neatly blocking his casual retreat. "Because you're a woman." It wasn't as if he hadn't been presented with the choice before. There had even been a single night—during the dreadful time when eligible noblewomen had been competing for the chance to marry him—where one competitor had snuck into his bed to wake him with her inept pawing at his clothes. Even though several months had gone by since then, he could recall the hungry, desperate look on the woman's face easily enough.

And Onella wore the same expression.

"Indeed," she said, her voice husky. Her hand slid up his chest, toying with the toggles holding his clothing fast. "How about I show you just how much of a woman I am?"

Panic squeezed his chest and closed his throat. He flailed behind him, blindly searching for the column that had halted his retreat and seeking to skirt around it. He side-stepped and—

Nothing.

His feet failed to obey the command to move. No matter how he tried to focus, his limbs were frozen in place. Had she used her magic to bind him? He couldn't feel any actual restraints.

"Come now," Onella purred. "It's better if you don't fuss. I promise, you won't regret it."

"I definitely dinnae agree." Regardless of his ability to physically halt her hands, standing here in silence whilst his sister-in-law molested him wasn't happening. He glanced around, searching for Darshan.

There. The golden flash of his husband's attire appeared in the brief parting of the crowd. Not far away. If only Darshan's back wasn't turned to him.

"And if *you* dinnae get your bloody mitts off me, I'll—"

"You'll... *what?*" Onella grinned. He'd seen friendlier smiles on a rabid boarhound. "Scream for my brother? Prove to everyone that you need him to save you? Even from his own sister? Let everyone here know how pathetically vulnerable you are? How easily they could take your life?"

Nothing appeared to restrain him from alerting Darshan with a yell. He could speak normally and breathe easily enough, so he assumed his voice was his own at a greater volume. That meant she had deliberately left him with the option to shout out, knowing that uttering a single loud word would draw more than Darshan's attention.

She slid closer, pressing her body against his.

He swallowed hard, tamping down the rising panic tightening his chest even as it screamed in his skull.

"Just how long do you think some weakling without a drop of magic could last in our court?" she hissed. "A month? A week?" She flicked open one of the toggles holding his overcoat closed. "You're lucky this is my soirée or I wouldn't have given you a day." She gave him a consoling pat on the shoulder. "Don't worry. I'm not yet interested in causing your death. Not when the court can handle that." She smirked. "Providing my brother doesn't tire of you first."

That's nae likely to happen. He was well aware of how smitten his husband was with him. "Even if that were true, it doesnae give you the right to lay your hands on me." She hadn't gone as far south as she had first threatened, but that was only a matter of time.

"Of course not." No longer did her smirk attempt to hide behind the veneer of civility. "But the fact you can't stop me does."

Hamish set his jaw. "If you continue down that path of thought, you'll regret it." Darshan might be under a pledge not to kill his half-sister, but Hamish was willing to bet there were a dozen other ways to make Onella's life uncomfortable.

"I haven't so far. Shall we see just how much my brother wants his newest toy once I've had my—what charming vernacular did you use?—*bloody mitts* all over it?"

After glancing back to where Darshan still stood, he fixed the woman with a hard stare. "You'll nae get the rise out of him that you're after."

She grinned. "Let's find out, shall we?"

Chapter 4

Darshan wove through the crowd gathering in the shelter of the balcony pillars, collecting a full glass of wine along the way. Keeping the brown-haired head of the dwarven woman in sight wasn't the easiest task whilst also side-stepping people and slaves, but the throng finally parted and allowed him the chance to stop at her side.

Like most dwarves, she was a strong-looking woman with a build that seemed familiar to the act of trekking through the forests for days on end. And tall, too. A little more so than himself. Her outfit was modest in design—a buckskin leather apron dress sat atop another dress of ashen brown. The sleeves just so happening to be a close match to her skin.

Both dress and apron bore embroidery along the cuffs and neckline in the typical runic symbols. The only concessions to the mellow shades of the forests were two apron brooches—discs of brass with the intricate tree sigils stamped into their faces.

"Madam Hedgewitch." Darshan pressed his hand to his chest and bent forward ever so slightly. He offered the woman only a dip of the head, but it was more than the surrounding nobles had gotten. "I had no idea my half-sister had invited you. What brings you through Nulshar?"

The woman smiled. "Nothing of note," she replied in perfect Udynean, her melodious accent lending a soft lilt to the words that rounded off the harsher notes of his native tongue. "I'm mostly biding my time whilst my escort gathers supplies before they take us east. There's a rumour of a ruin in the forests along the Demarn border."

Darshan smiled. *There always is.* Hedgewitches were dwarven scholars sent abroad to learn all they could about their ancestors. All that needed was just a sniff of being on the right path was often enough for them to set about hunting for what they had lost in the unfortunate outcome of meeting the first humans.

He sipped at his wine, considering the distance between Nulshar and the neighbouring kingdom. "Wouldn't it have been easier to travel through Demarn in the first place, Madam Hedgewitch?"

The woman snorted. "You don't need to call me that, *vris Mhanek*. Katarina will do fine." She grinned, a little sheepishly. "And you are correct. But my original plans were to return to Dvärghem—and I was on my way home from a sadly fruitless search in Stamekia—but one of your imperial scouts alerted his superiors of something dvärg in nature hidden in the forest." Her eyes widened, revealing their hazel hue; a common colour amongst the dwarves. "The Coven thought it might be the remains of something rare and best left alone, although the reports are promising on it appearing to be quite safe."

"Do be careful. As I understand it, there's a dreadful scuffle going on near the eastern border." There had been for as long as he had lived. Even beyond his grandfather's rule.

Katarina wrinkled her nose. "I believe the Demarners call it a war, *vris Mhanek*."

"Really? I've not heard any official declaration of such." Demarn was a small kingdom, populated by those fearful of magic who confined their spellsters in a giant prison. If the Udynean army was brought upon their borders, the Demarner army wouldn't last very long.

"From what my guide says, I believe one or two Udynean houses are contesting the land. And have been for some generations."

"I see." Scuffles between houses weren't uncommon. Bickering over boundaries was practically a hobby amongst the lower houses and the imperial forces were rarely employed to halt them. "Well then, I wish you luck on your expedition."

"If I may ask a favour of you, *vris Mhanek*?"

"Always." Whilst the hedgewitches asked very little, they knew the empire was happy to grant them favours. It wouldn't set right what humans had done to the dwarven population—no amount of favours done would be enough—but reparation had to start somewhere.

"My efforts would be improved if they weren't fighting at all."

Darshan hummed to himself. There had to be a reason why his forefathers hadn't sent people to halt this push against the border of the empire. "I shall see whose influence I can sway to make your expedition as comfortable as possible, Madam Hedgewitch." There was little he could do about the Demarn portion of this apparent war, but hopefully having their enemy withdrawing would suffice.

"If you are able, the Coven would appreciate the assistance." She went to turn away, halting only as he laid a hand on her shoulder.

"I didn't come merely to exchange pleasantries. I was wondering, your hedgewitches..." His thoughts drifted off for a moment at the glimpse of Onella in the crowd. *Where have* you *been hiding?* And what was she up to now?

Katarina cleared her throat. "There was something you wished to say, *vris Mhanek?*"

Her gentle enquiry jolted Darshan back to his current conversation. "The ancestral hedgewitches." He would have to be quick in getting the information he required, and then find Hamish before his half-sister did. "They were capable of communing with nature, correct?"

Katarina bowed her head. Although her brow was furrowed, there lurked a cold guardedness to her eyes.

"Do..." He rubbed at his neck. He couldn't push too hard on the subject. "Are you aware if they left behind any record of what that was like?"

"Sadly not. I don't think they ever considered a time when their abilities wouldn't be around." She cocked her head. "Why do you ask? Have you found someone?"

His gaze drifted out into the ballroom. "No, merely curious." Some months has passed since a bear had nearly taken Hamish's life. The man survived only because of Darshan's intervention. But that had involved sucking the life from the surrounding forest.

And ever since then, the world seemed that little more alive. He had grown accustomed to the whispers and the feeling of never being alone unless he sought somewhere deep in a building.

"I—" The explanation stilled on his tongue as his gaze settled on his half-sister. *'Nell.* She stood before Hamish. The chatter and whirl of the dancing crowd stole much from the view, but his husband was clearly uncomfortable with the closeness of Onella's presence. Was she—?

Indignance stole Darshan's breath for a heartbeat. Was she actually *groping* his husband?

Darshan laid a hand on the hedgewitch's elbow. "Do excuse me." He set his wine into her grasp and strode out into the crowd. The nerve of his half-sister, touching what didn't belong to her. And against Hamish's will. *I'm going to strangle her.*

No, such a death would be too swift.

Hamish's head jerked his way as Darshan exited the dancing crowd. Relief moulded his husband's face, but he made no attempt to move away. Just how long had Onella kept the poor man her prisoner?

Onella spun about before Darshan could speak, her eyes widening as recognition lit a feral glee in their depths. "Why, *vris Mhanek,*" she murmured, giving him the barest twitch of a curtsy. "I almost didn't recognise you with your new style." She gestured at her chin with the tip of her closed fan, clearly indicating the circle-shaped nature of his beard. "It certainly... matures you."

He folded his arms. No amount of pleasantries was going to have him forget what he had witnessed. "What do you think you are doing with my husband?" he growled, daring to glance Hamish's way.

Even with Onella's focus having turned from him, Hamish hadn't moved. The stiffness of his stance was clearly due to magic. *Her* magic.

"Release him this instant," Darshan demanded.

His half-sister smiled in that pretty display of coy innocence their father often fell for. "Such anger, brother dear. You really should keep that under control. What would the court think of their future *Mhanek* flying off in a rage at every little thing?"

"*Little thing?*" He took a few slow steps towards her, summoning an elemental wisp to balance on his upraised finger. To look at, it wasn't much more than a ghost of mist and a flash of lightning, but it packed a painful punch. "You were molesting my husband."

Onella scoffed. "There you go, blowing everything out of proportion again." She smiled sweetly over her shoulder at Hamish and added, "I do hope you know what you're getting into with him. He can be so... dramatic at times."

" 'Nell," Darshan muttered through clenched teeth. The wisp sputtered and sparked on the end of his finger. "Let him go."

"I mean, just look at him," Onella continued, clearly ignoring the order. She laid a hand on Hamish's chest, toying with one of the toggles and indicating Darshan with the tip of her fan. "So quick to resort to violence when I was merely showing you what a woman's touch was capable of."

"Trying to insert yourself where you're nae welcome, you mean," Hamish snapped back, disgust twisting his lips and roughening his voice. He had recoiled as much as her magic allowed, the veins in his neck bulging from the strain. "I dinnae need a woman showing me anything."

Her hand closed on Hamish's sherwani and, judging by his husband's wince, possibly some of his chest hair. A smirk took her lips, even as she fanned herself. Those hard eyes glittered with their usual malevolent glee over the lace edging. "Would that be because you have *him*?" She gestured to Darshan with a quick snap of her fan.

Darshan tightened his jaw. The elemental wisp grew hotter, forcing him to abandon it or burn his own clothes. *The very audacity.* He was *not* a replacement for a woman. That she would dare to use his sexuality in such a poor attempt of goading his temper spoke only of her desperation.

Scoffing, his half-sister resumed stirring the air around her face. "Don't look so sour, Darshi. You know what you are. Just as you know how I do so love playing with my big brother's toys."

Darshan wrinkled his nose. She couldn't actually be referring to the toys he'd been forced to leave behind during his journey to Tirglas, could she? *Possibly*. He would have to ensure every single one of them was destroyed once he reached Minamist. It didn't matter if she was lying or merely referring to Hamish, his half-sister was the last thing he wanted to think of when engaging in any sort of sexual intimacy.

Closing the space between them in two quick strides, Darshan fastened his fingers around her forearm. "I told you to release him." He focused on the flesh directly beneath his palm and let his fury have control.

Sparks of lightning leaked through his fingers, charging the air.

Onella flinched, her jaw jerking and her nostrils twitching with the effort to contain her voice. Her eyes narrowed, but she continued to hold his gaze, calling his bluff on how far he would push the punishment.

"Do it now," he grated. This close the heat radiating off her arm stung his palm. As much as he wanted to, purely to wipe the smug look off her face, putting any more magic into it would kill her.

"Fine," she finally spat from between clenched teeth.

Hamish stumbled as the magical binds restraining him vanished. He sagged, supporting himself against the column for all of a few hasty breaths, before jolting upright and bolting to Darshan's side.

Darshan withdrew his hand.

"Go right ahead and take your toy back," Onella said, her voice still strained. "I was done playing with him, anyway." She examined the damage, a sharp hiss slithering out her sneering lips as she peeled the diaphanous silk shawl from her skin. The seared and jagged cracks along his sister's skin were already starting to heal. "You didn't have to ruin my gown."

Clenching his hands in an effort to keep himself from blasting her with all his magical might, Darshan turned his focus towards wrapping both himself and his husband in a solid, if transparent, shield. She wasn't likely to directly strike out at him, but he certainly felt better knowing Hamish was securely out of her reach.

Onella's gaze lifted, likely sensing the charge of magic surrounding them. Smiling in that nasty little vulpine fashion she was so fond of, she flicked her unbound hair over her shoulder. "Look at you, protecting him like a mother hen whilst he huddles beneath your power. Do you really think you can keep that up?"

"When it comes to defending him from *you*? Always."

Giving an unimpressed huff, her gaze flicked to Hamish and back. "I must say, this seems to be an older model than what you usually play with." She flashed her teeth in a mockery of a smile. "Are we growing tired of keeping up with all the fresh young bucks? Starting to feel our age?"

He knew Hamish's slightly older age would amuse Onella. She was well aware that Darshan's tastes tended to gravitate towards men in their twenties rather than nearing their forties. "I—"

"And have you told him how much of a whore you are?" she continued.

Darshan glowered at her. "What I have and haven't told my husband is none of your business."

Onella ignored him, choosing to focus on Hamish. "Whilst I'm sure you know his tastes are only for men, are you aware of just how many my brother prefers at once?" She laid a forefinger on her lips in a display of innocence before grinning. "I'll give you a hint, he's very greedy."

"That's enough," Darshan snapped. "I suggest you conduct yourself with a little more restraint, before I see you escorted to your quarters and confined there for the rest of my duration in Nulshar."

Onella gaped at him. "You would dare to put me under house arrest?" she hissed. "In my own home!"

"You're the one obviously incapable of displaying proper decorum in a civilised gathering." Darshan gestured to the ballroom and the crowd who, for the most part, were doing a decent act of ignoring them. He tried to centre his emotions, to keep his expression neutral. If any rumours were to come out of this, he'd prefer them to cast Onella in the appropriate light for once. "Would it not be better for you to retire before you make a bigger fool of yourself?"

"*I'm* the fool?" She leant forward, stopping with her nose barely an inch from his shield. "I'm not the one touting a lover as my husband."

Darshan clenched his hands, focusing on keeping his hands cool or risk having the surrounding air burst into flame. "We are *legally* married." Did she honestly think he'd make such a baseless claim?

"Not by Udynean standards."

Darshan's jaw almost dropped before he managed to control the act. Months of not needing to cling to his expressionless mask had made it difficult to slip back into such a stance. She knew they had wed before they entered the empire? That could mean only one thing. "I see we've resorted to sending our spies out to collect gossip again."

Onella raised her chin. Her nostrils flared, but she said nothing more.

"Whether we took vows here or in Tirglas, they are still in effect.

As are the consequences if you harm him." Once, he couldn't set foot in the same city as Onella without her trying to kill him. She still tried from time to time, but in ways that made it extremely difficult to trace back to her.

Their father had forced this truce between them. If Darshan's death was proven to be her doing, her son would never get the throne. And that truce extended to their spouses as well as Darshan's twin.

His half-sister glared at him before her lips curved with contemptuous laughter. "You don't actually believe father will accept that claim?" She arched a brow at him. "Does he even know what you've done? What you're bringing home?"

"Father knows everything." Darshan had sent the missive himself the first day he set foot on Udynean soil. If her spies were any good, she would've known that. "If you're thinking you can surprise him with information about my husband, then I'm afraid I am very much full of disappointments tonight, dear sister. He is protected."

Onella shuffled from one foot to the other. It seemed she finally doubted her position. "Father would never validate—"

"What makes you think he already hasn't?" Whilst his announcement via the Singing Crystal hadn't been immediately contested, his father also hadn't sent any sort of acceptance missive. "He's well aware of my tastes."

"Indeed." She arched her brow at Hamish. "But how aware is your husband?"

"I ken more than you think, lass. Especially of how you're looking to dethrone me husband and put your wee lad in his place."

Stiffening, Onella snapped open her fan and fluttered it furiously.

"And how *is* my nephew?" Darshan asked before she could think of a retort, knowing full well that Tarendra would still be at the imperial palace and safe under his grandfather's doting gaze. Only once Darshan had returned to Minamist would the boy be sent back to his mother.

Onella silently glared at him, her mouth tightening. Her son was the only weak spot she had dared to suffer, but then he was also her sole chance to rule. Sometimes, Darshan wondered if she actually held any affection for the boy or only saw him as a means to the throne.

"I do hope you're keeping the estate healthy. Ren's going to need something to inherit."

"Especially once *our* son takes the throne," Hamish added.

The fan halted its fluttering, concealing half of Onella's face. "Son? With who?" Her gaze darted from him to Hamish. "*Him?*"

"Go," Darshan growled at his half-sister, hoping to turn her attentions from Hamish's words. It wouldn't take much for her to realise just how they planned on having that heir. That there was a means for two men to merge their bloodlines had been common knowledge since before he had left for Tirglas. "Out of my sight before you get burnt. And if you touch my husband again, I might just forget what I've promised Father."

She sneered. "I see married life has made a man of you." Frowning at Hamish, she turned on her heel and marched off into the crowd.

Darshan watched until she was out of sight before turning his attention to his husband. "Are you all right?" he asked in Tirglasian. "You look..." *Ashen.* "...frightful."

Hamish shook himself. "I'll be fine." He dusted off his sherwani and refastened the toggles, subtly rubbing at the point on his chest where Onella had grabbed him. "Think I might be sporting a bald patch for a while, though. She has quite the grip."

Guilt twisted Darshan's stomach. *I knew we shouldn't have come here.* He should've listened to his own feelings on the matter rather than deferring to Hamish's wishes. It was one thing to be reckless with his own life, but risking his husband's—and all on a whim—was another matter.

"I thought you were nae going to notice."

"It was a mistake to come here." Granted, there would be more rumours flying if he had stayed away than if anyone had spied Onella molesting his husband, but he could've weathered that. "We are leaving."

His husband remained silent, seemingly considering it.

Then Hamish breathed deep and shook his head. "Your half-sister cannae actually harm you, right? Nae if it can be traced back to her?" He waited only for Darshan to give a curt nod before continuing, "And the same protection goes for your spouse?"

"Clearly, that does not exclude her from other methods." The thought that she would even attempt to go as far as she had hadn't ever crossed his mind. "She does all of this just to get a rise out of me, to test my weaknesses for when our father finally passes on." Their truce stood only until Darshan took the throne. Then, Onella would attack. Just as she had promised for so many years.

Hamish tipped his head to one side. He eyed the crowd. Could he spot her? His height did put him head and shoulders above most. "She *did* seem a tad disappointed in your reaction. I think she was expecting something a wee bit more dramatic than a brotherly growl."

"Such as me storming out?" Yes, he could see how she would twist that little display. "But this is different. You were molested." And if she dared such again, she would get far more than a few harsh words.

"Say we leave. Then what?"

Darshan shrugged. "We head back to the imperial estate. Leave via lakeship in the morning." It was no different to what they had planned.

"More like hide and run," Hamish mumbled, shaking his head. "We're here. Our presence has been marked by all."

Darshan inclined his head. "That it has been." Whoever hadn't heard the initial announcement of his arrival would've definitely become aware of his presence during his little dance with Hamish. "I am not exactly flouncing off in a huff. Nor was the act a suggestion. We are leaving."

"Why would I give her the satisfaction of seeing me dash off with me tail between me legs?"

He laid a hand on Hamish's arm, gripping it reassuringly. "No one will think—"

"Your Crystal Court will. I'll be labelled as weak. A poor spouse for their *uris Mhanek*." He frowned at the crowd. "But a perfect target for *them*. Tell me that's nae the truth."

Darshan opened his mouth to deny it all. The words balanced on the tip of his tongue, the lie not quite willing to be said. When it came to magic, Hamish *was* weak. There was nothing to be gained in denying the simple facts. "I would never consider you as a poor husband."

Hamish gave a curt nod. "We're staying." He jerked his shoulders back, readjusting his sherwani. "I'll be all right, so long as she stays out of me way."

"It is your choice. If you wish to, we shall stay. Do not worry about her, she has been warned." She could choose to retaliate further, but it would be a foolish gesture now Darshan was fully alert. "If you insist on staying, then allow me to introduce you to Madam Hedgewitch Katarina. And I think there might be a few counts that—"

The meal gong sounded somewhere beyond the ballroom entrance.

In the sudden stillness of the ballroom, the tinny echo of the gong was swiftly replaced by the scurrying pad of feet before a figure appeared in the doorway. The man remained at the top of the stairs, clasping both gong and hammer to his chest. "My lords and ladies, my most humble of apologies in interrupting your enjoyment, but you are humbly requested to adjoin to the dining hall for—"

"Dinner!" Onella declared, the word echoing off the ceiling. "I do hope everyone's hungry." She beamed in their direction as if the last few moments hadn't transpired. "Especially you, brother dear, I had them cook your favourite."

No doubt laced with toxic delights. Forcing an amicable smile, Darshan inclined his head in acknowledgement before escorting his husband across the dance floor. Just as well they had agreed on staying, for leaving now would be a high insult. One that Onella would take great delight in using to chip away at any allegiances to himself.

Just a few hours. It would be necessary to sit through a few dinner courses and mingle whilst a little light entertainment was struck up. Then they could leave this place, and his half-sister, far behind.

Chapter 5

Hamish's stomach offered up a small grumble. He had eaten a fair bit back in the imperial estate, but the scent of roast bird—orange-glazed quail stuffed with garlic and crab set upon a bed of vegetables—was definitely working its way towards convincing his stomach that there was enough room for a nibble here and there.

Cannae touch. Darshan had been explicit on that fact. The food was piled high because the cooks also expected to be feeding any remaining morsels to other slaves. It didn't matter that neither Darshan nor himself had one at their side.

It had been the same for the other courses the servants plonked before them. The first had been a brown soup pungent with spices Hamish couldn't identify. Two courses of seafood had followed; half-shelled raw oysters, then a selection of whitebait and eel fritters.

On his right, Darshan remained stoic. His face had grown progressively stiffer with each course and his manner had turned cool. If Hamish didn't already know his husband's true nature, he would've been forgiven for thinking the *vris Mhanek* was an aloof man prone only to bursts of anger.

In the face of this course, Darshan kept his hands in his lap, clutching each other as if he was afraid they might act on their own accord. He hadn't even laid a finger on the array of forks and knives gracing either side of the plate.

The tables were laid out in one massive circle, following the shape of the room. Three young men danced in the corral the tables made. The candlelight gleamed off their oiled and sparsely clothed bodies as their limbs swayed and bent along to the soft music. The flowing movements halted only in the time it took for them to refill a noble's drink.

Darshan sat on one side of the circle with Onella and her husband directly opposite. She watched them through each course, almost disappointed neither Hamish nor Darshan had touched the food.

Such control wasn't echoed in other guests.

A young blond noblewoman seated halfway down the arc at Hamish's left had devoured each course as though her life depended on it, leaving little more than crumbs. She would mumble between mouthfuls, her words too soft to carry over the room's general chatter.

Her father occupied the seat next to her and had already apologised for his daughter's greediness whilst admonishing her. She seemed to pay it no mind beyond wrinkling her nose and carrying on in a dogged manner. Even knowing how spellsters consumed a great deal more than the average man, Hamish couldn't imagine where she was putting all the food. It was harder to tell seeing only the upper part of her torso, but she seemed short and solid. Perhaps her legs were hollow.

"Adya," her father groaned during a lull in the chatter. "*Please.* This is unseemly even for you. What of your new charge?"

The woman glanced over her shoulder at the equally young man standing close by. He was elven, like most of the slaves brought by the guests, and showed little in the way of expression. Hamish couldn't quite decide if the man had been brought here to look pretty or as added protection.

"I made sure he ate a proper meal before we left," Adya declared, her voice pitched to carry. "Am I expected to do *that?*" She gestured at the people sitting at the arc of tables across from her.

Hamish couldn't help follow the direction of her knife to where a lord was busily stuffing food into the portly face of an elven man. The slave, the flesh of his neck bulging around his collar, continued to scoff down the food being fed to him even though he looked ready to vomit.

Digging his fingers into the arms of his chair, Hamish turned his attention elsewhere. Although he had limited experience with elves— and that familiarity being with the few amongst the Tirglasian royal guard—he knew it took a lot of food to pile any sort of weight on their typically lean frames. For the poor man to be that rotund, his master had to be force-feeding him practically every day.

His gaze settled on the hedgewitch, Katarina. She had introduced herself on the way to the dining room and now sat a few seats down, chatting to everyone within earshot about all manner of topics. She paused between courses to scribble away in a little book, seemingly cataloguing what others said. Her meals lay half-eaten, a thoughtful frown furrowing her brows.

Hamish had met a hedgewitch just the once. *Years ago.* Back when he was still a teenager and delusional in thinking his mother wouldn't retaliate in response to him lying with a man if said man's duties had him lingering only briefly.

Looking at it from years of experience with her toxic behaviour, he had been such a fool. And lucky his fumbling hadn't led to a feud with the dwarves.

"Your highness," Katarina said in a clear address to himself. "I hear you've travelled through imperial lands for some months. What is your current outlook on it?" Although she spoke Udynean, the musical hint of her own language whispered through. A much softer melody than the last hedgewitch Hamish had met.

He swallowed the wine and considered the past eight weeks of travel from the distant port of Haalabof to here, of the seemingly endless roads winding along the lands and the villages small enough to barely warrant a mention on a map. "It has certainly been an experience." He'd been propositioned at least seven times along the way. Maybe even more that had been too subtle for him to notice.

The hedgewitch's eyes almost sparkled. "You simply must give me details, your highness. It's so rare to have an outside opinion on Udynea."

Hamish opened his mouth, his agreement balancing on his tongue, only to remain silent as Darshan laid a bejewelled hand atop his.

"I'm sure my husband is most eager to oblige the request, Madam Hedgewitch, but perhaps another time would be more suited?"

Her lashes fluttering, Katarina lowered her head. "Of course, *vris Mhanek*." She picked at the rest of her meal, perhaps looking for a reason to remain silent as she vibrated with an energy that reminded Hamish of his nephews when they sorely wanted to natter people's ears off.

A pang of longing turned his stomach. A yearning to embrace his sisters, to hear his nephews scheming and his niece's laughter. He would even take his brother's good-natured ribbing just for a chance to hear his voice.

Hamish swallowed, blinking furiously to stem the tears threatening to spill. He hadn't expected to feel homesick, but he'd never been beyond Tirglas before, hadn't even been more than a week's travel from Mullhind Castle for years. Now it was months away and there was more land to cover before they reached their destination.

A whole continent between him and his family; people he would never get to see again thanks to his mother's poisonous ire.

"Do eat up, brother dear," Onella purred, jolting Hamish from his thoughts. His sister-in-law gestured to the plate before Darshan, the rings adorning her fingers glittering in the candlelight. She had changed gowns, or at least the filmy topmost layer, and her arm showed no sign of Darshan's attack. "All that dancing must've worked up quite the appetite. I can't imagine the poxy inns you've stopped at during your travels had meals sufficient for a man of your power. You must be ravenous."

Darshan smiled. Hamish wasn't sure how his husband managed to seemingly detach the expression from his face, but the sight prickled his skin. "I think I'll pass, dear half-sister."

"But isn't quail your favourite?" Onella pressed. "Did all those stodgy meals up north affect your palate?" She leant closer to one of the men flanking her and continued on in a loud whisper. "I hear they do ghastly things like stuff sheep stomachs and eat them."

"They do indeed," Katarina piped up as grumbles of distaste trembled along the table. "And the stomachs of cows and pigs."

"There's little from an animal we dinnae eat or use," Hamish added, ferocious pride for his homeland's self-sufficiency puffing his chest. "And what's left goes to feed our dogs and pigs. We dinnae let a thing go to waste."

"Clearly, trade relations with a superior people isn't listed as one of those things." Onella sipped at her wine, her gaze boring into him. "But I suppose you're not privy to such matters, being dead and all."

A woman part way down the table flung her head back and guffawed.

"He seems very lively for a dead man," pointed out the woman sitting next to her as her neighbour continued to wheeze.

"Clearly not in the literal sense," Onella said, her gaze remaining firmly on Hamish. "But it would seem that the news of how the current queen of Tirglas disowned her younger son hasn't reached all present company."

Darshan straightened in his chair. "Has it not?" He took up his glass and tapped his forefinger against it, waiting whilst a servant topped up the wine. "What is the rumour mill coming to if it cannot keep up with such trivial concerns?"

Onella briefly pressed her lips together before a forced smile took them. "Well, if no one else is going to eat," she said, swiftly changing the topic. "I guess..." She motioned for the waiting servants to take the plates, just as she had done for the last three courses.

Hamish bowed his head, his grip on the chair arms tightening. *Slaves, nae servants*, he reminded himself. The collars adorning each neck might've been polished to shine prettily enough in the candlelight, but it did nothing to hide their true nature. These men and women were her property.

His husband silently laid a hand on his forearm. Darshan knew how he felt about this rotten part of the Udynea Empire. That he hated how engrained it was, how indifferent everyone acted about it and, most importantly, how he couldn't do a bloody thing to change it. He could feel his complacency slipping at times, especially the longer he travelled the empire. He would not become the same as these nobles and forget how these people didn't have the most basic of freedoms.

"I'll just take a nibble," insisted a nobleman halfway down the table before the lanky man standing at his elbow could take his food. "Aarav—" He giggled, grinning up at the man. "I mean *my slave* is going to need the energy. Aren't you, dear?" The nobleman ran his hand along the side of his slave's hip as the man murmured his agreement.

"Shameful," muttered the elderly man sitting the closest to Hamish's left. He eyed the loud-mouthed nobleman, sniffing into his napkin, as one by one, the rest of the seated party abandoned their meals to their slaves.

One of Onella's slaves removed the full plate from before Hamish. The man's eyes never strayed from the food, even as he daintily popped one of the carrot slivers into his mouth. Had she starved these people for them to look so ravenous?

Hamish forced himself to stare straight ahead, to not acknowledge their hostess or risk giving in to the temptation to strangle her. How could he do this? How did the Goddess expect him to witness this injustice every day and not retaliate?

The distinct smash of a plate hitting tiles whipped Hamish's head around.

A figure stood bent over in the doorway, clutching at their throat even as they fell to their knees.

Hamish stood, slowly as if in a dream. It was the man who had taken his meal. He was choking as if—

A scream erupted from the adjoining room. "My lady!" A woman raced through the doorway, neatly skirting the gasping man, to kneel at Onella's. "Save him," she wailed. "Please, he—"

Darshan had already vacated his seat. He strode to the gasping slave's side, reaching it before the man could finish collapsing. Steadying the man, Darshan laid a hand on the close-shaved scalp. Their heads bowed, almost touching.

Hamish settled into his seat as his husband's eyes closed. He knew that look; the determined furrow of Darshan's brow, the stubborn set of his jaw. He had seen it one time too many during his husband's ambassadorial stay in Tirglas.

He was healing the man. He would do a bloody good job of it, too.

Darshan's head snapped up once the deed was done, his face tight and flushed with rage. Hamish had witnessed that expression once, thankfully not directed at himself. There could be only one thing that could've affected the ailing man and anger his husband so thoroughly.

Poison.

Clutching the chair arms, Hamish pressed deeper into the back of his seat. The wood offered a faint creak of protest. *Me food.* The man had eaten only a small portion, barely a bite, and had succumbed before leaving the room.

If *he* had actually eaten it?

"You," Darshan growled, levelling a finger at his half-sister. Shimmers of heat radiated from the hand. "You *dare?*"

Onella flattened a hand upon her bosom. Shock and indignance widened her eyes and caused her mouth to gape like a stunned fish. She glanced in Hamish's direction, no doubt gauging his reaction to the attempt on his life.

Hamish faced the look with all the courage he could muster. The Goddess knew it wasn't much. Had this always been her goal? Or a backup once her poor attempt at seducing him had failed?

"You think *I* did this?" she hissed, bouncing to her feet. "How dare *you* accuse me of such a crass display." She tipped her head back with a sniff. "I am utterly insulted, brother dear, that you would think I could ever do such a shoddy job of it. Or that I would put my own slaves in harm's way. You ought to be ashamed. Your time in Tirglas must've addled your brains if you think I would risk them over something so trifling as a husband. I have greater concerns beyond where you moor."

Darshan bit out a few curses in what had to be Ancient Domian by the way much of the nobility gasped.

Onella merely offered another sniff. "There's no call for that language."

"Fetch Zahaan," Darshan ordered of the closest servant, who scuttled away as if his life depended on speed. Hamish couldn't be certain it didn't, his husband looked primed for murder.

The mention of Zahaan seemed to perk Onella's interest. "If you think I'm going to let your spymaster have unrestricted access to my mansion, you—" She turned to glare at her husband as he prodded her into silence.

"I'm sure we're all concerned as to who dared to attempt this vile act," Count Aagney said. Standing, he gave Darshan a deep bow. "All our resources are at your immediate disposal, *vris Mhanek*. In the meantime..." He waved his hand. "Please, dear guests, let us retire to the solarium whilst we wait for the *vris Mhanek's* good man to aid in the unsnarling of this unfortunate event. After all, we are the heads of an empire. How could we call ourselves such if we allow one little failure sully the evening?"

"An excellent idea, husband mine," Onella said, swiftly standing to take control. "I shall send for proper refreshments and a few of my favourite singing boys."

One by one, the nobles vacated their seats to follow like dazed ducklings after Onella and her husband.

Hamish slowly stood, his back feeling awfully exposed as thoughts of shadowy assassin's raced through his mind. They were never a thing he had to worry over in Tirglas. Not when it came to himself and not since his childhood.

What else could they throw at him? They had to know of their failure. Would that make them desperate or look to reassess their method? Would they have the courage to try with everyone on edge?

He squared his shoulders, doing his level best to keep his hesitance from showing. He fiddled with the edge of his shawl, the silk cool against his fingers. Mimicking the pose Darshan had effortlessly struck took some effort. *Strong. Confident.* Whatever his attempted killers tried, they wouldn't dare for a while.

"Your highness," Katarina called. She hastened to his side as he paused, cupping her hand in the crook of his arm. "Perhaps you've time to indulge me in your travels whilst we wait for the *vris Mhanek's* man?"

Hamish glanced his husband's way, hoping to catch the man's eye.

Darshan gave a barely perceptible flick of his fingers—little more than the glitter of light across his rings—before his focus returned to the man he had healed. A signal to carry on without him.

Of course Darshan would want to stay and monitor his newest patient. He took every attempt on someone's life as a personal affront. It would also keep him close enough to stop anyone from doing away with the man should he know anything.

Laying a companionable hand on the hedgewitch's shoulder, Hamish smiled. "I can tell you a wee tale or two on the way and, if the singing's nae too loud, a few more once we're settled again."

His gaze slid past her face to the man still hunched over on all fours before Darshan. *That could've been me.* He'd really have to watch what he ate for the rest of the night.

Katarina patted his hand, the attempt of a smile stretching her lips. "If you're not feeling up to it..." she said in near-perfect Tirglasian.

He shook his head. "Thank you," he responded in kind, "but I'm feeling well enough." Despite being the target, it hadn't been him who'd suffered a poisoning.

Clearing his throat, he wondered where to begin the tale of his travels to Nulshar. At the beginning of his journey across Udynea seemed the best place.

"Are you familiar with Port Haalabof?" he asked of the

hedgewitch, returning smoothly to the Udynean tongue and ensuring his voice carried enough to tweak the ears of certain stragglers. The more they thought of him as a witless oaf, the easier it would be to catch a crook unawares.

"I know of the place," she assured him. "But I can't say I've ever had a reason to venture that far."

He nodded. The port city was the closest to the border of Obuzan, the empire's oldest enemy. "They've *kofe* houses even all the way up there." He chuckled as she screwed up her face. "By your expression, I dinnae need to ask if you've had it before."

She wrinkled her nose further, the tip of her tongue poking out in disgust. He didn't need any more of an answer than that.

"It's nae a taste I've acquired either." He could be persuaded when the brew was more sugar than *kofe*, but even then, the bitterness crept along his tongue. How Niholians managed to drink the stuff on a daily basis was beyond him.

He continued talking of their jaunt through Haalabof and the sights he had witnessed. The stragglers slowly encircled them in an unthreatening manner. A few murmured as he spoke, gentle corrections or agreements. Their pace slowed the closer they got to the solarium. Most seemed reluctant to actually reach it.

By the time they entered the room, he was on his fourth story involving a barely dressed dancer who insisted he could touch his toes to his head, except his little-left-to-the-imagination trousers kept trying to leave even less to the mind's eye whenever he attempted the act.

Hamish halted in the doorway, stepping further into the room only because of Katarina's gentle tug on his arm. The solarium was easily thrice the size of the one back in Castle Mullhind, its roundness adding to the illusion. He had expected large windows, or a long panel of them such as was in the imperial estate, but the walls were entirely made of glass with thin supports linking the huge curving panels.

The candlelight obscured a lot of the view beyond the glass, bouncing their reflections across all surfaces, but he caught the shadows of trees swaying against the night sky.

His gaze swept by Onella, pausing upon realising she stared back like an enraged boar. Between his mother and Darshan, Hamish thought he had witnessed the full range of stewing anger, but this was a look that didn't wish for his death so much as demanded it.

Giving her a small bow of his head in acknowledgement, he settled in a wicker chair and returned to his tales—this time, of their journey through a little place called Oldunmere and the tavern's bard who'd been so far gone in her drink that getting it into her head that neither of them were interested had taken some convincing.

Movement coming from the entrance drew his attention for a breath. A bunch of young men—in their early teenage years if that— entered the room. Were these the singing boys?

With no introduction, the group scuttled over from the doorway to sit upon a pile of cushions propped against the glass window.

"Finally," Onella said, giving the group a stern look that had an odd motherly fondness to its edges. "As amusing as his highness' anecdotes have been, I'm sure we're all ready for some entertainment that's a little more appropriate to such a refined audience." She smiled sweetly at him.

Hamish returned the expression, waving his hand in a mimic of Darshan's magnanimous gesture for her to continue. Seeing her face darken was worth the extra ire she was sure to foster for him.

She composed herself quickly, turning to her singing boys and ordering them to begin.

The boys' voices were light and harmonised just enough for Hamish to make out the words. It sounded like a folktale. One Darshan hadn't acquainted him with.

Perhaps he could get his husband to. Most attempts to learn of the empire and her people had Darshan handing over a book and leaving him to it when Hamish would've preferred his husband reading the relevant passages to him. Not that he hadn't made an effort to learn the written language. But it was harder to keep the words from wandering—more so than Tirglasian—and he still struggled in reading it for more than a few words at a time.

Relieved of their previous entertainment, the crowd dispersed into smaller groups to gossip away. It also had the blissful effect of leaving Hamish alone. At least for a short spell as Count Aagney settled next to him with a weary sigh.

The man stared out at the gathering with all the energy of a grandsire although he was a year shy of Hamish's thirty-four years. "Can I ask a favour of you, your highness?"

"You can ask," he replied, knowing better than to leave the question at a nod as he had so often done back home.

"Please. *Please.*" He laid a hand on his chest, clutching the heavy embroidery at the front. "For the good of my heart and the sake of my sanity, convince your husband to have a child. Several. And *soon.*"

Hamish chuckled. Of all the things he expected of the man, *that* hadn't been on the list. "I take it you and your lady wife dinnae see eye to eye on a few wee matters?"

More people filed through the entrance bearing trays of glass goblets and jugs of what looked to be more pale wine. No sign of Darshan. What was holding his husband up? Should he be worried?

Aagney smoothed down the front of his outfit. "Not all of us are so willing to toss aside the natural order of things. But I fear my wife might do something foolish if left to her own devices for too long." He glanced into the crowd and grimaced, although Hamish saw nothing awry. "Excuse me, your highness. It would seem I have dallied too long at your side." Standing once more, he bowed low to Hamish and strode to his wife's side.

Onella was back to giving Hamish that murderous look.

"A glass of *sebzahaa*, my lord?" piped up a small voice at his elbow.

Hamish twisted to find a young elven boy standing beside him. The boy carried a tray of glass goblets. Candlelight glittered along the gold running around the goblet's rim and the chain adorning the boy's neck. *A slave collar.* It was studded with gems and delicately wrought in silver, but the little label at his throat made him no less free than those Hamish had seen bound by leather and iron.

The boy offered up a smile that sat woodenly on his face. His gaze dropping, he lifted the tray. "*Sebzahaa?*" he repeated, his voice warbling on the last syllable. His gaze seemed uncertain of where to settle, darting from Hamish's face to the crowd, the floor and back up.

Hamish took one of the goblets, gingerly grasping the stem. It felt so fine beneath his fingers that he feared the glass might snap if held any tighter. He eyed the liquid within; a cloudy, pale yellow like year-old hay. *Sebzahaa.* Whilst the latter part of the word eluded him, *seb* meant apple in the common Udynean tongue. He breathed deep and, sure enough, the sweet aroma of fruit tickled his senses. Cider, then?

"I see we're back to immersing ourselves in the festivities," Darshan said, halting at his side. "And so soon after someone made an attempt on your life, poorly executed as it was. It seems we'll make a Udynean out of you yet." His gaze fastened onto the goblet and the faint hint of a smile curling his mouth froze. "Have you consumed any of that?"

"Nae yet," Hamish admitted, raising the rim of the glass to his lips. He nodded at the servant as the boy melded into the crowd. "He called it *sebzahaa*. That's cider, right?" He went to take a sip.

Darshan gently lowered the goblet with a single finger on the rim of the glass. "I would not drink that if you value your life," he murmured in Tirglasian. "I would say it is indeed cider, but do you not remember what *zahaa* means?"

Struggling to find the translation, his thoughts flashed to the elven man Darshan had summoned. The word was close enough to Zahaan's name. On the other hand, the man's name could've come from another language, maybe even the elven one, and mean something entirely different. "Strong?" he guessed.

His husband sighed. "Any drink ending with *zahaa* indicates that it is poisoned."

First his food, now the cider. "Why would they tell me that?" What of the other drinks he had imbibed during his time here?

"Because the people drinking it are not actually looking to die. Announcing that it is poison allows those who do not wish to take the risk a chance to refuse. Why on my way back, I heard Lady Adhira refused a glass and she's always hunting for chances to show off her healing prowess." He peered into the crowd, that half-smile returning. "I dare say she looks a little plumper than the last time I saw her, too. Strong possibility she is pregnant despite no announcement."

"You almost sound happy about that."

"I will be if I am right. Poor woman has gone through three husbands trying to get an heir for her family's estate."

Hamish eyed his drink. "If people dinnae want to drink poison—" And he couldn't see why anyone would want to. "—then why make a poisoned drink specifically for people to do that?"

His husband gave a soft gasp of mirth. "Because it is fashionable and designed to display one's healing abilities." He plucked the goblet from Hamish's fingers and drained the contents in one long swallow. "The length of time taken to remedy a poison's damage is meant to prove one's—" He grimaced for a moment, the veins on his forehead bulging alarmingly, then everything seemed normal again.

"Idiocy?" Hamish finished.

Coughing and thumping his chest, Darshan flashed him a smile. "I was going to say magical prowess, but your reason is just as true. Doing dangerous things and seeing how unscathed you come out the other end of it is almost a sport." He raised the glass, inspecting the small amount of cider resting in the bottom of the goblet. "Given my half-sister's penchant for dangerous creatures, I would hazard a guess that this particular toxin comes from the flesh of a Stamekian spiny fish whose name translates as *one-bite death*. Nasty stuff. Just a mouthful of its flesh induces paralysis within the half-hour. Although, there've been stories of people lasting a whole day."

Was that what had been in his food? If the poison used was already in the kitchen, tracking just who was responsible wouldn't be as clean-cut as he originally thought. "Has your man found anything?"

"The venom of the Niholian hooded asp was popular when I left," Darshan continued with the shake of his head, his voice loud enough to still the closer gossiping groups. "It wouldn't have killed you, not through consumption, but a bite from one would've had you vomiting until you stop breathing within the first minute." He smacked his lips. "Had an interesting flavour, if I recall correctly. Better than this oily aftertaste. Although, I don't suppose you have snakes in Tirglas. Too cold."

"We've snakes," he drawled, trying to follow his husband's aversion of an answer. The snakes back in Tirglas were little ones that largely made a nuisance of themselves when they popped up during the summer and autumn months to hunt field mice. "Their bites cannae kill a man, though."

Darshan eyed him from the edge of his glasses, one brow twitching. "Surely a few have found their mark? Or perhaps I was misinformed of their lethality. Did they not have your people fleeing some years back? To hide between the old yews?"

Hamish frowned at his husband. What was Darshan on about? "Yews?" he echoed flatly. There were a great deal of them around Mullhind with the couple marking the forest run behind the castle being the eldest of the bunch. They had been the starting point of the second trial for Hamish's hand.

His question earned him another twitch of Darshan's brow and a flattening of his lips.

Those yew trees had also been where a distant ancestor of Hamish's had fled to after his family had been slaughtered. What did that have to do with snakes? The attack had been a collection of rogue clans and—

An assassination. One of the few in Tirglas' history.

By the look on Darshan's face, he had given away just where his mind had gone and, apparently, had arrived at the conclusion his husband was hinting at.

"Aye," he mumbled. "But it's rare for them to be found in Tirglas, let alone get as far as the castle."

"Truly?" He returned to examining the glass. "So you've no intimate experience in dealing with one?"

Snakes, yes. Assassins? "Nae really."

Disappointment wrinkled Darshan's nose and narrowed his eyes. A smidgeon of worry furrowed his brow.

Hamish wished he could've said otherwise, but if they really were talking about assassins, then lying would only see him dead that much quicker.

Shaking himself out of whatever dark thoughts plagued his mind, Darshan beamed up at him. "We shall have to remedy that once we reach Minamist."

They mingled with the rest of the guests, Darshan barely saying a word as the other party blithely chatted away. Hamish had always hated this part of any formal gathering. Back home, he would've pardoned himself with the excuse of too much drink. Sadly, the liquor on offer here was either poisoned or weak. But there was a lot of it.

Eventually, their trip around the solarium took them to a table where three women and a man played some sort of dice game.

Claiming the remaining chairs, Hamish tried to focus on the game in the hopes of learning the rules, but a far more pressing matter was making itself known. He bounced his leg, trying to ignore the urge.

Darshan laid a hand on Hamish's other knee. "Is something wrong, *mea lux?*"

Heat flooded to his cheeks. He hadn't needed to ask about the privy since he was a lad of four years. "I've had... I cannae even count how many... drinks since I got here." Coupled with the lack of further food—beyond a few squares of those powdered, gelatinous cubes that Darshan liked to gobble down with his evening cup of *kofe*—his bladder was not at all happy with him.

"Yes? And?" Comprehension swiftly rounded his husband's mouth. He clicked his fingers, summoning a balding human to their side. Darshan gestured for the thin man to bend close and whispered in his ear before addressing Hamish. "This is one of Zah's men. He'll show you the way."

The man turned to Hamish and bowed. He bore no markings that signified any ownership or loyalties; no collar or insignia. "Follow me, your highness."

Chapter 6

Hamish eyed the privy walls as he washed his hands, trying to spy where the pipes would be. Most of the places he had come across displayed them with something akin to pride, especially when they'd any option other than cold. But there was only dark wood panelling and a massive mirror.

If there was one thing from Udynea he could take back to Tirglas, it would be indoor plumbing. The ability to turn a tap and get not only running water, but for it to be *warm*, was unheard of. Much nicer than giving himself a quick scrubbing in freezing water.

Not that Tirglas didn't have the means to transport water, but there was only so much a hand pump funnelling directly from the source could do. It certainly couldn't turn icy water into something hot enough for a good soak.

It wasn't the same throughout the Udynea Empire. The outposts between villages and the smaller inns they'd spent the night at didn't all have these luxuries on hand—some were lucky to have indoor plumbing at all—but the presence of taps had become more common the further south they travelled. Enough for Hamish to see them as ordinary.

The toilet itself had been another matter. He hadn't come across anything more than seats with a hole for the chamber pot during their travels. This had been different, and not just because the bowl already had clear water in it. It had taken a bit of speculating on his part—largely via tracking the gilded pipe up from the bowl—and curiosity to realise the pull chain jutting from the box sitting near the ceiling was meant to flush everything away in a roar of water.

Drying his hands, Hamish glanced in the mirror at the box's reflection. It had stopped emitting little gurgles and blubs just a short time back. Did that mean it had filled up again? A cheeky little part of him itched to pull the chain and find out. The reasonable part stayed his hand and had him vacating the room.

He paused in the doorway, barely registering the body sprawled in the hall, before diving back into the room. Whether the man was dead or merely unconscious, he didn't waste time with checking. It meant the same thing.

Slamming the door shut, he searched the room for something to defend himself. Toilet. Sink. Bucket. A stack of clean towels and a hamper of used ones... No cabinets to rummage through. The walls had nothing on offer, being bare except for a mirror half the size of the door.

Bucket? He stepped away from the wall. Yes, there was one in the far corner, near the hamper. Metal and empty.

He grabbed it, testing the weight. It had some heft. Lobbing a bucket at his attacker would grant him one shot. At best, it would serve as a distraction. *Nae exactly ideal.* But if doing so saw him out of the immediate area, then it was better than nothing.

You won't last a week. Onella's words echoed through his mind. If he was going to survive in this world, he needed to learn how to tread through it. And he wouldn't be able to do that whilst hiding in a privy. He knew the way back to the solarium. Darshan could take it from there.

Flattening himself against the wall beside the door, he listened for any sign of someone on the other side. Had they seen him about to exit a moment ago? Did they know he was alert to their presence? Were they patiently waiting for him to show himself? They didn't seem keen on coming in after him. That spoke of wanting to keep their identity secret.

How long would it take for Darshan to notice he hadn't returned? Could he perhaps wait out his attacker?

Cannae risk it. They might be patient, and currently complacent, but if Hamish chose to hunker down for any sort of prolonged stay in here, then it could make his attacker wary. And an alert spellster would blast him at the slightest hint of movement.

Or maybe they wouldn't wait for a sign at all and choose to set the whole room ablaze.

The wall at his back suddenly seemed a lot less solid. If he was going to make a run for it, it would have to be now.

He opened the door. A figure stood on his left. A woman.

Hamish hurled the bucket at her and took off in the other direction. The surprised, and enraged, yelp chased him as he skidded around the first corner he found. As long as he kept out of direct line of sight, he'd be safe. More-or-less.

Trying to keep his breathing steady, he jogged down this new hallway. Most of the noblewomen didn't look all that fit—none of them would've been able to physically match his sisters—and his longer stride would be enough to keep him well ahead of his attacker.

The space between his shoulder blades prickled. Just like that time the man-eating bear had snuck up on him. Something was behind him. And gaining.

Hamish threw himself against the wall, barely missing being hit by the woman as she blew by.

The flare of lush silk and jewels glittered as Onella spun on her heel. Murderous rage widened her eyes and contorted her face, which still bore the impact of the bucket. "*You,*" she snarled. Something gleamed in her hand; a thick needle-like object. A hairpin? She brandished it as though it was a dagger. "You think a magicless fool like you could outrun me?" She dove for him, her arm raised.

He grabbed her wrist, straining to keep the pin from his skin. Whatever its original use, she clearly meant to use if for harm. "I thought you were nae interested in killing me," he growled, gritting his teeth in his effort to keep her in place.

How could she be this strong? She had to be bolstering herself with magic. That wouldn't last long, not if she wanted to avoid tearing herself apart. He just needed to hold out until then to have the physical upper edge.

"That was before." She flexed her fingers, trying to loosen her grip on the pin.

Hamish closed his hand around hers. If she managed to grasp the pin with her magic, he wouldn't stand a chance at dodging it. "Dinnae do this, lass." He fumbled for the pin. If he could wrest it from her grip, then it would be one less threat to deal with. "Think of your son."

"My son?" she snarled. "I think of nothing else. I do this for him. I do everything for him. I have already waited too long, sacrificed everything. I'm not about to let some backwater savage prince upset my plans. I won't let you take the throne from him."

The build-up of powerful magic tingled across his skin. Did that mean someone else was near? Or was she keeping her full power in reserve, ready to change tactics? Battling his strength against her magically bolstered power was one thing. Fighting a magical battle? Impossible.

The thin film of a shield stuttered around him. He forced it down. He couldn't deflect much with it, even after months of practising with Darshan to summon the barrier at will. Right now, it would be more hindrance than help.

Onella's eyes narrowed. "You *do* have magic," she hissed, jerking her head forward until their noses touched. Unbridled rage seethed in her eyes—hazel like Darshan's, if not as vibrant. "A weakling specialist. You're not fit to be the sire of a future heir. You're barely worthy as a toy."

Hamish quashed the urge to throttle her. His worth wasn't up for debate. Darshan had already chosen him. No matter what anyone else thought, his husband saw him as worthy enough to fight for. That was all Hamish cared about. "The throne isnae your son's to have anymore than it's yours to give. To him or anyone. Do you really think your father will let him inherit a thing if you kill your brother's spouse?"

"He doesn't have to allow anything. He's old. Once he's gone, with you out of the way and my brother dead, it'll come down to the eldest living male in the line. That *will* be my son."

Shimmering tendrils of purple light wrapped around her torso before he could think of a response. The coils bound her, tearing her from his grasp.

The pin bounced onto the carpeted floor.

"You *dare?*" Darshan's voice boomed along the corridor.

Hamish snatched up the pin before Onella could regain her wits, careful to keep himself from being pricked. He wasn't about to give her the satisfaction of succeeding in her goal, even if Darshan was close at hand.

"I gave you a chance to extract yourself from this," Darshan continued, storming down the hallway. Magic flared around him in arcing sparks and wisps. The tendrils confining Onella writhed from his hand like a nest of snakes. "And you *dare?*" The purple light flashed the glowing red of embers.

Onella drew her shoulders back. Pain danced in her eyes. It pinched her nostrils and clenched her jaw.

"My brains must be addled?" Darshan growled, echoing the retort she had flung at him only an hour ago. "I suppose I must be seeing things here, too." The tendrils no longer flashed purple, but seethed a gory red shade.

Smoke drifted up from Onella's dress. The stench of singed flesh and silk invaded Hamish's nose.

No more than a huff escaped her lips. Sweat trickled down her face and her body trembled, but she remained stoic.

"Stop," Hamish demanded, swinging about to face Darshan.

His husband stared at him incredulously. "She attacked you. *Again*. That demands retribution."

"Aye." Even though he had come to no harm, he couldn't afford anyone to think they could attack him and face no charges. "But nae like this. And you should definitely nae be the one to give the punishment." With only the three of them around, it would be their word against hers should she bring it up with the *Mhanek*. Having never met the man, Hamish still wasn't quite sure what sort of person his father-by-marriage was beyond being irrationally lenient to a daughter with clear murderous intentions towards her half-brother.

The tendrils that wove from his husband's fingers to Onella faded to purple as Hamish spoke before disappearing altogether.

A blast of wind whipped past Hamish, clawing at his clothes. It hit Onella and sent the woman tumbling back the way they had come until the wall stopped her. She landed face-first onto the floor and lay still. Alive? She was too far for Hamish to tell.

Darshan grabbed him, turning him back around. "Did she touch you?"

"I'm fine."

"Not an answer. Did she touch you with this?" He snatched the needle from Hamish and waggled it. "A prick? A scratch? Anything?"

Hamish shook his head. It swam. "Maybe," he conceded, feeling Darshan's healing magic washing over him before he could finish the word. He didn't recall the needle piercing him. Maybe it was the kind that didn't need to. "Why? What was it?"

"Poison. She must've realised you've not the same luxury as most spellsters in the court when I stopped you drinking the *sebzahaa*."

"How do you deal with her?"

"Carefully. I didn't expect her to try anything, not after the ordeal with the food. She often retires early, if she even deigns to show to her own soirée, but I spied her slinking out of the solarium and decided to tail her."

"I've nae had people wanting to kill me for a long time." Not since he was a child and certainly never within his own family. "If all your sisters are this opposed to me, then how will I ken which one to look out for?"

"Most of them aren't that direct and the younger ones are, typically, not aggressive without agency. You should be safe within the imperial palace, still... I generally don't trust my older half-siblings and would recommend you take a similar stance." He looked around them, his brows lowering in bafflement. "Where's the man I set to watch you?"

He pointed the way Darshan had slung Onella. "Unconscious."

"You're certain?"

Hamish shrugged. "I didnae exactly have time to check between lobbing a bucket at your sister's head and running for me life."

"You threw *what* at her?" Shaking his head, Darshan pursed his lips and quickened his step. "Never mind. Show me where. There may still be time."

"Left at this corner. You cannae miss him." Hamish peered at Onella as they reached the end of the corridor. Still no movement. She was breathing, at least. "What did you do to her? I've nae seen that sort of magic from you."

"Why would you? I've rarely been given a reason to use it."

"Nae even when you were attacked on our way to the cloister?" Seven men had sought Darshan's death, old guards whose minds were still poisoned by the old scripture's insistence that men who slept with men must die. They believed they were saving Hamish from corruption.

Darshan had slain six single-handedly. And gruesomely, with one immolated and the rest either impaled on jagged constructs or crushed under shattered masonry.

His husband let out a disgusted huff that sounded semi-serious. "I had an arrow in my chest at the time. Forgive me if finesse was not on my mind back then. And what would saving their lives have done other than delay their punishment for attacking my royal personage?" He halted, a small gasp slithering out as Hamish's escort came into view, before rushing to the man's side. He knelt and fussed with the man, no doubt checking for life signs a little more thoroughly than Hamish could ever be able. "He'll live, at least. Although, I don't envy the headache he'll get from Zahaan's disciplining later."

Hamish grunted.

Darshan peered at him from the edge of his glasses. He tried to hide it, tilting his head to obscure his expression

"Is something wrong? Besides the obvious."

Sighing, Darshan stood and adjusted his clothes. "It just occurred to me," he mumbled in Tirglasian. "That you would have been better off had you been born a Nulled One like your brother."

"Because being immune to direct magic would've kept me from being poisoned?"

His husband huffed out his frustrations, the blast disturbing the curls of hair threatening to drape over his glasses. "I suppose you are right there. But as things stand, you have magic... just not enough to protect yourself let alone defend against an earnest attack."

Hamish glanced over his shoulder at Onella's still form. Darshan didn't deem her attempt as earnest?

"It seems that I have taken you from a place where you are closely monitored and constantly escorted only to put you back into that very scenario." Regret clouded his eyes and flattened his mouth.

"I see one big difference." He wrapped an arm around Darshan's waist, drawing them closer together. "Back in Tirglas, I couldnae be with the man I love without fear of being caught, imprisoned in me room and—" His throat tightened. *And the life of that man being shortened.* So many men who dared to touch him had faced that very outcome. "Here? With you by my side? I am definitely better off."

Warmth deepened the wrinkles at the corners of those hazel eyes. "I certainly hope so."

He clasped Darshan's shoulder, squeezing in reassurance. "You'll figure something out. You have so far." They had managed to work within the rules of the union contest and Hamish's obligation to marry the person who won his hand in the trials. They could find a way around this obstacle.

Darshan beamed up at him. "Such faith you put in me, *mea lux.*" He gave another sigh, finally expelling the gloom that weighed him. "You're right. We will. Together." His gaze slid past Hamish and his brows lowered until they brushed the upper edge of his glasses. "And I shall start by dealing with my sister."

~ ~ ~

"You can't do this," Onella shrieked as Darshan continued to tow her down the corridor towards her chambers. She fought his grip, her magic flaring sporadically as she struggled to use it against him. "Putting me under house arrest? *In my own house?* You've not the authority."

"I'm confining you to your quarters," he snarled, jerking her towards the stairway leading to the stately wing and dragging her up when she refused to ascend. He would've preferred to do this with a lot less noise, but she was clearly set on making enough fuss to rouse the dead. "I ought to do worse." He had signed death warrants for lesser transgressions. Their father had ordered far worse punishments. "At the very least, you should be leashed."

Onella clutched at her neck, her eyes narrowing. "You wouldn't dare. Father wouldn't allow it."

"For attacking my husband?" He shook his head. Hopefully, Hamish had reached the upper studies by now. He would be safe and within sight of Zahaan's people. Not that they had managed to do much beyond alerting Hamish of danger. "Do you honestly think my husband didn't fall under the protection of our agreement? That Father would help you gloss over it? *Again?*"

She flinched at that. Did she think he was ignorant of her interference with his love life? Still, she rallied. "You're bringing home a specialist. One who's considered dead by his own mother. Father won't let this stand, you know."

"He will." He would make sure of it. Hamish had already crawled through the underbelly of creation to make it this far, he deserved to live out the rest of his life in blessed peace. Darshan refused to let anything bar his husband's path to that goal.

"And how will you maintain your court when anyone could hold him prisoner?"

"Is that a threat, *venefica*?" he snarled, spitting out the Ancient Domian insult. "You know how Father feels about those."

She wrinkled her nose. "Trust you to use your privileged upbringing to be vulgar. Does that mean it didn't occur to you before you brought him here? Just think, all those times you crowed about having no weaknesses. And here you are, trotting your biggest soft spot through my halls."

"He is not a weakness. And I will maintain my court the same way Father does." It wasn't uncommon for the Nulled Ones to shadow the *Mhanek*, or even himself and his twin. Having them watching over Hamish wouldn't be seen as superfluous.

"He's going to die. The court doesn't suffer fools or weak links. And he's both."

Two of Zahaan's men greeted them at the top of the stairs. They marched onwards to her chambers in silence where he slung Onella through the doorway like an empty saddlebag.

She stumbled a few steps before righting herself and facing him. "How am I supposed to host from here?"

"You should've thought about that beforehand." He stepped back, keeping her in his sights. "Hamish and I are departing. We'll be gone from Nulshar by the morning." He nodded at the guards and, slamming the door shut, turned on his heel. "You'll be free to host all you like then."

The unmistakable cry of a person enjoying themselves in the carnal fashion echoed down the corridor, overpowering his sister's frustrated scream.

Darshan glanced in the direction the sound had originated. *Someone's starting their own festivities early*. At least Hamish waited on the opposite side of the mansion. He would rather have the man back at the imperial estate before the typical orgy half of this soirée began.

A figure detached itself from the shadows as Darshan made his way to the upper studies. "Don't tell me I've just wasted several hours of my night," Zahaan groused, falling into an easy stride with Darshan.

"What did you uncover?" His own search had pulled up nothing beyond the obvious. Darshan hoped the several hours of combing the mansion hadn't been fruitless.

"A handful of new liaisons, an affair that I've filed away for future leverage, several threads of gossip that I shall set the network on confirming—"

"About the poisoning attempt on my husband."

Zahaan halted in the middle of the corridor. His head tilted, the tip of his ears twitching ever so slightly as he listened.

Darshan waited for the man to confirm they were alone. He picked up more cries of pleasure, wails that he couldn't quite tell were of delight or dismay and what felt to be a few magical pulses vibrating the air; no doubt the precursor to some wine-fuelled scrap. How Zahaan could pick out specifics was beyond him, but he had long since given up trying to understand it. It was an elven trait, plain and simple.

Eventually, Zahaan gave a satisfied nod. "I found the woman responsible." There was something about the man's face that spoke of what he had discovered not being satisfactory. "She was already dead. By the signs, the cause was the same poison that was intended for his highness."

"So, Onella *was* to blame." He gnawed at his thumbnail. Even as he spoke, something felt off. His half-sister picked her people so carefully. It just didn't seem like her to throw them away like this. Had his marriage made her *that* desperate?

Zahaan's lack of response drew his attention.

"There's something else, isn't there?" Something the man didn't want to admit.

"The woman's brain showed signs of recent spider web scarring."

Hypnotism. Nothing else could leave its mark on the brain in such a manner. Most likely done to mask the woman's actions from even herself as well as erase any hope of tracking just who else was involved. Or had it been to *give* the order? *Not Onella, then.* Who else? The list of those wanting him dead was a long one. "All right. You know who is in attendance. Tell me which ones might've been able to do it."

"None, as far as I know."

He peered at Zahaan. "As far as you know?" That sort of answer wasn't like his spymaster.

"They don't exactly announce what they're capable of," Zahaan growled before adding a diffident, "*vris Mhanek.*"

Darshan wrinkled his nose. That was true. Outside his close family, and a handful of trusted friends, few knew just how strong he was. "You know I hate it when you call me that," he said by way of apology. They were alone. Or possibly not, if Zahaan had fallen into using the address.

Zahaan chuckled dryly. After three decades in Darshan's presence, the man knew precisely what part of that address Darshan objected to hearing. "You'll have to get used to me saying the word eventually."

Darshan grunted. *One day.* When his father was gone. "What a horrid thing to suggest. Especially when my father has already insisted that he'll live forever." Shaking his head, he looked over his shoulder. A foolish gesture that he swiftly remedied, but all this talk of people being hypnotised into committing murder wasn't how assassination attempts usually worked. "Did anyone see who spoke to the woman before she handled Hamish's food? Someone who wasn't meant to be there?"

"No one. Although..."

Following the man's line of thought, Darshan nodded. Someone could've caught the culprit in the act and had simply been made to forget.

"Onella hasn't the knack for it."

Even though it wasn't a question, Darshan shook his head. Few would have the finesse.

Zahaan eyed him. The man knew the limits of his father's magic just as well as he. "You don't think the *Mhanek* sent her?"

"And implicate his own daughter in the process?" If they'd been on the road or staying in some inn, then it would've been a possibility. But during a soirée hosted by his half-sister? "No. Something else is afoot. Did you interrogate everyone?"

Zahaan bowed his head.

"Good." He returned to making for Hamish, a thread of fear quickening his steps. If the gods had allowed any harm to come to his husband in his absence... "I'm leaving." For the imperial estate now and for Rolshar as soon as their things were packed. He would've preferred to stay until morning, but Nulshar clearly wasn't safe. "I'm on my way to collect Hamish. Have all of your people—and I know you've brought everyone, don't give that innocent look—set up a controlled channel from the upper left wing to the side entrance." Hopefully, Hamish still lingered there.

"And the road to the imperial estate?"

"No." They hadn't the manpower for that as well. "Wait until we're out of the mansion," he amended upon seeing Zahaan's brow furrow.

The man bowed and went to leave to issue his own orders.

He clapped a hand on the elf's shoulder. "Oh, and before I forget entirely. Send out a royal decree to the eastern border. Apparently, the nobles there are scrapping with Demarn again. Remind them that my father is looking for peace and inform them that a hedgewitch is travelling through there in a few months. The way must be cleared."

Zahaan tilted his head, one brow twitching in curiosity. Dwarven studies had been his favourite as a child, just below espionage.

"Consider it done."

He pulled the man in for a hug, ignoring how the body in his embrace stiffened at the contact.

"Darshan?" Uncertainty wavered in Zahaan's voice. He didn't blame the man, physical affection hadn't been a part of their relationship since childhood. Not since the divide between him, the heir to the imperial throne, and Zahaan, a nursemaid's child and slave, had been made clear.

Right now, Darshan didn't care. "I've missed you," he whispered, the words barely a breath. "Missed my eyes and ears. I made such a mess of things in Tirglas."

"I know."

Chuckling, he released his spymaster. "Naturally."

"We'll get to the bottom of this." Determination skewed his lips and lowered his brows. "And quickly."

"I would expect nothing less." If there was one thing Darshan's spy network prided itself on, it was its efficiency. Zahaan was the likely cause behind that. "Let me know if you need any doors opening."

Zahaan fidgeted with the tag dangling from the *infitialis* chain hanging around his neck. "This serves as an adequate enough key."

"I can well imagine." Few bore the mark of the *vris Mhanek*. Only those he trusted with his life and no more. "But if I have to reassure one more noble that I did *not* send you to their lover's bed..." he warned.

A delighted squeal, a little louder than most, echoed down the corridor before Zahaan could respond.

The man's lips twitched in mild amusement. He likely knew precisely who that noise belonged to. "I'll go gather my people." Giving a final bow, he turned crisply on his heel and marched down the corridor.

Chapter 7

Hamish sauntered alongside the study's wide window, his gaze half on the dark scene of the garden far below and half on the reflection of those who shared this room.

A handful of the guests lingered near the low-burning fireplace, chatting amongst themselves on matters that seemed to have a local political air. They would largely natter about disturbances in the Pits—what he'd swiftly learnt was their charming name for the slums. Strange fires were apparently being set that had to be magical in origin, yet with a power that suggested strong bloodlines.

Hamish only idly listened. Although he'd no interest in the rumours, it was better than hearing the noises happening beyond the confines of this room. Squeals and delighted screams pierced the air every so often, akin to the sounds of a brothel. Whenever they did, a few more people casually vacated the study.

Was this why his husband had mentioned leaving early? Did this happen at every soirée? Had Darshan joined in, back in the time before they'd known each other? He had confessed to not being the tamest man and that his dalliances had been behind his ambassadorial position in Tirglas.

If Hamish had been a suspicious man, he would've wondered at the reason behind the delay in their regrouping. Having found the person responsible for the attempted poisoning seemed the likeliest option. Or perhaps Onella was proving to be more of an annoyance, if that was possible.

"...and that's why I think it would be prudent to open more schooling in the Pits."

Hamish's gaze swung towards the owner of the voice. The young woman, Lady Adya, had been louder than most whenever the topic of the Pits came up. Every time she spoke, it was with great passion.

If only there were a few more like her.

"Sweet-pea?" As he had done the entire night, her father laid a quelling hand on her arm. "Now isn't the time to speak of your pet projects. This is for more serious matters than educating the rabble."

"But, if they had access to the resources required to better their livelihood—"

"Child," her father growled. "You test my patience. I said, silence."

She huffed, folding her arms and glaring at her father for some time, before bouncing to her feet. "I guess bringing me here was a further waste of your precious resources. I'll leave you to atrophy with the rest of the geriatrics. My lords and ladies." She bowed mockingly to the rest before flouncing out of the room with her slave following close behind.

Groaning, her father turned to the rest of the group. "Do forgive her. She has been uncompromising ever since she brought that blasted man. I told her that pickings from the orchard dregs make poor personal servants, but she won't have it." He shook his head. "Now she's stubbornly clinging to the idea of educating him. What use does a slave have for higher learning, I ask you?"

Hamish bit his tongue as a series of agreeing murmurs circulated the group. Would it be possible for him to follow Adya? He couldn't flounce quite as spectacularly, but she seemed to have a few notions that he could get behind.

"I wonder," one of the men mused. "This young slave of hers. He *is* gelded, isn't he?"

Hamish didn't hear the answer. He strode across the room for the door before his anger got the best of him. *If they were nae spellsters...* As much as he wanted to rearrange a few of their features, he likely wouldn't get more than a single punch in.

The door flung open.

"There you are," Darshan said. He glanced about the room, grimacing in commiseration as his gaze alighted on the company. Leaning closer, he continued in a voice pitched low, "Have you been cooped up with them this whole time?"

Hamish swayed his head from side to side. "Nae really. Just since people started feeling each other up and leaving."

Darshan gave a sympathetic wince, which did a lot towards confirming Hamish's suspicions of this being the usual ending to a Udynean get-together. "I *had* hoped to extract you from this place before things grew heated." Casting another sideways glance at the group near the fireplace, he silently waved Hamish to join him out in the hall.

Without the added shielding of the walls, murmurs and giggles joined the other sounds of people enjoying themselves. He scanned their surroundings—both up the hall opposite the door as well as those leading left and right—letting out a breath upon finding they were alone in the corridor. After all the squeals and yells, he had half-expected to find the halls seething with naked revelry.

Darshan led the way down the corridor stretching directly ahead. It wasn't the way Hamish had come here, but he followed at his husband's heels.

"I should've warned you of how these soirées usually end," Darshan murmured.

"You mean of how they turn into orgies?" He had heard stories of it back home, usually from drunken traders willing to share a tale or two for a drink. He hadn't believed much of their nattering until now. *How many of those tales are true?* So far, it was a lot more than he had counted on. "Are all Udynean parties like this or just ones your half-sister hosts?"

"Most are. Some of the temple festivities, too. Once alcohol flows and people's moods are raised, lust feeds on itself until it burns out." His tone was neutral, as if he explained a force as inevitable as the tides. "The way down is clear anyhow. Zahaan will be waiting for us at the side entrance."

Hamish nodded. *That's a relief.* Bad enough that he could hear people carrying on as they strode by several closed doors, he didn't want to witness anyone in the act. He had managed his whole life without stumbling upon couples having sex back home. He wasn't planning on breaking that streak now.

The hallway Darshan had chosen seemed far longer than the one Hamish had taken to get here. Or was it his awareness of how simple wooden doors were the only barriers between them and the revelry going on in the rooms?

Was that what it sounded like to others when he was with Darshan? Hamish knew he didn't make much noise—a fact Darshan occasionally lamented on and vowed to change—but his husband was a different matter.

A door flung open, permitting exit to a woman and two men. All giggling like teenagers.

Hamish froze. They were all in various stages of undress. One man stripped only from the waist up, the other all the way to his smalls. And the woman...

He swiftly looked away, his face heating slightly upon realising her bosom was largely uncovered.

"Excuse us," the woman said, glancing down at herself. "Oh! Do excuse *me*." Her pale face grew steadily redder as she fumbled with tucking herself back into her undergarments. "I—"

"Fancy joining us, *vris Mhanek!*" one of the men said as the woman continued to blush and utterly fail to cover herself. "Your highness is welcome, too."

"Does he like women?" the second man enquired, his gaze flicking from Darshan to Hamish. Whatever expression the man saw, it seemed enough of an answer. "No? More for me, then." Growling, he wrapped his arms around the woman and buried his face into her cleavage.

"You cad!" the woman shrieked, ineffectively swatting at the man's head with her fan.

"It's an... interesting offer," Darshan said, tugging on Hamish's hand until they were moving again. "One I simply must decline." He persisted in towing Hamish down the hallway, his grip tightening until it squeezed Hamish's fingers together. "We've had a long day and many more to come yet. I fear we must depart for bed early. Get a good night's sleep and all. Give Onella my best if you see her."

"Of course, *vris Mhanek*," the woman managed.

"Sleep?" The first man nudged his companions. "*Sleep!*" He laughed, the sound chasing them around the corner.

The corridor opened out a little into what appeared to be the remnants of a foyer. The space left was a cosy little nook, big enough that his older sister would've turned it into a—

Movement to his left drew Hamish's gaze and halted his feet.

Two men, one with their trousers around their ankles whilst the other was fully stripped below the waist, were snogging up against the alcove wall. Besides the flash of a naked arse, it wasn't any raunchier than what he had witnessed in various taverns, both in Tirglas and during their journey. It looked to be the slave, Aarav, and the nobleman who had been so loud at the dinner table.

No sooner than Hamish had glanced their way, that the half-naked nobleman bent himself backwards and allowed Aarav to flip him upside-down.

"He just—" Hamish grabbed his husband shoulders as he twisted until his back was to the pair, putting himself squarely in the adjourning doorway whilst shoving Darshan into the corridor. His face felt hot enough to melt iron. "He just stood that man on his head." Whilst still inside him, no less. *How is that possible?* He shook his head, banishing the thought. He didn't want to know.

Shooting Hamish a puzzled frown, Darshan peered around him and shrugged. "He seems comfortable enough. I dare say the height difference helps."

Hamish bunched his shoulders in an attempt to further fill the doorway. "Dinnae look!" he hissed.

"What? Why ever not? If they wanted privacy, then I'm certain they wouldn't be doing it in a public thoroughfare."

There was perhaps a little too much truth in that, but… "You're a married man. You cannae just casually look at people having sex." He reached back and fumbled for a door to shut. His questing came up with nothing beyond more archway and wall. "And I thought you said the way was clear?"

"It *was* when I came through here. And if you're going to be prudish about it." He turned on his heel and resumed leading the way through the halls and down a flight of stairs. "Count Jeet is also married, by the way." Grinning wickedly, he arched a brow at Hamish. "And most certainly not to his slave." The expression froze, then fell into a sombre one. "Although, I think he would have been had Aarav's parents given their blessing."

"Wouldnae have thought a slave's parents had any say in marriage." Or that they *could* be married.

Darshan's brow creased in a confused frown before he touched a hand to his forehead. "Of course you don't know about the scandal." He cleared his throat. "Aarav's family is high nobility—higher than Count Jeet's. His parents refused to let him marry down and threatened to confine him if he continued the affair, so he sold himself to Jeet. They can't contest it beyond reclaiming him through the spoils of battle and Jeet's household is stronger in that respect thanks to his marriage to Countess Baani. And don't get me started on the gossip circulating about her and her personal maid."

It didn't surprise Hamish, according to the old rumours the sailors told back in Tirglas, Udynea ran on vice. He could even understand railing against parents who refused a union for political reasons, but it was a complicated way to go about it. "People do that?" He hadn't paid much attention to anything pertaining to the Udynean practice of slavery. *I should.* It would help in avoiding embarrassments and, maybe, also aid in Darshan's vision of seeing the end to its practice. "Sell themselves, I mean?"

Darshan nodded. "It is quite common. According to the last census, about a quarter of all slaves had sold themselves."

"Why?" He saw no reason to and didn't know a single person in Tirglas who would've ever considered it.

"I cannot speak for all of them, but most of those who sell themselves directly to the empire do so to clear their debts. They typically need only to work off what they're owed before gaining their emancipation writs. Even before we'd an empire, it was seen as a more effective method than permanent imprisonment, especially if the reason was over unpaid taxes." He gently combed a piece of hair back behind his ear. "Barring corruption, of course."

"What sort of corruption?" If people were selling their freedom, anything seemed possible.

His husband frowned. "Some officials think they're above the law and fiddle with the numbers to keep certain people around well after their debt has been paid. There are harsh punishments for it, but it happens more than the senate likes to admit."

Hamish grunted. He eyed the doors dotting the hallway as they continued to walk. Most were closed and little noise came from within. It seemed they had passed through the last section of unbridled debauchery. "Did you get involved in all this? In the past, I mean."

"The past being roughly a year and a half ago?" Darshan toyed with the edge of his shawl. "I did. Frequently. But, as you say, that was in the past. I have you."

"How many of them do you suppose are also married? Beyond Count Jeet?"

"About half, I would wager. And a handful who aren't are probably engaged."

"And you dinnae feel an urge to...?" The question died in his throat as Darshan shook his head.

"Even if you were amenable to the idea of finding a secluded spot to be intimate, *and* you hadn't also been the target of an assassination..." He straightened his sherwani. "Well, this is still my half-sister's house. That alone rather takes the shine off the idea."

Hamish nodded absently. In Tirglas, the royal family was expected to remain in Castle Mullhind, including adult children and their spouses. His childhood bed back in the castle would've also been his marital bed had he followed with his mother's wishes for him to wed a noblewoman. It wasn't the same in Udynea, but he supposed Darshan saw the idea of sex within Onella's estate as akin to doing the act in her very bed.

He tilted his head, eyeing his husband from his periphery, as he recalled something the woman had uttered about Darshan that also seemed to aim true. "Out of pure academic curiosity, how many *do* you prefer at once?"

Darshan gave a considering hum. "Don't let my sister's thoughts get into your head, *mea lux*. They'll never leave."

"I ken that. I just—"

"Can't stop wondering? For *academic purposes*?" He raised a brow suggestively. "Four Udyneans." Darshan grinned up at him. "Or one strapping Tirglasian."

"Four?" Hamish frowned, his thoughts bumping to a halt along with his feet. "How can you manage four? Dinnae tell me you can fit *four* in—" He fell silent as Darshan's laughter boomed down the hall.

"Gods, *mea lux*! Not all in the same place! What sort of man do you take me for?"

Someone who can take four men. He exhaled in a deep, blustery breath. "How am I equal to them? I cannae do the job of four men." He could barely do the job of one. Darshan was submissive enough on the rare times Hamish let the man ride him, but he was aware of just how little experience he had. At least, he thought he had been. Obviously not.

"I have never asked you to. Nor would I request you to be anything other than your gorgeous self. I've already been on the sour side of such deception. I would never do that to you."

Hamish grunted. *Four.* He knew his husband had advanced appetites. He had even experienced the man's near insatiable nature. He could handle the idea of toys—he had even enjoyed what little Darshan had been able to share of that desire—but *this*? All this time, he thought he had known the true extent of it.

The hall halted at the railing of a mezzanine that circled the room and led to a set of stairs.

Darshan spun on his heel, walking backwards for a few steps before halting between Hamish and the railing. "Look it has been years since I was so promiscuous and it was hardly a common occurrence when I was."

"You spent most of that time in Tirglas. With me."

"I said *years, mea lux.* Far longer than I've known you." He stroked his beard, his gaze dropping as it dulled. "I regret not telling you earlier as well as not thinking of Onella using that little snippet to goad us. But I have been with so many during my impious years, people I couldn't even recall the faces of let alone their names, that remembering every single act is impossible. You know all this."

He did. From the first time they'd slept together, Hamish had known he was sorely lacking in experience. "I didnae bloody think you did it as a group," he grumbled through clenched teeth.

Darshan cupped Hamish's jaw. "Dearest. My beacon. My light in the dark. If I didn't think we would both be happy together, I wouldn't have asked for your hand, much less have married you. No one could take your place, be it in my heart or in my bed."

"Nae *one*? How about four?"

"No matter how many there are on offer."

His shoulders sagged, releasing tension he didn't realise he'd been quietly stowing since those words first left Onella's lips. He pulled Darshan close, squeezing tight until he caught that little tap on his shoulder that was his husband's request for breath. They stood there, still in each other's embrace with their foreheads touching.

Finally, Darshan let out a soft sigh. "You know, I wasn't jesting when I warned you that a great many will try to pull us apart."

"I didnae think you were." Maybe he had done at first, for a little while. But he could see the truth now, especially when it came to Onella. His death might've been the quickest way to end their relationship, but it wasn't the only way. Not if she managed to pollute their love.

"I need you to trust me. Completely. If there is something you need to speak with me about, anything at all, simply say so. I will answer truthfully. There should be no secrets between us."

Hamish wet his lips. There were a few things he wanted to ask, but perhaps it was best to start small and work his way to the bigger questions when they were alone. "Did you manage to get what you wanted from the hedgewitch?" He knew that whatever it was Darshan sought from them gnawed at the man, but was it a secret?

His husband blinked up at him before shaking his head. "I was hoping to properly explain that when I had answers, but it is hardly of consequence. I can request the information once we reach Minamist."

"What information?" The hedgewitches shared much of their knowledge freely, claiming that it shouldn't be hoarded behind caste or coin, but even they held back what they didn't think the world needed to know.

Darshan's lips pursed. "I would prefer to speak of that in private," he replied in Tirglasian, warily eyeing the crowd milling on the other side of the mezzanine. "But if you truly wish to know…" He tapped the side of his head. "The noises. They are getting louder."

"What noises?" He didn't recall Darshan ever mentioning hearing things. Was it a spellster issue? A medical one? Did he need to get a priest? That was what had happened to a sailor back in Mullhind who'd raged through the central market raving about noises. He didn't know what had become of them.

Darshan's slightly uncomfortable expression twisted further, turning sour. "Remember when—" He cut himself off, staring across the mezzanine.

"—said let go of me."

Hamish followed his husband's gaze, swiftly spying a young woman struggling to be free of an older man's attention. "Dar…"

No sooner than he had alerted his husband, did an elven man speed from the shadows to land a punch straight to the older man's jaw. The struck man fell, releasing his hold on the woman. He recognised the woman's face. Their vocal dinner companion, Lady Adya.

"I guess that sorted itself out," Darshan murmured. "As I was saying, the day you—"

"You filthy vermin," the older man spluttered, getting back to his feet with surprising speed. "You will pay for this outrage! I demand blood. Flesh. Your life will be penance for laying your disgusting hands on me, elf."

Right. Hamish had rather forgotten not all Udyneans treated elves with the same deference he had witnessed from his husband. According to Darshan, the general outlook on elves in the empire was they were either slaves or part of the lowest class.

Hamish grasped his husband's arm, turning him. "They're *really* going to kill him?"

"He struck a noble." Darshan glanced down at Hamish's arm, twisting gently as if such an action might free him from the grip. "The sentence for that is death."

"For protecting the lass?" If anyone was to be punished, it should've been the nobleman.

Adya continued with her attempts to shield the elven man with both her body and an actual magical barrier. The first saw her shoved to one side, the latter was met with jeers and insults.

"You're the *uris Mhanek*," Hamish persisted. "Can you nae throw your weight around and stop them? They'll listen to you, right?"

Darshan raised a brow in his direction, but wouldn't meet his gaze. "You forgot to bat your lashes," he replied, a touch churlish. "Just for that extra pandering look."

"I wasnae trying to—"

"It's all right. Most who invoke my title are attempting to curry favour, not aid an unknown being." He eyed the group forming around the elven man. By the way things were heating up, there was no chance of anyone else defusing their rising ire. "I don't typically involve myself in these matters. The law isn't exactly on his side, even if he doesn't deserve punishment for protecting his mistress, and I've already let my personal feelings on a particular matter let myself get in the way of legalities."

His husband knew the outcome of Darshan's decision on that matter better than most. Having Darshan involve himself in the contest for Hamish's hand had led to their exile from Tirglas and the solvency of a treaty between their people, barely avoiding a war. Neither of them was certain if that threat wouldn't come to pass.

"This is different. You ken I wouldnae ask you to if I thought they'd treat him fairly. It may be the law, but it doesnae mean it's right."

Darshan pursed his lips. "Very well."

Hamish strode at his husband's side as they trotted towards the crowd.

No one appeared to notice their approach, being far too focused on the still ranting nobleman. A few urged the man on whilst a handful seemed apprehensive. Had they also witnessed the assault on the young woman? That could work in their favour.

"Just what is going on here?" Darshan demanded, easing his way through the crowd, who were quick to part once they realised their *vris Mhanek* was coming through. "I don't recall a public execution listed as one of tonight's entertainments."

The struck lord instantly whirled on Darshan. He swayed. Whether his imbalance was due to the punch or drink, it was hard to tell. "This *filth* dared to strike me."

"It's not his fault," Adya interjected. She remained planted between Darshan and her slave. The elven man was thin—enough so that Hamish thought the man would need to stand up twice to cast a shadow—and Adya's plump frame made an effective shield. Anger and embarrassment had painted patches of stark redness across her pale cheeks.

"And I suppose his fist leapt up to savage me of its own accord?" the lord snarled.

Adya clutched the front of her gown something fierce, but there was fire in her eyes and it drew her shoulders back. "He was merely protecting my person, *vris Mhanek*. From *him*." She stabbed the air in the direction of her attacker, as though he needed to be pointed out.

The lord jerked back, staring at her accusing finger as if it were a viper. He peered at her, calculating. "She's clearly trying to shield the bastard." He sneered at the gathering crowd. "Everyone here knows she's a sympathiser. We've all heard her natter on tonight about educating the poor and freeing slaves. I demand retribution for his actions."

"Demand?" Darshan echoed. The word might've been whisper quiet, but it rumbled through the air like a thunderhead. "Surely, you're not making such demands of me?"

The man winced. "Of course not, *vris Mhanek*. Just of the law, which states—"

"I am well aware of our laws, Lord Balvaan." Disgust twitched his nose, a crack in his usual emotionless mask. Pushing his glasses back into place, he turned to the elf. "What's your name?"

"Kaheran," the young man replied, shrinking slightly. Then he seemed to remember who Darshan was and bowed low. "My... uh... *vris Mhanek*."

"You will address the *vris Mhanek* properly, *elf*," one of the noblemen snarled, starting up a buzz of discontent amongst the crowd.

Hamish frowned. How could the man be expected to know if he hadn't been taught?

His husband seemed to have the same thought as he commanded silence with the flick of his hand. "You did remarkably well, for someone of your background."

There was a twitch from Kaheran's lip, the fight to restrain showing contempt.

"No formal training in combat, correct?"

The sneer fell a margin. "None, *vris Mhanek*."

Darshan inclined his head, then turned to Adya. "My lady, did you give Lord Balvaan permission to lay his hands upon your person?"

The wrinkling of the young woman's nose answered well before she spoke. "Not at all, *vris Mhanek*."

"That settles it then. It would seem the grievous error was on your part, Lord Balvaan."

The lord hunched his shoulders.

"Furthermore, it would be counter-productive to reward a man's loyalty with pain. This young man could've hung back, could've allowed all manner of harm to come to his dear lady." A twitch of a smile lifted one corner of his mouth as he turned back to Kaheran. "Instead, he chose to intervene. Lady Adya, did I hear right that you are tutoring him in... shall we say... less conventional activities?"

Adya nodded enthusiastically, a fresh bloom of pink unfurling in her cheeks. "You heard correct, *vris Mhanek*."

"May I suggest adding formal training in protectoral combat?"

Bowing low, Adya barely managed a strangled, "Of course, *vris Mhanek*."

"You're rewarding him?" Lord Balvaan blurted. "You can't!"

Darshan slowly faced the man, his eyebrows raised to their highest and a dangerous glint in his eyes. He silently pinned the lord with that sharp-eyed stare Hamish had witnessed only a few times. His hands unfurled from idly clasping each other to spread before him as if inviting the man to explain himself further.

"I—" the lord stammered. "I mean you *can, vris Mhanek*. Of course. It is, naturally, your prerogative to do as you please. I simply... *query* the rationality of such an act."

"I see," Darshan murmured. Never had Hamish heard anything spoken with such cool indifference than those words. "It would appear there's more than one person sorely lacking in base education around here." He turned from the man, the aloof mask slipping for a moment as he met Hamish's gaze. "*Mea lux*, I believe we have tarried long enough. Shall we depart to the imperial estate?"

Hamish eyed the crowd. Most were doing their best to look as though they were ignoring the show, peeking around fluttering fans or casually glancing over their drinks. Some even regarded Lord Balvaan with pity. "Aye, us leaving is overdue."

Grinning, Darshan practically swooped to his side. He took up Hamish's arm, wrapping his hand into the crook of the elbow. "Then let us be on our way."

Hamish glanced over his shoulder as they descended the stairs. Few outwardly watched them, just the elven slave and the lord he had struck. "Will it be enough?" They had saved Kaheran's life for now. "What'll happen once we're gone?" If Darshan ordered it, Zahaan's people could watch over them, but not indefinitely.

If we'd taken just a wee while longer... He didn't want to think about it, couldn't stomach the thought of that young man being punished in any fashion. All because he protected Adya from the lord's advances.

"He'll be fine as long as he doesn't strike another noble." He patted Hamish's hand, his smile not as comforting as he likely hoped. "I may be *vris Mhanek*, but there's only so much I can do."

He knew that. Darshan had stressed how the court had a greater role in the running of the empire than it did in Tirglas. Unlike Hamish's mother, the *Mhanek* had to work within the confines of the law as well as appease the senate if he wanted to keep his throne.

It didn't make the churning in his gut any less easy to bear.

Chapter 8

The carriage lurched, prompting Darshan to lean back into the seat or be thrown face-first into his husband's lap. Not that *he* would've minded, but Zahaan certainly would have.

He doubted Hamish would've currently welcomed such an act, either. Not with the way he eyed the mansion over Darshan's shoulder.

Hamish only moved to stare out the window to his left once the carriage had finally reached the road. "That could've gone better." Whilst there was no sign of concern on his face, it lingered in the way he held his shoulders and how he searched for the hunting knife that didn't hang from his belt tonight.

No doubt, the young elven man's fate still weighed heavily on Hamish's mind.

I should've done more. There was so little that wouldn't have caused his father more trouble. The only mercy he had came from having seen what provoked such a retaliation. He vastly would've preferred throwing Lord Balvaan into the dungeon. If the lady had struck first, he could have. But it had been her slave and the law allowed only so much there.

He could change it. That was the goal. But it took time. Minds would need to be brought around to a new way of thinking, enough that when the court came to a vote, those who were for change were in the majority.

"Better?" Zahaan's grunt filled the silence. "That's an understatement." He had spoken with his people before joining them in the carriage. It had been in low voices, but long enough for Darshan to know the man was aware of everything they'd done between leaving his side and now. "I would class it as an absolute disaster."

"It wasnae *that* bad. Dar stopped that elven lad from being punished."

Staring out into the darkness beyond their carriage, Darshan hummed to himself. *For the moment.* What Onella would make of it was a far more pressing matter. She would've already heard about his intervening and, undoubtedly, would be busy thinking of ways to use it against him. But what other information had she managed to garner from the night?

"Do you think that, maybe, we should've brought him along with us to keep him safe?" Hamish asked.

Darshan shook his head. "Doing so would've required his purchase." If the pin she wore wasn't donned in mockery, then she likely abhorred the idea. It was curious that she had a slave at all. Most of the freedom sect had long since forsaken the idea. Perhaps, like with those belonging to Darshan, she had been gifted the boy as a child and had only the law stopping her from using the emancipation writs. "She wouldn't have sold him."

"Nae even to the *vris Mhanek?*"

"Did you notice the pin just below her throat?" A series of dangling links representing a broken chain. He had seen a mere handful amongst the nobility, and none worn so openly. "She's part of the *libertas omnium* sect."

Hamish screwed up his nose in confusion and Darshan silently cursed the unconscious slip into the Ancient Domian language. The exertions of the night must've been getting to him.

"She's someone who seeks freedom for all beings," Zahaan explained before Darshan could dredge up the right words. "Or did you think the *vris Mhanek* was the only one with such a view?"

Hamish shrugged. "More a case of hoping there were others."

"There's not that many," Darshan murmured, idly scratching at the nape of his neck. "Not amongst the court. I'd recommend being careful when interacting with the few there are. Some can be rather... fanatical in achieving their goal."

"To put it mildly," Zahaan muttered. "Or have you forgotten that time one sprayed acid over your carriage?"

He grunted. "Not forgotten, just deeply buried."

Hamish eyed them as if they'd proposed jumping off a cliff. "They did *what?*"

"It was the celebration of my..." Darshan tapped his forefinger on the side of his face as he cast his mind back to that year. "...nineteenth year, I believe. Tradition demanded a ride through the city. Show off the might of the imperial throne and all that."

"You loved it," Zahaan teased.

He had. Back then, most of his excursions beyond the palace were kept to short distances and whilst surrounded by Nulled Ones. The carriage ride had been different. It had enabled him to see more of his homeland and still be considered safe. Until the vehicle was doused in a liquid that dissolved the wood and gnawed at the steel frame. "My shield stopped it easily enough." The driver hadn't been as fortunate.

That was often the way of the sect. *Freedom for all, no matter the cost.* It sounded pretty, but the cost was often the lives of those they sought to free. Most focused too much on getting those emancipation writs and not on the necessities a person needed to survive. When it came to afterwards? Most of the sect had moved on.

But after was just as important as before. The slave records were brimming with recounts of freed people selling themselves right back into slavery purely to survive. Laws had to be put in place. Safeguards to erase the flaws in the current system. But there was only so much he could do. *Once I'm the* Mhanek...

He sighed. Even then, he was beholden to the senate.

Somehow, he would find a way. It was the *Mhanek's* duty to lead the people—all of them, not just the nobility—into a brighter future. When his time came, he would not fail them.

Zahaan shifted in his seat. He kept glancing out the window, clearly agitated. Did he think another attack would happen? Not likely at this time of night.

Darshan twisted in his seat to address his spymaster. "You don't *have* to travel with us." It had become a habit for Zahaan to use such time on the road to brief him, but there was little he could add to their previous conversation.

"I'm fine," he grunted. "Stopping to let me out would present anyone following with a better target."

"Suit yourself." His gaze slid back to Hamish. Darshan had considered suggesting an earlier departure from the city, despite the hazards of sailing a lakeship from the docks at night. But, now they were in private, his husband looked rather haggard. Sleeping in a decent bed, even for one night, would do him some good. "*Mea lux?* How are *you* holding up after all this? Especially in regards to Onella?"

"I thought you were exaggerating," he murmured, his gaze unwavering from the lantern-lit streets. At this time of night, the high quarter was empty of all but the criminally inclined and the desperate. "That your half-sister would nae be the terror you described her as."

Zahaan snorted his amusement.

Darshan flicked the man's head with a wisp of air, earning a disgruntled sniff from his spymaster. Part of his attraction to Hamish had come from how the man saw the good in others, including the whirlwind mess that was himself. "I *did* warn you."

"Aye. Are they all like that?"

He gnawed at his bottom lip. It had been a few years since he'd seen some of them. "Most of my younger half-sisters are a little more congenial. Onella is the worst of the bunch, I'm afraid." He glared at the mansion's dwindling shadow. "I would apologise for her behaviour, but if I started that, I'd never be done."

Grunting, Hamish's brow creased in a thoughtful frown. "She said something before you intervened in the dance hall. I mean, she said several things, but this stuck out. I thought you said Anjali held the title of *vlos Mhanek?*"

Darshan inclined his head. "That is correct."

"Then why did Onella introduce herself with it?"

Darshan's brows rose. He glanced at Zahaan to find the man just as surprised. *"Did she?* Interesting. I must say, that's a new one for her." He would have to tell Anjali that little morsel once they arrived at Minamist.

Every one of the empire's royal titles hinged on how close their connection to the *Mhanek* was. There were four such titles when it came to the imperial children. As his father's only male child, Darshan had automatically been gifted the title of *vris*. It meant both eldest and heir. If his father had actually managed to sire another son, then they would've been a *vrissin.*

The title of *vlos* worked in a similar fashion amongst the women being that it meant the eldest living daughter. But Onella was only Darshan's oldest half-sister. And cousin, thanks to his father lying with Darshan's aunt—on his mother's side, although he wasn't sure if he'd put anything past his father if it got him another son.

"Do you think something could've happened to your twin?" Hamish asked.

"I would've told him," Zahaan replied.

"Succinctly put," Darshan said. True, for Onella to lay claim to the title of *vlos*, she would have to see to the death of the only sister older than her. That was Anjali. But for something fatal to have happened to his twin without him knowing? That message would've been first and foremost amongst those Zahaan had rattled off earlier in the imperial estate. "Although, I am sure Anjali will be so thrilled to learn of her apparent death. Onella is still only the first *vlossina.*" Already, he could envision an argument with his father over how he treated her. "And one of a great many who wish me ill."

"How many siblings did you say you have?" Hamish asked.

"I believe there are still a dozen living ones. Correct?" he enquired of Zahaan, smiling as the man gave a sharp nod.

There used to be a great many more. His father had sought for another son ever since the year Darshan's mother died giving birth to Anjali. He had only stopped trying five years ago, when Onella's son had come into the world.

"What happened to the others?"

"My other sisters?" Never anything good. "On the whole, they've been waiting for me to die."

"Although," Zahaan added. "The more impatient ones do attempt to expedite the natural process."

That they had. And always to their own demise. "Our right of succession is somewhat the same as yours; the eldest in line, then the next. Only with us, it's the next male barring no immediate heirs." Anjali might've been able to take his place if the court let her, but he didn't hold out much hope of her outliving his death. Certainly not if any of his half-sisters were involved. "However, marrying *you* rather upsets their plans."

Hamish frowned. "How so?"

"The way I'd been living before meeting you, I was on the path to die as an heirless emperor. But now? Even if we had no children by the time of my death, if you still lived then you would inherit everything."

His husband looked blankly at him for a moment before terror took his face. "Even the throne? But I'm nae part of *your* royal bloodline."

"It wouldn't matter," Zahaan said. "You'd be a human man in a ruling position."

Hamish's brow furrowed in disbelief. His gaze darted from Zahaan to Darshan. "And you didnae tell me this beforehand because…?"

"It hadn't crossed my mind," Darshan admitted. "Hopefully, it won't matter. I plan for us to have a child, or two, who can do the inheriting well before my father is feeling so much as a little poorly."

"Or *two?*" One side of Hamish's cheek fattened in a lopsided smile.

"Just to be on the safe side." There were easier ways to sire children than what Darshan planned, but his twin was the safest way to keep conniving claws out of it. "If Anjali is willing." A lot of his planning hinged on her agreement. He had no guarantee of her reaction. To his knowledge, she'd never had a lover. To ask her to birth his heir was a gigantic favour even for family. Without it, Darshan would be forced to choose someone who could carry his child and not use it as leverage.

The mention of Anjali had his husband's smile drop. "Does your father really ken how you plan to have this bairn?"

Darshan shook his head. "My father knows only that his heir has married a man who once claimed the title of Tirglasian prince." And he had yet to hear precisely what his father thought of *that.* "I intend to tell him the rest once I can speak with him face-to-face." His father wasn't going to like the idea of risking Anjali's life in an act that had killed their mother, but it wasn't his call to make.

"What's to stop your sisters from going after her?"

Zahaan snorted. Like Darshan, she'd been trained alongside them and knew the pitfalls within the Crystal Court, often using them to her advantage. "None of the *Mhanek's* daughters would dare an attempt on her life. Not whilst he lives."

Hamish peered at him. "Nae a single one of them has ever managed a serious attempt to kill Anjali? Nae even Onella?"

"None," Darshan assured. That didn't excuse trying to use her as bait or lure her to their side, but Anjali's loyalty to him was unbreakable.

"But they've tried countless times with you?"

"They're a little more cautious nowadays." Especially after two of his half-sisters got all tangled up in each other's plot when they both sent assassins from Niholia to end him. Unfortunately for them, the Nulled Ones foiled their efforts and exposed the two sisters. They'd been executed for their hubris.

"But nae Onella?"

"He's a touch lenient on her." If she hadn't been a product of his aunt and father... Or if his father didn't still have a soft spot for anything, or any *one*, related to Darshan's mother...

Zahaan hummed thoughtfully. "He *was* close to signing her death warrant the day she shot you."

Feeling watched, Darshan glanced at Hamish.

His husband stared at him, those blue eyes at their widest as they practically bored into the spot where the scar laid. "That's the old hunting accident, right? The one where she mistook you for a— What was it again?"

"A rabbit." Darshan pressed a hand to his chest. It had been years since he'd thought about the reason behind the old scar. "I was quite young," he murmured. Just eight. An age when his father still harboured hope of siring another son. They used to visit the northern retreat in the summer. "We were hunting small animals." It had been one of the rare moments his father had the time to focus on them individually. That most had been still too young to hunt helped. He barely recalled the time when his half-siblings could be numbered on one hand. "It was never meant to be anything *serious*."

"And yet, Onella still chose *infitialis*-tipped arrows," Zahaan reminded him.

"You're lucky it missed your heart," Hamish added.

"I know." It *had* punctured a lung, but that was a minor detail his husband needn't concern himself with. It was an old injury that had long since healed. "Fortunately, I had already completed my healer training—at my father's insistence, of course. He was convinced someone would try to rid him of his heir." He rather doubted his father had expected that person would be one of his own. "It still ached for a few winters after." The arrow tip being to blame there.

"And she wasnae punished?"

"I didn't say *that*." She had naturally claimed it as a mere accident, but her disappointment in the outcome had been crystal. Even his father saw through her usual manipulations. "There was no way to prove it had been a deliberate attempt on my life. Father had her spend a number of years at her mother's estate."

"A bad call on the *Mhanek's* part," Zahaan murmured.

"Indeed." His aunt had been sniffing around the throne ever since her sister died. That she had birthed a daughter rather than a son was likely the only reason he still lived for she certainly would've managed his demised if it could've elevated her own child.

"Do you think I could learn to heal?" Hamish asked, pulling Darshan out of his musing.

Could he? Hamish might have enough magic to have his arrows do the impossible, but he struggled with simpler tasks. "Others? Not likely. Not with your strength." Even a proper shield, a talent that any spellster should've been able to do at birth, seemed beyond the man. "Yourself?" Darshan wet his lips. Healing was an art. It required finesse over brute strength, so it was possible for weaker spellsters. The idea of Hamish trying something that volatile, of training long enough to gain the same innate ability as himself, terrified him. "I honestly have no idea if it could be accomplished safely. To my knowledge, no specialist spellster has ever managed before and lived."

Hamish frowned. "Me grandma managed to learn it on her own."

"And it killed her." Darshan had never met the woman—she'd been dead long before Hamish was born—but he had heard the story, he'd even agreed with his husband's conclusion that she was where the meagre magic originated. "Whether she knew of her power or not, she clearly didn't have any knowledge of what it was doing to her." He had seen what that sort of ability did to a person.

"So you've said."

Stretching across the carriage, he clasped one of Hamish's hands in both of his own. "I don't want that happening to you." The mere thought came close to stealing his breath.

"I ken that. I just—"

He squeezed his husband's fingers. "It's too dangerous to even think about."

Hamish laid his free hand over the top of Darshan's. "I'm nae about to run off and attempt anything. I wouldnae even ken where to start."

"I'm sure you'd eventually figure it out. I know how stubborn you can get."

"Stubborn? *Me?*" A puff of laughter escaped in a flash of teeth. "I'm naewhere near as stubborn as *you*." He leant forward, the carriage leather creaking, until he was almost close enough to kiss. Coils of his hair had come undone from its binding at some point during the night, they tickled Darshan's forehead. "I *promise*, I willnae try."

The tightness that had slowly been squeezing his chest eased at the words. He inclined his head in acceptance of the vow.

Zahaan cleared his throat. The elf had twisted his back to them to stare intently out the window, no doubt regretting his choice to join them within the carriage.

Darshan sat back. There was one thing he wanted to ask the elf. "Zah?" Even though he spoke quietly, the man still flinched. "Did you get the decree I sent to the palace? The one about the emancipation writs?"

He hadn't ever been entirely comfortable with technically owning the few people he felt closest to. His time in Tirglas had only rubbed those feelings raw. Freeing everyone under his ownership was a controversial move for any noble. For the *vris Mhanek*, it was unthinkable.

But it was the right thing to do. No matter how long it took.

Zahaan nodded. "I got it."

"And? Have you considered my offer?"

The man continued to stare out the window, fiddling with the tag at his neck. "You can't free everyone," he murmured.

Darshan examined the floor in the hopes that it might have the right words. The carriage turned, the subtle squeak of the suspension giving way to the crunch of gravel. They were almost at the imperial estate.

"I know the law," he finally murmured. Even though he had the funds to free every single person under his ownership, the law demanded he released no more than a quarter at a time. *And wait five years after.* Then he could free a quarter of those left. It would take decades and three would still remain.

Zahaan turned to face him, troubled thoughts clouding his gaze as he stared down at his hands. "With all due respect, I've made a lot of enemies over the years. Living under your ownership is the safest place for me to be."

Darshan scoffed. "You don't actually think I wouldn't give you the means to start a new life elsewhere?"

The man's gaze snapped up to meet Darshan's. "I don't *want* a life elsewhere. And Ma feels the same way."

"You mean Darshan's old nanny?" Hamish asked, sitting straighter. "She deserves—"

"A long and happy life where she is safe," Zahaan finished. "None of which she'll attain once the court realises she belongs to no one."

"Dar would still protect her." There was no hesitance in his voice. Hamish was certain that Darshan would do all in his power to protect the woman who raised him.

And of course he would. Daama held the same special place in his heart as his twin and Zahaan. But... "It wouldn't be the same," Darshan murmured.

Hamish frowned at him.

"Attacking a slave is akin to attacking the owner," Zahaan explained. "We who are under the *vris Mhanek's* ownership have certain privileges not afforded to any other group. Most of us would be fine if freed. Myself? My mother? And a handful of others close to him?" He swung his focus on Darshan. "You'd be signing death warrants if you freed us, not emancipation writs."

Darshan bit his lip. He didn't want to admit that Zahaan was right, but he could also clearly remember a good handful of times Daama had angered those in the court—and the one time she had slapped a nobleman—people who would take great delight in her suffering if she wasn't tied to him. "Are you certain I couldn't at least tempt you into journeying with us?"

Zahaan shook his head. "I'm needed here." He smiled fondly up at the estate's walls. Objectively, especially when Zahaan pulled that expression, Darshan could admit the man was a handsome one. Most elves were. He could certainly see how Zahaan charmed information out of people. "The network would fall apart without me."

Darshan scoffed. "Nonsense."

"You ken," Hamish rumbled. He leant back, his limbs spread wide until he filled the whole seat. He fixed that sapphiric gaze on Zahaan. "You've changed since this morning."

The man straightened, his shoulders tensing slightly; impossible to mark unless someone sat as close as Darshan did. "I've simply had a chance to reconsider your dynamic since we met."

Hamish's eyes flicked to Darshan and back before their crystalline blue hue was lost under the shade of his lashes.

"That's Zah talk for he considers you worthy enough of his trust," Darshan translated, nudging his spymaster. "Which he should already have known."

"Do you remember Lord Kanan?" Zahaan shot back, his tone light though his eyes sparkled mischievously. "You thought he was the centre of your world."

Groaning, Darshan tipped his head back again the carriage wall. He *did* remember. Had he really been that besotted with the bastard? "That was *years* ago. I was barely twenty-two. *And* it was for all of three days... then the bragging fool revealed himself to be a prick and an elf beater." Darshan had learnt a few things that day. Just how darkly satisfying it could be to mete out punishment with his own hands was the one that actually unnerved him.

"Wait," Zahaan said. "Were *you* responsible for those gods-awful wounds of his? You know, his nose never set straight."

"I'm aware." Half the man's jaw had also refused to mend properly. *They should've left him to die.* That's what Lord Kanan had planned to do to the poor servant the man had beaten. "But that's hardly a fair comparison to Hamish." Closing his eyes he stretched across the footwell to rub his ankle up his husband's calf. "Quite frankly, I'm insulted you'd think my flame eternal was anything like that scum sucker. I wouldn't marry just anyone."

"I shouldnae think so," Hamish murmured in Tirglasian. "We've names for people like that."

Darshan laughed. "I'm sure you do, *mea lux*. And I'm sure they're colourful." He leant forward, holding his husband's stare and giving him a wide grin. "And it's rude to talk in a language present company doesn't understand."

Again, Hamish's gaze settled on Zahaan. This time, Darshan caught a hard edge to the usual softness. "Then he can learn," he muttered, switching back to Udynean.

"Certainly," Zahaan replied as the carriage slowed, then stopped. "I can see a few applications where it would be of use, at least until the court learns it. It might take their networks a little longer, but that could work in our favour."

"Always thinking of ways to send the other spy networks scrambling, hmm?"

"A confused enemy is the best type to have, *vris Mhanek*," Zahaan teased. "Spy basics. I thought Ma taught you better." He hopped out, bowing low and keeping the door open as a valet should for his master.

The night air nipped at Darshan's skin. Not as sharp as the Tirglasian wind, but still bitter. He tugged his shawl a little closer. The steps of the imperial mansion glowed, beckoning them upwards.

He tried to keep up with the banter between Hamish and Zahaan, but other voices tugged at his senses. It carried a drowsy note of grumbling and mutters that drowned out all else. *The lanterns.* Their steady glow illuminated the courtyard and stairway, but it also kept the bushes and the trees awake. He would need to fix that.

"Are you all right?"

Darshan blinked to find he stood on the upper landing with only Hamish for company. Zahaan must've slipped off in his usual silent fashion. "Of course. Why wouldn't I be?"

His husband narrowed his eyes at Darshan. "Can I ask you something?"

"Always."

Sighing, his husband leant against the pillar and glanced towards the door. "You dinnae *have* to tell me, all right? But did you and him ever...?"

"Ever what?" Darshan frowned at his husband, trying to decipher what he was talking about whilst the buzzing in his mind persisted. Were the plants somehow sensing his presence? "You mean myself?" he mumbled. "With *Zah*? *Gods no.*" Yes, he had strong feelings for the man—something that would still be seen as scandalous if the court caught wind—but it was the same protectiveness and love he had for his twin.

True, Zahaan found men attractive and had slept with a number of them as readily as he'd lain with women. But the idea of himself being one of them curdled Darshan's stomach.

Hamish peered at him, those blue eyes regarding him with a faint gleam of disbelief.

Perhaps he once might have considered it. Way back in his youth, he had confused that growing seed of friendship for something else, but never had he thought to act on it. "Answer me this—" Even if Zahaan hadn't been gifted to him alongside the man's mother when they were both babies—as big a hurdle as being under Darshan's ownership was to metaphorically ignore—they had been raised together. Their relationship had started as being akin to siblings and remained that way. "—would *you* ever consider lying with *your* brother?" He certainly didn't see Zahaan in any other light.

Hamish grew still. "I think I just threw up in me mouth a little." Grimacing, he audibly swallowed. "Point taken."

Darshan hummed. If those sorts of questions were starting to surface in his husband's mind... "How much did you say you've had to drink?"

"Nae enough to get me drunk," Hamish shot back before the last syllable could leave Darshan's lips. "I wasnae that foolish."

"But enough to accuse me of lying with Zah." He pinned his husband with what he hoped was a firm look. "Who is still a slave regardless of his liberties. You know I don't do that." He had made that mistake the first time he had lain with anyone. Although he'd been unaware at the time, propositioning someone who couldn't refuse him was not an act he planned on repeating. Ever.

However much alcohol Hamish had drunk, he still had enough

sense to look embarrassed.

"Come on." Darshan wrapped an arm around his husband's waist, his heart skipping a beat as Hamish leant into the touch and followed him inside. The man had certainly become less guarded about how people might see even the smallest of intimate touches. "Let's get you into bed before you start accusing me of sleeping with my own father."

"I wouldnae go *that* far. But, if I believe all your stories, then you must've bedded every man in the Crystal Court."

"I think you underestimate the court's size, *mea lux*." He *had* lain with quite a few of them, but not all.

Hamish snorted his disbelief, but said nothing further on the matter.

Darshan really hoped he hadn't married a jealous man. That could get tricky to deal with, even with being open about his past. Especially if one of his old flings caught wind and sought to part them for the sake of petty revenge. "Nevertheless, we've an early start tomorrow and I think it's past time I got you out of these clothes and snuggled beneath some plush blankets." Only now he had his husband within his grasp did Darshan notice the man's subtle swaying. As much as he wanted to leave Nulshar immediately, having Hamish hurling over a lakeship railing was best avoided.

"Aye. Sleep is long overdue tonight."

He hummed his agreement. As much as he hated admitting it, using his magic to heal that slave and confine Onella had taken more out of him than it should have. *I'm losing my touch.* It was nothing that some rigorous training wouldn't fix, but it was disheartening to find a few months of low use could see him this rusty.

"It'll be nice to share a bed with only you for a change." Hamish ran a finger up the back of Darshan's neck.

Darshan shivered and trotted a few steps ahead of Hamish to get out of reach. "Don't remind me." He itched at the mere suggestion of the fleas they'd found in their last bed. He was certain he would've scrubbed himself raw if his healing magic hadn't also soothed his scoured skin. "I promise, the remainder of our travel won't involve any more poxy inns." That had been an error on his part.

Hamish halted just before the landing. It put them almost at the same height. "I dinnae mind if we camp under the stars every night, just as long as you're there when I wake, me heart."

His breath caught at the address, leaving him to stare wordlessly at his husband. Hamish said it so rarely, only when he was sure no one could overhear. " 'Mish," he breathed. He caressed Hamish's jaw with the back of a forefinger, mindful of his rings to keep them from snagging that luxurious beard even as he stroked it. "My shining beacon. I don't plan to be anywhere else."

Chapter 9

Darshan stared at the shore they were fast encroaching on. The *Gilded Cage*. It was just a spit of land. An islet, barely worthy of the name. A beautiful and miserable embodiment of the atrocities best left buried deep in the past.

He didn't think he would be setting foot on land so soon, not until they'd reached Rolshar's port. But this… this couldn't be ignored.

It had taken five days to sail this far, the normally short trip across the Shar hindered by a squall. And, like in his journey through the strait, he had spent the first few days in blessed silence from the moment he had stepped aboard the lakeship. Not so much as a single peep from leaf or root.

Except for one.

How it knew of his presence, he wasn't certain, but it had reached far across the water to summon him. *From here.*

The lakeship waited a fair distance from the shore. The captain had halted her southward journey at Darshan's request, but she wouldn't allow a single one of her crew near this islet. He didn't blame the woman. If it wasn't for the voice calling to him, he wouldn't have come near this shore either.

The rowboat bumped against the dock. Or what remained of it. Bits of wood sat beneath the waterline, fossilised in the slightly saline waters of the Shar, leaving only weathered stone and hints of rust spots on the granite where iron bands had once hugged columns.

Warnings assailed his mind the second he stepped onto the land; wails and pleas for them to turn tail and never come back. A sense of foreboding, of fatal danger, lingered on the edges and lifted the hairs on his arms.

Through it all was that call. No matter how the other voices tried to drown it out, it beckoned him.

"Remind me what we're doing here?" Hamish grumbled as he secured their rowboat. "You ken the sailors said this place is cursed?"

Darshan inclined his head in acknowledgement. He had heard the ship's crew muttering as they'd lowered the rowboat. The *Gilded Cage's* reputation for being haunted was a well-earned one. *And well it should.* So many innocent dwarves had met their end here. It had been centuries ago, but the earth remembered.

"And do you also ken what usually happens when the locals tell you a place is cursed? You bloody run the other way. Nae barrel head-on towards it." He had made similar objections aboard the lakeship. Despite them, he had still followed Darshan and, even now, tromped out of the rowboat to join him on the shore.

"It's not cursed." That was too mild a word for what they'd done here. "All those tales the sailors said of hauntings and monsters? They're just that. Tales. What really transpired was far worse." And the monsters had long since packed away their claws to terrorise the rest of the land. As most conquerors did.

"Is that supposed to make me feel better? Because that was the grandsire of all failures." Hamish looked around them, peering into the trees.

Darshan already knew what his husband was only now confirming. Civilisation sat but a short distance away, the eastern shore close enough for him to make out houses. It would take a few hours of rowing to reach should the lakeship abandon them.

But on the islet itself? There were only trees and scrub to greet those daring to land.

The suggestion of what might've once been a path shaped the layout of the trees nearer the dock. It was this that which Darshan struck out for. The islet wasn't terribly big. Whatever called to him couldn't be too hard to find.

"And where are you off to now?" Hamish demanded. "You havenae even told me why we're here."

To get answers. And, hopefully, set a few things right. "I need you to wait here for me." Whatever had called out to him, it had to be what the rest of the trees were warning him back from. The weapon, perhaps? But the last recording of the *Gilded Cage* being used against hedgewitches was over fifteen hundred years ago. It couldn't *still* be actively seeking anything.

"Wait?" his husband echoed, his usual pleasantly deep brogue squeaking slightly. "Nae bloody likely." He all but scuttled to Darshan's side, eyeing the foliage all the way. "These trees give me the willies. Nae come across a plant that I've dreaded being near before."

Darshan laid a hand upon a vine-claimed pillar. The stone

beneath was worn smooth from centuries of wind and rain. "Then, before we go any further, I need to tell you something." He wrapped a tendril of the vine around his finger as if it were a coil of hair. Or did the vine wrap itself around the digit? "Do you remember me mentioning how I'm hearing noises in my head?"

"You—? I dinnae..." Hamish trailed off, scratching the back of his head. "When did you tell me this?"

"At Onella's soirée." He didn't blame Hamish for forgetting a half-uttered conversation. A lot of things had happened during that time, and he still wasn't convinced that Hamish hadn't been more than a touch drunk by then. "Around the time that elven boy hit Lord Balvaan."

"Now *that* I *do* remember. But nae—" He rubbed at his temples with a thumb and forefinger. "That was *days* ago. You've nae mentioned it since then."

Whilst the days following their stay at Nulshar had been calmer, the lakeship didn't lend itself to privacy. Of any sort. Until he knew precisely what had happened to him, he wasn't prepared to let the whole empire know. And when the time finally did come? He wouldn't be spreading the news through a sailor's rumour. "I wanted us to be alone."

"And are we? Alone?" There was a wary softness to his voice. Darshan had heard it before, typically from those trying to quell an unleashed and magic-maddened slave. "Or are you still hearing whispers?" Hamish's expression lacked the thread of fear Darshan had witnessed from others in the past to those slaves, but the guarded concern wasn't much better. It pricked at his pride. He was neither dangerous nor unstable.

"*Don't* use that tone with me," Darshan hissed. What he heard was no different to being in a crowd and catching snippets of other people's conversations. Just with added impressions. Images. *Feelings.* "And don't look at me like that." Even if he was losing his grip on reality, he would never harm anyone. Especially not his flame eternal.

Hamish held up his hands. Be it to placate him or in surrender, it twisted Darshan's stomach all the same.

"You think I'm losing my mind, don't you?" Why wouldn't he? Who knew how they looked upon the same symptom in Tirglas? *The work of demons, most like.* That was the usual response to anything of unexplained origin. *Priests or the axe.*

"I didnae say that." Still, the lines of worry on his face didn't fade. "We've both been under a lot of stress. Your sister's party was enough to muster anyone's sanity off a cliff."

Snorting, Darshan shook his head. If Onella could cause this sort of stress, she would've been his demise years ago. "I'm not crazy. I'm just—"

"Hearing voices?" Hamish finished. "I'm nae questioning your sanity, Dar. But you cannae tell me that's normal."

"No," he whispered. Even in Udynea, hearing voices others couldn't was treated with caution. "It's not all the time." When they travelled, it was a murmur in the air, a whistle on the wind. The fields of wheat they'd ridden by only mumbled, what meagre memory grass possessed was buried deep within the roots. Memories didn't cling to leaves and blades.

The pretty gardens surrounding the estates were worse, full of complaints for space and water. He hadn't heard anything screaming since his first contact, not until coming across the freshly cut flowers in his chambers.

"How long?"

"You remember the bear attack?" He still recalled that dreary morning with startling clarity. Of how Hamish had deliberately taunted the beast into attacking for the express purpose of taking his own life rather than be forced into a marriage he didn't want by his mother.

They hadn't spoken much about that day. Certainly not the full outcome of how Darshan had healed him.

Hamish fingered his neck, sliding over the scars. One side of his mouth lifted in an attempt at a smile. "Bit hard to forget. But that was *months* ago. You couldnae have found the time to tell me between then and now?"

Darshan bowed his head. "I know. I should've told you." At the time, there'd been the pressing matter of keeping Hamish from ending his own life and winning the union contest. But after? He had no reasonable excuse for staying silent on the matter. "I thought it a temporary effect. That it would fade with time. I didn't want to worry you."

"Dar..." Hamish clasped Darshan's hands in his, squeezing. "Me heart. It's me duty as a husband to be worried about your wellbeing. You're nae going to change that."

His throat tightened at the declaration. He swallowed hard, trying to find the words that would free his tongue. It shouldn't have affected him this deeply. Of course his husband counted amongst the few who genuinely cared about him. "I know," he finally managed, squeezing Hamish's hands.

Hamish kissed the back of Darshan's fingers, exhaling even as his lips remained pressed to the knuckles. "All right," he murmured. "You've given me the when. What of the how?"

Still holding fast to his husband's hands, he spread their arms wide. The question of how was far trickier to answer. He could speculate all day long—he'd done so countless times—and be no closer to really knowing. "Do you remember what you saw when you awoke on that day?"

Hamish frowned. "You mean the dead grass? Aye."

Withered shells of a life gone. What he had done was worse than a field being bleached under the summer sun. It had been quick for the grass, the flash of a flame. Not like the bushes he had claimed. He still recalled their inhuman screeches. "I drained the life from them."

Pain. That's what he remembered the most. His desperation had led him to dragging the essence from hundreds of plants through his body and using the energy to replace the blood his husband had lost. It had set his nerves on fire. It had changed something in him. He could feel it in his core.

Whatever he had done had gifted him with abilities that he shouldn't have.

"Drained," Hamish echoed, the lingering note a question not quite asked clinging to the word. "I already ken that. You told me something along those lines back then, dinnae you remember?"

Darshan shook his head. They'd both been a mess near the end, but he had taken the worst of it. He had turned to the plants only after pouring so much of his own energy into mending Hamish.

"I thought you were talking nonsense. You jabbered quite a bit. I didnae ken enough Udynean then to understand you, but I didnae want you to stop, because—" He freed his hands from Darshan's grip to hug himself. "You were so cold. I thought if your talking stopped that... that the rest of you might follow."

"I very well might have." If they hadn't stumbled onto the road when they did, he would've died. Darshan bowed his head. "I think I did something no being should."

"You saved me."

"We both should've died that day. You were so close." The bear had nearly done the job. "You'd lost so much blood." Just a mention drew his mind's eye back to that day. Hamish lying broken on the forest floor, his lifeblood seeping into the earth. "I hadn't the energy within me to bring you back." He had healed the worst of the injuries easily, but Hamish had needed more and Darshan's magic hadn't been enough on its own. Not with him being the only source of raw energy. "Trying to heal you without help nearly killed me."

Guilt twisted Hamish's lips. He scrubbed at his neck. "I remember you saying as much."

"I—" He choked on the word. Tears welled, blurring his vision and fogging his glasses. "I couldn't let you go." He hadn't realised until Hamish was healed just how much he cared. What the warm fondness he felt in the man's presence really meant.

"It's all right, Dar." With the pad of his thumb, Hamish carefully wiped Darshan's cheek. "I'm nae going anywhere you cannae follow."

He knew that. Winning the union contest had given Hamish the chance to live without needing to conceal a part of himself. It didn't completely shake the darkness lurking in his husband's mind, nothing truly would, but its grip had weakened.

Darshan inhaled, trying to still the tremors memory rippled through his nerves. "To save you, I took fresh energy from the only source I had ready access to." The forest. "I funnelled it through me to mend you." The fire in his veins. The feeling of his very being burning at the core whilst he used himself as a conduit. Never in his life had he experienced such agony. "Ever since then, I can hear things I couldn't before."

"Like what?"

"Them." He waved a hand at the surrounding foliage. "All of it." It had been indistinct at first. Overlays of impressions and ghosts of whispers. Now? The murmurs were crystal. "It didn't happen right away. And it's not all the time, but it's there."

Hamish eyed the trees as if seeing them for the first time. "Do they speak to you?"

"Not usually." That one voice calling him here had been the first direct contact. "It's more akin to eavesdropping."

"Can you speak to them?"

"Can I—?" He had tried blocking out the noises with varying success. But to actually converse as if he was a hedgewitch? "I... don't know. I haven't tried." Where would he even begin? Speaking with plants had never been a spellster talent. "I'm no dwarf." Would they even listen? He knew they were aware of his presence and that he heard them, but if there was a consciousness beyond base needs, he had yet to find it.

Hamish leant back on the vine-enshrouded pillar, his weight setting off a faint complaint from the smaller shoots. "Nae even a wee bit?"

Darshan shook his head. Even if he couldn't trace his lineage back several centuries... "Dwarven and spellster bloodlines don't mix well. If I'd a dwarven ancestor, then I wouldn't have magic. In truth, I'm not sure what happened, only that the process of saving your life did something to me and I..." He held up his hands. The bands of his rings gleamed dully in the dappled light. They were the same hands that had done this to him. Or were they? "I'm not sure if I'm entirely human anymore," he whispered. Nothing about him looked any different. Would he have even noticed a change if it were slow enough? If it was still happening?

"Nae human?" Straightening, his husband crept closer. That sapphiric gaze locked on Darshan, keeping him rooted to the spot. Hamish slipped his fingers along the nape of Darshan's neck and drew their mouths together.

Darshan leant into the touch. The world seemed to still whenever they kissed, falling silent but for their breaths. Or perhaps it was the bliss that came from basking in the light of his flame eternal. Such a simple act certainly hadn't been as enjoyable before he met his husband.

Hamish broke the kiss first, still cradling Darshan's head in both hands. Those blue eyes bored into him. Whatever the man sought, it didn't take him long to find. "I see nae difference. I dinnae ken what happened to you, but I *do* ken you're still the same man I fell for and that's all that matters."

Warmth unfurled itself from deep within, banishing the chill gnawing at Darshan's extremities and tugging at the corners of his mouth until he grinned like an idiot. Trust his eternal flame to tease out the heart of his fears. He wasn't sure if anyone would be able to tell him with certainty if he had altered his very being or merely unlocked some power buried within all spellsters, but it hadn't changed him into a completely different person.

Stepping back, Hamish frowned at the canopy. "If you can hear them..." He trailed off, rolling the end of his beard between his fingers. The act was irksome to watch and left the hairs sticking out in all directions, but it seemed to be an unconscious act. "Or is it that you sense them?" He shook his head and continued before Darshan could answer. "Doesnae matter. However it is you ken, what are they saying right now?"

Saying? They *said* nothing. They screamed. If the trees could move, he had no doubts they would've bundled the pair of them back into the rowboat. "They want us to leave."

"Cannae argue there." Hamish tucked his hand in the crook of Darshan's elbow, turning them towards the dock. "How about we take their advice and head back to the lakeship?"

"Not yet."

Hamish's shoulders sagged. "I thought there might be more." Releasing his hold on Darshan, he folded his arms. The posture was one he had used on Darshan from the very beginning, especially whenever he wanted the unadulterated version of events.

Darshan was rather loathed to admit just how attractively imposing it made his husband.

"All right, out with it."

"There's something here." Mentioning it brought the call to the forefront of his mind. It hissed and cajoled within the same desperate breath. *Where* was that gods-awful call coming from? "It's been calling to me for about a day now." Growing steadily louder, and insistent, with the passing hours.

"And the reason we're nae going the other way is...?"

"I want to know what it is." Based on his current knowledge, it could only be a plant. Perhaps a tree. A very old one. Age seemed to factor into how strongly he heard the voices.

"*What?*" Hamish echoed. "Nae *who.*"

Darshan inclined his head.

Scrubbing at his face and muttering to himself, Hamish paced a few steps towards the dock before whirling back to face Darshan. "And we're here for *that* reason only?"

"For *answers.*"

"To what question?"

What indeed. He had so many. What had his desperate act done to him? What else would happen? Would the noises get worse with time? Would he wake one day to find his humanity had finally slipped away? "The hedgewitches of old were said to be able to commune with the land." Darshan slid his hand along one of the tree trunks. Life pulsed beneath the smooth bark, humming against his fingertips. "With plant life specifically."

"You think what they did is the same as what you're going through now?" Hamish looked around them, his arms spread. "And you're hoping to find an answer amongst... *this*? What *is* this place? Why come here when even the trees are telling you to bugger off?"

"It's known as the *Gilded Cage.*"

"A prison, then? For who?" His eyes narrowed. "Or *what?*"

Mirthless laughter snorted out Darshan's nose. "It was no prison." Maybe it had started that way, but the records going that far back were mostly dust. "This place was a death sentence for dwarves. The Ancient Domian people hadn't quite the same scruples as ordinary folk. They used to bring hedgewitches here. Hundreds of them."

He leant against the tree. If he focused, if he drew on the memory of that time—shared from the very earth—he could almost see them. One by one. Alone with the trees screaming for them to run even as their captors towed them to oblivion.

Some had escaped their captors' hold only to find themselves still very much trapped. The hedgewitches of old couldn't abide water. Being aboard a boat, losing their connection to the earth that they had been able to converse with since birth, had reputedly made them quite ill.

"Ancient Domian has been gone for centuries," Hamish pointed out. "The Udynea Empire saw to that."

They had. Like a plague, Darshan's ancestors had spread across the continent. That hadn't meant relief for the downtrodden. "And when that burgeoning empire claimed this land for her own? When Ancient Domian control over these sickening experiments was no more?" He sneered. "They took over."

"Why?"

Darshan bowed his head. "They wanted power, what the hedgewitch's had. They couldn't get it the usual way." No matter how many times imprisoned hedgewitches were subjected to carrying a spellster's child, it always negated the magic. "They couldn't understand where their abilities came from, not even the current hedgewitches know." He shook his head. After all humankind had done to the dwarves, it amazed him that the dwarves could bear to speak to them. "I believe the Ancient Domians came close to understanding the dwarven nature of speaking to the plant life, but they couldn't take that final step. They couldn't claim the power for themselves, but they *did* learn how to strip the hedgewitches of their power." In the tales, it left people as little more than husks.

"And you think that knowledge is here?"

"It *was*. There used to be a building. Maybe something survived." He couldn't be certain if any of the Ancient Domian preservation domes were in use. Or if the information hadn't already been handed over to the dwarves.

And there was still that pesky voice beckoning him.

"I dinnae suppose the hedgewitches reclaimed the place and we're meeting with one?" A desperate note warbled in Hamish's voice, peeking out through a veneer of optimism.

Darshan shook his head. How he wished he could say otherwise. "Hundreds of years have passed since the last true hedgewitch, a proper one with the power, touched these shores. The dwarves of today no longer have the abilities." Maybe if they did, they would've been able to tell him what he needed to do.

Hamish remained silent. He tilted his head, looking first over his shoulder, then the way Darshan had struck out for. Was he having doubts about journeying further? Darshan didn't think he would turn back, but also wouldn't blame him if he chose to.

Finally, he spoke. "This place isnae that big. If this building still stands, in any form, then it'll be near the middle." He pointed at the indent in the land that Darshan had taken as a suggestion of a path. "That curves the other way. We need to go straight through." He jabbed his finger at where the trees and scrub were at their thickest. "Force our way if need be."

That could be quite the problem. "I'd rather not carve a path through them." A shudder took his shoulders at the thought. Whilst he could do it swiftly enough, the memory of those dying flowers screaming was still fresh. He didn't want to know how wounded bushes and trees sounded.

"That bad?"

"They feel. And their screams are sharp."

Hamish linked their fingers and led the way to the section of trees he had previously indicated. "Then we'll pick our way through. It'll take time, though. How long will the lakeship wait for us?"

"Until sundown." That gave them several hours. Given the size of the islet, it should be more than they needed. Although, he hadn't factored in the denseness of the undergrowth they were to navigate. If they had to, he would return to the lakeship and somehow convince the captain to linger for another day.

Either way, he wasn't continuing their journey south until he knew the source of that voice.

Chapter 10

They picked their way through the undergrowth, diverting around the denser pockets of vegetation at first before it became all too clear that they would need to force their way deeper. Whatever called him sat in the heart of the islet and, no matter what angle they attempted entry to the centre, the way there was choked in scrub.

The deeper they pressed, the more the trees objected to their presence. They couldn't stop them—no matter how they protested, trees hadn't the ability to just up and move—but the winding path they were forced to take did chew up the hours.

If it hadn't been for that beckoning call, Darshan had no doubts that he would've swiftly lost his way. Perhaps that was what the trees intended, as foolish as the thought seemed to him. There was a deliberateness in their growth, a passive directing akin to what the Nulled Ones did in shielding the yearly royal street procession.

What they hadn't stumbled upon was any sign of habitation.

It was possible that the wilderness had long since reclaimed whatever structure the Ancient Domians had built. But he had expected to see a hint. Even a single slab of stone would give him some indication of where to begin a proper search.

"Do you have any idea what we're looking for?" Hamish asked as they slithered through a narrow gap between two trees. "Because it would help if we're both able to keep an eye out."

Darshan tugged his clothes back into place. He could've sworn a branch had deliberately snagged his collar. The trees were definitely growing tighter together, almost as one in some places, forming a wall with only a scant few cracks. It was a wonder they'd enough sunlight and soil to manage. Perhaps they had a way of sharing the required nutrients.

The call for him to come closer was fast growing stronger, enough to drown out much of the warnings from the surrounding trees. He was almost there. Whatever called out to him had to know for the call changed, growing exultant. It almost hurt.

"Dar? Did you hear me?"

He shook his head, trying to banish the noise enough to focus. "I heard. I don't know." Daama used to tell him horrid stories about the *Gilded Cage*. Of a monster confined in stone, tortured and bound in metal. "The tales didn't exactly give specifics. Every story seemed more interested in how they used to feed hedgewitches to this... *thing* they had crafted." The tales would refer to it as a beast. The historical records called it an abomination.

Hamish took another sweeping look around them, his chest puffing before he blew out in a mighty exhalation. "Well, that's just bloody grand."

Darshan flashed what he hoped was a reassuring smile. "You needn't worry. It has been literal centuries since then. Whatever it was is long dead now."

Absently nodding, Hamish poked his head between another pair of trees before shaking it and sidling off to his left. With the roots bunching together, secure footing was the hardest thing to find. "What else can you do with the plants? Besides hearing them?"

"I don't know."

"You havenae tried?"

"No." Even this extra sense of hearing them came passively. If he attempted anything at all, it was blocking out the noise. "Experimenting with strange new abilities without a mentor isn't generally the best idea." He didn't know if it was comparable to a spellster's power, but practising magic without knowledge often led to an early death.

Hamish glanced back, snarling as his hair tangled in the spindly fingers of a low branch. He snapped them off in an effort to deal to them.

Darshan winced as the tree hissed. At least the twigs had been dead.

"I dinnae suppose you can convince them to let us through?"

He paused in his surveillance of a possible path to shoot Hamish a confused look. "Of course not." True, they wouldn't have this problem of reaching the source of the call if the trees didn't press in so single-mindedly, but it was an impossible task. "Trees don't move."

Hamish scoffed. "Sure they do. How else would they be able to break down walls and spread across fields? It just takes them longer. I just thought that, maybe, you'd be able to have them do it faster."

"A nice thought." And it would certainly make things easier. That was often the way with impossible requests. "But no."

"Pity."

Returning to peering through prospective gaps in the wall of tree trunks, Darshan caught the familiar curve of a gate archway, the weathered stone stark against the green. "This way!" he called over his shoulder, squeezing through the opening. Thankfully, he'd the forethought to don the garb he had acquired whilst in Tirglas. It was bulky, and slightly on the warm side for southern weather, but the heavier wool and linen also protected him better than his silk attire.

The bark still scrapped his skin through his clothes.

He didn't care. His magic worked to soothe the cuts and abrasions even as he subjected his body to more. The gateway still stood. Maybe more did, too. Even if it wasn't what he was after, perhaps it would be worth something to the dwarves. Enough to exchange for the knowledge they kept closer to their chests.

He tumbled through the gap and rolled across a carpet of leaf mulch. He had made it. At last, he would find the source of that call and be rid of it.

Grunting from behind him broke his reverie, the sound followed by a frustrated huff. Darshan tore his gaze from the archway to the hole he had crawled through. He had barely made it. Whilst Hamish wasn't a rotund man, with much of his bulk being evenly spread across his torso, there was no chance of him fitting through.

"Wait there," Hamish ordered, fixing Darshan with a firm look. "Dinnae take another step until I'm next to you."

Darshan glanced back at the archway. The lure of taking even the smallest of peeks through the opening tugged at him. "It's close. Just through there." The call reached out to him, jubilant. It pulled at something within him.

He took a single step towards the archway. It hadn't been easy to reach here, what need was there to hold back now?

"*Dar.*" He barely registered the concern in his husband's voice. It gave him pause nevertheless. "Wait for me."

"It's right *there.*" His legs gave another shambling lurch. Just a few more steps and he would see what had called to him from out on the Shar.

"Stop! Dar, *please.* I dinnae ken what you're hearing, but stop moving."

His feet shifted of their own accord, drawn by that voice. "I need to get closer."

"Nae right now. Nae yet. Just let me—"

The call grew louder, drowning out all but its voice. The warnings screaming in the back of his mind from the surrounding trees at last faded. Other thoughts tried to invade his own, flashes of a hulking beast consuming all in its path, but these, too, were suppressed.

Darshan stepped through the archway and halted.

The call stopped. Silence followed in its wake, a void that sucked at his very soul.

There was no building beyond the archway, just the crumbled remains of bricks and tiny sections of walls, the layout suggesting an enclosed courtyard. A gnarled, dusty-grey willow stood in the middle. It wasn't tall for a tree, but it filled the courtyard. Branches with long tendrils of drooping leaves shadowed the ruins. Great tangles of roots had cracked the flagstones and crawled over the fallen chunks of wall.

Nothing else grew within that boundary. No grass. No ivy. Not even a hint of another plant poking its leaves into this artificial clearing.

Darshan ventured deeper into the space, finally stepping out from beneath the canopy of trees and into the noonday sun.

Something grasped his shoulders before he could venture further. They dragged him back under the archway, giving him no time to regain his footing.

He whirled, ready to retaliate, his shield snapping up.

Hamish froze, his hands outstretched. His eyes were wide and glazed with fear. Not for himself. He wasn't wary, but he was scared. *For me.*

Silence flowed around them for a few breaths, so still after the battering Darshan's mind had taken. He looked around them. If he wasn't certain they were the only two people here, he would've expected an ambush. "You made it through."

Hamish wet his lips. "Aye." His gaze slid to the still-standing arch of the gateway. Whatever he saw, it didn't give him any comfort. "I've nae seen a ruin that wasnae covered in moss before."

Darshan didn't want to admit he hadn't witnessed such a thing either. "Maybe it's the salt in the air." All the ruins he'd been allowed near had been dwarven sites, set deep in forests and far from any major bodies of water.

Hamish's lips disappeared beneath his beard as he pressed them together. He frowned, his gaze dropping to the ground. It was an expression Darshan had learnt meant his husband didn't agree with him, but also saw no advantage to arguing over it. "What did you say this place was again? A cage?"

Darshan laid his hand on the bare stone. "Amongst other things," he murmured. Cage. Prison. Executioner's block... It was all the same back then.

"And the beast that killed the hedgewitches is long dead?"

"It is." He eyed the willow over his shoulder. Why was it here? There were no other trees of its type on the island. Why place that one within the courtyard? What made it so special?

"So why are there fresh skeletons?"

Darshan arched a brow at his husband. They hadn't come across a single carcass in their winding travels through the trees.

Hamish wordlessly pointed at the flagstones.

There, amongst the twisted roots and tendrils of leaves, sat dry lengths of broken branches or... *Bones.* Darshan's questing gaze caught on the eye socket of a skull, then the elongated grin of what used to be an animal.

The longer he looked, the more signs he saw. There were plenty of skulls that suggested sheep or goats. Most likely, they'd been offerings from the nearby village to appease the so-called spirits haunting this islet. But there was also the spiralled antler of a plains deer. And, hanging where a branch had speared it through an eye, the gaping maw of a large predator. Big enough to be from one of the striped big cats.

Every single skeleton was devoid of flesh. The bones left to bleach and crumble in the sun.

Darshan took a step back and out of the archway. The warnings returned in full, screaming in his skull and blurring his vision. "*This* is the monster?" he whispered. He stared at the willow, barely able to believe it. The beast of history and legend.

Never had he thought the abomination everyone feared would be a *tree*.

"*That?*" Hamish said. "I thought you said it was dead? Is *this* what you've been hearing?"

Darshan shook his head. It couldn't be. "It's been fifteen hundred years." At *least.* "It *should* be dead." No willow lived that long. It should've rotted to nothing by now.

Yet the gnarled beast still stood. Like an aged dog, it slumbered in the ruins of its old cage. *Waiting.* Just as it had done for centuries. He could almost make out the pulse of life running through the roots. Sluggish. After so long, this thing had to be near the end of its time.

Was that why its call had been so insistent? A last desperate attempt to contact the hedgewitches who had been lost to this world?

The willow's vine-like leaves shivered. Their presence, *his* presence, had been marked.

A deep need washed over Darshan. A *hunger.* There was a hole within the willow, dark and endless. Never had he sensed such a thing in any other tree. It practically vibrated with the need to fill that space.

The willow creaked and groaned, unbending from its stoop to stand taller than the surrounding trees. Like eels, the tendrils of leaves slithered back. More skeletons came to light, yellow and cracked.

The remnants of a fence encircled the tree's base, the bars jutting through the trunk like spears. The bark nearer the fence was dark and puckered as if singed. The stories said the beast had been bound in iron; that was how they had supposedly controlled the monster.

Darshan squared his shoulders. If this was the abomination of legend, then there was only one thing to do. Be rid of its influence on the world. "Stay here." Hamish was right in the fact nothing growing on the archway wasn't normal. It could only be a sign. The willow could reach this far, but no more. "I have to get closer." He needed to examine the tree further, find a weak spot, before he struck.

Hamish shot him a wide-eyed stare. His mouth hung open for all of a few seconds before he shook himself. "*Closer?*" he screeched, grabbing a handful of Darshan's sleeve. "Did you lose a few arrows from your quiver along the way? That tree *eats* animals."

"I can see that." He jerked free of Hamish's grasp. "But need to destroy it."

A snarl reverberated through his skull and raised every hair on his body.

Hamish gaped at the willow, his face a mask of naked terror.

"You heard it, too?"

"The bloody dead could've heard that."

"It *has* to die."

"I'm nae disagreeing, but do *you* have to be the one to do it? We ken what it is, what it does. We can send others, a proper team, to do the job."

Darshan shook his head. "That would take time." He would need to convince the senate that it was a worthwhile task. And there was a risk someone would try to use it, just as they had done in the past. "We're here now. I can't just walk away. Look at it." He waved his hand at the courtyard. The space would've contained it once. Now it filled the area like an engorged leech. "What if it gets bigger? What if it takes over the islet entirely?" It was a small area, but still rich with life. "It reached me out on the Shar. That's with it like this. Who's to say it won't start calling sailors?" Maybe it already had. Maybe that was where the rumours of this place being haunted had come from. "I am not prepared to leave my people with that sort of danger lurking at their backs." Too many had already fallen into this monstrosity's clutches.

It stopped here.

"All right. How do we do this?"

"*We?*" All Hamish had on him was his hunting knife. As meaty a blade as it was, it would be useless against a tree.

Scoffing, Hamish rolled his eyes. "You ken what I mean. What's the plan? Even normal willows dinnae die easily."

116

Darshan shrugged. He was no arborist. What did those employed by the palace usually do with a diseased tree? "Burn it?" Even with its extraordinary lifespan and abilities, the willow was still made of wood. Fire should work. He would have to char it to the heartwood to be certain it was well and truly dead. Based on the sheer size, easily several stories, it would take an inferno to get it over with quickly. He didn't think he had that much power within him, but he was prepared to try.

He stepped back out into the old courtyard, keeping an eye on the willow as he edged closer. Once lit, any flame he created wouldn't be fully under his control. Whilst that worked in his favour in terms of the drain on him and his magic, he would need to contain it somehow least an errant spark ignited the surrounding trees.

Where to start such a blaze? Close to the base? After fifteen centuries, the willow would either be severely frail or like iron. Perhaps in one of the hollows next to the old fence. The area already appeared compromised.

He focused on one such spot, drawing to suck the surrounding heat into a single spark.

Something tingled in the air, humming in the wake of his magic. He knew that feeling. *Infitialis*. The magic nullifying metal. *The bars*. Not pure iron at all. An alloy? He hadn't heard of anyone managing to stabilise *infitialis* with anything—the metal being volatile at the best of times—but it was the only answer.

And something he could use to his advantage. He switched his focus from the humble spark to the much greater blast of a lightning bolt. If the alloy reacted anything like normal *infitialis*, then all he needed was one jolt and—

The willow cracked across his mind like a whip. It wriggled through his consciousness. Seeking. Probing.

Darshan struggled to shake off the pressure but, like a sea hawk, the willow latched onto something deep within him and sought to tear it free.

Fire seared his veins. Pain blinded him, the world a blur of pure light. Something on the left side of his face gave with a dull crack. Dust filled his nose and mouth. A tortured scream shattered in his ears.

A familiar warmth clamped down on his shoulder.

'Mish.

His husband grabbed him, hauled him up from where he had fallen face down on the flagstones. As soon as he let go, Darshan collapsed to his hands and knees, his head too heavy to do more than limply hang.

What had that blasted tree done to him?

Hamish laid a hand upon Darshan's back. "You still with me?"

He swallowed hard. His throat hurt. As did his face and hands. His magic was too scattered to soothe the pain. It didn't help that his head continued to spin. Keeping his eyes closed seemed to help. "Still here," he growled through the nausea. But not because he had managed to wrest himself back from the willow's clutches.

The damn thing had recoiled.

It hissed in his mind, wary and frustrated like a cornered cat.

"It tried to take my magic." His power buzzed through him, unsettled but still his. Was that what it had done to all those hedgewitches? Could it succeed with him? Or was it because his power didn't come from the same source? "I'm not what it expected." They could hear each other like it would've done with a hedgewitch of old, but it wasn't with the same energy. The tree had let go because it couldn't dig itself deep enough into him.

"It *expects?*"

Feeling that he could open his eyes without vomiting, he lifted his head to the view of a shattered world. *Ah.* That cracking sound had come from his glasses. Just the left. The lens remained in the frame, but it was a useless web of factures.

Darshan launched himself up onto his heels, his gaze swinging to the willow. It swayed gently from side to side as if caught in a breeze. Was it plotting? Could it plan?

"Get back," he snapped at Hamish, shoving his husband behind him with a gust of wind. Darshan had been the willow's main focus, but if it turned from him for even a moment, it would realise there was now another target within reach. Maybe it already knew. "Other side of the archway. Now! I can't focus if I have to worry about you."

Hamish glanced from him to the willow, determination hardening his face.

For one shuddering moment, Darshan thought he would have to argue, to waste time they didn't have. He staggered to his feet, planting them to keep his legs from caving, even as he considered how much air would throw Hamish back to safety without seriously injuring him.

Then his husband gave a curt nod. "Dinnae let it get its hooks into you again."

Hamish hadn't taken more than a few steps towards safety before falling to the ground with a pained yell. Further obscenities and curses erupted from him, too fast for Darshan to understand in full.

" 'Mish?" Darshan shot over his shoulder. He didn't dare tear his gaze from the willow, which sat as still as any tree, but he could see Hamish floundering on the edge of his vision.

"Dinnae fash about me. Deal to the bastard. Bloody—" The glint of a blade flashed through the air. "Get off!"

The willow snarled, annoyed but oddly triumphant.

Darshan whirled to find Hamish's foot had been ensnared by one of the willow's outer roots. He barely registered how his husband lay twisted, fending off vine-like leaves from fully entangling his legs. *No, you don't.* He had not brought his husband back from a bear mauling to let him be killed. And certainly not by a tree.

Fire poured from Darshan's fingers in a blaze of heat and rage. The leaves withered beneath the flame, turning to ash.

The willow's screech echoed in his mind. Far from being deterred, it sent more leaves slithering across the flagstones towards the still vulnerable target.

Darshan reached his husband's side first. Standing astride Hamish's still-bound legs, he slammed a shield around them. The vines hit the surface and started to climb, slowly encasing the shimmering dome. Thin tendrils snaked across the shield, seeking a way in.

He thickened the barrier's typically porous nature. It left them with only this pocket of air to breathe, but it also ensured that nothing, however small, wormed its way in. It didn't give them much time, but he needed all he could to think. "Are you all right?"

Hamish had freed himself, but hadn't gotten back to his feet. "I've certainly been better," he grated, pain creeping through the words even as he chuckled. "Damn root broke me bloody ankle."

Darshan reached down, blindly seeking the injured joint through the tendrils of wood binding Hamish's legs together. He had fixed worse than a broken bone before.

Hamish knocked his hand aside. "Nae now. Healing me will nae mean a thing if we cannae survive this beast."

"We'll be fine." At least, he hoped so. It had been a long time since he had needed to fend off an attacker whilst at a clear disadvantage.

"You sure about that?"

The leaves had almost fully enveloped his shield. The spindly, vine-like tendrils were slowly giving way to woodier coils, weaving this way and that in their quest to break through. Their weight pressed down on the barrier. The strain of keeping the shield firm dug sharp claws into Darshan's brain. He would need to deal with the vines to get a clear enough path at the willow.

He set the outer surface of his shield alight. A temporary measure, even if the willow screamed mightily in his head. It would take more than this to burn the main trunk. It would require a lot of energy. Drawing on enough to do the job and not endanger himself in the process was a fine balance to maintain at the best of times. Doing it whilst under attack wasn't an act he had much experience with.

"Dar," Hamish called, frantic. "The ground's moving."

Darshan felt the flagstones lurch almost at the same time. *Of course.* He hadn't thought about shielding the very earth they stood on. Nothing had ever attacked from that angle before. Now roots wormed their way between the cracks. Not as precise, but with the same zeal.

He pushed back, forcing the shield's bottom edge to twist and slide across the ground, shearing off the tips of questing roots along the way. The pinch of the unfamiliar move dug into his mind and blurred his already compromised vision. He knelt. It did nothing for the pressure in his skull, but it did keep him from collapsing.

If the willow continued to harry them like this, he wouldn't have the focus left to effectively retaliate.

His husband's broad hand laid upon his back, splaying between his shoulder blades. He leant into that touch, seeking its silent strength as he gathered the last of his.

One shot. He would need to clear the way first. Using his shield as a battering ram would be the most effective, but it would leave them vulnerable if he failed to divert the willow's attention.

Hamish certainly couldn't defend them. Not with the same strength. If he wasn't injured, he could've at least attempted to shield himself whilst returning to safety. But the same magic that came so easily to Darshan required heavy concentration from his husband.

This fight was all on him.

Planting himself, Darshan spread his arms wide. The gesture wasn't necessary for the magic to work, but it did help him focus and he needed every scrap of assistance. With the shield's surface still afire, he separated the back of the dome to fold and concave until it was a flat wall before him.

With a flick of his hand, he sent the wall crashing into the willow.

In his mind, the willow roared in pain. Outwardly, the shield had done little damage. A branch, caught square on, had broken and tendrils of charred leaves still drifted to the ground, but the shield had largely exploded in a cloud of cinders and smoke.

He had expected as much. The attack was merely to give him the freedom to put his all into a proper bombardment.

First target? The fence that had originally bound this monster.

He wasted no time in letting the willow recoup before blasting the trunk with lightning. The bolt crackled and spat, charring a line across the bark before anchoring on a bar. *Infitialis* ore took only the wrong touch of magic to explode. When worked, it took a continuous blast. An alloy? Darshan could only push everything he had into the lightning and hope it was enough.

Blue light danced from one bar to the other. A low hum

reverberated across the courtyard. The charge lifted his hair and sent the sane part of his thoughts screaming for cover. The rest of him sought for reserves. How much more of himself did he need?

The willow howled. Its branches swayed from side to side, the tendrils of leaves like smouldering curtains.

The bars arced and crackled, spitting sparks but nowhere near ready to explode. The buzzing climbed to the point of painfully shrill.

Still, Darshan poured more of his magic into it.

"Get down!" Hamish growled.

Before Darshan could react, he felt his husband grabbing his overcoat and hauling him onto his back.

The rods exploded in a brilliant plume of blue light, showering the courtyard with splinters and bits of molten metal. He fought to block out the squeal of breaking wood and the wail of a hundred voices all crying out at once.

Darshan cringed, realising he'd been hit with none of the debris when the absence of further pain finally registered. He opened his eyes, blinking away the after image only to have his gaze fasten on the familiar purple sheen of a shield. Not his own. " 'Mish?" He currently lay atop Hamish's chest, held there by his husband's enveloping grip. Such a position left him unable to see Hamish's face, but the man vibrated with effort.

Hamish grunted in reply.

"You can drop your shield." He needed to finish the job before the willow retaliated. He couldn't do that whilst confined in another's shield. He couldn't even move. At least it was permeable enough to let them breathe.

"Right," Hamish mumbled. "How do I do that again?"

"Focus on drawing the power back into you." Such a question had left Darshan dumbfounded the first time Hamish had asked. Summoning a shield, and its dispersal, was as instinctual to him as breathing. Not so for specialists like his husband. That Hamish had been able to extend the normally close barrier far enough to hold Darshan as well was a miracle in itself.

Slowly, the shield faded. Not smoothly, but in irregular patches that let in the residue of scorched air and charred wood long before Darshan was able to lift his head to examine the damage the explosion had done.

Once there was nothing keeping him in place, Darshan stood, absently dusting himself off as Hamish deftly started to untangle himself from the dead tendrils still binding him.

The willow remained silent. Had the blast been enough to destroy it?

Darshan lifted his focus from his husband to the tree and froze.

"By the Goddess," Hamish breathed.

The explosion had blasted a gaping hole in the side of the willow. Whilst Darshan had hoped for such an outcome, the powdery, rotten core it had exposed was an unexpected boon.

What rooted him in place was the sight just beneath the bark, in the healthy section of trunk between it and the core. *So many faces.* All seemingly carved into the wood and human in appearance, their expressions were twisted in horror.

Were these the hedgewitches the people of Domian and Udynea had fed to it? Was that what the willow had done to them? What it had tried to do to *him*? *Gods.* Had anyone known?

The willow groaned. The trunk twisted upon itself, closing up the hole. The expression on the faces also moved, shifting from horrified to enraged.

Darshan flung a fireball at the trunk. The flames spiralled across the courtyard, searing through the leaves easily enough. If a spark managed to reach within and ignite, the whole willow would be gutted with little effort on his part.

When it hit the bark, it left little more than a smudge.

Swearing under his breath, Darshan rolled his sleeves up. After the lightning, the fireball should've been enough. Did he have to throw the heat of a furnace at the thing?

At his back, the sound of sawing grew a little more frantic as Hamish fought to free himself from the last of the tendrils with his hunting knife. Darshan wasn't sure what difference it made. Even free, with a broken ankle, any bid Hamish made for safety would be reduced to a crawl.

Stretching out both hands before him, Darshan let forth with a continuous stream of fire. The air immediately heated, bearable by a fraction and no more. Sweat slicked his skin. The wind caused by the blast stirred up dust and ash, doing nothing to help cool him.

In his head, the willow's cry swiftly turned from anger to pain. It twisted tighter on itself, seeking to protect its core even as the tendrils of leaves burnt and the branches charred.

Darshan swayed, the fire under his control sputtering. The air grew cold, a warning he was putting too much of himself into the blaze. Gutting the willow required more power than he had.

Just a little longer. It didn't matter that what he had left wasn't enough. He needed to hold on, to give Hamish enough time to get to safety. He hoped his husband had taken this chance, broken ankle or not. He didn't dare turn his focus from the fire to find out.

Other sounds invaded his mind. They stretched out to him, offering themselves. He just needed to be within reach of one. They were too far. What if reaching them meant abandoning Hamish to the willow? *Not in this lifetime.*

Blindly, he reached back. Maybe if he—

His hand met the woody tendril of a vine. Darshan flinched. *Where—?* He brushed the thought aside as it wrapped around his wrist. There was no time for thinking.

Darshan latched onto the fresh source of power and drew deeply of the energy within. As soon as it reached him, he poured that power into the flames, calling upon all the wrath of an erupting volcano.

Black smoke filled the courtyard between him and the willow, fast obscuring his target. Heat warped the air and cracked the flagstones before him. The blast whipped the worst from his face, but it scorched his lungs. The skin on his outstretched hand blistered, reforming under the sporadic burst of latent healing only to restart the process. He bit his lip, then his tongue, tasting blood every time. Anything to divert the pain.

His face grew uncomfortably warm, his breathing laboured. The sweat that had poured down his skin now evaporated before it could cool. The sulphurous stench of burning fibres invaded his nose; his hair or his outfit, he couldn't tell.

Instinctually, a shield flickered around him, then failed as he took that power and refocused it. He could be safe later. He could heal *later*. He just needed to hold on for a little while longer, so there could *be* a later.

He didn't know how long he had been standing there, enduring the force of an inferno, before he realised the willow's wailing had stopped.

Letting his arm drop, he dispersed the remaining energy across his body, letting instinct take over to heal the damage as he fought to take a decent breath in the furnace-like air. Did the silence mean it was over?

He shook his free arm, checking the skin as his magic healed the last of the blisters and threading a tendril of cold air around his rings to aid in their cooling. At least the majority bore stones that could handle heat. His legs wobbled, barely holding him upright. He couldn't relax yet. Not until he knew the willow was no more.

The smoke thinned, revealing the dark outline of a stump and a few charred branches. Definitely dead.

Relief rattled through his body, quaking out of his lips in a burble of laughter. He had done it. The monster of legend was gone. The hedgewitches who had been fed to the willow were at last avenged. Their souls could now rest. But he'd gotten no closer to discovering where this new power had come from.

Or what other havoc he could wreak with it.

Chapter 11

Darshan waited a little longer for the rest of the smoke to clear, frowning when it didn't. He unwound his arm from the crumbling remains of the vine and removed his glasses to find they were covered in a fine layer of soot, shading the world. He gave the unbroken lens a cursory clean before abandoning the effort and returning them to their customary position.

Through it all, what remained of the willow stayed silent.

Keeping an ear out for any sign of retaliation, he moved on to examine his sleeves. They were intact, if a little scorched, likely only thanks to him rolling them further up his arm. The hair on his forearm was another matter, having been completely singed off. The hair on his face and head, from what he could feel, was altogether unharmed, if a little brittle in places.

Hamish groaned, the sound more distant than Darshan expected when the man had been right next to him. "Is it over?"

He whirled to face his husband, dreading the worst had happened.

What he found was Hamish cocooned in a mass of woody vines. *How?* His ankle was still broken. He couldn't have moved himself and that didn't take into account of how the vines—

Darshan's gaze lifted to the trees and he forgot all about Hamish's question.

Behind the man, the trees that had crowded the courtyard's old entrance were withered and stark. The leaves they'd borne only moments ago now mere husks carpeting everything on the ground, including his husband.

I did this. Just like the time he had brought Hamish back from the brink of death. Only this was on a far grander scale than a clearing's worth of grass and a few bushes.

"I'll take your silence to mean the deed's done?" Hamish sat up, sputtering and brushing away the vines. "Carnivorous trees," he muttered. "That's a first. Does anything in Udynea do *normal*?"

"I'm sure the hedgewitches could give you quite a few records on such phenomena. And not only from within Udynean borders." He glanced back at the charred trunk. Energy buzzed all around him, but none of it came from the willow's remains, nor from the trees he had sucked dry. "This was just weaponised."

Reaching his husband's side, he bent and turned his attention to the injured ankle. It was a clean break and easily mended with the little energy he had left.

Still, the hum of energy from all around called to him, tempting him to use it.

He pushed the desire deep into the dark and focused only on the methods he had been taught so long ago, of tricking the body into quickening its natural healing.

Hamish was on his feet and dusting himself off as soon as the bone was whole. "Do you still think there's anything on it here? There's nae much left of—" He halted upon facing Darshan.

Darshan held his breath. How he wished he could make out his husband's expression without being almost nose to nose with the man. "How bad is it?" His face didn't feel raw anymore, so his skin must've healed. Had he lost more of his hair than he realised?

"Your glasses..."

Scoffing, Darshan waved the concern away. "I'll be fine." Just impaired until they reached Rolshar, where he hoped the imperial estate still had a spare set. If not, then he'd be buying at least a close replacement before moving on. The city wasn't as big as its sister across the other side of the Shar, but it should have a decent glass smith. "Are *you* all right?" After healing Hamish's ankle, his magic hadn't found anything beyond a few extra scrapes, but not all wounds were so easily fixed.

"Aye." Hamish gestured to the vines. They were dead now. And seemingly came from the same source that had reached out to Darshan. "They were set on carting me away to safety. Almost made it until they up and died."

Until I killed them. Darshan stared down at his hands, finding it hard to swallow past the sudden prickly lump in his throat. Would he have taken Hamish's power—his husband's very life—if he had kept going? Would he have noticed? Or did he need to be linked to the source in some way? There was so much he didn't know about what he was doing.

"You sure you're all right?"

No. He needed answers, needed to know what he had done to himself and, most importantly, how to stop it before he hurt someone he cared about. "We should search the ruins. The Ancient Domian preservation domes were designed to withstand immense catastrophes."

Hamish stared at him—silent, considering—before shrugging. "All right, how do we open one if we find it?"

"There's a finite amount of commands they'll unlock for." If it came to it, and providing this theoretical dome was small enough, he'd simply bring the entire thing to Minamist with them and work on unlocking it along the way. "We should get started before the light drops any further." He didn't know if their journey to the shore would be as hampered as the way in, but it would take them a few hours.

Hamish lifted his head to the skies. Dark grey clouds still lingered overhead. "Are we sure the captain hasnae scarpered? Burning that tree put out a lot of smoke." Having been behind Darshan as well as lying flat on the ground, he'd been spared the worst of it, but ash still stained his clothes.

Darshan could only shrug. If they reached the shore and the lakeship wasn't there, then it was only a short distance to the nearest port. It wouldn't be the same as arriving at Rolshar, but he would have the means to journey onwards, as well as track down their mounts and gear. "We'll be fine regardless."

"I dinnae want to lose me horse. I've had her for near a decade."

"You won't." Neither Hamish's mare, nor the gelding Darshan had been gifted, were of a size or breed that could blend in easily with Udynean mounts. Tracking them would be an inconvenience, but not an impossibility. And there was always a chance they'd be confiscated by Rolshar's imperial guard. "I promise."

It would be foolhardy for the captain to leave them here, even if she thought they were both dead. Darshan's arrival was expected. Zahaan would've ensured of that as well as noting which lakeship they were due to be on. To have the lakeship arrive at Rolshar without her royal passengers would see the captain detained at best and executed at worst. Both after a lengthy, and likely tortuous, interrogation.

Hamish hummed, his brows lowering. He remained silent for some time.

Darshan thought he might insist they return to the rowboat sooner rather than risk being left behind.

"Where do you suggest we start looking?" Hamish finally asked, gesturing to the courtyard.

Only the flagstones directly before his onslaught had warped and cracked in the heat. The rest of the courtyard was in much the same state as they had found it, which was largely rubble. The preservation dome, if there was one, could be tucked under a mound of fallen stone.

He had no inkling of where to begin. One spot could be as good as another. "The right side, I suppose." The rubble on that side was less heaped upon itself. They should be able to eliminate sections relatively quickly.

Nodding, Hamish trudged across the courtyard. He toed a few humps of the willow's roots, eyeing the charred stump cautiously. "What do these domes look like, beyond the obvious?"

"They're pretty simple, mostly glass-like in touch and appearance." Some had elaborate designs etched on the outer shell, but most were rather unassuming given how they tended to hold objects of rare import. "You'll know when you come across it." *If*, he softly amended to himself. There was no guarantee that there was such an item here. The Ancient Domians could've easily taken both it and any documents. Or it could be buried deep beneath the ruins. They could quite possibly pass over the dome several times and never know.

Hamish grunted and clambered over the first mound of rubble.

They poked about the ruins, swiftly combing the right side and moving on to the left. Inspecting the layout gave Darshan an idea of what the structure had been before becoming a cage for the twisted willow. At least, it seemed to be the standard layout of an Ancient Domian asylum.

That brought up more questions he didn't want bubbling through his mind. What had become of the original inhabitants? Had the patients been the willow's first meal? It clearly didn't care what it feasted on. Was that why it had been abandoned? Because it had started snacking on those who tended to it?

Shuddering, he glanced at the willow's remains. Their search brought them ever closer to the charred stump. *Still nothing.* With the fire having gutted the tree's very heart, there was little left of the monster. *May it remain that way.*

Strange how a part of him expected it to erupt from the earth in a surge of wrath and strangle them.

"Over here."

He tore his gaze from the stump to where Hamish crouched near a snarl of the willow's roots. His husband poked at something amongst the debris. Upon closer inspection, it appeared to be the outer corner of a wall.

"Might be a cellar?" Hamish suggested.

"Indeed." Or the remains of one, at least. With the upper levels of the building destroyed, he hadn't held out hope for those underground. Nor truly considered them. "But the roofs would've caved centuries ago. They must be full of dirt by now."

"Only one way to be sure." Hamish brushed along the brickwork, searching for a weakness in the masonry with the tip of his hunting knife. The mortar crumbled in a few places. "I bet we can lever some of these out?" he suggested. "Have a wee peek to see if it's worth it?"

"I suppose." Darshan eyed the rest of the courtyard. How many underground rooms could this place have held? What of beneath their feet? Searching everywhere could take them several days. "We've only time to search a few more spots."

Hamish grinned up at him. "A blind man can tell you're curious." One brick came free with a grinding crunch that turned Darshan's teeth furry. "We could always have the captain drop us off at that fishing village across the way. Maybe set up lodgings and return here tomorrow?" Another brick dislodged. The dark gap it left was promising.

"And how do you expect me to explain our reasoning to the locals?" Bad enough for them to be coming from a place people clearly expected them to not return from. "This place has been considered haunted for far longer than it has been abandoned." Such superstition couldn't be overturned in a few days.

He had already experienced that when it came to his twin sister and the ridiculous notion she carried no soul because she was the other child in a multiple birth. Most newborns in her position died a few days beyond birth, if not hours. Anjali lived only because she was the *Mhanek's* daughter. Even then, she didn't exist to most outside the palace.

A third stone slid free. Along with the cracked dome of a skull. Human or dwarf, he couldn't tell.

Hamish jerked back, dropping the brick. Carefully pushing aside the skull, he peered into the gap.

Darshan wet his lips, trying to stem hope. "Anything?"

"Nae much." Feeding his arm into the space, his search for more was far too brief to come up with any extra news. "Feels like a slab fell against the wall when the ceiling collapsed." He tilted the skull back into position and replaced the bricks. "Poor sod must've gotten caught in the fall."

If that were true, then it was possible the being was of dwarven origin. The hedgewitches would need to be informed and a rotating guard contingent organised to be present the whole time the dwarves were busy unearthing the site. "If there's nothing here, then we should head back."

His gaze returned to the stump. *All those faces.* He hadn't paid much attention after the willow had retaliated and there wasn't enough left of the stump to leave an impression. Had he imagined them and their twisted expressions? *No.* He lifted his glasses and scrubbed at his face. Hamish had reacted to the faces. Those ghastly things had been there.

Turning his back on the willow's remains, Darshan headed for the old archway.

What would the hedgewitches make of such a tale? Did dwarves still feel a connection to nature even if they couldn't hear it? He couldn't imagine hearing about the willow's destruction would bring much sorrow, but would it open old wounds? *Possibly.* He doubted ancient records of the fallen would suffice. And what if there was no preservation dome? What else could be gifted to them? The islet itself?

A flagstone rocked beneath his foot. Quite a number of them had lifted or cracked during their scuffle. But this one was far from the willow's rampaging path and his retaliating blast. *Could it be?* He wouldn't have expected his own people to bury it in such an ambiguous place, but maybe the Ancient Domians had done so to keep their invaders from discovering the truth.

Darshan scrabbled at the dirt between the stones, searching for purchase. "Help me. I think—" He jumped back as Hamish's hunting knife dug into the dirt and scraped out a trench wide enough for their fingers.

Together, they were able to lift the flagstone to spy something smooth, hard and black lying underneath. Renewed hope flooded his veins, giving him that little bit extra to haul the slab free and toss it aside.

The dome. He knelt and clawed at the ground, doing little damage to the compacted dirt until Hamish started hacking at it with his knife. They unearthed the preservation dome swiftly. It wasn't much bigger than a cloche fit to cover a single meal, just the size to hide important papers.

He hefted the preservation dome out of its burial place, setting it down atop the very flagstone that had kept it hidden. Whatever metal made up its composition, it was immensely heavy. Far more so than he had expected. Thank the gods it had never fallen into the water or they never would've hauled it ashore.

He sat back and critically eyed the preservation dome's surface. Its outer shell might've been blackened by grime, and a little scuffed from the flagstone rubbing against the surface, but it appeared otherwise undamaged. He ran a hand over the surface, smearing the dirt to reveal a sliver of the original glossy sheen. How long had it been since any human laid a hand on it?

Hamish crouched next to him. "I dinnae see a keyhole. How does it open?"

"Magic," he replied, still stroking the surface. It hummed with the same energy of a shield. So many things in the Ancient Domian lands had relied on a spellster's power. That reliance had contributed to their downfall.

"Can you open it?"

Darshan shrugged. Had this preservation dome been accessible to every spellster here? "Let's see." He sent a small pulse of his magic through the dome's surface. He'd give it one attempt. If the simplest method didn't work, he wouldn't linger or waste more energy in trying others.

The preservation dome buzzed, clearly accepting the magic, but it didn't open.

Hamish sat back as Darshan shook his head, disappointment sagging his shoulders.

"I could try later, once we're aboard the lakeship." Recouping whilst they travelled would put him in a better frame of mind to figure out the code. It would be an unwieldy object to lug through the trees, its glossy surface offering little to maintain a grip on, but not impossible. Maybe if they wrapped it in Hamish's overcoat.

"Aye," his husband murmured, returning to his feet.

The whisper of a beat started up in his mind as Darshan went to follow. Four taps, followed by a pause, two thumps and a tattoo he couldn't quite keep track of. Over and over, it pounded through his head.

"Can you hear that?" he asked Hamish. "It's a—" It wasn't just a random string of notes. It was "—a tune."

Hamish paused, frowning and silently tilting his head to listen before shaking it.

Turning back to the hole they'd dug, Darshan knelt next to the preservation dome. He glanced at the willow's remains, then the surrounding trees. The sound came from them, vibrating across a million leaves. Not a single one of these plants could've been around since this dome was last opened, but could it be the key to unlocking it? He'd never heard of such a method. On the other hand, this *was* an unusual case.

Lightly touching the dome, he followed the beat, first with just the thump of his fingertips, then with feather-light pulses of magic.

The surface of the preservation dome resonated with him. Lines appeared in the originally seamless hemisphere. The sections lifted, spreading wide like a flower, before vanishing as the magic holding them dissipated. All that remained was a metal tray bearing a small book and a pile of papers.

Darshan held his breath, barely daring a wisp to escape his nose. He bent down, gingerly stretching a finger towards the topmost leaf of parchment. There was always a chance that the dome hadn't effectively preserved its treasure. If that were true, then the parchment could crumble at the slightest touch.

The top page was soft and supple, the lettering as clear as though it had been written yesterday. The dome had done an exceptional job. He just wished the subject it preserved had been a less distasteful one.

As expected, the words were in Ancient Domian and carried on for some time before suddenly stopping, the flow of the letters varying as different hands penned their reports. He'd seen that before on a number of ancient texts lifted from other preservation domes. Unlike those old documents, where his people had taken over the running of experiments or governing tasks, there was no sudden change to the Udynean tongue—the older variant, complete with archaic words and strange spelling.

He lifted a handful of sheets from the pile, glancing at each one. Most were records of prisoners and the willow's reaction. Only one bore the method of its creation.

Darshan glared at the willow's stump. Without this guidance of what the Ancient Domians had been doing, the Udynean people of old had continued to feed hedgewitches to that thing. All the while, being blind to the true meaning behind what they did. They had made it stronger with every meal, let the fences degrade and the forest beyond the courtyard grow wild until it was too late.

He set the final parchment alight. The world didn't need the knowledge to make another monster.

Beside him, Hamish crouched to examine the preservation dome, turning the metal disc over and tapping its base. "Handy thing, this. How does it work?"

Darshan shrugged. If anyone ever learnt the method, there'd be hundreds of them across the empire. "No one knows. Not anymore. My people have tried for centuries to unlock the secret." Perhaps, one day, someone would finally do it. When they did, they would undoubtedly become quite wealthy and famous.

"Nae one in all those centuries since?"

Darshan shook his head. He couldn't even reactivate this one. "Many have tried. They left these scattered all over the continent, including Tirglas." Like the old cloister that housed Hamish's younger sister, alongside other Tirglasian spellsters.

He hadn't seen that particular preservation dome, but it must've been the biggest to hold not only an entire room stuffed with books, diagrams and several jars of organs—including two brains. But there had also been three complete skeletons; human, dwarf and even one from the original elven settlers.

A twinge of guilt gripped him at the thought of that place. He had promised to send medical notes and herbs in exchange for a copy of their tomes. He still had quite a number of loose copies—a mere fraction of what resided in those old texts, yet still valuable to Udynea's academy of healers—but any further trade with Tirglas was no longer possible thanks to him winning Hamish's hand.

But if he hadn't competed? If he had let another, a woman, win in his place?

The memory of Hamish lying flat on the ground, his life bleeding from the multiple bites and gouges, surfaced from deep within his thoughts.

Darshan shook his head, scattering the image. He knew precisely what would've happened had he not been victorious. *Death.* First Hamish's, then a possible civil war amongst the Tirglasian clans.

As much as the council, and his father, would harp about losing the chance at a fresh surge of resources, he couldn't have walked away knowing the man he loved would be trapped in a loveless marriage and that Hamish would seek out any means to escape that fate. Even suicide.

Letting the last scrap of burnt parchment flutter to the flagstones, he gathered up the remaining pages. The dwarves would want these records. The hedgewitches might even be able to make sense of them and regain their power. "Let's head back."

"You sure? You didnae exactly find an answer."

"No," he agreed. But did he really need it anymore? It was clear to him now that this ability was his alone, born through the crucible of desperation and desire to not lose the burning beacon that was his flame eternal. A decision he would've made a thousand times over. "But I'm sure." His gaze slid to the willow, finally silenced after centuries. "What's done is done."

And he didn't need some dwarven hedgewitch with no power to tell him he wasn't like them.

Chapter 12

Hamish twitched an eye as a trickle of moisture rolled off his brow. Mercifully, the droplet hit his cheek and vanished into his beard. Sweat already soaked his undershirt. He had shucked his overcoat some time back but the breeze tugging at his hair and clothes did little to cool him, even with the approaching twilight hours.

Huffing, he adjusted his grip on the oars and returned his focus to getting them to the shore. His back ached, the muscles that had trained for decades at archery now growing weary after a day of being pummelled by a murderous tree and hours of rowing.

It would've helped if their destination wasn't so far away. The sun would set soon. He wanted to have solid land under his feet before then.

"I still can't believe they left us," Darshan moaned. "Where's the loyalty to the imperial line?"

Hamish glared disapprovingly at his husband and kept rowing. He should've anticipated the captain up and leaving with her crew. They both should have. "Maybe it vanished along with the bloody great cloud of smoke?" Although the blackness had faded, clouds still hung above the isle.

Rolling his eyes and giving a dramatic sigh, Darshan fell silent. He burrowed deeper into Hamish's jerkin and flopped back against the stern as Hamish continued to row. Darshan had offered to take over for a bit, but one look at how much the man shook and sagged without any additional exertion was all it had taken for Hamish to refuse.

It didn't matter how much Darshan professed otherwise, Hamish knew his husband had used too much magic.

He still wasn't certain what Darshan had done for the willow to finally perish beyond the immense heat, but it had taken a lot out of him. He even looked leaner than he'd been this morning. Hamish would've taken it as the light throwing odd shadows as it set, but that didn't explain his clothes. They might not hang in the same tailored fashion as the rest of Darshan's outfits, but they seemed looser.

Some food and a decent night's rest would hopefully see Darshan back to his old self. They didn't have access to a lot of other options.

Thankfully, it didn't appear to have left him drastically weak. *Or freezing*. Hamish had been warned in his own failing attempts at conjuring a fire to seek other sources of heat beyond his own body for ignition. After seeing the lifeless mass that had become of the trees near the gateway, there was no chance Darshan hadn't taken what he needed from them.

He eyed the *Gilded Cage*, the little spit of land getting smaller by the moment. His childhood had been full of tales about the evils of magic, of how it ate into a being's soul. He'd been sceptical ever since his younger sister was revealed to be a spellster. Even as a child, none of the people within the cloister seemed anything like the monsters he'd been warned about. As a teenager, their magic had saved his life. Twice.

Darshan, being both Udynean and a spellster, was meant to be all the evil a being could be. At least, according to Hamish's mother. He hadn't heard such words from his siblings or his father. But then, his attraction to men had clouded his mother's judgement. Even with Darshan barely using his magic within Tirglas' borders, he was considered dangerous and unstable.

Yes, Darshan *had* wounded men during his time in Tirglas. He had even killed a handful, but never without a clear threat to his life. *All because of me mum*. Men loving men was still a strange concept for most back in Hamish's homeland. It hadn't been considered immoral or a cause for execution for fifty years, but some people were more prejudiced than most, too stubborn for things like reason and logic.

The Mullhind dockmaster, Billy, had been the first to meet Darshan's magical might. That had been Hamish's fault for not considering how the man had always been a blustering fool looking for a fight. If Billy hadn't been as deep in his drink as Darshan, he might've been reasoned with. However unlikely that possibility could've been.

Whereas the old guards who had attacked them during their journey to the cloister? They'd been sober and well aware of who they targeted. *The man who corrupted me*. That was what they had believed. More poison spewed from his mother's mouth.

Billy had gained a broken jaw for his trouble, an injury Darshan mended as promptly as he had made it. Whilst the guards had paid for their transgression with their lives.

It hadn't been a pretty sight, especially the man Darshan had instantly burnt to a cinder, but there was reason behind their actions. Even in their flaws, those men had followed their logic.

What he'd seen on that isle?

Pure evil. No other description for it came close. That willow had been the old tales boiled down to their core.

Darshan tried to explain what the Ancient Domians had done to create the abomination. He had sounded so clinical, like the time he had recounted the tale of the original elves dashing across the stone bridge from Obuzan to Tirglas. Back when the former had still been a part of Udynea. For his husband, it had all happened in the distant past. The centuries were a chasm separating him from his ancestors.

All Hamish could think was of how the willow had only sat dormant for this long because it must have consumed those tending to it.

Frowning at Darshan's idly tapping feet, Hamish forced himself to row harder. The sooner they were back on land, the quicker they could catch up to the lakeship.

They better nae have sold me mare. Maybe his husband was right and their horses would be snaffled up by the imperial servants posted in all major cities and stabled in the estate, but he wasn't happy taking that chance.

"We're almost there," Darshan said, sitting up.

The familiar smell of the docks hit Hamish even before he stopped rowing to look over his shoulder. After spying the village from the shore of the Gilded Cage, he hadn't expected much. A homestead consisting of a few buildings and maybe a smithy or barn they could spend the night in. But there were ten distinct houses sprawled across the shoreline, a handful perched on stilts jutting from the water and what looked to be several bigger buildings set further back from the shore.

The docks were quieter than he expected with most of the boats rocking placidly at their moorings. He had grown up in a port city and the one place that always seemed to be bustling had been the waterfront, even in this dusky light. Rumbling stomachs didn't care for the time if it meant food and idle hands didn't get paid.

Only a few of the bigger boats had crews working at them, many unloading baskets of what he presumed were fish. Others roamed the docks, mending nets, carrying crates and baskets, or merely wandering back to their homes after a day's work. No one seemed to spot their approach. If they did, it was without dramatic gestures.

"Do you think they're friendly?" he finally asked. In Tirglas, he wouldn't have considered such a question for the answer was simple. Travelling through his new homeland had made him wary. Anyone he met on the streets—from lords to merchants, servants or beggars— could have magic. Not all of them would have the same sense of when to use it as Darshan, and more people than Onella wanted his husband dead.

Darshan hummed, playing with his bottom lip as he squinted somewhere into the distance. Whatever he saw through the mess of his glasses, it didn't appear to help with his assessment. "I don't see any sign of an imperial guard station."

They'd come across several in their travels, all very eager to aid their *vris Mhanek*. The buildings were distinct structures, tall and fortified against both physical and magical attacks. Nothing in the village came close. Did that mean he should row on? What were their odds of survival if they disembarked at some unclaimed shore and headed on foot across unknown land?

"I can't be sure," Darshan finally admitted, sitting back. "There must be an outpost nearby, but it could be a day's ride from here. The best we can do is trust them."

Hamish nodded and resumed rowing. If his husband thought it safe enough, he could only follow suit. Besides, they needed food and rest.

A cry went out as they neared. By the time the rowboat reached the shore, a group of fishermen had gathered. Their arrival was met with a mixture of perplexed greetings and questions of where they'd come from even as they helped beach the boat. Hamish let his husband do all the talking.

Darshan was quick with his tongue there, evading anything that even hinted at the Gilded Cage whilst giving vague ideas of a lakeship leaving them to drift. The exchange happened so fast that he barely managed to keep up.

Seemingly satisfied with Darshan's answers, the majority of the fishermen wandered off to their homes or returned to their own boats to resume working in the dregs of daylight.

A couple lingered and it was these men that Darshan sold the rowboat to. It wasn't much, maybe enough for a night's rest at a respectable inn and supplies that they might be able to stretch for a few days. Certainly less than the boat was worth.

They strolled through the village in search of a place to rest. The greying light threw odd shadows over the streets that grew darker as people slid curtains shut and blocked the meagre light leaking out their windows.

The village was definitely bigger than Hamish had first thought, but the inn was in a predictable position not far from the docks. The raucous of music and joviality lured them down the street until the scent of predictably fishy food hit his senses and set his stomach to grumbling. They hadn't eaten since the morning.

Like the surrounding structures, the inn was wood all the way to the ground. The music came from within, suggesting the place housed the usual pub. The scent of food grew stronger as they neared. His nose couldn't catch any hints of spices which was a bonus. As much as Darshan attempted to broaden Hamish's palate and tolerance to local dishes, his stomach still objected to all but the mildest variants.

The music and chatter stopped as they entered the inn. Patrons twisted in their seats to get a good eyeful of them crossing the room to the counter where the innkeeper lingered.

The inn's interior was no different to the dozens of others they'd lodged at. It was the smallest, though. The pub took up much of the lower level, with a narrow flight of stairs leading up to the next. The counter also sectioned off an archway where the smell of food wafted from.

The innkeeper was an older man, his dark hair shot through with grey. He eyed them up and down. His weathered face remained carefully neutral, but his stance slowly shifted. It was the same defensive position Hamish had witnessed from his husband, a move Darshan had learnt whilst training alongside the imperial guard.

They'd encountered a handful of brawls during their travels, both with and without magical involvement. Most of the former had been from a distance, typically amongst thugs or rivalling street gangs. The bruisers there had been sloppy, relying too much on their shield for protection and projecting their attacks well before they made them.

Hamish didn't doubt the innkeeper was a spellster, but the man also knew how to fight and was clearly expecting one. Had he been trained by the imperial army? Had he been one of them? If so, then they might have an easier time getting to Rolshar than Hamish had first believed.

"You two look like you've had a rough time of late," the innkeeper said, a slight guarded tone to his voice. His brow twitched with the suggestion of filling him in on the details of what had left them in such a haggard state.

With half his clothes in tatters and the other half partially burnt, Darshan almost looked like another person. At least he had forsaken his customary adornment of kohl around his eyes during their few days of sailing or he would've looked even more of a mess.

Rather than heed the innkeeper's unspoken request, Darshan leant against the counter and fixed the man with a firm look. Had he also marked the innkeeper's stance? "Do you have a spare room for the night? And bathing facilities."

The innkeeper relaxed, humming and hawing to himself. "That depends if you two are willing to share a bed."

Darshan's face remained still beyond a wisp of amusement lightly skewing his lips. "I think we'll manage." He placed a few coins on the counter, spinning them until they all showed the profile stamped on one side. After so many years in circulation, the coins bore the faces of the current ruler and heir. Had the coins been gold and copper— the latter gaining worth with scientific usage—that profile would've been the *Mhanek's*, but all they'd garnered from selling the rowboat were bronze and silver. The face on them was that of the *uris Mhanek*. "What of the bath?"

Grumbling, the innkeeper shook his head. "We've a tub in the shed out back that you can use. If you're desperate for a proper soaking, there's always the Shar."

Hamish repressed a shiver. Back home, he had once competed in the yearly spring race to shore in Mullhind's harbour on a dare. Swimming in freezing water had been an experience he never wanted to repeat. The lake might not be as cold given the steadily approaching summer, but his aching muscles still objected to the idea of plunging into any water that wasn't steaming.

"We'll take the room and make use of your tub," Darshan said, sliding over the money. He inhaled deeply and, wetting his lips, added a few more coins. "Plus a generous helping of whatever your most protein-laden meal is."

The man's gaze dropped, lingering a little too long on Darshan's bejewelled hand. Then he gathered up the coins, carefully counting them. "Would that be meal first, then bath, *uris Mhanek?*"

"That would be welcomed."

The innkeeper bowed his head. "Please, *uris Mhanek*, rest a while." He pocketed the money and handed over a chunky iron key. "I've a single room up top. I'll see to the tub myself whilst my daughter brings your food." He left the counter, swaying with every other step as he entered the kitchen.

Hamish turned in search of an empty table to discover they were still the focus of the pub's patrons. Their every step, from the counter to a table tucked into the far corner of the room, was tracked by a good half-dozen pairs of eyes.

A young woman came out from the kitchen at the same time Hamish's backside hit the seat. She carried a tray with two steaming bowls, chowder by the smell. It wasn't Hamish's favourite taste, not even after a childhood of eating little else during the middle of winter, but his stomach didn't care what his mouth thought. It was food and it promised to be warm.

Offering Darshan a shy smile, the woman set the food before them.

The bowls had barely touched the table before Darshan started scarfing down the meal, forgoing the spoon to drink directly from the dish.

"I'm afraid we've only cider to offer," the woman murmured, keeping her head down. The innkeeper had definitely told her who Darshan was. At least she hadn't fawned over him or made a scene over his title. "We *did* have beer, but the rats gnawed at the strops last winter and the rice wine from—" She fell silent as Hamish laid a comforting hand on her forearm.

"Cider'll do, lass." At least here, he could be sure that it wasn't poisoned.

The woman frowned. "That accent..." She flicked her gaze to Darshan as if expecting him to offer some insight, but Hamish doubted his husband even heard their conversation.

"I'm Tirglasian, born and raised," Hamish supplied. "That's what you're hearing. How about two of those ciders?"

Nodding absently, she scuttled behind the counter, returning swiftly with two mugs full to the brim before making herself scarce.

Hamish lost himself to the rhythmic motion of ladling spoonfuls of chowder into his mouth. Although it had the aroma of fish and leeks, there were barely any chunks of either to be found. *Trust us to get the dregs.*

The lack of solid sustenance didn't seem to bother his husband. Darshan finished before Hamish got halfway through his bowlful and eyed the remainder of that meal like a starved man.

Hamish pushed his bowl across the table. Magic took a lot out of a body, Darshan needed to replenish what he had lost more than Hamish did.

Darshan grimaced at the act. But rather than the usual blustering insistence of being content with what he had already eaten, he fell upon the chowder, lifting the bowl and draining it much as he'd done with the first.

Leaning back in his chair, Hamish nursed his drink and surveyed the room. The innkeeper hadn't yet returned, he wasn't sure if that was a good omen or not, but the group of men scattered around a nearby table seemed to be engrossed in some sort of game. The act of watching two strangers must've lost its shine when they did only normal things.

All the patrons were human. That wasn't uncommon in these smaller villages. Udynea boasted the largest elven population outside of the secluded realm of Heimat, but most of those elves were enslaved and toiling their lives to the bone on farms or mines far from prying eyes. The ones who were free lived in the poorer parts of the cities as even the smallest singularly elven community became a target for slavers.

The inn's entrance opened, admitting a man who looked like one of the handful that'd been working the docks earlier. He scuttled over to the group and, at first, looked to be heavily invested in the game. Then the low voices stopped completely except for one.

The six of them listened to the newcomer, occasionally glancing Hamish and Darshan's way before returning to their huddle.

Those looks had a certain air about them. *Trouble.* How he wished he had more than his hunting knife. If Darshan had been in better shape, it wouldn't have been much of a problem. As things stood? Well, it definitely wouldn't be the first time he'd been in a pub brawl, but his brother had been far better at defending himself without bloodshed. "Looks like we've already become ripe for village gossip." Not that they hadn't in other pubs, but most stayed back from the dapperly dressed noble and his taller-than-average travelling companion.

"That tends to happen to strangers," Darshan said between slurps. "Can you imagine what they would be saying if I wasn't wearing this?" He plucked at his overcoat. It had taken the brunt of the beating during their fight with the willow, the right sleeve a little charred in places with the rest being soot-stained.

He could. Even with Darshan wearing his plainest silk sherwani, his presence had a habit of drawing the eye and loosening tongues. It also made people wary. Like a lot of things in Udynea, coin was tied to magic and titles. Expensive clothes and jewellery meant nobility. Most people fell over themselves in an effort to accommodate them, more so once they learnt the mysteriously wealthy man standing before them was their *vris Mhanek*.

Frowning, Darshan pinched the skin between his brows. "This is going to be a bother." He took off his glasses and examined them, his lips pursing as he rubbed fruitlessly at the intact smoky lens. The other was clearly beyond repair, but he attempted to clean that as well with similar results. "I was rather hoping to reach Rolshar in a *day*, not a week."

Hamish lowered his mug. *A week?* Were they really that out of the way from their original path? "Rolshar cannae be that far." A day or two on the road at most.

"Not via lakeship. On foot?" Darshan shook his head and set the glasses down. "I'll see about procuring horses and supplies in the morning, but we still won't catch up."

"We dinnae have the coin for horses." They'd barely enough for a few days worth of supplies. Darshan had funded their journey ever since Hamish's mother evicted them from Castle Mullhind, first with the gems from his clothes, then with coin as they reached Udynean lands and he was able to access the vast coffers of the *uris Mhanek*.

But because Darshan could access his funds from multiple cities, they carried only a modest amount on them. All of that with their effects. *And me mare.*

He stifled the growl rumbling in his throat with another swig of cider. A week would give the captain plenty of time to sell her. Or even sail back to Nulshar with her on board. She was the last piece of his old home, to lose her before he even reached his new one…

He couldn't bear to think about it.

"Don't look so sour."

Hamish eyed his husband's glasses sitting forlornly on the table. Without them, anything beyond the length of Darshan's arm steadily lost detail until it was a mass of blobs. The table was definitely wider than that. Darshan might be able to distinguish Hamish from another man, but seeing any expressions would be beyond him. "There isnae any look."

"*Mea lux*, I can practically *hear* you pouting."

Grunting, Hamish leant against the table. He didn't pout. He had never pouted in his life.

"I promised you wouldn't lose your horse and you won't."

How exactly? He washed the question back down his throat with a deep swallow of cider. This wasn't the place for in-depth enquiries. They could discuss what Darshan planned later, when they were alone.

At the table, the newcomer had finished telling his companion whatever story they'd found so interesting. It didn't stop the looks, though. There was one fair-haired young man, a sight that grew less common the further south they travelled, who kept twisting in his seat to ogle them.

Hamish couldn't peg whether any of them were looking for trouble or merely after more to gossip about. Both seemed equally possible. The village didn't have the air of a place that saw a lot of change and he knew from personal experience that fishermen loved to natter about anything new. Even if it was just to complain about it.

But if it was trouble the group was looking to stir up…

Draining the last of his cider in a few heady gulps, Hamish motioned for Darshan to retrieve his glasses. His husband was in no state to fend off an attack and Hamish couldn't take on all of them alone. "Maybe we should—"

"Pardon for the bother, good sirs," the newcomer yelled, bouncing to his feet. He strolled across the room to lean on Darshan's side of the table. "Neither of you would happen to know anything about the incident at the *Cage*, would you?"

"What cage would that be?" Darshan replied, not even bothering to face the man or retrieve his glasses.

The man scoffed. "You might not be from around here, but everyone who goes near the Shar knows about the *Gilded Cage*." He dragged out a chair and straddled it. "You were on the water, I saw you row in. And you reek of smoke." The man breathed deep, wrinkling his pinched nose. "Both of you."

Surprised, Hamish sniffed the collar of his jerkin. After being draped over Darshan during their stint in the rowboat, the leather had grown a wood char odour.

"You know that place is haunted?" the man continued.

"No," Darshan replied, a mask of polite disinterest slipping across his features. He turned his shoulder towards the man in an obvious dismissal.

"It is," the man insisted. He tugged at Darshan's sleeve. "It goes way back. As far as the Ancient Domians. They experimented on people there, you know? Did *terrible* things." He leant in close, cupping his face as if revealing a great secret. "Some say their spirits became so warped that they're still there, luring people to the isle and sucking the flesh right off their bones."

"Bollocks," Hamish rumbled. If that had been true, their ancestors would've packed up for elsewhere a long time ago. The village might not have been on the main path south, but it looked hearty. Maybe even thriving.

The man frowned at him, bewildered.

"What makes you think the smoke was coming from the isle?" Darshan asked before Hamish could explain himself. "We clearly didn't get the rowboat from there."

"I heard the excuse you gave. Survivors from a sinking lakeship, right?" He chuckled as Darshan gave a curt nod. "And it left just the two of you?" The man shook his head. "I've seen a lakeship get itself into trouble. The only things their captains sacrifice is their cargo. There'd be more of you if any lakeship had come to grief."

"That's gloriously optimistic of you." Collecting his glasses, Darshan stood. An act Hamish eagerly mimicked. "But our day has been long and not without its trials. So, if you will excuse us?"

The rest of the newcomer's companions had also gotten to their feet. One stood at the fore, his arms crossed. He'd a weathered, weaselly face and eyed Darshan with greedy interest. "That's an impressive array of baubles you have on your hands. Where'd you get them?"

Darshan's hands slowly clenched. There were a lot of rings, at least one on each digit. Beautiful. *Deadly.* Arrayed together as they were, they hit like a studded gauntlet. Hamish had witnessed what damage they could do with a single punch.

"Not keen to talk about them? Perhaps you will about whatever's around your neck?"

Darshan closed a hand around the heart-shaped ruby pendant still concealed beneath his clothes. Instead of flattening the man or giving him some dry remark as he had done to so many at Onella's soirée, Darshan donned his glasses and turned for the stairs.

"Hey," the weasel-faced man snapped. "I'm talking to you. Don't you walk away." He lunged for Darshan's sleeve.

The faint sheen of a shield shimmered around his husband at the impact.

As one, the group let out a mocking drone of surprise. Hamish had heard such a cry before. Thugs were the same no matter where they were born.

The man scoffed. "You think a little magic is going to scare us off?" He laughed in a flash of yellow teeth. "Guess what?" The man flicked his hand, sending a spray of icy sparks across the shield.

Darshan tilted his head. Even in scorched clothes, with his glasses cracked and smoke-stained, he still managed to regally regard the men taunting them. "It would be unwise of you to persist."

The weasel-faced man laughed long and low. "Would you listen to that accent? It would be unwise," he echoed, a whingeing note creeping into the words as he mocked Darshan's velvety voice. "Who do you think you are?"

"Maybe he fancies himself as some high and mighty," one of the others answered.

The leader nodded. "Could be. Is that why you've got the bodyguard?" He sneered at Darshan, then thumbed his nose at Hamish. "You think he's going to be enough to take us on?"

Hamish squared his shoulders. "If I have—"

"He is my *husband*," Darshan snapped before Hamish could finish. "*Not* my bodyguard."

"That handsome hunk of muscle married *you*?" demanded the tallest of the group. He was broader in the shoulders than the rest, bulky and with sooty stains on his clothes. Likely the village blacksmith. "Friend," he said to Hamish. "You can do so much better than this scruff. I mean, I'm available. So's Kit." The man indicated the scrawny, fair-haired fellow to his left.

Kit flushed and, flustered, babbled out something that sounded like a denial.

Darshan's expression didn't change beyond the faint twitch of a cheek. It wasn't the first time someone had propositioned Hamish—a lot of men, and women, seemed enamoured with his height—but no one had insulted Darshan in the process before. "Do fishing villages throw children at strangers now?"

Kit's face managed to turn a deeper red.

Laughing, the blacksmith spread his arms wide. "I see no children here."

"I've been through my *Khutani*," Kit mumbled.

"When?" Darshan retorted. "*Yesterday?*"

Darshan had explained the *Khutani* several times during their travels, both the rite of passage into manhood and the act of removing the foreskin that the rite was named after. Even with it being one of the few acts observed all over Udynea, his husband had stressed that Hamish, being born beyond the empire's borders, wouldn't be expected to undergo the procedure. For Udynean boys, it was typically done between twelve and fourteen years of age.

Kit couldn't be more than fifteen at the outside.

"My husband hails from Tirglas," Darshan continued before anyone could reply. "You're just a *wee lad* to him."

Hamish shot his husband a glare that he was certain Darshan deliberately ignored. It was true that he didn't see the boy as anything but, that didn't mean he had to rub it in the boy's face, or mangle the translation of his language with such a dreadful approximation of a Tirglasian accent in a Udynean tongue.

The blacksmith shrugged. "More for me."

"Cool your dick, Yaash," the leader snapped, rolling his eyes at his companion. "He's not that pretty." He turned back to Darshan before the blacksmith could reply. "But if he really *is* your husband, then maybe *he* can persuade you to give up those baubles." He jerked his head Hamish's way and the men swiftly surrounded him. "Or perhaps you'll give up whatever's hanging from that chain around your neck that you're clearly protecting."

Darshan watched from behind his shield, his face like thunder. "Don't you dare touch him."

Hamish squared his shoulders. He might not have much in the way of magic, but they'd be foolish to use anything flashy in close quarters. "I'll be fine," he reassured Darshan in Tirglasian. He knew his way around this sort of brawl and even the biggest of the bunch barely reached his chin. Taking out the blacksmith alongside the stronger-looking ones would give the others something to mull over.

His assurance did nothing to change Darshan's expression for the better. If anything, it darkened further.

A rumble came from beneath them, shaking the looser floorboards.

The men stilled, their gazes dropping and their heads tilting like confused boarhounds before they started peering at the walls. A few shuffled their feet in uncertainty. Kit bounced from one foot to the other like a startled bird. None seemed willing to move from their little circle around Hamish.

Nevertheless, he took the opportunity of the distraction to slip through the gap between two of the men, halting as a hand clamped onto his wrist.

"Where do you think you're going?" a voice grated.

The faint crack of wood drew Hamish's gaze to his toe. Vines crept between the cracks, growing thicker as they wound across the floor. Like snakes, they slithered with purpose towards the men. None of them seemed any the wiser.

Hamish glanced at Darshan. There was only stark anger on his husband's face. Had *he* noticed the vines?

"What the—?" The leader lurched back, struggling to free his foot from a forerunning tendril.

"Gods!" Kit screamed, his voice cracking as he stomped on another grasping vine. "It's the *Cage*! It's come to kill us!"

His shriek drew everyone's attention to the floor where it became apparent that the vines were quietly ensnaring every one of them.

Chaos erupted from the group. They danced about, flames flaring and sputtering around them, as did the flash of blades. The vines placidly continued their advance, shrugging off the attacks. They didn't move with any great speed, but they were dogged in their task.

Hamish wormed his way free of their flailing, tripping and scrambling over several low-lying vines as the group continued to battle their unfeeling enemy. A mouse thrown into a busy kitchen would've caused less panic—his elder sister had done that trick when he had seen only five summers.

Reaching Darshan's shield, he pressed as close as he dared. The buzz of his husband's magic lifted the hair on his arms. Hamish paid little attention to it. Where *had* those vines come from? Why were they ignoring him and focusing only on the men, the leader specifically? Were they—?

A hand closed on his sleeve, tugging him through the gossamer shield and into Darshan's grasp.

The vines stopped their pursuit.

"What the hell is going on?" the innkeeper roared from his place in the kitchen doorway. "Have you all gone as mad as Jalaane?"

It took Hamish a moment to realise the man invoked the king of their gods—Darshan rarely spoke of Udynea's many deities. Jalaane was the one who had raged across the land after discovering his wife had fallen for a mortal woman.

"What are you fools getting yourselves into?" the innkeeper demanded of the group's leader. "Scrapping with the heir to the imperial throne like he's a common thug? Are you getting tired of having your head attached to your shoulders?"

"Is that who he told you he was?" The leader clicked his tongue at Darshan before the innkeeper could reply. "Impersonating the *vris Mhanek* carries a steep penalty."

Darshan leant closer to the edge of his shield. "I assure you, the punishment for injuring him is even steeper."

The leader frowned.

"Is that really a risk you want to take?"

Doubt flickered across the man's face before vanishing like a candle in a storm. "He's obviously an imposter. What would the *vris Mhanek* be doing in this backwater?"

"Less sense than a fish," the innkeeper muttered, shaking his head. "Whatever he's here for, it's not my business to ask. Nor yours."

"That only applies to the real *vris Mhanek*." He sneered at Darshan, who responded only with a cool look. "We all know it's punishable by death to impersonate a member of the royal family."

"Then he won't live long once the imperial guards catch up to him." The innkeeper folded his arms and gave a firm nod. "*If* what you say is true."

"But—"

"I've seen the ring. You won't trust his word? Trust my judgement. It's not worth your life. Or that of the rest. Yaash," he said, singling out the blacksmith. "You should know better. And Kit? He went through his *Khutani* only a month ago. What are the rest of you doing dragging him into a brawl?"

Like berated boys having been caught riding the farmer's sheep, the group bowed their heads and ground the toes of their boots into the floorboards.

"Kit's a man," the leader retorted. "If he's fit to steer a fishing boat, then he can fight alongside his crewmen."

"And *you* have enough years on you to be wiser than this. Go home. Sober up. They'll be gone in the morning and we will, by the grace of Araasi, all still have our heads. Kit, get yourself out back and scrub those plates. I won't ask again."

One by one, the men filed out the door whilst Kit rushed through to the kitchen.

Darshan's shield flickered and vanished.

"I hope you can forgive them, *vris Mhanek*, blood boils quick in the drier months around here. Not much else to whet their senses. The... uh..." The words fell into unintelligible mumblings and the ruddiness of his cheeks slowly paled as he eyed the vines.

The vines weren't moving, but the way they laid along the floorboards as if they'd been growing for years held the energy of a spider waiting in its burrow.

Shaking himself, the innkeeper gestured towards the kitchen.

"The bath is ready. If you would follow me?"

Bowing his head, Darshan indicated for the man to lead on.

Hamish followed, quickening his step as the vines slithered back beneath the floorboards with a gentle hiss. Wherever they had come from, he wasn't about to stick around and find out just how friendly they were.

Chapter 13

The offered bath wasn't as big as those back home, more of a
cottage's laundry vat than a tub of any decent size. Hamish had
gotten used to the lack of bigger amenities and normally made do
without any grumbling, but he longed to fully soak in the warm water
with its salts and suds. Getting his aching shoulders beneath the
surface required his legs to stick out into the chill air.

No doubt, Darshan would've had something to say about the sight
had Hamish not actually been alone in the shed. He wasn't quite sure
where his husband had popped off to, but as long as it was within the
inn's confines, he could be certain that Darshan wasn't getting into
trouble.

Whilst guiding them to the shed, the innkeeper had divulged once
serving in Minamist as a guard on the inner wall gates. He had
retired after a riot through the temple quarter had seen him lose the
full use of his left leg. Hamish hadn't understood half of what the
man prattled on about, but he did catch his loyalty to the throne and,
by extension, the *uris Mhanek*. He would ensure Darshan's safety
within these walls.

That might be of further help come tomorrow when they went in
search of supplies. They would only need to reach the next imperial
outpost, but considering how far from the main trading routes they
were, that could take a number of days.

The door creaked open.

Hamish cracked an eye to witness his husband slipping through
the doorway with a couple of clay bottles tucked under his arm.

"How are we feeling?" Darshan asked. His face was already clean
from having made brief use of the tub whilst Hamish undressed, but
he didn't look much better than when he'd left.

"Better." The truth, if by a small margin. He squirmed a bit, trying to right himself and failing the first few attempts before managing to find purchase on the wood. Water poured down his chest, swiftly turning his skin chill. "It would be nicer if I wasnae squeezed in like pork in a sausage."

"Indeed," Darshan hummed. "Rest assured, home has bigger baths. Although, I would love to get you into a public one."

"I'll think about it." His husband had suggested it a handful of times during the months of travelling, but always faced Hamish's refusal with a shrug before moving on.

The idea of sharing a hot pool with a few travelling companions wasn't unfamiliar to Hamish, especially when it was at the end of a day's trek. But doing the same with complete strangers? That was a different matter. *They'd stare.* He'd had confirmation of that particular concern from Darshan. Not just because of Hamish's height, but because of the difference the *Khutani* made. Even with magic to help the healing process, he still shuddered thinking about it. Such an act was unheard of in Tirglas.

"Are you getting cold?" Darshan asked. "I'm certain our room will be ready by now. I could go see?"

"What about *you*?" He couldn't say how badly the drain of magic affected the body, but a proper soak couldn't hurt.

Darshan shook his head. "Don't mind me." He settled on the lip of the tub and, grinning, waggled one of the bottles. "I'm just here to drink and enjoy the view." He took a long swallow.

"Is getting drunk in your state a good idea?" He'd never seen his husband get quite as intoxicated as the first time he tried Tirglasian ale, but Darshan had been tipsy several times. *And woke up every morning with nae a hint of a hangover.* Hamish knew that was due to healing magic, but he wasn't sure if the same magic helped Darshan whilst imbibing.

Darshan lowered the bottle. The grin returned, creasing the corners of his eyes. "This is fermented mare's milk, not wine. It's barely alcoholic."

"Mare's?" He hadn't drunk milk since he was young, but Udyneans seemed to enjoy downing all sorts of liquids. He had gotten used to being offered the different varieties, typically goat and sheep alongside cow, but never anything from a horse. Even those living on Tirglas' plains only consumed mare's milk the once, as newborns.

His husband nodded. "It's just the thing to aid in replenishing my reserves." He gestured to his feet where the other bottle sat. "There's some more cider for you, if you're of a mind."

"Maybe later." Resting his elbows on the tub rim, Hamish tipped his head back to stare at the candlelight flickering along the ceiling. "I've been thinking." When it came to the group in the inn, Darshan had barely acknowledged any of the leader's threats. He had clearly been bothered by the blacksmith's suggestion of not being good enough for Hamish, though. "I dinnae believe you've shown your jealous side before."

"My jealous side?" Darshan scoffed. "Why ever would I be jealous? Since birth, I've had everything I could ever want."

Hamish grunted his agreement. Beyond Onella, he hadn't been introduced to Darshan's family much less been able to get anecdotes on his husband's younger years. But it seemed pretty much idyllic. He couldn't imagine being able to grow up knowing he would be accepted no matter who he fell for.

"And now I get to share all that I have with my beloved light," Darshan continued.

"You still tensed earlier." Spying Darshan's brow beginning to furrow with confusion, he added, "When that man suggested he'd be a better fit for me."

Soft laughter parted his husband's lips. "That wasn't jealousy. I was irritated. If I had my full power at hand, I would've dealt him a good dozen blows to his backside for the impertinence. Do I have to strap a sign around my neck declaring you as my husband? Is it really so outlandish to believe a ruggedly attractive man such as yourself would be with someone like me?"

Hamish shrugged. "Aye, it would seem some have that very problem. I could always wear a copy of your signet ring." He hadn't mentioned it, partly because his banishment meant he could no longer claim a crest, but marriage between clan nobility in Tirglas involved the crafting of a merged crest along with matching rings.

Darshan gasped as though Hamish had suggested murdering someone. "I can't have you wandering around with the symbol of the *vris Mhanek* on your finger. That's entirely inappropriate and could get you killed."

"For wearing your mark?"

"*Mine?*" Darshan shook his head. "I don't have a personal mark." He raised his hand, examining the signet ring. "The symbol is of the crown for a reason. The *Mhanek*, and his heir, have no ties, no duty, to anyone and anything beyond the people."

"What of your clan?" In accordance with the old laws, much of Hamish's immediate family lived in the same castle, the exception being his younger sister, who resided in a cloister alongside other spellsters. He also had cousins, and others even more tenuously related, scattered around Mullhind and the surrounding royal clan lands. As singular as Darshan made the imperial line seem, they had to come from somewhere.

"We've... distant relatives. It's harder to track a line that melds into others once separated from direct inheritance. Of course, there's a slew of aunts, uncles and cousins on my mother's side." He idly rocked back and forth on the tub's edge. "Not that we have much to do with them. The reminder pains my father too much."

Hamish stayed silent. Never had an entire bloodline been shunned because they dredged up bad memories for the head of the clan. Not that there were many in his immediate family line who still lived outside the castle. His father's parents had died young and his grandparents on his mother side, the old king and princess consort, had succumbed to the last plague.

"But that's a different issue," Darshan said. Slapping his hands onto the rim of the tub, he bounced to his feet. "I'm sure, once we've settled in Minamist, that people will adjust to your presence at my side swiftly enough without me marking you as mine." He tilted his head, eyeing Hamish with an unnerving sharpness for someone who couldn't see properly beyond the length of his arm. "How are your shoulders?"

They ached and not only from the rowing. But if he told Darshan that, his husband would insist on using whatever scrap of magic he had regained to ease them. It wasn't the first time he had hit the ground at speed. The overworked muscles would eventually relax and the bruised skin would settle down without the aid of healing. "I said I'm fine and I am."

"But still sore, correct?" He nodded before Hamish could utter a word. "Shuffle a little more towards the middle, *mea lux*," he commanded, pushing his sleeves up and toeing off his boots. "I may not be able to heal your aches away, but I can still ease your pain somewhat."

He did as ordered, even though it meant scrunching his legs before him.

Darshan unbuckled his trousers, letting them drop to the ground, and stepped into the tub to resume sitting upon the edge. The sure press of his fingers ran along Hamish's shoulders and upper back, gently kneading.

Hamish leant into the touch as his husband worked to ease his tired muscles. This wasn't the first time Darshan had administered such a treatment, but it was usually accompanied by the prickling, tingling sensation of magic.

Darshan fell silent as he worked. His fingers tenderly sought out the knots in Hamish's muscles, whilst his thumbs and the heels of his hands dealt with each one. He just as gently adjusted Hamish's position to work at a troublesome spot, rubbing harder.

Unbidden, a low moan slithered out Hamish's lips.

"Goodness," Darshan replied on the breath of a laugh. "You don't even make this much noise when we're having sex."

With the way Darshan's touch stirred him, they might as well have been preparing to do just that. He tried to say as much, but all that came out was a slurred, "It's good."

"Is that an implication that sex isn't?" Even without seeing Darshan's face, he could picture the man's impish grin.

Hamish splashed water over his shoulder at him. "Bite your tongue. I dinnae say that. I meant—"

Chuckling, Darshan cupped Hamish's chin and coaxed his head back until their eyes met. "It's all right, *mea lux*. Your touch leaves me just as much at a loss for words." He kissed Hamish's forehead before sitting upright, his fingers releasing their tenuous grip on Hamish's chin.

Hamish captured his husband's hand before it slipped out of reach and pressed the back of the fingers to his lips.

The weight of Darshan's head gently settled atop his own. "*Mea lux.*" Cushioned by the bulk of Hamish's hair, the shift of his jaw was barely noticeable. "My shining beacon. If you want this massage to continue, you'll have to give me back my hand."

Reluctantly, Hamish let go.

Darshan returned to silence as he continued the massage, falling into small circles that kept Hamish's shoulders supple.

Hamish leant back, his eyes closing. He could happily fall asleep like this.

Sluggishly, his thoughts turned to the aftermath of the battle with the willow. Those vines that had broken through the inn floor, they had the same look as the ones on the islet, he was sure of it. "Can you still hear plants now the willow's dead?"

Darshan grunted. "Not at the moment, being inside helps. But that monster wasn't the cause of my abilities."

"You can still hear them even though your magic is taxed?"

"I don't think it's tied to my magic. If so, it's passive."

"What about controlling them?" The vines hadn't busted through the floorboards on a whim. The way they'd gone specifically after the men could only mean they'd been guided and it certainly hadn't been by Hamish.

"I don't believe so."

"Those vines back at the *Gilded Cage*, the one that dragged me out of the willow's reach and helped you..." His thoughts trailed off, taking his voice with it. He couldn't be certain, but the vines seemed to heed Darshan's bidding.

"What of it?"

He turned to look over his shoulder, grunting as Darshan's fingers found a lingering knot. "I—" But then, the willow had moved of its own accord. Who was he to say the other plants there weren't capable of it? "I dinnae ken." Perhaps things would seem clearer in the morning.

Darshan hummed. "I attempted to duplicate the phenomena before I came in. To no effect, I must add. Perhaps it was some residual power from the trees that helped me with the willow." He stared at his hands. "Whatever it was, it appears to have slipped beyond my control."

"Were they in your control to begin with?"

"I've been asking myself that. I believe the vines reacted to my temper. Beyond that?" He spread his hands wide. "It's curious though, that I was barely able to summon a shield, yet the vines reacted so strongly."

"It wasnae magic?"

"Not as I've been taught, certainly." He sighed. "It seems I will need to speak with the Coven after all."

The hedgewitches? Dwarves didn't have magic, not as spellsters did. They once had some affinity towards the earth, but that had been long ago. All the current hedgewitches had at their disposal were records, ones dating back to the formation of Dvärghem as a nation. "You think they might have records of others doing what you've done?"

Darshan bowed his head. "And possibly an explanation. I can't be the only one."

"What if you are?" Saving Hamish's life had involved a lot of pain on Darshan's part. It had drained him and brought him near death. If it *had* altered him as he feared, he might've also been the first to live through the transformation.

"I don't want to think about that."

"Dar? You wouldnae lie to me, would you?" He twisted in the small space to see his husband's confused expression. "You're nae trying to keep things from me? Right? You really dinnae ken what happened?"

Darshan smiled. "*Mea lux*, you are one of the few people I trust with all my secrets. I am truly keeping nothing from you."

Hamish grunted. "Except it took you this long to tell me you can hear plants." They'd been travelling for months.

"I thought it would fade. I thought I'd have answers by now. Clearly, I was wrong on both counts."

"Tell me again how it happened."

He shrugged. "There's not much more to tell. I was trying to keep you alive. Everything had healed, but your heart was failing. You had lost so much blood."

He didn't remember the attack well. Not like Darshan. It was mostly sensations. Fear. Pain. And a flash of those wet teeth coming for his throat.

Yet, the same question would slink its way up from the dark and always had him wondering. Would they be in the same place if it hadn't happened?

"*Mea lux?*" Darshan gently called. "You still with me?"

"Aye." Shaking himself, he resumed leaning back on his husband's knees as the question returned to the dark depths of his thoughts. "Just thinking." Hamish groped over the edge of the tub. "I'll have that drink now."

"Allow me." Darshan stood and retrieved the bottle.

Hamish turned around in the tub to face Darshan whilst they drank. He rolled his shoulders, testing his husband's handiwork. They didn't ache as much, but it made him no less knackered. "Careful, you might get me used to this."

"Of being waited on hand and foot? Pampered like a prized parrot?" Darshan swirled a finger in the water. "You should. After everything you've been through, you deserve the divine blessing of Araasi herself."

"That's the one who committed adultery with a mortal woman, right?" And turned the poor lass into a lick of flame to mount on her crown like a trinket when her godly husband found out. "The one who made the first Eternal Flame?" He tipped his head back to take a long swallow from the bottle. The angle gave him a decent view of his husband's face. "I dinnae think I need her blessing."

Darshan wrinkled his nose, the cracked lens of his glasses reflecting the candlelight at odd angles. "That used to be a perfectly romantic tale until you picked it apart." He gently flicked a spray of water at Hamish. "You... story-ruiner."

Hamish echoed the phrase with a chuckle. His husband was usually more inventive when it came to such things. "You must be bloody shattered." So was he, when it came down to it, but he could've come up with a far better insult than that.

Groaning his agreement, Darshan sagged, propping his elbows on his knees, his arms dangling listlessly between them. "What gave it away?"

Although it had been an educated guess, the confirmation was good to have. "Well," he teased, "I'm fully naked and you're nae trying to climb in here and have your wicked way with me."

A low bubble of laughter shook his husband's body. "Am I really so bad?"

"Aye." Over the years, he had heard a great deal about the bottomless depths of spellster stamina. Darshan's explanation of how the strength of their magic was said to tie directly to their sexual desire did nothing to contradict those rumours. Nor did the countless examples Hamish had been treated to during their travels. "It's been three whole days now, you usually cannae last more than one."

"My apologies for finding you so sexually appealing." Another hiccup of laughter, followed by a soft sigh, escaped his lips before he sobered. "But, even if my magic hadn't been so taxed, there's a lot to be said for being in the right mindset."

"And also nae discovering the beasts from your legend is a bloody murderous tree?"

"That, too." He upended his bottle, frowning and tapping the bottom for the last drop before letting it roll to the floor. "I tried to do it alone, you know? Fighting it. It took too much. Just like saving your life. I wasn't strong enough on my own. Maybe if I'd had someone to share magic with, I might've—"

"Dar..."

He scrubbed at his face. "There are stories—" He chuckled. "There's *always* stories. But they're cautionary tales to scare children. Like how the cackling owl will flit through your window at midnight and steal your tongue if you tell a lie."

"You and I definitely grew up with different views of what a cautionary tale is." The worst he had ever heard had been how to deal with arrowbacks, but that was because a bite from the females was deadly.

"My point is, they're not meant to be real. Can you imagine the tales being true? Not the owl one—that was always ridiculous—but the Stamekian fables speak of taking a life to renew another?"

He recalled the tales, or at least Darshan's version of them. Of people who'd been dead for several days being brought back after the killer's life force was drained and used. He hadn't thought much on the stories until now.

He'd seen the aftermath of Darshan taking with he needed from the plants, the brittleness of death. For it to be a person? It would be like that man Darshan had instantly burnt to the bone.

"I've wondered over the months..." Darshan's focus seemed to drift into the distance before he pulled himself back. "My people consider it as forbidden magic, but they also say it's impossible. It can't be both. So which is it? If it's impossible, then why forbid it? If it's forbidden, then it must've been possible at some point."

"Maybe it takes a lot out of a person to do," Hamish guessed. "Maybe it's only possible to a few and deadly to the rest."

Darshan's lips thinned in thought. "Perhaps. But those tales also mention people and animals as the source. Never plants. I fear I might be the first there." He leant back, rocking on the edge of the tub. "And, gods help me, I pray I'm the last. But one thing at a time. We must reach Minamist and that requires collecting our things at

Rolshar."

If they were still there. "How would we pay for horses?" They could restock their supplies at each outpost, giving them less to lug, but a horse would be a great deal harder to come by.

"They might accept a means of payment beyond coin." Darshan lifted his hand to examine the rings that had almost caused a brawl. "If they're eager to fight over these, then maybe they'll also trade for a horse or two."

"You shouldnae have to do that." They could walk easily enough and, if Darshan was right about there being an imperial guard post, then they wouldn't be on foot the whole way. "You've already given up several rings." Two had gone during their wedding, one to convince the Tirglasian priest to marry them, whilst the other had been resized for Hamish's hand.

"They're just gemstones and precious metals."

It wasn't as simple as that. There were so many, but Hamish knew the origin of each one. Darshan would never give up the simple band of silver with a crown carved in relief, that was the signet ring of the *vris Mhanek*. The one bearing a big oval ruby with small diamonds studding the outside was likewise off-limits as it had been given to Darshan at the age of twelve by his father after the *Khutani*.

Most of the others were also gifts from his family, some mere bands of rare ores, others great chunky things of metal with tiny gems cringing in the middle. The humble wooden band of his wedding ring sat amongst them, its surface now charred.

"Do they nae all carry meaning?"

"Only some. Most are merely pretty baubles gifted to me because it's an easy way for my half-sisters to pay lip service to their brother." He adjusted one ring, admiring it in the light. "Even if I'd as many arms as the Great Mother, I wouldn't have enough fingers to wear them all."

The Great Mother was one of the few goddesses widely worshipped by Udyneans. Hamish had seen a number of statues and reliefs dedicated to her, most depicted her as eternally pregnant, all showed her with six arms and eyes.

"But if it bothers you," Darshan continued. "Then I shall use the rest of our money for supplies and we'll walk to the outpost. However, it will make our journey longer."

The idea of lengthening their time from Rolshar's gates, and his mare, didn't sit well with him, but their choices out here were few. They'd no guarantee that any of the outposts would be willing to give up a pair of horses to their *vris Mhanek*. Maybe if they promised to send them back once reunited with their own mounts.

"For now, I think bed is in order." Darshan stood and briskly clapped his hands. "Out of the tub with you, it's my turn."

Hamish obeyed, shivering slightly in the chill air. He hastened to dry himself, well aware of how his husband's gaze lingered on his every movement. Before meeting Darshan, he never would've thought this mundane activity was at all enjoyable to watch.

By the time he was dry enough to pull on clothes, his blood had well and truly warmed to the idea of sex. He faced his husband, finding no answering heat in those hazel eyes. *He really* is *bloody knackered.* Hamish knew Darshan would respond favourably if he coaxed the man, but it would be far better for them to use the night to replenish their reserves.

Still, it felt strange to bid his husband a brief farewell and venture up to bed in the full knowledge that sleep would be all he got there.

Chapter 14

Darshan strode down the sparsely lit corridor, his footsteps echoing off the naked brickwork. The lanterns sputtered at his presence and also the lack of decent oil. Their light threw odd shadows along the walls.

He'd never been to the detention centre in Rolshar. It seemed a little different to the one sitting just within Minamist's walls, with the exception of these cells being underground. The sounds were the same, groans reverberating from somewhere deep within the twisting network of corridors, punctuated by the occasional boom of a door and the fainter impression of rattling chains.

There were *infitialis* cells set further into the building. The vibration of that much magic-nullifying metal in one place set his skin to itching. He shuddered at the thought of having his magic, the very core of his being, denied to him for more than a short moment.

At least the place didn't stink quite as bad as Minamist's detention centre. Or that might've been thanks to a week's worth of riding with little breaks. He had yet to change after seeing Hamish secure in the imperial estate and still reeked of sweaty horse.

But bathing would have to wait. He needed to find out what the imperial guards had done with the lakeship captain. The best bet was here, but few would be aware of just what prisoners were being held, and where, at any given time. Would they keep her in the special chambers? She might've had spellsters in her crew, but she wasn't one.

Given how many days they'd been missing, the interrogation room was a possibility. Not one that Hamish would've liked, but if the lakeship captain had been detained because of Darshan's disappearance, then she would've been questioned. Thoroughly.

A familiar shadow detached itself from the corridor wall up ahead and sauntered Darshan's way. Although the low light obscured most of the silhouette's features, their eyes gleamed in as only elven eyes could. There were but two elves who would dare approach him in such dingy surroundings without a hint of apprehension and only one could've reached Rolshar in the time he had been missing.

"Zah?" Darshan lengthened his stride to greet his spymaster.

"Do you have any idea of the stress you have put me under?" Zahaan boomed down the corridor. The man strode under a lantern, the light etching sharper shadows into a face that gave serious thoughts towards murder.

"What are you doing in Rolshar?" He had left the man back on the other side of the lake. It was a short distance by lakeship, but he hadn't ever been able to shift the man from the trade hub without a direct order.

"What am I doing here?" his spymaster echoed, incredulous. "What am *I* doing here? What do you think I would be doing when news of the *vris Mhanek's* disappearance reaches me? *Knitting?*"

"Of course not." Darshan pushed his glasses further up his nose. The frames didn't mould to his face quite as well as his destroyed pair, but they would in time. For now, being able to see properly was worth the mild annoyance. The lack of a headache also helped his mood. "I thought you might've sent your second in command to oversee—"

"*That* idiot?" Zahaan snarled. "You think I would entrust your life to *them?*"

"*You* trained them." Whilst their original purpose was to trace rumours and obliterate those plotting his demise, his spy network had been roped into playing the part of Darshan's personal guard a great many times.

Zahaan waggled a warning finger under Darshan's nose. "Do you know how many of my people are out scouring the Shar's shoreline for your corpse at this very moment?" His voice wavered the longer he spoke, cracking with a certain wet emotion.

The sound had Darshan's magic tingling along his skin. He hadn't heard such a noise since they were children. "I'd hazard a guess and say *all of them?*"

"*Dead,* that damn lakeship captain said," he continued as if Darshan hadn't spoken. "She fell to her knees and wailed it as soon as the servants couldn't mark you coming off her ship."

Darshan winced. If the rumour of him dying managed to reach the wrong ears, then he'd be in a race to reach Minamist before Onella dug her claws into his father's grieving heart.

"*Fortunately,*" Zahaan added with a scathing look. "One of the dock guards had the sense to drag her in for questioning. But I thought—" His voice finally broke, squeaking terribly as he scrubbed his face.

"Zah, I'm—"

His spymaster swiftly closed the gap between them and, before Darshan could react, threw his arms around Darshan's shoulders. Zahaan squeezed with a shaky might, soundless sobs the source of his trembling.

"Goodness," Darshan said, keeping his voice low and light as he patted the man's back. "Such familiarity with your *uris Mhanek*. Just as well we are alone or people might talk."

A soft hiccup of laughter bounced Zahaan's shoulders. "Arse," he murmured, the word lacking heat. "I was really worried. I thought you had gone and died on me. How was I going to explain that to Ma?"

He could well imagine how Nanny Daama would react to being told of not only the death of a man she had practically raised from birth, but of how his end had been through his own stupidity. For those words to come from her son would've only sharpened the knife.

Darshan gave the man's back one final pat. "I love you, too."

Zahaan laughed. "Don't let your husband catch you saying that, he might think the wrong thing of us."

Doubtful. Hamish had heard Darshan's romantic declaration multiple times, both with the phrase his husband understood and the Udynean variant. "He is aware of the custom." Whilst the Tirglasian words to denote close, romantic feelings might've translated to the same as what he spoke to Zahaan, the meaning behind them was different. A distinction Hamish would easily pick up on. His husband might be considered as lacking in certain ways when it came to the Udynean ideal of a nobleman, but his cognitive abilities wasn't one of them. When it came to the rest, as far as he was concerned, his husband's gentleness and compassion more than made up for his limited magical talents.

With a sniff, his spymaster collected himself, stepping back to put the usual respectful distance between them. "What were you even thinking in going to the *Gilded Cage?*"

Darshan readjusted his glasses. "I was... called there."

"*What?*" Zahaan shook his head, his face scrunching. "I don't—" He fell quiet as Darshan raised a silencing hand.

"I'll explain later." Hamish might've taken the idea of him hearing plants in stride, but his husband also had the oddest notions of what a spellster was capable of. Zahaan knew the extent of Darshan's abilities. He would demand to know how it was possible down to the last detail. Darshan needed time to think on how to explain to keep the man happy without giving him everything. The last thing he wanted was another person attempting to replicate his miracle or more deaths on his conscience. "Take me to the lakeship captain."

"She's this way." Zahaan indicated the corridor he had come down. "I was speaking to both her and the inquisitors when I received word of your arrival."

Darshan resumed marching down the corridor with his spymaster trotting at his side.

They encountered a handful of guards patrolling along the way who saluted as they passed. The main trunk of the inner corridors was largely relegated to transporting prisoners rather than confining those of import. The actual cells were situated in corridors peeling off from this one.

The closer they got to the interrogation room, the more Zahaan fidgeted with the *infitialis* chain around his neck, running the ownership tag up and down the links. Darshan was well accustomed to the action. There was something his spymaster wasn't saying that he knew would upset Darshan.

Questioning his spymaster would get him nowhere. Zahaan could be more stubborn than the prevailing winds of a monsoon. But silently waiting him out and letting the man work through his own thoughts often got results, a trick Darshan had picked up from Nanny Daama.

Sure enough, after a few more corners, Zahaan cleared his throat and announced, "You're not going to like what you find."

"I know what the inquisitors are like." They didn't exactly ask people politely. The lakeship captain would've been tortured. Mercilessly so. *Because of me.* He could've placed all the blame at her feet—she *had* chosen to flee before sunset, after all—but if *he* hadn't set foot on that islet, neither of them would be here. "I am prepared."

"Is that why your husband is remarkably absent?"

"Sort of." Darshan hadn't explored the full depth of Tirglasian legalities—not beyond those pertaining to trade—but he'd a sneaking suspicion they were rather blunt in their punishments. *He* might be able to stomach and eventually forget whatever the inquisitors had done to the woman, but Hamish would definitely not approve of their methods.

"Where is he? Somewhere safe?"

He gave an agreeing grunt. "I left him tending to his mare at the imperial estate." Not that he could've stopped Hamish with anything less than magical binding. The man had all but vaulted over the railing into the stall to throw his arms around the horse's neck. Surprisingly, the mare had whickered at Hamish's arrival, the soft and low sound booming in the confined space. "Did you find out anything new about the attempted poisoning on him?"

Zahaan shook his head. "Could it be possible that your half-sister *is* responsible? What if she placed the marks of hypnotism on that woman to eliminate her from suspicion?"

"Doubtful." She'd been after the throne for so long that she would have to know any foul play towards him or Hamish would see her as the first choice in a long line of suspects. "But I'll keep that thought in mind." Such a complicated plot was in her wheelhouse of tricks. And having him actually attend her soirée with his husband at his side had certainly seen her bold enough to outright attack Hamish.

Still, something felt wrong about it. If there was one redeeming bone in his half-sister's body, it was that she didn't purposely endanger her slaves. The man who had served Hamish was one of her favourites. And there was one other thing that didn't match her methods. "You've said remarkably little about the woman herself. Did she not belong to the household?"

Zahaan shook his head. "Not at all, she wasn't even under their employ. Before you ask, she wasn't with one of the guests, either. No one seemed to know anything about her."

That seemed even less plausible. Onella often boasted about the security around the mansion and, as much as it pained him to admit it, she was right. Not even Zahaan had been able to sneak his way in. The woman wouldn't have gotten beyond the front gates without express approval.

They speculated further on various scenarios as they walked, each one just as unlikely as the last. Worst still, there wasn't anything either himself or Zahaan could do to gather more information. Even if completely innocent, Onella wouldn't allow his spies to prowl through the mansion again. And he couldn't order it without cause.

"We're there," Zahaan declared.

The corridor looked no different to the dozens of others they had walked through. Even the closed door appeared to be the same sturdy metal panel as the dozens of others they'd passed. The exception was the three guards standing outside the entrance, one on either side of the door with the third in front.

Darshan quickened his pace. The sooner this was dealt with, the better.

The guards stiffened at his approach. He wasn't surprised. Only the inquisitors saw the prisoners unannounced. People like himself were expected to wait in the bright and airy rooms above whilst they brought the prisoner to him, which was ridiculous. What did it serve other than to give the guards time to prepare the prisoner for viewing, to hide the worst of what the inquisitors had done?

"Let the *vris Mhanek* enter," Zahaan bellowed.

Two of the guards dropped to their knees and saluted him as the third scrambled to obey the order and unlock the door. Darkness greeted them as the man slid the metal panel aside. If Darshan didn't know better, he would've thought the room empty.

Zahaan led the way inside, pausing in the doorway to set a spark off towards the right wall. A flame burst to life, speeding along a groove in the wall until the whole room was ringed in fire.

The scene it illuminated was one Darshan sorely wished he could snuff as quickly as the flames.

The lakeship captain sat in the middle of the room, naked and shackled at wrist and ankle to a metal chair. Her head was bowed in resignation and her chest barely rose with each breath. For a moment, he thought she was near death.

She lifted her head as Zahaan shut the door behind them. Her gaze fastened on Darshan. "You're alive? No." He got only a glimpse of her injuries before her head dropped, her unbound hair long enough to cloak her face in shadow. "You're just a figment, a ghost, here to torment me. I know my crimes." She clutched the armrests with shaky hands. Her fingers were caked in dried blood, the nails completely absent. "I am prepared to pay for my cowardice."

"I'm not dead." Darshan knelt before the woman. He laid a hand on her wrist, flooding her body with his healing magic. The inquisitors had been thorough in their methods, leaving but a few obvious outward signs of their handiwork. They had delivered all manner of injuries that would still keep her alive enough to talk. Their barbarism had already destroyed one kidney and, if he wasn't mistaken, broken and healed her fingers a number of times. "What you saw that day on the Shar. The smoke? That was me ridding the islet of its demons."

Her gaze slid upwards, not quite meeting his. Although diminishing under his ministrations, the faint swelling of her left eye kept it from opening as far as the right. She wet her lips, the bottom one freshly split.

He waited for her to speak again.

"You're lying," she finally croaked. "No one comes back from the *Gilded Cage*."

"If you had lingered," he continued. "If you had waited until sunset, you would've known. Neither of us would be here right now." She might've made the call to remain in Rolshar to ensure the trip back across the lake worthwhile, but he and Hamish would've been well on his way to Minamist.

"The crew..." She shook her head. "When that smoke rose from the trees, they were terrified. If I had told them to stay, they would've mutinied. I couldn't let that happen."

"I understand." He wasn't sure if the lakeships operated under the same code as the sea-going ships, but crews who mutinied, for whatever reason, were declared pirates and hunted as such. "Nevertheless, you abandoned us. You abandoned *me*." He dipped his head, holding her gaze until he was certain she understood just how far she had erred. Potential mutiny was nothing next to deserting the *vris Mhanek*, no matter how much he agreed with her course of action. "The law demands punishment. I cannot change that, only lessen the terms."

She turned her gaze from him, blinking furiously as tears ran down her cheeks.

Darshan got to his feet, his stomach knotting. She had already suffered enough. "You are to be stripped of your rank. The lakeship is yours no longer, it is now mine. Your crew shall be free to seek other employ, but *you* shall be imprisoned. Nine years ought to suffice, one for every day you thought me dead." Hopefully, it would be long enough for others to forget the reason behind her imprisonment and she could get a fresh start.

The woman bowed as much as the restraints would allow. "Thank you, *vris Mhanek*." She knew as well as he that the punishment should've been far more severe. Endangering his life, whether through a direct act or via neglect, was treasonous and there was only one punishment for that.

Darshan left the room, leaving Zahaan to snuff the fire as he strode through the doorway. He lingered just outside long enough for instructions to be sent to the detention centre's warden before carrying on. His spymaster would ensure his orders had been followed later, he just wanted out of this place.

Zahaan was unusually silent as they left the guards behind. He remained that way until they were alone again. "What the hell are you going to do with a lakeship?"

Darshan faltered for a step. *A fine question.* What *was* he going to do with it? He didn't travel across the Shar often enough to warrant owning his own transportation, although no one would think twice of the *vris Mhanek* having such an obvious extravagancy.

He stroked his beard, considering his options. It would be a pain to hire on a captain and train a new crew, but that task wouldn't be his. And where would he send it? Back to ferrying people and goods? "My copper mine, the one on the western shore? It's still productive?" He'd so many plots of land scattered across the empire, both in gifts and personal investments, that it was hard to keep up with those further afield.

"I've not heard otherwise."

"Then send it there. I'm sure Anavi would vastly prefer having access to transport I own rather than relying on others." As the mine's overseer, the reports he got from her were often peppered with complaints on shipping delays.

Recollection of the reports had him groaning. He had been away for almost a year. There was going to be a mountain of paperwork waiting for his approval even with Anjali handling them.

Zahaan's laid a hand on his chest and bowed. "I will see to it. Will you be staying in Rolshar long?"

"Tonight, at least." They'd not only pushed their horses—borrowed from the first outpost they'd stumbled into—but themselves to get here. A decent night's sleep in a bed that wasn't stuffed with straw would do both of them wonders. Perhaps Hamish would be interested in a little exploration of Rolshar's many entertainments. They didn't call the city a cultural hub for nothing. "For now, I just want out of here." He wouldn't be able to easily shake the image of the former lakeship captain from his mind, but a lungful of fresh air and some distance from the detention centre would ease his stomach.

Again, Zahaan bowed, this time gesturing for Darshan to walk ahead. "I know of a shorter passage."

~ ~ ~

Darshan found his husband in exactly the same place he had left him upon returning to the imperial estate, still fussing over the mare. Hamish had even led her out of the stall to run her around the yard as if the stablehands were incompetent.

Darshan lingered at the stall railing as Hamish finished cooling the mare down and grooming her already immaculate coat. "You know, there *are* people who are quite happy to do that for you." It was different when they were on the road or at an inn with barely enough room to house a single horse. The imperial estates had all the amenities a place could need.

"It's more personal if I do it," Hamish replied, the brush not even pausing. "Helps keep the bond strong, too. She must've been worried sick. Is that nae right, me wee lass?"

Being of Tirglasian stock, the mare wasn't *wee* by any stretch of the imagination.

Hamish coaxed the mare's head lower, rubbing her forehead and scratching between her ears. "I bet you missed your favourite being in the whole world."

Darshan smiled to himself. If there was one thing he could be sure of once they reached Minamist, it was that his husband would definitely get along with Anjali. Hamish could mother his mare whilst she cooed over her giant tortoise.

"Maybe you should try it," his husband suggested. "Might make him an easier ride."

"Maybe," he hedged. He eyed the black and white bulk of the gelding he'd ridden from Tirglas, currently munching his way through a pile of hay. Keet wasn't unruly, but he could be difficult. It didn't help that, whilst considered a pony in the animal's homeland, he was the same height and build as a moderately sized draught horse.

"It would also probably help if you stopped calling him an insect."

Darshan scoffed. "He doesn't understand Udynean." A point of annoyance when others dealt with him. He would need to have the royal stablehands taught the right phrases once they were settled in Tirglas. If nothing else, then for the sake of Hamish's mare. "And I don't see you calling your horse anything special. It's always *lass*."

"That *is* her name." He gave her shoulder a hearty pat. "It's nae the most original, I ken, but she doesnae seem to mind."

"You're starting to sound more and more like my sister." Anjali would say similar things about her tortoise, Mani. She had also deliberated on naming the animal for days as though it were her child, right before settling on what basically meant precious.

"There's a sickening thought. Quick." Hamish squared his shoulders, making him look even more of a mountain. "Give me a topic she wouldnae discuss with you before you start to think I *am* her."

Laughing softly, Darshan leant against the railing. "That wouldn't be remotely possible. She doesn't have anywhere near as luxurious a beard."

"Good, then I willnae need to assert me superiority there." He managed to hold a stern expression for all of a single breath before bursting into laughter.

Darshan swiftly found himself joining in until he was draped over the railing struggling to remain upright as his legs failed to support him. The image of his sister sporting Hamish's full beard was difficult to shake free, she'd hadn't the same sturdy features to pull off such a look.

It was some time before he could speak coherently again and once he had gathered himself, he was crying enough to have fogged his glasses.

He gave a final jovial sigh as he dried his eyes. "I was wondering, since we're planning on spending the night in Rolshar, how do you feel about going to the theatre?"

"What?" His husband had collected himself far sooner and now paused in brushing his mare to face him. "Like a—what do you call it?—date? You want to duck out with me?"

"In a fashion, I suppose I do." The one time they'd had anything close to a date had been sneaking off to laze atop a cliff whilst their escort set up camp. It had been spontaneous and foolish. But the memory of the setting sun enriching the fiery orange-red shade of Hamish's hair as he fumbled through a childhood recollection of their mythology still set Darshan heart aglow. The theatre wouldn't be anywhere near as romantic, but it would be enjoyable.

Hamish shook his head. "We're *married*. Couples dinnae duck out once they've tied the knot."

Oh. Darshan hadn't considered there might be certain customs that would still appear foreign to Hamish.

But they were far from Tirglas now. They didn't have to be bound by another kingdom's constraints. And besides... "When we were in Tirglas, we could barely step outside the castle together without an escort." Only once did they manage such a feat, to disastrous results. "I couldn't just be alone with you."

"We've been alone since leaving Mullhind."

"Yes. But this isn't riding down some dusty road or sharing a meal in an inn whilst the singers blare their version music at us." With him wanting to put as much room between them and the Tirglasian border—to reach home before the rumours of his time in the other kingdom could be warped beyond repair—there hadn't been many chances to show Hamish much of Udynea.

"I've loved those times."

"As have I, but this is a place I would've actually taken you to had we met in Minamist." He slipped through the gate and into the stall. "I was denied the right to properly court you because of your mother. I know we're already married, but I still want that chance."

"Court me?" Hamish returned to grooming his horse, the act poorly concealing his smile. "You'd do that by taking me to the theatre and do... *what?*"

The memories of his past visits to the theatres in Minamist flashed through his mind and heated his cheeks. There was a good reason his father had expressly forbidden him from attending them without family as company. "Relax?" he suggested. "We could watch a little opera, if you're musically inclined. Or see a comedy?" The latter performance was one he had already witnessed in Minamist a few years back. They weren't the best, but he would weather their unique sense of humour if it meant time at his husband's side that was neither in the saddle nor in bed.

"Just you and me?"

"That would be correct."

Hamish jerked his chin at the nearby archway where a handful of guards had sectioned off the stables. "And *them?*"

"I'm afraid so." The freedom they'd had travelling through a village would undoubtedly be curtailed whilst within city walls. "Zah will insist on the precaution." The man might even order his people to escort them all the way to Minamist.

"The burden of being married to the *vris Mhanek*?"

"One of them, yes."

Hamish looked down at himself. "I dinnae have anything to wear." His clothes, like Darshan's current attire, were travel-worn and desperately in need of a good wash. Something the estate's servants could take care of whilst Darshan and Hamish were elsewhere.

"Not true, *mea lux*." He must've forgotten that their effects had been unloaded from the ship along with the horses, but this was the perfect opportunity to show him one perk of having the *vris Mhanek* for a husband. "Finish up with your *Lass* and I'll show you just how wrong you are."

Chapter 15

Darshan's words continued to bounce around Hamish's head as they entered the quarters set aside for the *vris Mhanek*. The room, though a little musty from lack of airing, looked no different to the one they had been staying in at Nulshar.

The same couldn't be said for the wardrobe. The space looked to be of a similar size, but Darshan's clothes only took up one side, crammed along a railing that he could've sworn was bowing. The little shelves where his shoes and boots sat also seemed to be pulling double duty.

The other side wasn't completely empty. A familiar outfit cringed against the far wall, the shoulder of another peeking out from behind it. Had additional space been made for Hamish's things? Just how much did the servants expect the two of them to be lugging through Udynea?

Darshan gestured to the almost empty side as he ran a hand along his own selection of clothing. "Take your pick, *mea lux*, I'm certain they'll all look ravishing on you." He plucked a black outfit from the selection of his own clothes. "I'm off to bathe, although you could join me in that, too, if you'd like."

He needed a bath, no mistake there. He hadn't bathed solely with Darshan before, but if he did, he'd a suspicion that the only activity they'd be doing tonight was each other. "I'll wait for you to be done with it first. You ken what you're like."

Laughing, his husband conceded with a bow. "You don't need to wait, though. There's more than one. I'll use the *Mhanek's* quarters and send for someone to heat your bath." He gave a farewell flap of his hand over his shoulder as he slipped through the wardrobe doorway.

There was the subtle click of the door, a murmur of voices, then silence.

Hamish turned back to the clothes. *Take me pick?* He recognised the silvery outfit as the one Darshan had ordered for him in Nulshar. But what of the one behind it? Had the tailors made him another in the time he and Darshan had been missing? Not implausible given how swiftly they'd crafted the first. He eyeballed Darshan's vast collection. Did they expect him to own just as many? *I hope not.*

Sliding the silvery sherwani along the rail, he found not one, but two other complete sets, one in a shade of bluish-grey and the other in a muted golden hue.

Hamish stared at the trio of outfits laid out before him. *Which one?* He went to lift the silvery one off the rail.

"Your highness?"

He whirled about at the address. He hadn't heard the door, not since Darshan's departure, or the footsteps of anyone approaching.

The man standing in the doorway looked just as startled as Hamish felt. "Th-the bath?" he managed, bowing low. "It's ready for you, your highness."

He nodded his thanks and dismissed him with a flick of his hand, a gesture he'd witnessed Darshan use in Nulshar.

The man bowed again, backing away and out into the hallway. The purple banners hanging from the ceiling, depicting the *vris Mhanek's* crown in gold, softly swayed in the gust of the door closing.

Like in Nulshar, the chambers were a mass of luxury. The framed bed, with its gauzy curtains and piles of floppy cushions, took up a large chunk of the space. The short flight of steps leading to it also didn't help to make the bed seem smaller. Their saddlebags sat at the foot of the bed, retrieved from the lakeship and examined for clues, but otherwise undisturbed.

Beyond the bed, the room was lushly furnished. A chaise lounge sat near the window, its surface faded by the sun, along with a low table. There was another table in the far corner and a few chairs. They'd eaten a light breakfast at a similar spot in the other imperial estate.

There had also been a massive gilded mirror adorning the wall closest to the wardrobe door in Nulshar. Not so here. There *was* a third door, though. It had been closed when Darshan first guided him to the room, but now stood open.

The bath sat steaming and waiting.

Hamish sighed as he submerged himself. The race to Rolshar from the fishing village had been virtually non-stop. He wasn't a stranger to riding hard for days on end it, although he hadn't needed to for some time. His muscles had ached a little in the beginning, adjusting by the third day, but that didn't mean he was above enjoying a little pampering.

Scrubbing the travel dirt from his skin took little effort. Even with every inch of him clean, he wasn't quite ready to leave the warm water. After all that had happened at the soirée, the battle with the willow and the trip here, it was nice to just relax. Maybe he could convince Darshan to linger for a few days. They were already a week behind schedule, nothing they did would have them reaching Minamist sooner.

He clambered out when the water started to cool and dried himself. Throwing a towel around his waist, he padded back into the wardrobe gathering up his saddlebag along the way. If the tailors had the time to make two outfits, had they also crafted him some new smalls?

A quick search revealed the answer to be no. There wasn't any footwear to match the new outfits, either. That was to be expected. It didn't matter, the trousers hid most of his boots and he'd enough in the way of undergarments in his saddlebag to not be bothered. If Rolshar's servants were anywhere near as efficient as those in Nulshar, then his travel-stained clothes would be clean by tomorrow morning.

His hand landed on the silvery sherwani. Remembering a snippet of conversation with Darshan from the last time he had worn it—the pained look his husband had shot him at the suggestion of wearing the same outfit at two functions back-to-back—he slid the sherwani along the railing and picked up the bluish-grey one. The stark, geometric design embroidered on the shoulders and a third of the way down the front looked to be done in simple silver thread. No hints of actual blue.

He swiftly donned his new attire. In cut, it sat no differently than the sherwani he had worn in Nulshar. The buttons holding the front closed were fiddly. Difficult, but not unmanageable. There didn't appear to be any matching shawl, but he had seen Darshan go without for most occasions that he assumed the addition to be a formal one.

The click of the door opening alerted him to company.

Hamish paused in fastening the last few buttons to listen as the person drew nearer. He knew the owner of those footsteps quite well. *Took your time.* Or maybe his husband had also opted for a little soak.

"Slate is definitely your colour."

Hamish turned at Darshan's voice to find the man decked out in the same dark attire he had worn in Tirglas. Except... "Did you nae burn that with the others?" Apart from the attire his husband had bought whilst travelling through the colder climate of Hamish's homeland, Darshan had come away from Mullhind with only one of his original outfits. The rest had all been reduced to ash in an effort to salvage the gemstones for future trade.

Darshan eyed his outfit as if he hadn't ever seen it before. The black sherwani was trimmed in dark embroidery, the light glistening off small pieces of obsidian sewn into the design and a row of black pearl buttons that held it closed. "I've duplicates of my wardrobe all throughout the imperial estates. As do you. Now, at least."

"That seems grossly extravagant."

"And this isn't?" He gestured to the room. "Besides, not being burdened with extra clothing whilst travelling does mean I can travel faster via horseback rather than in a carriage."

Hamish grunted. He hadn't thought about that. When Darshan had first arrived in Mullhind, he'd come bearing a heavy chest, mostly full of clothing. Lugging it into the castle would've taken a pair of strong men. A good packhorse would've been able to cart the contents, but that likely would've also damaged them.

"You going to shave beforehand?" Hamish countered, pulling their conversation in another direction before his husband gave him that self-satisfied smile that set all sorts of notions fluttering through Hamish's mind.

Darshan had definitely taken the time to make himself tidy. His skin emanated a soft musk, his hair was combed, fluffed and styled rather than be allowed to fall naturally. He had even applied the usual lines of kohl around his eyes despite that no one but Hamish would see it tonight. But his facial hair was another matter. During their extended trip from Nulshar to here, the sides had started to fill in. It still wasn't anywhere near a properly full beard, but it was getting closer.

Darshan hesitantly rubbed at his jaw. "Do you think I should?"

"That's nae a fair question, you ken what I prefer." Tirglas was full of hairy men and he'd be a damn fool to think it hadn't affected his tastes.

"I must admit, it has grown on me, if you'll pardon the pun." He chuckled as Hamish rolled his eyes and groaned. "I think I'll keep it. I can always shave if it proves bothersome." He grabbed the still-unbuttoned collar of Hamish's sherwani and coaxed him closer. "The more important question is, how does it feel?"

Their mouths met, abruptly at first as Darshan practically collided with Hamish. Then there was just softness and the silken glide of his tongue against the seam, parting Hamish's lips, exploring as if they hadn't been travelling together all this time.

Hamish's legs wobbled. There was an old tale in Tirglas, of how a spellster's kiss could steal away a man's breath, his strength, his very soul. It was a little too late to worry about if it was true, but if every spellster kissed like his husband, he could see how such a rumour could start.

He didn't know what it was about the theatre that Darshan wasn't telling him, but it had definitely fanned that impish spark he loved in the man.

Not that this kiss was anything different to the other times. Hamish welcomed the familiarity. It was warm. It was comfortable. He was safe in the arms of a man who loved him wholeheartedly.

It was like arriving home.

With a sigh that slipped halfway down Hamish's throat, Darshan withdrew. "Well? What do you think?"

"That you're looking to start something."

Darshan grinned. "With you, *mea lux*? Always." He kissed Hamish again and, this time, there was a slight teasing quirk to his husband's lips. "But I'll settle for a pleasant, uneventful evening out with my husband."

"Then lead the way, me heart." Hamish bowed and indicated the exit with a broad sweep of his arm. He'd never been to a theatre like what Darshan had described. Travelling shows set on a makeshift stage, yes, but not something in a building dedicated to such entertainment. He was definitely eager for the chance to simply enjoy himself without any distractions, even if it meant they needed guards to shadow them.

But Darshan promised that Zahaan's people understood how to be discreet. *That I willnae even ken they're there.* He certainly hoped so. He didn't want their first official time stepping out to be like those morose stories Darshan told him. *Nae kidnappings. Nae deaths.* Just a simple night out like normal people.

~ ~ ~

Darshan sighed as the carriage finally came to a stop outside the theatre. They had rattled along the road, bumping down it so much that he suspected the driver was aiming for every pothole. If his backside hadn't already adjusted to the previous week's rough riding, it likely would've started smarting several streets back.

He made a mental note to have a word with the estate's overseer once they returned. If it had jarred his bones this badly, then who knew what damage it did to the carriage.

One of the guards opened the door, the rest fanning out along the street. Hamish eyed them, a faint wrinkle of distaste creasing his nose. The escort couldn't be helped. Zahaan had practically demanded it. All Darshan could do was insist on a modest retinue.

Offering Hamish his arm, Darshan strode up the stairs leading to the theatre with the guards spread out along the sides and rear. The building was old and not terribly well-maintained with the grey stone pitted and cracked from decades of weathering the elements. He had expected more from a place housing a supposedly angelic voice.

Nevertheless, Darshan could barely keep his excitement contained. "I have missed the theatre," he confessed. "Father forbade me from attending those in Minamist without his presence after the last incident." One that had seen a man dangling from the balcony railing with his trousers hanging off his ankles.

Hamish arched a brow at him, his gaze not stilling for a moment as it roamed all over the building. "Should I ask what happened?"

"Well..." His cheeks heated as memories of past lovers flapped about his mind like startled moths. "You know how noisy I can get," he hedged. That hadn't been the worst part—how could he have predicted the man would lack such a poor grasp of his own upper body strength?—but it had been a factor.

"You've done it in the theatre?" Hamish hissed in his ear.

Darshan nodded and hummed an agreement. Practically every time he went.

Finally, Hamish tore his gaze from the building to shoot Darshan a wide-eyed stare. "Is there anywhere you havenae had sex?"

"Council hall, slave market, judicial court..." he instantly rattled off. "That's just off the top of my head." He used to be able to declare to never being sexually intimate in the wilderness, but Hamish had put that admittance to rest about a month ago. It hadn't been the most mind-blowing sex they'd had—his thoughts being far too caught up in how they were utterly alone in the untamed forests of the north and could be interrupted by the local wildlife at any moment—but it *had* been fun.

They passed beneath the once airy patio, the wide arches now sullied by a screen of bars. Inside, the building had the atmosphere of once being a mansion. The foyer was huge, far bigger than those of the theatres in Minamist, the vast majority of the space taken up by another flight of stairs luring them upwards with dimly lit corridors leading somewhere into the dark on either side.

Groups of people dressed in their finest attires milled beyond the circle of guards surrounding Darshan and Hamish. A few dared to get closer, whilst the rest gossiped amongst themselves.

Evidently, news of him spending the night at the theatre with his husband had reached Rolshar's upper classes. He would need to speak with Zahaan about that. Loose tongues around the imperial estates could easily turn to poison in the cup.

A woman trotted her way down the stairs as they started up.

Judging by the worn state of her clothes, she wasn't a noble. At least, not one who ranked very highly.

She made it to the landing where the edge of the guards halted before falling to her knees. "It is an honour for the *vris Mhanek* to visit our humble theatre." She glanced up, swiftly took in Hamish, and bowed her head again. "And his highness as well, of course. I am Lady Aashi, Mistress of The Spectral Palace."

Darshan dipped his head in acknowledgement. He had chosen this particular theatre based on favourable gossip about the prima donna, but there'd been plenty of other rumours. If they chose to blatantly refer to the ghost who supposedly haunted this place, then there must've been a fair bit of myth surrounding it. "I take it that our box is ready?"

"Of course, *vris Mhanek*." Her eyes widened, as did her mouth. A pretty display of shock that looked too well-rehearsed. "Rest assured, I have seen to it *personally*." She gave a simpering smile that churned Darshan's stomach and reminded him of the other reason why he had stopped visiting the theatres in favour of the temples. The festivals might've been further apart than he would've liked, but at least the priesthood didn't fall all over themselves in his presence. She got to her feet. "Shall I show you the way?"

Darshan gestured for her to continue back up the stairs.

Lady Aashi resumed her talking with barely a pause. "If you are here, word of our Krittika has reached Minamist." She fussed with her bun, tucking wayward strands of light brown and silver back into place.

"Actually, I've been abroad for some time." How many months had it been? *Ten.* With another to go before he reached home.

The realisation hit him like a bull. Had it really been almost a year since he setting foot in Minamist? No wonder Onella had started referring to herself as the *vlos*. She probably thought his mission in Tirglas was a front for his exile.

Disappointment sagged the woman's bronze cheeks. "Oh," she murmured.

"Still, I have heard of this singer," he admitted. "The Jewel of Rolshar, so I am told."

At once, Lady Aashi returned to her preening and talking about the angelic singer as though she had personally birthed the woman. Darshan slowly turned his focus elsewhere whilst she waxed lyrical with barely a pause to breathe. If Darshan hadn't heard similar praise from less biased mouths, he wouldn't have believed a word of it.

Finally, they reached the entrance to the royal box. Darshan and Hamish lingered in the corridor with Aashi as the guards checked everything within, including a pitcher of wine already set out for them.

The corridor kept going, bending into the gloom. To where? He didn't know.

It seemed to bother the guards, too. A quick query by the captain had them dividing their strength between the two entrances rather than invade Darshan and Hamish's privacy by taking up position directly outside the box's entrance. Anyone who desired entry would be thoroughly questioned before they were allowed to pass.

"You dinnae look all that thrilled at her greeting," Hamish murmured as he watched a pair of guards escort Lady Aashi back down the corridor.

"I'd merely forgotten how much I detested the court's fawning, is all." Whilst they had encountered little in the way of disrespect towards his title during their travels, flinging themselves at his feet for no reason hadn't been an issue. It would only get worse once reaching Minamist. After so long away from his duties, there were no doubt countless nobles seeking his audience to aid them in their trials. "I shan't let it sully my mood." He strode into the royal box, beckoning Hamish to follow.

The royal box was positioned directly across from the stage, jutting out over the seats far below. Drapes that looked as though they hadn't been dusted properly in years edged the opening. The space was illuminated in candlelight, soft enough to see without being intrusive. The light played on the worn curves of the four seats and a pair of slim tables, the wood polished by years of casual touch. The wine sat on the left table, the two goblets already full.

Hamish leant on the railing—it barely even reached his waist— and gave a low whistle. "I dinnae think they could cram any more people down there."

Joining his husband, Darshan gave an acquiescing grunt to the assessment. Every seat was full, with others scattered up and down the stairs leading to each row. The people milled about, their combined chatter drifting up as mere noise. Did anyone notice they were being watched? A number of them seemed to glance this way, but it was difficult to make out people's faces from this distance.

Maybe they believed in the tales and how this was the ghosts favoured spot to watch. Not that he could blame the spectre, it was an excellent view.

There were other such boxes staggered along the wall, curving along the wall until they abutted the stage sides. It was a curious design choice. Certainly not one he had seen before. For now, they were illuminated for the guests to seat themselves. At least once the candles were snuffed, they would become shrouded in shadows.

Leaving the inhabitants perfectly private and able to enjoy the evening in blissful peace.

"Odd name for a theatre. Spectral." Hamish rolled the word around his mouth. It wasn't one either of them used all that often. "That means ghostly, right?"

"Amongst other things," he agreed. He indicated the theatre with a broad sweep of his hand. "This place is supposedly haunted." A ridiculous notion given that spectres and the like only existed in stories.

Then again, he hadn't believed in murderous trees, either. Not before encountering the willow.

"Haunted?" Hamish echoed. "I wouldnae have thought Udyneans would believe in ghosts. Thought having magic would've taken the mystery out of a lot of mystical things."

"Not really." Whilst having magic meant it could aid in solving mysteries, it didn't work for everything. "There are some things the gods clearly mean to remain unexplained." Spirits being one of them. If there was a ghost wandering the theatre, there was nothing anyone could do about it.

"So..." Hamish drawled as he settled into one of the seats. "Do you ken what this tragedy's about? Have you seen it before?"

Darshan arched a brow in Hamish's direction. Whilst he had needed only to briefly explain the idea of an opera—his husband claiming they'd similar theatrical works in Tirglas, if not as ornately housed—he hadn't realised Hamish knew anything about this particular piece.

Chuckling with only the slightest hint of smugness, Hamish leant back in his seat. "Dinnae look so surprised. I saw the banner flapping across the doorway when we arrived. *The Deceits of Love*? Cannae be anything but a tragedy."

"I cannot rightly say," he admitted. "I don't believe I've seen this one." Nor could he be entirely certain it was tragic. "It has been a long time since I've visited a theatre, after all, and I don't quite recall the specifics of each one." His mind had generally been concerned with engaging in more carnal acts. "But it hardly matters, they rather sound all the same to me." So many of tragedies and romances alike revolved around jilted lovers and misunderstandings that could be resolved if they just sat down and talked for a little bit. He much preferred action pieces, but they weren't as common.

"Then why suggest coming here?"

The stage curtains parted before Darshan could formulate an answer.

Silence trickled over the crowd until there was only the rustle of people hastily settling into their seats. A few squeaks of a flute issued from the music pit before stilling.

"Curiosity," Darshan said, snuffing the candles with a precise snap of wind, throwing them into darkness. One by one, the other boxes followed until the only light came from the stage. "A few of the nobles at Onella's soirée were telling me about the leading lady here."

"The one the mistress was on about?"

"The very same." He leant forward in his seat, searching for the prima donna as several women danced onto the stage. None looked dressed for the part, unless the character she played was meant to be from a farm. "She's rumoured to have quite the voice." A gift from the gods, many had said.

A man strode out into the middle of the stage, all the while belting out his woes. Largely about a woman his family forbade him to see, someone born far above his station.

Definitely a tragedy.

We should've gone to the other show. Even if he *had* seen the comedy more times than he had wanted to and didn't think much of it, Hamish might've actually had fun.

"Dar?" In the darkness, his expression was difficult to make out, but he sounded uncertain. "What—?"

He laid a hand on Hamish's forearm as the man left the stage and another figure swept in. A woman. This had to be the prima donna. "Relax, *mea lux*." He topped up his husband's goblet. "Try to enjoy."

The woman merrily glided across the stage, her voice smoothly skimming up and down the scales. She was pleasant to listen to, and something he might've thrown a few coins to if heard busking on the street, but hardly worthy of the rumours.

Perhaps her reputation came not from skill, but from others believing Lady Aashi's hype.

His attention wavered as the opera continued until he lost track of the story. What little he heard seemed like the usual arc of secret lovers being thrown into turmoil because of a jilted suitor, just with the death of the supposed heroic lover. Not that he saw anything valiant about dying in a duel.

He glanced at the stage as the prima donna raced out from the wings to dramatically discover her lover's death with a warbling tune. *Here we go*. If he had realised much of it would be woeful singing, he wouldn't have come no matter how unique a voice she had.

The woman lifted her head, her lamenting cries reverberating through the theatre.

Darshan's jaw dropped. "It would seem—" He jerked back as Hamish's hand landed on his chest, the fingers dancing upwards until they reached his face. "What are you—?" He fell into silence as the questing hand clapped over his mouth.

"Hush."

In the ambient glow of the stage lighting, Hamish's face was barely visible. But Darshan saw enough. Whilst the plot of the opera wasn't anything *he* hadn't heard before, the experience was new to his husband and it showed upon his face. *I really am a jaded fool.* Still, it was a delight to see his husband enjoying himself.

A portion of the stage lifted, slowly winding upward until the height was equal to their box as she sang her pleas to the heavens for her lover's return. Note after note filled the theatre, along with a faint ethereal trill squeaking through as her voice reached its peak before swiftly dropping again.

Darshan frowned. There was only one species he knew to have such a vocal range. *Elves.* Had he imagined it? To his knowledge, not even half-elves were allowed to perform in operas much less star in them. He wouldn't pick Lady Aashi as the type to risk her theatre and it did seem at odds with how she praised the prima donna.

Yet, what he had heard...

The music stopped, leaving the woman to vocalise the last few notes without any accompaniment. Darshan listened, seeking for that trill as she climbed the scales. Nothing. Perhaps he had mistaken the source and it came from one of the instruments.

The stage dropped from beneath the woman to the gasp of the whole crowd.

He sat up, clutching Hamish's arm as his husband lunged forward to grasp the railing as though he was preparing to vault over it and save her.

Those blue eyes glared at him. "What—?"

Darshan pointed wordlessly at where the woman hung in the air, clearly supported by a pair of ropes, and still singing with barely a warble. She no longer used the full range of her voice, no doubt hampered by the harness holding her aloft, but the lower range was still smooth and melodious.

The curtains slid shut, leaving the last note echoing in the darkness.

The crowd erupted into a cacophony of clapping and cheers.

Hamish sat back, breathless laughter shaking his body, as Darshan reignited the candles. "That was definitely different to what we have back home." He rubbed his right thigh. The whole leg had started bouncing through the last aria. "But what happens now? They cannae stop there, she still hasnae learnt what actually happened to her lover."

"Relax, it's just intermission." He waved his hand at the stage. "Gives them time to change the props, I suppose." And let everyone's heart settle from the scare.

"A break? Time enough for me to use the privy?"

Darshan inclined his head. "Best get one of the guards to show you the way. Although, may I suggest limiting the amount you drink next time?" He hadn't even realised until now how empty the wine pitcher was. He'd barely consumed his first drink, which meant the majority had gone down his husband's gullet.

Shrugging, Hamish stood. "Then get me stronger alcohol," he shot over his shoulder as he left. "I've barely a buzz."

Left alone, Darshan sat back and closed his eyes. He listened to the bustle below as others stretched their legs or had similar ideas as Hamish about relieving themselves. He had missed this gentle contentment. Much of his adult years had been bouncing from one bout of mindless pleasure to another. This carried the very domestic comfort he would've once scoffed at.

A feeling he was, embarrassingly enough, growing accustomed to.

Tamed by innocence. Who would've thought that he, the *vris Mhanek* everyone expected to find dead under a pile of naked men, would become enchanted by the gentlest of pursuits? *Getting syrupy in your dotage.* That was fine, too.

The pad of approaching footsteps reached his ears. Far too hesitant, and too soon, to be his husband returning.

He twisted in his seat to face the person, one hand raised in the scant chance that they were hostile.

The man standing in the doorway jumped, upsetting the tray he carried and almost sending the two goblets flying. Somehow, he managed to stabilise them. "M-my apologies, *vris Mhanek*. I... I didn't mean to—"

Darshan waved the man into silence and gestured for him to set the drinks down. There were only two ways in, he wouldn't have gotten here without the guards both questioning him and ensuring the drinks weren't tampered with.

"Mistress Aashi sends this with her compliments. She trusts you're enjoying the show."

Darshan took up one of the goblets. "It has been entertaining."

The man clutched the tray to his chest. Droplets of sweat ran down his face and his wide eyes didn't quite seem to settle on any one place for long. "Is there anything else I can do to increase your enjoyment of the night?" He bent over, his lids lowering. "Anything at all."

Darshan eyed the man over the goblet's rim. He hadn't imagined the thread of invitation woven through the man's words. *This place is one of those theatres, is it?* That explained the design of the boxes. *Absolute privacy.* He set the goblet down. "Perhaps you've not heard." He fiddled with the marriage band. It might not be the most materially expensive thing—or pretty for, as much as he had tried to polish the surface back to its original richness, the wood had charred deep—but its value was beyond comparison. "I'm rather spoken for."

The man shrugged. "Since when does that stop a person?"

"Allow me to put it another way, then." He fixed the man with a pointed stare, taking in the narrow nose and pinched features. "I'm not interested."

"As you wish, *vris Mhanek*." The man bowed, bumping the drink set aside for Hamish. Dark wine slopped over the rim. "Again, my apologies." He hastened to readjust the goblet and be on his way, his footsteps like thunder as he fled with a squeak.

The faintest shuffle of someone trying to avoid the man alerted Darshan to the presence of another at his back.

He glanced over his shoulder to spy a silhouette he had grown to know well. "*Mea lux*," Darshan purred as his husband re-entered the royal box. He clasped Hamish's hand as it came into reach, bringing the knuckles to his lips. "You're just in time. The final act will start soon."

Rather than sit, Hamish bent over him and, for a moment, Darshan was entirely disorientated by the sight of the great looming figure that was his husband. Hamish's forefinger slid beneath Darshan's chin, tilting his face up. Then those very kissable lips were upon Darshan, claiming his mouth in a possessive manner that all but took his breath away.

His heart quickened, blood rushing to all the usual places and making him dizzy. He curled the fingers of both hands around the goblet's stem, not only to keep his drink upright, but also to keep himself from tearing Hamish's clothes off then and there.

Hamish withdrew almost as abruptly as he had begun, leaving Darshan to dazedly stare at the stage's closed curtains, struggling to regain control over his faculties.

"Whatever did I do to deserve that?" Darshan breathlessly asked. And was it at all possible for him to repeat it? Especially if doing so garnered him another fervent kiss.

Shrugging, Hamish reclaimed his seat as if he hadn't just scrambled Darshan's thoughts with a kiss. "I learnt something new about meself."

"And what would that be? That you look good in slate?" He plucked playfully at the sleeve of Hamish's sherwani. "Because I already told you that."

Hamish grinned and, ducking his head, ran a smoothing hand down his outfit. "Nae that."

"You've decided you like the theatre? Fantastic. There's six in Minamist and at least one has a new performance every month." If he was with Hamish, his father couldn't possibly forbid him from going.

Hamish shook his head. "It's nae that, either. Nae to say this isnae nice." There was that tone, the hollow one that rang out of how he was merely being polite.

Darshan collapsed back into his chair. "You don't like it." A pity. There were precious few things Hamish enjoyed that he could indulge in once they reached Minamist. Darshan had hoped to introduce new likes to fill that void. "We can go." He went to stand, only to have Hamish clamp his hand firmly to the arm of the chair.

"Can we? Will the departure of the *vris Mhanek* before the final act nae shake the basket?"

Whilst no one would query them leaving, it would most certainly bring about gossip that could fall anywhere between the so-called ghost scaring them from the box to the performance being abysmal. He didn't fancy letting either one take root.

Hamish turned his attention to the dark curtains. "Besides, the thing I learnt was how much of a jealous man I am."

"You..." Darshan also stared out into the dark. Silence had befallen much of the theatre. The second half would start soon. "You saw him, then?" He risked a glance towards Hamish to find him staring back. "The man who..." He faltered, searching for the right word.

"Who propositioned you?" The softness of those jewel-like eyes hardened. "Aye. Bumped into him just at the entrance." Humour softened the firm line of his lips. "Thought he was going to choke on his tongue."

Darshan could imagine. The sight of his husband in the gloom was quite the imposing one. The sherwani only amplified it. "Nothing happened." It was a terrible response, he knew that the moment it left his lips. But it was the truth. "*Mea lux*, you know I would never do anything to harm you." The very thought that Hamish could even suspect him of adultery...

Well, he couldn't really blame his husband if the man thought the worst. He had alluded to, and outright mentioned, his hedonistic past a fair number of times.

Darshan opened his mouth, an explanation already balancing on his tongue. Hamish's reassuring squeeze of his fingers stalled his voice.

"I ken that." The hardness to his gaze mellowed. "And I heard you giving him his marching orders."

"He wasn't aware I was married." Not that it would've stopped the man had Darshan been inclined. Thankfully, he had left swiftly enough and not forced the issue.

"So your wild reputation precedes you, but nae your marital

status?"

"There's not much I can do about that." Sexual intimacy in Udynea was viewed differently than in Tirglas and Darshan had drunk deeply from the wellspring of debauchery. He had spent years cultivating a supposed taste for the decadent.

He'd even begun to believe his own tales.

"You dinnae have to look so ill, me heart. I trust you."

A weight lifted from his chest. This wouldn't likely be the last time a man approached him. If he was forced to trot out the same excuse every time? He wasn't sure if Hamish would ever stop believing the truth, but he wasn't prepared to take that risk.

"It's all the other buggers I dinnae trust," Hamish muttered.

"I can handle myself." It wasn't as if he hadn't spent a good deal of his adult years dealing with men, and the odd misinformed woman, who sought to curry favour. "I'm actually surprised he didn't attempt to extend his offer to your presence."

Hamish's nose wrinkled, confusion narrowing his eyes. "And have me do what? Watch?"

"Or participate."

"A man only has so many places to put it."

Darshan laughed heartedly, sobering quickly when Hamish didn't laugh with him. There were still certain areas where his husband's imagination didn't stretch terribly far.

"Well." He sipped at his goblet. "It would depend on what you wanted from it. Personally, I used to enjoy being sandwiched between two equally handsome men." The latter might've been a touch difficult to manage nowadays. His tastes had refined since leaving home, growing somewhat singular. "Of course, there's always the classic of pretending I'm a roast on a spit."

"What does spit roasting have to do with—?" Hamish fell quiet, his jaw dropping slightly.

Darshan waited whilst the man's mind finally caught up with the imagery.

His husband shot him a filthy look. "You're a bad man."

"Yes, *mea lux.*" Grinning, he swirled the remaining wine within his goblet. "But you knew that when you married me." The point was moot. The gleaming thought of having another man beyond Hamish touching him—be they riding him, thrusting into him or filling his mouth and emptying themselves down his throat—had long since lost its lustre.

Not that his old fantasies weren't there anymore, because that simply wasn't true, but the once faceless figures in them all looked like the same gorgeous blue-eyed man.

"I'll pass," Hamish murmured. "You're the only one I want, the only one I trust to be gentle."

"That—" Darshan's throat closed. He hadn't expected such a declaration. He'd never had anyone assert their utter trust in him before. It was oddly *sweet*. He cleared his throat and swallowed the last of his wine. "Never fear, my burning beacon, no other man will ever get the chance to try." And no man could replace his eternal flame. Be it in his heart or his bed.

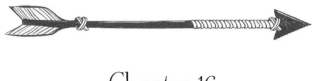

Chapter 16

The music started up and the curtains opened to display the second half of the opera. People danced and sang. There was even a dashing display of balance whilst sword fighting atop a plank that looked to be affixed to gimbals.

Darshan tried to focus on it all, but his thoughts kept cycling back to that kiss.

It had been over a week since he had touched his husband so intimately. He wasn't used to waiting so long—Hamish had the right of it there—but their dash to Rolshar had left precious time to think of a great many things.

Yet, here they'd time enough to slow down. Even if it was just for the remainder of the night. He could contain his desire until abed with his husband laid out before him like an offering, willing and wanting.

"Dar?" The word came hesitantly and with a hint of desperation.

He shook himself from his reverie to find his hand had alighted on Hamish's thigh. "My apologies." He snatched his hand back, cradling it in his lap as though it were a scolded puppy. "I must've zoned out." Darshan turned back to the opera and forced himself to focus.

Hamish silently scooted his chair closer until the arms abutted each other. "I'm nae some innocent wee lad, you ken? Nor am I fragile. I ken you. I ken where your mind's at. You dinnae have to hide it."

"I want you," Darshan admitted, keeping his eyes on the stage and its performance. "Make no mistake about that. I want to bend you over that chair and take you until you're screaming my name louder than her singing." He swallowed and took a steadying breath. "But I don't want to ruin this experience for you with my desires." Later. They could indulge in each other to their hearts' content once back at the imperial estate.

His husband fell back to silence, frowning down at the stage.

Darshan returned his focus to the singers and found he had rather lost track of the story. Why were there a half-dozen or so dancers waving streamers in the prima donna's face as they circled her? Why was she lamenting over the death of the villain? Hadn't she been told at the beginning of this act that he was responsible for her lover's supposed death?

"Is that all that's stopping you?" Hamish finally asked. His hand landed on Darshan's knee, sliding up as Hamish twisted in his chair.

Darshan sat back. He hadn't expected such a response from his shy little light. His husband was usually very particular about people not knowing they were having sex. "Aren't you worried someone will see us?" He had snuffed all the candles once there was other light to see by, but the glow from the stage was still substantial enough to clearly see each other. Which meant certain others might also have that chance.

He wasn't sure what rumours would come about if word spread of him being his old self with his husband, but they certainly wouldn't be good ones.

"I dinnae see how." Hamish leant forward, his head twisting one way, then the other. "I cannae make out anyone in the other boxes."

That was true. And some occupants would be using that to their advantage.

"Who would see us?"

"An elf?" Many employed them as spies for the very reason that, as well as having superior hearing, they saw better and further. That included in the dark.

Hamish shook his head. "They'd have to be up bloody high, maybe in one of the boxes near the stage. But they would also need to be looking this way at the right moment rather than watching the show or doing their job." He settled back in his chair with a shrug. "But if you dinnae want to—what was it?—bend me over this chair and take me..."

"*Mea lux!*" He fought to sound suitably scandalised even as he struggled to keep a straight face. "I am trying to be a gentleman here." Failing miserably, he knew, but *trying*. "And I can't expose you to Udynean culture if we're—"

"Dar," Hamish purred. His hand was back on Darshan's thigh, moving steadily upward. "We've a lifetime for you to expose me to all manner of things. Besides..." He flashed a grin that went straight to Darshan's groin. "I can hear them singing just fine and I'm sure I still will with whatever we do."

That was a challenge. There was no taking the goading in his voice as anything but.

Darshan licked his lips. Gods, he truly was beyond tempting. "I thought *I* was meant to be the bad influence between us?"

"Maybe you are," Hamish whispered, his breath warming Darshan's ear. "And maybe I really am just the poor, impressionable bastard who's going to regret meeting you at the end."

The notion that he might hurt Hamish, even inadvertently, wasn't one he wanted to linger on. "I hope not."

Hamish cupped one side of Darshan's jaw, running a thumb across his cheek. "You and me both, me heart. But right now?" His husband's other hand had wandered up Darshan's thigh to his groin, massaging through the thin layers of silk. "That's the least of me concerns."

Groaning, Darshan pulled Hamish closer, claiming his husband's mouth. He slid his own hand downwards, swallowing the hitch in Hamish's breath as he found his prize.

They remained that way for the whole song, sharing breath as he ground against Hamish's palm whilst likewise massaging the growing bulge in his husband's trousers.

All the while, Hamish offered little in the way of release. Darshan was being baited, he knew it. Just as his husband had to know the soft kisses and reserved groping wouldn't be anywhere near enough for him.

If he wanted more, he'd have to go after it.

Darshan pushed Hamish back into the chair as what had to be the opera's finale began. Clambering out of his seat, he knelt before his husband and slowly unbuttoned the bottom half of Hamish's sherwani.

Hamish shot him a puzzled frown before realisation lit up his face and set him fumbling to undo his trousers.

"I've got this, *mea lux.*" It wasn't as if he hadn't the experience of undressing his husband before. And, at this angle, he was in a far better position.

Darshan sat back, a small sigh escaping his lips as he pulled both trousers and drawers down enough to release Hamish's length. He had done this a number of times since leaving Tirglas, but there was something deliciously sinful in him, the *vris Mhanek*, kneeling before his husband to service him like a lowly lord trying to garner favour.

All whilst the opera carried on at his back.

"Dar?" Hamish whispered. "Are you going to do something other than stare?"

Whilst he would never stoop to so crass an act as staring... "Some things require proper admiration." His husband *did* look so very good framed in slate silk. Like a piece of art.

He wrapped his hand around Hamish's length, slowly stroking to the sound of soft and appreciative murmurs. Darshan coaxed the foreskin the rest of the way down, fully exposing the tip before delicately sucking on it.

On the edge of his vision, he spied Hamish's fingers tightening on the armrests. His husband shifted in the seat and, at first, Darshan thought he would stop this. But such a command never announced itself, leaving him to do as he pleased.

They both knew Darshan was the least experienced between them when it came to this act. Few men allowed him the opportunity, the vast majority being whilst he was also engaged in other acts, and none had been uncut. Hamish might've also been more sensitive than most, but Darshan had swiftly learnt what his husband liked and that was all he really cared about.

Even so, Hamish had admitted to never knowing what this felt like from the recipient's end until Darshan had shown him.

That night would be forever etched into his mind; the faint flap of the tent in the cool Tirglasian breeze, the smell and rustle of the grass beneath their blankets. And the exquisite way Hamish's body had responded, his husband's frenzied breaths filling his ears much as they did now.

Darshan basked in that muffled sound, shamelessly revelling in the fact that no one else had ever heard it or ever would.

This little piece of Hamish was his alone.

He slowly engulfed the rest of his husband's length. Hamish wasn't the biggest man he had attempted this with, but getting the whole thing down his throat took some effort. At least he could trust his husband to be gentle; there was never a time when the man wasn't. The way he continued to ensure Darshan's wellbeing bordered on emotionally overwhelming at times, but he loved Hamish all the more for it.

The encouraging noises continued to whisper into Darshan's ears like velvet. So soft and honest. Yet, so frustratingly quiet.

As much as he tried to bring out the more vocal side of his husband, years of seeking pleasure in secret had led to Hamish being a lot more restrained than what Darshan was used to, including being practically silent as he finished.

True to form, the only warning his husband gave before he tipped over the edge was the sudden clamp of his hand on Darshan's shoulder.

Darshan released his spent husband and sat back to catch his breath. He took in the sight of Hamish sitting there with his head tipped back and his chest heaving in an effort to breathe even harder than Darshan. *Stunning as always.* Even the way Hamish dug his fingers into his hair, mussing the heavy coils, was a wonder to behold.

A true masterpiece of the gods.

Yes, his admiration could've been fogged by lust and the prideful knowledge that *he* had been the one to bring his husband to this gorgeous state, but he didn't care.

He clambered to his feet, willingly throwing himself into Hamish's welcoming embrace. Their lips connected in a crush of breathless kisses. His own erection, having been blatantly ignored as he tended to Hamish's, insisted on relief. Darshan pressed against his husband, rubbing against the thigh he currently straddled. It wouldn't get him anywhere fast, but it felt good enough.

Hamish grew still, then pushed him back ever so slightly.

"Is something wrong?" He hadn't discovered many of Hamish's hard limits—and, quite frankly, dreaded the idea of stumbling into any more by sheer happenstance—but this couldn't possibly be that.

Unless he had seen something that Darshan couldn't.

Hamish softly shook his head. "Naething's wrong, me heart. I just realised you're nae done. Let me help with that." His firm hands grasped Darshan's buttocks, coaxing him fully onto Hamish's lap. Their mouths met again whilst Hamish slowly undid the ties to Darshan's trousers. Those fingers, calloused from years of archery, slid beneath the silk to wrap around Darshan's length.

Relief at the touch escaped his throat and persisted pouring out as Hamish moved his hand. As good as it felt, there was one teensy problem to his husband's solution. "If you're planning to work me towards an orgasm this way, I fear the aria will be done far before I am."

An exasperated huff left Hamish's lips, the blast warming Darshan's face. "How else would you expect me to do it?" Even so, his hand continued to move in languid strokes. Darshan's body might still be craving the high of an orgasm, but Hamish was steadily coming down from his. He was prepared to linger. "I cannae just take you. I'm spent."

"What if—?" he panted, his fogged mind straining for an alternative. "What if I took you instead?"

Hamish hummed as he kissed Darshan's neck. "Oil?"

"You mean, do I have any on me?" Darshan scoffed as his husband moved to nibble his ear. "Of course not." He had come to the theatre with completely innocent intentions. If anything, their current predicament was entirely Hamish's fault.

Hamish gave another considering hum, the vibration rippling across Darshan's skin.

Slowly, Darshan became aware of being tipped back. His shoulders touched the railing.

He braced himself as Hamish shifted his weight, clinging desperately to the wood. Gilding flaked off in his hands. He looked over his shoulder to the drop far below. If Hamish lost his grip on him, not even his magic would help him survive the fall. "I trust you've something good planned, *mea lux*."

Hamish remained silent, moving Darshan's legs to rest either side of his torso. His hands worked almost methodically as they slid Darshan's trousers and drawers off his hips, stripping him, just enough to—

Gods. A groan escaped his lips as Hamish greedily consumed him. Another followed on the tail of the last, then another, growing louder despite his attempts to silence them. He couldn't even muffle himself with a hand without risking his balance on the railing.

He tipped his head back, blearily seeing the illuminated stage as his glasses shifted. His body sang alongside the high notes, his husband's talented mouth driving him closer to the edge. Between the thrill of possibly being spotted from below, his precarious position and Hamish's ministrations... lasting before the final aria ended most definitely wasn't happening.

His magic buzzed through his body, seeking its own release. The wood beneath his hands grew hot. He shakily directed the heat to the nearest candle, which ignited and swiftly melted into a stub. He moved on to the next couple to similar results.

That wouldn't do. He needed to dispel his magic in a way that wouldn't set the royal box ablaze or bring it crashing down on those below.

"Wait," he huffed, praying Hamish heard him, relieved when his husband heeded the ragged plea.

With as much focus as he could manage whilst his mind still swam in that pool of pleasure, he raised a hand and sent his power out into the rafters to form a fine mist. It took a lot out of him and, in time, would drift into the crowd, but it was nowhere near as destructive as if he let his grasp on it loosen.

"Can I continue?" Hamish asked, already bent over him in anticipation.

Darshan barely got his affirmative reply out before that mouth was upon him once more. He really needed to find out what he had done to rile his husband this much.

The prima donna hit her highest note as his body reached its peak, the sound drowning out his lust-filled cry.

The curtain closed and darkness fell upon the theatre once more.

Hamish righted him as the crowd cheered the theatre's performance. Listening to them was quite the rush. Almost as if the people were praising this little private act.

He collapsed into his husband's arms, giggling and giddy. "I should bring you to the opera more often."

Hamish grinned, his laughter hissing between his teeth and shaking their bodies. "Oh aye? Just as long as we've our own private box."

"I'm certain that could be arranged. We should neaten ourselves up, though." He patted his husband's shoulder and wobbled to his feet to haul his trousers back into place. Properly attired again, he reignited the remaining candles. "It simply wouldn't do to have news of this leak out."

Hamish's mirth returned. This time, his laughter carried a wicked edge. "I'm sure it's nae as bad as some of the incidents you used to get up to."

Darshan smothered a laugh and reached for his goblet. "But I am no longer the dashing rogue now. A reputation must be maintained."

"Are you saying this still would've happened if you were courting me?"

"That's more than likely. Although, perhaps not as vigorously." Finding his goblet hadn't miraculously refilled itself, he swiped his husband's untouched drink and took a deep swallow. Sharp, acidic wine danced along his tongue. He grimaced at the taste. This was the best the theatre had to offer? Although, he could've sworn that his own drink hadn't been nearly as bitter. "Just you wait until I get you back to the estate. I'm going to have you seeing stars."

"Is that drink you're busily glugging down *mine?*" Hamish snatched the goblet from Darshan's fingers, lifting it to his lips.

Darshan's body quivered, fighting something dangerous recently introduced to his system. "Wait." He laid a hand on his husband's arm. "Don't." The feeling dissipated, nullified almost as soon as it became a threat, but he was certain of what he had felt. *Poison.*

He snatched the drink from Hamish's hands and downed the whole thing. Again, weakness flooded his body as his magic hastened to repair what the toxin sought to destroy.

Darshan stared at the few drops that remained. This wasn't like the alcohol back at his half-sister's soirée. The servants had been open about the poison within. This... this was malicious. Deliberate. Were they nearby? Waiting to see if the deed was done? Would they hear him?

"Dar?"

He lowered the goblet and staggered towards the exit. "I must speak with the guards," he muttered, switching to Tirglasian in the faint chance that someone was within hearing range. "I have just been poisoned." By a drink that was clearly meant for his husband.

Chapter 17

Hamish leant against the wall near the entrance to the royal box, watching his husband pace. Darshan muttered to himself, flipping a wisp-like spark from one hand to the other. In the corridor beyond, four guards barred the way. None of them were those who had guarded the two entrances further down the hallway. Zahaan was currently interrogating them.

"This is ridiculous," Darshan growled. "We shouldn't be sitting here waiting for answers. We should be leaving and doubling the guard on the estate."

"It's *your* spymaster who wants us to stay put," Hamish reminded him. "Did you nae say you trusted him with your life?" Zahaan had already ordered all of the theatre's entrances be blocked off. Whoever was behind the attempt to poison him had to be trapped within the building.

Unless they got out another way. He had seen plenty of windows just a floor up from the ground. Climbing down from them risked injury or worse, but it wouldn't be impossible.

Darshan pulled a face at him and went back to muttering under his breath.

Hamish didn't blame the man. His own mind wouldn't stop tumbling over how close he had come to drinking that poison. *If Dar hadnae taken a swig...* He shuddered. "What I dinnae understand is why they're only trying to bump me off now. We've been in Udynea for *months*."

Granted, a lot of that time had been with them on the move, never really staying in one village for longer than it took to sleep. Nulshar had been the first major city since their arrival in Udynea via Port Haalabof. And the lakeside city was the first one to house any of Darshan's family. The rest of the princesses were either in Minamist or further east or north than the path Darshan had chosen for their journey.

"Why?" The wisp his husband still played with flared and spat small forks of lightning. "Because she knows how serious I am about keeping you, as well as where we are."

"*She?*"

The wisp crackled. Darshan shook his hand and dispersed the wisp in a puff of grey-blue smoke. "Onella."

"You really think she's behind this one?" Hamish could understand the woman being the main suspect in the poisoning at her soirée, even if she did make a scene of denying it. And there was no mistake who was to blame when it came to her outright attack on him. But this? She couldn't have predicted they'd be here at this time. Not when they should've left the city a week ago.

"She generally is." His husband frowned out into the theatre, running a hand through his beard. "She's never sent assassins *this* careless, though. Maybe she's more desperate than I thought."

"I—" The abrupt stiffening of the guards just outside the royal box stilled his tongue. People were coming. Not a lot. And not with any hostility or they would already be dead. Most of Zahaan's people had magic and the poisoning had put them all on edge.

The guards saluted as the spymaster himself entered the royal box. All four of the men who'd been set to guard them during the opera filed in behind and knelt before Darshan. Hamish recognised two of them. One had escorted him to the theatre's privy whilst the other had remained at his post.

Darshan swung to face the group. "Well? What did you find?" he demanded of Zahaan before turning to the guards. "Where's the man? The one you let through between acts?" He had confessed to not knowing if the man who had propositioned him was also the one behind the poisoned wine, or if he was merely the unwitting carrier, but he had to know something.

The guards looked between them in confusion. "As we told Master Zahaan, *vris Mhanek*," one of them replied. "No one entered the hallway once you were settled."

"Impossible. I spoke with him. My husband saw him. Do you think we both hallucinated it?"

The question was met with a chorus of denials.

"Perhaps it was the ghost?" the same guard suggested.

Darshan scoffed. "There are simpler explanations to rule out before we reach for the paranormal. Did you check for any scarring?" he asked Zahaan who shook his head. "Then, let us see." He strode closer to the guards, touching each one in turn before returning to the second man in the row. He motioned his spymaster closer.

Zahaan tilted his head, his face expressionless as Darshan whispered in the elf's ear. He stared at Darshan for several long breaths. "Are you certain?"

"Look for yourself." Darshan gestured to the guard.

The spymaster did, cradling the man's head. "I didn't even think about the possibility. He's been hypnotised."

The guard rocked back, almost falling over. "I've been *what?*" He shook his head and mumbled a swift, "Sir?"

"You'll be fine, Ratik," Zahaan soothed. "Your magic will remedy the little damage it left."

Ratik's face scrunched in disbelief.

"Were you alone at any point?" Darshan asked the guard. There was a desperate edge to his voice, but the harshness had faded. If Ratik had been hypnotised, then he couldn't be blamed for what had happened.

The guard bowed his head, his ears steadily turning pink. "Briefly, *uris Mhanek*. When his highness appeared and Jaat escorted him to the privy."

Both Darshan and his spymaster turned to eye the guard who must've been Jaat.

The man nodded and uttered something. He'd been difficult for Hamish to understand when not startled. Now, the words almost flowed over the top of each other. It sounded like an affirmation.

Zahaan frowned at his guards, then turned to Darshan. "The scarring's not that deep."

"I noticed," Darshan replied. "I haven't seen that type of pattern before, though."

"Could it have been done in haste?" the spymaster suggested.

"It's possible."

"What if there's a wee chance something they didnae want him remembering slipped through?" Hamish asked. He'd no idea how hypnotism worked, but if it was any other sloppily done magic, then it could be possible.

Zahaan eyed him, then critically examined Ratik. "Report what you remember of the night. *After* the music started."

The man snapped a sharp salute. "Yes, Master Zahaan. I—" Panic twisted his face as the full realisation of what had happened seemed to hit him. "We took up position either side of the entrance," he mumbled, staring at the ground like a child attempting to recite history. "His highness came and Jaat left his post to escort him. Then... then..." He licked his lips, worry knotting his brows. "They came back?"

"Obviously," Darshan grumbled. He had started pacing again, this time, rolling his bottom lip between his fingers.

"How long were they gone for?" Zahaan pressed.

Ratik's neck disappeared as he lifted his shoulders. "I remember only their return, not the length of time."

"What of a man?"

The guard shook his head.

Hamish frowned. There was no mistake that the man he witnessed speaking with Darshan had been real, he had almost bumped into the bastard. But for the man to have left the immediate area would've meant passing one of the two pairs of guards in the hallway. Except he hadn't.

So where had he disappeared to? There were no other entrances in the hallway. Or were there? But if that was how he got in, then why go to the trouble of hypnotising the guard?

"What else can you recall?" Zahaan continued. "Anything at all."

"Yellow hair?" Ratik's face wrinkled with his confusion. "Pale, like straw. Cut short? No, in a bun. A woman, maybe? I can't—"

"That's enough," Darshan commanded. "Push any harder and the scarring will be permanent." He dismissed all four guards with the flick of his hand.

"The man wasnae blond," Hamish pointed out once the guards filed back out. The light hadn't been the best, but the man who had propositioned his husband definitely had darker hair.

"No," Darshan agreed. "This other person..." He flopped into a chair, stark resignation etching his face. "They must be the one who's behind the attempted poisoning and who hypnotised the guard."

Zahaan leant on the railing, staring out at the now-deserted stage and theatre seats. "My people aren't used to this sort of investigating. If we'd a body—some hint of where they'd come from, anything—then I'd be able to determine who had sent them. I can't pin anything down whilst chasing phantoms."

"Is it—?"

"—linked to Onella?" Zahaan finished. "I don't think so. It's a completely different poison from the other with origins far from here. How do you expect me to find out the culprit with nothing to show except for maybe a hair colour? And the suggestion of a man that both you and your husband have seen but is nowhere to be found." He threw up his arms imploringly towards the rafters. "Are you testing me, Chaal? Is that it?"

"Chaal?" Hamish enquired of his husband. It was clearly a deity, but he hadn't heard this one before. With Udynea having so many, Darshan had schooled him only the main ones.

"Patron God of Spies," Darshan supplied with a shrug. "I think he was originally a trickster god or something along those lines, although I could be thinking of different one."

"You're not," the spymaster said, finally facing them. "He was the Patron God of Nulled Ones once." He leant back on the railing as though the deadly drop behind them wasn't there.

"Nulled Ones." Darshan scrubbed at his face and fisted his hair. "What I wouldn't give for a few of them in your ranks. You should've asked my father for some."

"I tried years ago. He refused."

"Why?" Hamish asked. He knew little about Nulled Ones beyond them being born from the same stock as spellsters and were supposedly rare. But with them being immune to direct magic, no amount of hypnotism would've worked.

"All Nulled Ones born in Udynea are the property of the *Mhanek*," Zahaan replied. "As such, they leave Minamist at his behest alone. When I requested a handful be integrated with my people, the *Mhanek* said it wasn't a viable use of a precious resource."

Darshan grunted. "He would."

Zahaan patted Darshan's knee. "Sit tight a little longer. I'll have my people comb through the guests here. If our hypnotist truly is pale-haired, it shouldn't take long to find them."

"Really?" Hamish looked from one man to the other, trying to determine how hair colour would factor into the ease. "I would've thought—"

"This isn't Tirglas," Darshan said as Zahaan disappeared out into the hallway to speak with the guards. "There are very few with pale hair. Or red, for that matter. Most are varying shades of brown and black."

"That right?" Not everyone in Tirglas was blond or red-haired, but a great deal of the population was. He tugged a lock of his hair free from the tie, pulling until the coil had straightened a good foot from his forehead. "I didnae realise I'd be a rarity." He'd definitely never considered it as anything special.

"That would depend on where in Udynea." His husband leant back into the chair, closing his eyes. "I believe it's different further north and I'm uncertain if that includes the elven population, although I suspect not."

"Are you all right?"

A soft smile graced Darshan's lips. He had insisted his innate healing dealt with the poison as soon as he consumed it, but downing all except for the last few drops couldn't have done his body any good. "I'm fine, *mea lux*. I told you, the poison is gone. They're no more than random impurities I'll expel in the usual manner come morning." One hazel eye slid open to focus on Hamish. "Honestly, the worst I feel is weariness over all this waiting."

Zahaan strode back in as Darshan aired his woes. There was no chance the elf hadn't heard him. "Then you'll be pleased to be up and moving out, *vris Mhanek*." The words had a touch of a bite to them and the smile he gave Darshan seemed excessively toothy. "Shall I have the guards flank our departure or will they be carrying you out?"

Launching himself to his feet, Darshan muttered something that Hamish could just make out as being in the Ancient Domian tongue. It was a language that most of the upper nobility in the empire were fluent in, having being taught it as children. Hamish had tried to learn, but really saw no practical use beyond deciphering the ancient texts the civilisation had left behind, something he also had no interest in doing.

"Am not," Zahaan replied, scrunching his nose.

Darshan stuck out his tongue as he strode past his spymaster.

Zahaan replied to the childish gesture in the same language, which elicited a brief chuckle from Darshan.

Hamish bit the inside of his cheek and silently revised his decision on learning Ancient Domian, if only to be included in the jokes.

Three guards went on ahead as they walked through the hallways to the stairs, ensuring the path was clear, whilst four more tailed them. None appeared to have anything that resembled a weapon. He wouldn't have expected bows indoor, but he only now realised that not a single one bore a sword or even a short dagger. Were they all spellsters?

"Don't look so sour, love," Darshan chided in Tirglasian as they took the second corner. "Zah was simply suggesting I act my station."

"I dinnae see what's so funny about that. You should in public."

His husband grinned broadly. Maybe the poison had affected him more than he claimed. "*Mea lux*, could you honestly see me as some drab and dull man of the throne?"

"Drab and dull? *You?* Nae at all. But you could be more serious."

"Serious?" He stroked his beard, making a show of mulling the word over. "I can be serious."

"Nae if it's anything like your attempts at being discreet." Their extremely public snog in a Tirglasian pub had only been the beginning. Darshan's restraint wasn't completely lacking, especially after Hamish explained what had set off his mother's wrath, but he had still been far more affectionate than most unrelated men in Tirglas were to each other.

"I thought we agreed to put the indelicacies of that kiss behind us?"

As if Hamish would ever forget the first time those lips touched his, reigniting a fire he had resigned to being doused long ago. "*You* agreed. With yourself. I dinnae say a thing."

" 'Mish." Darshan gasped, splaying his free hand upon his chest. "My sweet light, I'm surprised at you. And mildly scandalised."

"Oh aye?" he replied, deliberately returning to Udynean. *"That's what scandalises you? Nae when I had you draped over the railing and—"* His jaw, all at once, refused to open and let him speak further. No doubt, his husband's magic was to blame there.

Darshan stared up at him, those hazel eyes wide and his cheeks steadily darkening. His gaze darted from Hamish's face to over his shoulder. "Not in public," he hissed in Tirglasian.

"Gods," Zahaan muttered. The tone in his voice reminded Hamish of the first time his own brother had stumbled upon him with a man. Not outright revulsion, but a certain familial distaste. "Can't you keep your pants on for *one* opera?"

"They *were* on," Darshan shot back. "What sort of debauched things do you think I get up to?"

The sort that sees you spread in front of me like a feast. The image of how his husband had been just an hour ago slithered through his mind. Hamish coughed. Not only to disguise his smile but also the growing heat in his face.

"So, it wasn't you who we found naked in the middle of the rubble that used to be Madaara's statue?" the spymaster teased.

Hamish pressed a knuckle against his lips. He already knew the tale of his husband's yearly involvement in the harvest festival. And how the festivals typically devolved into orgies once wine flowed.

Darshan's cheeks darkened further. "That—" He hunched his shoulders like a scolded boarhound. "That was an accident."

Understandable. There were times when they were intimate where Darshan had to step back and centre his mind or, so the man claimed, risk something dangerous happening to their surroundings. Hamish was always thankful for the breather it gave him to help keep up with his husband.

"You accidentally fornicated on it at every harvest festival?" Zahaan asked, the wickedness curling his lips whispering that he already knew the answer.

"Not *every* festival," Darshan mumbled, adjusting his glasses in such a way that hid his face from Hamish. "And I paid for their replacements."

Capturing his husband's hand in his own, Hamish squeezed reassuringly. They had discussed a lot of Darshan's past during their travels to ensure the Crystal Court didn't try to catch Hamish unawares. Nothing he had heard concerned him. It was in the past. It couldn't be altered, but he refused to have Darshan act as though none of it ever happened.

Darshan flashed him a charming smile, the expression eliciting a soft gagging sound from Zahaan before the man stiffened and motioned them to slow their pace as the hall opened out to the main entrance.

The guards swiftly followed the order, closing rank around them and parting the crowd in an effort to reach the main stairway even as their passage remained uneventful.

Hamish strained to hear what the elf listened for. He picked out nothing from the low murmur of the disgruntled crowd. He was well aware he had a severe lack of knowledge in how to conduct himself in a Udynean court, but he wasn't foolish enough to believe things couldn't easily change for the worse.

Mistress Aashi scuttled to their side as they reached the top of the stairs, her face flushed with anger. She glowered at them through the wall of guards, not foolish enough to try barging through. "I understand the *uris Mhanek* would have a very valid reason for barring my patrons from leaving, but I—"

"I do," Darshan snapped. He barely paused in his descent, forcing everyone else to follow. "Unless you can tell me where the short, dark-haired man with the wide, grey eyes vanished to."

Her mouth gaped for a few breaths. "I know of no one under my employ with such a description. But I assure you, if there is someone here, then he can be brought to you."

"What of a blonde woman?"

The theatre mistress pursed her lips, her brow creasing. "There is one, but she's—"

"Let her go!"

The demand cut cleanly through the drone of the crowd, snapping everyone's attention to the left side of the foyer where a dark-haired woman faced down one of Zahaan's people, who held another woman in his grasp. The screaming woman might've been tinier than the guard, but she faced him as though she was a moss-maddened boar.

Hamish's gaze slid to the woman still held in the guard's clutches. Her hair was the same straw-like shade Ratik had described. Could she be the one behind all this?

"Unhand her this instant," the dark-haired woman demanded, punching the guard's arm and clawing at his hand. Her efforts did little to free the other woman. The dark-haired woman appeared to be more elaborately dressed than the other, the skirt of her gown like a bloom of green at her hips and trailing several feet behind her.

Hamish had seen that gown, or one very much like it, during the opera. Was she one of the singers? Maybe even the lead. He hadn't expected her to be so petite, almost elf-like in proportion. She barely came to the guard's shoulder. Even Zahaan, a full-blooded elf, wasn't that short.

"Kris—" Mistress Aashi blurted before slapping her hand over her mouth.

The call was enough to catch the dark-haired woman's attention. "You there." She stalked their way, dragging the guard and the blonde woman. "I assume you're in command of these brutes," she snapped at Darshan, who faced the tirade with a neutral expression. "I insist you order him to let go of my friend."

"Insist?" Zahaan echoed incredulously. His brows had lifted so far up his forehead that they looked ready to make a run for his hairline. "Do you—?"

"I'm sure that whatever happened to cause you to lock down the entire theatre is justified," the woman continued, ignoring Zahaan. "But my friend isn't responsible. Honestly, it's appalling enough this targeting of half-elves every time something bad happens. It's so typical of the common guard, but I expected better of the royal ones."

Hamish reassessed the blonde woman. She was taller than the one speaking on her behalf, but now he was looking for the points in her ears, he caught them just peeking through the thick curls of hair.

Zahaan wrinkled his nose. It could've been Hamish's imagination, but he swore the man had just growled.

"Calm yourself, Zah," Darshan said. "I'm certain this misunderstanding can be sorted in a civilised manner." He smiled coolly at the woman. "Shall we start with introductions?"

"Certainly," Mistress Aashi said. She squeezed her way past the guards to stand at the woman's side. "This is Miss Krittika, Rolshar's—and the theatre's—greatest treasure."

"One that is well-kept, I'm sure." Darshan's smile wavered slightly as he bowed his head. The cold expression that flashed across his face didn't give Hamish much hope of Krittika making it through the night without further angering his husband.

Hamish eyed the woman. She was the prima donna? Granted, he had heard her and not much else, but he'd been expecting someone a little more solid rather than this slight young woman. He never would've imagined someone so small being capable of creating such a powerful voice.

"Miss Krittika?" the theatre mistress continued. "This is the *vris Mhanek* and his husband."

Deeply dark eyes blinked up at them, naked terror shimmering in their depths as Krittika mouthed the title. She patted her hair, paying curious attention to the thick curls covering her ears, and curtsied low. "It was an honour to sing for you, *vris Mhanek*," she mumbled. "I do hope you found it to your liking."

"The finale was certainly..." Darshan's gaze slid to Hamish as his lips widened into a genuine smile. "...orgasmic."

Hamish let out a harsh, blustering cough, his face steadily growing hotter. After how he had teased his husband earlier, he should've expected such a response.

Krittika's gaze slid his way, her brow briefly creasing with a puzzled frown, before she returned her focus to Darshan. "And I pray the *vris Mhanek* will understand why I cannot sit idly on the wayside whilst your guards drag my friend off to who knows where under some spurious charge."

"Spurious?" Zahaan echoed. "Child, you clearly have no idea what has transpired. I would suggest you be entirely certain of the people you choose to stick your neck out for." He turned to the guard who still held the blonde woman firmly by the arm. "How many have you found who match the description?"

"Just the one," the guard replied.

"I'm telling you Megala can't be responsible," Krittika said. "She was with me."

Zahaan scoffed. "Surely, that cannot be true. What of whilst you were on stage?"

Darshan hummed, his gaze drifting to the gathering crowd. "Perhaps this would be better discussed in private?"

Hamish followed his husband's line of sight. There was no doubt they had become the centre of everyone's attention. A gaggle of the theatre's actors and singers stood the closest, talking amongst themselves in tones too low to make out. Most of them looked terrified. For themselves? For the women?

Mistress Aashi also seemed to have noticed the scene they were making. "Of course, *vris Mhanek*," she replied before either of the other two women could open their mouths. "This way, please." She led them down the stairs to a door tucked beneath the main stairway.

The room held little in the way of furniture. A small, round table and four chairs took up the central space, all covered in a thin sheet. A handful of old posters decorated the walls—too few to disguise the peeling paint—and a threadbare rug carpeted the floor. A marked difference to the polished walls of the foyer or even the waxed wood of the doorway they had just walked through.

Zahaan took one look around before stepping out and ordering the guards to wait outside.

After the night's upheaval, Hamish's back prickled slightly at the lack of protection. *Dinnae be a fool.* He took a deep breath, reaching for reason. He wasn't alone. His husband was with him and capable of magic. If any of the three women tried something suspicious, they would be dealt with.

"If I may be bold, *vris Mhanek*," Mistress Aashi said as the door clicked shut, the words rushing out so fast that Hamish was amazed she had any breath to speak at all. "What is this all about? Can I assume the performance was to your taste?"

"I thoroughly enjoyed myself," Darshan confirmed. "At least, up until someone tried to poison my husband. With wine *you* sent up, I may add."

"Poison?" she echoed. "But I..." Panicked confusion creased the theatre mistress' face. "I ordered no wine to the royal box beyond what your guards had already tested. You have my word."

"The man I described to you on the landing? He has mysteriously gone missing. He clearly stated the wine was a gift from yourself. Or do you think I misheard?" There was a hard edge to his voice, one Hamish hadn't heard since confronting his mother. The only difference between then and now was the hold on his composure.

Mistress Aashi shook her head. "I'm sure the *vris Mhanek's* hearing is exceptional." She bobbed and fluttered around the room's small confines like a startled hen. "But as I said, there is no one within the theatre who bears such a description. And I would never—"

"Ghost," Krittika murmured.

A gasp emanated from the blond woman, who now stood at the woman's elbow.

A look of horror briefly twisted the theatre mistress' features before a smile reclaimed them. "I'm sure the *vris Mhanek* has heard the tales of how the theatre is haunted. The ghost... Occasionally, people die."

"Do I look to be in a gaming mood, Mistress Aashi?" Darshan demanded, his tone leaping from vaguely annoyed straight to enraged. "My husband almost died and you're claiming an apparition is responsible? I suppose this ghost of yours is prone to poisoning people's drinks as well?"

Mistress Aashi fell to her knees as though her legs had been cut. Her lips pressed together. Even before she spoke, Hamish could see the answer on her face. "Not at all, *vris Mhanek.*"

"The ghost would never," insisted Megala. "Not poison. It never uses poison. It's always blades and string. Isn't that right, Mistress?" She looked expectantly at the woman. Finding no backup from her, Megala turned to Krittika. "Miss?"

Krittika fidgeted on the spot. She tilted her head slightly as if listening to something beyond his range of hearing, before giving a curt nod. "That's right."

Mistress Aashi closed her eyes and prostrated herself before Darshan. "Forgive Megala, *vris Mhanek.* I'm afraid her tongue runs as freely as her imagination. She was a favoured pet of my brother's, you see? Left her with these nasty habits." She glared at the woman.

"Casually conversing with one's betters? Preposterous! I will see she is suitably punished."

Hamish tightened his grip on his husband's sleeve. He had been in the empire long enough to know what the punishment for that supposed crime would most likely be. If Megala was as innocent as Krittika claimed, then she didn't deserve a lashing.

"That won't be necessary," Darshan replied, gesturing for the theatre mistress to stand. "I have heard the tales of your ghost. *All* of them. Each death is precise, quick and clean. This attempt on my husband's life was nothing of the sort. I lay no blame upon your ghost."

Relief relaxed Mistress Aashi's face. She slowly got to her feet. "You have my unending gratitude, *vris Mhanek*."

"Your theatre, however," Darshan continued. "*That* is most definitely hiding something. I intend to discover what, and who, is behind it before anyone is allowed to leave."

The theatre mistress wet her lips, her gaze briefly landing on Krittika before she curtsied. "Whoever did this heinous act surely cannot escape your clutches."

"Indeed, they shall not." He swung to Megala. "I will start with you. Come."

Looking as though she might faint at any moment, the poor woman wobbled closer.

"I already told you—" Krittika said, falling into silence as Darshan fastened his glare on her.

"*I* will determine who is at fault. If she's innocent, she has nothing to fear."

Hamish bit his tongue in an effort to keep his expression neutral. Whilst he knew his husband would remain fair, he had heard that phrase from his mother one too many times. And few had been deemed innocent in her eyes.

Darshan laid a hand on Megala's shoulder, then immediately turned down the high collar of her gown a fraction. The purple sheen of *infitialis* gleamed from beneath. "You are leashed."

"Yes, *vris Mhanek*," the woman replied. "Have been most of my life."

Darshan had attempted to explain the leashing process once and Hamish had tried to understand it—something about the way worked metal reacted differently to pure ore and how it affected certain regions of the brain—before giving up. It boiled down to one truth: the leashed were incapable of magic unless their masters ordered it, then they were able to do whatever was within their grasp.

That alone didn't mean Megala was their culprit. But combined with the hair colour, it definitely looked suspicious. Surely, whoever owned her wouldn't have sent someone so easily picked from the crowd.

Unless that is *their plan.* It seemed counterintuitive to have the person responsible for the attempt on his life be so easily caught, but after the convoluted schemes he had heard Onella try in the past, he couldn't disregard the idea.

Darshan eyed the theatre mistress, his expression unreadable. "Did you say she is yours?"

"Sadly yes, *uris Mhanek.* I inherited her, along with the theatre, upon my brother's death. But I've never—"

Someone rapped their knuckles on the door, turning everyone's head.

Mistress Aashi flinched, a shield flickering around her for a heartbeat, before she shook herself and scuttled for the door.

Zahaan stood on the other side, the bad news he harboured practically plastered across his face.

"What did you find?" Darshan asked.

"The man, *uris Mhanek.* He's dead."

"*Dead?*" Mistress Aashi yelped.

"My people found him crammed into what appears to be a hidden compartment in the hallway not that far from the royal box. Poisoned. Most likely with the same stuff used in the attempt. And, yes, *uris Mhanek*" Zahaan added with a mighty exhale as Darshan opened his mouth, "he also has web scarring on the brain. Extensively so."

Darshan frowned, his bottom lip disappearing as he hummed in thought.

Mistress Aashi staggered back a step, one hand pressed to her temple. Megala scuttled to the woman's side to support her.

"A scarred brain means what exactly?" Krittika asked into the silence.

"It's a mark left by hypnosis," Hamish replied, earning him a glower from Zahaan. He pinned the man with a similar look. "Whoever this man was that tried to poison me, he wasnae acting under his own power."

"So it would appear," Darshan murmured, his attention having been diverted to Megala, who looked as ready to faint as her mistress. "And, judging by her reaction, this isn't the woman we're after. It seems they have mysteriously vanished."

"It would be best if we followed suit," Zahaan suggested.

Darshan sighed. "Regrettably so." He swept past the mistress of the theatre with barely a glance her way, bowing his head to Krittika as they left the room.

The spymaster had his people once again close ranks around them with a few crisp words. They were escorted out of the theatre under the intense scrutiny of many whispering faces.

Hamish stared back. Had the culprit really gotten away? Or could it have been one of these people? He frowned.

The man before him fell to his knees spewing apologies.

Hamish took pains to relax his face. *I am never going to get used to this place.* He was judged on his every movement and word, even his very expression.

How did Darshan manage it?

He knew the answer there. His husband had schooled his features to form a perfectly neutral mask.

Outside the theatre, night had claimed the sky. A row of lanterns illuminated the stairs leading down to the road, as well as their transport. It took all of Hamish's willpower not to run towards the carriage. He would've preferred walking through utter blackness to strolling down this clearly lit path. How much of a target did they make to those hiding in the dark?

"Relax, *mea lux*," Darshan whispered. Pressing close, he wrapped an arm around Hamish's waist. "You can't see it, but you're safe beneath my shield."

He glanced up. The transparent sheen wasn't perfect, not when they were on the move. It rippled slightly with each step, distorting the stars peeking out from behind the glare of the lanterns.

He stayed transfixed on those stars as he entered the carriage. Why couldn't the night have stayed pleasant? They could've mingled briefly with the crowd, then sauntered back to the estate and spent the rest of the time lost in each other.

"I don't like this," Darshan muttered once the carriage door shut. It was just them and Zahaan. "Hypnosis is a nasty thing. I've never once heard of a reason that was justified. To use it like this..." He grumbled further under his breath.

The spymaster grunted his agreement. "It was one thing for the woman behind the poisoning in Nulshar to be hypnotised, that wouldn't have taken much skill, but now one of my guards? *And* this man?"

That no one knew. Hamish sighed. "You believe they're connected?"

"Indeed." Darshan glared at the seat opposite as if it had done him a personal wrong. "Hypnosis where the victim forgets permanently isn't easy. To have them perform specific tasks once out of immediate sight is practically unheard of. I know of only one person capable of such skill."

"Onella?" Hamish guessed.

Zahaan shook his head, his lips twisting as if he had bitten something sour.

"No, *mea lux*," Darshan replied. "My father."

Chapter 18

The smell of cooking rabbit sat thickly in the air and set Hamish to drooling. He set his saddle near the campfire and sat down to test their meal. *Almost ready.* It wasn't the biggest feast, not like the rabbits back home. *At least we've one each.* Hamish had come across little else in the way of prey whilst traipsing through the woods and Darshan refused to go near any sort of civilisation.

His husband was against a lot of things lately, including an escort down to Minamist. Instead, it was just them in this little camp tucked far from the road. They'd snuck out of the imperial estate under the cover of night—and from beneath Zahaan's very nose—two days ago. Taking a meandering path through the wilderness that also put paid to any chance of sleeping in a bed.

Hamish had expected some of the spymaster's people, or the man himself, to catch up, but Darshan insisted no one was following.

Darshan stared into the fire, his arm moving the spit as though in a trance. He barely acknowledged Hamish's presence. He had been unusually quiet since leaving Rolshar, speaking only when prodded and never about the topic that clearly ate at him even though Hamish knew the source.

His father.

Hamish had personal experience in having an untrustworthy parent, his mother's absolute denial of him wanting men having been the reason they were travelling over land rather than by sea. *Would we have been safer?* Maybe in the short term, but unaware of this danger until they'd stepped ashore.

Were they even safe out here? The soft noises of creatures whistling and croaking in the trees filled the silence. He hadn't spent much time in Udynea's woods to get a feeling for what was dangerous, but he'd heard stories of cats bigger than any boar.

Neither of the horses seemed worried, the gentle tearing sound of their grazing remaining rhythmic. Normally, he would be confident of them alerting him of something coming, but they were used to dangers like bears and maddened boars. If big cats hunted anything like the castle mousers, then they could be too quiet for the horses to hear until it was too late.

At least it hadn't rained during this leg of their travels. The air still smelt wet. If it was Tirglas, he would guess a drenching wasn't far off.

"We'll have to find somewhere to restock our supplies tomorrow," Hamish said. The horses needed grain, such as what the pair would usually get once stabled at an inn. They might not have been pushing their mounts hard, but there was a limit to their endurance and they already found the more humid air difficult.

Darshan grunted. His expression was one of a man lost deep in his thoughts. He didn't even blink as Hamish took the rabbits off the spit. Or when he was offered one.

"Dar?" Hamish waved his hand before his husband's face. Rabbit might not be Darshan's favourite, but the man had never outright refused food. "You still with me?"

Darshan jerked back, blinking erratically until he took off his glasses and rubbed his eyes. "Forgive me, I—"

"Was doing some heavy thinking," Hamish finished for him. "I ken that." Sighing, he propped their meal near the fire to keep it warm. "I also ken you're worried about what happened, but I'm fine. I dinnae drink a drop and—"

"That was more through luck than my efforts to keep you safe. I should've known better. I should've been more vigilant."

He took up Darshan's hands, keeping them close to his chest. He hadn't been the target of an assassination attempt since his childhood. Even then, the men sent to kill him and his younger sister had been direct about it. "There were guards barring access to us on all entrances, you had nae reason to suspect that man had anything dangerous on him."

That Zahaan's people hadn't been able to catch the hypnotist responsible for the attempt on Hamish's life was a sore spot, for both Darshan and the spymaster, but inevitable if the person responsible could wipe the memory of themselves from a person's mind.

Darshan sighed. "You don't understand. There'll be other attempts. What sort of husband am I if I can't do something as simple as protect my spouse? And if I can't protect the man I love, then what does that mean for Udynea once I take the throne? Maybe they're right."

"They?"

208

"The council, Onella... They all expect me to fail. Even my father despairs it. *Mind's too addled in pleasure.*" His voice dropped, growing gruff as Darshan mimicked his father's voice. "I guess he's right. We should've stayed in the estate, but I—" He hung his head. "I was only concerned with showing you a good time. I gave no thought to our safety. All the precautions? They were Zahaan's idea. They should have been mine. I should've thought of your safety. I didn't. I should have, but I didn't and you..."

"Me heart..." He pulled his husband into a hug.

Darshan clung to him, his hands trembling as he grabbed fistfuls of Hamish's shirt. The breath he took was shaky and carried the soft wetness of unshed tears.

Hamish stroked his husband's hair, not daring to even whisper a soothing sound for fear that Darshan would return to silence. Now the man had dropped his inner shield to lay bare his uncertainties, it was best to leave the talking to him, to have him air out everything before it ate him up inside.

"You could've died," his husband mumbled against Hamish's bicep. "All because I was stupid enough to think—"

"Nae, me heart." He rubbed Darshan's back. The trembling was still there, but growing fainter. "It was a close thing, you'll have nae disagreements from me on that, but you're nae to blame. It's nae your job to guard me."

"I was supposed to be bringing you to safety, to where you could just be *you* without worry, without having to sacrifice yourself to someone else's ideal." He gave a small huff that sounded perilously close to a sob. "I feel like I'm marching you to your death."

Hamish bit his lip. The thought of his life ending whilst he was still young, still able to be him, had carried the lure of freedom not that long ago. It still whispered in the back of his mind, not strongly and lacking persistence. He had gone about his little existence in Tirglas for so many years that he'd forgotten what living without its insidious call was actually like.

Darshan pulled out of Hamish's grasp to dig his fingers into his hair. He stared at the ground as if the answers would come. "You are clearly being targeted and I can't—" He breathed deep, sitting back as though fully composed. His expression spoke otherwise, his olive-brown skin sickly in the shifting firelight and seemingly stretched taut across his features. "The only way to ensure your safety is to surround you with Nulled Ones, they can't be hypnotised by anyone. But they're all at Minamist."

Personal escorts. His life back in Tirglas had been shadowed by them ever since his mother found out he liked men. Always there. Always judging his every move.

He hated it.

But this would be different. The Nulled Ones wouldn't be watching over someone that thought of as a rebellious man who refused to do his duty to the crown, they'd be protecting the *vris Mhanek's* husband and father of the next heir. "What if you request for some to be sent our way?" Zahaan might've been denied having them scattered through his people, but surely the *Mhanek* wouldn't refuse an appeal from his only son.

"Even if my father agreed, it'll take them no less time to reach us than we would have to them. What are we supposed to do in those three weeks? Hole up here?" He waved a hand at the surrounding trees. "I can't keep you tucked away in the forest like a... a..."

"Pet?"

"Like a dirty little secret." He grimaced as the words left his mouth. "The alternative is to settle at one of the outposts. But if I can't even trust those I am closest to, then what hope do we have with common guards?"

"Then maybe we should do that, nae trust anybody." Something about the timing of it all nagged at him. "I've been in Udynea for months and it only started when we went to your half-sister's soirée. Maybe that's the problem. Maybe whoever's behind this has set traps where they ken someone of your status would go?" Only recently had they spent time in any place more extravagant than a common inn.

Darshan frowned, his lips pursing in thought.

"What if we go back to how it was?" They'd had no trouble at all coming down from the fishing village. And they would make better time if he could convince Darshan to return to the roads. "We travel anonymously. Skip staying at any imperial estates and lingering at fancy parties. If we head straight for Minamist, then they willnae be able to trap us, right?"

The furrow in his husband's brow deepened. "Depending on who is behind these attacks, it may be too late for that. What happened in Rolshar wasn't normal."

"And the attempted poisoning at your half-sister's soirée was?"

A small smile crept up one side of Darshan's face. "Yes, crudely done though the attempt was. But I know from personal experience that the art of hypnosis is fickle. It doesn't take much to break. My father is—was?—the best and, to my knowledge, his will doesn't last long enough for them to get far."

"So, you dinnae think he's the one behind it, either?" His husband had been so convinced as they'd left the theatre. Had the spymaster found some new evidence to change Darshan's mind? With the way his husband had insisted on leaving without anyone knowing, it seemed unlikely.

"More I see no reason why he would go to this length. It wouldn't be practical. If we were *in* Minamist, then maybe." Darshan rubbed at his temple. "But I know of no one else who would come close to his skill. The only way to truly be sure is to confront him."

And facing the *Mhanek* meant continuing their journey to Minamist, all the while hoping no other bugger made an attempt.

What else could their mystery attacker lob at them?

Huffing a wayward coil of hair from his face, Hamish picked up his rabbit and chewed as he thought. If they were being followed, then the culprit would have to know they'd get suspicious over any food or drink they hadn't personally hunted and collected. Buying supplies at a random stall could be risky, but Darshan could test for poison.

That left a direct attack, which wouldn't work in the opposition's favour unless they managed to incapacitate Darshan. Any failure there would put his husband on the defensive. Hypnotising random folks seemed the only certain way to keep them on edge.

Unless... Swallowing his current mouthful, he eyed Darshan. "Are you nae afraid that they'll hypnotise *you?*" If they could enchant a man to consume poison, then what of a spellster to attack someone dear to him? *I'd have nae chance.*

Darshan shook his head. "Firstly, these—" He ran a finger along the earpiece of his glasses. "—offer a small layer of protection. Not much, but enough to give me a warning and protect myself. Secondly, I know most of the tells and what it feels like."

"Why have you nae taught them to me?" Hamish grabbed the other rabbit and shoved it into Darshan's hands. "You eat, then you teach me." He scarfed down the rest of his meal and checked on the horses whilst waiting for his husband to finish picking at the last few pieces of rabbit. It wasn't that Darshan ate slowly, but he was methodical when it came to anything Hamish hunted, consuming every last morsel as though he was being starved.

Hamish considered himself fortunate to not have found a stream suitable for fishing. Back in Tirglas, fish would be gutted and grilled whole until the scales dropped off and the skin crisped. It might've been served with its head still on, but no one actually ate that part. The castle cook had considered it as only good for fertiliser.

Then Darshan had sat down at the banquet table and stripped a fish head to the bone. Hamish didn't think he could stomach watching his husband eat another eyeball.

Eventually, Darshan threw the last of the rabbit bones into the fire. "All right." He removed his glasses and settled cross-legged on the ground. Without the glittering silver of the frames and the kohl, his eyes seemed oddly small. He gestured for Hamish to sit across from him. "Shall we begin?"

Aware that he was likely a vaguely recognisable blob to his husband right now, Hamish plonked himself close enough for their knees to touch. He mimicked the cross-legged posture and the way Darshan held his hands, resting them palms up one atop the other in his lap. "What now?"

"In hypnotism, the first and more crucial element is maintaining eye contact with your target. If this link is broken at the wrong time or done in haste, then the chance of losing control increases."

"That simple?" He hadn't given a great deal of thought to how the hypnotist had actually managed to control the people beyond assuming it worked like Darshan's healing magic, which required touch.

"I did say it was fickle."

"So, if I dinnae look anyone in the eye for long—?"

Darshan fluttered his fingers as though shooing the suggestion aside before Hamish could finish speaking. "That might work with me when I'm wearing my glasses." He toyed with the pair in his other hand. "The lenses delay the effect, if only for a few seconds. However, a hypnotist skilled enough to erase memories could catch you in a glimpse." He leant forward, staring unblinkingly for a little too long.

Hamish felt himself relaxing. His head became fuzzy, like he'd had too much to drink. His eyelids lowered, blocking out Darshan's face.

Then the sensation slipped away, leaving him dizzy and slightly nauseous. "What was—?" He scratched at his head. His very brain itched. "Did you just hypnotise me?"

"Briefly." Darshan rubbed at his temple. "I'm not very good at it. Haven't exactly spent much time with the skill, not when I could always command people to do my bidding. Magical coercion seemed rather like a waste of energy. Still, I figured it was for the best if you know what it feels like."

He could see the point, but there was something else. Something Gordon had told him that had clearly been a lie. "You told me brother—"

"That I hadn't hypnotised you," Darshan interrupted. "Which, up until now, I had not. I still haven't, really. I just pulled you into a pliant state. It's all I've ever done during training."

Hamish frowned. "But you ken how to fully hypnotise a person?"

"If I wished it, yes. Just as you undeniably know how to kill a man, but the—" He tapped his lips with a forefinger. "What is that charming idiom? The bow without its arrow poses no risk," he mumbled in Tirglasian.

Hamish knew that phrase. He had grown up with it. "But it can be brought to bear in times of need," he finished. "Where did you hear that?"

"Read," Darshan corrected. "One of the books I used to study Tirglasian on the way to your homeland was a transcription of your people's philosophers. That one stuck. It's surprisingly similar to one of our own sayings."

"And you think a bow, with or without its arrow, is akin to the ability to ensnare someone's mind?"

"No, but I don't believe they had much to say about magic. At least, beyond it being an affront to the Goddess and would better serve the people once locked away."

Hamish grunted. His husband had the right of it. The Tirglasian view on spellsters was limited. Either they were shuffled off to spend their lives in cloisters or they were free, dangerous and dead soon enough. His own mother thought of her youngest daughter as an abomination. He didn't know what she'd make of them all having latent power, a trait his father had unknowingly passed on.

If I'd been anything like him. Or even his brother. According to Darshan, they were both Nulled Ones. Having immunity to direct magic would make him safe from any hypnotist's sight. Although, it would've also meant he'd have succumbed to his injuries in the bear's attack.

Or would Darshan have found a way around that?

He scrubbed at his face. He knew so little about how things worked. Not only his husband's new abilities, but magic in general. And, once they reached Minamist, he would be in the heart of a land that all but ran on that power.

"We can stop," Darshan said, breaking Hamish's musing. "If you'd prefer?"

"Nae." Hamish placed his hands back in his lap. He needed to learn. Even if Darshan couldn't show him everything, knowing something was better than ignorance. "You said eye contact was the first step, what's the next?"

"That would be when a hypnotist imposes their will on yours. This is also where skill and finesse comes into play over brute strength. There are two levels of difficulty in this, the easiest being asking a person to do things they would have no compunctions about doing under usual circumstances."

"Such as?"

Again, Darshan leant forward to hold Hamish's gaze. "Kiss me."

The fuzziness returning to his mind, the command wrapping around his thoughts like a warm blanket. *Kiss him.* A strange thing to suggest at this time and place, but he didn't see why not? His body moved without further thought, breaching the space between them to lay claim to Darshan's mouth.

No sooner had their lips touched did the order fade.

Hamish sat back, shaking out the feeling of not being in control of his body. It prickled through his flesh like the awakening of a sleep-numbed arm. "That was weird." Like watching himself move through a dream. "But nae exactly impressive." He would spend days kissing Darshan if he could.

Grinning, his husband gave a slightly wicked chuckle that shouldn't warm him but always did. "I did tell you it was the easiest." He picked up his glasses, unfolding the earpieces. "You'd rather I made you do something you wouldn't choose to?"

"Aye, give it a try."

Darshan smirked and lowered his glasses. "As you wish."

This time, Hamish could almost feel the threads of fuzziness slipping over his mind before he lost control of himself to it.

"Hit me. Right here." Darshan tapped his chin. "As hard as you can."

The suggestion fogged his mind and pulled back his fist before his thoughts caught up with the act. Even then, it seemed like a reasonable thing. Darshan could heal himself so it wasn't as if any damage would be permanent.

When it came to actually throwing the punch, the command's hold on him slithered off like an eel down the river.

He quickly lowered his hand, cradling it in his lap. "That was... nae as pleasant." If his punch had landed, he could've broken his husband's jaw. Just because Darshan's magic would've fixed it didn't make the act disappear. And who was to say the jaw wouldn't heal crooked? Or that some unseen injury wouldn't leave him dead?

Darshan returned his glasses to his face. "You did ask to see. I'll count myself fortunate that you hold no ill will towards me."

"You could've asked me to put me hand in the fire or break me bow." He wouldn't have been eager to do either, but burnt skin or snapped wood would've been less damaging.

"*Mea lux*, I would never consider asking you to do anything that would cause you pain."

"But if what you claim is true, then I wouldnae actually do it, so—" He let the argument drop as another thought came to him. "What of the people we found?" In both accounts, their deaths came by the very poison they had attempted to kill him with. The hypnosis had to involve eliminating them to keep Zahaan's men from finding the culprit. "You cannae tell me they wanted to die." He couldn't be certain of the woman in Nulshar, but the man in the theatre had definitely shut himself in that little nook in the wall and drank the same poison that would've killed Hamish.

"That cycles back to skill. The more adept a hypnotist is, the stronger their hold and the harder it is to break free of the trance."

He tapped the side of his head. "After all, tricking the brain into agreeing is the root of hypnotism. With the poisoning, it could've been a simple matter of not informing them of what it was."

"What about removing memories?"

Darshan shook his head. "I cannot do that."

"I thought—" He scratched his scalp. Why was it still itchy? Or had Darshan planted that idea into his mind and he simply hadn't noticed? "Well, I thought since your magic is strong…"

"Strength doesn't always equate to aptitude. I could have all the magic in the world, but it would be useless if I haven't the training. As for being capable enough to erase memories…" He puffed his cheeks, his breath gusting out in a mighty sigh. "My father learnt the trick from my grandfather. He won't teach anyone, not even me, and he has only used such knowledge once that I remember. Out of mercy."

"But if it isnae him as you believe and your grandpa's been dead for years." Not as long as Hamish's grandparents, but at least a decade. "Then this person has spent a lot of bloody effort harbouring this talent, waiting to use it."

Darshan nodded. "That's what scares me."

Why now? Was it because Darshan had little in the way of protection? But his husband confessed to sneaking out to festivals, to engaging in revelry that put him literally in the hands of others. If they were after the throne, there had been ample times to end Darshan's life.

Why target me? If he had entered this marriage with his mother's blessing, then his death could've started a war between the two lands. But she had declared him as dead to her. Some of the rumours even claimed his husband had killed him.

As things stood, the worst outcome if they succeeded in killing Hamish was breaking Darshan's heart.

Hamish stared into those hazel eyes, the ones that had first captured his attention all the way back in that dockside pub. In this light, he couldn't make out the rings of green and brown, but he remembered the way they sparkled with mischief, of how they lit up whenever Hamish shared his heart.

To imagine that spark growing dark with his death…

"I have something for you," Hamish murmured, getting up to rummage through his saddlebag.

Darshan remained silent, one brow lifting in query.

"I was going to give it to you on your birthday." That was still the better part of a week away, if he had managed to keep proper track of the days during their whirlwind journey. "But I figure you could do with it now." His hand finally closed around the small lump of carved wood, a mouse he had whittled from a chunk of walnut bark. After days of polishing, the surface was smooth as stone. "Here." He pressed it to his husband's palm.

Darshan examined the piece, the softening of his face instantaneous. "*Mea lux.*" His voice wavered. He dabbed at the outer corner of one eye. "It's exquisite."

"It's a field mouse." He knew Darshan already had a small marble version in his pack, bought as a gift whilst one of Hamish's nephews regaled him with the old fable of Great Ailein, where the Goddess sent two mice of ivory and onyx to help him survive a month of being trapped in the cave of the Grey Bear.

"So I see." Darshan ran a thumb over the head. It was hard to make out with the waning firelight on his glasses, but he seemed to be on the verge of tears. "It's beautiful. Did you make this? Was that what you've been doing these last few nights?"

Hamish nodded, his face heating. With the pair of them out in the open as they raced for Rolshar, he hadn't been willing to sleep without someone on guard. He hadn't been the best with wood and the only tools on hand was his hunting knife, but the nights had been so dull that he turned to carving simply to keep himself awake. "It'll bring you luck."

"I remember the tale. I didn't realise you could work wood so finely. You truly are a man of many talents. But I think you might need its luck more than I."

Hamish closed his hands over Darshan's before the man got it into his fool head to give the mouse back. "Great Ailein's mice are meant to be gifted, nae kept."

His husband's gaze finally lifted from the piece, his delight shining brightly through his smile. "You really didn't have to go through all that trouble."

"A man should receive gifts on his birthday and I couldnae think what else to give you that you wouldnae already have." He could almost see why Darshan's siblings resorted to trinkets each year. "I ken it's nae much. I dinnae have access to any money that's nae yours, so I couldnae afford any fancy jewels or—" He fell silent as his husband laid a hand on his shirt.

Darshan chuckled softly. "You really think I'd be concerned with you dipping into our coffers?"

Hamish shrugged. Back in Tirglas, his mother kept a tight rein on his allowance, never giving him access to much in an effort to keep him from affording anything beyond a little food or a cheap bauble. Outwardly, it was meant to foster frugality in him, but he knew the real reason was to ensure he couldn't leave her reach.

"My beacon, I freely share everything I possess with you, that includes money. You're free to spend it on whatever you desire."

"I dinnae want to look like some spendthrift." He didn't need to be told what the Crystal Court's rumour mill would do with *that* information.

"You'd have to empty my coffers to outstrip my own reputation there." Darshan ran a thumb over the wooden mouse's back. "After everything you've been through, having you well and alive at my side is a gift in itself. But thank you, *mea lux.*" He clutched the mouse to his chest. "I will cherish this." Curling his fingers into the linen, Darshan drew him closer and kissed him, almost tipping them onto the ground before his lips were in reach.

Hamish leant into the kiss, tucking his husband against him and mulling over the risks of suggesting they both retire to the tent. Although, given that they were travelling alone, the tent wasn't a necessity. He had rutted a number of times in the forests, back when he'd been young and foolish and his mother hadn't linked his excessive hunting to other activities.

Here, they'd the bonus of knowing the sky wasn't about to rain on them. The tent *did* have blankets to stop the ground from distracting them with its coarseness, but their clothes would do the same job at covering the grass and smoothing out the bumps.

Whilst his mind still hummed and hawed, his hands had wandered, slowly undoing the tiny buttons of Darshan's sherwani. He broke the kiss, nuzzling the underside of his husband's jaw, then the side of Darshan's neck to a small sigh of the man's pleasure that reverberated against his lips.

With the sherwani undone and his mind finally made up, he pulled at the undershirt as Darshan finished shucking his sherwani. Hamish slid his hands under the fine linen barrier. The skin beneath his fingertips shivered.

Soon, even the undershirt was no barrier, stripped and laid aside.

Hamish went to coax his husband to lie on his back to better rid him of his trousers when Darshan halted him, one hand on Hamish's chest to keep him in place.

Prickling silence sucked at his ears, draining the warmth infusing his body. The gentle sounds of the woods had halted. Even the horses no longer ate, staring off into the darkness beneath the trees, in the same direction his husband seemed focused on.

"What is it?" he whispered.

Darshan motioned him to silence. He clambered off Hamish's lap and to his feet.

Hamish took up his bow. This far south, he could rule out bears and boars. What other predators prowled this wilderness? *Big cats.* He'd only seen the remains of one and heard rumours. Could it be one of them? "Dar?"

The trees rustled, their branches twisting, although there was no wind to drive the unnatural swaying. Was his husband talking to the trees? Were they talking to him? Exactly how much were they aware of Darshan's presence? Had they sensed what Hamish had planned?

His cheeks heated at the realisation that he'd been ready to have sex whilst being watched over by dozens of plants. Maybe retreating to the tent would've been the better option. It couldn't be too unusual. There were hundreds of animals in the woods. They all bred the same way.

"*Tigris*," Darshan hissed, jolting Hamish from his musing. He swiftly threw a shield around them, the shimmering dome filling the clearing. "It must've smelt the horses. Or maybe our dinner."

Curious, Hamish peered into the darkness beyond the magical barrier. He recalled Darshan's warning about the big striped cats, but they hadn't encountered any in their travels.

At first, he saw nothing. Then he spied the green glint of eyes reflecting the firelight as the cat came closer. It was hard to tell with the creature blending into the darkness, but it looked as long as a horse, although nowhere near as tall and solid. Almost the size of a boarhound in height.

It stopped just before the shield and raised its head to sniff, then slunk along the curve of the barrier in a fluid gait, aiming for the horses.

That could be a problem. For now, both mounts seemed only spooked. If they got a whiff of the predator, then their only hope was in containing them. "Your shield's solid both ways, right?" He couldn't reliably create one, but he knew Darshan could manipulate his for all sorts of conditions. Watertight, airtight, even capable of lifting a person.

"Apart from letting air in, of course."

"Good." At least if the horses broke their tether, they wouldn't end up dashing out into the woods. He watched the big cat lope one way, then the other. Each step carried far more grace and power than any castle mouser. "Do you think you could scare it off?"

Darshan also tracked the cat, his brows lowering. "I'd prefer not to hurt it."

"I'm nae suggesting that. Just... persuade it to go elsewhere." He went to step closer, to get a better look at the animal's striped coat, but couldn't lift a single foot. Looking down, he found vines twisting around his boots. "I thought you said you couldnae summon these wee buggers?"

"I can't. I didn't." He knelt to examine the vines. They shifted at his touch, winding around his hand like an affectionate puppy. "I don't *think* I did."

"Can you get them off me boots?" Even with Darshan's shield shimmering in all its purple glory around them, he felt a little exposed being rooted to the spot...

"Hold on. Let me just see if..." Darshan tugged on one tendril and the vines slithered away. "Remarkable," he breathed. "I—"

The scream of a horse split the air like tearing metal. Hamish's mare reared and kicked out, fighting her tether. The gelding was likewise stirred up, but nowhere near as vocal.

Hamish hastened towards them. He needed to calm them down before they keeled over from stress.

"Hold," Darshan ordered. He raised a hand towards the cat. Lightning crackled from his palm, landing just in front of the massive paws. The flash illuminated the clearing in pale blue light.

In the midst of blinking away the glare and trying to shake the muffled sensation from his ears, Hamish barely caught the cat racing back into the woods.

That's one way to scare the bugger off. He had thought Darshan would try something less dramatic.

With his balance a mess and his ears still ringing, Hamish staggered the rest of the way to the horses. With Darshan's help, they soothed their mounts as best they could, not leaving their side until they had fully calmed down.

Darshan reignited the campfire as they returned to the tent. "I think it's best if I keep watch tonight. You try and get some sleep."

"You cannae keep that shield up all night." Not without rest. "What if it comes back?"

"It won't. It's hungry, not foolish. Most won't come near a campfire unless they're desperate. Judging by the size, I would say it's a young female looking for an easy meal. Now she knows we're not it."

"You sure? It looked bloody interested to me."

"Oh, she would pick our flesh out of her teeth with our bones if we gave her the chance. But Udyneans have been living alongside the animals for several millennia, they've learnt we're a difficult meal. Although..." His attention slid to where the cat had fled back into the shadows. "Perhaps it would be prudent if we return to spending our nights in the local inns."

"Aye." He would definitely feel better knowing they were safely behind solid walls and locked doors. Most of the inns they'd stayed at seemed to have very tall fences, too. He hadn't given it much thought, but a cat that big would need an equally large barrier to keep it out. "It's just—"

"We'll be fine, *mea lux*. I've got this, I promise. Just get some rest. It won't do to have both of us exhausted."

Hamish slipped into the tent and settled on the blankets. Sleep would not come easily, but Darshan was right. One of them needed their wits about them tomorrow, even if Hamish didn't know the first sign of being stalked by a *tigris*.

Hopefully, he wouldn't need to know, just as he prayed to the Goddess that all would go back to normal once they returned to spending their nights as unknown travellers in quiet village inns.

Chapter 19

Darshan flopped back onto the bed. The mattress greeted his spine like a brick. *Lovely.* At least it seemed free of parasites. Although, the stain on the floor near the foot of the bed was suspiciously rust-coloured. Blood or something less sinister, he didn't want to know.

They had travelled for nine days, with each inn no more luxurious than this poxy place. He missed the beds with broad mattresses he could sink into, the cuisine that his tongue didn't register as mere mush, and the people who ensured his every need was attended to. He might've done without all those things for several months, but it had only taken a few days of old normality to rekindle the yearning.

Yet such absences came at a price Darshan was quite willing to pay.

There'd been no attempts on Hamish's life since sticking to these backstreet places. Few seemed to even recognise their *uris Mhanek*, an added bonus that also let him see his empire unfiltered by the lens of rehearsed greetings and fearful gestures.

"Almost seems like home," Hamish said, shuffling their gear into the corner farthest from the door. They hadn't come across anyone attempting to steal their stuff yet, but Darshan saw no point in objecting to the precaution. "Although, I suppose this wasnae how you imagined your birthday going?"

Chuckling and expending as little energy as possible, he levered off his boots, letting them drop to the bare floorboards. "Actually, I vastly prefer this to being the subject of countless saccharine blessings and gifts from the court." The official celebration required nothing from him but to sit upon his throne and nod in acceptance at each gift. Usually, they were slaves that the noble had tarted up after culling them from their under-performing.

And the statues. The palace grounds were overflowing with his visage, carved in all manner of stone, with the rest in storage. There were an additional twenty-one scattered about the city squares, but those had been commissioned by his father. One for every year after his *Khutani.*

"Is it really that bad?"

Darshan rolled onto his side to stare gobsmacked at his husband. Bad was too poor a word to describe the stuffy formal ceremony that served as a reminder to all that he was another year older, and still without a spouse or heir. "It's *ghastly.* Anjali is hardly ever acknowledged without it sounding like an afterthought." Those few who remembered his twin always announced their offering to her with an insufferable smugness as if they had uncovered some secret ticket to winning the *vris Mhanek's* favour.

"So, how does Darshan celebrate his birthday after the *vris Mhanek* is done?"

Resuming his recline on his back, he grinned up at the ceiling. His celebrations beyond the formal were rather singular in design. "By falling to the usual pastimes of drunken revelry and orgies." With him as the centrepiece in a pile of naked men, waking up hours later and having no memory of how he had gotten there.

Hamish gave a considering hum. He leant over the bed, his head hovering above Darshan's. "What would you say to celebrating this birthday in the Tirglasian style?"

Since starting their journey to Minamist, he had accepted the simple fact he wouldn't arrive in time for a proper celebration—and he hoped that meant fewer garish gifts to sort through once they *did* reach the capital. He was prepared for a quiet night in Hamish's arms, even looked forward to it, but if the man had something better to offer... "What would it entail?"

"Getting drunk off our asses at the nearest pub and dancing terribly to whatever music they're playing."

"Sounds divine." It truly did. He had originally considered spending the night doing that very thing, followed by tumbling his husband into bed to ravage him senseless. That had all been before Nulshar and the events after. "But we best not lower our guard until we've reached somewhere a little safer."

There were reasons beyond protecting Hamish's life to be wary of getting drunk in these unassuming villages dotting the countryside. The inns they stayed at were the sort where people didn't ask too many questions. Whilst it worked in their favour, it came with its own risks and, more than once, he had been forced to pay extra to ensure them and their horses remained undisturbed.

"Come on, a few drinks willnae hurt."

"Absolutely not."

"It's your birthday." Hamish knelt on the floor, resting his chin on the blankets like a pleading child. "One drink with your husband?"

"I just want us to get home. Alive." They'd been careful not to mingle too much. It was a delicate balance. Overt secrecy drew unwanted attention just as quickly as if he cavorted through the streets. When it came to his husband's life, he wasn't prepared to risk anything.

Hamish rolled his eyes. "I ken you're worried, but all of the attempts on me life have been in fancy places; your half-sister's soirée, the theatre—" He waggled a finger at Darshan. "I'm nae counting the tree. That one was on you."

Darshan inclined his head in acceptance of the fault.

"We've been travelling for over a week now. There's been nae sign of trouble in all the other inns and pubs since Rolshar. All I'm suggesting is one drink and then come back up to sleep."

"Fine. One drink and that's all." Although, if he had his way, sleep afterwards would not be on the immediate agenda.

~ ~ ~

Darshan peered down at his mug. One drink had turned into quite a few more. How many did this one make? He had rather lost count after the third. Or had that been his fifth? Did that mean this was his sixth? His seventh? The swill they called beer was quite weak and he'd been doing his level best to match his husband mug for mug.

He peered at Hamish. The man certainly didn't look anywhere near as drunk as he would be after so many. Maybe *this* was their fifth, then. Whatever the number, it certainly had to be enough.

They'd taken up residence at a corner table away from the larger bustle of the tavern. Only the servers broke their isolation, generally with another round that Hamish had signalled for.

Setting his half-full mug aside, Darshan lurched to his feet. His legs objected to the sudden weight, not fully caving but slightly uncertain. "We should head back to our room."

"One moment," Hamish mumbled from the depths of his own drink. He tipped the mug back to drain the dregs before following Darshan in leaving the table.

They sauntered through the crowd, aiming for the stairs and doing their best to avoid bumping into anyone who looked primed for a fight. Most were occupying their time in dancing either by themselves, in pairs or in small groups, all to the lively tune played by a trio of musicians.

The woman amongst them sang a bawdy song he'd heard a great many times, of a young maiden and her five lovers, whilst she banged a tambourine against her hip to the soft shiver of metal. Behind her, the two men played a flute and a disc drum.

Had this been any other time, he would've joined the dancing. But they'd an early start tomorrow. After drinking so much, his magic would be working hard to deal with the after-effects without him needing to rely on it in the face of trouble.

A man on the edge of the crowd gyrated up to Hamish, his movements so overt that his intention could only be to, as his husband called it, show off the goods. He placed a hand on Hamish's chest and uttered something that, although too low for Darshan to hear, was definitely a proposition.

Hamish stumbled back a few steps with his hands upraised. "I appreciate the offer, but I'm married." He swept Darshan into his grasp, positioning him between them like a shield. "To this gorgeous man right here, in fact."

Darshan pinned the man with a scathing look, daring him to question it.

The man's face paled, recognition lighting his eyes. "My apologies, *vris Mhanek*," he mumbled, bowing low. "I did not realise." He hastened outside, almost falling over himself as the door swung easily into the street.

It might've been the drink—it could've also been the possessiveness brewing in his gut—but Darshan gave little thought towards dragging his bewildered husband into the middle of the dancing.

"I thought you wanted to head off to bed?" He paused for a beat, long enough for Darshan to glance incredulously over his shoulder. "Nae that I'm complaining."

"Good." He twirled into his husband's arms—with, by the way Hamish chuckled, less elegance than he had assumed. Undeterred, he led them on a merry little dance across the floor, just barely missing bumping into people.

Hamish rested his hand on the small of Darshan's back, abruptly halting them before they collided right into a rather solid-looking table.

Taking the hint, Darshan ceded control to his clearly more sober husband. He rested a hand on Hamish's hip and the other atop one huge bicep, running his fingers over the sleeve and absently smoothing the wrinkles. Warmth soaked through the soft linen, setting his skin to tingling.

Winking playfully, Hamish effortlessly took the lead. He guided them between the couples and groups all without missing a beat.

Darshan did his best to follow with as much grace, stepping forward when Hamish stepped back and trailing along whenever the man turned. No matter how much they danced together, it always amazed him whenever Hamish led. The way he felt every movement his husband planned, the when and how. Dancing with him like this, where neither of them were concerned with who watched, was as easy as breathing.

Disappointment briefly flooded his senses as the song came to an end and Hamish let go with a flourishing bow. They parted for a short while, dancing alongside each other as the sultry music of an elven lap harp took place of the woman's voice.

The trio's playing continued, gaining speed and energy.

A few of the tavern's patrons leapt onto the table. The room was a buzz of cheers and laughter. Darshan watched as their feet kept time with the beat. For a few seconds, it appeared as though the people were hovering above the stained wood. It looked like fun.

Slowly, he guided Hamish towards a vacant table and hopped onto one of the chairs. It put them at around the same height. With his husband's face so close, all scrunched in bemusement, Darshan couldn't help but kiss him.

From the chair, it was a simple matter of stepping onto the table. His head spun as he straightened, but the table was wide enough to accommodate his staggering as he regained his balance.

"Dar!" Hamish hissed. "Get down."

Someone else joined him on the table, a woman with a shocking amount of rouge and eyeshadow. "Steady, lovely," she said, her voice a deep gravelly tone. "Let's not wreck that pretty face of yours." She wrapped her arm around his waist, pulling them hip to hip. "Like this." She moved her feet in a blur of bare toes.

Darshan fumbled atop the table in his attempt to mimic the woman, taking a few tries before he got the hang of it. The music blithely played on, unconcerned if he kept in time.

Lifting his gaze from his feet, he found Hamish watching with a look of consternation. Darshan blew his husband a kiss and, releasing his hold on the woman, spun towards Hamish. His momentum flung him right off the edge of the table.

He landed in Hamish's grasp, laughing as the crowd cheered his recklessness. Then he was back on his feet and up onto another table, whisking through the dancers as Hamish trailed along.

He caught glimpses of people cheering and whistling, for him alone or the others he didn't know or care. He hadn't felt this free since he'd been a young man newly introduced to the wonders of the adult world.

A hand clutched his as he went to climb onto yet another table, drawing him back until he was pressed hard against a familiar chest.

The tension in the air vibrated just as much as the lap harp's strings, singing a beguiling tune that flowed through his veins and straight to his groin. Darshan pressed closer, grinding his backside against his husband's thigh.

"I dinnae remember that being part of the moves they showed you," Hamish said, his voice heavy.

"*Mea lux.* Love. Darling." He hooked his fingers into Hamish's belt and drew him closer. "Light of my life."

"Aye? And just what are you after?" He bent over, the words a whisper purring into Darshan's ears.

Grinning, he cupped his husband's crotch to the glorious reaction of those sapphiric eyes widening. "I think you already have a fair idea."

Rather than the blushing and scandalised reaction Darshan expected, Hamish laughed and languidly leant into the touch. "Well, you're nae exactly subtle."

Darshan wet his lips. Whilst there truly was something about the way the lap harp sang that stirred his blood, if Hamish kept speaking like that, neither of them were leaving this room with their clothes on. "Subtle clearly doesn't get me laid."

"Greedy," Hamish breathed. "As if you didnae get any last night."

A wistful smile tugged at his lips. Last night had been amazing, as always, but there was one important factor. "I didn't *get* anything. *You* got." He poked his husband's chest with a forefinger, swaying slightly as the hulking figure before him didn't move. "*I* gave."

Humour plumped Hamish's cheeks regardless of how he tried to hide it. "And *you* are definitely drunk."

"It's also my birthday!" Darshan spread his arms wide and shouted the declaration to the rafters to the chorus of cheers. He returned his hands to Hamish's belt buckle, seeking to undo it. "And I'm invoking my right to make long, passionate love to my husband."

"Oh, are you now?" His lips skewed into a crooked grin that almost had Darshan jumping the man then and there. "Well, since you're so eager..." Hamish guided them out of the dancing throng. "How about we head up to our room before you undress me?"

"I thought you'd never ask." He was more than ready for the intimacy of a bed. Darshan led the charge towards the stairs, a thought occurring to him as they reached the first step. "I wonder... would you be willing to indulge your husband if he made a special request?" Whilst he didn't mind men riding him or being ridden, Hamish's preference wasn't quite as fluid. His husband leant more towards being the one penetrated.

Despite the man's insistence of being no good at it, he always performed beautifully, but had admitted to not enjoying the act as much, certainly not on the same level as Darshan did. Even with being physically bigger, dominance didn't come naturally to the man.

However, Hamish would play the part readily enough if asked. Darshan tried not to abuse that, requesting sparingly and never with great insistence.

"Well," Hamish drawled. "Since it *is* your special day..." His hands landed on Darshan's hips.

A brief sensation of weightlessness overcame Darshan before his stomach alighted on his husband's broad shoulder. He lay still for as long as it took for his mind to acknowledge he'd been slung rather like a sack of grain. "You utter savage," he managed between bouts of inelegant giggles. He squirmed, seeking a way to free himself without much luck. "Put me down!"

"Nae bloody likely." He gave Darshan's rear a hearty pat that warmed more than mere skin. "Off we trot."

"You did *not* seriously just smack my backside." And he most certainly hadn't felt his body tingle at the contact.

"I'm going to do a lot more to it than that once I get you upstairs," Hamish growled.

"Help," Darshan pleaded to the crowd, unable to keep the grin off his face or the laughter from his voice. "This foreign brute is carting me off to his den to have his wicked way with me." He could certainly hope that was what Hamish had in mind.

His announcement was met with a fair number of drunken roars and cheers. A few had the audacity to whistle and he caught a couple of lewd suggestions that, judging by the way Hamish ducked his head, his husband had definitely understood.

Hamish made his way up the stairs. Where Darshan was certain he would've struggled to carry a person thusly on the flat, his husband took each step with little show of using any effort. He made his way down the hall with the same indifference towards the extra weight.

Draped as he was, Darshan could do little else but hope his head didn't bump against the ceiling or doorframes they passed through. But in this, too, Hamish was remarkably skilled in avoiding such obstacles. "Why do I get the distinct impression you've carted someone off like this before?"

Hamish chuckled breathlessly. "A few times," he admitted. He reached their room, ducking as he entered. "Nae with the same intentions, though."

Of course not. Hamish had always been the receptive party back in his homeland. Whilst he hadn't been entirely innocent when it came to sex, he had lacked certain experiences beyond being bent over a barrel and used. A space where he had been free and safe to experiment with his desires was one of many things Darshan couldn't imagine living without.

Darshan was still deep in his musing when he found himself landing on their bed hard enough to bounce. He didn't mind terribly much as it left him sprawled atop the moonlight-drenched blankets for Hamish to do as he pleased.

Hamish roughly undid the ties to his shirt, discarding it without a care. His boots were next, then his trousers.

Darshan tried to muster a clever retort at the eagerness in which Hamish undressed, but found himself speechless. Propped on his elbows, he barely breathed as he watched. He had seen his husband undress multiple times, but this was different. Standing right before him was the stuff of his dreams, of his fantasies. All soft around the edges as his drink-blurred eyes refused to focus. It was the image he had envisioned on the nights where there'd been only self-gratification.

Now? It was his reality. It was...

My light.

Only when Hamish straightened before him, clothed just in drawers that failed to hide the extent of his arousal, did Darshan realise he was no less dressed than when they'd headed into the tavern.

Hamish eyed him critically, his breath heavy, then gave a wolfish grin. "Guess I'm stripping you, too."

Heat took Darshan's face. A quick glance downwards confirmed that, yes, his clothes hadn't miraculously shed themselves whilst he continued to gawk at his husband like a man new to the ways of pleasure.

Darshan swiftly aided in the removal of his garments, unbuttoning his sherwani and undershirt as Hamish relinquished him of his footwear and trousers. It was rare enough for his naturally submissive husband to slip into the dominant role without making it difficult for him.

They tugged at each other's drawers, the attempt to remove them altogether hindered as Hamish half-climbed on the bed.

Then, after a few muttered curses and the total collapse of his husband onto the mattress, there was just bare skin as they fumbled and kissed their way up the bed.

His hips lifted, aided by Hamish's grasp on them. Their lengths brushed against each other and a desperate moan rumbled in his throat. *Gods.* He wrapped an arm around his husband's waist, steadying the haphazard pressure.

Hamish bent closer, his shoulders trembling slightly as he lowered his glorious weight, pushing Darshan deeper into the mattress.

Their foreheads met, both already slightly damp from dancing. They panted into each other's face, sharing breath and soft groans as each minuscule movement had them rubbing against each other.

Hamish tilted his head and slowly blanked most of Darshan's thoughts with a long kiss.

Darshan dug his fingers into the hair carpeting his husband's chest. He'd never known a man to be so hairy, but the sensation of it rubbing against his body was divine. He slid his hands downward, tracing the taut muscles, grabbing Hamish's backside and squeezing to the decadent sound of his husband's growl.

Hamish indolently rolled his hips and heavenly friction undid the rest of Darshan's mind.

They continued that way for a while, hands and hips bringing them closer to the edge until Darshan couldn't take anymore teasing. " 'Mish," he pleaded, his body keening to continue this gentle bliss and for more at the same time. "I want you in me."

His husband hoisted him up until he was positioned for an inward thrust that would give Darshan precisely what he had asked for.

Then all movement stopped.

"Where do you keep the oil?" Hamish asked.

"It doesn't matter." It might be a little uncomfortable at first without preparation, but his magic would make things right after. "I can—"

"*Dar...*" A warning warbled on that syllable. "We've talked about this." They had. At great lengths.

Between them, Hamish had all the experience when it came to being taken dry and he was determined not to do anything that came close. All of Darshan's counters didn't matter. His magic. The fact he was too excited to possibly feel it until later. Nothing would move his husband.

It was the one definite limit Darshan had found in the man and one argument he would never win.

"*Where?*" Hamish persisted.

"Side pouch. It looks like an oddly rolled scrap of cloth." Darshan stretched out on the bed as his husband clambered off the side and onto his feet. At least the cessation gave him time to recover his strength. And possibly last longer than a repressed teenager new to sex.

The view was a bonus, the moonlight might've drenched the bed, but it reflected just enough to illuminate that glorious backside as his husband rummaged through the saddlebag.

Darshan sighed. The things he wanted to do with that man. But if he started down that path, then *he* wouldn't be the one getting his arse thoroughly pounded tonight.

"Got it," Hamish announced, standing upright and turning around. He halted.

Darshan waited, anticipation slowly turning to impatience, then fluttering on to concern. " 'Mish?"

Hamish shook himself and quickly returned to the bedside. "Look at you," he purred, kneeling between Darshan's ankles at the foot of the bed. The angle had him backlit by the moonlight. "Glowing like a gift from the Goddess."

Darshan peered through his lashes at the dream bent over him. "You're quite the vision yourself."

Although Hamish's face was in shadow, the answering brief chuckle sounded slightly on the embarrassed side. He slid closer, further spreading Darshan's legs. "How do I do this?"

"*Mea lux*," he chided. "This is hardly your first time." He had been there for that gorgeous revelation.

"I ken that, but usually... Well, you've generally already prepared yourself. How do I ken I'm nae hurting you?"

"You won't." He cupped Hamish's jaw, luxuriating in the softness of that beard against his palm. "Just take it slow and trust yourself."

Darshan reclined on the bed, fisting the blankets and concentrating on his breathing, whilst his husband set about preparing him. Not an easy feat with the way Hamish's finger moved inside him, teasing him by not going quite deep enough. The man's other hand, calloused from years of weapon training, gripped Darshan's length, each firm stroke slipping him further down the spiralling path to ultimate pleasure.

Darshan pushed back on the finger in him, seeking more of the man, arching as a second finger entered him. He bit back the demands of *want* and *more* and *now*. Hamish wouldn't proceed until *he* was satisfied Darshan was ready, no matter Darshan's insistence.

Not that Darshan could bring himself to mind the time it took. He was no stranger to having his body worshipped, even if it was usually lustful and intense, but this was on a whole other plane of existence.

A mortifying keening noise tightened his throat when Hamish finally withdrew his fingers, the sound halting abruptly as the gorgeous, shadowy bulk of his husband leant over him.

"You are damn near vibrating," Hamish whispered, the warmth of his breath slinking along Darshan's already sweat-slick skin.

With his spine feeling as though it had turned to water, Darshan dug trembling fingers into his husband's hair and brought Hamish's mouth to his own. He sucked and nipped at Hamish's lip, delving between them with his tongue to play, moaning as his husband replied in kind.

Hamish wordlessly cupped Darshan's backside, the friction of those calloused fingers sending extra sparks of pleasure right to his groin.

Heeding the command, Darshan lifted his hips enough to allow for a pillow to slip beneath him. Another thing that Hamish insisted upon. Usually, Darshan wouldn't bother. He'd had his fair share of sprained and cramped muscles over the years. His magic dealt with the pain almost as soon as it appeared, rendering the caution Hamish gave as superfluous.

Still, he hadn't the heart to object if his husband found the act beneficial.

Hamish propped himself on one outstretched arm, his other hand guiding him in with the faintest of inhales. Curse him and his silence. It didn't matter that Darshan made enough noise for the both of them. He certainly couldn't help the moan that left his lips at Hamish's entry or the groan that sighed out once his husband's pelvis was nestled against his backside.

This connected, Darshan easily sensed Hamish's weight shift before the mattress had a chance to move. A finger traced its way up his chest, stopping only when it could cup Darshan's jaw.

"I love you," his husband breathed, the declaration sending Darshan's soul spiralling out on a dizzy loop.

"*Mea lux*," he thickly replied, nuzzling his husband's palm and kissing the heel of his hand. "My beacon."

Hamish dropped his head, claiming Darshan's mouth with infuriatingly slow kisses. His hips rolled, withdrawing unhurriedly, then driving back in with equal speed.

Darshan had experienced sex in so many different fashions, be it in groups, pairs or singles. He had spent long nights doing little else that had left him wobbly and slightly hesitant to sit despite his healing magic. He'd had lovers who would attend to his every whim and more, frequently. But not like this.

Not in the deep, core-stirring fashion that left him shaking and unashamedly moaning.

Never.

He clung to Hamish, digging his nails into that broad back, feeling the muscles beneath shift with each thrust. He breathed deep of his husband's skin, the scent turning his already giddy mind to utter mush.

The bed creaked through more than just his husband's movements. His magic quaked through his veins, seeking an outlet. Darshan struggled to suppress his power. He really hadn't thought everything through when he asked for this. They weren't in some little clearing in the woods or a sturdy mansion designed to withstand the forces of unfettered magic.

If he let himself go, he could very well send them plummeting to the ground floor.

Hamish must've caught the change, for he slowed his hips from indulgent to languid. "You all right?" The hushed, thickly rich desire soaking the words thrummed through Darshan's whole body. "You want me to stop?"

Gods. Darshan swallowed, trying to find the words to speak. If his husband kept talking in that same tone, then he wouldn't need to concern himself about whether Hamish stopped or not. "Perish the thought," he managed.

Giving a wicked chuckle that would definitely find its way into Darshan's dreams, Hamish resumed his rhythmic movement, growing steadily faster with each thrust.

Noises escaped Darshan's lips, deep pants that his husband cheerfully compared to an animal's mating call. It had his face heating every time, but he couldn't control it. He had tried, but it was so hard to concentrate on the *nos* when every part of him screamed *yes*.

"*There's* me stag," Hamish growled, his teeth clenched. "Is he going to bellow for me?" His thrusts gained more power, shuffling Darshan up the bed. Affectionate but strong. Filling Darshan perfectly at just the right pace to leave him breathless.

There was no hope of containing his voice after that.

Darshan reached the edge with a roar. Lightning danced down his spine and white light flashed before his eyes. He arched beneath his husband, his heels digging into the mattress, his head thrown back as his body succumbed to the orgasm. His magic thrummed through the air, the lingering scent of wet earth overlaying an almost storm-like aroma and the musk of lovemaking.

Hamish's soft grunt warmed the air between them. His hands clamped onto Darshan's waist, lifting him off the pillow in an effort to keep them together as he silently reached his own climax.

Darshan shivered. In this hyper-sensitive state, he was certain he could feel every emptying twitch of his husband's length inside him. He panted, his lungs seemingly wanting all the air they could hold at once. At least he saw more than twirling lights.

Slowly, Hamish relinquished his hold, allowing Darshan to slip back onto the bed. "Better this time, then?" he breathed.

Darshan grinned, recalling how concerned his husband had been about his performance the first time he'd taken control. "A marked improvement."

"I figured as much since you went off before me."

"For someone who professes they don't like sex this way, you're damn good at it."

"I nae said I dinnae like it, I just prefer it the other way." Hamish shifted, leaving Darshan where he laid to shuffle off the bed and onto his feet. "I need a drink, then I think a bath is in order."

"A bath does sound delightful." Darshan stretched, relishing the satisfaction buzzing through his body. "Do you suppose you'll have the energy to repeat the act?"

"Again? In one night?" Chuckling, Hamish shook his head. "Greedy."

"Well, it *is* my special day," he purred, echoing his husband's words back in the tavern.

"True as that is..." Hamish spread his hands. "I'm nae like you. Me magic isnae strong enough to bolster me libido."

"I hardly think magic plays that big a part in it." True, the mixture of strong magic and lust tended to feed on itself at the best of times—and strong magic only heightened the effect—but it wasn't the be-all and end-all.

"Really? Well, maybe it's me age that only allows me to get it up once in a night."

Darshan scoffed. Given a few more decades and such an excuse might've been plausible. "You're four years older than me." Technically, three and a half. "I would hardly consider that as ancient."

"Maybe," Hamish murmured, pouring himself a cup of water from the jug. "If you ask me nicely, I might be persuaded to suck you off." He glanced over his shoulder, flashing a wicked grin before downing his drink.

Wetting his lips, Darshan stifled a moan at the thought of that exquisite mouth engulfing him.

The cup shattered as it hit the floor, followed swiftly by Hamish.

Darshan sat upright, a shield stuttering around him. " 'Mish?" The room was locked and, in the faint glow of his shield, he made out no other figures. They were the only ones here. Not a direct attack, then. He flung a globe of light out into the middle of the room to properly assess the situation. "What—?"

Hamish lay sprawled on the floor, arching and kicking alarmingly. He gurgled and sputtered, foam bubbling from his mouth and down his beard.

No! Darshan flung himself off the bed, tripping over his own feet in his haste to reach his husband's side. He clasped Hamish's shoulder, holding tight as his magic delved in and discovered multiple organs failing.

Lungs. They needed to work, to bring in more air, but his heart struggled to keep a regular rhythm.

"Hold on, *mea lux*." He sank to his knees, cradling Hamish to his chest. *Heart first*. If it stopped, Darshan hadn't the luxury of seeking aid elsewhere.

He pushed himself, sending a spark through Hamish's back to shock the man's heart into a stronger beat. It pumped harder, matching Darshan's frantic pulse, but wouldn't stabilise unless he fixed the rest. Hamish's lungs still strained to keep up with the demand for air, but only because his throat was closing. Darshan turned his focus to that, shuddering as his magic tugged him in yet another direction.

There was too much to concentrate on all at once, he'd never do it all trying to manage every minute thing.

Pressing his lips to his husband's clammy temple, Darshan released the hold on his magic, letting it seek out what was damaged and aid Hamish's body in the purge. It was crude and sucked most of the energy from him, but it was faster than he could ever hope to be.

He bent over Hamish, concentrating only on his breath and his heartbeat. *Please, be enough*. He didn't know what he would do if he needed more power. Could the vines that had helped him at the *Gilded Cage* reach him? *Be all right. Please*.

After what seemed like an age, Hamish pushed out of his grasp. Hunkered on all fours, he retched up a terrible dark green goop.

Darshan knelt where he had fallen, slouching. Weary but not fully drained. "How?"

Panting, Hamish gestured towards the overturned jug. It had fallen along with the cup; whole but with most of the contents staining the bare floorboards.

Darshan crawled close enough to sip at the water remaining within the jug. It wasn't the cleanest, but there was nothing sinister about it. Yet, there was no doubt Hamish had been poisoned.

What could they have—?

His gaze fell on the shattered cup. The clay shards lay all over the floor, the inner curves glistening with an unnatural oiliness. He selected one of the bigger pieces, sniffing it. A familiar aroma tickled his nostrils and spun his brain. He licked the inside curve.

Instantly, his magic prickled through his body, healing what the toxin tried to damage. *So much for being safe*. He knew he should've insisted on staying in the room rather than cavort through the tavern. "Leave?" he suggested.

"Aye," Hamish rasped. His breathing seemed to have steadied. A good sign that Darshan's magic had done its job. "Before the bastards come to check on us."

Darshan wished the culprit would. Now that his husband was safe, his body itched for violence. If he encountered those responsible for this attack, they weren't coming out of this night alive.

Chapter 20

They raced down the stairs, stumbling on the landing and picking themselves up to carry on. Darshan glanced behind them, seeking any sign of them being followed. It might've been the middle of the night, but someone had clearly marked them as people of interest. If they were any good, then they would be watching to ensure the job was done.

Or finish them.

The tavern was empty save for the innkeeper and a few workers cleaning up, all of whom stopped to gawp at them. Could one of them have been responsible? Not a one appeared any different to the dozens of other men and women Darshan had seen working in such places. But any decent assassin would blend into their surroundings.

"My lords," the innkeeper said. "Is something—?"

The scream of a horse echoed out in the courtyard.

Hamish's hand landed heavily on Darshan's shoulder. He grabbed fistfuls of cloth, dragging Darshan towards the exit. Their saddlebags were tossed aside in the rush.

"What in the—?" The innkeeper snatched up a cudgel from behind the bar and made for the door. "I swear," he growled. "If it's those damn horse thieves again..."

Out in the courtyard, the horses' distress became louder, punctuated by the bang of something heavy against wood and a lot of swearing. Torchlight flickered from within the stables.

Darshan's stomach flipped. Their horses were the only ones being housed within. Had the people who'd tried to kill Hamish also targeted the horses? *They wouldn't, surely.* It would be a foolish move that few assassins worth their coin would attempt. It had to be horse thieves. *Please, be right.* Thieves he could deal with.

Hamish raced ahead, his longer legs far surpassing Darshan's strides no matter how he struggled to keep up. The drain on his body from both sex and the overuse of magic in such close succession didn't help, but he couldn't let Hamish face whoever was in there alone. If he did and it was the assassin, then he'd be handing their target to them on a platter.

The innkeeper hastened alongside him in a similar puffed state, brandishing his cudgel like a sword and muttering dark threats.

"Bastards!" Hamish snarled. "Get away from her!"

Darshan rounded the corner to a scene of madness. Four people clad in dark clothes filled the small stall containing Hamish's mare. A woman dangled from the horse's halter whilst two men attempted to haul the animal back to onto all fours. Another clutched a small bottle, their back turned to them. Every time the mare lowered herself, they tried to force the neck of the bottle into her mouth.

Definitely not mere horse thieves.

Hamish lunged for the closest figure as they turned, collecting them with a solid punch to the back of the head. They crumpled to the dirt floor without a shred of resistance.

The others swiftly abandoned the mare. One of the men aimed for Hamish, the other two skirting around to face Darshan and the innkeeper. *Even odds.* That was something. Darshan doubted he could take on more than one in his current state.

The heat of a flame flashed by his head and out into the courtyard.

Darshan flung up a shield as another blast came closer to its mark. He couldn't use equally destructive magic without risking setting the stables alight. If he wasn't so drained from healing Hamish, he could've secured them with a construct from the very—

Of course. *Air.* He rarely used it, but it took less energy.

He focused his power into a gust, hoping to knock his opponent over. Dust kicked up before him, blinding both himself and his target but nowhere near strong enough to knock the man over. At least it kept them out of the skirmish.

He glanced towards Hamish, watching his husband battle the other man through a haze of disturbed dirt. Hamish swung his fist at his opponent, jerking back at the last second as the man brandished a dagger. He hastened to free his belt knife, ducking the man's swipes.

"No, you don't," the innkeeper snarled. He whacked the blade away with his cudgel and dealt the man a swift blow to the face all in one smooth move.

One less to deal with. But where was the woman? Darshan searched his surroundings, squinting through the dust coating his glasses. Had the innkeeper already handled the last assassin?

His eyes caught a spark flare on the far side of the stables.

"Look out!" The warning left Darshan's lips the same time as the women flung a spear construct towards them.

Hamish grabbed the innkeeper, putting himself between the attack and the man even as he turned to position his back to the construct. The shimmer of a shield stood out in the haze, holding but barely. All the woman had to do was keep pummelling that gossamer barrier and it would fall as cleanly as a spider's web.

Darshan pushed more of himself into the gust holding his opponent at bay. If he had just a little extra energy to call upon, this fight would be over. Where were those gods-forsaken vines when he needed them? *Please.*

Movement on the edge of his vision drew Darshan's attention. Two more men. From where, Darshan didn't know. They crept up on Hamish as he was harried further, their blades poised.

No!

Darshan raised his hand, the haphazard spark of lightning sputtering to life in his palm before he let it die. He couldn't use it. The mare stood right behind them, snorting and kicking the sides of her stall in panic. If he missed the men, he would kill her.

He needed to protect Hamish. Needed something more refined, but that took time and—

Vines erupted from the ground, entangling the duo like a constrictor. The men's eyes bulged, their faces reddening, before a wet crunch turned them limp.

"What the—?" the innkeeper blurted.

Hamish's shield stuttered and dropped.

No! The danger wasn't over. Beyond the man Darshan held back, there was still—

Her. Darshan swung his focus to the woman who had only momentarily paused to stare agog at the vines. He barely finished the thought before another vine, thicker than the rest, erupted behind her and swatted her to one side like a midge. She hit the stall pillar and stilled.

Without him blasting the final opponent with wind, the majority of the dust had settled. The man blinked and rubbed at his face. His shield clearly hadn't been dense enough to block out the side effects of Darshan's attack. He gaped at the scene, slowly dawning horror twisting his brows.

Darshan peered at the man. Could he willingly call upon the vines to do the same to him as they'd done to the woman? He wasn't a threat just now, but he would become one. All he needed was to be restrained until they'd saddled the horses and were off.

Instantly, fresh vines lashed out within the circumference of the shield. It caught the man around the leg and pulled him to the ground with a heavy thud and a surprised yelp.

With the threats quashed, Hamish wasted no time in entering the stall with his mare. "Easy, Lass," he murmured. She still snorted and panted, but stopped trying to kick her way out of the stall at his calm voice.

The bottle the assassin had been attempting to feed to the horse lay near the stall door, its contents split across the dirt.

Darshan knelt before it, scooping up the bottle to gingerly touch the tip of his tongue to the opening. As he had expected, his magic hummed at the presence of a deadly toxin. "It's the same poison they gave you." Amateurs. Possibly hired because they were expendable and not easily tracked to the one behind all this.

"The bastards," Hamish growled.

"Poison?" the innkeeper blurted, his brows almost rising off his head. "What sort of madness..." He kicked the man he had knocked unconscious. "I cannot apologise enough, my lords. I'd no idea I had employed such scum."

Darshan absently nodded. Whether the innkeeper knew or not was irrelevant, he could even be part of the whole operation. Although that seemed unlikely given how the man kept staring at the crushed bodies and swallowing heavily. "Could you please retrieve our saddlebags?"

"At once." Giving one more glance to the bodies, the innkeeper trotted back to the tavern.

Hamish continued to pat and rub the mare's neck, soothing her with small noises, as they waited. Seemingly content she would remain calm, he slipped into the stall where the black and white gelding should've been. "Dar..."

Dread crept into his gut at the warbling note to his husband's voice. Darshan dared to enter the stall and discovered the gelding already on his side, his flanks sleek with sweat.

"Do you think...?"

"Yes." He wasn't sure how long the gelding had, but it didn't look as though the animal would survive. They would have to purchase another, but not tonight. Such a transaction would draw attention. What they needed right now was to gather their things and leave before the wrong person discovered they were still alive and had them tracked.

Hamish knelt next to the gelding, stroking its neck. "Can you heal him?"

"It's a horse." Learning to heal people without killing them took years. To his knowledge, no one had ever used that talent to heal an animal.

His husband's jaw squared. Stubbornness drew his brows together. "Can you or nae?"

Darshan knelt next to the horse's trembling shoulder. Even after months of travelling, he hadn't grown all that attached to it. His father advised against him having pets lest they became leverage. That didn't mean he was prepared to watch them suffer. "I could probably end it faster." And with less pain.

"Try helping first," Hamish pleaded.

He laid a hand on the sweaty neck. *Help.* How? He'd never been taught a horse's anatomy. *Heal.* He closed his eyes. *Try.* The worst he could do was kill the beast, and the gelding was already on his way there.

His magic responded listlessly. No matter how he pushed, he didn't even have the strength to begin a proper delve. But he knew where there was energy close at hand. "Drag one of the vines in here," he ordered Hamish, who was quick to obey, lugging a thick tendril into the stall.

Darshan grasped the woody vine. The energy within pulsed to his heartbeat, extensive and immense. How did he do this? He'd been exhausted and desperate the first time, his ability to funnel the excess power akin to an overflowing river.

Yet, to reach into that unending stream of power and deliberately direct it? Did he have the strength to not get pulled in along the way? The time he had drawn Hamish back from the brink was a memory of pain, searing its mark into his soul that he still quivered at the memory. He had done it for Hamish's sake, promising to never do it again. Healing the horse would mean breaking his word, even if he didn't count what had transpired at the *Gilded Cage*.

What was his alternative? To let the animal die without trying? Was he that kind of man?

No. Never. The gelding—his argumentative pest of an overgrown pony—needed help, and *he* needed the extra energy. There was no alternative that wouldn't see one of them dead without doing this.

Breathing deep, he cleared his mind until only the feel of the vine in his grip remained at the forefront. He could sense something within that thrum of power. If it had been an animal, he would've called it curiosity.

Help me.

The vine shifted under his fingers, curling around his wrist.

A surge of energy jolted through his body, stiffening his muscles and pulling a shuddering gasp from his lips.

"Dar?" Hamish's voice came faintly.

There was no fighting, no need for him to force the power from the vine. Like a seed seeking nourishment from the earth, he asked and was given until that faint pulse of another world thundered through the core of his very being. It roiled within, flooding every inch of him until he felt fit to burst.

He funnelled that energy into Keet's failing body, delving deep in the search for something familiar to even begin an attempt at healing. *The heart.* It was massive and frail, struggling under the stress. He had heard of animals dropping dead not from injury, but the shock. Was this the beginning of that?

Darshan relaxed his stranglehold on his magic, letting a thin vein slip off to mend what it passively could as he focused on getting the animal's heart back into a normal rhythm. Not the easiest. In every other attempt, he'd had his own heartbeat to measure by.

The lungs. There was a lot more of the organ than expected. He'd had no idea how much of the horse's body was lung. And, like in Hamish, they were slowly filling with fluid. Drawing it out required a little more effort, but Keet's sudden and strong cough reassured him he headed in the right direction. *You better not die on me.*

He kept going, not daring to open his eyes lest it disrupted the flow. It grew harder the longer he pushed it. *More.* Each plea rippled precisely that through the vine, the constant exchange further exhausting him.

But it was working.

Finally sure he had done enough, Darshan withdrew his touch from Keet's sweaty neck and leant back on the vine. It was finally over. Strange that, this time around, he felt slightly rejuvenated. Was it the difference in injuries or the fact the power had been offered rather than torn from the source?

He broke the connection to the vine, his body shuddering at the absence.

The source. He had thought of it a wellspring, but it was more an ocean stretching far before him. If he turned his full focus on it—

"He's nae getting up."

Hamish's declaration swiftly pulled Darshan's attention back to the stall. "He should be better by now. *You* were." All that remained was the same type of goo in the horse's stomach that Hamish had expelled on the inn room floor. He told Hamish as much.

His husband gave him a look that suggested he was dense. "Horses cannae throw up."

They couldn't? That certainly posed a problem. If the sludge remained, Keet would just fall sick again. "Then I'll have to do it for him." Forgoing the connection with the vine, he delved back in. The difficulty was a simple one, a ring of muscle that contracted around the top of the stomach. It seemed quite strongly sealed, remaining shut even as gas distended the horse's belly.

Would forcing it open harm the animal? He wished he knew the answer there, if only to prepare himself for the worst.

He would have to try either way.

Keet kicked out with a hind leg as Darshan tried to carefully convince the muscle to relax and form a small opening. He had no idea what was going through the animal's mind, but this had to be a strange sensation. Hopefully, it wasn't a painful one. Although, judging by the way his magic buzzed slightly along the stomach lining, that hope could be in vain. *Just hang on a little longer.*

With the muscle open enough to let air escape, he swung his focus towards the gas and used it to sluggishly help push the sludge up the horse's long neck. The gunk bubbled out Keet's nose and mouth, setting the gelding to snorting and coughing.

Darshan waited until the animal had stilled again and threaded his healing magic through the horse for a final check. Apart from the dwindling hum around the areas he had just aggravated, the gelding appeared healthy. "Done." He absently dried his hand on his trousers and rocked back onto his feet.

Keet slowly rolled off his side, clambering to all fours where he stood there and blew deep breaths. He eyed them with his usual indifference, before sniffing the contents that had previously been in his stomach and wrinkling his nose.

"Aye, me wee lad," Hamish said, cradling the massive head in his arms and rubbing the gelding's ears. "It's a vile thing. You'll be all right, though. Will he not?"

Darshan nodded.

"Why go to the trouble of poisoning them?" Hamish raised his hand. "I'm nae arguing about them nae choosing a quicker method, I'm just saying I ken how to put down a broken horse and do it swiftly. I've seen it. It would've been faster for them to slit their throats."

"Faster, most certainly." It also would've been messy and led to questions. "On the other hand, what would you have concluded if you'd been a young stablehand encountering two dead horses during your morning shift?"

Hamish squinted into the distance as he continued to rub the gelding's ear. "Sweaty, churned bedding, blood and foam around the nostrils..." He shook his head. "There's a number of ailments that can do that. Poison wouldnae be me first guess."

And therein lies the answer. The tactics weren't something he had come across. They were sloppy, almost suited to the way the Obuzan guerrilla troops fought the Udynean army along the eastern border. But they couldn't be Obuzaners, especially not the ones with magic. The neighbouring realm—having once been the origin of Udynea before it became an empire—was well-known for the barbaric practice of burning their spellsters alive.

Perhaps the group had fought Obuzaners, learnt from them by way of sheer survival.

The only way to know that was to interrogate them. "Do you think any of our attackers would have useful information?" He could wake one up.

"Maybe the one you threw to the ground or the one I punched. Dinnae think the lass the innkeeper smacked will be able to think straight, or the one you swatted like a fly. Definitely nae the two the vines crushed." His voice dropped to a whisper and he eyed where the vine had been lying placidly in the stall door. Gone now. "I really think we need to figure out how they keep appearing."

Darshan nodded his agreement, although there was no *we*. The vines responded to him alone. It was something *he* needed to decipher. Alone.

They exited the stall to find the innkeeper had returned with their saddlebags. The man stared at the blood-soaked ground, his eyes huge and his face pale.

Darshan looked around, immediately spotting a certain lack. "Where are the bodies?" He couldn't imagine the ones who'd been knocked out had spontaneously regained consciousness and wandered off in their confusion, but it was a faint possibility. However, even the dead bodies were gone.

The man pointed at the spot where they'd been. "The vines," he murmured, dazed. "They were like water snakes. Just wrapped around them and *voop!*" He threw up his hands as the noise squeaked out. "Sucked them into the ground."

Darshan's stomach churned. Was that where the energy had come from? He pressed a hand to his gut, hoping to still the wave of nausea threatening to immobilise him. Was that also why he felt so much better? In the process of healing the horse, he had renewed himself by using the life force of others?

But they hadn't all been dead. Two, certainly. And it could've been argued that three of the others might not have woken, but the last man he had dealt with had still been breathing.

Steadying himself, he turned to Hamish. "Grab our bags, we're leaving now."

The innkeeper shook his head, still clearly struggling to comprehend what he had witnessed. "Who were they? Didn't you say they were poisoning people? What did they want with *you*?" He scratched at his cheek and frowned at Darshan. "For that matter, *who* are you? I ain't ever seen magic like that. How did you summon those vines?"

Darshan pursed his lips, considering his options. There were a number of questions he really would've preferred not answering. If he remained silent, then the man would come to his own conclusions. Without an incentive to keep his mouth shut, he would talk. Maybe even directly to the person responsible for the attack.

If word got out they were here and had survived...

He drew himself to his full height. There was only one way to ensure their presence remained a mystery. "I want you to know that I shall regret doing this, especially given how you were an exemplary host."

The innkeeper's eyes widened. He backed away, his hands raised as his focus darted from Darshan's face to the ground. "Forget I said anything. I've decided I don't want to know anymore."

On his periphery, Darshan spied his husband dropping the saddlebags. "Wait..."

"I won't breathe a word of it to anyone," the innkeeper insisted.

"No," Darshan agreed. "You won't." Not until tomorrow, at least. Close enough to touch the man, he gave a gentle tap to the innkeeper's forehead. It was an old technique, but an effective one that sent a soft vibration through the body, convincing it to sleep.

Hamish squawked and dove to catch the man, falling short as the innkeeper toppled backwards onto a pile of straw that looked a little on the used side. "Did you just kill him?"

"What? Of course not!" He'd never take a life without good cause. "He's just unconscious. Look." He nudged the innkeeper with the side of his boot, rolling the man slightly until his face was clear of the straw. The innkeeper's chest rose in a steady rhythm. "We need him to stay quiet until we're out of the village. If I had let him go, he would've told his tale to the first person he saw."

"Aye, he likely would have. But you sounded so ominous." Hamish rubbed at the back of his neck. "I thought you were trying to scare him off. Or hypnotise him."

Either option would've seen them with someone on their tail within the hour. "Let's just saddle up and get out of here before someone comes looking for him." Heeding his own words, Darshan grabbed the gelding's gear and marched towards the stall.

Hamish followed, scratching at his beard. "I dinnae think it'll be wise to ride him right now. He might stumble and throw you."

"Then I'll ride double with you and have him carry his gear." That wasn't the best option, either. But they hadn't the time to linger whilst the horse recuperated.

After months of travel and doing the same tasks every day, they swiftly secured their gear to the horses. Darshan deliberately left the girth on Keet's saddle a notch looser. He wouldn't be riding him, anyway.

Affixing Keet's lead line to the mare's saddle, he clambered up behind Hamish.

The instant Darshan swung his leg over the horse's back, he regretted his decision. The mare was broad and straddling her back stretched muscles he hadn't been aware he owned. He adjusted his seating, then again, wrapping his arms around Hamish's waist for stability. It still wasn't the most comfortable, but they wouldn't have to travel this way for long.

They left the inn courtyard with only the placid clop of the horses' hooves on the cobbles disturbing the silence. Were they being watched? He didn't know. Beyond the torches, the only light was the moon filtering through the clouds.

"Where do we even go?" Hamish asked over his shoulder once the inn was out of immediate sight.

Darshan considered their options. The village was small. They'd a governor who would happily put up the *vris Mhanek* for the night, but would that be the expected path? "There's an outpost not far from here." It sat an hour's ride away. No one would consider them travelling the distance in the dark. "That way." He pointed out the direction, clinging tighter as the mare's back swayed under Hamish's instruction.

"Are you sure?"

"They won't let anyone but us in." Especially if the *vris Mhanek* commanded it. The outpost's gate would also be watched over by several guards, limiting the chance of hypnosis working in their adversary's favour. It wasn't something they could rely on all the time but, with whatever sliver of luck they had left, those behind the kill order wouldn't know of their survival until they were beyond reach.

For the moment, he could only hope he directed them to safety.

Chapter 21

The outpost had been more than accommodating once Darshan showed his *vris Mhanek* signet ring, the captain going so far as to offer his room to them for the night. The place wasn't the most spacious—barely enough space for a single cot and a chest of the captain's personal effects—but it had the bonus of being high up in the outpost's tower. The spiralling stairway to it and the surrounding guards definitely put Darshan more at ease.

Darshan nudged the door into the room with his hip as he walked backwards through the opening, the majority of his focus on the bowl of chicken broth he had carted all the way up from the kitchen.

Hamish already sat on the cot, his weight bowing the whole frame. He eyed the bowl, ruefully shaking his head. "When you said you were getting me some nourishing grub, I was thinking something heartier. Maybe roasted?"

"At this time of night?" The broth didn't look the most appetising, being thin and oily, but they were lucky the guards had it already brewing for the night shift or the meal would've been a modest fair of unleavened bread and rice. "I'm sure they'll prepare enough for you to stuff your stomach to bursting in the morning, but you need something in it now. Magic only goes so far and—"

"Half the healing toll was on me body," Hamish muttered, finishing the sentence with a roll of his eyes and a good-natured smile.

"If you remember that, then you'll know why you need to replenish your reserves with food and rest. This broth will suffice for now." He handed over the bowl. There had been a spoon, but he lost it part of the way up the stairs. "Don't worry, I tested it. It's a little on the salty side, but serviceable."

Hamish's nose wrinkled as he stared at the broth. "I'm just a wee bit light-headed. I've had worse after a night of drinking, you dinnae have to fuss over me."

He fixed his husband with a stern look that would've undoubtedly made his old nanny proud. "*Drink it.*"

"All right. All right. You can put the bloody glares away. I'm drinking, see?" His husband took a sip, grimacing and gagging like a child tasting their first bitterroot. He even gave a similar pouty look of betrayal. "You could've warned me it was chicken."

Darshan arched a brow at the man, barely holding his uncompromising expression.

Hunching his shoulders, Hamish offered up a few longer slurps of the broth before lowering the bowl. He dabbed at his beard and leant back on the cot. "I'm sorry for ruining your birthday. This cannae be how you were wanting it to end. In fact, I'm bloody certain it wasnae." His lips twisted into a rueful smile. "I should've had you test the water before I let a drop touch me lips."

Darshan shook his head. If anyone should've been sorry, it was him. He shouldn't have allowed his judgement on staying in their room to be swayed. "Testing the water wouldn't have helped. It was the cup. They'd coated the inside with miner's wax." Even though he'd only ever seen the substance in solid form, he wasn't mistaken about the oily residue he had tasted on the inside of the clay cup. "They generally dip raw *infitialis* into it to make the ore safer to transport."

"So, nae a typical poison, then?"

"I didn't say that." Unable to stay still, he paced the small room. "This is my fault. I shouldn't have let you talk me into going downstairs, then they wouldn't have been able to poison you."

"You dinnae ken that. It could've been done before we stepped into the room. Besides, without the alert, we might've woken up to find the horses dead."

Darshan paused. He hadn't considered that possibility. "That man in the tavern recognised me. He must've been sent to target you." If only he had his network. Digging for answers without a proper direction would only serve to further fray his already frazzled nerves. The best he could do was send a missive to Zahaan and hope his spymaster could uncover a few more titbits. Everything else would have to wait until he had reached Minamist.

"Why me?" Hamish asked. "Why nae you?"

"The miner's wax..." He rubbed his chin, trying to think of terms to explain without delving heavily into the realm of elements and toxins. Beyond the uses of a few rudimentary plants and ores, such topics weren't part of a Tirglasian prince's schooling. "The usage is specific, but the ingredients are cheap, easily accessible and difficult to trace." He had personal experience in that from his time attempting such after someone poisoned one of his slaves. "The fact it's useless against those with healing abilities means they would've known their target couldn't easily mend themselves." How many were privy to that knowledge? Who would've told them?

He wished Zahaan was here. Wished he hadn't opted to leave Rolshar in the middle of the night.

But what if bringing the spymaster with them had made things worse? What if Zahaan had been targeted? What if the man ended up hypnotised like the others and, whilst under that influence, took the very poison used to harm Hamish?

He refused to sacrifice one man to save the other. He couldn't.

"Could Onella be to blame for this one?"

"I don't know." That the attacks on Hamish had only started happening since the soirée in Nulshar was suspicious, yet it could've been to the simple fact that no one had a point of reference for his husband until that night. "But she would be foolish to try when she's aware we are legally married." In their father's eyes, it would be tantamount to her attacking Darshan and that was something their father swore would lead to her son never inheriting the throne.

But if his father was behind the attacks…

There'd been no acknowledgement after Darshan had sent his father word of his marriage. He knew the unconventional way they'd gone about it would upset his father, but surely not enough to have Hamish killed.

"Have you had anything to eat?" Hamish asked. "Any healing that took that much out of me must've had some effect on you."

Darshan's thoughts slid to the pools of blood staining the stable floor. The vines had dragged the bodies under, both the dead and the merely unconscious alike. Those people would've been absorbed to feed the demand his healing had asked. No one deserved that kind of death and he'd done it without even knowing.

"Dar?"

He shook himself and paced the room, shutting the door in the process. "I have recouped enough. Just drink up." He leant against the window sill, staring out into the dark forest as Hamish begrudgingly drank.

The trees were silent, still slumbering beneath the last few vestiges of moonlight.

His mind wouldn't stop thinking about those bodies. If they dug through the soil beneath the stables, would they have found merely bones? The flesh stripped bare, but the clothes still intact?

There were stories. Old tales. Ancient, really. They spoke of spellsters living for years, centuries, on the lives of others. *Monsters.* Demons wearing the likeness of humans as a suit.

248

Had he done what they once did? Was that what he was? A monster? He didn't feel like one, but had they? How would he tell if he started down that path? Whose opinion could he trust?

Darshan glanced over to where his husband still sipped at his meal. He trusted the man's sincerity, but this was magic; a topic Hamish had admitted to knowing only what Darshan had taught him. He needed the palace library with its vast array of ancient knowledge, needed his twin, his Nanny Daama. They would know, they would see if he—

"Me heart," Hamish murmured. "Are you sure you're all right?"

How was he supposed to answer that? *With the truth*. Which was what? That he was terrified of turning into a monster? That his every effort to keep Hamish safe only put them in more danger? That he didn't have all the answers? "You know what I find interesting?" Darshan waited for a response. A word. A grunt. Some acknowledgement that he had been heard.

What he got was more of that patient silence his husband was so good at.

Nevertheless, he cleared his throat and continued, "You didn't appear to suffer from any nightmares whilst we're on the Shar. Does the rock of the ship soothe you? Or perhaps you've a connection to large bodies of water?"

"Or maybe I've gotten better at hiding them."

"Don't say that." Darshan whirled around to face his husband. "I don't ever want you to think you need to hide things from me." His stomach twisted as the words left his mouth, the bitterness of his hypocrisy tainting his tongue.

Hamish fell quiet, draining the last of the broth as he eyed Darshan over the rim of the bowl. His brows lowered as he uttered a soft, "Aye."

Gods, I'm turning into my father. How many times had his father expected utter transparency from Darshan and his siblings whilst keeping his thoughts and motives entirely to himself? It was one thing to maintain his aloof guise in front of the masses, but to his husband?

"I'm not all right," he blurted.

"I ken." Hamish held out his arms, imploring Darshan to enter their embrace. "Come here."

He did, connecting with his husband hard enough to knock the man back and leave them lying partially draped over the cot. "I'm scared." The admission slunk out in a whisper, almost ashamed to be heard. He had been trying not to think on it, trying to keep everything bottled up, trying to be the strong and detached *vris Mhanek* everyone expected him to be.

He couldn't. Not here. Not with his beacon.

"Scared?" Hamish echoed as he stroked Darshan's hair. "Of what? Losing me?" Darshan bounced slightly on his husband's chest as a soft bubble of mirth shook Hamish. "That's nae going to happen." He pressed his lips to Darshan's temple. "You brought me back from the brink once, I have faith in you being able to do it again."

Darshan shook his head, trying to find enough purchase to lever himself up, but his husband's grip around his shoulders made any act beyond lying there impossible. "It's not that."

"The vines?"

He nodded and hummed in affirmation. "I can't control it. I don't know what I'm doing, where it's coming from, how to make them stop. What if something bad happens? What if I hurt someone I don't mean to? What if—?" Darshan's throat closed on the question. *What if I hurt* you? He trembled at the thought.

"I'm nae an authority on magic, but the vines seem to follow your whim. I dinnae think you'd be capable of harming anyone unintentionally. Nae with them."

Darshan wished he could believe that. "I did more than kill those men. I took what shouldn't have been taken. I used what should never be touched." He hadn't known. Not at the time.

It hadn't been that way on the islet. Beyond his husband, there'd been only plant life to draw from.

Why hadn't they taken Hamish, then? The man had been injured, but the vines had dragged him out of danger instead of using him in their attempt to aid Darshan, even as they had died.

"Some of the people weren't even dead." Although, they had been mercifully unconscious. Was that why the vines hadn't targeted Hamish or the horses? "I stole every last scrap of life from them. To save Keet, to replenish myself."

"You took the energy from the vine. Where they got it from wasnae your decision."

The vines... Such an easy excuse. An escape. *Absolution.*

He couldn't take that route. To free himself of guilt would be just another step down that path to tyranny. "They respond to me, to what I wanted the most. And if it's a case of me merely having to think too poorly of something for it to react, then it'll get worse." He couldn't march into the Crystal Court with such a raw nerve. He'd wind up killing half of them.

"Worse?" Hamish mumbled. "You've killed with your magic before."

He had—most recently, the old guards in Tirglas who had tried to kill him—but he'd been mastering his magic since he was a child. "Untrained spellsters have been known to burn down whole streets at a single upset. I refuse to become such a statistic."

"What of when I was poisoned in Rolshar? If the vines are tied to your emotions, then why did they nae burst through the floor like they did in that fishing village off the shore of the Shar?"

Why? That was a good question. He had been livid. Even the memory of their night in Rolshar was tarnished. "For the same reason I couldn't hear the plants, I suspect. I wasn't in close proximity to any earth at the time. But I can't hide myself away in my chambers and I won't suffer having this *thing* flailing around unchecked. If it *is* connected to me in some way, then it shall have to learn to obey my will." That would take time he didn't have.

"Are you sure it's obeying anything? You dinnae speak of your magic as a separate entity. I ken you dinnae like to admit it, but your life was flagging just as much as mine the day you saved me."

That was true. Even though the reason behind it had been due to the overuse of magic in an effort to replenish the lethal amount of blood loss Hamish had suffered, the strain on Darshan's body had almost stopped his heart.

"You *did* say you were nae sure what had happened. What if you're right? That you're nae fully human anymore? What if, in using your power to pull the life out of plants, you left part of yourself in them as they did into you? What if those vines are *your* roots? When you cannae hear the plants, when they cannae respond, it's because you're nae near viable soil?"

Darshan propped himself up on outstretched arms to gawp at his husband. "You can't be serious. You think I'm part plant? *Mea lux,* that cannot be possible. That's not how magic works." Certain things remained in a fixed state. How a person came into being was how they remained until death. There was no magic in the world that could alter such a fact.

"Nae how it works? You took the essence of a plant, funnelled it through yourself—at least thrice over now—and then used that power to bring me back from the brink of death. Where in that am I supposed to see how magic doesnae work?"

"That's not the same as this. Those vines. When they attacked in that village, when they wrapped around your legs in the forest, during tonight... I wasn't using any magic. Not for any of it." That made it even more dangerous. At least the drain on his magic would eventually lead him to stop if he ever went berserk. With this, what would keep him from levelling a whole city in his rage?

"You said there were stories of people doing similar things."

"Yes. To other people—human, dwarves..." Not elves. The species as a whole hadn't arrived on the continent during the age those ancient tales were set. "There was no mention of using animals let alone plants."

"Then you're never really going to ken the truth. Who would be able to tell you?" He enveloped Darshan in a hug, squeezing just enough that Darshan couldn't escape but was still able to breathe. "Me heart, whatever has happened to you, we'll find a way to control it. Together."

"I know." Maybe he wasn't capable of harming Hamish. Even in his weakest moments, the vines hadn't sought out his husband as a means of energy. Was that because of what he had done to heal the man? Was he connected as well?

Sitting upright, he silently gnawed on his thumbnail. He'd too many questions with no way to answer them. Who could? *No one.* Hamish was right. He might've been able to seek guidance from the hedgewitches of old, but that hadn't been an option for centuries.

"So, sleep?" Hamish murmured, tugging the cot's blanket out from under his backside to drape it over himself. "We'll be safe here, right?"

Darshan shrugged. Was anywhere truly secure? "Safer perhaps." For the night, at least. "We shall have to be more vigilant in our mingling, especially if we continue with our plan to stay incognito. I cannot be eternally by your side to heal you if they strike again."

"I understand."

"You rest. We'll leave in the morning." He didn't know where they would bunk the next night. Clearly, being a pair of unassuming strangers casually renting a room in a nondescript inn was only marginally safer than announcing their presence to all.

Would they draw less attention if they entered inns separately and paid for individual rooms? It would take some adjusting to find peace without his husband's snoring lulling him to sleep, but if it kept Hamish safe...

Maybe they'd fare better using the outposts? They weren't as numerous, with lone ones like this staggered between villages. Would it increase their attacker's desperation? Surely, they had to be anxious to have sent thugs to do an assassin's job.

Perhaps making it harder to reach them might reveal the culprit.

Hamish half rose out of the cot. "You're nae coming to bed?" He glanced down at the blankets and grimaced. "Such as it is."

"In due time. You're not my only patient tonight." They hadn't pushed the horses and the gelding had shown little sign of distress after his ordeal, but Darshan wanted to be sure. "I'm going to check on the horses, then I'll be back up."

Resuming his recline, Hamish chuckled. "Told you he'd grow on you."

Darshan grunted in agreement. "Like lichen." No point denying he had felt a twinge of concern for the animal during their journey to the outpost.

"You would've cared if he had died," Hamish insisted.

"Sleep," Darshan said, slipping out of the room.

Every guard he encountered saluted as he made his way down into the modest stable. No one questioned his movements or made to stop him, which meant word had circulated through the entire outpost. Not that he was surprised. The place was small, the garrison holding perhaps two dozen guards at best.

The stable was a little over half the size of the courtyard. Unlike other outposts they'd stopped over in, it wasn't a separate building but rather a section of the towering structure. No one else lingered here. The absence of people also meant an absence of light for the horses.

Darshan threw up a softly glowing globe to illuminate the way.

There were six stalls in all. The outpost's mounts occupied half of them, their slight frames dwarfed by the new arrivals. They stirred at the far end of the stable, mere shadows in the gloom.

Hamish's mare stretched out her neck as he sauntered by her stall, snuffling his shoulder in search of food. He gave her nose a brief rub before guiding her back to the rack of hay she'd been munching. "I've nothing on me, my lady." Hamish was sure to be down come morning to check on her and spoil her with whatever treats he pilfered from the outpost's kitchen.

The gelding was less interested in garnering anyone's attention. He watched Darshan from the back of the stall, snorting and pawing in a warning to keep back. His hoof clipped the wall, taking a few chunks of old wood with it.

"Easy, my little pest," Darshan murmured. "I rather doubt I have it in me to heal you again so soon."

There was no chance the gelding understood a word without being spoken to in Tirglasian, the language the animal was trained under, but his ears swung in Darshan's direction and he stopped pawing at the ground.

Darshan quietly leant against the stall door and observed the gelding. He might not have been the best judge of such matters, but the horse seemed more uncertain than unwell. "I suppose I am glad you still live." Perhaps Hamish was right in that he had gotten used to the gelding's presence. He certainly would've missed that stubborn demeanour had he failed to heal the animal.

After a short while, Keet shuffled close enough to sniff Darshan, blowing hot air into his face.

He tentatively stroked the gelding's neck. "I'll take that as a thank you. You've certainly been a first." Would others be able to replicate what he had done? Did they already do so and he was simply ignorant? *Doubtful*. Anjali would've alerted him to such abilities. She would've been among those willing to learn. He knew a number of her pets had succumbed to injuries magic could easily mend. How many could've been saved if they'd gotten proper treatment?

Closing his eyes, he let his magic slip into the gelding. There appeared to be no lingering physical effect to the ordeal.

Keet snorted. He shook his whole body and shuffled beyond Darshan's reach to lazily lip at his hay.

"I'll leave you to your rest, then." He checked the stall one last time to ensure the gelding had everything. There was a water trough that appeared to be shared with the neighbouring stall and an overturned tub Darshan assumed had contained the hardier feed he recalled Hamish requesting from the guards.

Darshan vacated the stable by the main entrance leading out into the courtyard, the cool night air caressing his face.

How late was it? Definitely beyond midnight. Perhaps several hours before dawn. He wasn't a stranger to being up this late, but rarely for anything more than mindless merriment. He didn't feel the least bit tired, but Hamish and the horses needed rest.

How safe were they here? Could they linger for a few hours after daybreak? *Possibly*. The guards certainly wouldn't object. What of a whole day? Whoever had sent those thugs would need to learn of their failure as well as track their passage out of the village.

A whisper on the wind drew his attention to the walls.

Guards marched along the battlements, too high up for their mystery hypnotist to target. A pair stood either side of the gate with a third holed up in a small recess off to the side. Whilst the one on gate duty was responsible for who the gates opened to, those controlling the mechanism could also opt to refuse should there be any sign of coercion. He wasn't certain if every outpost between here and Minamist was laid out the same, but if so, then staying in them could be the safest option.

He strode towards the building's main entrance. If they were staying for the day, then he had best inform the captain and give the man time to make arrangements.

The murmur upon the breeze tugged at him as he reached the door. There was no call for him to step beyond this cage of stone and dead wood and yet...

Darshan craned his neck to take in the outpost's height. The imperial palace was taller by far—even the estates could claim such—but the lack of girth in the building lent a certain loftiness to the structure that was stifling.

Darshan turned from the entrance and headed for the gates. He needed to be beyond its confines, out where walls held no meaning.

The woman sitting within the recess near the gates trotted out to greet him. "Can I be of help, *vris Mhanek*?"

He barely took his eyes off the gates to acknowledged her. "Open them."

She glanced over her shoulder at the two men standing watch atop the wall, then back at him, eyeing him as though he had taken leave of his senses. "The captain said your orders were to—"

"Not allow entry to anyone else. I wish to step outside. Open the gates."

The guard hesitated, once again glancing over her shoulder.

His gaze lifted to the men. They would undoubtedly open the gates at her word. What of at his? "Your *vris Mhanek* demands you let him pass," he yelled up to them. "Now."

The men scrambled to obey and the gates ponderously opened enough for him to slip through, immediately closing at his back.

Darshan took a deep breath. The world before him seemed too still. Quiet. Slumbering. He wiggled his toes, his footwear suddenly stifling. He bent to unlace his boots.

There was the ear-splitting wail of a hinge in need of oil, then a guard's face appeared from a hole in the wall. "Is everything all right, *vris Mhanek*? Should I rouse the captain?"

"That won't be necessary. Everything's fine." He peered out into the darkness. Like all outposts, a clearing had been carved from the surrounding woods. Nothing lurked in it. Nothing dangerous, at least. "Stay vigilant nevertheless." Stripping his feet bare, he sauntered across the clearing, aiming for the nearest line of trees.

The grass brushed his feet like dozens of reverent hands. Out here, the trees slept soundly beneath the half moon. They creaked and groaned in the darkness, their leaves sighing against each other in a shiver of sound that could be mistaken for wind if he hadn't heard it in his mind.

He settled cross-legged on the ground and closed his eyes. *Focus.*

The throb of raw power beat all around him. Soft and steady. Tempting.

Ignoring the lure, he turned his attention inwards until his world encompassed only his mind. *No sight. No sound.* He let all thought slip into the ether, leaving him floating in the darkness of his mind.

This technique had been first taught to him by Nanny Daama, back when he'd manifested his first flame as a child. He'd learnt later that the method had originally come from Stamekia. Quite a few years had passed since the last time he'd felt the need to seek out its calming qualities, but if these vines were somehow a manifestation of his subconscious then he needed to learn control before he hurt someone again.

Slowly, he allowed himself to be aware of his surroundings. The steady beat of his heart and the measured rhythm of his lungs, both cyclic and calm. The subtle flow of blood through his veins whispered in his ears. Above it, he picked up the distant snort of a horse in the still air, but otherwise, the edge of the clearing remained silent.

He moved on, focusing on the way his hands, capable of raw violence, now sat serenely in his lap. Of the slight stoop in his shoulders because of his lulling head. He adjusted his stature and continued, seeking the inevitable end to the exercise.

His senses spread, stretching beyond himself. The birds sleeping peacefully in the trees, their little claws clinging tight to the branches. The insects that nibbled at the leaves and made their homes beneath the bark. There was the flare of pain from an oak that was more hole than tree and the pines that cringed from a campfire far from here.

It was all connected, from the lingering hollowness at the *Gilded Cage* to the ancient vibration of what had to be the mother tree all the way in Tovehalvön. *The world*. He could feel it all.

He inhaled deeply and it was as though the world breathed with him.

Carefully, he retreated from the sensation, drawing himself back into his body. He opened his eyes, staring into the shadows beneath the trees. *This power*. There was nothing normal about it. What he felt, what he was connected to, was something far bigger than himself. Yet, it bent to his will.

What have *I done?*

Chapter 22

Hamish tilted his head back to take in the full majesty of the temples dedicated to this and that god. There were a lot of them. Every deity, no matter how small, had a temple in what Darshan had cheerfully called the cleric's quarter. The majority of the buildings had a swath of land surrounding each one. Most were cultivated, the trees and bushes having a purely ornamental look rather than the private gardens the priesthood grew back in Tirglas.

The last few weeks of travel had gone by swiftly and with nary a sniff of anyone looking to attack them. It could've been because Darshan had them sticking to the outposts, sometimes having to ride on by the light of a globe to reach one.

All that didn't matter now. They were finally at their destination.

Minamist.

Hamish had known two things about the city he was to call home: it was the largest on the continent and sat at the mouth of a river that wound down from distant mountains. He hadn't asked Darshan what it was like, preferring to wait and see firsthand. Now he wished he had. Maybe then he wouldn't still be gaping at how the place was nothing like the port city he had imagined.

They'd entered the outer parts of the city around midmorning and had wandered the streets since, on horseback to begin with, but now on foot like everyone around them. He hadn't realised how everything would glow, be it the natural sheen of stone and glass, or how the shop signs blazed like lanterns.

Were the other places in Udynea like this? They had spent only a short time in both the Shar's major port cities. Nulshar had a beaten and rusty exterior whereas its sister city, Rolshar, had been in drab shades of grey. Minamist felt like he had stepped into a completely different realm.

Beyond the temples, buildings crowded for space, climbing upwards until they were enormous towers dwarfing the streets. Some had bridges connecting them to other, equally tall buildings. He wasn't sure how the land managed to support the weight.

Magic fluttered everywhere. It lifted crates and barrels that would've taken several men to move back in Tirglas. It guarded stalls and shielded carriages. It shone as signs in eye-catching blues and purples, indicating places that would otherwise have been lost in the shadows.

Hamish wiped his brow, unsurprised that his hand came away damp. They could've done with a few of those shadows now. The sun had definitely gotten hotter with the passing hours. The lack of breeze between the buildings didn't help.

His mare plodded obediently at his heels, her head low. Sweat darkened the usual light brown of her coat in patches.

"Are we almost at the palace?" he asked Darshan, who sauntered at his elbow. The layout of the city was hard to distinguish whilst in its streets, but they had to be near.

Hamish had seen glimpses of the city several days before their arrival. Islands broke the wide river mouth into a series of smaller channels leading down into the harbour. The city sprawled across every island, the sections connected by broad bridges.

"Not far now, *mea lux*," Darshan replied. "There's a bridge on the other side of the cleric's quarter that leads directly to the main gatehouse."

From what he'd seen as they rode down towards Minamist, the inner section of the city was situated on an island large enough to lose the Tirglasian capital several times over. Hamish had thought them already on it, but if they'd another bridge to cross... "Maybe we should find some shade and rest of the horses for a wee while."

"I am aware of the toll it's taking on them." Darshan gave his gelding's muzzle an affectionate rub. Keet didn't look any more enthusiastic than Hamish's mount, but he had recovered well from the poisoning. "They'll have all their needs cared for soon enough."

The crowd grew thicker as they approached what appeared to be an impromptu market square. The bustle filled Hamish's ears. Chimes and gongs sounded all along the streets, hawkers and priests fought to be heard over each other whilst the communal chatter of the crowd continued to buzz all around them.

Darshan beamed at the commotion. "I didn't realise how much I missed this place until now." He inhaled mightily. "Can you smell that?"

Hamish nodded. How could he not? His every breath was choked by the pungent mixture of incenses invading the air, all caught up in a faint seaward breeze. His eyes watered with their combined strength.

Trying not to breathe too heavily, he peered at the merchants to see just what they were selling. There were no fancy stalls, or even the plain wooden ones he was used to. Everything was spread out on the ground, sometimes on a simple rug or blanket. The items they were selling seemed like simple things; food that he wasn't certain hadn't begun to spoil, scraps of cloth and clothes that both looked like they'd seen better days, other people had what Hamish could only guess were trinkets or wards.

"I'm surprised the priests allow goods to be sold in front of their temples." No one would've dared hawk anything outside the temples back in Tirglas. The priests would've considered it sacrilegious and had the offender whipped.

"Not many do. The desperate, mostly." Darshan politely declined the insistent request of a hawker with a gentle shake of his head. "Except for the monthly market hosted within the palace grounds, this is one of the few places a person can sell their wares without belonging to the trader's guild. And the only place you can sell without paying a levy."

Hamish eyed the people. Most of those in the crowd looked well-dressed, a stark difference to those attempting to sell whatever item they had on hand.

The flash of bare flesh caught his eye. He glanced through a fleeting gap in the crowd, spying a group of women. To a one, they walked down the street with their breasts bare. "And is indecency also common here?"

Darshan turned to him, his brow furrowed. "Depends on who you ask. Why?"

Looking everywhere but in their direction, Hamish pointed as Darshan strained to see over people's heads. "Those women are nae wearing any clothes."

His husband must've spotted them, for he settled back onto his heels with a breathless chuckle. "You mean the priestesses of the High Mother? Well, I beg to differ with you there. They are most certainly wearing skirts."

Hamish rolled his eyes. Yes, if he dared another glance their way, their lower halves weren't bared to the world. It wasn't like that in Tirglas. There, women showed no more than an arm. A man might witness the briefest glimpse of a breast when a woman nursed her hungry infant, but that was it. "If they are priestesses, then why are they nae in something more modest?"

Darshan hummed. "Because that's what those priestesses wear? I've never really asked. It's probably symbolic, most of the priesthood garb is. Did you see me enquiring as to why your priests wore robes?"

"Nae, you dinnae do that." He hadn't given it much thought, either. It was merely what the priesthood wore. "But—" His heart galloped into his throat. "Sweet Goddess," he muttered, turning on his heel. The women were coming their way!

The priestesses effortlessly wove through the crowd, finding little resistance as the masses parted for them. They stepped fluidly by those who had the appearance of owning little in favour of those who clearly possessed a lot.

A young girl, clothed right up to her neck, trailed them. She balanced a large basket, bearing fruits and bread, on her hip. Occasionally, she would pause to serve one or the other to a seller.

The leader of the group halted before Darshan. Bowing low, she extended her clasped hands, opening them as they neared his chest. "Alms for the bosom, my lord?"

Hamish frowned. He couldn't have heard that correctly.

"Of course." Darshan practically tore his coin purse open to rummage through the coins. He momentarily withdrew a gold before dropping it back in. "You know? Just take it all." He pressed the whole purse into her hand.

Unadulterated gratitude lit up the woman's sun-browned face. "Thank you, my lord. May the High Mother smile her blessings upon your children."

"We are all her children," Darshan murmured, bowing his head as the group continued on.

Hamish learnt close and whispered in his husband's ear, "You gave her alms for the what?"

"Breast," his husband replied in Tirglasian. "I know it is not a word you have heard a lot of during our travels. Did you not understand her accent? Those from the north-western border do tend to talk quickly."

"I understood the words just fine," he mumbled. "The meaning nae as much." Shouldn't they be collecting for the poor or needy? Aiding the Goddess in reaching those who truly needed her guidance was what the priests back in Tirglas did.

Darshan tipped back his head, pressing the heel of his hand to his forehead. "Of course. Like I said, they're priestesses of the High Mother. Their whole existence revolves around caring for children. They largely take in orphans. Abandoned babies, mostly. Small children, too. Maybe a mother on occasion."

The idea of orphans wasn't a strange one to Hamish—a lot of children had lost their families during the last plague that had taken his grandparents and put his mother on the throne—but the thought of them wandering the streets was foreign. There was always a farmer or craft master looking for an extra pair of hands to lighten the work. Those who couldn't labour outside a house worked within and if they were still too small for those chores, they were usually the cause of them. "And what she said?"

"They typically feed the babies with their own milk. I can't quite remember why." He fell silent for a breath, the tip of his tongue running along his upper lip. "Something about bringing them closer to the High Mother."

"And what happens to the babies once they're older? Or should I nae have asked?"

"From what I hear, they're trained for priesthood. I don't know about the girls, they may choose to remain in service to the High Mother, but the boys join other sects. There has been quite a few tales of mass clashes arising from the cleric's quarter over who got the apprentice priests."

Hamish sighed. "For a moment there, I thought you were going to tell me they sold them."

Darshan shook his head. "The priestesses would never allow it. They ensure each one of their children is taught according to the old ways. That makes each child beyond the value of those sold in a common slave market. Even if the buyer was on the hunt for a clerical scribe, they'd have to tow a child away by force and those priestesses are not ones to be trifled with."

"Oh?"

His husband snickered as they turned down a street that guided them towards a bridge leading out of the cleric's quarter. The people crowded around them, shoving each other as they crammed themselves onto the bridge.

Hamish drew his mare closer. She snorted and bumped him with her nose, but walked at his side readily enough. Her size kept people away. "What's funny?"

Darshan shook his head. "Just a memory. The next time Zahaan is here, remind me to have him tell you about the altercation he had with the First Priestess of the High Mother involving a young woman set to take their oaths." He smiled off into the distance. "I honestly thought he had lost the ability to stand straight when he returned."

The press of the crowd lessened as they flowed off the other side of the bridge.

"I dinnae see how—" With his gaze lifting to the scene before him, all words fled his mind.

The area on the other side was the largest square Hamish had ever seen. Makeshift stalls dominated much of the paved area, leaving just enough space for handcarts to move between them. There were trees everywhere, they seemed to mark the huge sections of land reserved for gardens. Statues depicting what Hamish guessed were past rulers also dotted the area, although one bore a striking resemblance to Darshan.

And overlooking it all, sat a gatehouse as tall as the cliffs his childhood home was built upon. The walls were no less as grand and stretched for miles on either side. Banners bearing the *Mhanek's* emblem flanked the gatehouse, marking the otherwise grey surface in red and gold.

Hamish's thoughts slithered to the castle of his childhood. It had been the biggest building in Mullhind, not counting the old cloisters that were often repurposed from Ancient Domian structures. If the walls and gatehouse were this large, then what of the palace it shielded? *It must be enormous.*

"So wide-eyed, *mea lux?*"

"I expected it to be big," he confessed. The way Darshan spoke of his home always carried a broad sense of scale. "Just nae like this."

"This is just a gatehouse. The cloister we visited in your lands was bigger."

It had been, but that was also a whole building carved high up in a mountain. This stood far from any such landmarks. *Where'd they get the rock?* Had they used magic to raise it from the very ground? That was possible.

Like most things in the southern part of Udynea, it had a familiar feel. And, the closer they got, the more he noticed the lack of certain details. The walls had no discernible gaps, no marks of where the slabs would've been put together. It looked as though made from a single length of stone.

The craftsmen of Ancient Domian had done well in leaving their mark all across the continent as they searched for the eternal answers.

Although the gates stood open, everyone seemed to avoid the area directly between here and the palace entrance. Now that he was closer, Hamish spotted a ditch surrounding the wall. *A moat?* Some Tirglasian castles had them. He wouldn't have thought it a viable defensive structure against spellsters.

He peered into the ditch as they strode over the wide bridge. It was indeed filled with water. Brightly coloured fish swam in its depths alongside eels.

Movement from something much bigger had Hamish tracking a brown and spotted creature swimming away from them. *A shark?* It was a little smaller than the ones the fishermen back in Mullhind lugged ashore in winter, but the body shape was similar, if not the weird board-like head.

A guard stepped out of the shadows as they neared the gate. "Who goes?"

Darshan lifted his hand, sending a spray of sparks that danced on his palm and formed a symbol before the guard. Hamish had seen it before, although usually adorning his husband's signet ring. The sign of the *vris Mhanek*.

The guard instantly fell to her knees. "Forgive me, *vris Mhanek*. I was unaware you were due back."

Grimacing, Darshan gestured for the guard to rise. "That was the idea," he muttered before clearing his throat and speaking louder, "Inform my father I am here."

"At once." She dashed off through the gates ahead of them, another guard swiftly taking her position at the entrance.

Hamish couldn't help glancing at the great section of stone hovering above their heads as they passed through the gate. *As thick as a cart.* Not something to easily pass through or scale. Whoever had been after his death, they surely wouldn't get through easily once the gates were closed.

The amount of space inside the walls looked little different to that outside, beyond the lack of stalls. People still bustled about, whether they were carting goods or guards patrolling or even the occasional person hurrying for this and that reason.

Two men came to their side, bowing and offering to relieve them of their mounts. They left almost as swiftly as they came, uttering their assurances towards maintaining the wellbeing of the horses all the way.

Hamish barely heard them. His gaze had landed on the building set in the centre of the square. That had to be the imperial palace. Objectively, he knew it would be big, but much like Minamist, it surpassed his expectations.

He gestured to the building. "You didnae tell me you could fit the whole of Castle Mullhind's complex in your palace." No wonder Darshan had found his Tirglasian accommodations quaint. *I've been living in a bloody hovel.*

"That's the council hall and official throne room. The imperial palace is behind it. I'll show you." Taking up Hamish's hand, he led the way up the stairs of the gatehouse until they were atop the structure.

The front half of the palace grounds stretched before them. The walls which he had assumed were the main defensive structures between the city and the palace appeared to be inner fortifications sectioning off this courtyard from the rest. In an attack, any breach of the main gate would turn the space into a killing ground.

"There."

Hamish peered in the direction his husband pointed. Whilst not as broad, the roof of another building peaked over the council hall. It gleamed in the afternoon sun.

A shed. Not a hovel. The castle he'd grown up in had been a damn shed.

Darshan pointed out other buildings, from the right where the main barracks, stables and training arenas lay, to a swath of green and blue dominating the left side that was supposedly a garden. Even more sat further back—the guest palace, the library and study halls, kitchens.

He couldn't make out everything Darshan spoke of, but there would be time for him to familiarise himself with the layout. He had literal years. "It's like a village within a city," he murmured. A man could easily spend his whole life here and never feel the need to venture further.

"Come on." Darshan once again grabbed his hand and dragged him towards the stairs. Mercifully, there was only one way to go. Once they had reached the ground, Darshan aimed for what Hamish now knew was the left inner wall. "I want you to meet someone before my father demands my presence. And I think I know where she'll be."

Chapter 23

Darshan kept his husband's hand tucked firmly into his own as he led the way across the courtyard and through the gate separating this more-or-less public space from the rest of the palace grounds. It had been all he'd known of the world as a small child. Everything he could've wanted had once resided in these walls.

The tranquil gardens were huge, ornamental and often overrun with Anjali's menagerie of pets. His twin spent much of her time here, her status as first princess leaving her with little duties to otherwise occupy her time. She would be keeping an eye on his affairs, but any action out of the norm would require his authority.

The plants hummed at his passage. Bushes shaking their leaves and trees bending just that touch too much for it to be the wind. Even the grass and flowers strained to make themselves known. His feet itched to be rid of their leather prisons, to feel the grass caressing his soles.

Deeper into the garden and the plants grew less wild in nature, but also more vocal. Flowering bushes that the gardeners had arranged in pleasing patterns moaned about the lack of shade. Hedges that were fastidiously trimmed into shapes griped about the inability to extend their branches.

Darshan tried to ignore it all. What could he do? Demand the garden be left to grow wild? What would that help?

Hamish slowed the further they got from the second gate. At first, Darshan thought his husband was simply taking in the sights, but the more they walked, the more the man seemed to be dragging his feet.

"Are you all right?" Darshan asked. They had pushed themselves these past few weeks, trying to make up for the time lost. Just stepping into Minamist had loosened the band of apprehension that'd bound his chest. If Hamish felt the same, then perhaps introductions could hold off until they had rested.

"Truth be told, I'm a wee bit nervous meeting your twin. What if she doesnae like me?"

Soft laughter escaped unbidden from his lips. Was that all? "You'll be fine. Zah would've been in contact with the imperial palace from the first time we set foot in Nulshar." Possibly even earlier, if he knew his spymaster. "He would've already given what he thinks of you to his mother as well as Anjali. And, I assure you, his opinion is a favourable one. Anje will think no less once she has met you."

"What of your other sisters? Your father? Do their thoughts nae matter?"

"Why should they?" There were only four people whose opinion he valued and not a one could alter his point of view when it came to his husband. He didn't need a soul to tell him he had found his flame eternal. After the confrontation with Hamish's mother, he wasn't about to let anyone come between them.

"I get that you and your father dinnae leave things on amicable terms, but he's still your parent as well as the *Mhanek*. What he thinks must have *some* weight."

"Not since he started pushing for an heir from me." Darshan had actively fought the idea of becoming a parent for so many years that it had become almost second nature. Only in watching Hamish interact with his nephews had Darshan found himself facing the uncomfortable truth that, given the right spouse at his side, fatherhood wouldn't be such a terrible thing. "Besides, I'm sure you remember Tirglas was to be my punishment." Who could've predicted that he would find his beacon there?

The murmur of a familiar voice reached his ears as they neared the pond. Anjali spent a lot of time with Mani, her giant tortoise. Was it perhaps time for the creature's monthly bathing?

His musing was confirmed as they entered the lawn surrounding the pond. His sister and her giant tortoise sat near the water's edge, her decked in a plain loose tunic and trousers befitting a farmer and buffing Mani's shell as though she cleaned the mesh-delicate exterior of a vase whilst the tortoise munched on a selection of vegetables.

"Is that the tortoise you spoke of? It's bloody massive."

Darshan left forth with a sharp whistle, the tune one they had made up at a young age.

Anjali whirled about on one foot. "Darshi?" Beaming, she threw aside her rag and raced over to hug him. The dampness of her clothes soaked through his sherwani. "I knew you were coming, but I didn't think it would be today." Her attention flicked to Hamish and back. "Is that him?"

Darshan nodded.

Straightening her clothes, Anjali turned to address his husband. "Greetings, my new brother by marriage."

Darshan stared agog at his twin. When had she learnt the man's native tongue?

The tip of her nose twitched, a habit from her childhood that she hadn't really lost. "I am pleased to finally meet you." She sounded almost like another person. Had he been that stiffly formal upon first arriving at Tirglas?

Hamish's brows shot up. "You speak Tirglasian?" he responded in the same language.

Anjali smiled. "Of course! When I heard my dear brother was bringing home a husband from another land, I simply had to learn the language." She bit her lip. "Did I say it right? I am afraid there is still much to learn, so I do hope you will forgive me for any transgressions."

"That's all right," Hamish replied, switching to his Udynean. The man might've been missing a few words from his vocabulary, but it was near perfect. "You dinnae have to speak Tirglasian if you nae feel up to it."

"You speak—?" She shot Darshan a baleful glare. "You could've told me!"

Darshan spread his arms wide. When would he have had that chance? "You didn't think I would teach him the language that everyone around him would speak?" There might be a few capable of conversing with Hamish in Tirglasian, but he was far safer knowing what everyone said without relying on a translator. His husband had even insisted on learning Ancient Domian for that very reason.

"*You?* Teach? I thought you might have Nanny do it, but not you."

Pouting, he folded his arms. "I happen to be a very good teacher, thank you. I even started before we left Tirglas."

His husband chuckled and bumped Darshan's shoulder. "Try before you got it into your head to marry me."

Darshan grinned. "It was." Almost from the moment they'd met, he had attempted to establish Hamish as the long-needed ambassador for Tirglas. It was a position that would've been required in court, had the trades relations with Tirglas gone smoothly.

The muted plop of something falling into the pond caught Darshan's attention.

He glanced towards the tortoise to find Mani standing over an overturned basket of fruit. He elbowed his sister. Clearly, she hadn't learnt from the last time the animal got itself involved in food. "Your greedy reptile's at it again."

"Mani," Anjali groaned, exasperated. "Now the waterfowl are

going to get it." Muttering a few curses in the animal's direction, she marched back to his side to set the basket upright and load the bigger chunks of food back in. "Just look at you. Bits of mango squished all over your mouth. I hope you didn't swallow the stone." She searched their surroundings, plucking the mango stone from between Mani's forelegs before clutching the animal's head in both hands and rubbing her nose against his. "Who's a greedy little monster?"

"Little?" Hamish echoed. "You were nae joking when you said that thing's bigger than a boarhound."

"You can feed him, if you like," Anjali offered. "It'll keep him from overturning the basket again."

"Do we have time?" Barely pausing for Darshan's affirmative nod, Hamish all but ran to the tortoise's side to offer Mani a papaya. "I wish Mac could see you," he murmured, smiling sadly as the animal ate.

"That's one of his nephews," Darshan supplied before his sister could ask. He hadn't spent a terrible amount of time with the trio, but the youngest of the three had a particular fondness for all things tortoise related. *I wonder if he ever got that statue.* Darshan had definitely seen the merchant back in Mullhind trot off towards the castle with it. Perhaps the better question was whether or not the thing was still in one piece given the boy's apparent preference to clamber aboard all animal statues as though they were steeds.

"You could always invite your family to Minamist," Anjali said. "I am certain they would enjoy themselves."

"That wouldn't be possible," Darshan replied as his husband grew quiet.

"Aye." Hamish shook his head and selected another fruit. "Nae unless me mum was dead."

Anjali turned to seek an answer from Darshan, her brows raised to their utmost.

"We rather burnt a few bridges on our way here." Aiding his sister in gathering up the fallen fruit, he explained their time in Tirglas, starting with his arrival on the shores and his first encounter with Hamish, the man still bloody from hunting a dangerous boar, and their first kiss in a dockside pub that led to a brief fight with the locals. He skimmed over the journey to the cloister where he had discovered Hamish's magical lineage, as well as the bear attack, in favour of the trials he had gone through to secure Hamish's hand.

Strange to think how it had all happened only five months ago. *Not even a full year.* Standing in the heart of his homeland, he could almost imagine it had all been a dream.

"I'm sure there's still time to mend the divide," Anjali said once Darshan was finished. "And Mani will just get bigger. Much. Give him another decade, or two, and he'll be strong enough to carry a person. At least that's what Jin said."

Darshan remembered the man. He had come from the Independent Isles several years back looking for a royal bride. And if he had chosen anyone but Anjali, he probably would've left with one. As it stood, it had taken two years, and countless gifts, before he accepted her refusal. "Was that the not-so-subtle hint of how your *grandchildren* would be able to ride the tortoise once Mani was fully grown?" he needled. The look on her face back then had been hilarious. How Jin had gotten back to his ship intact was still an enigma.

Rather than the customary punch to his shoulder or a well-aimed cuffing of the head by magic, his sister pursed her lips and cast Hamish a sideways glance.

Darshan stood. He knew that expression. She knew something and hadn't yet made a decision to reveal it. Was it of some news that hadn't reached them? Of the poisonings? Had Zahaan discovered the culprit and sent his findings? "What is it?" he whispered in Ancient Domian.

Anjali scrunched her nose at him. "Nothing."

Cupping her elbow, he led her a short distance from Hamish and the tortoise. His husband seemed too engrossed with feeding the animal to notice. "Don't try to fob me off. I know that look. That's not *nothing.*"

"It's just—" She fluttered her hands as if dispersing butterflies. "*What* is that thing attached to your jaw?"

"What?" He pulled back, evaluating her for any sign she had been compromised, then running his gaze across their surroundings. They seemed to be alone. "You mean *this?*" Grinning, Darshan stroked his beard. Whilst being nowhere near the luxurious example his husband wore, it was a fair bit more facial hair than he had left home with. "Don't you like it?"

She screwed up her face.

His grin grew wider. "*Hamish* likes it."

"I shan't be commenting on *that*. Although... I see what Zah said is true."

"Oh?" He tried to keep his voice light and nonchalant. Maybe Zahaan had discovered something. The man certainly wouldn't use the Singing Crystals for idle conversation. "And what gossip have you been sharing with our darling spymaster?" Something not fit for idle ears by the way she was acting.

Anjali returned to watching Hamish. "That you haven't smiled this much in a long time."

"That is true." Extremely. "I don't see the significance. I am content, am I not permitted to show it?"

"Content?" She gave a little laugh that could've easily been mistaken for contempt. "Well, great gods above, someone alert the guards, I do believe my brother is..." She pushed her face closer. Her eyes sparkled with a hint of mischievous glee. "...happy."

No matter how much he tried to contain it, the grin that stretched his lips would not be denied. "Very much so."

Anjali squealed. "Look at that smile."

"Not the face!" He recoiled from her grasp too late.

His sister grabbed a generous pinch of his cheeks and cooed as though he was a baby. "I'm just so happy to see my brother smiling."

"If you don't let go," he grated, "I might never do so again."

"You're so adorable with him. He's very sweet. And tall..." She pulled another face, sticking out her tongue like a child eating lemons. "And hairy. Not that you need my approval."

"But it's nice to have."

"I thought you didn't like your men sweet?"

Darshan grimaced. He *had* said that. A great many times, too. "What I detest is the mawkish way men in the court attempted to woo me to further their own gains." His gaze slid to where Hamish knelt before the giant tortoise, now feeding the animal a cabbage leaf. "But I've come to appreciate the finer qualities a certain gentle nature presents."

Anjali leant against him, draping her arm on his shoulder. "So let me guess, things went the usual route? You saw him, decided you wanted him and got him?"

"Not exactly." Yes, he had taken one look at Hamish and let lust take control for a moment. But once he had spoken to the man, had seen the light residing in Hamish's soul, he'd been done for. "Pretty sure I fell first." Embarrassingly quickly, too.

Silence had him returning his attention to his sister to find Anjali staring at him with a soft smile curving her lips.

His spine tingled at the sight. It wasn't usually a good sign. Mischief tended to happen in the wake of that expression. "What?"

"Don't mind me. I'm just trying to remember the last time I saw you so smitten." She wrapped her arms around him and squeezed until he was certain his ribs creaked. "It's good to see you happy again."

Grunting Darshan prised himself free to put his clothes back in order. "Perhaps old age has mellowed my taste in men."

Anjali stiffened. "Are you calling me *old*?"

"Of course not, I wouldn't dare. I'm calling myself old."

She dealt him a hearty thump to his upper arm. "We're the same age."

"Are we? Fancy that." He tweaked her nose. "Pretty sure I've a good two hours on you." That was how long it had taken for the birth of the future *Mhanek's* children to turn from a happy affair into a sombre one.

No one blamed Anjali for their mother's death. Not him. Not his father. Not even the senate. Their mother had been surrounded by the most skilled midwives in the empire and even they hadn't noticed her slipping away until it was too late.

Sometimes he would wonder, if their mother hadn't been a purist obsessed with the idea of using magic only when absolutely necessary, would she have been able to save her own life?

The sole person capable of answering that had been dead for thirty-four years.

Anjali glared at him, pouting and with her arms akimbo. "Well, excuse me for forgetting two whole hours of difference."

He patted her on the shoulder. "It's all right, everyone makes mistakes. Mine was not realising my eternal flame was patiently awaiting my arrival in Tirglas."

"Really?" A duck waddled up to them, unconcerned with their conversation. Anjali picked it up and snuggled the bird close to her chest. "You think he just sat around waiting for his saviour? Have you slipped that much to believe he was sent there for you?"

Darshan scoffed. "Of course not. That would be foolish. He's four years my senior. Clearly, the gods placed *me* here for *him*." Who else could've won his hand in a contest against his mother's wishes but a powerful ambassador from an equally impressive empire? "And it would definitely be less sitting and more hunting." Even imagining his husband lazing about required a fair bit of bending his nature. Hamish wasn't the type to spend a lot of time inactive.

Stroking the duck's neck, she seemed to be a world away when she asked, "And Father hasn't met him yet?"

He shook his head, pressing his lips together in an effort to keep any emotion from peeking through. "*I* have yet to see him. Although, I'm sure his request to see me in private will find me soon enough. When it does, I was hoping you'd stay with Hamish... just for the moment. I don't fancy having him wandering the grounds alone just yet. Not when someone's targeting him."

"Targeting?" she echoed. "Of course they are. He's your husband. What did you expect would happen?"

"It's nothing like what we're trained to detect. The culprit is hypnotising people."

Anjali gasped. "Hyp—" She stalled the shriek escaping her lips with her hand. Glancing around, she whispered, "You don't think Father is...?"

"I don't know." He didn't think their father would stoop to something as low as having Hamish removed whilst they conversed, but he also hadn't believed their father would have the original ambassador to Tirglas assassinated just so Darshan could take the position.

And if he *was* behind the attempts on Hamish's life? It would be the final unforgivable act he ever did.

"Regardless, it has been a while." He had changed in the months since leaving Minamist. No one needed to tell him, he felt it in his bones. Maybe it was Hamish's influence. Or the act of seeing the empire he would rule through a lens unclouded by his title. He didn't really care. "I'm not sure how Father's going to react."

Anjali hummed. "You know, most of the court knows about your husband. The rumours circulating... The speculation of just what would make the *vris Mhanek* finally chose to settle down." She gave him a wicked grin. "Of just how big he is."

"I can imagine." Sometimes, the court gossip was more sordid than any brothel.

She snuggled her face against the duck's back. "And?"

Heat blazed across his cheeks. "I..." It had been years since they'd been that open with their personal lives. "I hardly see how that matters."

Anjali scoffed. "After all those years of saying—what did you claim?—the bigger, the better?" She scrunched up her face, peering at him through narrowed eyes. "Or is he really tiny?"

The heat grew to encompass his face and neck. "Shut up. And no. Not that it matters. We don't... have sex that way very often."

"You mean he's a taker?" She giggled. "But he's got to be a foot taller than you and he is *built*."

"So?" Some positions were a little awkward, but it was nothing that a little resourcefulness couldn't fix.

"I always thought the shorter man in a couple was the receptive party."

"Shows what you know about sex," he snipped. "Maybe you should try it for once."

Anjali wrinkled her nose. "You mean let someone stick their bits in mine? With all those wobbly bits and fluids?" She pulled the duck closer. "Ick. Why would you even suggest it? Nothing is going up there."

Shrugging, he returned his attention to the giant tortoise. "Nothing necessarily has to, but who knows." His twin had always the same reaction to the idea of sex, at least when it involved herself. It had led to their Nanny Daama's casual observation that he seemed to have enough interest in it for the both of them. And, maybe, she had the right of it. "I believe Mani has grown since I last saw him," he added, hoping the usual deflection of his sister's attention to her animals worked.

"He has." Anjali beamed like a proud parent. "And he'll keep growing for decades to come. He'll probably outlive us." Snickering, she set down the duck. "The throne will inherit him."

"I'm sure my son will be thrilled," he murmured absently. The words were out before he could regulate the thought.

"Son?" she squeaked, her eyes wide. "Did you—?" She pointed at Hamish. "Can he—?"

"Carry children? Gods, no." It would've uncomplicated matters if Hamish could and was willing, but neither of them were built to bear children.

Anjali shot him a puzzled frown. "Then how do you have a—?"

"I don't. Not yet." Raising a brow, he glanced at his sister. He might as well ask before speaking with their father. If Anjali wasn't willing, or able, to be a surrogate for them, then maybe she knew of someone who could be. "I am in need of an heir. Father is most explicit on that, he has been for years. I have a husband with a healthy bloodline, if not a strongly magical one. And Niholia already offers the use of their healers for those with the coin to try for magical fertilisation."

"But you would need someone to carry it," Anjali finished. Her eyes glittered as she pressed her face close to his. "And you want *me* to be that someone?"

"If you're amenable?" he drawled.

"Yes! By Araasi, yes." Squealing, she threw her arms around his neck and squeezed. "Why are you even asking? Of course I will."

"Air," he wheezed. "Breathing. Fond of."

She bounced back with no acknowledgement of having nearly strangled him. "I'm going to be an aunty!"

"You already are one." Several of their half-sisters had children. The living ones were all nieces, with the exception of Onella's son.

"But *not* to my brother's children."

"Children?" His spine iced over at the thought of having a brood of little hims running around. "A single son will suffice." He wasn't greedy and they were both well aware of the risks behind childbirth, even for a spellster with strong healing magic like his sister.

Anjali scoffed. "You'll get what I give you and like it." She clapped her hands over her mouth and, through her fingers, mumbled, "Does your husband know?" She erupted into a bout of bubbly laughter before he could answer. "Sorry. I'll get over the fact you're married eventually."

Darshan inclined his head. "We have spoken about it."

Even with her mouth obscured, the breadth of her smile was obvious. "My brother becoming a father." She grabbed his arm. "What do you think he'll look like? Your son? Will the child favour you? *Him?* Will he have your husband's hair?" Anjali all but bounced on the spot with excitement. "He will look so *cute.*"

"In all honesty, I haven't given it much thought." Even whilst explaining what he knew of the Niholian method of conceiving, he had stressed that it might not be possible. Whilst Anjali's willingness was a large factor, it hinged on more than that. The compatibility of their blood mattered far more and, if that couldn't be mixed, then they would have to find an alternative. "I'll be happy with a healthy child." And preferably a spellster. That could also be a concern given how many Nulled Ones were in Hamish's immediate family. A Nulled One couldn't rule the empire. Not for long.

"Healthy?" His sister cooed unintelligibly and pinched his cheek. "Look at my brother being all paternal."

He prised himself free, forming a shield around himself to keep her at bay. "Stop it or I'll change my mind."

"No, you won't," Anjali replied in that infuriating sing-song tone she got in her voice whenever she knew she was right. She tapped on his shield, sending little shivers through the diaphanous surface. "And you have to dissipate this eventually, then those cheeks are mine." She made little pincer motions with her hands.

Darshan rubbed at his cheeks. His magic had already fixed the aching of the previous pinching, but the memory lingered. He inched towards his husband, who still seemed engrossed in feeding Mani. "I only need to wait until you're not around."

Cackling, his sister trotted back to her tortoise.

Hamish stood as they neared, grinning boyishly. "Shall I take all that squealing as her agreeing to carry our bairn?"

"No," Darshan teased. "She thinks it's a horrid idea and how dare we ask her to carry our child."

Hamish chuckled.

"Don't laugh," Anjali said, gently whacking Hamish's stomach with the back of her fingers. "You'll just encourage him."

Darshan grinned wickedly. He had spent a great many years annoying her with bad jokes and harmless pranks. "Too late," he replied, mimicking the very tone she'd used on him.

His sister's mouth dropped open in a dramatic display of horror. "Gods, now he's never going to shut up."

Someone cleared their throat.

Darshan whirled to find his old nanny, Daama, standing on the path leading to the pond. "Nanny!" He raced to her side, throwing his arms around her slight frame. After months apart, she had grown in his mind's eye. Seeing her anew, he was stunned by how short she was. Objectively, he knew—she was an elf, after all. But her full height barely brought her to mid-chest on him.

"It's good to see you to, my boy." She effortlessly slid out of his grasp and stepped back to put a respectful distance between them. "Although, I do wish it could've been under better circumstances."

"Father?"

She inclined her head. "He awaits you in the throne room."

"Serious," Anjali murmured, giving Daama an eye-fluttering grin as the old woman fixed a stern look at her.

"Should you nae get going, then?" Hamish asked.

"Yes." Darshan clasped his husband's hand, squeezing in the hopes of stilling the sudden churning of his gut. *He'll be all right.* Anjali's magic was strong and she could wield it with the same aptitude as the elite guards. It would be no different than if he were to protect the man. "I shan't be long."

Anjali shook her head. "I can barely believe what I'm seeing."

"That I'm off to clash with Father? That's hardly new."

"Sadly," Daama muttered. "I would have to agree with you there."

"That you're fighting for the right to marry this mountain of a man," Anjali clarified, jerking a thumb at Hamish.

"We're already married," his husband growled.

"Indeed." Unlike in Tirglas, no one had disputed or even looked sideways whenever he announced the status. Still, his father could object on a handful of grounds. "If there is any squabble to be had over the fact, it'll be because of his stubbornness in accepting it."

"Then go!" Anjali made little shooing motions at Darshan with her hand. "I'll keep an eye on your husband."

Giving Hamish's hand one final squeeze, Darshan followed his old nanny out of the garden.

Chapter 24

Hamish watched his husband depart, dread settling in his gut. The man walked as if he was being led to the gallows. "He doesnae seem at all happy to be off."

"Father can be particular about my brother's interests."

"Aye." He'd heard about the *Mhanek's* attempts to get a grandson from Darshan. It had done little but set the man on a path of self-destruction. "I suppose Dar's reputation for excess doesnae help." After witnessing Onella's soirée and how certain things in the theatre weren't considered unusual, he could imagine an impressionable and fragile young man finding plenty of bad examples to follow.

Anjali hummed thoughtfully. "I didn't realise he would've divulged so much of his past to you, although I suppose he would think prudently there. It wouldn't do to have his own husband be caught unawares. And people *will* try to use his past against him."

"I've noticed."

A flicker of remorse crossed the woman's face. "They've already started, then? That is unfortunate. However..."

The breeze stilled. The world seemed muffled.

Hamish looked around, detecting a slight distortion in the air. "Why did you shield us? Did he tell you about the attacks?" She was supposed to be one of the few Darshan wholeheartedly trusted and warning her seemed like the sensible thing his husband would do. It would also explain her sudden jitteriness. But they were in the palace grounds. Weren't they meant to be safe here?

The front gate is open. With plenty of guards keeping watch. And they had passed through a second gate to get here which had definitely closed at their backs. The person hounding their every step wouldn't get any thugs through and attempting to poison him with everyone on the alert would be a foolish move.

Anjali's dark eyes narrowed. "Darshi didn't give me an in-depth explanation of what's going on—I was hoping you would elaborate—but he did mention hypnosis. That's a dangerous thing for anyone to play with. Whoever it is, they'll slip up eventually. Your safest bet is for Father to assign Nulled Ones to guard you. In the meantime, we should keep moving." She companionably linked her arm into the crook of his elbow. "I wouldn't want you to come to any harm, especially now that I've decided I like you."

"And that wasnae certain before?"

"Not at first." Anjali picked up her skirt and escorted him down a path leading deeper into the garden. "All manner of people have attempted to wheedle their way to my brother's side for their own gain. But you? You make him smile."

One of his own curled his lips as he glanced over to the flowered archway his husband had vanished through. He recalled Darshan saying that it was a rarity for the court to witness him being happy.

"Keep up with that look and you might become my favourite brother."

His grin broadened. "And me making Dar smile is your criteria for liking me?" Lots of men must've done that in the past, before Darshan had grown jaded.

"But he adores you."

"I should bloody hope so."

"Why don't you tell me what's been going on whilst we walk? Starting with the ghastly debacle my dear half-sister dares to call a soirée."

He regaled Anjali with the events at Onella's mansion. She admitting to having heard snippets of what had transpired that night—mainly of how Darshan had taken an elven slave's side in a dispute and the announcement of his marriage—but not the poisoning or Onella's attack on Hamish. And definitely not of how Onella announced herself to him as the current *vlos*.

"The little thief," Anjali hissed. "Bad enough she won't give up her title, she takes mine as her own? I knew she was a snake, but I didn't think she'd be an eel." She waggled her finger, the movement shimmying through her clothes. "That's one transgression Father won't put up with."

Hamish grunted. His husband had implied as much. Darshan had also stated that the punishment wouldn't be anywhere near the same severity as it would've been had one of the man's other sisters made the claim. Being the mother of the *Mhanek's* sole grandson made Onella practically untouchable.

That would change once Darshan made the necessary arrangements with the Niholia Empire. And Onella knew it.

"I still can't believe it," Anjali murmured, smiling up at him. "The rumours of my brother being actually married are true."

"You thought his spymaster was lying?"

Chuckling, she shook her head. "More I never thought I'd live to see the day. You must tell me all the details. How did you meet? I assume he made the first move, given your kingdom's history and all. Whose idea was it to marry?"

Thrown by the query, he stared unseeing at her for a breath or two before realising she was waiting for an answer.

She grimaced. "I promise not to pry too deeply. I'm just curious as to how you managed to win his heart."

Hamish sighed. He had been expecting the probing questions to start the moment they were alone. Whether they were from Tirglas or Udynea, siblings were the same. "Dar did." The idea of marrying Darshan hadn't crossed his mind—and he would've been content simply being lovers—until the man suggested it.

"Really? I can't imagine..." She snapped her fingers. "I bet it was terse and clinical. Almost businesslike, right? Darshi does prefer to keep his emotions buried three feet under."

Hamish grinned. What she suggested sounded more akin to the usual Tirglasian marriage arrangement. Far from something his expressive husband would do. There'd been hints of that outward demeanour here and there, but he had yet to see Darshan fully don the emotionless mantel of the *vris Mhanek*. "Actually, it was sweet. He proposed. On one knee and everything." It had surprised him at the time, for they didn't announce their intentions to marry like that in Tirglas.

"Darshi did that?" Anjali pressed. "*My* brother?"

Still grinning, he nodded. "He has also been courting me the whole way through Udynea."

"*Darshi?*" she repeated, clearly stuck on the point. "He hasn't ever courted anyone in his life. I didn't even know he *knew* how to. He thinks romance is inane and fit only for ignorant saps." She peered at him, suspicion turning her eyes into dark slits. "What have you done to my brother?"

He shrugged. The only change he had witnessed in Darshan was the lack of suppressing his affection for Hamish around others. The man had been so guarded in Tirglas, more so after being banished from Mullhind. But Darshan had expressed his distaste in hiding how they felt. He had remained discreet only for Hamish's sake, until he had won the union contest and not a second more.

"I can scarcely believe it." Her gaze flicked to him and she gave that same charming smile Darshan would flash. "Not to imply you're lying, forgive me if I gave the impression, it's just—" She whirled on her heel, her slippered feet barely making a sound as they traversed a gravel path between two hedges. "Who could've thought that my brother, the personification of hedonism himself, would be harbouring a romantic streak wide enough to drive a carriage down."

There was that word again. "You ken, I've had a few people describe him as such." Including Darshan. "But I've yet to see any sign he was ever like that."

"Of course you haven't. Look at you." She indicated all of him with a sweep of her hand. "Why would he look for fun elsewhere when he has this all to himself?"

Their aimless wandering led them through a small maze. Lush hedges hemmed them either side. Any intersections they came across were covered in lattices festooned with vines and blooming flowers. Bees and butterflies, too. The former hummed merrily as they flew from bloom to bloom.

Statues also dotted the landscape, be it the centrepiece to a flowerbed, filling this or that niche or merely placed as though the gardener had run out of places to put another. Most appeared to be depictions of Darshan. It had been the same at every imperial estate.

Hamish stared up at the current statue of his husband. There were five surrounding a fountain, occupying the flowerbed in what appeared to be the middle of the maze. An entrance into the area stood on the opposite side of the one they'd walked through. Nothing beyond birds and insects appeared to be around. "Dar sure has a lot of statues." The one in the middle of the area held a bowl full of water aloft and appeared to depict his husband as he would've been in his early teenage years.

Anjali nodded. "He gets at least five gifted to him from the court every year, much to his dismay. He can't refuse them, either. Not unless he rejects all of them. Can't be seen playing favourites." She bumped his thigh with her hip. "Just wait. Once they learn of you and your birthday, you'll start getting them."

Hamish eyed the statue. He hadn't a direct comparison to how Darshan used to look, but some of the statues bore only a faint resemblance, if that was who the figures of stone were supposed to be. "That would be interesting. I've never had one before."

"They don't do statues of the royal family in Tirglas?"

He shook his head. The only statues were of the Goddess and legendary heroes. "Even me mum doesnae have any." It was blasphemous for a mortal being to have their image carved, although he never understood why.

"That's a shame. Sometimes, all that remains of us are the impressions we leave behind and—" She fell silent upon glancing to one side where a group of guards strolled along the path her and

Hamish had taken. "Darshi's summoning you already? That was quick. *And* without any explosions. The masons will be pleased." Anjali acknowledged the guards with a wave, just as he'd seen Darshan do.

Unlike the guards his husband had greeted, these people didn't even pause at her address. They drew their weapons and continued their silent approach.

"Stand down," Anjali shouted, her hand raised before her in warning. She stood between him and the oncoming guards. A shield flickered to life, encompassing Hamish as well as herself. "Your *vlos Mhanek* demands your obedience."

The guards kept coming, their weapons at the ready. Whatever orders they'd been given, it was definitely the kind requiring lethal force.

Hamish clutched his belt knife. It wouldn't do much against those fanciful curved swords, or even a hand axe, but it stilled the dread fluttering in his gut. They were supposed to be safe here. Who had sent them? The hypnotist? How had they gotten in? Were they even palace guards?

Anjali appeared unfazed by their advance, her shield remaining strong around them. "If you continue this threatening procession, I shall be forced to retaliate. This is your last chance to stand down."

There wasn't a flicker of acknowledgement amongst the group that she had spoken.

One of the guards raised his axe and lobbed it towards them. The weapon bounced off Anjali's shield with a dull ringing note.

"So be it," she snarled. Lightning crackled from her hand, burning its mark through the hedge and grass. It struck the guards, bouncing from one twitching body to the other.

To a man, they collapsed like puppets with severed strings. Wisps of smoke drifted from their clothes. Hamish didn't dare to look any closer. He had seen men struck by lightning before, both the natural and magical kind. It always did a thorough job.

All that mattered now was that the guards weren't a threat.

Hamish relaxed his hold on the hilt of his belt knife. "We should go." He went to take the opposite entrance when a remembrance of Darshan's past actions tugged at him. "Can you check if they're—?"

Movement drew his eye, coming from the same direction the guards had appeared.

Another group raced their way. Seven in all.

Hamish drew his belt knife. These new guards didn't have their weapons drawn—and they appeared to have the same variety as the first group—but that could change.

"It's all right," Anjali murmured, placing a hand on his wrist. "I know them."

"To be frank," he snapped back. "Whether or nae you ken them doesnae mean much. If they've been hypnotised—"

"*That* would not be possible. They're Nulled Ones."

Grunting, he sheathed his blade. Given his luck, he wouldn't be surprised if their stalking hypnotist was capable of scrambling a Nulled One's brain. "They make the wrong move, say the slightest wee thing that I deem out of kilter, and I slit their throats."

"Duly noted." Humour tinged the words and plumped her cheeks.

The Nulled Ones slowed as they drew even with the dead guards. Unlike the others, they all appeared to be women and wore a bright red overcoat with dark trousers. Most of them stopped to check for signs of life whilst one marched to kneel before Anjali.

"Our apologies, *vlos Mhanek*," she bowed her head. "We came as swiftly as we could. Are you injured?"

"Not at all," Anjali replied, gesturing for the woman to stand. "However..." She waved her hand at the stricken guards.

"Oh dear," said one of the Nulled Ones examining the bodies. She let the arm she was holding flop back to the ground. "Would you look at that?"

A third woman shook her head and tut-tutted. "It would seem the poor souls fell down dead in the middle of insulting you, your highness."

Hamish frowned. Could they not see what Anjali had done? The marks had to be deep within flesh and cloth. It even scarred the very ground they trod.

"The *vlos Mhanek* is truly dazzling," the first woman said, eliciting a chorus of murmured agreements.

"Flattery, Oja?" Anjali turned back to the leader. "Find out how they got so close. *And* who had contact with them before they were recruited? Also, check to see if they're linked to any assassination contracts. Inform the guild of the repercussions should they be less than willing."

Oja bowed. "It will be done, *vlos Mhanek*. Do you wish for us to dispose of them in the usual manner?"

Hamish fought to keep his expression neutral. How many times did Anjali get attacked for there to be a usual method of disposal? Had they been here for her? *That cannae be right*. It seemed too much of a coincidence. And those targeting a spellster would know to use surprise, not a direct attack.

Anjali hummed. "I've heard rumours of cadavers coming back and wandering about after I've dealt with them, but I would so hate for them to go to waste." She rested her chin upon her upraised hand. "Perhaps see if the gardener isn't after more compost?"

The Oja's gaze flicked to him, her stern expression hardening further. "And the insubordinate?"

"Hmm?" Anjali turned back to the group, confusion twisting her lips. "Oh! Of course, you've not yet been introduced." Laughing, she laid a hand on his arm. "This is Prince Hamish, Darshi's husband."

Like a felled tree, the Nulled Ones collapsed to the ground with their arms stretched before them.

"Forgive us, your highness," Oja pleaded. "We were uninformed of your attendance in the garden."

And probably his looks, too. "On your feet, lass. All of you," he added to the rest of them.

The group bounced upright almost as fast as they'd fallen. They milled around him, expectant. What did they want from him? Darshan hadn't mentioned anything special about the Nulled Ones beyond them being trained to serve and protect the *Mhanek*.

What would his husband do in his place? "Your suspicion is commendable as is your eagerness to protect me new sister." He gestured to Anjali, who smiled back. Hamish took that as encouragement. "But—"

"Perhaps it would be best if a profile is sent?" Anjali suggested. "The *vris Mhanek's* spymaster recently sent me a portrait. It should still be in my chambers. Cycle it around the other Nulled Ones and let them know the royal guard has been compromised. Discreetly."

Oja bowed and turned on her heel as the rest of the Nulled Ones started hauling the bodies away.

"Before you trot off with the evidence," Hamish called after the woman, relieved when she commanded her people to wait. "How did you ken we needed help?" The surrounding hedges were high enough that even he couldn't see over them no matter how he tried. Those up on the wall might be able to make out figures moving through the maze, but little else. And they wouldn't have arrived as promptly.

"Word of his highness' arrival reached the main barracks. These new recruits..." Oja frowned at the bodies as though they were a puzzle. "They heard about you and just walked away from their training."

"How new?" Anjali asked.

The woman shrugged. "A couple of months? The commander likes to have them enter in batches."

Hamish turned to Anjali. "I ken how odd this request is going to sound, but can you check them for scarring on the brain?"

"You don't really think they've been hypnotised?" she replied.

"I do." In all the attacks, it had been the one thing in common.

"Hypnotised?" Oja echoed. Her brows lowered, her dark eyes darting from Anjali to Hamish.

"It's a long story," Hamish warned. "And I'm sure you'll be briefed on it soon enough."

"But if they've been in the palace for months," Anjali said, "then—"

"With all due respect, *vlos Mhanek*," Oja interjected. She stood squarely, her hands clasped at her back. "The guards aren't prisoners of the palace. They take leave. Visit family. If someone hypnotised them, they would've had ample opportunities."

With worry creasing her brow, Anjali knelt before the closest guard to examine him. She cradled their head in her hands, closed her eyes and pursed her lips.

Hamish waited in silence, sure of what the woman would find.

She gasped, her eyes flying open. "It can't be." She scrambled to another body, almost slithering along the ground. "This one, too?" Shaking her head, she practically dove to examine a third. "They..." She wasn't so hectic when it came to the fourth, fifth and sixth.

"They've been hypnotised," he announced before she was done with the last.

"Every single one," Anjali agreed. "But how? The guards are—" She clapped a hand to her mouth. "Oh dear. They weren't even in control of themselves. I should've tried to break it."

She could do that? Darshan hadn't mentioned his sister having the ability. Would the guards have been able to give any details, maybe even the culprit's identity? "So the hypnotist is in the palace grounds?" Hamish thumped his fist into the palm of his hand. *So much for safe.*

Darshan was going to lose it once he found out.

Anjali shook her head. "The scarring..." She touched the woman at her feet again. "It's old. Hypnosis can't hold a person for that long."

Hamish grunted in acknowledgement. His husband had said something similar of how the *Mhanek's* hold could last only a few days at best. Even without Darshan admitting it, he got the feeling that their shadowy hypnotist had surpassed the *Mhanek*. "What if it wasnae clinging on? What if it was more like a trap?" He turned back to the guard. "You said they left once hearing about me?"

Oja gave a curt nod. "And no amount of ordering brought them back. We've had deserters before, but these people didn't even hesitate."

Hamish had figured as much. "What if those words, the news of me arrival, was the tripwire?" This whole time, he'd gone along with Darshan's assumption that they had been followed. It hadn't made sense, but he'd seen no alternative until now. "What if this hypnotist laid everything out in advance?" And the times they were attacked were because they'd been where people expected them to be.

Except for the theatre. That had the air of hurried plotting. Did that mean the hypnotist was ahead or behind? Following them to Rolshar would've been easy, especially when it had taken them longer than usual to get there.

Anjali shook her head. "They would have to be the most skilled hypnotist to have ever lived. That sort of talent doesn't hide itself. Not in Udynea. They would've made themselves known well before now and targeted the throne."

"Aye." His husband had made the same comments. The very thought of being in the middle of a coup where the most stalwart of companions could switch sides at a single instruction chilled Hamish to the core. But something must've triggered the attacks. "What if the person doing this didnae want the throne? From what Dar and me have witnessed, they can erase memories."

Anjali gasped, outright terror contorting her face. "That's—" She placed a finger to her lips as if it would call back the word. She nibbled on a thumbnail, her brows knitting together. "It can't be possible," she mumbled. "Only spellsters of legend could do that and everyone knows those are only stories. No one actually believes them."

Dar had. And without that belief, Hamish might've become worm food that fateful day in the forest. "I've seen it with me own eyes." Maybe not the scarring everyone alluded to—only a spellster trained in healing ever would—but the alarmed bewilderment of missing memories. "Whoever is responsible for this, I dinnae think they've any interest in ruling."

Oja bowed, her fist pressed to the centre of her chest. "I am afraid, *vlos Mhanek*, I must insist on leaving two of my people to watch over you."

"Of course." She linked her arm with Hamish's. "For now, I think it would be best if we adjourned to the imperial gardens. It's far prettier, anyway."

Hamish looked around them. The hedges hadn't vanished like some illusion. The insects still buzzed and hummed, the birds continued their calls. "I thought we were already there."

Oja made an abrupt display of clearing her throat. Her amusement poorly veiled.

Anjali laughed and patted the back of his hand. "My sweet brother hasn't shown you much of your new home, has he?"

"Just a wee bit," he confessed. "But I'm guessing a proper tour of the grounds would take most of the day." Especially if they were as sprawling as it had seemed from atop the main gates.

"It would, and probably then some, if you wished to peruse more than the outside of the buildings. Fortunately, the route to the imperial gardens won't take more than a few hours." Anjali led the way down the path, keeping him close as they skirted the still smouldering bodies.

Hamish eyed each one, searching for clues even though a part of him knew he had no idea what to look for.

"I've never seen anything like this," Anjali confessed in a hushed tone. "Multiple hypnotised people? Wouldn't have imagined it in my worst nightmares."

"Seems normal to me."

She gave him an incredulous look. "What has Darshi been telling you? No." She held up her hand before he could speak. "I rather think I can guess there. It's not all assassins and hypnotic mayhem. Not usually, anyway. The people who make an attempt on our lives know what they're getting into. They're aware of why they attack. Even the assassins, doing their job for coin, know the risks." She gestured to the bodies, her expression sober. "Those guards didn't. They were innocent people. Pawns."

"Tools," Hamish added. Just like the woman in Nulshar or the man at the theatre. Neither one had been aware of their actions, maybe not even in death. Had these guards known? He doubted it. *Why me?* What did they gain from attacking him?

Was he merely a convenient target to warn the throne? Did they seek to drive Darshan mad with grief?

A madman wouldn't be considered fit to rule in Tirglas. Did they have the same law here? He would've assumed so, but Udynea also had the senate. Someone who'd lost touch with reality could be manipulated. Could it be one of them? He hadn't heard any speculation along that vein from his husband, but Darshan could be blinded by familiarity.

It could be a simple matter of eliminating who had the title of *vris Mhanek* without actually killing the man and sparking his father's ire.

And Hamish knew the first person who would benefit from his husband's removal. *Onella.* Darshan claimed she hadn't the abilities, but that didn't exempt her from buying the talent of those who could. It was a theory they hadn't considered and one to bring to Darshan's attention. Together, they could pick apart the probabilities.

For now, it was best to keep the idea close to his chest, remain vigilant and trust no one.

Chapter 25

Darshan tried to see the world he had always known with fresh eyes as he walked the open paths and covered walkways leading to the council hall. It wasn't easy. Months of nostalgia had eroded the stark lines of the buildings and softened the gilded panels into a homey glow. It did nothing for the size, but years of familiarity shrunk the space and the heights.

A village within a city, Hamish had called it.

That was truer than his husband likely believed.

Beyond the walls corralling the main entrance, more fortifications sectioned off vast complexes; each with their own guard barrack, servant and slave quarters, stables and gardens. It overtook most of the island the palace grounds sat upon.

The actual imperial palace, where the *Mhanek* and his unmarried children resided, sat in the middle like a spider atop its web. Walled off one more time with its own little set of side buildings. The gateway loomed on his left as he followed Daama.

Strange that his father didn't wish to see him in the comfort of the imperial palace. True, beyond calamity, the *Mhanek's* schedule should've put him within the council hall, but Darshan had seen multiple members of the senate wandering the courtyard. His father had clearly dismissed them.

"You caused quite the stir in the court, you know," Daama said, ducking her head to mask the movement of her lips behind her fan. He didn't think it warranted out here, but the move seemed so ingrained that she likely didn't even realise. "Everyone's talking about this new man of yours."

Darshan smirked. "I bet they are." All no doubt making their own secret wagers on how long it was before Hamish left, be it alive or not. Nothing could be done about that. "Tell me, is the current mood favouring a casket or an urn?"

"Neither." She gave her fan a few languid flaps. The swing of bracelets glittered and clattered along her arm with each movement—crude gifts crafted in their youth by Zahaan, Anjali and himself. He had almost forgotten a time when her movements didn't have such an accompanying rattle. "Few believe he's here to stay."

"That's fair." He'd had lovers before. Typically, not for long. A week had been his last record, before finding that man in bed—Darshan's bed—with another. For the first time in a long while, the memory didn't sting. It still carried a bitterness around the edges, but that was also fading.

"*Is* he here to stay?" Daama asked, her tone far too light.

He breathed deep and put on his best smile. "Considering I *married* him, I certainly hope so." If Hamish did leave these walls for good, it wouldn't be *his* doing.

Darshan eyed the council hall as it loomed over them. He hadn't considered the comparison to anything beyond the imperial palace before, but it truly was larger than the entirety of Castle Mullhind. Although it had always been a space for the senate to gather and the *Mhanek* to host his official greetings, it had also once held a war room. His great grandfather had repurposed the area as a place to deal with the vast trading council.

What did Hamish really think of it all? He hadn't a chance to fully gauge his husband's reaction. Was he intimidated? Humbled? He didn't want the man feeling either for his new home. *I should've prepared him for the size.* But how? There were so few places that came close to Minamist's glory. Nulshar perhaps. Or its sister city across the lake.

Except neither one had afforded them time to rest in peace, to let him just be with his husband as a mere man.

They trotted up the stairs and entered the council hall. Darshan's gaze refused to settle. The marble hallways were conspicuous in their silence. Cold stone greeted him wherever he looked.

Where were the messengers who usually scuttled about whilst the senate and the *Mhanek* conferred? Or the servants and slaves who saw to the passive running of the palace buildings? Even though they'd been told to keep out of sight, he could usually spy a few peering around a column or statue.

Daama strode along at his side as if nothing was out of place. Maybe it wasn't. Maybe it was merely his paranoia getting the better of him. *He's safe with Anje.*

"I read my son's reports," Daama said as they ascended the stairway leading up to the throne room, the steps muffled by the thick carpet and their passage watched over by the massive statue of

Araasi sticking out over the stairs. "Of the attack in Nulshar and the Rolshar theatre, as well as his assessment on your husband." There was a soft hesitance before she uttered the word, more bewilderment than outright disbelief. "You should not have brought him here."

"Where else was I supposed to take him?" He glanced over his shoulder, noticing the lack of anything within the shadows. Still no sign that anyone beyond them walked these halls.

Had they perhaps been sent away? Such precautions suggested his father expected Darshan to react unfavourably to what he had to say. *Foolishness.* He hadn't destroyed anything in anger for some years. Not anything structurally related, at least. And he most certainly wouldn't give his father such satisfaction now.

"How will he defend himself?" Daama asked, drawing his attention back to their conversation.

Darshan squared his shoulders. "Other nobles have non-magical spouses." Not many and none high enough in the ranking to be considered a threat by others.

"But none of those people are the *uris Mhanek*. Your very existence is challenged on an almost daily basis. How do you expect him to live through that?"

"I—" *Forgot.* It was that simple. He'd never come across an attempt on his life that wasn't child's play to defend against or negate. But after months at sea travelling to Tirglas, of the torturous weeks spent there and the rest of the time he'd used up traversing the empire to return home... he had forgotten how toxic the Crystal Court could be.

His gaze lifted to the statue. One of the major stories surrounding the Queen of the Gods was that of her and the mortal woman who became her lover; the first Eternal Flame. *Only after being hounded by Jalaane.* Surely if she could outwit the King of the Gods and protect her lover, then he could keep Hamish safe.

"How?" Daama pressed.

"I don't know," he finally admitted. "I guess I thought the Nulled Ones would keep the worst at bay." He hadn't expected to face a hypnotist, but they would do just fine against such magic.

Daama pursed her lips. "You guess? Has your time abroad scrambled your brains?" She sighed. "He'll need monitoring."

"He knows." Did she think Darshan wouldn't have broached the subject with his husband? Hamish wasn't all that keen, but he wouldn't outright refuse such protection.

They reached the top of the stairs. The hallway between them and the throne room was also devoid of servants. And guards.

His father definitely expected him to lash out.

"And if the Nulled Ones are to do the guarding, then you'll need your father to command it," Daama pointed out.

Darshan sighed. "I am aware." There was little he could do about that. The Nulled Ones served to protect the *Mhanek* and his close kin. If Hamish was capable of carrying a child, then they would give up their lives to keep him safe just as they would for Darshan. As things stood, it would take a lot of convincing with no guarantees.

Getting his father to order them was going to be like weaving moonbeams.

They reached the throne room where their entry was barred by a pair of massive doors. The wood was pale, echoing the marble flanking them. Much like the entrance to the main hall back in Onella's residence, the visage of a tree took up the panels. But rather than the carved and chunky display back in Nulshar, this tree was made entirely of gold inlay.

Where Onella's tree had been crafted to impose, this was designed with elegance and wealth in mind. Each branch was laid out in intricate curves and whorls, reaching for the doorframe as if to brace itself from ever opening. Gemstones in varying shades of green made up every leaf. Flashes of colour that Darshan had always assumed were meant to be fruit, dotted the canopy—the crafter responsible for it had used all sorts of precious stones as well as the silvery rainbow of mollusc shells to fill out the variety.

The roots stretched out and beyond the wood, merging with the pattern of gold and ebony adorning the floor. Darshan paced across the carpet running down the hallway, further flattening the pile with his impatience.

With the lack of servants and guards, he had expected the doors to be open. Was his father still with the senate? Was he supposed to wait like some minor lord with no appointment? Why summon Darshan if he wasn't free?

Was he even here? Had it been a means to part him from Hamish?

He placed a hand on the door. It hummed with magic. His father was definitely inside. Did he anticipate Darshan bursting in? *He's testing my patience.* His father used to assess all of them throughout their childhood in a similar manner.

Darshan was not in the mood for such games.

He turned on his heel. "Kindly inform my father that, if he wants to talk to me, I shall be with my husband." At the very least, he could show Hamish around the imperial palace and possibly how to find the stables so the man could visit his mare.

Daama stood off to one side, her hands clasped in front of her. She made no move to heed his wishes. "You are aware that your father spent the better part of a decade working on establishing trade relations with Tirglas? All that was required of you was to ensure the final negotiation went smoothly."

Darshan grunted. He was well acquainted with the upheaval he had caused. It wasn't as though he had gone into Tirglas looking to start a war. He had tried to act civilly. But after that first drunken kiss with Hamish, after learning that Queen Fiona planned to marry her son off through a contest of arms, of how she loathed Udynea...

He had simply stopped caring about trade.

How could they have trusted any treaty made? She didn't trust them. As far as Queen Fiona was concerned, all Udyneans were cheats and liars. Spellsters doubly so. What guarantee did they have that she would keep her word?

Yes, there had likely been a number of people salivating over the thought of getting their hands on Tirglas' rich copper deposits, but the lack of trade relations left them no worse off than before.

"And now we've missives from their queen claiming you killed her son."

Naturally. Darshan had expected such news ever since hearing the first rumours. "Except I obviously didn't." She had declared Hamish dead right to the man's face before flouncing off to mourn. "You saw him talking to Anjali."

She inclined her head, her brow furrowing. "The *Mhanek* still won't be pleased."

That's an understatement. Everything that'd gone wrong—the trade that was now beyond of reach and the ire Tirglas' crown now had for Udynea—might not have been entirely his fault, but he could concede he wasn't blameless. "The *Mhanek* will have to live with it." What did his father expect him to do? Queen Fiona would likely accept nothing less than the return of her son to marry off. He wasn't about to send Hamish back into her clutches. Not for anything.

Daama pursed her lips, her gaze drifting down the empty hall. "You are worried what he will think."

"I'm not." His pacing had been born of impatience. If his father could not, or would not, see him now, then he would return to Hamish's side and confirm the man was still in one piece. He wholly trusted Anjali, but she hadn't been there for an attack, hadn't encountered the dogged persistence that came from the hypnotised and the desperate.

"You're twisting the sapphire ring on your left little finger. You're worried."

He quickly lowered his hands to his side. "Don't be ridiculous, 'Ma."

"It will be fine, my boy." Striding to stand before him, she cupped his cheeks as though her full height was quite a bit more than the little over four feet that she actually stood. "Your father might be upset, but he forgives easily."

Because I'm his only son. The royal bloodline wouldn't grind to a halt if Darshan chose to remain childless, but his father was very particular on just who should inherit the throne. Right now, the sole other option was Tarendra, Darshan's nephew and Onella's child. That would change.

Perhaps learning that an heir could soon be in the making would soothe his father's temper.

"I just hope you've an adequate explanation as to why you thought eloping with a foreign prince was a good idea." By the slight tightening of Daama's lips and the subtle twitch of her brow, she struggled to understand it herself.

"I love him." Was it so hard to imagine?

Daama gawped up at him. "You say that so easily." She balanced on her toes to press the back of her hand to his forehead, the clatter of her bracelets sliding down her forearms filling his ears. "Are you certain you're not sick?"

He gently removed her hand. "I don't get sick, you know that." His innate healing did more than mend injuries and nullify poisons. It kept any illnesses and infections at bay. Even the sun had been unable to mark his skin as it had in his youth, no matter how many hours he spent outside. "I'm returning to my husband. Please, let father know that if he still wishes to talk, he'll have to wait."

The doors swung out, forcing Darshan to step back or be swept aside. The gaping alcove that was the entrance stood open like a big cat's maw.

He waited for some sign of people stirring within only to be greeted by silence. No grumblings of a disbanding senate, no messengers scuttling out to deliver whatever missive they'd been given. Had it been just his father this whole time?

Like on the outside of the door, there were no guards inside the throne room. *Odd.* The *Mhanek* was always attended by the Nulled Ones. "Are you certain he's here?" he whispered.

Daama silently gestured for him to continue, clasping her hands and following on his heel as he stepped through the doorway.

Chapter 26

Their steps made no sound on the carpet running the length of the throne room. *Red and gold.* Like much of the decor within the palace. *Red because it is drenched in our past*, his grandfather's voice echoed in his mind. *Gold like the light to show the way forward.* Like the banners adorning the archway walls, the colours clashed terribly with the gilding and black marble already present in the room.

White and silver would've been better. He still recalled how his grandfather had mocked the suggestion, of how silver in a banner suggested a purity the crown could never possess. And white? That colour belonged to the old Goddess of the Void, of destruction, she whose name had become anathema centuries ago and since forgotten.

The archway ended and the throne room opened out, stretching in all directions. Like a theatre, ascending stairs sat on either side, tilted to face the middle of the room rather than the throne. *All empty.* His father truly had adjourned the senate in preparation for Darshan's tantrum.

Light streamed in from the windows set high in the walls. At this time of day, the rays fell neatly along the carpet to warm Darshan's left side. It also robbed him of the ability to see anything on that side of the room. Not that it mattered. His attention was entirely taken by the dais at the far end.

Rather than some garish flapping banner, the symbol of the *Mhanek* had been etched into the wall. The gilding glittered in the yellow light of four globes that also illuminated the stairway leading up to a pair of thrones. One was marked by the crown of the *vris Mhanek* and sat rightfully empty. The other?

His father sat proudly in his seat of gilded wood. Once, Darshan had thought it to be solid gold. *Such a disappointment.* Like so many other things in his life.

"So." His father's voice boomed down the room. "You finally choose to come home."

Darshan kept his mouth shut. He needed to talk, quietly and civilly, not yell across this expanse.

"No words for me, my son? That would be a first."

He clenched his hands. He hadn't mistaken the thread of disdain in his father's words. Heat radiated from his palms. The scent of steadily warming silk drifted into his nostrils.

"Tread carefully, child," Daama whispered. She walked so silently that he had almost forgotten the woman was at his side.

Bit by bit, he reeled in his magic and relaxed each muscle until his pace wasn't so stiff. *For 'Mish.* He wouldn't get anywhere, wouldn't have his father's approval or the aid of the Nulled Ones, if he retaliated poorly.

"If you're not going to talk, then perhaps you will listen." His father stood as Darshan reached the midpoint of the room. "Do you have any idea how much work you've made for me?" he demanded, his voice bouncing off the vaulted ceiling. "I'm already placating the senate about the lack of an heir from you, and now you bring home a foreign prince *and* claim he's your husband? Are you aware that his mother has declared you to be his murderer? Have you heard what sort of talk is circulating?"

Darshan bit his lip, tasting blood for a brief moment, then the tingle of magic as his body healed the injury. He knew precisely what they were saying about him and Hamish. His spymaster might not have been able to track down the hypnotist targeting them, but he'd been most enlightening in regards to the rumours.

"And you have the audacity to flout him across the empire as if—"

"Why shouldn't I?" he blurted, unable to remain quiet any longer. "I thought you wanted me to get married? To settle down—"

"And *have children*," his father snarled.

He breathed deep, clinging to the phrases he had recited in his head since first marrying Hamish. The hardest part would be in getting his father to listen. "I am doing precisely what you've always wanted from me." He reached the first step up to the dais. "And I believe I—"

"What I wanted?" his father echoed, incredulous. "*This* is *not* what I wanted."

Darshan rocked back, his heels balancing on the edge of the step. His father's words bounced off more than the walls, they rattled around his head, disturbing long-buried emotions. Moisture pricked at his eyes. Old fears tightened his chest and clogged his throat until his voice barely squeaked out. "So not only must I be *what* you want, but also *how*? What happened to being open about those I chose to sleep with?"

"And I have been, even to the detriment of the empire. But *this*? This charade, this *mockery*, has to stop."

Darshan blinked the tears away as fury took over his tongue. "How dare you," he hissed. He raced up the steps, taking them two and three at a time until he stood nose to nose with his father. The shimmer of heat drifted around them, as did the scent of scorched silk and the crackle of tiny forks of lightning grounding themselves at his feet. "How dare you stand there demanding some godly standard from me when *you* couldn't even spit in its general direction."

His father straightened, his palms pressed together before him. To anyone who didn't know him, they would think him about to pray. But Darshan knew that stance. It was a defensive one, designed to focus any attack back on the aggressor. His father expected him to lash out with more than words. "It is a parent's duty to ensure their children do better."

"Was that what you were doing when you had me bundled aboard that ship and carted off to Tirglas like cargo? What did you tell me? *There are no men like me there*." He sneered as he recited the phrase. "If you had known the reason why they kept themselves hidden, you wouldn't have let me set foot on that land. Did you know they had only stopped killing men like me fifty years ago?" They probably still did, no matter that the practice was illegal now. Those old guards in the outpost stuck in the middle of nowhere had certainly tried with him.

How could the vaunted *Mhanek* have possibly thought it would've been safe to send his heir?

His father jerked back, his features briefly slacking with surprise before the stern mask slipped back over them. "Clearly, I was misinformed."

"Misinformed?" Had his father really just admitted he was unaware of something? "*That's* what you call it?" He glanced at Daama to find the woman standing passively beside his throne. "Did you hear him, 'Ma? *Misinformed*. Of a kingdom he wished to broker a treaty with." He would've deemed it as wilfully ignorant.

His old nanny gave a barely perceptive shrug, her head drooping to obscure her face in shadow. As she had done during the many other times he clashed with his father, she would likely do little more than stand there and wait for things to blow over. Then mollify his bruised pride.

He couldn't let that happen this time.

Darshan breathed deep, trying to quash his anger with reason. "Actually, all things considered, I don't mind that you shunted me off there. If you hadn't, I rather doubt I would've met the man I love." It was beyond doubt. Had he arrived at any other time, in any other fashion, Hamish would've been married off to some noblewoman. *Or worse.*

It definitely would've been worse.

His father scoffed, shaking his head. "There you go again. How easily you make the claim. And just how many have you supposedly fallen for now?"

"One."

His father laughed in a harsh blast of contempt. "For a moment there, I thought you were serious. I see we at least expended some energy on the lie this time."

His chest tightened. The hope to have a civil conversation, for his father to listen and understand, fizzled and died in his gut. *So be it.* He forced himself to take steady breaths, to show no weakness. "I am being serious and I speak the truth."

"*You?* Who was it who mocked the very idea of marriage and commitment?" His father sneered, twisting his features into a ghastly mask. "It is *lust.* Same as every other man you've brought home. I've seen no change in your behaviour to believe this man is here to stay."

No change at all? What sort of reports were his father's spies sending him? Hadn't they noticed the difference? Everyone else seemed to. Had his half-sister seeded doubt in their father's mind? He wouldn't put it past her. "I have remained within the boundaries of proper decorum and am no longer fooling around." Both old points of contention between them.

His father scowled. "So the reports of your debauchery in the Rolshar theatre or the unseemly display in the tavern during your birthday were falsified?"

"I am forbidden from sex now?"

"In *public.*"

"No one but your spies saw us in Rolshar." Their romp in the theatre hadn't been planned. He hadn't even expected Hamish to respond positively never mind with such gusto. "And as for my birthday..." He balled his hands as a new thought surfaced. Had his father actually been responsible for both poisoning attempts? "...it *was* private."

"Having your current toy carting your drunken self upstairs?" His father gave a contemptuous little smile. "Yes, utterly private."

Fire flickered on the edge of his thoughts. *Just one little flame.* He bit his cheek in an effort to keep himself calm. "I am *married.* He is my *husband.*"

"*Not* by imperial standards. Some backwater ceremony does not equate to a royal wedding."

Darshan's jaw dropped before he could control the expression. "All this talk of peace between lands, of unity and common ground, and you won't even honour a single custom that isn't ours?" He should've known better. His father would use any loophole as leverage.

"You wish to speak of honouring customs? What of the mess you left in Tirglas? Participating in their marriage rite? Causing mass panic?"

A blast on derision whistled through his nose. "There was nothing honourable about that union contest." Much of Hamish's family had rallied to *keep* him from that life, one that would've been greatly shortened had Queen Fiona gotten her way. "And I still won it."

"Don't be ridiculous. You and I both know—"

"What I *know*," he snarled. "What is only clear to me because of him, is that I *thought* I knew love." Looking back, he knew nothing else had been true. *Just fun.* Infatuation. Even his burgeoning feelings for his close friend, Vihaan, hadn't pierced the wall around his heart during adolescent. There'd been no ease, no calmness of his soul.

But Hamish? Darshan had spent years balancing his true self with the persona people believed him to be and one look from those blue eyes had shattered his defences. Hamish had seen through all the lies almost immediately. He had blazed into Darshan's dim life and shown him what it was to live in the warm glow of another's affections.

If that wasn't real love, then it didn't exist.

"I was wrong before," Darshan admitted. "All those other times hadn't been right. But it is now. You test me—you test *him*—and I'll fight it." Whatever his father attempted, Darshan would protect his beacon. "If Jalaane could not convince Araasi to give up her Eternal Flame, nothing you say will convince me to give up mine."

His father shook his head, his frustration palpable. "What did I do wrong?" He threw his arms up to the ceiling in an overtly dramatic display of supplication. "What deity did I anger that they would see fit to send me an unruly son like you?"

Darshan flopped into his throne, chucking a leg over one of the arms. "Don't they have some Goddess of Discord up north? It was probably her."

"Don't sass me, boy," his father growled. "You nearly started a war."

"And sit straighter," Daama snapped, slapping at Darshan's dangling foot with her closed fan.

Grumbling under his breath, Darshan obeyed the woman. "I don't see why you're so surprised at *that* outcome," he said to his father. "Isn't a war what the senate wants?" He spread his hands wide. "Why else would they make no objections to you sending me?"

"I am *not* in the habit of just giving in to the senate's desires."

Of course not. For the *Mhanek* to be a soft touch would only invite assassins—more than the usual amount, anyway. But his father couldn't be seen as always in direct opposition to the senate either. That would cause even more problems.

"I cannot believe what you did," his father continued. "How could you have been so callous as to throw away years of careful negotiations? Was it to punish me? I thought you were smarter than this, that you were past childish retaliation. Did you even stop to think about the repercussions of your actions?"

"*I* think you're forgetting I'm not a child," Darshan muttered under his breath. "We don't need their trade." Other lands had the resources Udynea sought, if not in similar abundance.

His father held up a silencing finger. "*Fourteen* years," he stressed. "Fourteen damn years it took us to get this far in our negotiations. And you overturn it all in four weeks—*less*, if my reports are to be believed."

"Yes." When it came to the task he had been sent there for, he would admit to a lack of attendance. It wasn't as though he hadn't tried. "But—"

"It was a simple task. Get the numbers, finalise the details and come home. But you had to put your dick in it, as per usual." He shook his head. "I see I was wrong to believe you were fit enough to handle an ambassadorial mission. Especially one as sensitive as Tirglas."

"Because the sensitivities of that ambassadorial mission was precisely what you had in mind when you shoved me aboard that ship—carefully crewed entirely by women, I might add. Were you expecting me to wind up tumbling them because I couldn't find a more suitable bed partner?" It was the sort of screwy plot his father would come up with. "And whilst we're on the subject of the treaty, it wouldn't have lasted long. Their Queen only accepted in the first place because she believed war was the outcome of refusal. She's rather distrustful of spellsters." Queen Fiona hadn't exactly warmed to him even before his rather public kiss with her son.

And after? She had shown her true poisonous self.

His father grunted noncommittally. "According to my sources, *you* attacked the castle guard. Unprovoked." One stern brow lifted. "With magic."

"I did *no* such thing." He had attacked men, true. He had even killed a handful. But not unprovoked and not where any more than a handful of people had seen it. The only other time he had dared to use magic had been at the end, when... "Queen Fiona was going to have me arrested."

"And *why* were they trying to arrest you?"

Because he had upset her plans to have her son married off against his will to some noblewoman. Because he had made it through all three trials to win Hamish's hand. "All I did was put up a shield to stop the guards from touching me."

"And the show of your power instilled fear in the people. You caused a mass panic, which in turn, caused multiple injuries."

Darshan ground his teeth. He hadn't known anyone had been injured, although it didn't surprise him. The crowd had fled in a rush of screaming bodies. But only once he'd shown himself willing to defend.

Even then, he had found it odd at how the people had been merely wary of the fireball he had inadvertently caused during the archery portion of the trials.

His father slumped into his throne, suddenly seeming a lot smaller and frailer. Just when had he grown so thin and pasty? "You'll inherit all this one day." He gestured to the room, still empty save for the three of them. "But how can I be sure you've the people's best interests in mind when you're more concerned about what's good for you? The empire follows their *Mhanek*. How can they trust a leader who is only interested in where their next orgasm comes from, regardless of the consequences for his people?"

Darshan bowed his head. There was no point denying he had made a mess of the trade negotiations with Tirglas. It was true. Every word. He still wasn't sure of the full consequences or how far-reaching they would be.

"And you return from that debacle with a husband."

He lifted his head a fraction. All the fight seemed to be draining from his father. Perhaps he would finally listen. "Have you not said I should settle down?"

"With a woman. Or, at the very least, someone capable of giving you an heir." He rubbed at his temple. "This is almost as bad as that time you chased off that Vihaan fellow."

"*I* did no such thing. That was *you* scaring him away with talks of children." The last mention had seen Vihaan fleeing the Crystal Court, terrified the *Mhanek* would order them to breed. Darshan occasionally wrote to the man, even though he had never once received a reply.

Just like that, he had lost a close friend, the rarest thing in his life. All over his father's stupidity. He couldn't even be sure Vihaan was still alive.

"You need an heir, he had the parts. He could've given you one."

That didn't mean Vihaan was willing to carry a child. Most

paalangik, at least the handful of men Darshan had conversed with, found the idea nauseating. "We have been through this. I am not having this argument again."

"You can't sire a child by spilling your seed up some man's back passage."

Darshan scoffed. Did his father think he didn't know how making babies worked? That Daama hadn't ensured both he and her son sat in on every class she taught Anjali? "Is that all you care about me being? Another link in the chain? What would Mother say to that?"

His father's face creased at the mention of his long-dead wife. "No." He sagged further in the throne, the colour draining from his already pallid face. "But you are my only son. Even if your sister had been a man, the senate would never have accepted her as *vris Mhanek* whilst you still lived."

Given that Anjali was entirely repulsed by the idea of sex, he doubted either his father or the senate would've had an easier time convincing her to sire a child.

"This is what I get for turning my back on what the gods decreed in marrying your mother," his father continued. "She paid for it with her life."

Darshan stared out into the throne room. The shadows had moved since his arrival, almost touching the first row of seats. "The gods didn't kill my mother, her lack of healing did." He wasn't supposed to know the full story. *She died of complications.* That was all anyone ever said. *Difficulties.* Like it was a minor snag in the greater plan.

The midwives who'd assisted her had been sworn to secrecy, but Darshan had seen the records tucked away in the royal files like a dirty secret. *Spontaneous self-restoration.* He'd seen the outcome. Could imagine how an already weary body would struggle to heal itself with the training to guide it.

And without such knowledge?

His mother had been a purist, one who rejected most usages of magic. An uncommon stance amongst the nobility, but one she had clung to with an almost fanatic fervour. Healing without guidance, without years of training, could lead to the magic running amok with no way to stop it.

The *complication* had been his mother's body cannibalising itself in an effort to mend itself.

"Perhaps not," his father agreed. "But that still leaves me stuck with you and your insolence."

"You cannot tell me *you* didn't do anything against your father's wishes." They were both aware he knew otherwise. "Or do you believe Grandfather failed to express his opinion of the wife you lost?" The old man had been very vocal in the years before his death, about a lot of things Darshan would prefer to forget. His father had tried to shield him from the worst of the abuse, but he hadn't always been there and his nanny could only do so much against the *Mhanek*.

"*I* didn't place the threat of war over the people's heads."

Darshan rolled his eyes. "He's not dead." Queen Fiona may have declared Hamish as such, but she wasn't delusional. And, however upset she might be, she wouldn't risk her people in a war with an empire that could swallow her kingdom whole.

"I can see that, unless you've managed to pervert the laws of nature and reanimated a cadaver. But it changes nothing. Did you honestly believe you could just saunter on home, declare him as your husband and everything would be fine?"

"Considering several of my sisters have done just that, yes." Suravi had known her husband for a week prior to their marriage. Darshan had at least spent the better part of a month in Hamish's presence before announcing his feelings. And marriage? They'd done that shortly before leaving Tirglas. "Hamish and I have deliberated quite a bit on the matter of settling down, which is just as you've always said I should do."

"One edict." He waggled a forefinger in the air in emphasis. "Just *one*. That's all it would take to have dozens of fertile young women lining up for you to choose from. Just one night of not being so damn stubborn is all I've ever asked from you. The gods know how I have tried to make you see that."

"You know that is never going to happen." To think, his father had become desperate enough to let any woman into his son's bed.

"Yes," his father sighed. "You made that abundantly clear the night you set your bed alight."

He could still see that night in his mind's eye, of walking into his bedchamber to find two naked women fornicating on his bed. *Those poor women.* They had done only obeyed commands, even inviting him to join in because that was what the *Mhanek* had ordered.

He would have to get a new bed again. Burn the old.

At his side, Daama grumbled under her breath. She had been livid upon learning of it, had wanted nothing more than to give his father a piece of her mind. Rarely heard of, the desire of a slave to berate those higher than their master. Only being explicitly forbidden to do any such thing had stopped her.

Sometimes, he wondered if it would've helped.

"And what do you suppose set me off?" Darshan asked. "Or shall we talk of the time you tried to hypnotise me instead?" Not permanently, his father hadn't the strength for that, but enough to make him suggestive. *If Anjali hadn't found me...*

The hold on him would have broken. Hypnotised or not, he

wouldn't have done anything. Not with a woman. Or would he? Was his father as adept as the hypnotist who stalked them? Would he have come around only to find he had done the unthinkable?

His skin quivered at the thought.

Heedless, his father rubbed small circles into his temple. "That was a temporary lapse of judgement brought on by stress." He threw his hands up. "Must you always mention it?"

Yes. "Until the day you stop pushing and accept I will not change. You know my preference. You knew back then."

"And I have already apologised for—"

Darshan slammed his fist down on the arm of his throne. The heat radiating from his hand further singed the already scorched wood. "You will never apologise enough for then." He knew all about the stresses his father had been under; the sudden decline of Darshan's grandfather, the assassin that had finally managed to pick him off, the hunt for them, the calamity around a hasty crowning of the new *Mhanek*. None of it could ever excuse what his father had done. "Or for all the other lapses of judgement. I'm not changing who I am." Not even for a night. "I am a lover of *men*. You've had ample time to accept that."

Daama crowded at his side. She laid a hand on his shoulder. The soothing wordless whispers of old trickled from her lips.

The sound prickled his skin. How had he never noticed the thread of magic weaving through the notes before now?

His father shook his head. "My resistance towards your dalliances has never been because they were men. Keep your new toy, if you must, but you *need* an heir. You know you do. You should have at least one at your age. It wouldn't take much."

"Just one edict, right?" Darshan sneered. "Do you even think of what you're asking of me when you say that? No matter how you view the legality of my marriage, Hamish is still the man I love as deeply as you did my mother."

"That doesn't change his worth. He has no alliances, no ability to give you an heir and, even then, no magic."

"No alliances?" Darshan rocked back in his seat, his contemptuous laughter bouncing off the walls. "You dare to berate me over that? How hypocritical of you. Or has age addled your memories of how you were just as bad when it came to my mother? I remember Grandfather's stories. He was very explicit."

"You mean the man who would refer to you as the defective brat and Anjali as the waste of good breeding?" His father sneered. "How quick we are to forget such slights when it's convenient."

He hadn't forgotten. That taunt had seared itself into his soul. There'd been *Mhanek's* in the past who'd preferred men, but they'd also produced heirs the traditional way. As far as Darshan could figure, he was the first to outright refuse. "Every story he told me about you was true."

"From the perspective of a bitter old man."

Darshan grinned down at his rings, casually admiring the glitter of the gems in the light. How did his father not notice he was starting to sound like his own parent? "You badgered Grandfather into letting you marry my mother despite the minor influence her house had. How is my marriage any different?"

"*Mine* produced children. No matter how much you claim to love this man, you cannot do that with him."

Not alone. But there were other ways that didn't require him to lay with someone capable of carrying his heir and still be certain that the baby was his. Even if he wasn't entirely certain having a child with anyone would be the wisest when he didn't know how his new abilities had affected him.

He wasn't about to bring up *that* little wrinkle.

His father waggled a forefinger at Darshan as if berating a toddler. "I know precisely what this is all about. You think you can hide behind this play of a marriage, pay lip service to your responsibilities whilst you actually run from them."

"I'm not—" If he thought his father would remain silent long enough for him to explain everything they had gone through to get here, he would have. "I am married and planning to have a child." Both things being something he had sworn he would never want to participate in. "How am I running from my responsibilities?"

Daama gasped. "A child? Dear boy, you never mentioned anything about a child."

"I'm still working on that." He was fully prepared to pay for the Niholian breeders out of his own coffers, but it was the act of having them within Udynea that needed the *Mhanek's* approval. He swung back to his father.

For once, the man seemed to be listening, even if he eyed Darshan with suspicion.

"I plan to have an heir with my husband. Using the Niholian method," he hastily added before his father thought Hamish was capable. "It will require a third party and your permission for—"

"Niholia?" his father growled. "Magical conception? You plan on putting the future of this empire into the hands of Niholian breeders and their experimental procedures?"

True, the Niholians kept the secret of their conception magic closely guarded, but it was far from experimental. Their tsarina's wife had birthed two daughters using the process. "Their methods have been proven to—"

"With *women*. I've heard all about their precious magical means of creation. You think I wouldn't consider you taking that route? When it comes to two men, it's still considered experimental."

"I'm sure they've improved on it by now." Their success rate had been labelled as reasonable since before he had left for Tirglas. Surely, more men had tried in the duration.

"And you would choose to dilute your magic bloodline with *him*? Someone who has no magic?"

Darshan bit his tongue on that. If his father found out his husband was a specialist, it would be worse. "He comes from a strong bloodline." And adding new blood to the royal line wouldn't hurt. The gods knew the upper nobility was inbred. Even before his grandfather had fallen to an assassin's well-placed blade, the man had been weakened by an illness in his blood that no healer could mend. Darshan wasn't entirely certain he and his father weren't destined for the same fate, although the addition of his mother's lower noble line might be enough to spare himself.

His father shook his head. "You would need a surrogate. That's a political disaster waiting to explode."

It would've been had he not the perfect person for such a task. "Anjali has already agreed."

"No." The word rang through the room as his father's hand sliced through the air. "I know you are a selfish one, but I never thought you would wilfully endanger her."

"It's her choice." She knew the risks as well as he. Perhaps better. "I didn't cajole her." She could've rebuffed his request just as simply as she agreed and they both knew he wouldn't have pushed the matter.

"I refuse to let you use your sister in such a manner. I will not have her wind up like her mother."

All at once, it struck Darshan that, of course, his father would've known just how his mother died. There wouldn't have been time for the midwives to couch her death in pretty terms or tuck the true reason safe into history.

His throat tightened at the thought. "Then I'll find someone else." Whilst having Anjali as the surrogate would've been the best choice, it wasn't the only one. If there were dozens of women willing to be with him when they knew he could never be interested in them, then there'd had to be hundreds more who would loan him their ability to carry a child.

"*Who?*"

"I don't know," Darshan growled, flinging up his hands. He hadn't given any serious thought to anything beyond asking his twin. "Could be anyone! A lower noble, a priestess, one of the thousands of civilians. Even a servant." Not a slave. He wouldn't dare ask something so personal of someone who couldn't refuse him.

"Do you have any idea as to the upset that would cause? What if your chosen bearer decides to use the child as a means to further herself in the court? Did you think of that?"

He had and more. "Which is precisely why Anjali was my first choice." He lurched to his feet. "But I don't even know why I'm arguing this with you. She has already agreed. That's all I need." If his father wouldn't give permission for the Niholian breeders to enter Udynea, he would travel to Niholia and have the procedure done there.

"I know that look," his father declared. "I forbid it. You will not put her in any danger."

"If that's all you have to say on the matter, then I shall be returning to my husband. Do excuse me." He bowed mockingly before stalking off the dais with Daama trotting at his heels.

A blast of air whipped past Darshan. It slammed the doors shut and curled around him, pushing him back towards the thrones.

"Did I say you could leave?" his father bellowed over the roar of the wind. "I am not done talking."

"Evidently not," Darshan shot over his shoulder. He countered the pressure with a gust of his own, dispersing the air into little eddies, and whirled to face his father. "But I am done listening." He wrapped a transparent shield around himself like a cloak, protection lest his father tried to grab him. "I suggest you summon me again only once you've seen sense." With a flip of his hand to send the doors flying open, he strode out of the throne room.

No one was going to tell him how to live his married life, especially not his father. If he was to sire a child, then it would be his way or not at all.

Chapter 27

"And that's why the back section of the council hall is a completely different colour," Anjali concluded her tale.

"I still dinnae see it," Hamish mumbled. He looked over his shoulder and across the courtyard to where the council hall stood. In this light, the difference in colour to the newer brickwork was muddied by shadow. "Dars' nae the type to go off like that." He knew his husband had a temper. Just as he was aware that Darshan came from a strong magical lineage.

But he had also experienced the man's compassion, his gentleness, the eagerness to assist others. What he knew of Darshan clashed with the idea of the man being a temperamental young prince who was reckless with his magic. He certainly couldn't see the man blasting a hole in a building that size, no matter his wrath. If that had been true, then Tirglas would've been down a castle after Darshan had one brief conversation with Hamish's mother.

They halted before the gates leading to the imperial grounds. The two sections stood closed and were oddly shaped, resembling open fans. Hamish couldn't be sure if they were solid metal or merely encased in such, but they gleamed in the sunlight. Whatever they were made of, it definitely wasn't ordinary steel. He knew what sea air did to that.

"Of course you don't see how my brother could be so out of control," Anjali said. She sent up a spray of twinkling lights, forming a symbol that Hamish supposed was her insignia. "You've been privy only to the product of him restraining his magic for years. He has, of course, mellowed with age and it would likely take something immense to upset him to that level now."

The gates parted enough to allow them entrance. The stylised fan-like sections weren't merely ornamentation. The separation revealed the fans to be harbouring huge spikes that pointed towards any who dared enter. *Friendly.*

"Did anyone die?" Hamish asked. There were few things Darshan shied away from talking about when it came to his past. Being the cause of a death would definitely be something the man would mention.

Unless Darshan's fury had been enough to have him forget his actions. Hamish had never experienced that sort of blindness, but had witnessed others affected by it. His brother, Gordon, upon learning the fate of his wife. His hunting companion, Cam, after a boar took out one of the woman's hounds. His mother and her rabid reaction to Hamish's admission of loving Darshan. They had all lost their senses, their ability to reason, to comprehend.

But none of them had magic.

Anjali shook her head. "Fortunately, the day was much like this one with very few in the area and the handful who were there also managed to shield themselves in time. A couple of slaves were crippled, though. One lost her leg despite Darshi's attempts to save it." She fell silent for a while as they walked through the gap in the gates. "I think she works in the palace library now."

Guilt. That was why Darshan hadn't spoken of it. Without those injuries, it would've been another flippant tale of how the man had destroyed more expensive stonework thanks to his emotions. Although, exploding part of a building due to rage was leagues ahead of turning a statue to rubble and dust during a climax.

The gates shut behind them and his gaze lifted to the building looming over them.

His feet stopped working. *The imperial palace.* After seeing it from afar, he had expected it to be huge, but this was gigantic. It dwarfed the walls that were designed for its protection.

Forget the shed. There was no comparing Castle Mullhind to this gargantuan. The once impressive hulk of brick and mortar, the solid wooden beams and arches... All the things that made up his home, withered in his memory. He might as well have been living in a cave.

A hand touched his bare forearm, the fingertips firm but not quite callused.

Blinking, he tore his gaze from the building to acknowledge Anjali standing before him looking worried. Strange how her hands were so obviously used to work but her brother's were smooth and soft.

"Are you all right?" Anjali asked.

Hamish shook his head, trying to think clearly beyond the shine of wonder, before realising how the action could've been interpreted. "Aye. I just..." He stared up at the imperial palace. "It's bigger than I thought."

"Did my brother not talk about home?"

"He did." Sparingly and often with derision. "Just nae how big it all was." Hamish doubted his husband gave the size any thought or was even aware. "I'll get used to it." He might get lost for a little while, but if his sense of direction could get him through a forest, then it wouldn't be long before he was navigating this place like he had always lived here.

People bustled about the courtyard, their focus clearly on their tasks. A few paused to acknowledge Anjali with a low bow, before returning to whatever duty they were about. It was the sort of activity Hamish had grown up around. The familiarity soothed the tightness in his gut. *Nae too different*. Just scaled up.

They skirted the palace. Windows opened and heads peeked through the gaps, swiftly disappearing whenever he acknowledged their presence. He'd become accustomed to being ogled at during their journey as those in the southern half of the empire really were a fair bit shorter than the average Tirglasian.

The imperial gardens were less wild than the one they'd left and nowhere near the size, despite the massive pond and fountains dominating the centre. There *was* more attention to detail. Squat hedges and blooms of flowers grew in elaborate patterns that Anjali assured him created stunning images when viewed from the imperial suites.

"Not that you'll have much time for gazing out a window," Anjali added with a sympathetic smile. "I'm sure they'll have you bounced from one task to another once Darshi has finished talking with Father."

"They who?"

"The tutors Father will no doubt insist on."

Tutors. Of course the *Mhanek* would demand that. What was the schooling Hamish had been through in his youth compared to all this?

She glanced up at him and grimaced. "That came out wrong, didn't it? What I meant was that you've spent your whole life with Tirglasian customs and laws. Learning ours would be the bare minimum the senate would demand of someone married to the future *Mhanek*, especially when you'll be ruling at his side."

"Ruling?" he echoed. Objectively, he knew Darshan was the next in line—that was why his father was so adamant on him siring an heir—but Hamish hadn't given it much thought beyond that. Back home, the king or queen ruled with their own opinions as law, their consort was there for one reason.

It wasn't as though he hadn't been educated with designs of taking the throne. His mother had been very keen on impressing their history and how it had taught them that being even at the bottom in the royal line was no safeguard to never wearing the crown.

It had all seemed so distant. A vague possibility that he had prayed would never happen.

Except...

He had fallen for Udynea's heir. He had entered this marriage knowing that his husband would become the next *Mhanek* and their son after him. Hamish would be expected to step forward as Darshan's prince consort. To take up whatever role hadn't been filled since the death of the current *Mhanek's* wife.

A position he had never been prepared for.

The sporadic breeze jolted him from his musing. He blinked several times before realising the blast came from Anjali's fan fluttering furiously in his face. It took the edge off his flushed cheeks, but did little else.

"Are you *certain* you're all right?" She peered up at him, her hand outstretched as though her slight frame could keep him from toppling over.

He swayed slightly, his head spinning as though he had drunk too much. *Poison?* His heart thudded heavily in his chest. A symptom of something he should worry about? His stomach churned, but there wasn't any pain.

Hadn't he been shielded during the attack? *Aye, by Anjali.* And the woman hadn't given the guards any time to even attempt to graze him.

That didn't explain the light-headedness, the exhaustion or the sudden sweating.

"I need to sit for a moment." He shuffled along the hedges, halting at a stone bench set within an alcove. The late afternoon sun blazed above, carrying far more heat than he ever remembered it showing in Tirglas. Or even through the rest of Udynea. *Where's a sea breeze when you need one?*

Anjali laid a hand on his arm and the familiar sensation of healing washed over his body, slightly pricklier than Darshan's touch. "You don't seem injured." One side of her mouth hitched up. "Tired, though."

"Aye." He slumped over, resting his elbows on his thighs. "I suppose it *has* been a long day." Between the ride into Minamist from the last outpost, the walk through the city and all that had happened within the palace grounds, he was ready for a solid night's sleep.

Giving an exasperated gasp, Anjali plonked herself next to him on the bench. "You should've said." She flapped her fan a few times, barely stirring the hot air. "Would you like some refreshments? I can send for them. Although, judging by the sweat on your forehead, we should retire to the gazebo first."

Hamish examined the structure sitting in the middle of the pond. It looked sheltered enough to relieve him of the heat. He silently stood and made his way to the closest of the four bridges leading to the gazebo.

Anjali trailed along. As did one of the two Nulled Ones, the other hastening off to what looked like a barracks set against the wall.

The imperial palace wasn't the only building taking up the space. Another, although less enormous, sat on the far side of the gardens. A quick query revealed it to be the princess palace. Without asking further, Anjali gleefully filled him in on all the details Hamish was sure Darshan would've gotten to in time. Traditionally, it would've held all the *Mhanek's* unwed daughters, leaving them only seeing and being tended to by women. The practice had been disbanded generations ago in favour of having the entire royal family under one roof, the princess palace now relegated to housing visiting relatives.

Hamish eyed the single Nulled One trailing them. The woman remained a respectful distance; far enough to stay out of earshot, but within reach of still being useful if their lives were threatened again. "I take it that the scuffle in the maze wasnae the first time you've taken a life."

"Not at all. I've been the cause of people dropping dead in front of me before. It's all part of having the *Mhanek* for a father."

Hamish nodded as he undid the upper half of his overcoat. He'd been on the receiving end of that sort of grudge. "They didnae just drop dead, though," he pointed out. "You killed them."

She remained silent as they stepped onto the bridge, Hamish's boots drowning out the delicate steps of her slippered feet.

Fish, in bright colours he never would've imagined they could be, swam everywhere he looked. Their passage set the clear water rippling and shimmering in the sunlight.

Anjali spoke again only when they were halfway to the gazebo, "Did my brother not tell you that I am his twin?"

"He told me." Along with the list of names and political sway all eleven of his living half-sisters carried. Hamish had forgotten most of it. No doubt, he'd get a reminder when he was introduced to the rest of them.

"Then you must be aware that I am considered to have been born without a soul."

"Aye," Hamish grunted. He didn't understand the reasoning. In Tirglas, births that produced more than one child were seen as the Goddess' blessing. Here? Custom had long dictated that the soulless were to be put to death and there was supposedly only one soul gifted in each pregnancy.

The only reason Anjali had avoided infanticide was because of her father.

"Because of my unprecedented living state, the senate decided that I technically don't exist and my presence is supposed to be treated as such. I may be *vlos Mhanek*, but I hold none of the political power such a title should bestow upon me." She shrugged. "Which isn't as horrid as it sounds. No power means no assassinations beyond those looking to use my death as leverage with Father."

Hamish frowned. The one assassination attempt he had faced as a child had been to end his life, along with that of his younger sister, not threaten it as a means to influence their mother.

Would that be his life now? Bounced from under the protection of one lot of guards to another because he couldn't defend himself against magic? It couldn't be what Darshan had intended for him.

They stepped beneath the gazebo's shade. Without the sun heating him, his skin pebbled in the slight breeze. Rubbing his arms, he stared out at the water.

He glanced over his shoulder to find the second Nulled One had returned, along with two more garbed in red. They stamped onto the bridge—saluting to Anjali and Hamish without a hitch in their strides—and took up station at the far end of each bridge, ensuring no one could approach without notice.

"How do you expect me to believe you dinnae exist in the eyes of the court?" Hamish asked. "These women clearly acknowledged you." He hadn't been mistaken about their deference to her either. They knew precisely where she stood in the royal hierarchy. "As did the servants."

Anjali laughed and waved to one of the women now standing at the other end of the bridge. "They do. Although, I'm certain they've grown tired of having to pretend that any act I undertake comes seemingly from nowhere. Aren't you?" she yelled across the pond, grinning as the question was met with silence. "They're here to protect *you*, anyway. Wouldn't matter if I trotted off right now."

He eyed the distance between him and the Nulled Ones. Back home, his mother's lackeys had been practically breathing down his neck whenever he left the castle grounds. These women seemed to know how to guard and remain distant, if they could do discreet better than Darshan, then maybe being tailed by them wouldn't be so bad.

"It's the same reason why no noble within the empire dares to court me, anyone I married would still be considered unwed." She gave him a sly smile. "And any children I birthed would be miraculously born without a mother."

"Ah." Hamish leant on the railing edging off the pool. The damn barrier didn't even reach his waist, but it gave him an unimpeded view of the imperial palace. Once Darshan was done talking to his father, he would have to appear from that direction. "So that's why Dar suggested you as his preference to carry our child."

Anjali beamed. "Not only *that*. I am the only choice that he can guarantee Onella won't try to tamper with for fear of upsetting our father. Or try to use the child to start a coup."

"And you dinnae mind?" It had been months since Darshan first mentioned the idea of having his twin carry their child. "I might nae fully understand the whole process—" He had been taught about conception when it came to a man and a woman, but that wasn't what his husband proposed. "—and Dar did say it's still considered experimental." For two men, at least. Given that the Niholian method of fusing two bloodlines into a viable child had started with their empress and her wife, it made sense that their efforts would've focused on how two women could have children without the biological intervention of a man.

Anjali flapped her hand as she draped herself over the railing. Her head tipped back until she looked to have lost it. "Darshi has been away for some months, and he had only vague interests in the notion of children to begin with. It is my understanding that the healers in Niholia are beyond the experimental stage." She lifted her head to stare in the opposite direction of the imperial palace. "Nevertheless, you shall need one of them to be involved and it'll take some time for arrangements to be made. A month at the earliest. By then, they might've further improved on the method."

And if those methods didn't work? *He said there were other options.* Ways that wouldn't require either of them to lay with a woman. But would the child be Hamish's as well? He had always longed to be a father and would raise their son as though the boy shared his blood, just as he had done with his sibling's children. But a part of him had become enamoured at the thought of seeing a chubby face like his nephews with the dark hair and hazel eyes of his husband.

Shaking himself out of his musing, Hamish looked around them. With the pool hemming them in, the world sparkled under the sun. Almost like a sunny winter's day back in Tirglas. The warm breeze skittering across the water spoiled the sensation a little. At least it remained cool in the shade.

"How long do you think he'll be?" he asked of Anjali. He couldn't think about how much time had passed without his stomach knotting. With their walk through the palace gardens, the attack and subsequent relocation to the imperial grounds, he thought Darshan would've caught up with them by now.

What was going on? Why hadn't Darshan returned?

She hummed, her lips thinning in much the same way as her brother's when deep in thought. "It's hard to say. It depends on how difficult Darshi and Father choose to be with each other."

I should've gone with him. How much waiting would be necessary before the concern sickening him became justified? What if Darshan's guess on who the hypnotist was wrong and the *Mhanek* was it? Would the man hypnotise his own son? *Maybe.* Would Darshan expect it? "Dar said he'd been hypnotised once before. Did—?"

"—our father do it?" Anjali finished in a rush. She breathed deep, her whole face telling him the answer before she gave it. "Yes. Just the once." She turned from him. "Once was enough. I doubt he would dare it again. Besides, Daama will be there. She would cuff Father over the head faster than you could blink."

"Your old nanny?" He had seen her only briefly, and from a distance, but the elven woman didn't look strong enough to swat a fly. "She would attack the *Mhanek*? Isnae that treason?"

"For Daama?" Cackling gleefully, Anjali shook her head. "She has done it more than once in the past, usually when Darshi's not fast enough to stop her." She patted his arm. "Don't worry, they've been at this for years, you're in more danger than my brother."

"That's nae as comforting as you think." Darshan wouldn't be blind to the same fact. Worrying about Hamish could hinder the man's judgement when it came to dealing with the *Mhanek*.

"But it *is* truthful." She flicked open her fan and lazily flapped it in her face. "Relax. The worst you'll face at the moment is boredom."

Sighing, Hamish turned to stare out at the princess palace. He was all too familiar with boredom. He'd had spent years doing the same tasks day after day, be it helping the farms surrounding Mullhind, hunting to aid in feeding those who couldn't, or collecting the common folks' grievances. It had kept him busy, but it could be tedious work.

Still, it was nothing compared to the days his mother would confine him to his quarters like a criminal for merely looking at a man. There were only so many arrows he could fletch.

Somehow, this waiting was worse.

The murmur of other voices drifted on the breeze. A woman stood on the bridge opposite them. She spoke with the Nulled One at the far end, but her words seemed to have no sway. Back home, her brightly coloured clothes would be considered too fine for a servant, but that didn't exclude her here. And if she was a servant, then she might carry news from Darshan's meeting with his father.

And if she meant harm? It was one person. Between Anjali and himself, Hamish was sure they could subdue her until the Nulled Ones reached them.

"Do you ken that woman?"

Anjali beamed. "I do. 'Mika!" She waved her hand, giving the gesture an extra flourish with her fan. "Let her through!" she ordered the Nulled One, who obeyed begrudgingly.

'Mika made her way up the bridge. Her garb was similar to Anjali's in cut—the tunic billowy and unbound at the waist and long enough to reach her knees to reveal loose trousers—but the green fabric was speckled in floral designs.

She bowed deeply before Anjali, who objected at the action loud and long.

Hamish silently evaluated 'Mika as the two women chatted. She was lightly suntanned, which suggested only moderate days outside. Perhaps a merchant's wife. But the clothes seemed more like those of a noblewoman. The little he'd learnt of Udynea during his childhood schooling told him that all nobles in the empire were spellsters, a fact Darshan had since confirmed as largely true. His husband had also taught him that a proficient healer had the innate ability to repair their own body without thought, which included the usual effect of sunlight on paler skin.

None of that told him just how much of a threat she might be. He could only go along with Anjali's judgement.

"Allow me to introduce Prince Hamish of the Mathan clan."

Hamish stared at Anjali, jolted out of his musing by the address. He didn't realise the woman knew more than what they'd spoken about.

"Darshan's infamous Tirglasian husband?" the woman replied. Her eyes dominated a great deal of her face, a look that wasn't helped by the harshness of her tied-back hairstyle. "It is an honour to meet you." She snapped open her fan, fluttering it slightly as she bowed. "I am Rashmika of the Faljaaha household."

He bowed his head in acknowledgement. He knew that name. Darshan had spoken it in one of the many tales about his past. Which particular one had involved her? "Are you the same Rashmika who was to become Anjali's handmaiden?" Was that right? It felt right.

Rashmika's brows rose. Her fan stopped moving for a moment before returning to its fluttering. "I see our illustrious *vris Mhanek* has been talking."

"Of course he has," Anjali quipped. "My brother hardly ever shuts up."

Hamish cleared his throat to keep from laughing. There were times when he was certain his husband just liked the sound of his own voice. *That makes two of us.*

"To answer your question, your highness," Rashmika said. "I *was* in training for it, but that was some years ago." She studied him anew, her already slim lips thinning further. "What else did he tell you about me?"

"That he was going to marry you." He couldn't remember the full reason, or if Darshan had even told him, but his husband had alluded to a need to keep her safe. "And you refused." Thankfully. With marriage being forever amongst those in the Udynean nobility, they both would've wound up stuck.

Rashmika smiled. "He did. And I did." She resumed looking him up and down. "Interesting."

Hamish gave the woman a politely enquiring look.

"Forgive me. You're not the type he typically chases. The *vris Mhanek* has cultivated a reputation for pretty men."

"And I'm nae pretty?" he goaded, flashing his teeth in the ghost of a smile. He knew all about Darshan's reputation of having an appetite for younger men.

"Handsome, perhaps," Anjali offered. "In a scruffy kind of way."

Rashmika hummed, pressing the tip of her fan to her lips. "Eh," she finally squeaked. "Handsome is too subjective a word. He *is* hairier than most, though."

"Darshi's quite hairy, too," Anjali chipped in, grinning like a mouser who had cornered a rat. "Or have you not seen him in a bathing pool?"

I have. Although, the last time they'd been in any body of water together, it had been in Tirglas, along with his brother and a trio of trusted guards. As much as Darshan teased about dragging Hamish to a Udynean bathing pool, his husband had yet to try.

Blushing, Rashmika swiftly fanned herself. She side-eyed Hamish and her fan doubled its efforts.

"He's gotten hairier, too," Anjali continued, wicked glee curving her lips.

"Oh? Gone full barbarian, has he?" The considering look she gave Hamish didn't change. "Then, perhaps, our *vris Mhanek* has been influenced."

"Definitely." Anjali cupped her hand over her mouth, the act doing little to muffle her voice. "I hear he's also older than Darshi."

Hamish struggled to keep his face neutral. He had heard that teasing tone too many times to count, typically from his brother. Although his sisters did try to keep up with Gordon's jibes, Hamish was closest to his brother and that gave the man a better insight to work with.

Except, that would never happen again.

He bit his lip as a twinge of homesickness twisted his gut. He had thought himself finally used to the idea of never seeing his siblings. *Nae whilst Mum lives.* He had known that for months, since before they left Tirglas. Yet, he tried not to think about it. Even Darshan rarely mentioned Hamish's family and did so briefly.

It was like they had all died.

"Really?" Rashmika said, still in her conversation with Anjali. "He usually rejects offers from the older men. Says they've not the stamina. What makes this one so special?" She arched a brow. "Or is the answer to that rather simple?"

Anjali leant on the other woman. "He makes Darshi smile."

"How sweet. But it doesn't answer my question. After all, lots of men have made him smile."

Hamish wasn't entirely sure of her assessment on that. He clearly recalled the shocked whispers at Onella's soirée and he was certain it hadn't been because of his dancing. Even Darshan had admitted the court wasn't used to seeing him happy.

"Not like this," Anjali insisted.

He rested back against the railing. Did either of them remember he was standing right here?

"And where *is* Darshan?" Rashmika asked. "I wouldn't have thought he'd go far."

"He's talking to Father," Anjali replied before Hamish could clear his throat.

All at once, the other woman's light-hearted expression fell. "Has he been a while?"

"Aye," Hamish growled.

Anjali flapped her hand in the air. "But that's nothing new. Darshi and Father have never been able to have a single brief conversation between them. It always degrades into yelling."

"Not *always*," Rashmika said, giving Hamish a smile that he guessed was supposed to be reassuring but just made her look like she was suffering from gas.

"A vast majority of the time," Anjali continued, seemingly oblivious to the other woman's attempt to still the conversation. "I don't even need both hands to count the moments where it hasn't."

"And you dinnae expect this to be different?" he interjected.

"Not at all," she replied with a firm nod.

Not having the *Mhanek's* blessing could be problematic, but he had prepared himself for that. Where his husband's temper might get the best of him whilst talking to the man, Hamish already had all the relevant information to offer in a calmer manner.

Darshan had won the union contest, maybe not fairly, but by sheer chance of being the only suitor Hamish was interested in. Under Tirglasian law, Darshan had every right to take Hamish's hand in marriage. When it came to the matter of children, they had discussed at least two methods of producing an heir. And there were others they'd yet to explore in full.

And, once his homeland was under Gordon's rule, then they might be able to broker a new alliance. One that would see trade and knowledge exchanged just as the *Mhanek* had wanted.

If Darshan couldn't get his father to see that, then maybe Hamish could.

Chapter 28

Darshan grumbled under his breath as he stalked through the imperial gates, barely noticing the genuflections from the servants and slaves in his wake. *I can't believe I have to hunt them down.* Did he not tell Anjali to stay put? Did she expect him to chase them across the palace grounds like a child playing some sort of seeking game?

What was she even thinking dragging Hamish into the imperial grounds? If his father had given the order, the Nulled Ones stationed there would've slaughtered his husband and she wouldn't have been able to stop them.

Daama caught up to him by the time he had reached the imperial garden. She muttered her usual thoughts on his behaviour and how he should have conducted himself.

He barely heard a word. His sister stood in the gazebo, chatting to Rashmika.

He saw no sign of Hamish.

The pair regarded his approach with unease. "Why are your clothes singed?" his sister demanded. "Did you fight with Father again?"

"My husband?" he grated, ignoring her question. "Where is he?"

Anjali and Rashmika shot each other equally worried looks.

"He was summoned by the *Mhanek*," Rashmika said, shielding her face behind her fan.

"We thought you were still with him," his sister added. "Darshi..."

Darshan waved her into silence as he turned on his heel. "I have to go." Whatever his father planned, he needed to stop it before it was too late. "Anje?" he called over his shoulder. "My memory of you knowing how to reverse hypnosis is correct?" He knew it wouldn't be easy. That sort of magic was tough to shake and their father was amongst the best.

His sister trotted alongside him. She bit her lip, worry clouding her eyes before she nodded. "I'll try."

"What were you thinking?" he muttered. "I expected you to at least stay in the region of the garden."

"I wasn't lingering anywhere near where we were attacked."

"Attacked?" Darshan echoed, stumbling to a halt. "*Within* the palace?" He had caught no mention of an attack when roaming the gardens in search of them. "Was it the guild?" He could deal with that. He would prefer some mundane assassin testing the waters compared to the attacks they had faced getting here.

Anjali shook her head. "By a group of hypnotised new recruits to the palace guard."

He rubbed his chin, digging into his beard. He had ruled out Onella quite some time ago. His father wasn't so clean cut, but he didn't think the man would send his own guards to their deaths. The upper nobility didn't seem likely. He had considered all of them during his travels and, if any had this ability, they would've struck before now. The same could be said of the lower nobility but with less certainty.

Still, it had to be someone with such ties to get within the royal barracks. What was he missing?

He turned to find Daama standing nearby, right where he expected her to be. "Any unusual marriages since I've been gone? Any vacuums of power?"

Both Anjali and his old nanny shook their heads.

"There has to be some sort of change. It must be found. Go through every record," he ordered Daama. "Something is amiss." He would get to the bottom of it.

But first, he needed to deal with his father.

~ ~ ~

Hamish subtly examined the Nulled Ones escorting him through the council hall. Just three, but the men and woman carried themselves with a stiff demeanour absent in the previous ones he had met.

With the woman walking in front and the other two flanking him, he felt less escorted for his safety and more as though they were leading him to a dungeon.

What did they know about him? Had some nasty gossip spread that neither himself nor his husband knew? Or did these three Nulled Ones act more on the *Mhanek's* feelings about him?

Were there dungeons on the palace grounds? The idle thought

slithered to the forefront of his mind. He was well aware of the prison situated on the outskirts of the city—Darshan had pointed it out to him whilst identifying other larger buildings—but there had to be a few cells near the main barracks. Something to keep supposed criminals contained in the time it took to establish guilt.

Or was Udynean justice less refined in that respect? The crowd in Nulshar had been awfully eager to punish that elf when the man had only been protecting his mistress.

Am I being led to me execution? The notion bounced around his head, echoes of the terror his mother had wrought on the men he had lain with. Darshan hadn't mentioned any of his past lovers falling to the block, but Hamish was painfully aware of how ignorant he had been of his mother's actions when it came to dealing with those he rutted with.

They halted at a gigantic door bearing the glittering image of a tree. Seeing it, he was instantly thrown back to the crude likeness in Onella's mansion. As extravagant as that had been, he could see why Darshan had mocked the effort. There really was no comparison to the original.

Why a tree? He had asked Darshan that very question back in Nulshar and hadn't gotten much of an answer. Udyneans didn't regard trees with any sort of reverence like the dwarves. It couldn't be Ancient Domian, it would make the wood hundreds of years old. He'd seen what happened to heavily used doors after just one century. He couldn't imagine these ones surviving longer.

"Through," the woman commanded, her deep voice carrying a hint of menace.

Hamish leant on the door, expecting resistance, only for it to swing out of his way with barely a whisper from the hinges. His skin prickled as he stepped into the short tunnel-like archway just beyond the doorway, fully aware that the Nulled Ones weren't following.

The throne room, with its ascending rows of seats facing a central aisle, looked more akin to a meeting hall or temple. Two thrones sat at the far end, illuminated by magical globes of light.

As expected, the *Mhanek* filled one of the spaces, silently watching. He was a pale man. Not as much as Hamish's mother, but certainly lighter than the olive-brown tone Hamish had expected after meeting three of the man's children.

There was no sign of Darshan. Or of any other person beyond the two of them. *Odd.* Hadn't his husband said the *Mhanek* was always watched over by the Nulled Ones?

Hamish sauntered up the aisle, surveying the top rows of the seats and the shadowy corners of the room. They were definitely alone.

He had walked halfway across the room when the door slammed

shut.

Jumping, Hamish spun to face the only exit. There was no one on this side. Pulling it shut with such force wouldn't have been possible. Magic? Not from the Nulled Ones, but from the *Mhanek*. Maybe even in an effort to remind Hamish of the strength he lacked. *Nae the best first impression.* Still, after a lifetime of living with his mother's theatrics, he had learnt a great deal when it came to dramatic intimidation.

If Darshan's father was looking to scare him off, he would have to try harder than that.

"So, *you* are the one my son has been crowing to all and sundry as the man he married."

"Aye." It wasn't a question, but Hamish answered anyway. He turned back to the *Mhanek*, determined to see the man as he was: A father unsure if the person his had son brought home was the right choice for him.

After hearing about the lack of concern Udyneans as a whole had for a couple's sexual preferences, he had believed they would face little opposition in that quarter. That hope had increased after meeting Darshan's spymaster and siblings. He hadn't considered that there might've been other factors.

The *Mhanek* straightened in his seat as Hamish reached the bottom of the stairs leading up to the dais. This close, the similarities between the man and his son were more evident. It was there in the way he held himself, the proud set of his clean-shaven jaw and in the hook of his nose. The *Mhanek's* hair might've even once been the same dark brown as his son, but age had whitened it at the temples and raked grey through the rest.

The man tilted his head and peered down his nose at Hamish. Darshan had definitely learnt that gesture from his father. "I see nothing in you that would have me believe you are his flame eternal."

Hamish stared incredulously at the man. "I dinnae think that's something you get to decide, your Imperial Majesty."

The way the *Mhanek* arched his brow and the sharpness in his gaze was also eerily like his son. The contempt that flickered to life in his eyes and curled his lips was not. "Do you even know what that phrase means?"

Hamish wet his lips. He did. Or, at least, he had listened to his husband explain the meaning behind it. His people had their own term. *Chosen by the Goddess.* The meaning differed, but it was close enough for the idea to not be a completely foreign one. "Dar believes our fates were meant to become entwined."

There was another twitch of the man's brow. "Dar?" the man murmured. "Already so familiar with my son's name."

"We *are* married." He was familiar with a lot of Darshan. And in ways those closest to his husband seemed to lack.

"So I have heard." The *Mhanek* stood and marched to the top of the stairs to peer down at Hamish, his hands clasped at his back. "And what do you think of the fate you've been dealt?"

"It could've been kinder." *To the both of us.* When he thought of all the things they wouldn't have had to suffer had they just met earlier in life...

Would they have found each other compatible back then? His husband swore Hamish wouldn't like the younger him, would've found him too brash, but Hamish wasn't so certain. How much could Darshan have changed over the years?

"Indeed." The *Mhanek* rocked back on his heels, further tipping his head up and giving Hamish a good view of his nostrils. "I wonder if you'd be so good as to tell me just how you two managed it, given your kingdom's utter lack of acceptance to a union such as the one you've forged with my son."

Hamish frowned. Of all the questions, he would've thought that one to be well and truly answered before now. "Did you nae hear the stories?" The tales had been widespread by the time they reached Onella's soirée. He had assumed the news had already reached Minamist. Had he been wrong?

"I've heard quite a number of tall tales since before you had even likely left Tirglas. Several times over. And with each report differing from the next. I'd like to hear it first-hand and, since my son refuses to speak with me civilly on the topic, I was hoping you'd be able to tell me the truth."

Hamish inclined his head. If the man was after the truth, then he was prepared to give it. "It's a long story," he warned.

He spoke briefly of Darshan's arrival, of how his husband had diligently done his duty in negotiating the trade agreements—ones that his mother had casually thrown aside because of her bigotry. He glossed over their trip to the cloister, leaving out the attack by rogue royal guards. He also omitted the bear attack that had almost cost Darshan his own life whilst trying to save Hamish's.

Through it all, the *Mhanek* listened in bored silence, perking up only when Hamish mentioned the union contest and how Darshan had gone through all three of the trials to lay claim to Hamish's hand. "I believe I understand now," the man said, gesturing for Hamish to stop. "You were a challenge."

Hamish feigned a cough, fighting the desire to bite out a few obscenities at the man. When the urge died, he managed a strangled, "I'm a *what?*"

"A refreshing change of pace, if you will. There are few people, beyond myself, capable of denying the *vris Mhanek* what he wants. And he ignores even them for the most part. But *you*? You were denied to him until he put in the effort."

"That's nae true." He had omitted a fair bit more of their time in Tirglas than the attacks—the idea of describing the sexual side of their relationship to his husband's father set a cold shiver down his back—but they hadn't been chaste. Careful, perhaps. And maybe someone outside of his homeland would've considered a handful of intimate moments as a glacial pace, but when he had spent the better part of thirteen years abstaining from any sort of sexual contact, it had felt like every night.

"I know my son. He might be all sweet words and promises now, but he bores easily and will be done with you in due time. It has happened with multiple men."

He knew what *Mhanek* spoke of. Darshan hadn't grown bored with them, he had been aware of which ones were using him and, in the handful of moments he had let his guard down, had been betrayed by the man or his own father. "Then you didnae ken your son as well as you think."

The contempt returned to the man's lips, skewing them slightly. "Your loyalty is commendable. I am sorry he dragged you into all this."

"I wasnae dragged."

"But it seems my son has learnt nothing in his time abroad." He tilted his head, squarely meeting Hamish's gaze for the first time. "I am a patient and generous man, you know?"

Hamish folded his arms, staring down the man even as the base of his neck prickled. "It has been me experience that those who have to state what they are also fall short of their claims."

The *Mhanek* gave an unimpressed hum. "If I was looking to punish my son, I would have you sent far away. After offering a discreetly large sum, of course. I'm not a barbarian."

Money? The man thought riches would be enough to lure him away from the man he loved? Hamish flexed his fingers in an attempt to keep them from balling. If they closed into a fist, he wasn't certain if he would be able to stop himself from letting them swing.

"If I was feeling particularly cruel about it," the *Mhanek* continued in a soft tone. "You wouldn't leave this room alive."

There was something about the glint in the man's eyes that squeezed Hamish's throat. He swallowed hard. The briefest flicker of his shield formed around him, sputtering out before it could solidify.

The act didn't go unnoticed. "My word, did I see an attempt at magic? That does explain a few things. But there is so much rumour dancing about, it's hard to tell reality from fairy tales. To that end, I wonder if you'd be able to answer a simple question."

"Is this a test?" He couldn't shake the feeling he was being toyed with.

"You can think of it that way, if you'd prefer, but there is only the truth."

Hamish stepped back, considering his options. Fleeing wasn't viable. All the windows were set high up and the only door was the length of the room away. "What do you want from me?"

"Something very simple. What do you think is going to happen if you remain at my son's side?"

"Did Dar nae tell you what he intends to do?" After all that time, had Darshan not been able to speak to his father about producing an heir? "We—"

"He has." The *Mhanek* sneered. "Do you know our family's bloodline can be traced all the way back to the First Arrival?"

"The First?" he echoed, dumbfounded. "As in humans stepping on the continent?" That was thousands of years ago. Several wars had happened since then, along with the rise and fall of multiple kingdoms. "Didnae that happen here? When it was Domian?" That's what Darshan had told him, that his people believed humans had first landed in what was now Minamist. It clashed with what the Tirglasian priesthood taught, but it sounded less mystical and more logical than humans being created from the earth by a Goddess.

That did also bring the sticky thought of his own ancestors being the same. But Darshan had mentioned dwarven records speaking of many ships landing up and down the shores. Perhaps already warring factions had landed elsewhere. "You're Udynean, nae Domian."

Derision twisted the man's lips. "Do you think that the two bloodlines never merged? That we'd allow powerful magic to slip quietly into oblivion simply because we had conquered it?" He straightened, peering down his nose at Hamish. Not as imposing a sight as he likely hoped, given that he was at least a foot shorter now he had descended the dais. "The royal line is the oldest still standing. We are the last of an ancient line. Darshan's son is to be the next. And he wants to sully that imperial blood with you. A *specialist*." He spat out the word. "I will not allow it."

"I really dinnae see how you've a say in that matter." Darshan was adamant there was nothing stopping them from being together. Not even this man.

The *Mhanek* sighed. "You no doubt believe that due to the many liberties I have afforded my son over the years, ones that undoubtedly set him on this very path. Although, I am equally certain you have no qualms with the outcome there."

Hamish ran his tongue over his teeth in an effort to remain silent. He was well aware of the upset Darshan had caused—both here and in Tirglas—as well as the ripple effect he had made on Hamish's life.

"If he kept you as a lover, I could've overlooked this. If he had picked someone of noble blood, someone with *strong* magical lines, I might've been persuaded to announce your marriage as valid."

"It *is* valid," Hamish snapped. And, his weakness in magic aside, he was still from a hearty family. A royal one at that. He brought new blood.

The *Mhanek* continued without a hint that he had heard anything, "But it was a foreign ceremony in a kingdom we have no alliances with. You are *not* bound by Udynean law."

"That may be true." Hamish balled his hands, squeezing them tight until his arms shook, trying to keep his temper under control. After everything they'd been through, *this* wasn't going to stand in the way. "But we can get married again. Right in Minamist." He'd seen the array of temples and the various deities. Surely one of them would officiate.

"And then what?" the *Mhanek* queried, his expression far too calm. "Seal my daughter's death?"

"What?" He staggered back a step. How did Hamish marrying Darshan lead to the death of the *Mhanek's* daughter? And which one? The man had a dozen at last count. "I dinnae—"

"Anjali," the *Mhanek* snarled. "Or do you not know what my son plans to do?"

"Have her carry our child." Although claiming not to know the full extent of what it entailed, Darshan had spoken at great length about the process that would see their bloodlines merge without either of them needing to lay with another. *Why would that bother his father?*

"I will not see my daughter fall to the same fate as Falak."

Ah. That was a name Darshan always spoke in reverent tones, the woman who had died birthing them. This man's long-dead wife.

"I won't," the *Mhanek* grated. Their eyes locked, the man's seething with old grief and power. "Not again. Falak gave up her life to bring our daughter into the world. I swore that sacrifice would not be in vain. Anjali will live for a great many years still and I refuse to have you, or my son, do anything to endanger that."

The fog of ignorance lifted from Hamish's thoughts the more the man talked.

The *Mhanek* was right. What had Darshan been thinking? Asking his sister to risk herself in childbirth like that? How utterly selfish. And with *him*? With his ability barely recognised as magic? That made even less sense.

"You will leave this city," the *Mhanek* continued, the might behind his words thrumming through the air. "You will tell Darshan that he was wrong, that you cannot possibly be his eternal flame and you are leaving him as is proper. Understand?"

"Aye." He saw it all so clearly now. Of course Darshan was wrong to make such an assumption. Why would the gods put *them* together? It was a ridiculous notion, they were far too different. It would never work in the long term.

"Go." The *Mhanek* settled back into his throne. "Do it now."

Bowing his head, Hamish turned from the man. Now would be better. No point needlessly stringing Darshan along when they couldn't be together.

Then why were his legs leaden? What was this niggling feeling in the back of his skull? This wrongness.

He was halfway across the room when some unseen hold on him slithered off his mind. He halted, shaking his head. *What was that?* His brain felt as though it had been slapped.

"Go," the *Mhanek* ordered. "Why are you—?"

The ground shook. Hamish lurched to one side. *Just an earthquake.* Although, it didn't feel like any tremor he had experienced before. None of the usual rolling movements that made it impossible to stand. Yet, the room continued to shake, cracks appearing in the tiles.

The doors opened with a deafening boom.

"You *dare?*" Darshan roared. He strode across the room, a half-step from lurching into a run, with a finger levelled at his father.

The wall behind the thrones exploded. Huge chunks of brickwork bowled across the room, embedding themselves into the walls and crushing the seats. Hamish dove to one side, further rolling out of the way of one such piece rumbling by. Dust drifted in its wake and blanketed the room.

Coughing, he clambered to his knees, stilling as a hand alighted on his shoulder. *Nulled Ones?* Would *he* be blamed for this?

"Are you all right?" Anjali asked, her slight frame steadying him as he finished getting to his feet. They were cloaked in her shield, the dust within settling faster than the cloud without. "Your mind is your own again?"

"Aye." What had he been thinking before all this? He grasped for the thoughts, which vanished like mist under the sun. Had they even been *his* thoughts? "What happened?" He peered through the shield. Dust obscured much. It was settling, slowly. That it also seemed attracted to the shield's surface didn't help.

In the distance, he made out a figure stalking towards the space where the thrones had been. Something big seethed in place of the wall.

"My father hypnotised you."

That explained the fuzziness in his brain. What had the *Mhanek* intended? He couldn't remember.

"I finally, *finally*, found someone I love," Darshan continued to bellow, his voice cracking at every other word. "Someone I could *trust*. Someone who wouldn't *use me*. And you try to send him away?"

The dust thinned a little more, revealing the trunk of a massive vine. It warped and twisted on the spot. Smaller tendrils snaked across the room, digging into the walls, burrowing through the floor.

The *Mhanek* stood in their clutches. The man currently kept the full pressure of the vines at bay with his shield, but he couldn't hold it forever. His face darkened with every breath and, soon, that wouldn't be possible. Still, he seemed quite calm for a man ensnared from foot to neck. "My son, I was only trying to protect you."

"I don't *need* this kind of protection!" Darshan screamed. "I don't *want* it!"

The vines tightened around the *Mhanek*. Thorns sprouted along their length, growing sharper.

"What's happening?" Anjali demanded of Hamish. "Where did all these vines come from?"

These were the same ones that had dragged him towards safety at the *Gilded Cage*. The ones that had ensnared multiple men at a mere irritation in a village. That had crushed several more to death and absorbed the energy of the living along with that of the dead to fuel Darshan's flagging energy in that stable. "Dar..." They responded to his husband's need, his desperation.

His fury.

Anjali shook her head. "He's never been able to—"

"He can now." If the vines were reacting to his husband's rage, then they wouldn't stop until Darshan calmed down or the source of his anger was destroyed. "Let me out." He slapped his hand against the inner curve of the shield. The surface tingled against his fingertips. "I need to reach him." Darshan wouldn't listen to his father, not in this state. Maybe not to Hamish, either. But he had to try.

Anjali twisted her hands into her skirts, pulling the fabric taut. She glanced from him to her brother and back. "If you get hurt..."

"He willnae hurt me."

Grimacing, she squeezed her eyes shut. "All right, then." The shield flickered, then vanished.

"Dar!" Hamish wasted no time in waiting to be acknowledged. He raced to his husband's side, cradled the man's head and forced those hazel eyes to focus on him. "Come on, look at me. I'm all right. You can stop."

The monstrous face that glared up at him slowly transformed into the man he loved; his brows lifting, the wrinkles on his nose smoothing, the bared teeth disappearing beneath his lips. " 'Mish?" Darshan stared at him as though waking from a nightmare.

"Aye, me heart." Hamish pulled the man into his arms, holding him tight. "You need to calm down." He risked a glance at the *Mhanek* to find him still entangled in thorny vines. It didn't look like his appearance had changed anything there. "You dinnae need to do this. I'm safe. It's all right now."

Darshan stiffened in Hamish's grasp. "It isn't," he grated.

The vine tightened, groaning as more wrapped around the *Mhanek's* shrinking shield.

"I ken what he did." *If this was any other person...* What did Darshan expect him to do? Stand aside and let him murder the man? "But I also ken you and this isnae the way. You dinnae want to do this. That's your father."

"Exactly!" his husband bellowed, shoving himself free. Tears wet his face and fogged his glasses. "Of all people, he shouldn't be the one I have to fight to prove I can do this, to prove I know what I'm doing, to... to—" Whatever else he was going to say was lost in the wet hiccups of his sobbing.

Hamish drew his husband back into his embrace, keeping one eye on the vines as he stroked Darshan's hair and rubbed his back. "You dinnae have to prove anything, me heart. Nae to me. I already ken it all."

"I would've lost you," Darshan said, the words muffled as he spoke them into Hamish's chest.

"Never." With his husband's body still quivering against him, Hamish fixed his full attention on the *Mhanek*. The shield was all but gone, dwindled to a mere sputtering purple glow that outlined him. "*You*," he snarled, "would do well to sit your arse down, keep your yap shut and *listen*."

The man's brows lifted, his face darkening further. "You dare speak to me in such a manner?"

How many people raised their voice to the ruler of the most powerful empire on the continent? *A few, surely.* But how many of them weren't his relatives?

"*Sit*," Hamish growled.

The vines wrapping around the *Mhanek* twisted, throwing the man onto the trunk that had taken over much of the dais. The bark shifted and splintered, holding the man's arms down.

The *Mhanek's* face grew darker still, taking on a plum-like hue. "You—"

"Nae me," Hamish snapped. "I cannae do it. But that's nae

important right now. Truth is, when I was in Tirglas, Dar told me of how accepting Udynea was when it came to who a person laid with." He had since learnt the whole truth, that the genders within a couple were irrelevant because the species and class differences divided them far deeper. "But it turns out you are nae less controlling than me mum." She hadn't attempted the same acts as the *Mhanek*, but she had done unspeakable things in the name of saving and protecting him. Countless innocent lives had been taken because of her obsession with him marrying a woman and siring a child. "I willnae have more fighting over who I choose to be with. You want me to leave? I'll go rightly enough."

The man straightened in his throne of splintered wood and vines.

Darshan's grip tightened, his fingers digging possessively into Hamish's jerkin.

He laid a reassuring hand over the top of his husband's. "But I swear, if I go, then I'll be taking your precious heir with me. Dinnae think he wouldnae give up the throne to be with his eternal flame." It was a gamble. He knew that even as he spoke. Darshan forfeiting the throne would mean that his nephew got it. That, after years of fending off all of Onella's schemes, she would win.

The *Mhanek's* gaze shifted. Only then did Hamish realise Darshan still glared balefully at his father.

"Of course," Hamish added, trying to attain the offhand tone his husband was so good at. "If you want Onella ruling the empire until her wee lad is old enough…"

"I see," the man murmured. "It would appear I was wrong. You must forgive me, my son has been known to let his whims hold sway over his actions far too readily."

"I dinnae have to forgive shit. You should've believed him, believed *me*." He had seen it in the man's expression earlier, the doubt. He had hoped it a product of ignorance in the situation, not a lack of faith in his son's character. "I told you he fought for me hand, of the trials he underwent. Did you think he would continue that scuffle on a whim?" It hadn't been easy. Even with Darshan's magic to balance the odds of his inexperience to the other contestants' training, he could've lost in any of the trials.

The *Mhanek* regarded him with a coolness that almost had Hamish forgetting the man was still bound. Could he still hypnotise people from that distance? Would he dare with the vines holding him? "It would seem he isn't the only one willing to fight for this union."

"Bloody oath," Hamish growled. What sort of husband would he be if he stood back and let Darshan handle all their battles?

"Nor are you what I thought you would be." The man nodded as if to himself, relaxing against the massive vine trunk. His gaze dropped to the tendrils still keeping his hands in place. His fingers flexed, the slight sputtering of sparks falling from the tips like heavy dust. "I believe I understand what he sees in you." His brows lowered. "But that doesn't give you the right to endanger my daughter."

Hamish sucked at his bottom lip. He had heard the story of Falak's death, the how and why. He understood the man's concern when it came to his daughter's safety, even though he wasn't sure if it was necessary. Darshan claimed his mother might've survived had she not been a purist and actually studied healing long enough to gain the innate ability most nobles possessed. They would never know the truth of it.

Yet, Anjali seemed confident in her healing abilities.

The boom of a lightning bolt crackled across the room. It struck the floor to their left, flinging small chunks of stone that were easily deflected by Darshan's shield. The vines slithered off the *Mhanek*, forming their own protective barrier between them and whoever had flung the bolt.

Hamish craned his neck, trying to see through a writhing mess of vines, to make out who else still shared the throne room.

Anjali stalked towards them, the dangerous glint in her eyes reminding him of the striped big cat they'd met in the forest weeks ago. "You swore, Father," she snarled, levelling a forefinger at the man. "When it came to me bearing children, you swore to keep out of it. I am doing this, no matter what you command. If you don't allow the breeders into Udynea, I *will* go to Niholia. Don't think I won't."

All the fight seemed to drain from the *Mhanek* as she spoke. "Treasure..." Shaking his head, he sank into the makeshift throne. "You will die. I'll lose you just like I lost your mother."

"That won't happen." Anjali settled beside him on the trunk to throw her arms around her father's shoulders. "I'll have the best healers in attendance and—"

"So did your mother."

Hamish opened his mouth, the suggestion of an alternative ready on his tongue.

His husband spoke before Hamish could creak out a syllable, the first words he had spoken since Hamish had stopped him from trying to kill his own father. "Mother didn't have my expertise." His voice sounded strained, but stable. He straightened, finally loosening his hold on Hamish to face his father. "I'll be at hand and ready for whatever goes wrong. If I can bring my husband back from the brink of death, I'm certain I can keep my sister from it."

Hamish desperately pushed down the hollow fluttering in his gut. He hadn't mentioned any attacks, not even the poisoning. Although he knew Darshan spoke of the bear attack in Tirglas, the *Mhanek* would assume his son meant a time within Udynea.

Sighing, the *Mhanek* bowed his head. "I truly have no choice in this?"

"None," Anjali agreed.

"So be it." The man pushed himself to his feet. Seeing father and son standing close to each other, the *Mhanek* couldn't have been more than a mere finger-width taller than Darshan. "It appears that I've also no choice but to bless your union and the upcoming nuptials, especially if his bloodline is to be a part of your future heir. Although, I maintain my stance on having your sister be the surrogate."

"Upcoming?" Hamish echoed. "Didnae I tell you we're already married?"

"You did." He fixed his son with a stern frown. "And *him*. At great lengths. But as *I* have already said, you're not joined under Udynean law. It isn't just me who needs to acknowledge your marriage, but the senate."

"I doubt it'll bother them as much as you claim," Darshan replied. "But I can easily arrange an official appearance in the cleric's quarter. I'm sure any of the clergies would be overjoyed to perform a quick ceremony."

The *Mhanek* staggered back a step, his expression one of horror. "My son? Marrying in the first temple he stumbles into like a drunkard? Absolutely not! No son of mine will be content with a little ceremony in some tinpot chapel. Bad enough you eloped with your foreign lover. If this is your choice, then it will be done properly. He will *not* be considered as your husband until you are wedded right. And that includes having him in your suite." With an adjusting flourish of his shawl, the *Mhanek* marched off the dais.

Hamish watched the man continue his passage out through the open doors. He leant closer to his husband, unsure who could be listening. "What just happened?"

Darshan grimaced. "I cannot be entirely certain, but it would appear my father insists on us having a wedding befitting of a *vris Mhanek*."

"That cannae be a bad thing, can it?"

"I suppose it all depends on how you feel about a three-day ceremony," Anjali said. She bent to examine the vines, poking the still tendrils as though they would spring to life.

"*Three?*" Hamish echoed. Even the royal weddings in Tirglas lasted a day. The celebrating always flowed out into the following week, but that wasn't ceremonial.

"I doubt Father will go for anything less than a full traditional wedding for his only son." She waggled one of the vines at her brother. "What is all this?"

Now that he didn't have to worry about Darshan murdering his father, Hamish could take in what the main trunk had done to the wall. It hadn't ploughed its way straight through from the other side—the outer bricks still seemed intact—but it angled from beneath and completely destroyed the dais in the process.

"It's a complication," Darshan muttered, scratching the underside of his jaw. His features were stark, drawn as though he hadn't eaten in days. "A dangerous one at that. Seems it was just as well you managed to clear Hamish's mind quickly. I don't know what I would've done."

I do. Hamish had a very vivid image of vines squeezing the life out of those bandits. He didn't think any amount of healing magic could bring a body back from that. "She didnae clear me mind." He'd been hypnotised rightly enough, but the effects had pooled in his thoughts, then slid off like rain on a roof.

Anjali shook her head. "He's right, I didn't need to. There's not even a hint of scarring. If Father did hypnotise him, it didn't stick. Kind of like my question. These vines, Darshi." She indicated Hamish with a jerk of her head. "He said they're your doing, but you've never had this ability. No spellster on record has."

Darshan scrubbed at his face. "I did something in Tirglas that I fear has fundamentally altered me." He righted the throne bearing the symbol of the *vris Mhanek*, only for one of the legs to give and send it crashing back down. Wrinkling his nose in disgust at the throne, he returned to the vine trunk. "In fact, I shall require your healing prowess to confirm for me."

"Confirm what?"

Swinging to face them, he settled in the same spot on the trunk that had held his father. The wood shifted beneath him, smoothing the splintered patches and moulding the seat to his body. "That I am no longer fully human."

Anjali stared at her brother, her mouth gaping. "What?" she asked, uncertain laughter bubbling out with the word. "Stop talking in riddles. What could you have possibly done to think that?"

Darshan stared down at the shattered remains of the dais. Was he only now taking in the damage the vines had caused? "What have I done?" he whispered, the words low and threatening. When he looked up again, cold anger still seethed in his eyes. "Something utterly forbidden."

Chapter 29

F orbidden.

Hamish stared blindly at the guest room he'd been escorted to. He hadn't heard Darshan call his new gift as such before. He hadn't really taken in what his husband had done in full until hearing the explanation Darshan gave to his sister.

Shaking his head, he examined his accommodations under the yellow light cast by a small array of lanterns. The furniture seemed standard to both the imperial estates they'd briefly stayed at. The bed was a mattress on a raised dais surrounded by gauzy curtains and with a headboard that had holes the size of a fist bored into it. Plush rugs littered the stone floor, a welcome addition as he tugged off his boots and burrowed his toes into the softness.

The bed faced a series of massive windows big enough for an entire horse to leap through. *At least, that'll nae be happening*. Or maybe it could. It was probably best to not assume anything.

A little fiddling with the latches revealed one window was actually a door leading out to a small balcony. That would've been a worry, had his room not sat several stories up.

With the size of the imperial palace, he had expected there to be a guest wing. But they'd a whole other building, set within the palace grounds, but outside the imperial one. Other visiting nobility also currently used it and they had eyed Hamish with a stillness of witnessing a ghost. The rumour of his death was one he could've done without. Hopefully, it would fade with time and his very-much-alive presence.

Darshan had objected to them being parted during the night, at great lengths and relenting only when Hamish accepted the terms. This was to be his quarters until their second wedding. Along with setting up a contingent of Nulled Ones to guard Hamish, the *Mhanek* had also insisted they sleep apart. It would take a few nights before he adjusted to Darshan's absence, but it wasn't impossible.

He wasn't utterly alone, either. A pair of Nulled One's stood guard outside the only entrance, keeping him safe.

Hamish eyed the door, tapping the key to it against his lips. It was hard not to liken being locked in here to how it had been back in his quarters in Tirglas. His mother had set guards outside his door for years to keep him in line, to imprison him, night after night.

The duo outside this room remained purely for his safety, not to monitor him. They would undoubtedly follow him if he chose to leave—just as their comrades had done with Anjali and himself earlier in the day—but there would be no interference to his actions beyond keeping him alive.

He poked about the rest of the room, first investigating a door opposite the windows to find it led to a bath, with another door hiding the privy. He considered the broad tub. It had two taps, which suggested warm water on demand. Would that still be true now twilight stretched her fingers across the world?

A quick fiddle with the taps swiftly gave him a favourable answer. Shedding his clothes, he slipped into the bath to scrub away all the dirt from their travels. Once clean, he laid back and let the warm water slowly ease his muscles. This was definitely a luxury he had gotten attached to.

He remained submerged up to his neck until he caught himself nodding off a handful of times. Drying himself, he padded around the bedchamber, snuffing lanterns along the way, before slithering beneath the sheets.

He tracked the patterns painted on the ceiling, fidgeting as he sought the relaxing lull of sleep. The bed was softer than he had grown up with, the bedding cool against his bare skin and steadily growing warmer with his body heat. Neither stopped him from sinking into his dreams.

It was the silence.

Darshan didn't snore, not loudly, but the rhythm of his breath had always been there. A lullaby to remind Hamish that, even in the dark, no one could drag him back to his mother.

Rolling over, Hamish squeezed his eyes shut. *It's only for a couple of months.* Magic could see invitations to their wedding reaching the farthest estate in a day, but it would take no less time for the people to make their way down to Minamist.

He could survive that bloody long without Darshan at his side.

The creak of something moving had his heart making a valiant attempt to pound its way out of his chest. Thoughts of assassins swirled through his mind. He stared out into the night.

The moon was up, its light barely illuminating anything. Perhaps it was nothing. The palace was old. Even if well-maintained, it would make all sorts of squeaks and moans.

He lay still, listening for the soft pad of a foot, a hastily stifled breath, something to tell him he wasn't alone. Was that rattling at the windows really the wind? Did the shadows in the corner actually shift or was it just his imagination?

Hamish slowly lifted his head, curling his fingers into the pillow. It wasn't the heaviest object to throw at a person, of there truly was someone else in here, but he'd nothing closer. Should he start sleeping with a weapon?

The thud of a figure stumbling into something heavy in the dark caught his attention. They stood on the edge of the moonlight, slumped over a chair.

Flinging the pillow in their direction, Hamish threw himself over the side of the bed. He bumped down the stairs, tangling in the gauzy curtains hanging around the bed. *Shit!* He had forgotten about the bloody useless things.

He clambered to his hands and knees. No use in being stealthy now. His intruder knew they'd been caught. How had they gotten in? He had locked the door, which still looked to be in the same state. What were the Nulled Ones up to? They had sworn nothing would get past them.

So who was sneaking through his room? And what were they after? It couldn't be to kill him or he would already be dead.

Peeking over the bed, he grunted in disgust at finding the pillow he lobbed had also collided with the curtains and flopped back onto the blankets. Where had his intruder gone?

" 'Mish?" Darshan's voice called from the dark. Soft firelight flared to life on Hamish's left to illuminate the room in a ruddy glow. "Are you all right?"

Hamish squinted in the sudden light. He definitely wasn't hallucinating. "What are you doing here?" *How* had the man gotten in? Was there another way? Did the Nulled Ones have an extra key? "I thought we were meant to be sleeping apart until the wedding?"

His husband laughed in a low and wicked timber that never failed to shimmy its way to Hamish's groin. He lit a nearby lantern before letting the fire in his hand disappear in a few licks of flame. "You don't actually believe I was about to let my father get between us like that?" He sauntered across to the bed, perching on the side as Hamish got to his feet. "As if I'm going to let anyone dictate when I see you. I am unconcerned that we're not married by Udynean standards, you're my husband. We should be together. Besides—" He cut himself off, suddenly seeming invested in the gauzy curtains.

"Aye?"

"You snore," he said, plucking at the blankets. "It's atrociously loud, but I've grown used to the sound." He rubbed at his arm. "And it's very quiet in my room."

"You *miss* me snoring?" His brother would often compare his snoring to that of a carpenter sawing wood whenever they used to travel. He knew it was appalling, having woken himself up with the rafter-rattling sound. For Darshan to find comfort in the sound was a welcome change.

His husband scoffed. "I miss having you near." He leant back, stretching out on the edge of the bed. "And I still can't believe you went and spoke to my father alone. He could've killed you."

Hamish spread his hands. "Nae dead."

Darshan peered at him for some time. "I suppose..." His gaze sauntered down Hamish's naked body, clearly enjoying the sight. "You *are* a bit too realistic to be a construct. Father certainly wouldn't have paid any attention to how you hang to replicate it perfectly."

"That's nae a thought I ever want to consider again."

"What did he speak to you about?"

"Nae much. Asked how we came to meet each other and the truth behind all the rumours."

His husband fidgeted as Hamish spoke, sitting up and toying with his rings before reclining to start all over again. "I see." He jumped up from the bed as swiftly as he had seated himself. He paced along its width, then between it and the window.

Finally, he stepped out onto the balcony to lean on the railing.

The wind nipped at Hamish's extremities as he joined his husband. The brief idea of retreating to at least throw on some smalls slithered along his thoughts before his pride got the better of him. He had seen Darshan weather similar states. He could do it as well.

He leant on the stone railing, staring out at the palace garden far below as he waited for Darshan to speak further. Not a single cloud darkened the sky, leaving the world illuminated by the moon. The pond shimmered with the light, more than the small orbs of yellow dotting the pathways through the garden.

From this height, he could see over the palace's outer walls. The moonlight glittered along the ocean, cool and impassive. The hazy spray of stars twinkled out beyond the moon's glow.

Seeing that his husband wasn't going to offer up any information, Hamish asked, "What's wrong? I thought you'd be happy your father has blessed our union." Or was he mistaken about that?

"I *am* happy about that—overjoyed, in fact—but..." His fingers dug into the railing. "He sought confirmation from you, even after I had spoken with him, even when I—" He sighed. "After everything we've been through, I thought I had figured it all out, that my father *had* sent those assassins, that *he* was the only one behind all these attacks and it would stop once we got home." Darshan hung his head. "But he's not."

"Is that nae a good thing?" The *Mhanek* could've hampered any chance of a peaceful life if he chose. More than anyone else.

"It is nice to have him approving for once, if begrudgingly so. But if the attacks weren't his doing, then someone else is targeting you. Someone we know nothing about." He stared up at Hamish. "I've been protecting you from the claws of a phantom. And it won't stop until we find them." The moonlight blanched his olive-brown skin, putting a deathly hue to the worried expression. "I'm used to risking my own life. But others?" He shook his head. "Not like this, not knowing they couldn't defend themselves. And certainly never against people who aren't in control of their actions."

"Hush, me heart." He cupped Darshan's chin, tilting the man's head until that hazel gaze met his. There was pure dread in those eyes. Not even the gleam of the moonlight across his glasses could hide it. "There'll be time for panicking later. Now isnae it. We're finally home. Sure, we might have a few more steps to go through before we can fully settle into lifelong happiness, but they're wee problems."

One side of Darshan's mouth hitched upwards. "You think assassinations from unknown quarters are small things?" He chuckled, the sound quivering with the dregs of fear. "You're already starting to sound like a Udynean."

"I wouldnae say *that*." He could never face danger with the same brazenness as his husband, but he had something that the man seemed to be lacking in the here and now. "I *do* have every faith in you, though."

Darshan ducked his head, but not before Hamish caught the unabashed smile. "You're right. We *are* home. And safe for the moment."

Hamish trapped his tongue between his teeth. Had news of the attack by the hypnotised guards not reached Darshan? Or did his husband mean only now the Nulled Ones watched over him? He would ask later. Right now, he needed to get Darshan out of this mood.

He bent to kiss his husband.

Darshan practically melted into his arms. He sighed, the wisp of his breath slipping down Hamish's throat, before he straightened again. "I suppose the only actual obstacle is in having an heir and that is largely a matter of waiting."

"Then, how about a wee private celebration for arriving at our destination in one piece?" He inched back towards the bed, towing his husband. If he could get Darshan there, all the fuss of the day would fall off the man's shoulders.

"And where do you think you're taking me?" His voice sounded lightly innocent, but the quirk of his lips whispered that he already knew.

Even so, Hamish felt compelled to answer, "To bed."

"To *sleep*?" The flash of a wicked grin briefly marred the otherwise perfectly formed wide-eyed innocence of his expression. "You know," he whispered, resting the back of his hand on one cheek as if divulging a great secret. "We're not supposed to be sleeping in the same bed right now. *Mhanek's* orders."

"Aye, I remember him saying something along those lines." And, clearly, Darshan had already chosen to ignore the decree. Hamish drew his husband hard against him, whispering in the same conspiratorial tone the man used. "But what if we didnae actually sleep?"

A feral grin took Darshan's mouth. It gleamed in his eyes and rasped his breath. He ran his tongue along his teeth, eyeing Hamish as if he planned to devour him. "Have I ever told you how much I love you, *mea lux*?"

"Many times, me heart." It was a declaration that he prayed to the Goddess he would never tire of hearing.

Darshan ran a finger down Hamish's chest. "But you are already fully disrobed." His lips twisted into an insincere pout. "Half the fun of foreplay is in the removal of clothing."

"That's fine." The back of his heel grazed the first step. Hamish swung them about, coaxing Darshan up, relishing how it put them closer in height. "We can still enjoy the other half." He flicked open the top button of Darshan's sherwani. "And there's still getting you to the same level of naked." He bent to suck on his husband's neck as he blindly sought out the rest of the buttons.

Darshan moaned. His roaming fingers slid all over Hamish, digging into the hair on his chest and up to glide over his shoulders. He aided briefly in shedding the sherwani, and the shirt beneath, before completely disengaging to throw off his footwear and remove the rest of his clothes.

Hamish sat on the end of the bed, parting the gauzy curtains to inch himself into the middle. The sheer fabric fell back into place and shrouded the sight of Darshan undressing in a pale mist.

With them both naked, his husband took the steps leading up to the mattress in a flurry of movement. He flung open the curtains and launched himself onto the bed to clamber across the blankets, halting only once he straddled Hamish's outstretched legs. "We'll have to be quiet. Your current guards won't be as forgiving of my trespassing as the last shift were."

"Is *that* how you got in? Bribery?"

"I would never stoop to anything so crass." His gaze dropped and his tongue—the one Hamish had felt upon him so many times—peeked out to wet his lips. "I simply told them I wished an audience with my husband."

"And they let you in?" Could anyone have done it? What if he wanted to sneak into Darshan's chambers? Would they let him? Or was them turning a blind eye a privilege they extended only to the *vris Mhanek*?

"Of course." He slid his hands up Hamish's chest, the slight press of the tips as they sank into the hair drawing a shuddering gasp from Hamish's lips. Darshan stretched atop him, his whole body hot and taut as he strained to capture Hamish's mouth in a needy kiss that spoke of weeks of separation rather than the mere handful of hours it had truly been.

Darshan sat back, his fingers sliding back down Hamish's abdomen. The same slight pressure traced the hint of his muscles and stopped only once his fingers reached the base of his shaft, where his touch became a silken glide thrumming with the faintest hint of magic.

With that soft rhythm, his husband silently coaxed him ever closer to the edge, his palm hot and getting hotter.

"Dinnae you burn me," Hamish grated, struggling to keep the image from his thoughts and ruin everything. Whilst his husband was more than capable of righting such a wrong, that didn't mean Hamish was open to getting intentionally hurt.

"*Burn?*" Darshan snarled. "You think I—?" He inhaled deeply with a grumble. "I. Am. *Not*. Going. To. Burn. You." His hand snapped up and down Hamish's length at every word.

Despite his declaration, the heat radiating from Darshan's hand grew, sitting on the edge of discomfort.

A familiar tingling sensation suddenly infused Hamish. *Healing magic.* It buzzed along his skin, burrowed beneath, reinvigorating tired muscles and soothing small twinges he hadn't even noticed.

Hamish sank into the feeling, floating. He tipped back his head, instinctively muffling his groan. No matter how many times Darshan did this, Hamish would always find himself on the cusp of losing control.

" 'Mish?" The call came so softly that Hamish first thought he had imagined it. "I don't suppose you've any oil amongst your things."

He shook his head. Somehow, Darshan always wound up being the one to carry that. "It'll be fine without it." Hamish had lost count of how many times he spoke those exact words. It wouldn't be the first time he had done without such an aid, although his husband refused the idea even after weeks of travelling across Tirglas. Hamish had learnt a lot about sexual intimacy without penetration during that time.

But the possessive gleam in Darshan's eyes told Hamish that his husband wouldn't be satisfied with anything else.

Rather than give the usual refusal and bring them both to a climax another way, Darshan nodded and moved into position. He still prepared Hamish, using the only lubricant they had at hand.

Hamish bit his lip as Darshan silently positioned them, his breath rasping. His past was riddled with enough instances to tell him this wasn't ideal, but Darshan would stop if it became too much. *Better than letting him mope.*

He winced at his husband's abrupt entry. It wasn't the first time one of them had been that little bit too eager, but where had the usual warning gone? The silent reassurance that Hamish's needs weren't a secondary concern?

Even Darshan's movements were strange. Gone was his gentle husband, the man who had shown him that sex didn't have to mean pain. There still was little beyond a dull ache, but the being who had taken Darshan's place was far too single-minded. Not needlessly rough, but his every thrust carried a force that brooked no objections.

There was none of the little kisses and caresses that usually came with sex either. Darshan lay propped on his arms, his head drooping, his face obscured by hair and the heavy rasp of his breath heating Hamish's chest.

"Love," Hamish managed between thrusts. "Slow down." They weren't huddled in the back of a tavern storeroom, hoping no one came upon them. Or holed up in Castle Mullhind, desperately praying that his mother's guards didn't discover their actions. "We have all night." He didn't want it to be over this soon.

Darshan lifted his head, staring at him with the same expression as a rabid boarhound. "You are *mine*, you know." He punctuated every other gravelly word with a body-trembling thrust.

"Dar—"

"No one is taking you from me," his husband grated. "Your mother couldn't. My half-sister failed. As did my father. I'm not letting this blasted assassin succeed."

"*Darshan,*" Hamish grunted through gritted teeth. "Me heart..." Gathering himself, he hefted them over, pinning the man beneath him. "You need to stop." He cupped either side of Darshan's face. Only then did he notice the tears wetting his husband's cheeks. "I'm nae going anywhere, love. But if you keep this up, you're going to break something." Possibly Hamish's pelvis.

"I—" Darshan rubbed at one eye, setting his glasses askew. "I'm sorry. I just— I'm sorry." He peered up at Hamish, his other eye still closed. "Did I hurt you?"

"A wee bit," he admitted. It was the familiar ache of his youth. Nothing he couldn't bear.

Horror took Darshan's face. He slid his hands down Hamish's sides, clasping Hamish's hips. Warmth emanated from his palms. It burrowed into flesh, seeking out the source of the pain and mending it.

"I think," Darshan murmured as the healing magic faded, "we shouldn't pursue sex any further tonight. It would appear I am in the wrong mindset to do so safely."

"Aye."

"I cannot apologise enough, *mea lux.*"

Hamish wrapped his arm around Darshan's shoulders, drawing his husband onto the blankets beside him and tucking the man's head beneath his own chin. "I've had worse experiences."

"That's no excuse. I should've conducted myself better and done something else, despite your assurances. I'm ashamed to have put my pleasure over your comfort. It will not happen again."

"I ken that." He kissed the top of Darshan's head. "For now..." Hamish shuffled along the blankets. "Sleep would be best."

His husband squirmed in his grip. "Wait! Let me remove these first." He unhooked his glasses from behind his ears and laid them on a small shelf jutting from the side of the headboard. "And get under the sheets." A bit more wriggling finally had Darshan slipping into bed and snuggling up against him, his head pillowed on Hamish's bicep.

"Better?"

Darshan's soft sigh warmed Hamish's neck. "Much."

Hamish lay still, his gaze settling on the railing that held the gauzy curtains. The room was still illuminated by the lantern Darshan had lit, yet he hadn't the will to snuff the light. He listened to the gentle whisper of wind slipping through the open balcony door. *We should've shut that.* He didn't know if it would get any colder—the room was on the hotter side—but he didn't fancy waking up because he had frozen his arse off. "Can you hear the plants from up here?" He knew that Darshan would shut himself inside to keep the voices at bay.

Darshan shook his head. "It's too far from the ground."

Hamish grunted his acknowledgement. He hadn't thought them that far up. "Are you going to summon a hedgewitch?" That had been Anjali's suggestion after hearing how her brother had come into his new power. She had been insistent.

"In all honesty, what's some 'witch with no power going to do?" Darshan had asked the same of his sister. "The best they can do is coo over me like some remnant of their past. This isn't their power. *I* did this to myself. *I* must learn to control it. No one can teach me that."

"So what if they cannae do it themselves? Who's to say they dinnae also have the resources to teach you? What harm is there in trying?" At worst, Darshan would be precisely where he was now.

His husband exhaled a long, slow breath, then uttered a soft, "All right. If that's what you would have me do, then I shall."

They returned to silence. Despite the trials of the day, sleep was not about to come easily. They might've agreed to stop when it came to sex, but his body wasn't having a bar of it. It grumbled its complaints on lacking the promised release.

Darshan appeared to be having the same trouble. He shuffled and adjusted himself continuously, huffing every so often.

Hamish's mind also refused to still, with rogue thoughts galloping about his head like wild horses. "Why did you chase me?" That question in particular had started bouncing about the darker parts of his mind ever since listening to Anjali and her friend's speculations on the subject. He knew the two women had only been teasing, testing his resilience, but he still wondered. If he was really that far outside the range of men Darshan usually preferred, then... "Why'd you marry me?"

"I love you. Should I require a reason beyond that?" Darshan sat up, staring worriedly down at him. "Are you certain my father didn't get hold of your mind?"

"For nae more than a wee moment," he assured the man. Anjali had checked him thoroughly, muttering how it was impossible for him to be lacking the customary scarring that magical hypnosis caused. He hadn't known what to say to that. "These thoughts are me own."

"I don't know what to tell you that I haven't already." He ran a hand along Hamish's bicep, his fingertips barely grazing skin. "When we first met, it was like seeing something step out of a dream."

Hamish rolled his eyes. "Poetry? Really? I'm being serious here."

"So am I." He lifted Hamish's arm, clasping it to his chest. "I used to dream of men like you. Big. Strong." Darshan pressed his lips against Hamish's palm at each word. One side quirked up as he said, "Able to split me in two with a single thrust."

"I dinnae think I can do *that*." He wasn't even prepared to make the attempt. He'd been on the receiving end of a similar act. It had been his first experience. An extremely unpleasant one.

Darshan chuckled. "Not literally, *mea lux*."

"You married me because of that?"

"I got you into bed because of it. I married you because, as I've said before, you're a good man." He pressed his cheek to the back of Hamish's fingers. "A sweet and gentle being. The rarest thing in the empire. I'm sure there are plenty out there who would insist I don't deserve you, but am thoroughly selfish enough to want you all to myself anyway."

"I'm glad. It saved me life." He truly would've been dead, several times over, if it hadn't been for his husband. The man had done more than free him from an existence barely worth living for. Darshan had shown him what it was to truly live.

He had almost forgotten how.

It wasn't the only thing that would've been different without Darshan. Having helped raise his sibling's children, Hamish had always wanted some of his own. The reality of what was necessary to get them had been the only thing holding him back. Darshan had given him another option there, too. "You ever wonder what they're going to look like?"

"Hmm?" Darshan flopped back on the mattress, resuming using Hamish's arm as a pillow. "Who?"

"Our bairns. You said you wanted more than one. You ever wonder?" Hamish had, from the very moment Darshan explained what he knew of the process.

"My father would've barely sent the message. Conception of any child won't be possible for at least another two months. And that's if the Niholian breeders begin their journey right away by ship, which would hopefully not fall astray of pirates."

"I ken that. But I cannae stop picturing their wee faces." All chubby cheeks and big eyes. Just like his niece and nephews.

"With your eyes and hair."

Hamish scoffed. "May the Goddess nae be so cruel." He didn't mind sharing his eye colour. But if what Darshan said was true about his hair being a rarity in southern Udynea, he would've preferred his children to not inherit it. He fingered his husband's dark brown hair. "What about your wee curls?"

"Too common. The *Mhanek* should stand out like a bonfire."

"They'll stand out as it is." It would be a long time before any child of theirs took the throne. At least, he hoped so. "We do breed them big, you ken."

"Oh gods." Groaning, Darshan rolled onto his back, dramatically touching the back of his hand to his forehead. "I'm going to be the shortest of the lot, aren't I?"

Laughter bubbled through him. Brushing a kiss across his husband's upraised forearm, his gaze slid to one of the sections cut out in the headboard. "Since you're here, I wonder if you can answer one more wee question."

Darshan lowered his arm. "I shall certainly do my best."

"Why are there holes in the headboard?"

"Holes? Oh." He tipped his head back to eye them, grinning. "Put your hand through one."

Hamish reached up, hesitating just before the opening.

"It won't hurt, *mea lux*. I promise."

He shoved his hand through and the bottom seemed to fall out of his stomach. There was a strangeness to the world. *Muffled.* Like it was cloaked in snow. *Dull.*

Shuddering, he withdrew his arm and the room popped back into normality. "What was that?"

"So he *can* feel it," Darshan murmured as though in a daze. "Even as weak as he is, it still nullifies. Fascinating."

"Dinnae talk about me as if I'm nae here. What is it?"

His husband reached up to caress the inside curve of the hole. "There are thin rings of *infitialis* embedded in each section."

"I thought you said it was rare and volatile?" Why were they putting bits of it into headboards?

"It *is*, if still in its raw state or worked wrong."

"Why is it in there?" It obviously wasn't done to immediately nullify whoever stayed in their guest room otherwise they would've hidden it better. But what other purpose could it serve?

"It's an aid. Some find controlling their magic during sex a chore. The layer in each ring is paper thin. A veneer. If it was thicker, I would feel the effects of being near it, but like this it only suppresses magical abilities for the duration it encircles a person."

"During sex?" He recalled Darshan stating something along the lines of not being able to maintain a shield during the act. But he didn't remember the man having any trouble keeping his magic from manifesting during sex.

No, that wasn't entirely true. He recalled the servants back in Castle Mullhind had spoken of a window in the mezzanine bearing heat-warped stone and finger indents. Hamish had been deep enough in his drink to remember only flashes of that night, but he had supposedly pleasured his lover orally whilst Darshan sat upon the sill.

Once. Not a bad record considering how many times they'd been intimate. "I dinnae recall you having many problems there." Then again, there *were* all the stories of shattering temple statues during festivals. Tales Darshan freely admitted were true. He had claimed to be drunk during those times as well as being the centrepiece to an orgy.

"What I've *had*," Darshan said, "is practice. *Lots* of it."

If Hamish thought about the night they'd spent on their journey down, there would be the odd impression of a handprint seared into a bed railing or headboard that he was certain hadn't been there prior to them having sex. Nothing anywhere near the destructive potential of the rumours. "I think you're talking bullshit. You've clearly nae had enough practice, nae judging by tonight's wee performance."

Darshan's gasp warmed Hamish's shoulder. "Such insolence," he breathed, a lazy grin widening his mouth. "I'd like to see you do better."

"Nae a chance."

"Well, putting penetrative sex aside, there are other things. If you're still interested," he added, almost as an afterthought.

What sort of question was that? *If I'm still—* He chuckled to himself. Was a bloody stag interested in rutting during the spring? "What did you have in mind?"

"We could—" Darshan sat up, gnawing on his bottom lip in thought. "No, we can't, can we?" He grumbled something that sounded like a disgruntled agreement before Hamish could ask. "Gods, I wish you still had my gift."

The leather toy Darshan had presented him with one morning back in Tirglas had vanished from Hamish's effects somewhere between leaving the dock at Nulshar and them finally reaching the city on the other side of the lake. *Shame.* They'd used it a number of times to varying degrees of success. He did prefer the real thing, though, no matter how much Darshan made the crude copy buzz and vibrate with his magic.

"How about this?" Darshan stretched out a hand, running his fingertips down Hamish's arm. A wisp of magic tingled across Hamish's skin.

"I thought you didnae do sex magic?" he teased.

"What I said is that we don't call it that, not that I didn't do it." His hand slid lower, creeping beneath the sheets and down Hamish's abdomen to halt with his fingertips barely brushing the base of his shaft. "Do you want me to or not?"

Bastard. There was no way he was about to beg, no matter how much Darshan wanted to hear it. He flung the blanket's back, baring both of them to the night air and putting his full erect length on display. "What do *you* think?"

Once again grinning like a boy being told he could have all the honey cakes he desired, Darshan bent over him. "Remember," he whispered, the rasp of his breath pebbling skin in the brief moment before those lips started kissing their way along Hamish's collarbone. "We still have to be quiet."

Sucking on his bottom lip, Hamish tried to muffle the groan

tightening his throat as his husband's hands glided back up his chest. The buzzing of Darshan's magic running along his skin certainly didn't make staying quiet easy. Pain he could bear in absolute silence but pleasure, especially when given by someone who knew his body, threatened to draw all sorts of sounds from his lips.

The Nulled Ones guarding his room would forgive them if they made a little noise. Wouldn't they?

And what was the worst thing that could happen if they didn't?

The thought vanished quicker than a summer's mist as his husband's hand completed a second downward journey, this time brushing over Hamish's length. The light vibration tingling through it sent his breath shuddering from him. His hips rose towards the touch, deepening the sensation.

He turned his head, desperately catching Darshan's mouth with his own. His heart pounded mercilessly in his chest, battering against its bony prison.

Darshan broke the kiss first. He nuzzled Hamish's neck, sucked at his collarbone and slowly made his way south. "Still eager as ever to see me, I see," he whispered. Wrapping his fingers around Hamish's length, he dipped his head. His tongue wet the tip, circling in small motions that had Hamish biting his knuckles.

Mercifully, Darshan spared no time with his usual teasing. He drew Hamish deeply into his mouth, moving his tongue in a manner that Hamish could never quite mimic. His hand continued its roaming, massaging Hamish's backside and toying with his balls.

A finger, humming with magic, glided between his butt cheeks. It slipped inside him, working deeper to the rhythm of Darshan's bobbing head.

Caught by surprise, the gasp that left Hamish's mouth was louder than he had intended.

Chaos erupted from out in the hall as the two Nulled Ones stationed there all but broke down the door. They sprang into the room, weapons at the ready. "What—?"

The wet pop of Hamish's length leaving Darshan's mouth silenced everyone. His husband calmly sat back on his heels, as if he hadn't just been bent over Hamish in the middle of orally pleasuring him.

Hamish remained frozen, very much aware of the digit still deep within him. His chest tightened, his breath almost nonexistent and his heart beating hard enough for him to feel in his temples. His face burned. If he could've moved, he would've buried it in the pillow he still clutched.

The Nulled Ones seemed to take all of this in and, without even a glance towards each other, backed out through the doorway.

Regaining enough of his senses to move, Hamish lobbed a pillow in the wake of their retreat. It bypassed the curtains surrounding the bed and landed squarely against the closing door.

His face continued its inferno-like state. He buried it in his hands, muttering obscenities to himself. How much had they bloody seen? Whilst the original pair guarding the door had both been human, there were elves amongst the Nulled Ones. And the moon had crept a little further around in the sky, its light illuminating the bottom half of the bed.

But the curtains turned everything hazy. Could it be that they'd seen only outlines? Except they must've known it was their *vris Mhanek* in here with him, otherwise they would've investigated further.

Darshan shifted, crawling up the bed to kneel beside him. He laid a hand on Hamish's chest and the soft hum of healing magic seeped into his body, likely sensing the still-rapid heartbeat and flushing. "Relax, *mea lux*. We won't be disturbed any more tonight, I promise."

True to his word, no one else did intrude, leaving them to enjoy the rest of the night in peace until they lay tangled in each other, exhausted and satisfied. Hamish curled himself around Darshan, pressing as close as he could. His fingers wandered up and down Darshan's arm as their lips brushed each other in drowsy kisses.

As he drifted off into the fog of sleep, he barely registered that the moon had faded from the sky.

Chapter 30

"Hamish?" The voice called him as though from somewhere far in the distance.

He stirred at the sound of his name. His eyelids fluttered, not quite ready to let him wake. Pale, cool sunlight leaked between his lashes. Was it morning already? But the sun in Udynea was somehow richer, a deep golden colour. A light globe, then.

"Sweetie, can you hear me?"

He knew that voice, the way the rolling inflections of his native tongue were spoken in soft notes. It was the voice that had once dictated his every movement.

"Mum?" he rasped. At last, his eyes opened at his command. He stared up at the figure hovering over his bed. It looked like his mother, rightly enough. But a lot younger, the wrinkles not as pronounced on her face and the grey in her blonde hair wasn't as widespread.

The worry wrinkling her forehead quickly smoothed. She stroked his hair, brushing aside the coils to run cool fingers across his brow. "Welcome back to the waking world, sweetie. You gave everyone quite the scare." She grinned. "But it's good to see your senses havenae suffered."

After everything she had said, after claiming he was dead to her, he didn't think he would ever see her face again. "What are you doing in Udynea?" Had she decided that declaring him as dead wasn't enough? Had she come to make sure he actually was? *I'm still alive,* he reminded himself. If she had wanted him dead, he never would've awoken.

His mother laughed, a light sound that almost perfectly masked her contempt. How had he mistaken it in the past? "We're nae in Udynea. Dinnae you recognise the place?" She indicated the room in a sweeping gesture.

He did. It was the old cloister, the one they had taken Hamish to after the stablemaster left him broken and bloody. *I thought it was destroyed.* He remembered pointing out the ruins to Darshan. Had he been wrong? "This isnae possible." He struggled to sit up.

"Careful." She adjusted something on his chest, shifting fabric as though arranging a festive table.

His gaze slid from the cloister walls to the bandages wrapped around his torso. Blood had seeped through some of the layers. "What's going on? What have you done?"

"Dinnae you remember? You were attacked by a bear."

Hamish fingered the bandages. Something about it tugged at his thoughts. "Aye." He doubted he'd ever be rid of the image of it barrelling towards him, a wall of fur, claws and teeth. Of pain.

Of the darkness that had sucked at his very being.

Dar had been there. The thought hit him like a stroppy ram. *That* was what nagged in the back of his mind. The man had blasted the bear off Hamish and then charred the animal before it could choose to flee or fight. He had also healed the injuries completely. The act had altered his husband beyond anyone's full understanding. Hamish had no need of bandages afterwards. "What's really going on? Where's Dar?"

"Who?" His mother looked genuinely confused for an instant before perking up. "Oh, you mean the Udynean lad." She smiled, the soft expression one he hadn't seen directed at him in a long time, since before the first time he had been a patient of this very cloister. "He's long gone. Took the signed treaty papers and boarded a ship headed Udynea way. Dinnae you remember?"

Nae. That didn't seem right. His mother had destroyed all chances of a treaty with the Udynea Empire whilst she still lived. For his husband to have left him behind was beyond imagining. "Dar would never—"

She scoffed. "I did warn you that spellsters are nae to be trusted. Doubly so for Udynean ones." She reached out to cup his jaw. "It must be hard, waking up to such betrayal."

He recoiled from the touch. There *was* a betrayal going on here, but it wasn't Darshan's doing. *This isnae real.* That was the only logical explanation. He had definitely been travelling across land with his husband. To wake up back in Tirglas? That would've been an enormous feat.

The world wavered at the edges of his vision.

What was it, then? Not a simple nightmare. He'd had enough of those to sense a difference, a solidness that almost felt right. Was this some sort of hallucination? Some magical trickery feeding off his nightmares?

His mother's smile froze. "You need time. I understand." She stood, her hands clasped before her in a pose he had long ago deciphered meant she was displeased with him. "It'll be all right. Your wife will help you adjust."

Wife? The heat drained from him. He shook his head, wincing as the shudder took his body. Dream or reality, the pain in his chest felt real enough. "I dinnae have a wife." The only marriage vows he had ever spoken had been to Darshan.

He swung out of bed, grunting as the pain in his chest increased at the strain. If this was some spellster's doing, he was going to kill them. "I dinnae ken what's going on, but I'm married to Darshan. He is me husband. He wouldnae just up and leave."

"Him leaving immediately was a stipulation of the treaty." That admission sounded closer to his mother.

"You're lying."

The world shuddered.

His legs buckled. Hamish grasped for the bed only to find it had vanished. As had much of the room. The light filtered through a single grubby window, illuminating the room in its proper derelict state.

Wake up. This was clearly a nightmare, he just needed to jolt himself out of it.

He slapped his cheeks to no effect. Why wasn't he waking? *Come on!* What were his alternatives? *The tower.* Jumping off the top should be enough.

He strode out through the remains of a doorway, heading for the only set of stairs heading up. Even if this dream turned out to be real, then leaping to his death from the tower was better than any alternative his mother offered.

Even after leaving her behind in the infirmary, his mother was waiting for him at the top of the stairs. She stiffly strode to stand before him, blocking off any further chance of ascending. She stared up at him, her face thrown into shadow. Like most of his family, she was nowhere near as short as Darshan and came to his chin. "No more wandering off on a whim, 'Mish. You will conduct yourself as a proper prince of Tirglas. That includes ensuring your wife has plenty of children."

"Never."

His mother straightened, her height stretching to match his, then surpassing it. Or was he shrinking? "What was that?"

"A wife and children was always *your* path for me. I refuse to take it."

"Ungrateful little rat." She grew further, her frame bulking, her shoulders hunching. Her face changed with every breath. Her jaw shifted, stretching into a muzzle full of sharp teeth that glistened in the meagre daylight filtering through the boarded up windows and dust.

Hamish stepped back, his heel teetering on the edge of the top step. His heart pounded, stuttering on the brink of failing. *This is a dream. Wake up. Wake up!*

Throughout the change, his mother's ice-blue eyes remained the same. The glare she levelled at him harsh enough to cut through steel. "Waste of air," she growled. "I should've let the winter take you. You're good for nothing else."

His chest tightened. His breath non-existent. *It's nae real.* Not once had his mother ever expressed that option. Not even when he'd been at his wildest.

"If you're not going to behave." She raised her hand, her *paw*, the claws gleaming. "Then you can send my regards to the Goddess!"

The paw swung. It hit his chest with a bone-crunching thud and sent him plummeting off the stairs.

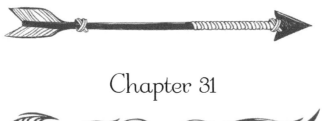

Chapter 31

Hamish sat up, his heart hammering and a distinct unsettling feeling in his gut. He felt his chest, his fingers finding nothing unfamiliar. Just hair, naked skin and scars. The latter was all that remained of the actual bear attack. He rubbed his chest, feeling the slight indents of the scars. No matter how quick a spellster healed their patient, such marks would remain.

He let out a shuddering breath and lifted his gaze to take in his surroundings. Rich, golden light filtered through a screen of curtains, turning the world beyond the bed hazy. Where was he? Not the old cloister. Was this another dream?

Shaking his head, he searched to free himself of the blankets. It didn't matter where he was, only that he needed to leave, needed to be anywhere but here in this strange bed with—

" 'Mish?"

Perched on the edge of the mattress, he twisted to face the owner of that velvety and sleep-slurred voice.

Sure enough, his husband lay sprawled across the other half of the bed, his face still partly scrunched into the pillow. One eye had settled on him, the gleam soft in the pale light. *"Mea lux, what is it?"*

"It's all right, I..." His attention drifted to the room. *The suite in the guest palace.* Nothing had changed beyond the time of day. He was in Minamist. His mother was far from here and powerless to alter his path. He flopped back onto the bed and scrubbed at his face. "Just a bad dream." He hadn't had them for a month now. He had hoped they were gone for good. None of his other nightmares had been that vivid. "It doesnae matter."

Darshan wriggled onto his side, extending one beseeching arm. "Come," he said, his voice still on the croaky side. "Lie next to me and tell me what you saw."

Slinking into his husband's arms, Hamish recounted all he remembered. Most of the details had faded like a spring mist, but the important ones remained.

When he was done, he remained in that calming grasp. He was safe here. Protected. Loved unconditionally.

It took a while for him to register the lack of noise. Beyond the low hum of his husband's soothing words and his own harsh breath, silence reigned. No screeching of birds or the muffled clatter of guards changing posts.

Just them.

His stomach grumbled. His mouth also tasted as though he'd been swilling swamp water.

What time was it? He eyeballed the sunlight. Dawn had definitely made its arrival known. How far from daybreak was another question. Maybe midmorning. "I think we slept in a wee bit," he murmured.

Darshan's hand flapped. A soft shushing escaped his lips like wind through the trees in winter. His hand continued to wander, seeking along the sheets until it found Hamish's forearm where he gave it a few uncoordinated taps.

Giving the hand an answering pat, Hamish clambered out of bed to stretch the kinks from his body before going about his usual morning routine.

His husband remained in his semi-dozing state. That always amazed Hamish. He'd never been one to loaf about once the sun was up. There had always been something to do back at Mullhind, be it in the castle or the surrounding farmland. He liked staying busy. It kept his thoughts from running in circles.

But now they had finally reached their destination. There was no need to be up at first light because they wouldn't be spending the day travelling.

What was he going to do with all that time? In Mullhind, he had officially been the unofficial go-to person for the local farmers. Someone they could air their grievances to whilst his older sister oversaw trade and his brother, Gordon, commanded the guard. But he couldn't do that here. Could he? From what he'd seen of the Udynea's citizens, they were quick to complain but hesitant to speak to authority figures.

What advice could he give those people, anyway? The farms closest to Minamist all seemed to grow rice. He had little experience with crops.

Did the court expect him to just bumble along, show up at the appropriate gatherings and generally be a trinket draped on his husband's arm? Darshan wouldn't expect him to be content as a glorified bauble. That couldn't be his lot in life.

A sharp, no-nonsense series of knocks rattled the door, jolting him from his musing.

Hamish waited a few seconds for some sort of announcement, but all he received was another door-shaking knock. "Keep your hair on," he muttered, hastening to open the door before the person on the other side pounded it down.

An elderly elven woman stood in the doorway, her fist still raised and her other hand occupied with fanning herself. Several other servants stood across the hall from them, one holding a silver cup, another bore a stack of papers and yet a third carried what looked to be clothes.

"About time," the old woman snapped, her fan closing with the same abruptness as a pair of shears. "I thought I was going to have to look for the key. These louts certainly haven't got it." She jerked a thumb at the two Nulled Ones standing sheepishly nearby. Neither one appeared to be of the original pair who had guarded him or the other duo who had burst into the room last night.

Hamish gripped the doorframe, crowding the space. "Can I help you?" The old woman looked familiar, but he'd seen a lot of elves wandering the palace grounds. Should he trust her? Judging by how the others winced, she carried some clout. What of the trio at her back?

The woman peered around him, her eyes narrowing and her lips puckering sourly. The guest room was gloomy, but her elven sight no doubt saw him clearly enough. "You make an exceptional impression of a door, but kindly stand aside."

"You are?"

The woman blinked up at him. "I'm Daama, personal attendant of the *vris Mhanek.*"

Daama. Hamish knew that name. *Dar's old nanny.* He'd vague memories of a woman following the man out of the palace gardens yesterday. She had looked bigger then, and her demeanour had been less abrupt.

"I believe this should suffice as proof." She fished out a fine chain of purple metal from beneath the high neck of her tunic. A golden disc swung on the end, stamped with Darshan's personal seal. *Ownership tags.* Darshan had described them.

Hamish hadn't expected them to be so unremarkable looking.

"That's a very fine collar." Especially next to the bulkier leather versions he'd seen elsewhere. If it wasn't for the disc labelling her as his husband's property, he never would've guessed. His fingers twitched. One jerk of the hand could easily snap the chain and see her free. "And, if I'm nae mistaken, it's *infitialis?*" That meant she was also a spellster. He understood why leashing a criminal would be required to make them safer, but the woman who had nursed and raised the *vris Mhanek*?

He eyed the Nulled Ones flanking the doorway. They looked slightly wary of Daama. How would the pair react if he broke the collar? Something else nagged in the back of his mind. Hadn't Darshan mentioned something about the metal? That it was unstable? *Aye, in its raw form.* But also, if tampered with. His husband had meant by magic, but what if Hamish used brute force?

He sighed. *Nae worth the risk.* If the chain exploded, it would kill her before she had the chance to shield herself. Hamish stepped aside, allowing all four of the servants to enter.

Daama marched into the room and over to the bed where Darshan still slept soundly. "Get up!" She prodded his shoulder.

His husband rolled over, peering at the woman. " 'Ma?" he mumbled, rubbing at an eye. The act further smeared the already streaked kohl. "I'm married. You can't just walk in. 'Mish doesn't take kindly to people marching in on him when he's naked and—" His gaze alighted on Hamish, likely taking in the fully dressed state. "What are you even doing here, 'Ma?"

"I ask that of myself, child," the woman wearily replied. "There I was, entering your chambers, when what do I find?" She jabbed a finger in his direction and, to Hamish's amazement, Darshan flinched. "*You* right where you shouldn't be. What do you think you are doing?"

"Sleeping," he grumped back. "Before you woke me, at least."

Daama swatted at him with her fan, landing a deft clip over the back of his head. "Don't sass me, child." She gestured for one of the other servants to come forward with the silver cup.

Darshan's eyes lit up at the sight. "*Kofe!*" He reached out for the cup. "Nanny, you truly are a spirit of hope."

With a twitch of her brow, Daama backed up to the balcony and tossed the cup's contents out the window.

His husband stared slack-jawed. "Why? That was—"

"It *was* perfectly drinkable *kofe*," she corrected, the sharpness of her voice bringing up memories of Hamish's childhood tutoring. "That would've been about an hour ago, when I had it first brewed. *If* you had been in your own chambers, it would not have turned into a cold, bitter mess not even fit for the birds. Now, get up," she commanded with all the sternness of a guard captain.

Darshan glowered at her, folding his arms like a child and remaining unmoving in his seated position in the bed.

Unbelievable. Did the man always act like this around those he was close with? He could understand the hostility and ill-tempered lashing out at Onella—the woman had been just as bad in that regard—but to speak to an elder in such a fashion? Especially one who had raised him. *Unthinkable.* Definitely so in Tirglas.

"Am I not allowed to be alone with my husband, now?" Darshan snipped back at his old nanny, earning another thwack over the back of his head with her fan.

"Nae really," Hamish said before the woman could. "You ken that being here is in defiance of your father's orders." Was that the reason behind the sudden shift in his behaviour? He seemed to recall the man's twin warning him of such displays. *And his father.* Although, the *Mhanek* had less warned and more stated that few could deny Darshan anything. "If you've a problem in waiting until this other wedding is done, then maybe you should ask for your father to revoke the order instead of lashing out like a blind pup?"

"Oh." Daama clapped her hand against her cheek. "You found someone with *sense.*" She smiled fondly at Hamish.

A soft pang of sadness further hollowed his already empty stomach, brought on by faded memories of his grandparents before the plague. His grandfather used to have the same expression whenever Hamish or one of his siblings showed him a new talent. Even if they failed. Especially then.

Sniffing, he scrubbed at his face with a hand. "Get up," he gruffly commanded his husband. "I'm hungry." Food wouldn't chase all of the hollowness away, but it would take the edge off.

"I'm sure you are both starving," Daama said. "The midmorning meal should be ready by the time you reach the dining hall. I'm sure your family would be overjoyed to have the pair of you there," she added to Darshan as the man scoffed.

Sighing, Darshan clambered out of the bed. He trotted down the stairs, not even attempting to conceal his nakedness from the others sharing the room, and into the bathing chamber.

"Midmorning meal?" Hamish echoed. "Dinnae you mean breakfast?" During their journey, they'd eaten at dawn and dusk, with the odd stop in the middle of the day, but back in Tirglas, most ate after the morning chores were done. He couldn't see how palace life would require either schedule.

"Has no one told you that spellsters consume a lot of energy?"

"Aye." His husband had revealed to him—along with their entire escort party during their journey to the cloister—that magic was more than summoning miracles from the very air and manipulating objects. Doing anything beyond a shield took the same energy to fuel the body as physical labour. If the man hadn't told him, he never would've come to that conclusion. Most Tirglasians had appetites that could easily match Darshan's.

"Five meals a day is standard around here." Daama eyed him critically. "And I'm certain it takes no small amount of food to keep someone of your stature going."

"His nephews could certainly given several of those in the court a challenge," Darshan said as he returned from the other room. Still lacking even undergarments, he crossed over to where the servant carrying a pile of clothing stood rooted to the spot. The servant extended her burden for Darshan to select an outfit from and don.

"Whilst I have you here," Daama said, ushering the last of the servants closer to pluck a page off the sheaf of papers they clutched nearly to the point of destruction. "There are a few matters that you must attend to. Shall I?"

Darshan paused in tying his trousers and gestured for her to continue.

"The first matter is a simple case. Lord Aarus wishes to barter Mylen for one of his own."

Barter. It almost sounded like a request Hamish would've heard from the Tirglasian farmers about putting a bull to stud. Was Mylen a person? An animal? Daama's expression said little beyond being annoyed and there could be a number of reasons behind that.

"Tell him no," Darshan said. "I don't trade people."

"I did. Several times. It would seem he insists on a face-to-face refusal."

"And he shall have it." His husband's reply was muffled as he slipped into a clean undershirt. "Set up a meeting in the council hall this evening. Then see to it that the guards show him the inside of a cell for a few months. That should soften his arrogance."

Daama bowed her head. "As you wish." She slipped another page off the pile. "The next matter..."

Hamish relaxed into one of the chairs, only marginally listening as the pair communed. A lot of what they discussed seemed to be the tail end of agreements that required Darshan's ruling. And politics.

Hamish would be the first to admit he hadn't the head for such matters. *I'll need to learn.* It hadn't been expected for him to have more than a rudimentary knowledge of the law in Tirglas—if he'd ever been in a position to gain the throne, he could've changed it as he pleased—but Udynean law was a little more rigid. Not even the *Mhanek* could bypass it.

In some ways, that was a relief. He'd seen what absolute authority led to. His mother could still decide on a whim to chase him down. She might not get far now he was beyond her influence, but it didn't rule out the possibility of a war. Likely, the only thing keeping that at bay was his brother's reasoning. But if she chose to, nothing short of the clans uprising would stop her.

" 'Mish?"

Jolted by the address, Hamish straightened in his seat. Had something happened? A quick survey of the room had everything looking fine. No guards. No people beyond his husband, Daama and the three servants. "Aye?"

"The charities, *mea lux*." His husband handed over the paper. "I asked what one you would choose."

Hamish stared at the words. The list. The curls and whirls that made up the main bulk of Udynean script shifted the longer he looked. Uncertainty creaked out his mouth in a wordless sound.

Darshan blinked. "Is Maari's penmanship really that bad?" He turned back to Daama. "I thought his hands had stopped aching. Didn't the healers fix the problem?"

"Old age is a difficult disease to stem," the woman softly replied.

"It's nae that," Hamish insisted. "I—" He wet his lips and ran a quick eye around the room. Not only did Daama still share the space, so did the other three servants. Sure, they bustled about, gathering up Darshan's discarded clothing and cleaning already spotless furniture. He could hardly admit he couldn't read half the words in front of all these ears. "I just cannae choose."

His husband's lips flattened. He nodded. "It *is* a puzzler, isn't it? There's the usual requests from the temples, of course. Always is. But take these two." He singled out the charities with a forefinger, the rings glittering as he tapped each one. "Do I help the orphanage feed its charges or assist in the repair of a healer's building in the Pits?"

"Can you nae do both?"

The servants paused in their work, sharing surprised glances amongst themselves.

Daama's brows rose. "Perhaps you do not understand how this works. If the *vris Mhanek* donated to every charity asking for aid, he'd have beggared himself by the beginning of the wet season."

"I wasnae asking him to do that." He might not have needed to pitch in more than his own labour when it came to charitable work in Tirglas, but he knew how donations operated. "Two instead of one," he said to Darshan. "Can you do it?"

His husband stared at the paper, stroking his moustache with his other hand. "I believe so."

"But—" Daama started.

"One decent payment to aid in the building won't beggar me, 'Ma. I'm sure I've saved a fortune by not being at the festivals this year."

Hamish discreetly cleared his throat to keep from laughing. Judging by the woman's face, she knew precisely what her charge got up to at each festival. And likely how many statues the man had broken during the revelry.

"Make sure the court hears of it, too," Darshan added. "Discreetly, of course. Who knows, it might get some members to donate in lieu of their usual grousing about the state of the Pits." He signed the bottom of the paper and handed it back to the woman. "Also, kindly inform Elke that there might be an increase in production from the copper mines on the western shore of the Shar. That should help."

Copper? His husband had mentioned owning a mine as they crossed the Shar. He had pointed it out, although Hamish had spotted nothing but trees and hills. He hadn't realised the ore they mined was copper. It was one of the resources Udynea had desperately wanted from Tirglas.

Daama wrinkled her nose as if she caught a whiff of spoiled milk. "Zah told me about the lakeship. And I believe he, too, questioned the wisdom of it. The costs of running such a vessel are—"

"—minor in comparison to the hiring of one and its crew whenever we need to ship goods," Darshan cut in. "Anavi has been pestering me for years about purchasing my own lakeship. Now she has one." He stood, stomping his feet into his shoes. They weren't the hardy boots he'd been wearing since Tirglas. More like the slippers the servants wore. "Shall we retire to the imperial palace? I would very much like to reach the dining hall before all the food is gone."

Before anyone could answer, Darshan tucked his arm into the crook of Hamish's elbow and escorted them out of the room, trailing Nulled Ones and servants in their wake.

Chapter 32

After travelling through Udynea for some months, the dining room was about what Hamish expected; a wide-open space with huge windows running down one side. Like the many *kofe* houses they'd visited, the floor was recessed, although the majority of the space was taken up by a long and low table rather than just a pile of pillows.

The *Mhanek* sat at the far end with Anjali already seated at his side. And circling the rest of the table?

He knew that Darshan had twelve living siblings. All of them half-sisters bar his twin. He had met one in Nulshar and expected a handful would still be living in the palace, especially given that the ages of the last four ranged between nineteen and ten. When it came to the rest, he assumed they would be with their new families as was the Udynean custom.

He hadn't expected to face all the siblings he had left to meet.

Ten pairs of eyes turned as their entrance was announced. Ten faces regarded him with the same cool curiosity.

Hamish gently wiggled his fingers in acknowledgement. "You didnae tell me they would *all* be here," he hissed to Darshan in Tirglasian. He had been prepared to greet the four youngest at once, but more? *Maybe with a wee bit of a warning.* Maybe not the ideal situation, but it wouldn't have been the first time he had mingled with large groups of women he had barely known. At least these ones weren't likely to grope him.

"Where else did you expect them to be after hearing about you?" his husband replied in the same language before beaming at his family and switching back to his native tongue. "Forgive us, he's a little overwhelmed by all your absolutely charming expressions." Tucking Hamish's arm firmly under his own, Darshan guided them to a pair of empty cushions.

The *Mhanek* sniffed loudly, a forkful of pink-fleshed fish raised halfway to his mouth. "So good of you to join us, Darshi. Suuk tells me you spent the night in the guest palace, despite my ruling."

Darshan clucked his tongue. "Sending your spymaster to follow me about? What a waste of talent. Don't you have better things for her to do? Like find out who attacked my husband and Anjali?"

A few of Darshan's sisters cast worried looks at each other. Another couple whispered between themselves. *Word doesnae spread fast, then.* If this had been anywhere around Mullhind, his mother would've known within the hour.

The *Mhanek* frowned. "This recklessness is precisely why I decreed what I did. This is no time to go gallivanting across the palace grounds on a whim. What if one of these mind-addled assassins had gotten into the room?"

Hamish chewed on the inside of his cheek. The man had a point. Although the *Mhanek* had added his own network of spies to the task of hunting down the one responsible for the attacks, they wouldn't have had enough time to learn anything.

Scoffing, Darshan sat down on the cushion nearest his father, urging Hamish to join him on the other with a tug at his sleeve. "There were still Nulled Ones guarding the door. Or are you suggesting they would be substandard in their task?"

The *Mhanek's* face reddened. He straightened in his seat, pushing out his chest. "There is no such thing as substandard amongst the Nulled Ones."

"I thought as much." Darshan casually went about spooning rice onto his plate. He plucked a circle of flatbread from a basket, tore a chunk off and smeared it across a bowl of green paste before popping it into his mouth. "I find it ridiculous that you would demand me to act responsibly," he said between chewing. "Then you seek to bar me from my own husband."

"I distinctly recall stating you were to be considered as engaged. Or have we chosen to ignore that as well?"

Hamish bit his tongue, much as he'd done after hearing the *Mhanek's* statement. It might be a nuisance to not have his marriage acknowledged, but it wasn't forever. He could bear being considered as Darshan's betrothed until their second wedding.

Darshan clasped his hands, resting them on the table. "Why should I ignore the vows I've already freely given?" He fiddled with the wedding band Hamish had slipped onto the man's finger back in Tirglas. No matter how many times Darshan tried to clean it, the attack at the *Gilded Cage* had irreversibly blackened the wooden surface. "Would you rather have me not be a man of my word?"

Sighing, the *Mhanek* put down his fork. "The gods certainly saw to it that you were a challenge when they allowed you into this world."

"I do try," Darshan replied, earning a snicker from his twin, who swiftly smothered the sound after a cool glance from their father.

"Whilst I'm on the subject of challenges, what am I supposed to do with the mess you've made of the dais? The vine is too big to burn and none of the gardeners have been successful in making more than superficial cuts on the damn base."

Hamish had forgotten about the vine Darshan's rage had summoned into the throne room. He had thought that, like the other vines, it would've slunk back into the ground after a while. But then, the base of this vine had grown far larger, thickening until it was a veritable tree, with ever shifting tendrils snaking along the wall or winding themselves around the closest pillars.

"Why would you do anything with it?" Darshan settled back into his cushion. "Just think how impressive it would look to the council."

"Excuse me for interrupting," Hamish said, laying a hand on Darshan's shoulder. "But maybe if you could get it to back off a wee bit, have it looking more like a throne and nae an octopus ready to spring."

Darshan frowned, stroking his chin. "I can't promise it'll work, but I'll see what I can do."

The *Mhanek* stared at his son for some time before speaking again. "So be it, see that his things are brought into your chambers. I can't have my son sneaking around the palace grounds like a thief. But, as custom dictates, he will return to the guest palace before the wedding begins. And I *will* see that the guards outside your suite are doubled."

Hamish silently bowed his head in agreement. He didn't think their attacker would be capable of sending another group of armed people their way, but having more than a couple of Nulled Ones on guard seemed prudent.

Darshan's eyes bulged. *"Doubled?"*

"They can be tripled, if you think four of my best isn't enough. Although I'm certain it would be an adequate final defence." The *Mhanek* eyed Hamish as though he was a prospective bull out for stud. "He will also need a great deal of schooling before he is fit to take an official position at your side."

Hamish knew himself to be ignorant on a few things, but the *Mhanek* spoke as though he was absolutely inept.

"Maybe on small matters," Darshan countered. "I've taught him a great deal about our customs and he's already proficient in courtly etiquette."

"For a Tirglasian court, perhaps."

Hamish bristled at the remark. Tirglas might have different methods when it came to teaching, as well as what was more important to learn, but he wasn't uneducated. His mother's obsession with the old tales ensured he'd been taught a great deal about running a kingdom, alongside clan history and customs. Udynea might be big enough to swallow his homeland four times over, but ruling it couldn't be that different.

Darshan laid a reassuring hand on Hamish's arm. The palm seemed hotter than usual. "Yes, the Tirglasian court," he said to his father, the slight strain in his words matching the twitch of his fingers. "Do you think him completely incompetent? He might need to be brought up on the current dynamics of the nobility, but I shall require that knowledge myself. Any other wisdom that needs to be imparted, I'm sure I can teach."

Hamish nodded in agreement with his husband. Everything he had been taught about Udynea—the real empire, not the old tales his land told that were designed to scare children—from the very language to the broad history and its varied customs, he had learnt from Darshan.

"*You* have your own duties." The *Mhanek* skewered a cube of fruit from the closest bowl onto his fork. There were a lot of such bowls scattered down the table, full of sweet melon and berries. "You cannot expect your twin to look after your responsibilities indefinitely."

"Then allow *me* to fill in the holes in Hamish's schooling," Anjali offered, earning a glare from her brother. An abrupt gust of wind flicked her hair.

"No, my darling child," the *Mhanek* said dismissively. "I think their monopolisation of you is quite enough."

"Why?" asked one of the younger women. "What have they done?"

Darshan twisted in his seat to eye his siblings, who all strained to hear the reply. "It was so nice of you to herd all my sisters into one place for introductions," he muttered to his father before a frown furrowed his brows. "But I do note the rather empty seat."

Hamish had also noticed the spot. It sat one place down from Anjali. He had thought it symbolic of the *Mhanek's* absent wife.

"Where's my nephew?" Darshan's tone was too light for him to not have an ulterior motive. It might've been no more insidious than seeking to turn the conversation away from their plans for children, but it still made him look suspicious.

The *Mhanek* glared at his son.

"What?" Darshan regarded his father with wide-eyed innocence, a hand splayed on his chest. That definitely wasn't going to help. "I haven't seen him in over a year. I merely wish to extend my greetings. Or have you been taken in by one of Onella's lies? You know I'd never cause him harm."

Grunting his agreement, the *Mhanek* fell back to his meal. "He should be along shortly. *And,*" he continued in a tone that put to rest all thoughts of arguing. "Regardless of who winds up schooling your betrothed, I'll ensure it waits a day or two for him to settle in."

Hamish followed along as his husband inclined his head in acceptance.

At Darshan's insistence, Hamish silently loaded his plate, piling on whatever was closest. As he had expected after seeing the surrounding lands, there were a lot of rice-based dishes. And fish. Some wrapped in leaves, others sitting atop rolls of more rice. Very little of it looked familiar.

Now I ken how Dar felt. During the first dinner the man spent in Tirglas, Darshan had looked upon the roasted meats and heavy pies as though it might leap up and savage him.

He scooped up a spoonful of what looked to be some sort of yellowy fish stew. Previous encounters of similar dishes had led to him preferring a heavy helping of rice with each meal, but the stew was absent of the usual heat. *Sweet.* But not sickly like those powdered gelatinous cubes his husband was so fond of.

The others also settled into eating. The room soon filled with the soft clink of utensils against plates and the murmur of requests for a certain dish to be passed over. Snippets of conversation also reached Hamish's ears. Bland talks of past events or recent rumours he had heard repeated elsewhere.

"He's huge." Low though the declaration had been, it neatly pierced the relative silence.

A few of the women giggled and chuckled into their hands. A couple of them snapped fans up in front of their faces, failing to conceal their mirth as their shoulders bounced in silent laughter.

Hamish glanced down the table to spy a small girl clapping her hands over her mouth. Her eyes widened, her tawny complexion growing increasingly redder. She looked to be the youngest at the table, which would make her Aditi, if he had remembered Darshan's family tree right. Whilst her years might've barely been measured in double digits, her small size had her seeming younger still.

"Tall!" the girl shrieked, the word echoing off the ceiling. "I meant *tall*, not fat. Big. St-statuesque." Her face scrunched as she fought to say the last word.

"I certainly hope that's all you meant, young lady," the *Mhanek* said. "I wouldn't like to think your older sisters have dirtied your mind already."

"Knowing our dear brother," said one of the women in a whisper designed to carry. "He's likely the other thing, too." She jostled her much younger sister with her elbow, further darkening Aditi's cheeks.

The girl likely knew not every man was built the same—a trip to one of their public baths would reveal that—but surely they didn't teach those so young about sex. The way her face crumpled in confusion suggested she was more regretting being under her sister's scrutiny than aware of where the conversation had gone.

"*Asmee*," the *Mhanek* snapped, aghast. "Such crassness is unbecoming of a *vlossina*. I will *not* have you corrupting your sister with your crudeness."

"Indeed," Darshan added, the squish of a grape between his teeth punctuating the word. "What would the court think of you putting such thoughts into a ten-year-old's mind?"

Aditi puffed out her chest. "I'll be *eleven*, soon. The High Priestess of Araasi said I was a promising acolyte."

"Araasi, huh?" Darshan popped another grape into his mouth, his brow creasing as he chewed. "Priesthood demands a lot of scripture. A lot of adherence to rules, too."

"I am familiar with both." She straightened in her seat. Any further and she'd be hovering. "And I've already got the three main tales memorised."

"Well done, lass." Hamish knew of the one tale, and only in brief, but Darshan and a number of the girl's sisters looked suitably impressed, so he assumed the praise well-earned.

"There'll be a lot of early mornings, too," the *Mhanek* reminded his youngest daughter.

She ducked her head. "I'm working on improving my morning routine."

"And failing," blurted the pale-haired sister sitting directly across the table from her. "The commotion from your nanny trying to rouse you this morning echoed all the way to my chambers."

"For your information, I had been practising the passing of the darkened moon a few hours beforehand. It must be done at moondown or not at all and Nanny never wakes me in time if I sleep first." She narrowed her eyes at her sister. "And, at least, *I* wasn't trying to sneak out a boy."

The pale-haired young woman leapt to her feet, one clawed hand raised. Blue fire flickered to life between her fingers. "You—"

"Jheel?" the *Mhanek* murmured, lifting his cup to his lips. "What have I told you about magic at the table?"

Whatever words she had been about to spew at her sister, she visibly swallowed them. The magic sputtered and died as she spun to face her father, clutching her skirts. "I can explain."

"That won't be necessary. The Nulled Ones caught him trying to creep out the gates. He's currently enjoying a rest in the barracks."

I was right. The palace grounds *did* have a jail within its walls. It was likely lined with *infitialis*, too.

"Honestly," the *Mhanek* continued. "I am disappointed in your complete lack of regard to security. What if he had been an assassin rather than a glass merchant's son? What if he had attacked one of your sisters?" He took another sip at his drink. "I should have him executed just for being on imperial grounds."

Jheel gasped. "No!" She hastened to the man's side, tripping over the cushions and scrambling on her hands and knees for half the length of the table. "Father, please. *I* brought him into the imperial palace. Punish *me*."

"It *would* be punishing you."

Hamish's stomach churned, the few mouthfuls he had eaten threatening to come back up. Objectively, he knew the *Mhanek* had to be careful with his children, especially who they chose to interact with. Marriage opened avenues for leverage; kidnappings, assassinations and the like. But to threaten a young woman with the possible death of her lover? *Just like Mum*. She might not have paraded her orders before him, but there was no doubt that she had considered it as his punishment.

All along the table, the young girl's sisters bowed their heads. Had they been subjected to the same stiff decisions?

"What it *would* be," Darshan muttered, "is an utter waste."

The man's father slowly turned his dispassionate scowl on him. "Is that your official opinion, *vris Mhanek*?" The address Hamish had heard so many times uttered in reverence now cracked through the air.

Darshan straightened in his seat until the cushion could've easily been a throne. "I merely meant Jheel could do worse."

The *Mhanek's* brow twitched in the smallest hint of curiosity.

"Glass merchants generally operate as family establishments—the Niholian barons prefer it that way—meaning he would've been trained to help run the business as soon as he had his *Khutani*. And anyone who trades in glass also isn't lacking in wealth, which would keep Jheel comfortable in a manner she is familiar with. In addition, he managed to reach the imperial gates before being caught, correct?" Darshan barely paused for the *Mhanek* to agree. "That suggests cunning and smarts, which would serve him once he inherited his family's business." He shrugged. "Like I said, there are worse options. Unless, of course, his courtship isn't serious."

As one, the man's siblings turned their attention to Jheel.

The young woman fumbled with a string of beads dangling from her wrist, producing a simple thong with a glass flower. "He gave me this last night. It was why I snuck him in, to tell you. Then Aditi's nanny started hollering at her to wake up and I thought—"

"That you had been caught," the *Mhanek* finished for her. He took up the trinket, closely examining it. "If his intentions were pure, he would've come to me directly."

"You're the *Mhanek*," Darshan said as if it wasn't the most obvious thing in the world. "Most glass merchants aren't even low nobility, he would be waiting for years just to get an audience."

The man's brow creased, his already slim lips thinning further. "I will consider it," he said, returning the simple cord to his daughter's wrist. "*After* I have questioned him."

Jheel bowed her head, resting it upon her father's lap. The man stroked his daughter's hair, bending to speak in a tone that didn't carry. Soon, she returned to her place at the table, whilst the rest of the sisters continued with their meals.

Hamish tried to follow, but found himself more moving the food around and eating only when Darshan nudged him. He couldn't shake how close the glass merchant's son had come to being executed. How it might still happen. *If Dar hadnae been here.* Would the *Mhanek* have listened to his daughter if Darshan hadn't interrupted? *Doubtful.*

What if they'd been late? A single day of bad weather, or an attack, could've held them up.

The tap of another's fork on his plate jolted him back into the world. He glanced up, following the drifting utensil across the table and into the hand of the woman sitting opposite him. She looked to be one of the older sisters, and heavily pregnant.

"Hamish was it?" she asked, waiting until he answered the question with a curt nod. "We don't get many visitors from the northern lands. Have you interacted much with the Udynean people? Or has Darshi been keeping you all to himself?" A fond smile lit up her copper-toned features as she spoke the last sentence.

"I've been in a few places." Hamish gulped down a swig of water to moisten his throat. If this enquiry went anywhere near the length of the similar one he had back in Nulshar, they'd have him talking for some time. "Taverns and pubs, mostly. Then the outposts as we got closer to here."

"Because of the attacks?" Anjali interjected, earning a few gasps and shocked whispers amongst a few of her siblings.

"Aye. Before then, we didnae stop until it was too dark to travel."

"Then, you've had little interaction with the court," the other woman pressed.

"Only the party Onella threw for Dar."

The woman beamed. "*Dar*," she softly echoed, her grin turning mischievous. "I thought you hated being called that?"

He does? Not once had Darshan given any indication of disliking the moniker.

Darshan silently withdrew his fork from his mouth. He fixed a bored look on his half-sister whilst he chewed, then he twitched a brow at her and a haughtiness took his features. "I don't mind it, so long as it comes from *him*, and him alone."

Issuing a small cooing sound that Hamish had only ever heard uttered towards babies and half-grown mousers, the woman laid a hand atop her bosom. "Always knew you were a soft touch, brother."

Darshan chuckled. "I've clearly been routed by your powerful deduction, Vin-vin." Smiling, he jerked his chin at her. "How's the child? I didn't even know you were pregnant. You must be due any day now." He leant closer, an impish light glinting in his eyes and skewing his lips. "Or did the desserts finally win out?"

Vin laughed. "Why can't it be both? The gods know it'll be born with an appetite for sweet." Like every other expecting woman Hamish had met, she cradled and stroked her belly. "It won't be soon, though," she added. "The midwives say before the second full moon. And the priests predict it'll be a boy."

"You know their predictions aren't worth the coin they ask for," the *Mhanek* half-heartedly scolded. "Look at all the beautiful daughters the gods blessed me with." He gestured down the table. "Every single one of you was supposedly another son."

"I hear you're planning on having one of your own," Vin continued, her dark eyes fixed on Hamish. "With your husband."

"Is he a *paalangik*," blurted the same young girl who had tattled on Jheel.

Hamish frowned. He recalled Darshan using that word before—it had no Tirglasian equivalent—but he couldn't recall what it meant. *Something about men.* A particular type. Were they the ones born with the ability to carry children if they chose? And often didn't, from what he could remember.

"It would be no business of yours if he was," Darshan snapped back at the girl. "But, if you must know, we are in the middle of making arrangements."

Someone at the entrance cleared their throat. The man waited until all attention was on him before announcing, "Lord Tarendra of the Praash Household."

The boy walked into the room, grimacing much as Hamish had done at the formal address upon their own entry. Onella's child resembled his father in the roundness of his face more than the boy's overbearing mother. Like many of the children he'd seen running around the streets, the boy's dark hair was cut short, the curls forming around his ears further softening his features.

How old is he? Hamish toyed with a piece of fish trapped between his teeth as he tried to remember. Darshan had told him. *Twelve?* That couldn't be right, the boy looked eight at best.

Tarendra bowed as he neared their end of the table, then he spotted Darshan and beamed. "Uncle!" He raced along the room, halting a few steps away and bowing. "I mean, *vris Mhanek*, I am glad to see you have returned from your ventures."

A small amused huff escaped Darshan's nose. "Your mother's not here."

The grin returned and the boy bounded into his uncle's arms.

"How have you been, you scamp?" Darshan ruffled the boy's hair, giving the curls a look that spoke of being dragged through the undergrowth.

"*Bored*," Tarendra unashamedly announced. He wriggled out of his uncle's grasp and rounded the table to take his place on the empty cushion. "They wouldn't let me out to the last festival. Do you know how hard it is to get a good view of the sky sparks when there are giant walls in the way?"

"That's because *I* wasn't here."

Hamish hid his smile under the pretence of having a drink. His husband had expressed multiple times that he'd be a poor father, even when Hamish continued to disbelieve every word. And it seemed he'd been right to. Maybe Darshan wouldn't be the perfect father—no parent ever could—but he'd the makings of a caring one and that matter far more.

"You know it's harder to protect you in the city," the *Mhanek* added.

If Tarendra had heard his grandfather, he offered no sign of it. Instead, Hamish seemed to have captured the boy's attention. "It's really bright," he mumbled. "Like fire."

"He's *tall*, too," said one of the women, eliciting a snicker from a few of the others and the boy's confused frown.

"Are you really from Tirglas?" Tarendra asked, jabbering out more questions before Hamish could open his mouth. "What's it like up there? Is it as cold as they say? Do you really get snow? Are you actually married to my uncle or is that just a rumour? Is it even legal for you to do that?" He rolled his eyes at his own question. "I mean, I know men marrying is legal, but how would inheritance work if you're both princes?"

Hamish couldn't contain his amusement, grinning broadly as the boy continued his barrage of questions without waiting for the answers. It sounded so much like Mac. He had lost count of how many times his youngest nephew had driven his mother to the point of exhaustion with his endless chatter.

Tears blurred his vision for a few blinks. Of all the things he didn't think he would ever miss. The boy would be nine by now. Had he improved on his archery in that time?

Would he ever get to see any of his nephews whilst they were still boys?

Tarendra continued talking as he piled his plate high with everything in reach, barely pausing even between bites. His questions moved on to querying yesterday's attack and swiftly drew Anjali into his querying range. A few other aunts sitting nearby also chimed in.

"I trust you've been causing lots of trouble for your grandfather?" Darshan managed to ask during a lull in the boy's questions. He flashed a wicked grin at the *Mhanek*, clearly seeking to stir the pot.

"He couldn't be any worse than you were at his age," the man answered with the twitch of an eyebrow and the whisper of a smile curling his lips.

"At *his* age, you had me go through the *Khutani*."

Hamish stiffened. He knew little about the supposed rite of manhood other than it entailed the removal of a young man's foreskin. He'd seen the outcome close up, and it didn't seem to cause Darshan any discomfort or reduce his pleasure, but the idea of letting a child go through such an act was barbaric.

"And the priests also deem Tarendra as old enough."

Hamish reassessed the boy. Maybe he'd been right in remembering the age as Darshan had been twelve when he'd gone through the rite. Tarendra didn't look anywhere near that, but if it was true, it would put him around the same age as Hamish's middle nephew. "What's the rush to make him a man?" Adulthood wasn't a consideration in Tirglas until a child had weathered their sixteenth winter where they still needed to prove themselves capable of fighting and providing for a family. "Can it nae wait?"

" '*Mish*," Darshan warned, the word a hissing breath above a whisper.

"I will kindly ask you to keep your nose out of this topic," the *Mhanek* snapped even as Hamish went to question Darshan further. "This isn't something you need to concern yourself with. Nor do *you*, for that matter," he added, pinning his son with the same stern look.

Hamish tried to hold his tongue, managing a few heartbeats before his ire got the better of him. "And when it's me own son? Will it concern me then?"

The *Mhanek* sat back, his face carefully neutral.

"Say I refuse to let some priest cut a piece off his dick? What then?" He swung to his husband. "You ken things are different in me homeland. Have you even given it a thought?"

"This is not the time for such talks," Darshan replied in

Tirglasian.

"When will be the right time? When me son's twelve years old and sitting on an altar with a priest ready to mutilate his genitals?" He folded his arms. "I willnae let that happen."

Darshan got to his feet. "I think I'll take him on a tour of the palace, so he at least knows the way to our chambers." He grabbed Hamish's arm and, with a feat of strength that could only have been magically assisted, hauled Hamish upright. "If you will excuse us." Maintaining his grasp on Hamish, he led the way to the exit, pausing only to bow to his father before marching out of the room and down the hall.

Chapter 33

Hamish's boot heels echoed as they strode down the hall, punctuated by the rapid slap of Darshan's softer shoes. Even though he didn't know where they were going, he continued marching ahead of his husband, barely heeding Darshan's direction. Why should he care where they ended up in these massive halls?

He dragged me out of there. Towing him out of sight like a bad-tempered child or disobedient pet. Not once, throughout all the mistakes he had made during their first few weeks in Udynea, had Darshan seemed ashamed of him. This wasn't the first time they had disagreed on subjects. Was it the audience? Did Hamish's unwillingness to sit passively aside at the idea of having his son irreversibly altered make Darshan look bad before the *Mhanek*? *Tough.*

" 'Mish," Darshan said, his voice low enough to not join the echoes. "Could you please slow down so we can talk?" He spoke only in Tirglasian. No doubt, the change was to keep the servants from eavesdropping.

Hamish eyed the other people sharing the hallways they trod. Human or elven, most went about their business in a brisk manner. A few nattered away in corners or alcoves, pausing to watch Hamish stride by. Any one of them could be a spy. Darshan had to know that even if the man didn't know who.

He slowed to a pace that Darshan's shorter legs could easily match. As much as the petty side of him would've preferred to stew somewhere in bitter silence, he knew they'd have to talk about it at some stage. "I'm nae an idiot," he growled. "I ken you dragged me out of there to keep me from making a scene." Was this the true side of it all? Would he be forbidden from making *any* decisions on how to raise his own child?

Darshan sighed. "I am aware it is a big ask for you to accept something you do not fully understand. You do not grasp what the *Khutani* means to my people. And, honestly, I did not expect you to."

"Because I'm stupid? Uneducated?" He regretted the words the moment they leapt from his tongue. Others had called him that, even his own mother. Never Darshan.

"You are neither of those things and you know it. I escorted you out of the dining hall because we needed to talk and some discussions are not suited to be had in public. My father is right in that we do not have a say in what happens with Ren, though. He is not ours."

"That's nae how it's done in Tirglas." A sibling's children were every uncle and aunt's responsibility. It kept children from being put under draconian pressure by a single couple. Mostly.

How different would things have gone had his father not been an only child? Or if his grandparents and the uncles on his mother's side hadn't fallen to the plague? Granted, the illness left one of the latter alive, but it had stolen the man's strength, leaving him with barely enough to breathe. Hamish hadn't seen him since childhood when the healers had taken his uncle to a cloister, somewhere in eastern Tirglas to be under their constant care. He didn't even know if the man had made it.

"I know this is not how your people do things," Darshan said. "But you must understand that the *Khutani* is deeply engrained in our culture. It is ancient, harking back from before we were an empire. Through all the changes Udynea has undergone, that rite has been our constant. It is part of who we are. I was halfway through my twelfth year when the priests deemed me ready to become a man."

"You've told me." The words snapped out before he could stop them. Hamish breathed deep and released his frustration on the exhale. If neither of them remained level-headed about this, it would only degrade into bitter words that they'd regret but, ultimately, never be able to take back. "Whatever you're going to say that you think will change me mind, it's nae going to work."

"I wish you could understand how I felt back then. Before I met you, I had never been happier than I was on that day. I was so full of pride, so determined to prove I was as ready as they had said, that I barely felt the knife. One slice and, nine minutes later, I was a man."

Hamish winced. "Nine minutes?" That seemed a long while to wait. "You can lose a lot of blood in that time."

"The priests know what they're doing. No one dies during the *Khutani*."

He tried to imagine it, but just the thought of a blade anywhere near his privates had him feeling as though they'd crawled up inside. *Nae for anything.*

"And you want our son to go through life with the knowledge that he has not taken the rite where he would be considered as a man? It is not something private that only his lover would see. One trip to a public bath and everyone would know."

Hamish knew that. Tirglas might not have the same carefree attitude about nudity between genders, but within them was perfectly acceptable. Darshan had even shared a hot pool with the group travelling to the cloister. And, despite Hamish insisting no one would stare, it hadn't taken the others long to notice the difference. "The same could be said of me. Am *I* still considered a wee lad?"

Darshan bowed his head. "Of course not. But you are not Udynean. Whilst the priests would welcome your participation in the rite, no one would judge you differently under our customs if you chose to remain as you are."

"But you'll force those same customs on me son?"

Aghast, his husband halted in the middle of the hall. "There would be no *force*. Participating in the *Khutani* is always a *choice*. If you refuse when the priests deem you as ready, no one drags you there against your will and ties you down. Is that what you thought?"

Hamish shrugged. He hadn't considered that part of it at all. "Sort of?"

"That—" Darshan shook his head and gestured for them to take the next turn in the corridor. "No one put me on that altar but myself. And no one will force our son to take that step."

No one except the Udynean society as a whole. He understood the pressure to be just like everyone else. He had lived with it for so long.

"But he *will* be born in the heart of Udynea," Darshan continued. "He will be raised alongside other Udyneans. How can you expect him to understand his people if you deny him a chance to be a part of the culture that unites us?"

"What of me own customs?" They might not be something their son was exposed to from the outside world, but he had been looking forward to sharing everything he remembered of his homeland with his son. The idea that he wouldn't be able to squeezed his heart. "Am I barred from teaching them to him?"

Darshan clutched Hamish's arm, staring up at his with a horrified expression. "Of course you wouldn't be," Darshan said, slipping into his native language before clearing his throat and continuing on. "I assumed that you would teach him everything you can of his Tirglasian heritage. Never would I have considered asking you to do otherwise." His hand fell along with his gaze. "But we both know he will never be able to set foot there whilst your mother still lives. Tirglas would be as foreign to him as it was to me."

Aye. The thought of his son reaching Tirglas and seeing it as he had first seen Udynea chilled him to the core. He could teach the boy everything he knew and it would still be about 'that place over there'. *All because of me mum.*

"It did not occur to you until now, did it?"

Hamish shook his head.

Darshan rubbed at the side of his jaw, then chuckled. "Look at us, arguing over how to raise a child that we have not even conceived."

"I wouldnae call *this* an argument." He'd seen enough of those, had been the cause of so many, to identify them.

"A heated discussion, then." His lopsided grin melted into a sombre expression. "I'm sorry. I clearly should've discussed this with you sooner." He clasped his hands, fidgeting with the rings. Hamish couldn't help but notice it was the wedding band. "I actually planned to once we were settled and the preparations were in hand."

"There's nae reason why we cannae have that conversation now."

Darshan nodded and indicated another hallway. "In private."

The corridor Darshan directed them down led to a pair of doors bearing the symbol of the *vris Mhanek* between them. Even if that obvious mark hadn't been carved into the rich brown wood, the four guards dressed in the red uniform of the Nulled Ones would've given away just who dwelt here.

The group bowed as Darshan marched up, casting a few glances between them. "One of your slaves delivered his highness' belongings an hour ago," one of them said.

Darshan bowed his head in acknowledgement. He parted the doors with a slight flick of his hand and entered the room.

After the imperial quarters they'd stayed in, both at Nulshar and the brief moment in Rolshar, he had expected it to be luxurious and he wasn't disappointed in that respect. The gauzy curtains Udynea seemed so fond of were everywhere, gracing the massive windows and surrounding the bed. Other, more opaque, drapes nestled against the wall, framing carved panels of scenes that Hamish couldn't be sure were exaggerated pieces of Darshan's life or sections from myth.

A huge rug covered much of the floor. Despite its tight weave, there was a well-worn path from the main entrance to the bed where another rug climbed the stairs leading up to the mattress. The bed looked to be sitting higher than one he had slept in last night.

Beyond the entrance, three solid wooden doors led off this room. One was likely a massive wardrobe akin to the space in Nulshar's imperial suite. Another likely led to a bathing room or, at the very least, a privy. He had no idea what could be behind the third one.

"All right," Darshan said as the door shut, returning to Udynean. He planted himself in the middle of the room, his arms folded. "Allow me to throw a hypothetical at you. Say he doesn't go through the

Khutani at the same age as myself. Say we wait until he's... sixteen or so. You would consider him a man then, correct?"

A prickliness settled in Hamish's gut. He'd a feeling he knew where this was going. "Aye."

"What if he chooses to go through with the *Khutani*? Would you restrain him?"

"You would let him choose?"

"I should've explained the rite fully weeks ago," Darshan said as he settled on the end of the bed with a groan. By the way he sank into the mattress, it was softer than the one they'd shared in the guest room. "The *Khutani* echoes the *Khotuno*, the bleeding women go through," he added, clearly catching Hamish's confusion. "Am I correct in that they *do* teach men about that in Tirglas?"

"I've two sisters," he reminded the man. Whilst Caitlyn would've been in the cloister by the time she was old enough, their older sister could complain enough for two. "But they do that naturally." There was no rite, no celebration, of the act in Tirglas. If it was announced at all, the news was met with grunts of acknowledgement before people returned to their business. The priests definitely didn't get involved.

"The majority do, yes." Darshan leant back, keeping himself from fully collapsing onto the mattress by propping himself on his arms. "When the priests announce you are old enough, they consider you as being capable of withstanding the *Khutani* in both mind and body. You always go of your own free will, at a time of your choosing. Most choose to go through the rite as soon as they can."

Hamish understood that sort of eagerness. Whilst participating in hunts wasn't a rite of manhood, boys back in Tirglas often saw it as such and clamoured to be allowed to join almost as soon as they could reliably handle a bow. "Do any ever refuse?"

"Some—I would be lying if I said otherwise—but it is rare. You don't go alone. The men in your family, along with the male friends you consider as being close to you, join you in the temple. They're supposed to chant alongside the priests, but not many do more than hum."

That sounded awfully like the days his mother used to bring Hamish and his siblings along to the mass gatherings within the temple. Few actually went to them regularly, the land dictating when they'd the time more than the people, and when they did, the understood the meaning behind the scripture more than the words.

"You enter the main temple naked," Darshan continued. "Along with the male members of your family. Your father, or whoever you chose to take that position, presents you to the priests who confirm that you are indeed ready. They lead you to the altar—I cannot be sure if they all are, but the one in Minamist is carved from marble—and you sit upon it with your legs spread for about an hour or so whilst the priests chant and prepare the knife."

"Naked?" The cold stone would swiftly numb the buttocks and the position could also affect the legs. It would also leave certain parts exposed.

Darshan nodded. "The head priest waves strong incense in your face just before making the first slice, which I'll admit is likely an intoxicant to help manage the pain. Afterwards, you sit there bleeding in silence for nine minutes. I think that's supposed to be some symbolism for each month spent in the womb.

"Why in silence?" Pain was meant to be weathered only in battle. All other times, it wasn't considered weak for the wounded party to be a vocal one.

His husband shrugged. "I never thought to ask. I'm not even sure if the priests know the answer."

"I suppose the priests heal you once the nine minutes are up?" He had seen the precise work of such magic. If Darshan's *Khutani* was typical, then the cut would seamlessly merge with little hint of a scar. But his husband had also learnt healing magic before taking part in the rite.

Something else nagged at his thoughts. If they were supposed to wait, how did they stop spellsters from instantly repairing the damage? He was afraid to ask.

Darshan nodded. "Of course they're healed once the ritual is over, the priests aren't sadists. They then anoint you with the blood you've spilt upon the altar and assist you in rejoining your family."

Hamish swallowed. It still sounded barbaric. "You dinnae regret it?" It must've changed something. Or maybe it had been too long ago, the memory muddied by the passing of two decades.

"Not at all. Had I the chance to choose again, my actions would not have changed." Darshan dropped back onto the bed and groaned. He remained still for a while, long enough for Hamish to seriously believe the man had fallen asleep.

Uncertain if he should wake his husband or not, Hamish returned to examining the room.

Now he had gotten used to the glitz of the gilding and the way the light played through the sheen of the curtains, it seemed sparse. Unlived in. Little in the way of Darshan's personality touched the room. The spaces where Hamish would've crammed gifts from his siblings' children were left bare. And there wasn't much furniture. Beyond a few shelves, there was a chaise lounge, a table and two chairs over by the window.

Like the guest room, there also appeared to be a way out onto the balcony. Was the view was as grand? The guest palace wasn't hemmed in by a high wall, but the imperial palace sat head and shoulders above its barrier.

Hamish went to find out just what could be seen from the *vris Mhanek's* chambers.

"Where are you off to?" Darshan rolled onto his side.

"I thought I'd leave you in peace. You looked like you were asleep. Remembering how comfortable your own bed is?"

Darshan chuckled. "I've never slept on this one. I commissioned a new mattress for when I arrived. Consider it waiting to be broken in." He bounced a little, frowning. "Could be firmer, I suppose. But I was merely thinking." He sat up. "Not that you aren't welcome to roam unescorted—this *is* also your room, after all—but you won't find much joy out there. Unless a view of the pool is to your liking. And the wind at this height is ghastly."

"What's behind the other doors?"

"You've the wardrobe." He pointed to the double doors on the right. "They should've made arrangements to set up your clothes on the left. You can get to the bathroom from there, but also through the other set of double doors. The privy is also off that."

Hamish nodded. It was as he had thought. "And that one?" He jerked his thumb towards a single door on the far side of the room.

"That's my study. Well, *ours* now, I suppose." Darshan perked up like a freshly trained boarhound eager to show its tricks. He took the steps leading down from the bed in one leap. "Would you like to see it?"

Ordinarily, he would've refused. Nothing bored him faster than a study or library. But it was always hard to refuse whenever his husband's interest was piqued and the man practically vibrated with keenness. "It's off your bedchamber?" His mother's study had been virtually across the other side of the castle from where she slept. He took in the room anew. "You could spend days here and nae have to leave except for grub."

"Daama typically ensures I don't starve." He opened the study door. To Hamish's surprise, it wasn't locked. Although he supposed it would be difficult to sneak into the room with the Nulled Ones guarding the entrance.

Hamish followed his husband, halting after a few steps into the room. He had expected the shelves of books—he had always known Darshan was the bookish type. The writing desk and a cabinet of scrolls sitting near the sole window were just as commonplace.

What caught his eye was the shelving along the right wall. It looked like an apothecary's shop with a vast array of jars and boxes filling every nook. The framework of metal and glass tubing taking up the nearby table wasn't anything he had ever seen, though. The air between them at the table seemed to shimmer. "What is all this?"

"My hobby." His husband bounced onto the balls of his feet and back down. "Ever since witnessing one of my people fall ill to an assassin's poison, I've spent time learning how to produce and counteract most of the main culprits." The air rippled like a disturbed curtain as he stepped up to the table. "*This* is why I wanted to get to Minamist quickly." His voice was muffled.

"What?" Hamish took a step closer and bumped into the unforgiving, faintly humming, surface of a shield.

"My apologies." Darshan hastened to his side, his voice returning to its full richness once he was back through the rippling barrier. He clasped Hamish's head, examining it as he continued babbling, "I forgot it's warded. It has been so long since anyone new has come in here."

"You keep a barrier up around your poisons?" That sounded prudent, especially given that the room itself didn't lock. "Wouldnae that put a strain on your magic?" How was he even able to maintain it? He thought spellsters needed to be able to see what they were doing when it came to such tricks?

"No, it's done via old Stamekian methods. I'll show you." He turned, only to be greeted by Daama standing in the doorway, clutching an armful of loose pages. "Another time, it would seem. What's still left for me to take care of?" he added to the woman.

"A few minor matters, child. And one hundred and thirty-four emancipation writs that require your approval and personal signature to be valid." She dumped the papers onto the desk.

Sighing, Darshan nodded. "Of course. Forgive me, *mea lux*." He grinned ruefully and patted Hamish's arm. "Duty calls, it would seem."

Hamish inclined his head. He might not like dealing with it himself, but he wasn't a stranger to the paperwork that came with overseeing a kingdom. For an empire the size of Udynea, there had to be mountains of it even without emancipation writs.

Hamish gnawed on his lip, watching as Darshan signed a page, melted a little wax onto the paper with his bare fingers and stamped it with his signet ring.

The current law permitted Darshan to free a quarter of the slaves he owned every decade, even if he could afford to do more. For there to be so many, it meant his husband had literal ownership of over five hundred people.

Darshan glanced up, seemingly surprised to find him still there. "I'm afraid this shall take a while. You don't have to stay. I could ask if Anjali is free to show you around the palace? I'll make it up to you later on, I promise."

Hamish leant against one of the huge bookcases. "I'm good." After the excitement of yesterday, a quiet day in a safe place sounded like paradise.

With a shrug, his husband returned to signing and marking the papers. He had gotten through five before setting the pen down. "I seem to recall there being a gorgeous little sheltered spot up on the back wall that gives the best view of the sunset over the ocean. What would you say to an evening repast there? Just you and me?"

"I'd like that," Hamish replied.

Grinning, Darshan doubled his efforts.

Hamish turned his attention from his husband's furious signing to silently examine the bookcases. The shelves weren't full of just books. All the things he had expected to find in the other room, the bric-a-brac and adornments that were Darshan's alone, were displayed neatly on the shelves. There were even a few paintings, largely of other people—his twin, his nanny, a few other faces he couldn't place—but there was one of when his husband was a boy.

He picked it up, absently wiping the faint layer of dust from the frame. The subject included two others alongside Darshan, a girl who had to be Anjali and an elven boy who was all ears and teeth. *Zahaan?* He couldn't imagine the vaunted *vris Mhanek* being allowed the familial closeness the picture depicted with any other elf. Not as a child.

"You never told me you were this cute as a lad." The cocky grin was there. And the confidence. He wore glasses even back then, the frames taking up half of his face.

Frowning, Darshan glanced up from his task. "Ah." His cheeks darkened slightly as his gaze settled on the picture. Even through his embarrassment, his lips curved slightly. "I had forgotten that was there."

"How old were you?" The image of Darshan looked around the same age as the man's nephew, but Hamish wasn't prepared to assume after misjudging just how old the boy was.

His husband's head dropped, along with the smile. "That was the day of my *Khutani*."

"I've never been prouder than I was on that day," Daama murmured, running the back of one long finger across Darshan's cheek. "Especially after hearing how well you weathered the nullifying."

"What?" Hamish had wondered how they stopped a spellster from healing themselves within the timeframe, but his husband hadn't mentioned his magic being nullified.

"They wrap a chain of *infitialis* around the torso," Daama

supplied. "Or so I hear."

"Rather apt that I became a man whilst bound in chains, don't you think?" Darshan quipped.

With a huff, Daama lightly smacked Darshan's arm.

Hamish replaced the painting on the shelf. "I would've thought there'd be a bigger portrait."

"There is. It's in my father's study." Darshan pointed at the painting with the butt of his pen. "That was a mere sketch I insisted they complete."

"And just as well that you did," Daama said, chuckling. "It's the only picture I have of Zah. He never stayed still for long as a boy."

"He hasn't improved with age," Darshan said, returning to the papers. "I've been trying for years to get him back to Minamist and take up your position, give you a much-deserved retirement, but he's always fluttering off to aid his people in jobs they are perfectly capable of doing unsupervised."

Daama's smile widened, revealing a hearty set of teeth, including the longest canines Hamish had ever seen on an elf. There were rumours that pure elven bloodlines could be determined by such markings. He hadn't put much faith in them. Perhaps they *were* true.

"It's probably for the better," Daama said. "What would I do with in retirement but grow old?" She pointed a finger at Darshan in warning before he could fully open his mouth. "Watch your tongue, child."

"Have *you* considered taking up the offer of freedom?" Hamish asked the woman. If she wasn't bound to Darshan, there were dozens of places she could settle and live in peace.

Daama shook her head. "I've done a lot of things in my service under the *vris Mhanek*, and his twin, things that would've seen me killed had I not their protection. I don't regret a single choice, do not mistake me there, but I'm also not looking for a swift end to my life."

He nodded. Her son had said something similar.

"You could've *not* slapped Lord Shaam," Darshan said, glancing up from the papers. "That would be one less grievance I have to deal with."

"He deserved worse for propositioning your sister."

His husband's lips twisted sourly as he returned to his signing. "You're right. You should've fed him his balls."

Hamish's brows shot up. He hadn't heard such language from the man before. "Isnae that a wee bit harsh? Is your sister nae allowed to have some say in who courts her?"

Darshan's pen paused. "We were *eight*. And Lord Shaam was the same age I am now."

"You've those types here, too." Hamish had hoped that, with the freedom people had with their sexuality, none of them preyed on children. "Is that why she'll nae let you free her?" He couldn't deny that it would be difficult for her to live a normal life having to constantly watch her own back.

"It is part of the reason, yes," Daama replied. "Kindly do not speak of me as though I'm not here."

Hamish grimaced. "Sorry, Mistress Daama," he said, catching Darshan wincing at the address.

"If it helps," his husband said before the woman could open her mouth. "Think of 'Ma as being under indentured servitude."

"It doesnae help." The way people placed themselves under indentured servitude in Tirglas were treated was nothing like the position Daama was in. "What about your magic?" he asked the woman. He didn't know exactly how the collars worked, but he knew they nullified a spellster's ability to use their talents unless given permission by someone with authority over them. "Dinnae you want to be able to use it without having to ask?"

Laughter escaped the woman in a soft gust before she stifled it. "I already do." Daama fondled the chain, running her thumb up and down the purple links. "This dear man here." With her other hand, she ruffled Darshan's hair as though he was a small boy, earning her a flat glare and a wrinkled nose. "He insisted on giving us leave to use our magic however we see fit practically as soon as his *Khutani* was over. Just as I gave the rest similar permission with the proviso that they not use it to harm their *vris Mhanek*."

"Us?" The idea of Daama having reign over her own magic wasn't a surprise, but who else would his husband trust so freely?

"My son, Zahaan, and myself."

Of course. He had forgotten the elven spymaster was also leashed and one of Darshan's slaves. The man didn't act like it.

"I would've done more," Darshan murmured. "Had you let me. Just as I would've written these decades ago."

Daama frowned, her lips flattening. She smoothed back the man's hair. "You know that wouldn't have been wise."

"Why?" Hamish asked. If they were seen as belonging to Darshan, then what could've stopped him from freeing as many as he liked?

Darshan paused in the act of drying the current paper he had signed. "I was twelve. The *Khutani* might've given me full control over my possessions, but I was still young and idealistic." Grimacing, he gestured to the stack of signed papers. "Emancipating even this small selection at such an age would've suggested that I, the *vris Mhanek*, would grow into a weak and sentimental ruler."

Hamish ran his tongue over his teeth. He hadn't thought about it might look to those who didn't know Darshan. "And now?"

"He would be considered as eccentric," Daama replied, narrowing her eyes at him. "Or possibly swayed by his foreign lover."

Yes, he could see the court jumping to that conclusion, but he hadn't suggested Darshan do anything. He knew there were laws and even rulers had to follow them. Or at least, be seen as doing so.

Which would be better for the court to believe? That Hamish had or hadn't insisted on the change? He was content being painted as the demanding fool but only if it didn't make things difficult down the road.

"So what'll happen to *them*?" Hamish nodded at the stack of emancipation writs. "If it's safer being under your ownership, why do so many want to be free of their shackles?" He didn't think he was wrong about Darshan not being a cruel man, but that didn't exclude ignorance to trouble.

"Simply put, I'm not giving these people a choice in the matter." He marked yet another page with his signature and seal. "You were right about how I must proceed. All my talk of abolishing the slave caste? Hollow words if not backed by action." Another page joined the ever-growing stack of signed ones. "I may not have bought a single soul throughout my life, but I own many." He shook his head. "I will see it all change in my lifetime."

"A big task," Daama murmured.

"But a worthy one. Besides..." Darshan flashed a cocky smile at the woman. "Tsarina Viktoriya oversaw the deconstruction of the serfdom in the Niholian Empire well before she ceded the throne to her son."

Hamish remained silent. Tirglas had little to do with the small southern empire and he knew even less of Niholian history. Or of its current state.

"Yet, she still couldn't manage to stop the glass barons from illegally acquiring slaves for their factories."

Darshan grunted his acknowledgement of her fact. "*I* will do better."

Chapter 34

"Viscount Vishal wishes an audience," Daama said.

Darshan sighed and set down his spoon, his appetite for breakfast waning. If he could've asked the gods to make one thing vanish during his time away from home it would've been the morning reports. Rarely did they bring good news, especially nowadays.

Thirteen days had passed since his return to the capital. And, every day, there'd be another small pile of missives from this or that member of the court wanting to speak with him. A scant handful of them bore legitimate reasons, most were an attempt to cosy up to him. It was as though his absence over the months had erased their memory of how he dealt with most requests. Or, perhaps, they thought Hamish's presence had filed down the sharp edges.

He would need to remind them that, just because their *vris Mhanek* had chosen to settle down, it didn't mean he had grown soft.

As aggravating as it was to start his reputation anew, it did give his spies a chance to flush out the leeches who would've otherwise remained tucked under their rocks. At least the only threats to Hamish's life were the usual testing of the waters by some of the nobility. It muddied the investigations, by Darshan's own network as well as his father's, though.

In that time, Daama had started her tutoring of his husband, under the pretence that if she was sufficient in raising the *vris Mhanek*, then she was good enough to tutor Hamish.

He was rather pleased at how swiftly his father latched onto the idea. It ensured that Hamish's schooling remained accurate as well as eliminating the chance of his weaknesses being leaked.

"Viscount Vishal?" Darshan mentality ran over his recent dealings with the viscounts. The name wasn't familiar, but he didn't know most of the border lords. They tended to spend much of their time on their own estates, sending only ambassadors to the court. Due to the nature of being the first defence from any outward attack, most estates along the western border had a great deal of autonomy. Even if they did bicker more amongst themselves than with the empire's actual enemies.

At times, he was certain many considered themselves as independent kingdoms.

Darshan stirred his spoon through the congealing mess of what had been a creamy millet porridge not that long ago. "Has he specified on what?" Ambiguity on the reasoning for the audience was often the first clue that they were looking to boost themselves up the social ladder.

With those from the border, it could also mean something dangerous. Those requests were typically sent to his father, but if the viscount suspected foul play from someone close to the *Mhanek*, Darshan could be a likely ally to the man. It wouldn't be the first time a son had overthrown his father.

"He says you've a debt to pay." Daama frowned at the letter. "You recently interfered with internal matters on his estate?" She shuffled through her notes, pulling a small slip of paper from the stack. "Something about a border dispute. He wouldn't elaborate further."

"I did?" He didn't recall ever having interfered with the running of another's estate, be they on the border or otherwise, and definitely not recently. "Which border?"

"I believe his estate is situated south of the mountains near Demarn. Would you like me to get the map and confirm?"

"Wasnae that where you said that hedgewitch was headed?" Hamish piped up before stuffing another forkful of poached egg into his mouth. "You ken, at your sister's party."

Darshan frowned at his breakfast, trying to remember their time at his half-sister's soirée. He had spoken with a hedgewitch. She had expressed concern over ancient dwarven artefacts being potentially destroyed in battle. *The Demarn border.* The imperial army wasn't responsible for any fighting there, but the viscount... "Tell him I refuse, that I am aware of how he was in breach of his holdings and to consider himself fortunate I don't intend to strip him of said land." He wished he could, but that power lay with his father and the senate.

"He won't be happy about that," Daama warned.

"I don't care. My father—my *grandfather*—has sought to instil peace with those who share our borders. We'll never manage it with Obuzan." The entire country was so fanatical about ridding the world of spellsters that they'd rather wipe out anyone who'd ever heard about magic than come to an arrangement over the cessation of a war going back as far as the country's creation. "But how can we hope to extend a hand in peace with Demarn if petty border lords like him won't pull their heads in and stop nibbling at foreign lands as though it's their right?"

"The viscounts maintain that, if they were to stop their defence, the Demarners will take it as weakness and claim the land."

"You mean *reclaim* it." It hadn't ever belonged to Udynea to begin with. "Father should've forced the viscounts to give it all back years ago."

Hamish mumbled something around his current mouthful that sounded like an agreement.

"There are already multiple Udynean settlements in the area," Daama pointed out. "Some of those citizens would be spellsters who, if they remained in their homes, would be at risk of imprisonment in that ghastly tower of theirs."

His husband made a low squeaking sound, hastening to lower his drink. It led to him spilling some the contents down himself. "Is that an actual thing?" Hamish asked, juice still dribbling down his beard. He swiftly mopped at his chin and shirt with a napkin. "I thought the Demarn tower was just a story. Something to make Tirglasian spellsters feel better about being in a cloister."

"Sadly, no." Darshan had grown up listening to horror stories of a mighty tower sitting in the middle of nowhere. Whilst Tirglas and Demarn confined those with even a hint of magic to buildings far from ordinary people, Tirglasians still used their spellsters for healing—it was all they were trained to do.

But, for Demarn, magic had one use. *War*. He wasn't certain what happened to the rest, likely stuck in that tower until their dying breath, but he'd seen a spellster who had reputedly come from Demarn's army.

Darshan had been a boy back then, barely nine years old. The power radiating off the woman had been more than he'd ever felt from his own father. If she hadn't been leashed with *infitialis*, if she had been able to bring her magic to bear during a battle, even for self-defence, she might not have been captured. Or, at the very least, made her capture costly.

But the Demarn army used their spellsters like glorified weapons, pushing until they were exhausted. They couldn't even refuse. All because they'd the misfortune to be born with magic.

To think Demarn still threw her people away like that.

Darshan pushed away his bowl. The thought of eating another mouthful made him want to wretch. "Are there any other reports?"

"Nothing important." Daama rifled through several pages, muttering to herself. "I found these transcriptions amongst your things. They look medical. Do want them filed with the rest of your records?"

Of course. Darshan leapt up from his seat to take them from her. "They're healer records from an Ancient Domian cache in one of the Tirglasian cloisters." With the commotion of his arrival and settling back into his routine, he had almost forgotten about them. There had been far more back at the cloister than this meagre selection, but he hadn't been able to carry more than this.

He flicked through the pages—much of it had to do with the ancient civilisation's studies on the inner workings of the brain, a subject few in Udynea dared to tread—before handing them back to Daama. "See that they're catalogued with the rest on the topic. But have them copied and sent to the Knitting Factories first."

Daama bowed and, gathering up all the paperwork, left them to enjoy the rest of the morning in peace.

He didn't know how much the healing academics could glean from a fraction of a much larger study, but it was a start. Maybe it would eventually mean ailments of the mind, such as what had taken his grandfather, could be slowed or halted, if not reversed. Having access to the rest of the study could've improved those odds. *If only I had secured that treaty.*

Darshan's gaze slid to his husband, who still shovelled down his meal. He could only hope that involving himself with Hamish had merely postponed such a union until such a time as when the man's brother took the Tirglasian throne.

Should he have felt guilty that his interference also meant he had possibly delayed the advancement of a cure? *A little.* It might not be possible even with all the resources in the world.

Someone knocked on the door, the rapid taping a Nulled One code that spoke of a messenger's arrival.

"Enter," Darshan called.

One of the men that he recognised as someone the Nulled One's regularly used as a messenger trotted in. The man halted before them, kneeling and holding out a letter to Hamish. "For your highness."

Surprise took Hamish's face as he straightened in his seat. "Me?" He claimed the letter, staring for some time at the name emblazoned upon the front. "I've only been here a few weeks."

Darshan tried to cover his amusement, failing as it huffed out his nose. "That's more than enough time for the entrepreneurial members of the court to seek your allegiance." Those who remembered Darshan wasn't the easiest target would naturally seek his favour by soliciting his husband to speak on their behalf. "Open it, *mea lux.* Let's see who dared first."

Groaning, Hamish parted the already broken wax seal and

withdrew the letter from its envelope.

A pungent and slightly sweet aroma wafted across the table, almost hidden by the scent of fresh ink. Despite the vaguely familiar smell, Darshan couldn't place it. *Perfume?* The page wouldn't be the original— Darshan had commanded all messages for his husband to be translated into Tirglasian by his own scribes—but the envelope would be. Had one of the court ladies sought to dangle their fruits before the man?

Darshan smirked into his cup before draining the last of the *kofe*. Any woman who tried would swiftly find their efforts wasted. He plucked a grape from the bowl in the middle of the table, rolling it between his fingers whilst his husband read the letter.

As always, Hamish's expression constantly shifted, scrunching in confusion in one second, then softly mumbling at the letter in the next. There didn't appear to be much in the way of writing on the page. It might've taken him a while if the letter had remained in Udynean, but his native language? Had his scribe mistranslated?

The messenger fidgeted from one foot to the next. "Is there a response I can send, your highness?"

Darshan watched his husband, all food forgotten. Was the man swaying ever so slightly in his seat? " 'Mish?" He plucked the letter from Hamish's unresisting grasp. It was a simple request for his presence by the Kaatha household. Although, the allusion to a debt to be paid carried the hint of a threat about it.

That familiar scent tickled his nose again, stronger and having his magic humming to nullify the effects.

"Leave us," he commanded the messenger who bowed and swiftly made his way to the door. After so many days without any incidents or attacks, he had begun to think they were finally safe. *Fool.*

Maybe he *was* getting soft.

"Wait," Hamish cried, leaping to his feet. "I was just about to—" He braced himself on the table, sending several dishes crashing to the floor. "I dinnae feel so good."

"Come with me." Latching onto his husband's sleeve, he towed Hamish towards the study. "Get Daama," he added over his shoulder to the Nulled Ones waiting by the doorway.

"What's wrong?" Hamish demanded.

Darshan remained silent, unsure just who might be listening outside the door. *Poison.* It wasn't a strong one, though, its effects further diluted by the removal of the original letter. Had it been a warning, then? What could Hamish have possibly done to warrant that?

Striding through the barrier protecting his assortment of poisons and antidotes, Darshan came to an abrupt halt as Hamish failed to follow. *Of course.* It had been so long since he had needed to modify the shield to allow another—all the others he trusted with the shelves' contents had gained his confidence years ago. "This'll be briefly uncomfortable." He plucked a hair from Hamish's head and, unearthing the small urn that kept the barrier going, dropped the strand in to join the handful of others. "You can enter now."

Hamish took a hesitant step, passing through the barrier to lean upon the metal table. "What was that?" He rubbed at where Darshan had plucked the hair. His gaze briefly alighted on the urn. "Some Ancient Domian trick?"

"Not quite." Keeping one eye on his husband, Darshan rummaged through the shelves of jars and bottles. The antidote had to be here somewhere, he was certain. "It's a Stamekian variation on the preservation domes," he continued, hoping that talking would keep Hamish focused enough to remain calm. "It does a terrible job of preserving anything, of course. But once activated, it'll allow no one to pass who hasn't left a piece of themselves within the vessel."

"Would make a handy prison."

"That's the original use." A barbaric practise that typically involved leaving the confined stranded in the middle of the desert.

Hamish sagged further against the table, the whole metal frame shaking along with the man. "What are you looking for? I ken something has happened. I feel like I've drunk a whole keg of beer."

"You've been mildly poisoned."

"And you're rifling through jars instead of using your magic to heal me like last time because…?"

Darshan flattened his lips. *If I'd been quicker.* He hadn't thought about such obviously weak attempts. "The toxin affects the mind." Had he put the concoction in one of the blue jars? He balanced on his toes, peering over the cork tops to find any of such colour. "Once you become dizzy it's no longer a simple healing fix." His own magic had stopped the effects before it could get that far. *I have to be more vigilant.* He would need to remind the Nulled Ones. They'd spent so long guarding those who could heal themselves. Too long. "Using magic on the brain is risky."

Hamish nodded then, groaning, placed a hand to his temple. "I remember that. But how? I've nae eaten a crumb or taken a sip without it having been by your father's testers. Do you think something got past them?"

"No. Do you recall a sweet smell when you opened the envelope? I mistook it for perfume, but that was the toxin. It would've been in the ink of the original letter." Did the antidote require a clay housing? He had less of those. "When wet, the toxin is harmless. Once dried… well, you can feel the effects."

"The ink? You mean they got me through a letter?"

He hummed his agreement. Where was that blasted mixture? "Fortunately, you haven't inhaled much, just the residue of it left in the envelope." His scribe likely thought she had nullified the risk or she would've sent the translated letter with only the seal. "If I can just find—" The gleam of a green bottle caught his eye. "Ah!" He plucked the bottle from its place cringing in the back corner of the upper shelf. "This ought to counter it." Uncorking the bottle, he held it up to Hamish's face. "Deep breathes now."

Hamish followed his instruction, taking a great lungful of the mixture's fumes. He coughed, gagging.

"Sorry. I know it's not a pleasant smell, but it should work quickly."

"I've been near cesspools that've smelt sweeter," Hamish grumbled. Nevertheless, even though his nose wrinkled something fierce, he continued the cycle of deep inhalations and slow exhales until Darshan's seeking magic could no longer find any hint of the toxin in his husband's body.

Darshan corked the bottle and returned it to the shelf. It would be useful for Hamish to be able to seek out such antidotes himself. He would need training, though. The same heavy studies himself, his twin and Zahaan had undergone.

The ability to find the right mixture quickly would also help. Even Darshan had struggled there. *I really need to catalogue these better.* He hadn't seen a need before. He was no physician with endless folksy remedies and tonics being doled out to the populace. Every single jar and bottle might've had a use proven by scientific research, but only he and three others knew which was good for what.

"Has the dizziness gone?" he asked of his husband.

"Aye." Hamish stared at his fingers, rubbing the tips along his thumbs. "Me hands are tingling, though. Is that normal?"

"A mild side effect," Darshan assured. "It'll fade shortly. But what about your eyes?" He picked up the letter and held it at a natural reading distance. With the fumes of the antidote still in Hamish's lungs, there was little any lingering toxin could accomplish. "The poison affects sight first." And he hoped it had been nullified before then. "Are you having any difficulty seeing up close?"

All at once, his husband's shoulders bunched defensively. "I can read it. It's from a..." His voice creaked, drawing out in that same low rumble he always fell into whenever Darshan attempted to teach him written Udynean. "Lady Keahto. And she wants to extend an invitation to—"

"That's enough." His gaze flicked to the letter. His original perusal wasn't wrong. It was indeed an invitation but not from Lady Keahto.

There was no such person. "I thought the trouble you were having with written words was in it being a foreign script, but you struggle to read your own language, don't you?"

Hamish opened his mouth, a clear objection on his tongue, before his shoulders sagged. "Aye."

"What is the problem, exactly?" He leant back on the table, half-sitting as he thought on all the times Hamish had done little more than glance at a book. Not once had he witnessed his husband open one of his own volition. Was there a deeper reason behind him merely not being much of a reader? "Is it your eyes?"

"My what? Eyes? What are you—?"

"Clearly, you can see words." The distinction between the real name and what Hamish assumed wasn't far off. If Darshan squinted, he could see how some of the letters could be misinterpreted. "Are they not in focus?" That was a simple enough fix. Although, it might take his husband a while to adjust to the idea of using reading glasses.

"It's nae that, I can see them clear as day. The letters just…" He grimaced and rubbed a hand across his chin. "They dinnae stay still, all right?"

"Pardon?"

"I said I *can* read," Hamish growled, his shoulders squaring again. "Once I ken the word, it isnae as bad picking it out again. It just takes me a while to… pin down the right letters. It has always been that way."

Darshan let the letter slip from his hand. He should've seen it earlier. Hamish had picked up speaking the Udynean language quickly when Darshan first started teaching the man during their travels through Tirglas. But once they reached Udynea and began working on the written word? Any progress was glacial. "Why didn't you tell me?"

"Because it's better to let people think you're ignorant or slow than—"

"No!" Darshan slammed his palm onto the table. "I have been torturing you for months in an effort to ready you for a life at my side, only to discover now that there's a reason you avoid the task." His husband read only at Darshan's insistence and never with any sign of enjoyment. But he took immense pleasure in listening to Darshan read the same texts aloud. "Did you think I would judge you differently if I knew the truth? When I need these—" He gestured to his glasses. "—just to see the world beyond my own nose?"

Hamish rubbed at his arm. "This is different. Those glasses are to help you, but whatever's wrong with me eyes—"

"It's your brain, actually," Darshan gently corrected. He scrubbed at his face. Was that also why his father's hypnotism didn't hold? His father had admitted to the act, but Hamish showed no signs, not even a hint of scarring.

Would one of the high healing academics in the Knitting Factory know?

"Me brain?" Hamish silently settled onto the leather stool set before the table. "Nae me eyes? Are you sure?"

"They're completely fine. And, clearly, work better than mine do unaided."

"And you ken this how?"

Darshan shrugged. "Healer training isn't considered complete until we're taught about every organ. We can't do much with the brain." Learning more than how to mend skull trauma and removing excess fluid from the cranium cavity was often as far as most tutors went. "But the study of differences is a complicated one and something that has always fascinated me."

"So, me brain's scrambled?"

"No more than anyone else's, I'm sure. Just built differently."

"And there's nae easy fix for this? You cannae just..." He wiggled his fingers. "...magic it away?"

Darshan shook his head. "There's nothing *to* fix." When it came to the brain, few were willing to attempt anything beyond the most severe of cases. "But we *can* find a better way than having you struggle through every letter." There had to be something out there that could help, he would have to put out feelers. Discreetly, for Hamish's sake. But his husband likely knew better than he when it came to dealing with this. "In the meantime, I will see to it that any correspondence is sent to my study for you to peruse at your leisure. We'll work on the rest, however long it takes."

"Thank you."

He hopped off the table and cradled his husband's head in his hands. "You don't need to keep secrets, *mea lux*. There's very little you could confess to that would see me re-evaluating my love for you." He bent to pick up the letter. "This is certainly nothing to be ashamed about."

Hamish grunted. "Tell that to me mum."

Something twisted in Darshan's chest, crying out for violence. *Curse that woman.* He'd been close to ending Queen Fiona's life after finding out what she had done to Hamish because he liked men, to discover she also berated the man for this difference only made Darshan wish he hadn't held back.

Taking a deep breath, he reined in his anger. "I have more than a few choice words for her." He linked their fingers, coaxing Hamish to follow him back out into the main bedchamber. "You should rest for a bit. Take a bath and clear your lungs with a little steam. And maybe get the stink out of your beard." Daama would be back shortly, he could ponder over the letter with her whilst Hamish recovered.

It took little time to see his husband ensconced in a bath of steaming water. Hamish leant back against the side of the tub, breathing deep. "Who do you think is trying to kill me this time? Someone new? Or is our hypnotist behind it?"

"Hard to say." He didn't know much about the Kaatha household beyond them being a small estate situated east of the Shar. "I don't think the hypnotist originated from there." If the household had anyone with such abilities, the whole family would've stopped being more than a minor voice in the courts years ago.

"So," Hamish drawled. "Am I soaking alone or you joining me?"

"Tempting." His own hair had a hint of the antidote lingering in the strands. And, judging by the suggestive curve of his husband's lips, there was more than a quick wash on offer. He hadn't attempted any sort of intimacy in a tub since his early twenties. "But I've a few matters to attend. Besides," he added, trying to alleviate Hamish's crestfallen expression. "I fear you'd cause me to sink."

"Sink you?" Hamish gave a broad grin that had Darshan wishing he could linger. "Oh aye, I'd sink in deep." He briefly bobbed his eyebrows.

Caught off guard by the unexpected innuendo, a harsh bark of laughter escaped his lips. "Tease," he wheezed. Did either the toxin or the antidote have a side effect he hadn't been aware of? He'd check on that later. Restraining himself, he flicked a spray of water at his husband. "I do have to leave you for a bit, though."

With Hamish's amusement still echoing around the room, Darshan left the bathing chamber to find his old nanny waiting.

"What was so urgent that you had to call me back?" She peered past him, her elven hearing no doubt able to distinguish any further hiccups of mirth from behind the closed door.

"Don't mind him." Darshan dabbed at the side of an eye in an attempt to keep his amusement from ruining his kohl. "He's just clearing the last of the toxins and antidote from his lungs." As swiftly as he was able, he recounted all the details, including the precise wording of the letter.

Daama examined the letter after he was done. "Curious."

"That they tried to kill my husband? Hardly." That they would be so overt in their methods was the more surprising thing. "I want the head of their household brought in for questioning."

"I'm afraid that won't be possible. The Kaatha estate was attacked by the neighbouring lands. They slaughtered every single one of that bloodline. Children and adults."

"When?" He might not have heard anything whilst travelling, but there'd been no announcement during his time back in Minamist either.

"A few months ago. Possibly around the time you arrived in Tirglas."

"Then who sent *this*?" He snatched the letter from her and waved it in her face. The seal had been genuine or else his scribe wouldn't have bothered opening it. The letter couldn't be old or the toxin would've become inert. "And why are they using a dead household to target my husband?"

Daama shrugged. "Retribution?"

Against Hamish? *No.* That was stupid. No one thought of his husband as a threat. "They think I caused those deaths?" It was the only logical path. What could he have done to be a party to the annihilation of an entire household? Especially unknowingly. "What ties did we have with them?"

"You mean, beyond your little fling?"

He frowned at her. "That doesn't exactly narrow it down." She knew that. She must've wasted years of her life berating him over his promiscuity. But what had been the point in saving himself? It had even worked in his favour. If he'd been chaste, his father never would've sent him to Tirglas.

"You were found with the man. The upset saw two households break off a wedding." She peered at him as though he was drunk. "Do you remember none of it?"

"No." That wasn't entirely a lie. He had slept with a fair few men in the months leading up to his departure for Tirglas. He didn't recall them all. That he was discovered with the possible lead narrowed it down a smidgeon. "Which one was he?"

"Scrawny fellow. Didn't look like he'd ever grow into his hands."

Darshan shook his head. He didn't spend near enough time mingling with the lower court to recall every face. But he *did* remember quite a bit of the dalliance that had ultimately seen him sent to Tirglas as punishment. The man had been engaged to a noblewoman. *She* had stumbled upon them. He remembered barely getting his shield up in time to block her fiery retaliation.

The man hadn't mentioned his household, though. Not in name, at least. *He asked for aid.* Darshan had assumed the young lord wanted an imperial troop to help in fighting a rival for him, just as so many had asked before.

Had the man actually come to his *vris Mhanek* not to curry favour, but to seek protection for his family?

And I used him.

He settled heavily into his chair. Gods, had he really become so used to the court trying to get what they could out of him that he had grown numb to sincerity? Or had he registered the truth and simply not cared? *All because it granted me a few moments of pleasure.* One that led to this vendetta. To dozens of deaths.

The extinction of a household.

He stared at the envelope abandoned on the table. *A vendetta.* That meant one of the Kaatha's was alive. Or a close ally. It wasn't much of a lead, but it was a start.

"I want the guards on alert. Hunt down whatever allies they had, any contracts with the guild they might've made." He would find them and, if they were also behind the other attacks, they would pay. Not only for the life they tried to take, but for the ones already taken. He would not see any more people suffer even another day over it.

And if *his* mistake was truly at the heart of it, he would make his own recompense.

Chapter 35

Hamish took in the space sprawled before him, the glitter and gilding. *This is a banquet hall?* Daama had told him it was the third biggest room in the council hall after the throne room and the ballroom, but he hadn't thought it would be this big. It certainly wasn't as imposing as the throne room with its large windows allowing plenty of natural light. He couldn't say much about the ballroom, given that he'd only heard about it.

It had been nineteen days since the poisoned letter. Longer than the last breather they'd had between then and the attack in the garden. There hadn't even been any caught attempts. Perhaps they were finally free of the culprit's reach.

Or maybe, as Darshan suspected, they were biding their time, waiting for everyone to let down their guard.

Servants bustled about him, making the final preparations for the engagement party in three days time. Throwing a small celebration after such news wasn't a foreign concept in Tirglas, but even his siblings hadn't commemorated the occasion with this level of grandeur.

The whole court wouldn't be in attendance. That would happen at the wedding. Most would still be travelling for the event. This party was merely for the few who were already here. It was still a lot. There was the senate, a few in the upper nobility and even more further down the hierarchy.

He was meant to be helping, even if that help was in delegating to those who could've done the job faster without his meddling. But he was there to select the entertainment, the decor, the seating... all the dull tasks designed to keep him busy and confined somewhere safe whilst others sought out the source of the last poisoning.

The people doing the actual work all suffered his intervention with identical genuflections and murmured agreements.

He hated it. He longed to be elsewhere, out in the city, or the surrounding lands. He'd been here a month and hadn't stepped beyond the palace grounds. Couldn't. At least he was allowed to leave the imperial grounds now, although, between these mundane tasks and Daama's tutoring, he rarely got a chance to and never without an escort.

No matter how much space the palace grounds held—definitely more than the entirety of Mullhind—it didn't make the walls any shorter or constricting. He wasn't stupid, though. As much as he wanted to see more of the city, exiting any of the palace gates wouldn't be safe, especially it was to some pub in the middle of the night.

Sadly, sharing a few pints with the palace guards wasn't the same. It didn't matter if he had chosen to hunt down the mess hall and imbibe amongst them in a place where they could rest, they were always careful to remain proper.

The Nulled Ones constantly flanking him probably had something to do with that.

It would've been more bearable had he been able to spend his time with Darshan, yet the man had his duties on top of managing his people. They were reunited every night and awoke together each morning, but his husband was often tired during the former and in a rush to begin his day in the latter.

Worst still, none of the man's networks had found anything close to a lead. They'd a dead household that no one would admit to associating with, no one within the assassin guild had contracts targeted either Hamish or Darshan—he was still getting used to the fact such a place existed—and the hypnotist hadn't left their mark anywhere else for them to start a fresh search.

Every day, Hamish woke wondering if this would be the day that changed things. But no. If their mystery hypnotist was near, they were clearly biding their time. *For when?* The engagement party? The wedding? Hamish would need to leave the palace grounds for the latter. The journey to the cleric's quarter might not be far, but it would leave him exposed.

Even embroiled in his own duties, his husband had noticed Hamish's eagerness to be somewhere not confined by walls. They might not have been able to properly duck out, but Darshan had promised him an evening of just them. *A date.* Just a private meal atop one of the towers in the outer wall whilst the sun set over the harbour. An enchanting alternative to full freedom and one Hamish looked forward to.

That still left him having to weather the day here.

Daama cleared her throat. "Whilst I am aware that the task leaves much room for idle thoughts, it would go by quicker if you refrained from disappearing into your own head."

"Sorry, Mistress Daama," he mumbled.

The woman's lips pursed, as they always did when he addressed her in such a fashion.

He couldn't help it. She was tutoring him and years of past lessons had led him to be respectful of such a position, but she was also under Darshan's ownership where any title was unnecessary or even frowned upon.

Sighing, Daama shook her head and returned her focus to the papers secured to a board she always carried about. "Part of your duties as the *vris Mhanek's* spouse will be to step in and make arrangements where he is unable to. Ensuring the soirées done in his name are exemplary is but a small part of it and they are more than mere parties thrown to amuse the masses. Many use them to strengthen current alliances as well as foster new ones."

"So I've been told." He had witnessed his share of houses doing a fair bit of fostering and strengthening of alliances at Onella's soirée. "It's also a place to spot potential enemies." Neither was a foreign idea. Most clan gatherings carried a similar air about them, just not as plainly stated.

"He ensured you knew that? Good. Then you shan't need me to repeat it."

"I just dinnae see what that has to do with us *being* in the banquet hall?" If he was merely delegating tasks to others, he could do it anywhere. Just as Darshan did. As Hamish's mother had.

She sniffed and adjusted the pen tucked into her bun. "The *Mhanek* has already ordered for the soirée honouring your engagement to be within certain boundaries. You must be *seen* complying with that request." She rifled through the pages on her board. "Now, the *vris Mhanek* would obviously already know the court's mood. But, as he is busy, he has asked me to help you oversee the seating details." Daama twisted until he could see the page over her shoulder, a simple diagram of the tables and seats in the same position the servants were setting them into. "Consider it a test of how well you've been paying attention to your lessons in Udynean politics."

If there was one drawback to being with Darshan, it was the court. He'd had little in the way of interaction with them, but it was still more than he wanted.

Sometimes, he wondered if his threat of tempting his husband into a simple life out on the edge of nowhere was possible.

"Let's get this over with." Hamish strolled through the room, eyeballing the tables. Although he had always known where to sit back in Tirglas, he hadn't really given much thought to how the other clans' nobilities were arranged. There must've been a knack to it that the head of the castle had known. And there were a lot more noble households than clans to contend with.

He paused in the centre of the banquet hall, turning on one heel to once more take in everything. The table where the royal family sat was obvious, it was the only long table in the room and tucked against the wall opposite the floor-to-ceiling windows. The round tables set near them would be for the upper nobility and those favoured by the *Mhanek* and Darshan, all of which would have their own feuds to consider.

Daama trotted at his heel as he continued navigating the tables, marking down the households he selected for each one. She didn't say a word about his choices—her only utterances being to add a few of the households he had forgotten—but the firm press of her lips suggested he'd done well enough to keep the soirée from erupting into chaos.

"Now that is done..." She gestured for a servant with a pitcher to come forward, waiting for the man to pour them a drink and taking a sip before continuing. "What colours were you thinking for the main decor? Do keep in mind that the *vris Mhanek* has—"

"Blue." The word was out before he could stop to think. Whilst certain combinations of colours weren't attached to particular clans like in Tirglas, they did have some strange meanings. The only one he could recall being bad as anything beyond an accent piece was white. Had it been something about a void? No, a goddess.

Still, he couldn't imagine blue having similar connotations.

Daama pursed her lips against her glass. "That isn't his favourite colour."

Nor was it Hamish's. He detested the colour on himself especially, but... "I think you'll find his opinion has changed a wee bit there."

She tilted her head, examining him just long enough for his feet to twitch. "It wouldn't happen to be a crystalline blue? The colour of our rarer aquamarine stones?"

"Quite likely." That was the shade his husband compared Hamish's eyes to. *Along with the harbour*. He hadn't seen enough of the city outside the palace grounds, much less the ocean, to judge whether the comparison was at all accurate.

"I see." She scribbled more on her notes. He couldn't be completely sure that they held only details for the engagement party, but he suspected she used this to determine just how much he knew about the man she had raised. "I never would've guessed he had a romantic side."

How would she? From what Hamish had learnt of the court, there weren't many Darshan would've felt comfortable enough around to woo.

"I suppose most men would be overjoyed at the idea that they had brought a new facet of their lover to light."

"It's nae new to me." The only change there had been from the man he first met all those months back were the public displays of affection, and he was certain the threat of his mother had been the reason Darshan curtailed those whilst in Tirglas.

Daama smiled sadly at her notes. "It seems he has spent so long hiding his true self, it became his nature to shield it even from those he was closest with."

"I'm sorry."

"No." She patted his forearm. "It's good that he's able to be himself with you." Clearing her throat, she adjusted her papers. "About the rest of the decor. I'd usually suggest fresh-cut flowers at this time of year, but the *uris Mhanek* seems oddly opposed to them." There was a hint of a question in the words.

"Aye." Having the room lavishly decorated wasn't something he had witnessed in Tirglasian banquets and, even then, it involved a lot of trophies from their hunts or those of ancestors. A detail Udynean decor seemed to lack entirely. "How about..." He struggled to think of Onella's soirée, of what he'd seen there that seemed as though it might be commonplace. "Feathers? Silk?" He'd seen so much of it hanging from the ceilings that the walls here looked bare. "Maybe some of those little light globes."

Daama wrinkled her nose at the final suggestion.

He shrugged. "Just a thought." He knew the last suggested needed the constant attendance of a spellster, but if any place had magic to spare, it was here.

"Perhaps we should mull over a few more ideas before settling on something."

They went back and forth on the details, him suggesting everything under the sun whilst Daama queried the logistics. Servants continued to scuttle about, most adjusted the seating and laid out little name plaques, some brought him swatches of blue cloth to choose from and a handful trotted in with refreshments that were eagerly fallen upon.

Noon had well and truly gone by the time they finalised everything.

Hamish returned to the imperial palace. He'd a few hours left to prepare before the date with his husband. Often when he had time to spare like this, he spent it in the stables, grooming and exercising his mare whilst the stable hands fussed outside the stall or at the gate to the working pen.

Did he have time now? Darshan would probably forgive him for turning up to their date reeking of horse sweat and dirt, but arriving properly groomed was the least he could do after the man worked to make this time for them.

Besides, he saw his mare more days than not. His husband was becoming the rare being to have more than a brief moment with.

At the steps, he waved off the Nulled Ones who had escorted him. There were plenty of their kin in the building. If he needed anyone to be his shadow, summoning them wouldn't be a problem.

He sauntered alone through the hallways. At least, as alone as he could be with a stream of servants scurrying by who were so absorbed in getting to their task that they almost bumped into him on occasion.

How they missed his presence was beyond him. With so many being elves, he towered over most. *Almost like being surrounded by half-grown people.* His youngest nephew must've topped the tallest of the bunch by now. The boy had been growing like a tree.

Swallowing the gentle welling of homesickness, Hamish climbed another flight of stairs.

There were fewer servants the higher up he went. Here, the public rooms dropped off and whole sections were reserved for each princess. Darshan and his twin's residences sat higher still.

Hamish trotted up the second-to-last set of stairs between him and the *vris Mhanek* suite. He would hate to be the fools who chose to storm this place. Every level seemed designed to expose an incoming hoard.

Like the stairways. Airy and broad, leaving an enemy open to attack from above. Nothing like the tight stairwells of Castle Mullhind that barely allowed the room for a descending party to swing a sword. Although, when the enemy lurked in the shadows, preferring to nip at the heels rather than face them head-on, structural defences seemed meaningless.

He was halfway to the final stairway when a soft voice called out to him. "Excuse me, your highness."

Hamish turned, spying a slight, blonde woman standing at his elbow. There was no one else in sight. Not a single servant or guard.

Dismissing the Nulled Ones no longer seemed like a good choice.

The woman stared up at him, her dark eyes huge and unblinking. "I don't suppose a tall man such as yourself could help me?"

"Lass, that would depend on the—"

A fuzziness swept over his mind, paralysing his body. He tried to look away, to close his eyelids, but found himself transfixed. *Those eyes.* So deep. Endless like the night sky.

"I thought you could," the woman murmured, her lips curling in self-satisfaction before the corners fell ruefully. "I want you to know that I *am* sorry. You *are* a mere innocent bystander, after all. But so was my betrothed. So were our families." She clutched at her chest, her fingers possessively clawing around a brooch. "And what did they get?"

He shook his head, struggling to clear it. Something nagged on the outer curve of his thoughts. It lifted his hair and sent prickles across his mind.

"Look at me," she commanded.

Try as he might to do otherwise, he couldn't refuse. His eyes burned from not blinking.

"Listen carefully." She beckoned him closer. "You are to enter that room you share with *him*. You will take that dagger of yours and slip it straight into your precious lover's heart."

Dagger? Did she mean his hunting knife? He fingered the handle. His insistence on wearing it around the palace grounds was often met with condescending smiles and chuckles. He knew it wouldn't do much against a spellster, it was designed more as tool than a weapon, but the blade was no less sharp. It would enter a man swifter than gutting a boar.

"Now go."

Hamish turned towards the stairs. *Plunge me knife into Darshan's heart.* That was...

Nae. His head spun. *Nae him.* He staggered a few steps. Never his husband. Hamish steadied himself as the hallway continued to spin, holding back the sudden urge to vomit.

With her feet barely making a sound on the tiles, the woman rushed to stand before him, pinning him to the spot with her crazed expression. "Do it!" she ordered, pointing at the floor above. "Kill him! Butcher that disgusting creature just like he did my Zia!"

The command settled on his mind like fog. *Kill...*

Her hold slipped off as quickly as water down a ravine.

"*You*," he snarled. All this time, all the chaos sewed through their travels. The stalling of his peaceful life with his husband. The *deaths*. It was because of this woman.

He lunged for her, his hand closing around a fistful of clothing.

In a flash of fire, she slipped out of reach. Before he realised she was loose, the woman was down the hallway with the swiftness of a horse thief and off around the corner. All without making a sound.

He threw down the scrap of cloth and gave chase. "Shut the entrances!" he bellowed to the first servant he came across, who hastened to obey. "Alert the guards!" There were only so many ways into the imperial palace, each entrance watched over by Nulled Ones.

She would *not* easily escape.

~ ~ ~

Darshan hastened towards the imperial palace. *I can make it.* The sun wasn't too low in the sky. He would have just enough time to bathe and be waiting at the base of the tower to greet Hamish. *Blasted senate.* If only his dealings with them hadn't gone in circles, he'd be well and truly ready for tonight.

He had thought his arrival, and the presence of a spouse, would've kept the senate from prying into the sudden emancipation of the people he had been gifted over the years, but he supposed having several hundred no longer tied to him in such a manner would be hard to ignore.

It was only natural for the senate to be worried. On the outside, it likely looked as though Hamish had coerced him into ordering the writs and that could lead to bad choices later on, when he was the *Mhanek*. Convincing them that Hamish had no part in the idea had sapped much of his enthusiasm.

How difficult could it possibly be to understand *he* had made the decision without any exterior influence? Did they not think him capable of such ideas? *Probably not.* The senate likely saw him as a puppet just waiting for their strings.

Darshan trotted up the stairs leading to the main entrance to the imperial palace.

He reached the closed doors as the bellow of a familiar voice caught his attention. *'Mish?* The man sounded positively feral. Clearly, something had upset him enough to—

The doors burst open, admitting his panting, snarling husband. His nostrils flared with each chest-swelling breath. Sweat tricked down his face and there was a faint red flush to his nose and cheeks.

Darshan wet his lips and pushed down the immediate urge to jump the man. He was quite certain the memory of his enraged being would be enough later on tonight. Providing he could calm his husband in the interim. "*Mea lux?* What is wrong?"

Hamish peered at their surroundings. His fingers twitched as though he held a bow and arrow, ready to loose at any second. "Did you see her?" he growled.

"See who?"

His husband glared down at Darshan as if thinking he lacked sense. "The wee blonde lass with the soul-sucking dark eyes. About this high." He drew a line across the midway mark of his chest with his thumb, around nose height for Darshan. "Bloody woman tried to hypnotise me."

Darshan's heart thudded an extra beat. She was *here*? *In* the imperial palace? "Are you certain?" A foolish question, he didn't need Hamish's dumbfounded expression to tell him that. "What was she attempting? Do you remember?"

"Aye. She wanted me to kill you."

"That doesn't make sense." He grimaced. "I mean, it makes perfect sense." He could count on one hand the household who weren't covertly trying to ensure the imperial line ended here. It was just how things were. "But I thought she was linked to the attacks on you. If she's after me, then—"

"It's like Onella said," Hamish interjected. "I'm a gap in your armour. A weak spot." He prodded Darshan's chest. "One that's positioned right over your heart."

Darshan closed his eyes. It was true. And with a single soirée, he had exposed his vulnerability to the court. There was little he could do about that bar removing Hamish from his life and that wasn't an option he was prepared to consider for a second.

And yet, if they found this woman and eliminated the threat hanging over their heads, maybe it would also convince the other households that his husband wasn't a weakness to be exploited. "Do you remember any other descriptors?" If they could find her swiftly enough.

Hamish grunted an affirmation. "She looked to be in her early twenties. Had a snooty air about her, too. Nae dressed in anything fancy, though. She wore a brooch, but I couldnae see much there. Was ranting about someone called..." He frowned. "Zee? Nae... Zee... Zia! Does that mean anything to you?"

He shook his head. Apart from the name being more common further north, he knew of no one significant with it. "The garb could've been a disguise." Even in the palace grounds, noble clothes drew attention.

"Fit her well enough." He swore low and long. "I tried to grab her. Got her sleeve, too, but she bloody seared the bit off and slipped out of me grasp. I drop the cloth when I was chasing her. It's probably still on the floor."

Or, far more likely, collected by the palace cleaners. If they had the piece, they might've been able to match any patterns or alert the laundry of any clothing appearing with holes that matched the scrap. "Do you remember much about it?"

Hamish shrugged. "Soft. Kind of a watery green, I think. It wasnae exactly the thing I paid the most attention to."

Lower nobility. The only other option would be a wealthy merchant, but only the glass merchants had the wealth to match a lower lord's coffers. But who? Clearly someone who carried a grudge.

He'd little to do with the lower households.

Darshan shoved his husband towards the very doors the man had erupted through. Sweat soaked through the silk and linen to dampen Darshan's palms.

Hamish halted, the abruptness almost tearing Darshan's arm from its socket. "Where are you taking me?"

"Inside. We have to—"

"Find her?" He jerked his arm out of Darshan's grasp and charged on. "Good idea. The palace still needs to be swept. If the trail is this fresh, we may be able to catch her."

"No! You were attacked. *Hypnotised.*" And had broken free of the woman's hold. *Just as he did with Father.* How? He still didn't have a confirmed answer there. Was it perhaps a specialist trick? "You need to be checked over and the guards must be alerted."

"The guards *have* been alerted. And *you* can check me right here." He halted, spreading his arm wide in an invitation.

Darshan placed his fingers onto Hamish's forearm. That was clammy as well. "Did you run the full length of the palace stairs?" Nevertheless, apart from the effects of obvious exertion, his husband seemed normal. No hints of scarring on his brain. *Same as last time.* Maybe he didn't have to worry about Hamish being compromised.

But there was still everyone else.

"Now will you let me help search?" He held up his hand before Darshan could voice his objections. "I've already given the guards all the details—and I promise nae to go anywhere without a Nulled One." He jutted a finger into Darshan's shoulder. "But I'm nae cowering under some guard. Nae after this. Bad enough she's ruining what was promised to me tonight."

"There's nothing to say we couldn't continue with our date." What better way to show themselves as unfazed with the attack than to carry on as if nothing had transpired? All whilst his network silently hunted their hypnotist. And he *had* worked hard to clear his schedule of all the important matters to give them this time. With the hypnotist desperate enough to target Hamish directly, who knew when they'd have another chance to be truly alone in the short term? "I can even get extra guards put on all the tower entrances."

Hamish narrowed his eyes, clearly giving it some consideration, before shaking his head. "I want her caught." He frowned at the imperial palace. "She's trapped."

Darshan wasn't quite so certain of that. He had snuck out of the palace plenty of times. Still, aiding in the search was the better option. "We'll have to be thorough." It would take hours to organise the Nulled Ones and send them sweeping through the palace.

It ruined his carefully planned date but, with luck, the

overhanging threat of their hypnotist would be over before the engagement party. Being able to finally relax was certainly worth the upset.

Chapter 36

Where is he?

Hamish paced before the closed doors leading to the banquet hall. This was the royal entrance, reserved for the *Mhanek*, his heir and their spouses. Everyone else was currently filing into the room elsewhere.

But even Darshan's father had left this quiet little anteroom for the bustle awaiting them on the other side of the doors.

He knew his husband would be taking extra care at making himself presentable for the engagement party, but how much time could that possibly take over his usual routine? He already looked perfect without further primping.

Was he even in the building? What if something had gone wrong? They hadn't found the hypnotist. What if she had grown desperate enough to target Darshan directly?

He's safe. The Nulled Ones would see to that.

Still, his feet itched to go search for his wayward husband. *A bad idea.* He didn't need anyone to tell him that. If Darshan was in trouble, there was little Hamish could do except put himself in harm's way. *If he doesnae get here soon...*

The whisper of a gasp tore his thoughts to shreds.

Hamish spun to find his husband standing in the opposite doorway.

"*Mea lux*," Darshan breathed. He didn't take his eyes off Hamish as he crossed the room, Hamish wasn't even sure if the man blinked.

Without thinking, Hamish tugged and straightened the hem of his sherwani. He might've commissioned the outfit some weeks back, but this was the first time he had done more than try it on for sizing. It was light grey with a faint bluish tint that balanced the sea-blue piping and embroidery. He hadn't asked for the buttons to sport similar beads but, after having a decent look at himself in the mirror whilst his husband bathed, he had to admit they definitely complemented his eyes.

"You look like a feast."

"And *you...*" Hamish took Darshan's hand in his and pressed the bejewelled fingers to his lips. Those rings weren't the only thing that sparkled. The glasses Darshan wore looked to be new, the rims gleaming gold. There was also a dusting of silver powder to the man's eyelids that made the customary kohl seem darker. Hamish had seen plenty of people at Onella's soirée with such makeup, but never his husband. "You look like the heavens."

The faint creases around Darshan's eyes deepened. "You really didn't have to wear that, though," he insisted, still eyeing Hamish's chosen attire.

He smiled against his husband's fingers. He should've known the man would spot any new outfit amongst Hamish's scant collection. "And have us nae looking like a matched set?"

Where Hamish's silver attire had blue accents, Darshan's was the reverse. He rarely saw the man in darker shades that weren't black. His husband was aware of how good he looked in ivory and his clothing choices favoured that in various shades. But the way the silver threads in the sea-blue silk caught the light definitely gave his husband the look of an ethereal water sprite.

"Perish the thought," Darshan murmured, running a hand down Hamish's front, adjusting the buttons and smoothing the fabric. "I guess we're both going to break a lot of hearts tonight."

"I can understand why some would be broken up over *you*, but nae meself." Everyone invited had to know this soirée was to celebrate their upcoming wedding. To that end he was, as his brother would say, off the market. On top of that, he didn't think more than a handful would consider him as the catch his husband somehow saw.

"The Crystal Court does like to pine over what they cannot have."

"Speaking from experience?" His husband had admitted to lusting after Hamish almost as soon as they had met.

"Absolutely not." He grabbed Hamish's collar, coaxing him to bend down. "The difference being," he breathed, their mouths close enough for their moustaches to touch. "Is that *I* got what I wanted."

"Aye," Hamish agreed, aware that his voice had grown a little on the husky side. "And more than you bargained for, I'd wager." Not that either of them could've envisioned their trip through Udynea would've included a vengeful hypnotist.

"I'll take my chances there." In one smooth movement, Darshan released Hamish's collar, readjusted the sherwani and tucked his hand into the crook of Hamish's arm. "Shall we?"

Hamish bowed his head in agreement.

With a flick of his fingers, Darshan set the doors swinging open, startling the announcer waiting on the other side.

"His imperial highness," the woman screeched before regaining her composure and continuing in a more dignified tone. "Darshan *vris Mhanek*, and his betrothed, Prince Hamish of Tirglas."

Hamish barely heard the woman, catching only the amendment to his address before the room caught his full attention. Even though *he* had done all the selecting, he hadn't seen his choices for the decor put together until now.

Darshan halted in the doorway. "Oh," he breathed. *"Mea lux."* He beamed up at Hamish, blinking furiously as his eyes took on a glassy sheen behind the lenses. "My gorgeous beacon."

The walls glittered. Curtains of beads and chains of silver and gold shimmered against a backdrop of rich blue silk the colour of the harbour on a clear day. Bubbles of light danced along the chains, not magic, but fizzing from a row of vases set against the walls.

Feathers—some he knew were plucked only yesterday from the very birds they were to dine on—adorned each table in a festoon of iridescent shades. The vases flanking the royal table held the longest tail feathers Hamish had ever seen, their tips blooming into an array of eye-like emblems.

Up and down the banquet hall, people had stopped to bow or curtsy at their entrance. They remained that way even now, waiting for them to fully enter the room.

Hamish tugged slightly at Darshan's arm. "Come on, me heart. I think we've lingered long enough."

Somehow, his husband's smile managed to widen further. "Lead away."

They made their way to the royal table. The people straightened as the door behind Hamish finally swung shut, some genuflecting anew as the path they took drew them closer to a few of the tables. Darshan barely acknowledged them, smiling at a select handful. Hamish tried to keep in mind which ones were considered as his husband's allies. He had the names, but very few faces to attach them to.

"Do you see anyone who looks like they might be our little hypnotist?" Darshan asked in Tirglasian. There were guards at all the entrances, both the ordinary kind and Nulled Ones, but it couldn't hurt to be thorough.

Hamish squinted into the distance. There were a handful of nobles taller than the average Udynean, but he still had a clear line of sight. It didn't help much. There were quite a few veiled heads amongst a crowd of black and brown hairs. "Nae so far." If he had been the woman, he would've opted to lay low and let people's minds drift to other matters.

And what guarantee did they have that she wouldn't disguise herself now Hamish had seen her face? A little dye in her hair, a little powder and paint. The only thing she couldn't change were those dark eyes and he didn't fancy getting close enough to recognise them again.

They reached the royal table, bowing their heads in greeting to Darshan's sisters and father, who were all seated and waiting. The *Mhanek* replied to his son in kind as the *vlossinas* all bent to place their heads inches from the table.

Hamish's stomach twisted a little at the display. So different to the bubbly way the women usually greeted their brother. The act would be expected of himself, too. Less once the wedding was over and he was considered as more than Darshan's betrothed.

The *Mhanek* got to his feet as they finally settled in their seats. "I thank you all for making the effort to join us in celebrating this momentous occasion..."

Hamish fought to stifle a sigh as the man continued. He hated speeches. His mother was fond of them, always using it as an excuse to boast about her children's many accomplishments and, in Hamish's case, prove how fit of a husband he would be. At least there'd be none of the latter here.

His attention slid down the rows of chairs at the table. There were vacant places down the table, spots that would've been filled with other family members had they been able to arrive in time. Members like Onella and her son.

But nae her husband. That last detail had been a shock when he'd first heard it. Married couples were meant to remain together during these sorts of parties and, like the rest of Darshan's married sisters, Onella should've been considered only as the matriarch of her husband's household. That she was still treated as an unmarried *vlossina* at all was thanks to being the mother of the *Mhanek's* only grandson and Darshan's bachelor status.

Hamish could see why she would attempt to eliminate whatever threatened that position. He didn't agree with her methods, but he was coming to understand her a little more.

What did her son think of it? Tarendra had to know that, for him to take the throne, his uncle would need to die. Hamish had only seen the boy during meals shared with the family, but the fondness he had for Darshan seemed genuine. Like Hamish's own nephews, he didn't think Tarendra would be willing to participate in the active usurping of Darshan's reign.

Hamish glanced back down the table, confirming that his eyes hadn't betrayed him. The boy was nowhere in sight. He discreetly scanned the front row of the tables facing them before leaning closer to Darshan and whispering in Tirglasian, "Where's your wee nephew?"

Darshan plucked his wine glass from the table and, whilst casually acting as though he was taking a drink, replied, "He *should* be resting in preparation for his *Khutani.*"

"Ah," Hamish managed, returning to silence. He had forgotten that particular ceremony was in a few days. He had been invited to attend, even though he wasn't technically considered a part of Darshan's family until their second wedding. As much as he wanted to decline, he couldn't refuse Tarendra's pleading eyes that, although were a lighter brown, reminded him so much of his own nephews.

The *Mhanek's* speech finally came to an end, eliciting a smattering of polite claps. The very way everyone seemed to be on edge had him biting his lip to keep from laughing. *It's dinner with me family all over again.* Except *he* wasn't likely to be the target for the *Mhanek's* wrath.

Servants trotted out with trays of appetisers, sitting the glass cloches on the table with practised precision. Steam fogged the cloche's inner surface, all but obscuring the meal within. *Eel pie.* His favourite dish back home, served with a heavy coating of white sauce that helped each bite slide down just right.

He swallowed to keep himself from drooling onto the table.

Confused murmurs drifted up from the tables as the cloches were lifted. No doubt, the people expected the usual fanciful array of birds stuffed with herbs or complicated rice-based dishes.

Darshan got to his feet, the act stilling all talk. "I can see some stirrings of bewilderment amongst you all. In honour of my hus—" he grimaced. "My *betrothed's* heritage, tonight, we shall be dining Tirglasian style. Including their custom of clearing their plates, so I hope you all have big appetites."

Those amongst the crowd exchanged looks that varied from mildly perplexed to outright panic.

"Because of this," Darshan continued, "the usual decorum of holding back food for your servants shan't be observed tonight. You might've noticed the absence of the ones you have brought. Be assured they are quite safe in the hall below and being adequately tended to. Enjoy!" He sat back down and immediately fell to eating.

Hamish took a bite of the pie and let out a mournful sigh. The white sauce was too heavily spiced, overpowering everything, and the inside of the pie lacked the jellified texture he'd grown up with.

"I'm sorry, *mea lux,*" Darshan muttered around a mouthful, his upraised hand shielding much of his expression. "I had hoped the cooks would be able to replicate it."

"It's nae your fault." It wasn't bad. A few would likely say it was an improvement. However, even if he closed his eyes and pretended, there was no chance of it tasting like home. "I should nae have expected it to be the same." Regardless of where the recipe came from, the dishes were still made by Udynean cooks. The rest of the courses were likely the same, tempting him with memories of a land he couldn't return to. He took another mouthful, more prepared for the disjointedness between looks and taste.

The rest of the table ate in silence. It was hard to determine their thoughts—each one seemed to have the same training of maintaining a neutral expression as Darshan—but they cleaned their plates with almost military precision.

A few of the other nobles were having a little more trouble finishing. Many had, no doubt, already eaten their fill before leaving the guest palace, just as Darshan and himself did back in Nulshar. "Is it nae cruel to ask them to eat every last bite?" This was only the first course. There were various baked goods, then a selection of roast animals to follow.

"A little," Darshan replied.

"But it's fun to watch," Anjali added, leaning against the table to poke her head around her father.

The *Mhanek* cleared his throat, quietening both of his eldest children. "Perhaps a little intermission will aid in giving them more room for the rest of tonight's feast." He beckoned one of the servants standing by the wall, whispering in the man's ear, before dismissing them back to the others.

One by one, the servants peeled off to flit around the tables. They gathered plates and filled glasses, all whilst delivering whatever message the *Mhanek* had given to the first man.

"I hope you don't mind," the *Mhanek* said. "But I delayed the second course. Just for another hour or so. Give people a chance to mingle and the like."

Hamish took a steadying breath. He had yet to fully integrate himself into the Crystal Court and his dealings with most of the nobles had come before any formal tutoring. He could excuse any blunders by playing the ignorant foreigner, but that wouldn't be an act he could fall back on for long.

"I think I'll excuse myself from any mingling," Darshan said. He waggled his empty glass at a passing servant, waiting until it was refilled before settling back into his chair. "Interacting with the court is rather like mining for *infitialis*." He didn't need to finish the other half of the sentence, Hamish had heard his husband say it enough throughout their travels.

It explodes in your face at the slightest upset. Some days, Hamish wondered how the Ancient Domians managed to work with the metal for long enough to discover its magic nullifying properties. They couldn't have known about the paste that the Udyneans now used to transport it.

The rest of the court clearly didn't have the same outlook on mingling. They swiftly started to chat amongst themselves, some sectioning into small groups to gossip. He caught a few of Darshan's married sisters amongst them. Did they seek to put out the fires of rumour or fan the flames? Hard to tell without eavesdropping.

No one dared approach the royal table. That was different from the Tirglasian court. Clan leaders could barely wait for their last mouthful to hit their stomach before they swaggered up to his mother.

Before long, cheers came from the far end of the room.

"What's happening over there?" Darshan craned his neck, attempting to see past the mob crowding the doorway to a balcony.

"Daama said there are typically games at these parties. I thought I'd give them a wee taste of Tirglasian sports."

Another cheer went up from the crowd.

"Don't tease me, 'Mish. What is it?"

"Archery," Zahaan supplied, causing Hamish to jump. Darshan's spymaster had arrived a week ago and promptly spent the majority of his time hunting for clues about their hypnotist. He was now here as an extra pair of eyes to train on the guests.

But he hadn't been behind them a moment ago.

Hamish clutched at his chest, his heart hammering at twice its speed. "Are you trying to do the bloody hypnotist's job?"

"My apologies, your highness," the man said, sounding no more remorseful than a rock. "I shall remember in future that the announcement of my arrival is important enough to interrupt the *Mhanek's* speech."

"My word," Darshan murmured, staring into his wine glass. "Someone is being extra catty tonight. What tweaked your ears?"

Zahaan sniffed, his narrow nose crinkling slightly. Looking down on his master, he seemed every inch a prince. "This soirée is foolish. You leave yourself open to attack."

"Don't be ridiculous. We're surrounded by just as many allies as foes."

"And if they all turn on you? The hypnotist has already proven herself capable of holding whole groups under her thrall."

Hamish held his tongue despite seeing the point the man made.

Darshan scoffed. "She can't control the Nulled Ones and they are alert." He gestured to the doorways, where people stood in the uniform Hamish had become accustomed to seeing everywhere he went.

Unlike the common guards who aided in keeping the doorways secure, the Nulled Ones also stood in measured distances all around the room. *Like statues.* Each one carried a sword, much like Zahaan did when he had met the man outside the palace grounds. He thought the weapon would be obsolete against magic, but even the strongest spellster had a healthy respect for a few feet of sharpened steel.

"There are a lot of people here," Zahaan pointed out.

"There'll be more at the wedding," Darshan countered. "If we cannot keep him safe here, then how can we hope to maintain security come the final day? We'll be out in the open, then. Or have you forgotten?"

Zahaan fell silent.

Hamish tried not to think about that last part. The beginning of the three-day ceremony was twelve days away. There were moments when the time between felt as though it rushed at him whilst, in other days, the wedding seemed so distant. All the preparations didn't help. His tutoring was often interspersed with fittings for his wedding attire alongside extra lessons on court etiquette and household standings.

He still had the rehearsals of their vows to worry about. He was less concerned there. A few words wouldn't be hard to memorise and he'd have Darshan's help if he stumbled, but did it really matter when all of it could be thrown into chaos by one woman out for revenge?

And over what? If they'd one solid idea to chase, then they might be able to catch the hypnotist. They had theories, but no one was certain. Darshan's people confirmed that everyone from the Kaatha household had died in the attack. And old allies had buried ties or refused to admit their connections.

Would they find her before the wedding ceremony started? Even with the size of the palace grounds, there were only so many places a person could hide. *Nae in the imperial grounds.* Not anymore. The Nulled Ones had searched every inch after her attempt on him. *Nae the guest palace.* Yesterday, they had ushered everyone out in a top to bottom purge that had flushed out a few spies, but not the woman.

That still left a big area with a lot of buildings. There wasn't the manpower to secure everywhere at once. If only the palace grounds were smaller...

"So," Darshan drawled, twisting in his seat to give Hamish a puzzled look. "You've given the court a taste of archery games, have you? Does that mean there's a target on the balcony? Is that safe?"

Hamish shook his head. "Nae if *they* are doing the aiming." He figured that only a handful of arrows would actually miss a static target, but that wasn't what sat out there. "We usually aim at wee straw figures or lob stones into pots, but I saw those paper lanterns from the last festival." It had been a small and solemn affair within the palace grounds. Nothing like the cavorting Anjali spoke about in teasing tones. "And, well..." He shrugged. "I figured there's enough spellsters around if something goes wrong."

"Has anyone actually managed to hit one?" Darshan asked of his spymaster.

"A couple of them," the man replied. "Although, I suspect a small amount of cheating going on."

Hamish had anticipated it might be a challenge and the court did seem to have a competitive streak wide enough to herd a flock of sheep along.

Grinning, Darshan got to his feet. "Come on, *mea lux*. You simply must show them how it's done."

"I didnae exactly have any intentions of joining in there." Nor did it seem fair. From the little he knew of the Crystal Court, few would have the training to properly loose an arrow. Still, he trailed behind his husband as Darshan strode through the hastily parting crowd. It had been a while since he had used a bow and his own sat on a rack in their bedchamber. His preference towards daily practice had been stifled by tutoring and the upcoming ceremony.

"Will they nae be able to tell I'm a spellster?" No one beyond Onella and the *Mhanek* had shown any disdain towards his specialist nature. And even the latter didn't grumble about it these days. But Zahaan had suggested they didn't make a show of it.

Darshan paused, then laughed, drawing the attention of a nearby trio. "*Mea lux*, most barely know how to use a bow, much less what skilled archers are capable of. All they'll think is that you are magnificent." He smoothed the front of Hamish's top, his fingers curling a little too possessively as they slid down Hamish's abdomen. "Which you are, of course, but I want to rub their noses in the fact."

"By showing off your most prized possession?" He knew Darshan saw more to him than the mere adornment on the arm, but that wouldn't keep Hamish from teasing the man.

Darshan hummed. "More in the realm of flouting what my stunning husband is capable of."

"*Stunning?*" Men had called a lot of things over the years, but never that.

"Gods, yes," Darshan growled, a familiar gleam lighting his eyes. "You certainly left *me* an incomprehensible mess when we first met."

Heat took Hamish's face. He was aware of catching Darshan's attention at the first glance, but not to that extent. "I still doubt they'll be impressed with me archery skills." What he could do with a bow and a few arrows seemed mundane next to the wonders Darshan wielded.

"You'd be surprised."

They reached the balcony where people still attempted to hit the targets. Those content with watching bowed and murmured their greetings as Darshan neared.

Hamish's attention was drawn to the targets. The lanterns bobbed in the breeze, tethered by way of a long rope treated in some sort of fire-repelling solution. *Four.* Zahaan had been right about some of the arrows striking true.

"Go on," Darshan insisted, handing him one of the bows. "Show them the skill and might of a Tirglasian warrior."

Hamish plucked an arrow from the stack, feeling the flight and peering down the shaft. *Nae exactly well-made.* His next choice was the same, as was the third. Did the fletchers in Udynea not know how to craft a proper arrow?

The bow was much the same, the string was fraying and the wood was rough and so light it felt as though he held nothing. *These have to be practice bows.* Even then, the ones his niece and nephews used were of better quality.

What he wouldn't give for his own weapon right now.

Still, he nocked the arrow and drew back, cringing slightly as the wood creaked. It was going to snap, he was sure of it. Aiming at the closest lantern, he let the arrow fly. The tip shot through the paper sides with ease and flew out into the courtyard, the area kept carefully empty for tonight.

Impressed murmurs filled the crowd.

"I don't think they're quite convinced," Darshan said. He gathered up three more arrows. "What's say you put down the last ones?"

"If you insist." It felt good to have a bow back in his hands and he definitely longed to use it again. Although, the way the lanterns moved reminded him of ducks on the water. He needed something with a degree of difficulty to really scratch the itch. "But make it interesting and cut the ropes."

With a wave of his hand, Darshan wordlessly severed the tethers and the remaining lanterns drifted off in three separate directions.

Hamish caught the first easily enough as it shot upwards. The second drifted off to his left. He whipped an arrow from Darshan's hand and caught the lantern before the first could begin falling. "Give me a bloody challenge," he growled.

A blast of air whipped past him, catching the final lantern as it lazily floated off on the breeze. It twirled in the sudden gust, travelling far from the balcony to bob around like a drunken chicken.

It sat almost beyond reach of his own bow. He didn't think this one could have an arrow make the distance but, having asked for a challenge, he was determined to at least attempt it.

He pulled the bowstring back, keeping his focus on the lantern. The bow vibrated in his grip, the shoddy wood protesting at the stress he put it under.

The bowstring snapped as he loosed the arrow.

It didn't matter. The arrow flew on, levelling out too short, then continuing to defy gravity by travelling dead straight to skewer his last target.

All around him, the crowd politely clapped whilst his husband crowed as though the efforts had been his doing.

Hamish ducked his head. Never had he heard anyone display such pride in his talent with a bow, not even his brother, who would assert Hamish was the best archer in the world. He tried to hide the growing heat in his cheeks by examining the bow, surprised to find the string wasn't the only piece to give. He turned it over, tilted the belly of the bow towards the light. Those cracks hadn't been there earlier, he was sure of it.

Darshan wrapped an arm around Hamish's waist, the grip carrying a slight possessive touch. "Come, *mea lux*. I think we've given them an adequate taste of your prowess with a bow. Although, perhaps we should have someone fetch your own next time." He delicately plucked the broken bow from Hamish's hands and tossed it to one side for a servant to snatch up. "Shall we leave these people to their entertainment?"

"What entertainment?" He had taken out all the lanterns and the dancing wasn't until much later.

At the smallest gesture from Darshan, a servant raced to the balcony's edge and ordered the people below to release more lanterns. It wasn't long before they drifted up, glowing warmly as they bobbed about in the waning twilight.

"You ken, if you get someone to fetch me bow and some decent arrows, I could probably hit those blindfolded." And with more accuracy than anyone else in the court.

Laughing, his husband nudged him away from the balcony. "So competitive. Let the others have some fun, *mea lux*." He snagged a glass of wine from a passing servant, eyeing Hamish up and down as he took a long drink.

Hamish felt the strangely loose collar of his sherwani. The button had, somehow, come undone. He went to fasten it again only for Darshan to draw his hand away.

"Leave it. You look far more delectable with it this way."

"I hope you dinnae plan to undress me in front of the whole court."

416

There were children here; Darshan's own siblings and nephew as well as a handful of others.

Scoffing, his husband rolled his eyes. "Of course not. I'll leave that for when we're back in the safety of our chambers." Once again, his gaze ran over Hamish, the heat behind the look less covert. "Doesn't mean I cannot enjoy the view in the meantime. It's going to be a long night as it is."

"I'm sure you'll manage." Like at Onella's soirée, his husband certainly appeared to be in his element amongst the crowd.

Even now, as they crossed the room, he seemed uncaring of how the people watched them. Some came up to speak with him and it was as though a different man walked beside him. The neutral mask hardened Darshan's features whenever one of them spoke and he never gave a definite answer to any question that didn't pertain to their recent travels or the upcoming wedding.

Hamish wasn't sure how the man managed it. He would've flushed to his toes attempting such evasiveness.

Through it all, he spied his husband's drink getting steadily lower. He turned to grab another glass from a passing servant and walked straight into a sandy-haired nobleman. "Sorry, I—" The faint coolness of liquid soaking into his trousers drew his attention downwards. Sure enough, a growing wine stain marred his left thigh. The source from the two drinks the man carried.

"Forgive me, your highness." The man hastened to step out of the way, slopping more wine onto the polished wood floor. He grimaced, his shoulders hunching. Although he was one of the taller people in the crowd, Hamish still topped him by a head.

The man looked familiar, too. *Where from?* He couldn't recall. Not in any of the attacks. All those involved were dead or imprisoned and he didn't seem dangerous. The theatre? There hadn't been many there with that pale a hair colour.

"Count Aarav," Darshan brightly exclaimed. "Without your collar, I see."

Onella's soirée. The memory of stumbling upon Aarav and his lover having sex hit Hamish with full force. His whole face steadily grew hot. The man hadn't been a count then. And there been markedly less clothing.

Aarav touched his neck. It bore the faint impression of where the band of metal links had sat, but little more. If Hamish hadn't seen the collar himself, he never would've believed it had happened. "Yes, *vris Mhanek.* Jeet..." The man's gaze slid to a nearby table where the much shorter man sat engaged in what looked to be a spirited conversation with others sharing the placing. "The situation changed."

"Your father," Darshan said, nodding sadly. "My condolences. For both you and your husband."

Aarav's gaze dropped. He hooked one foot behind the other. "Thank you, *vris Mhanek*. You are too kind. May I bid you farewell for now? My husband—" A faint smile creased his eyes at the word. "—is waiting for this." He held up the remains of the drinks. "Or at least what's left of it." He swung back to Hamish. "I'm truly sorry, your highness. I'd offer to amend my error, but I'm still getting used to having my magic again."

"I'm sure I can manage," Darshan said, gesturing for the man to take his leave before turning to tend to Hamish's damp trouser leg. He gently dried the silk, muttering under his breath. "I guess we can be fortunate that it wasn't red wine. Just imagine how it would look if you disappeared to change."

Hamish was less concerned about that. He was certain that his husband would come up with some excuse if he left alone. If they left together, then the rumours would be predictable and hardly scandalous no matter how the court considered the status of their relationship.

He bent close to his husband's ear, eyeing the count over Darshan's shoulder. "His father died?" He couldn't recall all of what had happened with Aarav, only that the man was of noble blood and had given up his freedom to be with his now-husband in the first place.

"Indeed. He took his own life about a month ago. Left everything to his son despite the circumstances. Jeet emancipated him a few days after. They married last week." Darshan stepped back looking pleased with himself as he eyed Hamish's trousers. "That should suffice for the remainder of the night."

Grunting his thanks, Hamish continued watching the count. The man had settled at the table next to his newly-wed husband. Jeet beamed up at the man, seemingly unconcerned that he'd only half the drink he should have.

Darshan glanced over his shoulder, then back at Hamish. "You're still not able to get the last time you saw them from your mind, are you?"

"They were half-naked and screwing in an alcove," he reminded Darshan, his face heating anew. "So nae really." That wasn't what kept his attention. It was Lord Jeet and the way he looked at his husband, all besotted and radiant.

Was that how he looked with Darshan? He'd never seen such a sight amongst men before leaving Tirglas.

It was everywhere in Udynea. Men... women... *And betwixt*. He still wasn't sure what that last one referred to, but had heard more than one person mention it whilst addressing crowds. *I should ask Daama.* She'd flash him one of those looks that queried his intelligence—an expression Hamish doubted the woman realised she made—before patiently explaining with as much detail as he requested.

Darshan swirled the remainder of his drink around the glass. "I need to take you to a few festivals. That might cure your embarrassment. The gods know I've been ignoring them."

"We observed one just a week ago."

His husband's nose wrinkled. "I mean a *proper* one, *mea lux.* Out amongst the people in all their revelry. Not some dry version of priestly prayers."

"As long as we stay away from any statues. And you dinnae drink yourself stupid." Carrying his drunken husband up a few stairs to bed was one thing, lugging him all the way to their suite was another.

Darshan spluttered around his drink, coughing and thumping his chest. "It was one time. *Two* at the most."

"Nae according to Anjali." His husband had originally admitted to breaking a few due to drunken exuberance when the topic first came up, but his twin spoke differently. For most of the temples, this was their first festival in some time that their *vris Mhanek* hadn't shattered the very statue he had replaced the year prior.

"Oh *really?*" A dangerous glint took Darshan's eyes and sent a shivering tingle down Hamish's spine. "And what else has my darling twin been telling you?"

Hamish opened his mouth and shut it as movement through the crowd caught his eye. The *Mhanek* was coming their way. The people didn't scurry to get out of the man's way as they did with Darshan, but more as though the man was a boarhound moving through a mindlessly parting flock of sheep.

"Darshi," the *Mhanek* said, halting before them. "I'd like a word." His gaze flicked to Hamish. "Just you and me."

Darshan stiffened, clearly ready to object.

Hamish laid a hand on his husband's shoulders before either man could say another word. "It's all right. I should do a little mingling with the court on me own, anyway." There were a few households that, although unwilling to be seen making a direct connection with the *vris Mhanek*, might broker a smaller alliance with his husband. At least, according to Daama.

He had intended to test those waters during the wedding celebrations, but there was no reason to not put in a little legwork tonight. Maybe he could even discover some links to the dead household used in the attempt to poison him.

Chapter 37

Darshan watched his husband wade into the crowd, silently lamenting the removal of his gorgeous presence. With the man's stature and fiery-red hair, Darshan could at least be confident that he wasn't about to lose sight of him. "All right," he grumbled at his father. "What's so important that he couldn't stay?"

His father remained silent for a moment, no doubt checking that those nearby weren't prying whilst he sipped at his wine. "It's disappointing that Onella chose not to come."

"I'm a touch surprised she chose to hide behind the facade of an uproar brewing in Nulshar," Darshan admitted. "But it's not as though this is the first time she has snubbed my accolades." His half-sister had also chosen to ignore her father's summons to join the celebration of Darshan's *Khutani. And* the day he graduated from the healer academy. "I am, however, sure you didn't dismiss my husband—sorry, my *betrothed*—to make snide comments about my eldest half-sister."

"No, but it *is* bad manners to commend someone with them standing right there. I assumed you didn't want me embarrassing him in public."

Commend? His father hadn't praised him or any of his partners since childhood.

"I fear I may have misjudged him. Misjudged *you*."

Darshan squirmed under the uncustomary display of his father's affection, waiting and dreading for the conversation to turn sour. *Not now.* It always did eventually. *Not this, please.* He sought out his husband in the crowd, not difficult with that banner of fiery-red hair flapping above everyone. Just the sight eased the tightness in his chest.

If there was one thing he knew he had done right, it was falling for a sweet man like Hamish.

"Especially your intentions when you chose to marry this one," his father continued.

There it was. *The poison in the soup.* He had hoped it would remain absent. "What is that supposed to mean?"

"When you get to my age, Darshi, you've heard enough stories of envoys and ambassadors, merchants and soldiers. How they disappear to far-off realms and come back married or, may the gods bless us—" He made the customary gesture to the heavens. "—with *children.* Then they're home and settled and..." Sighing, he shook his head. "It never lasts."

"You thought I had become one of those statistics?" It made sense on the outside, he supposed. His father certainly hadn't sent him to Tirglas with the goal of forming any relationship outside of a diplomatic one. "Do you really think I'm lacking a brain?"

Marriage in Tirglas lasted for two years barring the birth of a child within that time. He had told Hamish that, in Udynea, it was forever. That was true where it counted. Divorce wasn't unheard of, but that was a luxury commoners had. The law was different for nobles. Alliances couldn't remain stable if people were able to part ways so easily.

And for himself?

Whoever he married, the choice would reflect on the crown. A spouse who boasted good looks but no brain suggested a weak *Mhanek* who sought only the comforts of rule and would make for an easy target. If the choice was a spouse strong in magic, but who was mediocre in other ways, then the *Mhanek* cared only for power and that threatened the senate's standing. Few rose to rule under their might alone and any who directly opposed the senate found themselves with few allies.

What did his choice for a kind, gregarious foreigner say to the court? Hard to tell. Such a move was as unprecedented as a *vris Mhanek* marrying a man—those who had preferred men in the past married women for the sake of heirs and kept paramours. An unfair solution for everyone.

"Lacking?" his father echoed. "Not completely." His lips tilted into the faintest hint of a good-natured smile, enough for Darshan to know he jested. "But you *do* have a history, my boy. One that is long and not exactly stable when it comes to lovers."

Darshan knew that better than most. Even before he realised how deep his affections for Hamish had grown, the man had become his longest relationship. The one prior to that lasting a mere week, terminated upon the discovery of his lover in bed with another man. "It's different."

His father clasped Darshan's shoulders, the act so foreign that Darshan had to suppress the urge to shield himself. "I know. He is—" He froze, staring at something over Darshan's shoulder for some time.

Darshan twisted in his father's grip, expecting danger, only to find his nephew slithering his way through the crowd. The boy spied them and waved, then jerked his hand down as his face took on a plum hue.

"I shall take my leave." Giving Darshan a final pat on the back, his father glided off into the parting crowd.

Tarendra halted before him, bowing low as most nobles did. Although, the customary respect shown was slightly marred by the boy's grin.

Nevertheless, Darshan replied with a tilt of his head. "I thought you would be in your chambers. Or is fasting before the big event no longer mandatory?" He faintly recalled the process. To think he once found having to refrain from such things as torturous. He had already been the target of Onella's so-called archery accident by then and yet, to his twelve-year-old mind, abstaining from food and magic for much of a day had been worse.

His nephew wrinkled his nose. "I'll be starting tomorrow. Once midnight arrives."

"And will your father be in attendance by the big day?" He didn't mind that neither of the boy's parents had arrived in time to attend this soirée—he was enjoying the lack of drama their absence caused—but their reasons lacked proof. His own network hadn't caught wind of anything drastic stirring in Nulshar.

He suspected that feigning a problem in the city was Onella's doing. A small slight towards Darshan.

Tarendra shook his head. "Grandfather offered to take Father's place, but..." He fell silent, fidgeting on the spot.

"I understand." Even though Darshan disagreed on a number of topics with his father, he wouldn't have wanted anyone else to take the man's place in the ceremonial presenting of himself to the altar. Having a guide was a tradition almost as old as the *Khutani*.

If Onella was truly behind keeping her husband away from Minamist, her son would never forgive her.

"I was wondering," Tarendra continued, his fidgeting worsening until one leg looked as though it was about to twist right off. "If I can't have Father there, then maybe *you* would take his place?"

"*Me?*" he managed, all other words failing him.

Nowadays, it was the father who presented his son to the priests. It had been that way for countless years. But it wasn't how it had originally been. The old ways considered it as more than a simple task done once. Those who presented the child were meant to be the most trusted, the one the child came to for advice and assistance. Their guide for life.

"I'm honoured. Of course, if that's your wish."

Tarendra smiled broadly. He flung his arms around Darshan, burying his face into Darshan's shoulder.

"Ren," he gasped, still catching his breath. "Show *some* etiquette." The boy's act definitely would've caught everyone's attention. A glance at those closest confirmed it. *And there goes the gossip.* What would they say this time? That he had accepted his nephew as his heir? Involving himself as the guide in the boy's *Khutani* would worsen matters, but he wasn't about to deny his nephew on such a basis. "I'm quite certain your mother didn't raise you in a swamp."

With his grin less broad, and slightly sheepish, his nephew stepped back into being the respectful distance from the *vris Mhanek*.

Darshan straightened his sherwani. "How about you go take what joy you can from the night? I recommend stuffing yourself stupid. If you're planning on fasting, you've only a few hours left."

Still unable to keep the smile from his face, Tarendra raced back into the crowd.

"Is it wise to encourage excess in someone so young?" questioned someone at his back. A voice he hadn't heard in years.

Vihaan. Darshan whirled about to find the man standing before him. A little older, a little less flamboyant, but *here.* "You came." He flung his arms around his friend's shoulders, squeezing until Vihaan grunted in his ear. "You actually came." After Darshan's own outburst over his father's interference of their relationship, he had begun to fear the worst had happened to his friend.

"Steady on," the man said, chuckling. "People might think we're still involved."

Darshan gave the man's shoulders another squeeze. "And there's the wit I've so sorely missed." He plucked a stray brown hair from Vihaan's shawl, too long to belong to his friend. Had he brought someone special with him? "It has been *years*, my dear. How have you been? You don't write nearly enough. Or at all."

The delicate pink hue already staining Vihaan's buff-coloured cheeks rapidly darkened to one reminiscent of a fine wine. At least the man had the grace to look embarrassed about his silence. "I figured your engagement banquet was the safest time to show my face short of the actual wedding."

"*Where* have you been hiding yourself?"

"Up on my family's northern estate. The one close to the Cezhorian border," he added before Darshan could ask.

"I sent letters there." He had sent them everywhere he could think Vihaan might've been.

"I..." The man fiddled with the stem of his empty glass. "I got them."

"You never replied. I thought the worst." He had mourned for months thinking his friend was dead because of him.

Vihaan flashed an apologetic grimace. "I know." He bowed his head, sighing. "After what the *Mhanek* suggested, I figured it was better to keep connections to a minimum. Just in case he insisted."

"Well, now I'm offended." Linking his arm with the man, he drew Vihaan closer to the wall. Here they could converse away from the flapping ears of the crowd. "You can make it up to me by divulging just what you've been up to." Normally, he would wait for a quieter moment than this to catch-up, but he had no guarantees that his old friend wouldn't disappear back into the shadows come the dawn.

~ ~ ~

Hamish wandered alone through the crowd, chatting politely to those who welcomed his company and taking note of the ones who made excuses to avoid him. None seem to react to any mentions of the Kaatha household, beyond a few wrinkled noses which could've meant anything. How Zahaan managed to get anything out of these people was a mystery.

It didn't help that a few eyed him like he was an anomaly.

After the months travelling, he had gotten used to the wary looks and uncomfortable fidgeting that came with his presence. Most seemed far more comfortable when he sat, for he did unintentionally loom over all but a handful, but he couldn't remain seated whilst moving through the room.

And, whilst he had grown to understand that some might've been intimidated by his size, he recognised a few of the faces from the last soiree. *They* couldn't still be wary of him. Or was it as Anjali had explained to him? Of how his opinions were a mystery, his alliances nonexistent. Could he really be that much of a puzzle?

"Would you just look at the audacity?" a voice asked.

Curiosity tweaked his ear and turned his head. He paused in his search for a servant who still carried a few nibbles to snack whilst waiting for the next course.

Two women stood by a pillar not that far from him, obviously unaware of his presence. Their attention seemed to be trained on his husband, who had thrown his arms around a man Hamish didn't recognise. Darshan hadn't greeted any other of the nobles in such a fashion, only those he considered as trusted family.

Was that who the man was? *Nae another nephew.* The nobleman was definitely too old for that. A cousin? They seemed to be speaking warmly with each other, Darshan's relaxed stance suggesting none of his actions were for show.

"I know," the other woman replied to her companion. "Wearing so much silver? *Him?* Who does he think he's fooling?" She fluttered her fan, covering the lower half of her pale face with a splay of feathers as black as her hair. "Been a long time since there was anything *pure* about him."

Both women giggled behind their fans.

Hamish wasn't new to the idea of a blank colour being used to symbolise a particular ideal, Tirglas used it all the time in banners and clan insignias. But when it came to clothes, the combinations only mattered if it clashed with another clan's colours.

He'd been amused to hear how seriously the court took it here. Daama had been thorough in his understanding during the days between his choices in decorating this very room.

Some of them didn't differ too far out of his old understanding. Green, for example, had a different meaning depending on the shade—dark meaning the mountains and light representing hills and fields—but any variant here meant land. Whereas blue meant magic and water, in Tirglas it was all forms of liquid. The lighter shades would've meant a lake or river and the darker, the sea.

Purple was a shade he'd never seen in cloth before he arrived in Udynea. His homeland didn't have an equivalent, not in dye or paint. Getting it required a plant that grew just on the border that the Udynea Empire shared with Obuzan. Harvesting it was risky and few could afford the luxury, which was how it became synonymous with wealth.

Strange that none of Darshan's outfits bore that colour—he had checked them all. Perhaps his husband didn't think he suited the shade. Or he objected to the supposed death surrounding its harvesting.

The royal colours were red and gold, red meaning blood and power—also a similar notion to home—and gold alluding to the world's first light. *The sun.* The Udyneans had a myth that the first nuggets of gold came from drops of sunlight. It was a belief shared by the neighbouring Stamekia Empire.

Tirglas had no such tales. Everything was a blessing from the Goddess. Most of the time, the children didn't even need the priests to respond to their queries. Ore in the ground? The Goddess' doing. The formation of clouds? The Goddess. The tides? The weather? Goddess.

Learning what the Udyneans were taught left him with an increasing number of questions.

Then there were the rhymes taught to Udynean children about

silver being a gift from the moon. Not a deity, but the literal disc. On a banner it *did* mean purity, like white did for Tirglas.

He had almost chosen the latter colour, before recalling what it meant here. It was the blinding of the senses. The obliteration of all. The ultimate ending.

The light before death. He had seen it. Back in Tirglas. A flash of pure white just before his consciousness faded away.

Yet, the stigma didn't extend to clothes. Or rather, white could be worn, but not on its own. The addition of colour was key. Darshan had arrived to Tirglas in a sherwani of silvery-white with a heavy amount of embroidery.

"I hear his betrothed arranged the soirée," the first woman said, drawing her companion in close as if she uttered a great secret. "Do you think that perhaps his highness doesn't know what it means in formal terms?"

The second woman seemed to mull over this piece of information, slowly twisting a curl of dark hair around her finger as she peered into the distance. Or maybe at Darshan. "Could it be to indicate himself? I hear the Tirglasians are a very prudish lot. Maybe he's a virgin."

Hamish nearly swallowed his tongue in his effort to remain quiet. He hastily signalled over a servant who carried full glasses of wine. Not his preferred beverage, but a few glasses wet his throat all the same.

"That would be a bit boastful, don't you think?" the first woman continued. "From what I've heard, he doesn't seem like the bragging type. My cousin met him at Onella *vlossina Mhanek's* soirée. Said he was very polite."

The dark-haired women sniffed. "With all due respect to your cousin, she's not the best judge of character."

"I hardly think it's fair to critique her on that. It's not *her* fault that her husband ran off with a fire dancer. And I hope you're even less right about his highness. If he really is pure, it would be very much like throwing a pig to a *tigris*."

Hamish had to agree with the woman. Even with the limited scope of experience he had gained as a teenager, he hadn't been prepared for the lust of a spellster or the vast knowledge Darshan had eagerly shared.

"Maybe his highness thinks his dear betrothed is purer than he is," the first woman suggested.

The other one gasped, snapping her feathery fan shut to stare incredulously at her companion. "You think the *vris Mhanek* lied to his future husband? How scandalous."

"Not *lie*, dearest, stretching the truth. They do it all the time in brothels. *Oh my,*" she continued in a mocking tone. "*I've never seen anyone as big as you. Do be gentle, it's my first time.*"

Her companion chuckled, returning to hiding behind her fan. It did little to mask her reddening cheeks. Her gaze flicked his way and her expression slowly morphed into one of shock. "H-how would *you* know what they do in brothels?" she stammered to the other woman who tipped her nose into the air.

"I own several in the upper quarter. I thought *everyone* knew that."

Caught eavesdropping, Hamish finished the dregs from his third glass of wine and stepped closer. "Well, *I* didnae ken." He smiled at the pair of them. "Is that nae an oddity around here?" They'd something similar to brothels in Tirglas, but they weren't as obvious or as many. The one in Minamist was widely known as the tidy-looking house near the docks owned by an elderly woman who simply happened to have a lot of guests. Any noble back home would've been horrified at the mere idea they had walked by it, let alone having a direct connection.

The pair instantly started fanning themselves as though the breeze might whisk them away.

"I couldn't help but overhear the last scrap of your conversation," he apologised. "I hope you'll forgive me."

Having seen his approach first, the second woman recovered faster. "Of course, your highness," she murmured, curtsying deeply and elbowing her companion in the ribs, causing a shield to briefly flicker to life around the other woman. "It is *us* who should ask your forgiveness."

"We were merely parsing out idle gossip," the first woman insisted. "Nothing was meant by it. We've heard much about your coming. It's an honour to finally meet you."

"Me mum always says that spreading gossip was akin to letting a demon have reign of your tongue."

"What a charming phrase," Anjali interrupted. She halted at Hamish's side, along with Rashmika and a man he hadn't met, even though his face looked strangely familiar. "But then, Tirglasian is a colourful language." Anjali turned to the two unnamed women, who quickly curtsied deep enough that Hamish was impressed they didn't fall flat on their faces. "I don't suppose either of you ladies know any of it?"

Equally wide-eyed, both women shook their heads. They talked over each other in their haste to apologise for not having the foresight to learn his mother tongue.

Hamish tried to maintain a neutral expression, but it was difficult to keep the sourness from his thoughts. By their own laws, Anjali shouldn't possess the title she claimed, yet these two were clearly scared out of their minds by her presence. Just what had his sister-by-marriage done to warrant such a reaction?

Was it even *her* they feared?

He glanced Darshan's way. His husband had drifted into a quiet corner, still nattering to the same man he had hugged so warmly. The *Mhanek* sat at the table, observing the room with a sleepy idleness that had to be for show. How fast would either of them react to Anjali's cry?

The two women swiftly took their leave, addressing first Anjali, Hamish, the man at Rashmika's side and, finally, the woman herself. The way the pair curtsied with every backwards step had them looking like bobbing geese.

"Lower nobles," Anjali said with the hint of a sneer once the duo was out of hearing range. "Best you avoid any interaction before the wedding. They'll seize any opportunity to gain a higher status." She grinned at him, clapping her hands together. Unlike every other time he had seen the woman, she dripped with jewels and precious metals. Her hands and arms were no exception, although the rings were nowhere as many as the copious amount Darshan always wore. "Have we been enjoying ourselves? A little different to your last soirée?"

"You mean *boring*, my *vlos Mhanek*," Rashmika piped up, one high-arched brow twitching higher still. "I haven't witnessed Darshi make one scene or flirt with a single man that he isn't engaged to. Are we certain the right *uris Mhanek* came home?"

"Play nice, 'Mika dear," murmured the man at her side. "I'm sure we all know the wonders a good individual can do for the rudderless." He smiled up at Hamish. "And from what I've heard, the saving of self has been mutual."

"Aye?" He took in the man's clothes and fancy jewellery, coupling it with the way he stood. *Nae a personal servant.* Nor a bodyguard. That left him being a noble or emissary. Either way, he was clearly close to Rashmika and that made him a possible ally of Darshan's. "I'm Hamish, by the way." He held out his hand in the customary greeting.

The man eyed Hamish's extended hand as if expecting sparks to burst from his fingers before he mimicked the gesture. "I know," he replied distractedly. "Everyone knows his highness' name."

Rashmika gave a mortifying gasp. "Forgive me, your highness. I forgot you two haven't met. This smug man—" She bumped his hip with her own. "—is my husband, Sachetan."

The man managed to give Rashmika a cheeky wink as he bowed. "It's a pleasure, your highness. I'm also one of the *uris Mhanek's* cousins from his mother's side of the family." He grinned at his wife, who stuck out her tongue. " 'Mika always forgets to mention, even though he's the reason we're together."

"Dar played matchmaker?" Hamish had vague memories of his husband mentioning something along those lines. He assumed Darshan's involvement had been at a distance. And certainly not to a cousin.

"Something like that," Sachetan replied.

Rashmika fanned herself. She looked slightly queasy as if knowing one of them would tell the tale of how she met her husband and dreading it at the same time. "You are aware I've known the *vris Mhanek* for a long time?" She waited for Hamish to nod before continuing. "Well, he wasn't happy with how my father treated me."

"He wasn't the only one," her husband muttered through gritted teeth. "I'm glad the *vris Mhanek* had him assassinated. Man was a menace."

"*What?*" Hamish demanded. He knew Darshan had given orders to capture criminals, had even killed people, but to order the death of a friend's parent?

Anjali cleared her throat. "Abusing those beneath you may be frowned upon in current society," she murmured from behind her fan. "But it's not considered illegal. Not even when it comes to beating your own daughter."

"The lower courts are pushing for domestic incidents to be treated just as seriously as attacks on neighbouring houses," Rashmika said. "But there has been resistance towards putting it before the senate."

"Makes you wonder about those opposing it," her husband grumbled.

Hamish mentally ran over the conversation he'd had with his husband about Rashmika. There hadn't been any mention of the woman's father abusing her. Or of his death. "Dar had him assassinated because—?"

"Officially," Rashmika said, snapping her fan open before Anjali's mouth as if the simple lace could stop the other woman from speaking. "He was selling *infitialis* weapons to Obuzan."

"It is official because it is the only reason," Anjali countered. "He died for treason."

"Officially?" Hamish echoed. He examined each of the trio's faces in turn.

That definitely wasn't the real reason.

"It's a shame he betrayed his people like that," Sachetan murmured as he glanced over his shoulder. "Is that who I think it is?"

Hamish followed the other man's gaze to where Darshan still talked to the brown-haired stranger. "They've been like that for a wee while. Is he another cousin?"

Rashmika glanced in the same direction, turning back with a smile. "No. He's an old lover."

Anjali gave the woman a tap on the shoulder with her fan. "Don't stir the pot. That's just Lord Vihaan. Darshi and him were dear friends in their late teens. I didn't think he'd show his face, though. He has been somewhat reclusive when it comes to visiting Minamist since the incident."

Rashmika pressed her lips together in a disapproving hum.

Hamish examined Lord Vihaan. *A past lover.* Like most of the younger men, the man was clean-shaven. It was a look that reminded Hamish of his pre-adolescent nephews and added to the man's youthful appearance.

Darshan had been starkly honest with the extent of his sexual history, including the handful of men he deemed as lovers out of the many flings. "I think Dar told me about him." The *Mhanek* might've sent a fair few prospective lovers packing, but Vihaan was the only one to flee from the idea of being the *vris Mhanek's* husband.

In the wake of Darshan's refusal to bed a woman, the *Mhanek* had figured anyone capable of carrying an heir was good enough and Vihaan fit that description. That the man might not have been receptive to the idea apparently hadn't come into it. And that lack of thought hadn't sat well with Darshan.

"Naturally," Sachetan said. "Especially when rumour spoke of them becoming quite close just before Vihaan up and fled to his father's estate."

"And the gossip that flew around after Darshi's tirade at the *Mhanek* must've lasted at least a month," Rashmika added.

Hamish adjusted his clothes and neatened his hair. "I think I'll go introduce meself."

"This should be entertaining," Anjali said. She took a few steps towards the pair, stopping as Hamish levelled a finger under her nose.

"*You* are nae invited. None of you are, in fact. I'm not some actor in one of your little operas." If he had to perform, then so be it. But when and how would be on his terms.

"But—" His sister-in-law's protests cut off as Hamish gave the same warning hiss he would use on his nephews in their younger years. In Tirglas, the ruler might have sole governance over the kingdom, but their children weren't given half of the leeway he had witnessed Anjali breeze by with.

"Dinnae make me set your nanny on you." He'd learnt early on that there were two people Anjali paid any heed to, Daama and the *Mhanek*. Not even her own brother numbered amongst them.

Hamish would though, especially if she was to be carrying their child. She would learn he tolerated far less than her brother and that reining in her childish impulses was the only option, even if he had to put her over his knee and paddle her backside like what happened to every unruly child in Tirglas.

Realising how aggressive he looked to anyone paying attention to them—and he felt a great deal of eyes on him—Hamish gently bopped the end of Anjali's nose with a single finger as though she was his niece, then left the trio to join his husband.

Glancing over his shoulder, he spied Anjali with her mouth gaping like a caught fish and the other two watching on as if frozen in place. *At least I can still be unpredictable.*

He didn't need Daama's tutoring to know that would work in his favour.

~ ~ ~

Darshan tapped a finger against his empty wine glass, the golden band encircling the digit giving a musical tinkle. After hearing Vihaan's story, he was at a loss for words. "I can't believe you've been through so much." He had thought their relations with the northern kingdom of Cezhory to be neutral at worst. No one in the court or the senate ever mentioned trouble up there.

Vihaan's account of the passing years was a stark difference. The man's father commanded one of the imperial army's larger troops and he spoke of enslaving gangs running unchecked along the border, especially near the mountains. The guards spent most of their time dealing with them, leaving other factions—the wrong ones—to take up power. Stopping the cities from devouring themselves kept a lot of the nobles busy.

We should send more troops. Convincing his father they were a necessity would take time, and he wouldn't be able to act until his nuptials were over.

Maybe if he asked for command of a thousand soldiers as a wedding gift. He hadn't ever been interested in having that many armed men at his disposal as Zahaan's network had always been more than enough, but if it eased the situation up north...

"What of *you*?" Vihaan needled. "Last I heard on the rumour mill, you were leaving for Tirglas and now, not only are you back, but you're suddenly getting married?" He stepped closer, seemingly a moment away from checking if Darshan was ill.

Darshan brushed aside the concern in his friend's voice. True, it was sudden. Courtships amongst the nobility lasted at least a year and he hadn't even known Hamish that long. "We're already married.

Technically, this is our second engagement." Not that they'd the pleasure of a first. Queen Fiona would've quite likely preferred chewing off her own tongue than announce one of her sons as being engaged to a man.

Never before had he been so thankful for Udynea's blasé approach to the matter.

"I love Hamish and he feels the same, waiting until it was proper seemed ridiculous." How many actually adhered to that old custom? A handful? Less? It was originally designed to give a wooing couple time to ensure they were a good match before permanently uniting.

He already knew there was no one else he wanted more at his side than Hamish.

Vihaan hummed his disbelief, but remained otherwise silent on the matter. "I wouldn't normally ask this, but the court is buzzing with the rumour that you two will be expecting after the wedding or that you already are. Does that mean you found a betwixt to carry your child?"

"Not at all." It was slightly baffling how everyone assumed Hamish would be the one carrying their child—or that he already was—as if they could think of no other reason for Darshan to be marrying. "It's more complicated than that, but he's not betwixt." As far as he was aware, none of them *could* carry. Or were *paalangik* men choosing to carry children under the guise? He knew most were born with the means, but after his time with Vihaan, he had assumed that childbirth would be the last thing they'd want to go through.

Vihaan frowned, clearly unsatisfied with the answer but also willing to let the topic drop. "So, what exactly happened in Tirglas? The rumours speak of you competing for his hand, but that doesn't sound like the man I knew."

"Actually, the rumours are surprisingly accurate." He doubted anyone could be more amazed than himself about that. "I did indeed—" He fell silent as Vihaan's focus was drawn to something at Darshan's back. A familiar presence filled his left periphery. "*Mea lux!*" He turned smoothly on one heel to face his husband. "Allow me to introduce Lord Vihaan. This is—"

"—Hamish." He stuck out his hand, a gesture of greeting not typically used in the lower regions of Udynea.

Darshan hadn't considered informing his husband of such as being particularly important. Now, he rather wished he had as presenting an open palm to a spellster could be construed as a threat.

Fortunately, Vihaan had grown in the utmost northern section of the empire. He readily clasped Hamish's hand, the tendons standing out as he tried to reply in kind to Hamish's effortlessly firm grasp.

Did his old friend also notice the roughness of Hamish's skin as

Darshan had the first day he met his husband? Did he wonder how a prince had the hands of a labourer? Would he mention it in different company, leaving Zahaan and his network to stamp out another ridiculous rumour?

A sigh whistled out Darshan's nose. He didn't mind when the gossip was about himself. He could handle being labelled as a whore, a brat and a lush. But Hamish? He didn't want his husband having to weather the same barbs.

It would be foolish to think he could stop every rumour, but he would've preferred they kept to a manageable level.

"Your highness," Vihaan said, bowing slightly over their hands. "I've heard much about you."

"Likewise," Hamish replied.

"Only the good things, I trust." Vihaan winked at Darshan, flashing the same cocky grin that used to twist his insides and make his knees all watery. It carried no such power over him now.

Once, he had thought he'd found his beacon in the man. Never had he been more wrong about anything.

"I wouldn't know," Darshan replied. He mentioned Vihaan amongst the rest of his past lovers, but never in any great detail. Not that there'd been much to tell beyond it being a brief, and chaste, gambol.

"I get most of me knowledge about Dar's past from Anjali and Rashmika," Hamish answered, confirming Darshan's suspicions. "And a wee bit from Zah when he has the time."

Darshan silently lipped at the remaining droplets in his wineglass. So, his inner circle gossiped about him to his husband? Including his previous relationships? *Traitors.* At least *he* had already divulged the worst of it before the man had come into contact with anyone else.

He eyed his husband and Vihaan as the pair immediately fell into talking about the northern lands. Not for the first time he considered himself fortunate that Hamish wasn't a man prone to violent jealousy.

True, his husband had admitted to feeling possessive of his position around those who dared proposition Darshan, but that was mutual and Hamish had to know nothing would come of their requests. In the past, Darshan whored himself out only because the prospect of settling down hadn't presented itself. With Hamish in his life, he had no reason to seek hollow pleasure elsewhere.

It was also a blessing how easily the man got along with the rest of Darshan's inner circle. *Perhaps a little too well.* He would have to enquire just what his twin had said to the man.

The gong rang, announcing the next course was about to be brought up. If he recalled his time in Tirglas correctly, it would be a series of roasts, pre-carved to limit the amount of fuss from the court.

"*Mea lux*," Darshan purred, winding his arm around Hamish's. "We should adjourn to our table. I believe our next course involves roast venison." Amongst other things.

Vihaan bowed and, murmuring his farewells, hastened to do similar.

Hamish perked up at the mention of what had been a staple food source back in Tirglas. Then he deflated just as swiftly. "It's nae going to be the same, is it?"

"Probably not." The seasoning would be off. The cooking method likely differed, too. At least the beer would be serviceable. "Regardless, don't stuff yourself, I rather fancy a bit of dancing when all this is done." Between his duties and the preparation for their wedding, moments like tonight were few. He planned to enjoy himself to the utmost.

Sadly, the ballroom was off limits, his father insisting that it was less defensible. But if they moved the tables to one side, there was more than enough space here for slower dances where he could press close to his husband without causing a scene.

And after the soirée was over, he intended to have Hamish whilst the man still wore that delectable outfit. Or maybe he would drive his husband over the edge whilst slowly peeling off every layer.

"Let's not dawdle, love," Darshan rasped, quickening his pace to the royal table. "I'm *starving*."

Chapter 38

Hamish rubbed one bare foot against the back of his ankle, watching as the other men around him casually doffed their clothes and slathered themselves in water out of a trough that looked no different to the ones the farmers back home fed their pigs from. All of them stood in the entranceway to one of the High Mother's temples, waiting to be granted entry.

This was the place where every boy in and around Minamist underwent the *Khutani*.

When Darshan had explained the rite to him, his husband had left a few details out. Like how the cleansing of their bodies in sanctified water was required before they entered the temple.

This wasn't the first time he'd been in the presence of naked men. He had even shared a pool with a handful in the past, including Darshan. But never before with those he didn't know. Or in the presence of someone far younger than himself.

He hadn't even been walked in on by his own nephews, yet these people mingled amongst each other as if still fully clothed whilst they waited for the signal to enter the temple.

There were more people here than he expected. The way Darshan spoke of his family, Hamish had been under the impression that the man had few male relatives. That was true through the royal line, but there were a bunch of them on his mother's side. Beyond the boy's father, Darshan and the *Mhanek*, several of his husband's cousins had arrived to stand witness to another in the family becoming a man.

He glanced over at Tarendra. Several of the boy's cousins and uncles encircled him, some ruffling his hair as though they hadn't seen the boy in years, others cracking jokes about the upcoming ceremony, whilst a couple remained silent.

Those last ones prickled Hamish's skin. Especially in the way they'd occasionally look over at him. Maybe it was the dimness of the torchlight—he hoped so—but their eyes seemed dark and flat. Vacant.

He couldn't even be sure if they objected to his presence or if it was his uncut status, but the latter definitely didn't warrant multiple glances to confirm. Perhaps he should've considered himself lucky to not have submitted to Darshan's suggestion of bathing in a public pool.

At least the *Khutani* ceremony only involved men.

Darshan joined him in the quiet corner of the entranceway. As the boy's chosen guide, he'd been one of the first to unclothe and wash himself. Even though the rest had set aside all other jewellery, his husband still wore a few pieces. Apart from two rings—his wooden marriage band and the *vris Mhanek* signet ring—the heart-shaped ruby Hamish had given as his favour back in Tirglas hung almost proudly around the man's neck. No matter the situation, Darshan didn't seem to take it off. It glittered in the torchlight, almost as if the gem had a pulse.

"Are you going to be all right?" Darshan whispered in Tirglasian. "You look like you might be sick."

Hamish pressed himself deeper into the corner. "I'll be fine." He could've remained in the palace to study with Daama or train with Zahaan, but Tarendra had requested his presence in a rite where only family members and close friends who'd gone through the *Khutani* were invited. Not even Darshan's spymaster was allowed here, the man being relegated to waiting outside.

Refusing hadn't seemed like an option at the time.

It had also gotten him beyond the palace walls. He hadn't seen much during their carriage ride into the cleric's quarter, the curtains had remained closed and the guards escorting them had been many. With both the *Mhanek* and his heir here, he should've expected that.

At least we're safe. The guards encircling the temple consisted of spellsters and Nulled Ones. They'd ensure no one got close enough to disrupt the *Khutani*. If the hypnotist dared to show her face, she wouldn't get far.

A gong rang, reverberating through the entire entranceway. The door to the inner temple opened, admitting them passage. A sooty light illuminated the space beyond, barely touching the vaulted ceiling. The pregnant, many-armed statue of the High Mother sat opposite the door, the light hardening her usually serene features.

Hamish's skin prickled. The temple looked more like a crypt.

"Ready, Ren?" Aagney asked of his son. The boy's father had arrived that morning, huffing almost as much as his horse. Even so,

Tarendra had insisted on keeping Darshan as his guide for the ceremonial presenting of the boy to the priests.

Nodding, Tarendra drew himself up to his full height.

The men shuffled into a single line with Tarendra at the head and Darshan just behind the boy. Hamish positioned himself at the back, right behind Aagney.

Like guards on parade, they marched through the door.

Incense drifted thickly through the air, its vapour adding to the smokiness of the room. The room wasn't as round as the outside suggested. The angle of the walls, along with their flatness, suggested some manner of polygon. None of the walls had any windows and, beyond the door they had walked through, only one other way out.

This place could easily become a killing ground.

He shuffled along with the others, realising they were spacing themselves out on a circular platform surrounding the altar. The edges were marked by candles, yet no one was halting precisely before them. Hamish took that as an invitation to space himself from those on either side as he saw fit. One of the cousins he didn't know stood some distance on his left, whilst Aagney took up position on the right.

Darshan and his nephew stood before the altar. Tarendra looked relatively calm for someone about to take an irreversible step.

The slap of hands coming together once boomed through the temple. Priests filed in from the other doorway, all as naked as the rest of them. Some more so, having shorn their heads as well as their faces. A few looked to have rid themselves of all hair and one—

Hamish swiftly diverted his attention to the altar where the high priest communed with Darshan. *I thought...* He tilted to one side to whisper in Aagney's direction, "Dar said there wouldnae be any women here." He had only glimpsed, but one priest was definitely different to the rest.

Aagney frowned at him, then at the priests before shrugging. "If they're here, then they must be a man."

"*Paalangik*, then," he half-murmured to himself. He hadn't quite understood Darshan's explanation of the word in the past, but a lot of it was beginning to make sense.

Aagney's brows lifted in surprise. "I wasn't aware Tirglasians knew the word. But yes, that is likely correct."

The confirmation eased the tightness in his chest. He wasn't flashing his privates in front of some woman.

It *did* have him wondering about an old Tirglasian tale he vaguely recalled of the bearded warrior woman who tamed the eastern horses and amassed a herd that'd stood ten thousand strong. Could the woman of legend be *paalangik*? Did the clan who claimed her as their ancestor know either way?

After what seemed to be a murmur of acceptance from the high priest, Tarendra clambered onto the altar to straddle the marble top. Hamish thanked the Goddess his placement in the circle put the boy's back to him.

Why did I come? He should've refused Tarendra's request.

It was too late to do anything about it now. Leaving would disrupt the ceremony. And, if he left the temple altogether, it would split the guards' attention, endanger everyone.

With his close presence no longer required for this part of the ceremony, Darshan departed from his nephew's side to join the rest of the circle. He grinned at Hamish, trotting over to stand on his left and whisper in Tirglasian, "You are doing so well. I am glad you chose to come and see a *Khutani* firsthand."

Hamish pressed his lips together and bowed his head. He hoped his presence here didn't mean his husband thought he would go back on what they had agreed in regards to their future son.

The priests fanned out, taking up position on the platform to complete the circle. They began to chant as their leader gently draped a small chain around the boy's torso. The links glittered purple in the torchlight. *Infitialis.*

Hamish looked down at the ground, trying hard not to think on what was about to happen. *The lad wants this.* Tarendra had been waiting at the carriages, as eager as Hamish's nephews had been for their first hunts. The boy had practically shoved them into their seats.

He likely would've raced them to the temple had the *Mhanek* permitted it.

But Tarendra was also only twelve. One of Hamish's nephews was the same age and Bruce's half-thought ideas still got him into trouble. Those decisions were nowhere on the same level of permanence. How could anyone expect a child of this age to have the proper understanding to make this decision?

In the lull of the priests chanting, the soft gasp of pain reached Hamish's ears.

He glanced up.

Tarendra sat bolt upright on the altar with his head tipped to the sky. His shoulders trembled, every muscle straining in the effort to remain silent.

The only sound was the throaty chanting.

Nine minutes. That was how long Darshan had told them they were meant to bleed. One minute for every month they'd been in their mother's womb. A taste of the pain they'd caused just coming into the world. In the case of those who had attained the innate healing, the cut would've mended well before the time was up. The chain stopped that.

To think his husband had wilfully gone through this at the same age. That his son could choose to do the same.

He stared at his own member, trying to imagine sitting on the cold stone whilst some priest sliced off a piece of him. Only once had he experienced pain in that area by way of an elbow to the end whilst roughhousing as a boy. That had been excruciating enough and yet, no patch on what all these men had willingly put themselves through.

The chanting came to a halt.

Hamish lifted his gaze to the sight of the boy—the young man—hopping off the altar. Tarendra grinned as though he had just arrived home with his first boar. It twisted Hamish's insides with an unexpected longing for Tirglas.

The cool air. The scent of horse and earth. The laughter of his sibling's children as they played at hunting him across the courtyard.

He sniffed back the emotion threatening to spill down his cheeks, the act gaining him a cloying lungful of incense-laden air.

Once again, the gong rang. Its vibrations boomed through the room. A second gong answered it from beyond the walls, signalling to those waiting outside that the ceremony had been completed.

Abrupt movement on Hamish's right drew his attention. One of Darshan's cousins rushed towards him, pushing Aagney to one side. A ball of fire flared to life in his hand, blue and seething. It sputtered briefly as he aimed at Hamish.

Aagney righted himself, jerking the man's arm upward. The fireball sailed towards the ceiling, fizzling out as it hit the stone. He continued to wrestle with the cousin, wrapping his arm around the man's neck and pinning him in place with the knuckle of his thumb to the side of his throat.

The cousin froze. His face was a snarling mask of hate.

"You've got him?" Darshan enquired. Hamish hadn't noticed his husband putting himself between Hamish and the pair during the struggle. The air had the slight warp that suggested a shield enveloped them.

"He's not going anywhere," Aagney replied.

The crack of breaking stone drew Hamish's gaze downward. Vines crept through the floor, winding themselves around the man's legs. "Dar..." he whispered. "The vines."

"I see them," his husband replied. "Do not worry. I'm in control."

"Stand down," the *Mhanek* commanded, gesturing to a group of guards rushing through the entrance. "There is no danger." Despite his words, he stood firmly between the cousin and his grandson. The faint shimmer of a shield encapsulated them.

Tarendra peeked around his grandfather, terror widening his eyes. Had he ever seen his father in such a situation before? "Father?"

Without taking his eyes off the cousin, the *Mhanek* reached back and patted his grandson's shoulder. "It's all right. No one is going to get hurt."

"You dare interrupt this sacred rite of peace and family with violence?" the high priest bellowed, his sun-weathered skin turning blotchy with rage. He levelled a finger at the still-snarling cousin. "Your death should be swift."

"No!" Darshan cried, drawing everyone's attention. "I think..." He combed his fingers through his hair. "Check he isn't hypnotised first. Beyond 'Mish and one of my spymaster's men, we've no one who has met this hypnotist and lived. He might have more information."

"Unlikely," the *Mhanek* said.

"Please?" Darshan beseeched his father. "Check first."

Pursing his lips, the *Mhanek* let his shield dissipate. Ensuring Tarendra didn't follow, he wordlessly approached the cousin to lay a hand on the man's head. He nodded.

"Can you break her hold on him?"

The cousin blinked, his brows furrowing. "What—? *Mhanek?*" He bit his lip, trying to move with the vines still holding his legs. His eyes rolled back as he attempted to see behind him. "Aagney?"

"You can release him," the *Mhanek* said.

Aagney wordlessly withdrew his knuckle from the man's neck.

Like a discarded puppet, the cousin collapsed to his knees, still bound at the ankles by the dwindling vines. "I don't understand," he mumbled.

Darshan crouched before the man. "You were hypnotised," he explained. "I would say by the woman who has stalked us halfway across Udynea. I know you're probably confused right now, but I need everything you can remember about her. What she looked like. What she told you. Anything."

The man shook his head. "I don't... A scarf? Pale. It had a pattern on it. Stamekian design." He frowned. "Maybe."

"There's not much we can do with guesses," the *Mhanek* remarked. "Give it a moment," he suggested to Darshan. "His brain has been thoroughly scrambled."

"Is he saying a Stamekian is behind it?" Aagney exclaimed. "Are they after a war? I thought they were still recovering from their God Emperor's reign."

Darshan shook his head. "I don't think it's them."

"He waited for the *Khutani* to end," the *Mhanek* mused aloud. "That suggests she knew an apt trigger. A Stamekian wouldn't be as familiar with our rites."

"Wait…" The cousin held up his hand as to halt them. No one had moved. "That's what she told me." He perked up. "Yes, that was it. Wait until the gong strikes a second time and then—" Understanding finally settled on his face. He searched the men surrounding them, halting once his gaze landed on Hamish. "Then…"

"Kill me," Hamish finished for the man. She might've tried to have him slay Darshan, but every other attempt had been on his own life. If Darshan's death was her goal, she clearly wanted him to suffer first.

He eyed his husband. *What did you do?* No one just woke up with a burning hatred for someone else. There had to be a reason.

His gaze swung to Aagney. The man was crouched before his tearful son, reassuring Tarendra that he was perfectly fine. It reminded Hamish of his niece whenever her father returned from solo journeys that lasted more than a day. But she had lost her mother and older sister to a bear attack. What made this young man so fearful of losing his father?

Hamish quietly approached the pair to clap a hand onto Aagney's shoulder. "Thank you for saving me life." There was no chance his shield would've protected him, if it had materialised at all.

Aagney glanced up, his jaw slackening with shock. "Of course!" He bounced to his feet. "What man would stand by and let another be slaughtered before him?" He grimaced. "Although I suspect my wife will be less than pleased at my intervention once the news reaches her."

"You think you could teach me that move you did?" Hamish mimed the action on himself. He didn't know how the man had managed to hold someone bent on murder so effortlessly, but it had been effective.

Aagney grinned. "I don't think it'll work without magic."

"Ah." He hadn't considered more than pressure might be involved. Made sense. The man must've bolstered his strength like Darshan had done that time Hamish wound up dangling out the window. Only those able to summon their abilities to heal were capable of it. "Never mind then." He turned back to the group surrounding the cousin.

From the garbled words he caught, they seemed to be explaining the recent events to the high priest. Hamish hadn't paid much attention to the man before now. He was old, his back bowed and his shoulders drooping.

"Hypnosis?" the high priest mumbled, shaking his head. "An evil thing to bring into a place of peace. Damnation lies at this woman's feet. The High Mother will see to that."

Something about the phrase tweaked Hamish's memory of home. The Goddess he had grown up with was sometimes referred to as the First Mother, and he wondered if there could be a connection, but now wasn't the time. There was another similarity that he hoped they shared more.

"In Tirglas," Hamish said to the high priest, "our holy men knew a great many people. Could it be that you know of someone with the skill to keep people under her thrall long after they've been hypnotised?"

Darshan glanced up from where he still knelt at his cousin's feet. The vines appeared unwilling to release their hold on the other man's ankles. "Udynea is far bigger than your homeland, *mea lux*. It would be impossible for one priest to know everyone in the empire."

Hamish knew it was a slim chance, but if hypnosis really was a skill as rare as his husband claimed, then anyone that strong would garner attention. If the clergy here were anything like back home, they gossiped amongst themselves more than drunken fishermen.

"This strong…" The high priest stroked his chin, wisps of grey hair dangled from his face like cobwebs. His already narrow eyes disappeared beneath a sag of wrinkles. "I have heard rumours of one such woman, but it cannot be her."

"Why not?" Darshan demanded, instantly at his feet.

"She's dead, *vris Mhanek*. As is the rest of her family." He sniffed disparagingly. "My peers up in Nulshar say it was savage work. No doubt some mercenary company's idea of thorough."

Darshan's shoulder's sagged.

"*Really?*" Aagney queried. He tucked his son behind him, even though the threat was over. "I came from there. I've heard no such tales."

The high priest regarded the man coolly. "Then I suggest you enquire about the Jhanaar family who used to live on the outskirts of Nulshar, my lord. The priests will be able to lead you right to what used to be their doorstep." The man drew himself upright, his bowed shoulders snapping back. "But if you are suggesting I lie…"

Aagney quickly shook his head, clasping his hands before him.

Dead. Hamish eyed the once-hypnotised man. *Nae dead enough.* What if someone had revived her? *He* had been brought back from over the brink, after all. Darshan swore death hadn't touched him, but Hamish wasn't so certain.

Or maybe she had evaded the killing blow.

He thought back to the blonde woman and her attempt to hypnotise him. She might've failed in keeping him under her control, but she had ensnared his mind faster than a flushed hare. Could she have done the same to her attacker? He knew what would it take to halt the swing of a sword, but if the blows had been magical in origin?

The image of her had grown fuzzier as the week progressed. No longer could he remember her face. Just those eyes. Huge and dark.

Hungry. Burning with hate and desperation, living only for revenge.

"It's her," he said.

Darshan frowned, his nose scrunching and shifting his glasses. "You heard the priest, she's—"

"Nae dead." Not physically. The rest was another matter. "But whoever ordered her family killed, she clearly blames you."

His husband's brow furrowed further. "The Jhanaar family," he mused, biting his lip. The name didn't seem to spark any recognition. "I'll have Zah look into it. If you're right, if she truly blames me, we'll find out why soon enough."

Chapter 39

"As this flame..." Hamish stilled, the remainder of the vow balancing on his tongue. He peered up at the gazebo shielding them from the morning sun, his gaze sliding along the beams as though the answer was hidden in the shadows.

Even without the attack at Tarendra's *Khutani* yesterday, this was supposed to be a day of reflection and rest for others in the young man's family. And it *had* started off that way, until the priestess called them in the early hours of the morning to rehearse their vows.

Now he was out here, lying in the shade whilst practising and waiting for Zahaan to arrive with any news on the maybe deceased hypnotist in the north.

He groped across the nearby table until his fingers found the plate of biscuits. They weren't like any he'd ever had, being small, hard and slightly tangy. But they were dangerously moreish.

There never seemed to be a shortage of food in the palaces. Back in Tirglas, everyone ate heartily, but also with an eye to consuming enough to satisfy and no more. And, unlike most spellsters, the excess wouldn't be consumed simply by using his magic.

If he kept up eating everything set before him, he was definitely going to need to train more often.

"Go on," Darshan urged.

His husband sat at his side, weaving paper flowers into Hamish's hair. More lay strewn around their little pile of cushions and blankets, kept from scattering on the wind by the man's magic.

Although Hamish had never seen anyone wearing the floral adornments, Darshan swore it was an equally common sight amongst men as it was with women, especially whilst courting.

It was easy to forget the way their union came about was considered an unnatural progression by Udynean standards.

Marriage amongst the Udynean nobility wasn't left to chance like in Tirglas. Houses arranged things for their children, expecting solid alliances to form before worrying about details like love. Hamish had laughed mightily when Daama pointed out they should've been partway through a year of courtship, not preparing for a wedding.

He hadn't thought their whirlwind romance and subsequent eloping as anything strange. Any Tirglasian man who dared to court for so long would've been suspected of having a wife elsewhere or hiding a bit on the side.

And Darshan clearly wasn't concerned about following his people's traditions. Or with what the Crystal Court thought of him returning with a husband.

But the imperial household was another matter. They weren't above heeding the same steps the rest of the court danced to. The *Mhanek* might've left his daughters to seek their own paths, but he stepped in to arrange marriages for those requesting it. He would've done the same for Darshan, had the man not been aggressively opposed to the idea of marrying a woman.

So Hamish suffered having paper flowers woven into his hair, half-heartedly objecting in the beginning that he didn't need to be courted, only to find himself cut down by the softness in Darshan's eyes. Being able to lie out in the fresh air was a rarity these days, especially with his husband being the single other person in the immediate vicinity.

The flowers were still going to be a pain to take out later.

"I really don't see the problem you're having," Darshan said. "We speak our vows, which you've been correct in reciting so far, promise ourselves to each other for all eternity and—"

"Eternity," Hamish echoed around his biscuit.

"That isn't what's bothering you, is it?"

"Nae." It might be a huge difference to the terms of their current union, which hinged on the appearance of a child if it was to last beyond the second year, but he preferred the idea of their marriage being a permanent thing. "It's nae the words either." After a little practice, remembering his vows was easily done.

It was the actions.

One piece involved each of them lighting a candle to produce the very flame he was to swear upon. That he was incapable of the task had baffled, then infuriated, the priestess. "How am I supposed to light the wick?" It wasn't that he didn't know how it was done. Darshan had sought to train him in it before trying to see if Hamish was capable of a shield. "I mean, look."

He plucked a paper flower from his hair, holding it aloft. It was no wick, but it would burn just as well.

Relax. Darshan's advice echoed through his mind.

Hamish closed his eyes, focusing only on the feel of the paper in his grasp, seeking to draw on the heat in the air, to concentrate it around his fingertips. It sounded simple enough. Even in the shade, he felt the sun's warmth on the breeze.

But it had been the same the first time he tried. And all the others after...

He sat before their campfire, focusing on the dry wood. He could almost picture the flames licking at the tinder and hear it crackling along the bark.

"Don't try too hard," Darshan cautioned. "Creating heat is the easiest magic your body can do, more so than directing an arrow. I'm amazed it didn't come first. It generally does. Through frustration, anger, passion—"

"Fear," Hamish mumbled. He ran a hand through his hair, feeling for the scar lying beneath the thick coils. His younger sister, Caitlyn had been eight when her magic showed. To others, at least, he had never thought to ask if she'd known before that fateful day.

Darshan had been surprised at the age. Old he had called it. But then, strong spellsters had vestiges of magic from birth.

Hamish and his younger sister had been in the forest below the cliff, horsing around with the new targets his father scattered about the trees. Men from another clan had come, they'd grabbed Caitlyn first, threatening to gut her like a pig.

He had tried to hold them off, but—

One of the scunners had hit him from behind. He wasn't entirely sure what happened after that. There'd been screaming, first from his sister, then the men. And heat. The power of a furnace. The memory of it had seared into his soul.

He had awoken to find his brother kneeling over them with worry in his eyes and the bastards a charred mess.

Hamish cracked open an eye and examined the flower. Nothing. Not even a hint of heat affecting the edges. "Useless," he grumbled. He flung the flower to one side, rolling over to watch the wind carry it out onto the water. Darshan, Anjali, Zahaan... Even his own sister. They all made it look so easy. His husband could even summon images within the flames and make them dance.

Darshan glanced up from the flower he was in the middle of crafting. "I don't want you overexerting yourself for this. You're a specialist."

"So you've told me," he muttered bitterly. He hadn't considered just what that meant to begin with, being far too upset with the notion that his marksmanship was due purely because of magic. Now he knew it meant he was effectively useless as a spellster. To be unsuccessful at summoning fire? No spellster he knew would consider it as a possibility. It was *supposed* to be effortless. Children often manifested it first. It was known as the easiest of magics for a reason. *And I fail with all me might.* Every scrap of his power honed to one task and not a single spark to show for it.

"If you remember that, then you'll also recall how very few of them are ever able to perform more than the one feat. You struggle to form an adequate shield. I doubt you'll be an exception any more than I could've hit that target without my glasses." Darshan took up Hamish's hand, kissing the back of the fingers. "Just light the candle as those without magic do, *mea lux*, off the Eternal Flame itself."

He had heard of the Flame and how it blazed like a furnace behind Araasi's altar. Just standing beside a smaller version for a short time had him starting to sweat. How was he meant to last an entire ceremony there? Or light the candle without it melting. "What if I just do it off the one you light?"

"You could," his husband agreed, one side of his mouth hitching up. "Although, the court would dine on the symbolism for months." That hazel gaze examined Hamish critically as Darshan entwined yet another flower into Hamish's hair. Even under the gazebo's shade, the pupils had shrunk to small dots of black, letting the rings of green and brown dominate. Hamish could've sworn the colours were more vibrant than when he had first met the man.

Hamish absently brushed along his beard, plucking a flower from the strands. When had Darshan put one there? "You ken I've already said you dinnae have to court me."

His husband's lips curved into a gentle smile. "And what was my response, *mea lux*? Why should it matter if I choose to court you for the rest of my life? Would you truly bemoan my ability to do so now that we are out from beneath the scrutiny of others?" He flung his arms wide, gesturing to the gazebo, still empty save for them.

There were Nulled Ones at the far end of the bridge, of course. And Hamish was certain that, if Darshan called for one, a servant would pop up from somewhere. He wasn't entirely sure they didn't do it with magic.

"Whilst I'm on the subject, I must know what you said to Anjali this morning. I haven't seen her so obedient since Daama reprimanded her for over-purchasing when we were eleven."

Hamish resumed lying on his back, grinning up at the roof. "It wasnae anything of consequence, just that she should keep her nose out of any business that doesnae involve her and that, twin or nae, you dinnae need a second shadow."

His husband's small smile grew, as did the faint creases around his eyes. "She does linger a tad," he conceded. "I swear she has the best possible intentions."

"Aye." He didn't bemoan the woman wanting to keep her brother safe. "But you've a slew of bodyguards." The Nulled Ones were trained to do nothing except keep the *Mhanek* and his immediate family in one piece.

That same protection currently extended to Hamish purely thanks to the *Mhanek's* courtesy. They didn't listen to him, though. Only watched and waited. Once they were married, he'd be able to command them as Darshan did.

Darshan leant over him, plucking a biscuit from the plate despite having the ability to levitate any number of them into his grasp. "If you think you've your vows sorted, we could work on history?" He bit the biscuit in half with a snap. "What century does Daama have you up to?"

"The fifteenth." The last thing the woman taught him had been the coup that saw Darshan's family take the throne.

That was also when he learnt that ruling noble households stopped being relevant as a separate entity. To every Udynean commoner, the royal line had officially remained unbroken throughout history. All because the *Mhanek's* continued with the outward belief that they held no family allegiance to any household.

"The last few centuries are easy." Darshan leant over Hamish once more. This time, gathering a handful of biscuits before settling back. "Most of the wars had stopped, leaving just petty squabbles between noble households."

"I dinnae want to focus on me schooling." Not now. Not here. "And I definitely couldnae stand reading another thing." Even outside with the slight salt tang on the breeze tickling his nose, it was too stifling.

Darshan gave a thoughtful hum. "You know what you need?"

"To go hunting?" It had been months since he'd drawn his own bow.

His husband blinked at him, pushing his glasses back up his nose. "No, I was going to suggest—"

Hamish lightly poked the man's stomach. "*Hunting.* I want sunlight and fresh air." He stalled upon realising he already had both of those things and wasn't satisfied with them. "With nae walls!" Somewhere he could take his mare and roam the land.

Goddess, me wee Lass. Being confined to the imperial grounds for his safety also meant he hadn't been able to go near the stables. It didn't matter that Darshan insisted the servants were taking good care of her, she was his horse. He had always taken care of her.

But if they went hunting, he could take her out, stretch her legs.

He stood in a rush, toppling the small table and sending the remainder of the food flying. "Let's go. Quickly."

"Go?" A soft laugh lifted one corner of Darshan's mouth into an uneasy smile. "*I* have duties to attend."

Hamish scoffed. If any of the man's duties had been important, he would've been off doing them instead of lazing about here. "You've a few lords wanting an audience with you this afternoon. They can wait." It had already been months for some of them, another day wouldn't hurt. But a chance to be alone with his husband and out from under scrutiny was precisely what he needed.

"Then let me gather up some of the Nulled Ones." He gestured towards the couple who Hamish hadn't spied quietly resting in the shadows.

The pair straightened, waiting for their *vris Mhanek* to signal an approach.

Hamish shook his head. "You cannae go hunting with a contingent." His brother, Gordon, tried that once, hoping to impress a Cezhorian emissary. The whole group had returned empty-handed. "You might as well go stomping through the undergrowth blaring a horn the whole time."

"We also cannot leave the imperial grounds without some type of protection."

"Who's leaving the imperial grounds?" Zahaan asked.

Hamish glanced over his shoulder to find the spymaster approaching them with a stack of papers. Given the superiority of elven hearing, the man must've heard more than Darshan's objection.

Dusting off his hands, Darshan smoothly got to his feet. "*We* are, apparently. Go grab your bow, *mea lux*, we'll meet you at the northern gate."

Finally. Hamish didn't know where the gate led, they'd entered the palace via the eastern one, but he hastened to obey before something else appeared to change Darshan's mind.

~ ~ ~

"This is a bad idea," Zahaan muttered. Despite being within the palace grounds, he examined their surroundings as if expecting swarms of enemies to descend upon them.

Unlike the other gates, the northern one opened out onto a small dock. Cut off from the harbour by the east and west bridges, the only vessels here were smaller ones designed to ferry people to the rest of Minamist without braving the streets. Whilst the palace could get supplies via this route—and had done so in historic sieges—much of the palace's requirements came through the main gate nowadays. It left this little dock relatively quiet.

"This woman who's out for your blood will get more desperate," his spymaster reminded him. "Your betrothed has seen her face. She likely knows that we are aware of her name."

"How could she possibly be *that* informed?" They'd only learnt of her family yesterday. "Do you think she has operatives within the palace?"

Zahaan shook his head. "We would've found them by now if she had. I'm merely operating under the principle that she's been hypnotising people for information. She might even know we are here and what you have planned for this afternoon."

Did that mean he should have gone with Hamish? *He'll be all right.* Getting here would take time, especially when there were all those stairs to climb, then the trek back down the imperial palace and across the palace grounds to the docks. And his husband was being closely guarded by Nulled Ones who had orders to suspect anyone daring to approach the man.

What else could they do? Cower in their suite until she was caught? His pride refused to blithely walk into an even smaller cage.

"Hamish has left the palace grounds once since we arrived," he pointed out. Did Tarendra's *Khutani* even count? They'd travelled by carriage both ways and had been in the temple for the rest of the time. "As have *I*, for that matter." No sneaking out in the middle of the night to cavort amongst the whores. No parading himself naked around the temples, lost in a drunken bliss. Not even the simple pleasure of strolling through the market squares.

The Nulled Ones shadowing him must be thinking he had turned into a right bore.

During their travels, he had dragged Hamish into this and that place, boring the man to the point where he had zoned out several times. This day was well overdue.

Zahaan rolled his eyes. "You've spent *days* within your chambers in the past," he pointed out.

"True," he conceded. But that had been *before*. He hadn't the whispers of life slinking into his mind at every opportunity, hadn't a longing to be out barefoot in the wilderness, hadn't felt the walls as some stifling construction.

And if *he* felt like this, how trapped did his husband feel?

" 'Mish isn't used to this sort of life. I freed him from one cage, I refuse to lock him in another."

"Now you're just being dramatic," Zahaan sneered.

"Mullhind is surrounded by forest and he was out in it practically every day." If not there, then in the streets mingling with the townsfolk. "This poses far less risk than reaching somewhere suitable on foot." Even with an escort, he couldn't give Hamish the freedom to wander Minamist, not until they'd found the hypnotist. But to hunt with just the three of them?

That he could manage.

"I have news, you know," Zahaan said. "About the woman you had me look into." His spymaster didn't need to tell him it wasn't favourable, his expression said that readily enough.

"Later." Right now, he couldn't care if the world was waiting to drop around his ears. Bad news could wait. He would have this quiet afternoon of hunting with his husband first.

After some time, Hamish appeared through the gate, his bow already strung and slung over his shoulder and what looked to be a second one in his hand. He slowed upon stepping onto the docks, eyeing the boat as one would a viper.

"What is it?" Darshan asked. Had the man spotted something amiss with the boat? Admittedly, he knew less than he should about such transport, given that he had spent most of his life surrounded by water, but their chosen vessel seemed to float well enough.

"I had hoped we were travelling on horseback," Hamish confessed.

A soft pang of guilt twisted Darshan's stomach. He had forgotten about his husband's horse and the connection the man shared with the beast. He didn't really pine for the mount he'd ridden on the way down from Tirglas. Nor did he feel the desire to check up on the animal, knowing full well that any imperial beast would be treated like royalty.

Beyond the last few weeks, Hamish had the entirety of the palace ground to roam, even if he did spend much of his downtime in the stables. But there were no such accommodations within the confines of the imperial grounds or even a suitable place to house a creature of such size. "It wouldn't be safe to travel the streets." Maybe, when the wedding was over and things had settled, he could convince his father to let them travel to the winter estate.

"It's been over a week, me heart."

How dangerous would it be to allow Hamish access to the stables? The mare was no doubt regularly worked and groomed by the stable hands, there'd be no lack of people ready for the task, but she likely missed her owner just as much as the man did. "I'll speak to Daama and Oja when we get back about bringing Lass into the imperial grounds and giving you time with her."

A boyish grin took his husband's face. Hamish swept him into a hug, squeezing tight as Darshan's feet left the boards.

"Honestly," Darshan wheezed, trying to ignore the creaking in his ribs. "You should've told me it was bothering you, I would've asked sooner." With fewer obstacles in his path than there currently stood.

Would his father care if Darshan had the courtyard around the palace torn up? There was more than enough space between the two palaces for a small herd to roam, but little in the way of food beyond the hedges. The grass might take some time to grow in the heat, but the stable hands could tend to a single horse's needs easily enough.

Shelter was an issue. Would it be worth the trouble to repurpose one of the ground rooms of the imperial palace into a place suitable for a few horses? It would definitely eliminate the risk of Hamish entering the palace stables every other day.

Zahaan cleared his throat. "Are we going hunting or not?"

Hamish set Darshan back onto his feet. He didn't seem any less certain about their chosen method of transport. "I've only been on a boat this wee once before, when I rowed us onto the *Gilded Cage* and back off."

Zahaan frowned at the mention of the islet. Although Darshan had explained their time there at great lengths to him, the man still didn't seem entirely convinced he had heard the whole truth.

"And we were on a *lake*," Hamish continued. "A big one, aye, but still a lake. Even the fishing boats are bigger back home and they never left the harbour. Are you sure *this* is safe?"

Darshan examined the vessel. It *was* a lot smaller than anything he'd seen docked at Mullhind, but this type was common here. "I wouldn't have suggested travelling this way if it wasn't. It's also the fastest means of reaching our hunting destination from here." Without travelling over the water, they'd be forced to use the bridges, which would leave them exposed to any hostile party for far too long.

One by one, they lowered themselves into the boat. The vessel rocked and swayed as Hamish settled in the middle, but remained no less buoyant.

"How will it move?" he asked. "I dinnae see any oars."

"Oh dear," Zahaan murmured from his position at the stern. "You better hang on." He dipped his hand into the water, the surface slowly started to bubble.

A plume of water arced behind them and the boat leapt forward with all the exuberance of a puppy. It bounced along the water's surface, weaving erratically as Zahaan fought the rudder, before they slowed slightly and continued across the harbour with the reeds bordering the shore their destination.

"This is bloody fantastic," Hamish roared over the sound of the water jet propelling them. "How come they didnae use this method on the lakeship?"

"It's easier on the crew to let the wind do the work," Zahaan answered. "But I can manage this little boat just fine."

Twisting to face the front, Darshan held tightly to the boat. He closed his eyes as the sea air blasted in his face and threatened to stop his breath if he didn't keep his head at the right angle. How long had it been since he indulged in such an innocent pleasure? Years? Decades? He must've been a boy. *So long.* He should've thought of this well before now.

Others shared the water. Most of the people aboard them fished, their boats bobbing in place as they hauled in lines or nets. Some of the vessels carried cargo in the form of people or nondescript sacks, the former were typically folk who could afford their own boats and men.

None sped across the water as swiftly as they did.

"*Where*, exactly, did you plan on hunting?" Zahaan shouted, his voice thin on the breeze.

"There." Darshan pointed at the reeds. If their hypnotist had sent anyone after them, they'd have a harder time if they were aboard a boat.

"Are we nae going on land?" Hamish asked.

"Don't tell me you've never hunted on a boat before."

Hamish shook his head, his lips twisting into a bemused smile. "You've seen the land surrounding Mullhind. Where would I have found a body of water big enough?"

"The sea?" Even now, cut off from the ships by bridges as they were, this water was part of the massive harbour they shared with Stamekia.

"What would I have hunted? Fish? Maybe with a spear." He peered over the side of the boat. "The waters back home are a wee bit deeper."

"Then, I'm glad to gift you with this new experience." Darshan had faced a lot of his own during their travels, it was rather refreshing to find something pertaining to the outdoors that his husband had never attempted.

Their passage across the water slowed.

Darshan glanced back to see Zahaan withdrawing his hand from the water. The spymaster shook it as steam drifted off his fingers. Even with the jet no longer propelling them, their heading remained steady.

A flash of purple blinded Darshan for a second. By the time he blinked away the afterimage, his spymaster held a perfectly straight pole he had constructed out of pure magic. "Show off!" he teased the man.

Zahaan stuck his tongue out. They both knew the elf to be the better one when it came to constructs. Darshan's were always adequate for their task, but they lacked the same finesse.

The elf dipped the pole into the water, pushing the boat through the reeds. It wasn't as fast, but it was quiet.

Darshan relaxed as they made their way through the channels cut in the reeds. He brushed his hand along the tops of the stalks. The response was murky and sluggish, nothing like when he walked through tall grass, but still strong.

A skim along his extra senses told him there were no other boats within the reeds for miles. Just fish, eels and plenty of waterfowl. The perfect place to unwind and forget about their troubles, even if it was just for a few hours.

Chapter 40

T hey drifted through the reeds as the sun reached its zenith and
began its descent. All around them, birds chirped and whistled,
insects buzzed and skimmed on the water. Fish swam beneath their
boat, surfacing to pluck a meal from the water's surface.

The only disruption to the peace was of their own making.
Darshan flushed all manner of prey out via a small thrum of air
running through the reeds, followed by a low flicker of sky sparks.

Hamish had downed several ducks quickly enough, despite
insisting that the mottled black and white birds couldn't possibly be
related to the same species back in Tirglas. Darshan had seen several
of the shovel-billed birds during his time there, and had to admit they
held a minor resemblance to the bulbous-beaked fowl in these waters.
They tasted the same, though.

The latest flock he had disturbed flew overhead, scattering in all
directions.

Darshan nocked an arrow into the second bow his husband had
brought along. There was no chance Darshan could fully draw the
beast Hamish used, but this smaller one looked promising. He picked
one of the ducks, hurrying to line it up before the bird was out of
range, loosed his arrow...

And missed.

He hastened to try again with another to similar effect.
Meanwhile, his husband had hit three more, all caught and guided to
the boat by Zahaan's magic.

The spymaster hid his laughter behind a poorly imitated cough.
"Your archery certainly hasn't improved from when we were young.
How, exactly, *did* you win your betrothed's hand?"

"By cheating," Hamish replied without an ounce of shame.
Another duck fell to his arrow. Again, it was caught in mid-fall by

Zahaan. "He might've held the bow and loosed the arrow, but it wasnae *his* skill that got it to the target."

"On one very crucial task," Darshan stressed. "I got through the other two trials on my own."

"Really?" Hamish teased. "Me nephews led you through the forest, that's nae on your own. Nae to mention how you used magic to whip up a wind in an attempt to dust-blind your opponent *and* bolster your strength during combat."

Zahaan sniggered behind his hand. "You've mentioned trials before. As have the rumours. Is that what they entail? Romps through the forest and brawling like hoodlums?"

Hamish shrugged. "In a roundabout way, aye. The first is a battle of arms, traditionally with a sword. The second is a test of stealth and evasion."

"They sent us through a designated section of forest and lob bladders full of dye at us," Darshan elaborated. "You're right," he added to Hamish, "I never would've made it through without your nephews guiding me most of the way."

His husband grinned. "The third test is usually chosen by the prize as something they're good at. Naturally, I chose archery."

"And he cheated at them all," Zahaan said.

Darshan scoffed. Of course, his spymaster would think that.

Zahaan flashed a smile at him, showing off the full length of his canines. "I know for a fact that your swordsmanship is just as appalling as your archery."

Hamish stiffened in his seat. "Gordon did say Dar was lousy with a blade in the beginning," he conceded. "But it's nae true anymore. Nae after me brother trained him."

Darshan nodded. The training *had* improved his technique in both sword and bow, but he never would've gotten far if he hadn't utilised his magic in the battle of arms. Even then, he had very nearly lost, being fortunate only in a lucky blow happening to break his opponent's hand.

And the archery contest? He had loosed the arrow, no doubt there, but Hamish's magic had kept it steady. At least, up until the point where Darshan's nerves set it on fire. Along with the target.

The flap of wings heralded another bird presenting itself. This time, Darshan didn't bother raising his bow.

"Got it," Hamish announced as he loosed his arrow.

As always, it struck true.

The bird fell swifter than the others, plopping into the water and vanishing between the reeds before Zahaan's magic could seize it. "Damn," the man muttered under his breath. "You're downing them faster than I can keep up."

"I'll fetch it," Hamish said, quickly stripping to his drawers.

Darshan's gaze meandered down his husband's body. Although strong, Hamish wasn't chiselled or lean like those who fought naked in the wrestling arenas. If anything, the outline of his abdominals were a suggestion lightly padded with decades of hearty food. Years of archery had put a fine set of shoulders on him, though, and sculpted his back into a powerful display of asymmetry.

He could happily spend a lifetime etching it all into his mind.

A soft noise came from his left as his husband slipped into the water and waded through the reeds. He turned to find Zahaan leaning on the side of the boat, his head resting on an upraised hand and his eyes fixed on where Hamish had stood with a familiar glazed intensity.

"Avert your eyes, *meretor*," Darshan snarled at his spymaster. Bad enough everyone had been sneaking glances at his husband's naked form during the *Khutani* yesterday, he didn't need open gawking. Especially not from Zahaan.

Zahaan's enraged gaze snapped to Darshan. "*Excuse me?*" he growled back. "*Meretor?*"

He stared at the man. Had he really sworn at his spymaster in Ancient Domian? They'd both learnt the language around the same time and, with his superior elven hearing, there was little chance of him having misheard. "I—"

Zahaan's nose wrinkled, his lips curling back to further expose his fangs. "I have not, nor would I ever, prostitute myself. I have sex because I want to, not because I was ordered to, be it for money or otherwise."

Darshan hunched his shoulders, clinging to the side of the boat should the man's rage culminate with a blast that would send him overboard. "I know." Unlike some people, he refused to force those under his ownership into any sort of relationship. Whether they formed platonic companionships or more, he vastly preferred it happened on their own terms. "I'm sorry. I don't know what came over me." Zahaan had never been interested in the same men Darshan chased.

But then, Hamish wasn't anything like them, either. He was quiet, gentle, sweet and loving... All the things Darshan had sworn in the past as being boring.

Hamish also wasn't the kind of man who would actively stray— Darshan had encountered enough of them to know their type—but there were plenty in the court who would gleefully seek to have his husband down that path before the man recognised it for what it was.

Gods. Darshan scrubbed at his face. He had sworn to himself that he would never be a possessive man.

His spymaster glowered at him. Then he sighed and ran a hand through his hair. "Fortunately for you, I understand. You met him in a place where loving men is discouraged. You were already rare and exotic as a spellster. But then you probably flirted with him and that was exciting, plus a little dangerous for the both of you."

Darshan shrunk tighter into himself. *It had been.* Although, he hadn't realised just how unhinged Queen Fiona was at first. "I don't recall flirting." It hadn't helped that he had gotten drunk on their iron-tasting beer. He must have because he *did* recall crushing his lips against Hamish's. And being kissed back.

"But that didn't matter," Zahaan continued. "To either of you, I'm guessing. Then you were alone for a while. You dropped your guard, likely had him learning more about your quirks than you really wanted. And now? You're here, where the only perk of you being the *vris Mhanek* is that it has almost gotten him killed. Several times." His gaze slid out into the reeds.

Darshan mimicked the elf.

Hamish wasn't within sight. Darshan could hear where he was, though. His splashes were faint and didn't sound like he was in trouble. Zahaan would catch the change before he ever could.

Taking a deep breath, Darshan adjusted his bearing to display some semblance of dignity. "I hate it when you do that."

"You mean when I'm right about everything?" Zahaan flashed a grin before his expression returned to its usual seriousness. "Then let me see how close I can hit this one. To top it all off, you might be married, but it's in a union that will become void without a child."

"We *are* remedying that." A Udynean wedding might suffice, but his plans would ensure a child was born within the Tirglasian timeframe.

His spymaster bowed his head in acceptance of the fact. "*But* he could change his mind in the meantime. Maybe decide the risk to his life isn't worth it. And, deep down, you're terrified he will."

Darshan opened his mouth to object.

The smug certainty on Zahaan's face halted his tongue. Was the man right? He'd never been afraid of losing anyone before.

He'd never been in love, either.

Had he not been the one to suggest in the past that Hamish was free to take another lover? *Foolishly, yes.* But that had been at the beginning, when his concern had been more in getting Hamish away from the man's controlling mother.

So many things had changed since. His spymaster was right there, too. He *had* dropped his guard. Grown comfortable. Become *domestic.* He regretted none of it. He might've returned to the place of his birth, but Hamish had become his home. "He's my Flame Eternal." His beacon in the dark.

And yes, at his core, he supposed he was terrified of losing that. Of being left to wander blind through the cold abyss once more. Of having to rebuild walls his gentle husband had unwittingly taken down brick by brick.

"That's why you're out here," Zahaan said. "You hate hunting, but here we are. You haven't given a care towards horses in the past, but you do now? All because you want to keep him happy."

"Why shouldn't I?" When he thought of all the years Hamish had languished thanks to the man's mother, of the life her smothering had almost snuffed...

He still couldn't think of it without his throat tightening. A life of undisturbed happiness was long overdue. He longed to wrap his husband up in everything good and chase out all the dark thoughts. "Or are you saying I should only concern myself with his feelings in our bed?" He grinned, already knowing the answer there.

Splashing preceded his husband's reappearance through the reeds.

"Found it!" Hamish shouted, sending a flock of birds bursting into the sky. He held the duck aloft like an eager puppy as he waded back to them. "Bloody thing's nae that easy to spot amongst the reeds." He clambered into the boat, splashing water everywhere.

Zahaan's eyes widened before he swiftly looked away. But not before the coppery hue of his cheeks gained a ruddy tint.

The water had thoroughly soaked Hamish from neck to toe, lending him a holy gleam. It also had the soft, white linen of his drawers clinging to his skin, leaving even a casual observer no doubt that he was an uncut man.

"For gods' sake, *mea lux*, give me your drawers." Darshan held out his hand, waiting patiently for Hamish to strip. The reeds weren't high enough to completely hide their boat, but only an industrious elf would be capable of making out more than a trio of blurry figures.

His husband eyed their surroundings, seemingly coming to a similar conclusion. He untied the string holding his drawers up and, gesturing for Zahaan to continue looking the other way, hauled them down.

As expected the material was saturated.

"All right, Zah," Darshan sighed as he rang out his husband's drawers and focused on drying them. It required a balance of heat, too much and the item would combust, not enough and he'd be at it for hours. "You might as well use this time to tell me what you've managed to uncover about this dead Jhanaar woman." He hoped Hamish's hunch was right. With his father ordering a fresh search for the hypnotist after yesterday's attack, their resources were getting increasingly thin.

If there wasn't a connection, he would've wasted even more of his spymaster's time.

He couldn't fathom where a merchant's daughter would've acquired money, especially with her whole family dead. Had she been accruing favours left to the Kaatha household? Nobles typically had an extensive network. It definitely would've given her access to resources otherwise beyond her reach.

"Well, I've confirmed what the high priest said," Zahaan replied, still keeping his back to them. "They were indeed a merchant family. Dealt in *kofe* specifically. Not terribly wealthy, but comfortable enough to have land either side of the Shar. Few enemies as far as I can determine."

Kofe. It was a favoured drink of the wealthy, but the beans didn't fare well in Udynea's climate. Only Niholia could reliably grow them, but transporting them between the fields and Udynea wasn't cheap. The merchants could practically demand their price. And their connections stretched right across the empire.

"They must've had at least one enemy for their entire household to be killed," Hamish pointed out. He had settled on the opposite end of the boat to the spymaster, the rest of his clothes resting on his lap.

Darshan couldn't help but wonder if the darkening in his husband's cheeks was because of his current naked state or because Hamish had caught the elf staring earlier.

Zahaan shook his head. "I have poured over all the reports I could gather in such a short span. There are absolutely no survivors of that attack. It wasn't mercenaries, though."

Darshan took an educated guess. "Assassins?"

"Indeed," his spymaster confirmed. "The guild claims they had perfectly legal contracts."

"And they refuse to tell you who." Such was the way with the guild. Once contracts were fulfilled, they were kept for future blackmail or, far more commonly, disposed of. "What of the Kaatha household?" Darshan asked. Two households, both slaughtered to the last being. Both situated north of the Shar. That couldn't be a coincidence. "Have you found any links to the guild also attacking the Jhanaar family?"

"Not as yet."

"What of any other allies?" Someone had sent that poisoned letter to Hamish. Someone with access to the noble household's insignia.

"If they had any, they are continuing to distance themselves."

Darshan grunted. Bothersome, but expected. It wasn't every day that an entire household was extinguished. Not anymore. Maybe back when fights over land were common. His grandfather had taken a dim view of such methods and his father followed the same path.

"It doesnae make sense," Hamish mumbled. "Even if someone was avenging this Kaatha clan, why would they target Dar if he wasnae the one behind the attacks?"

"That is what we're trying to determine," Darshan said. No survivors meant retaliation couldn't have come within the household. But for a threat of retribution to appear without clear allies to back them could only suggest a survivor.

Zahaan suddenly jerked upright in his seat, the action rocking their little boat. "I might know that, actually. It's possible you could've thwarted the Kaatha household's extermination."

Darshan's focus on drying his husband's drawers sputtered and died. "Explain."

"I was looking through the death records and a name leapt out at me. The son. He came to you about three months before you were sent to Tirglas. I don't know what you two spoke about, but..." He grimaced, suggesting otherwise. "Could it be possible that he knew of the forces advancing on his household and sought your aid?"

"I don't recall any such audience." Those of the court who required military aid sought the *Mhanek* and his army. Darshan's only armed force beyond his father's was a network of spies.

Zahaan's gaze flicked to Hamish before drifting out into the reeds. "I believe it was more of an intimate encounter."

"Ah." He'd had quite a few of them in the months before his mission to Tirglas. Most of them had been with lords scheming to boost themselves into the upper court. Ever since Daama pointed out the connection, he had tried to remember them all, wondering if he had mistaken a genuine plea for something shallower. "Was that the one which started a feud between houses?" He had sent an official apology to both parties, but it had been largely ignored.

"Nae the one he got sent to Tirglas over?" Hamish enquired.

"No," Zahaan said, his brows lifting in surprise. "*That* man was higher up in the court ranking. The Kaatha household is—was—quite probably the lowest. Barely nobility."

It wasn't the man Darshan thought it was? The circumstances clearly weren't much different. They had come to him for aid and he had mistaken their intents, at least with one.

The one that counted.

"Their son was a bucktoothed fellow destined to marry a merchant's daughter," Zahaan continued.

"The Jhanaar family?" Hamish said, echoing Darshan's thoughts.

He'd been focusing on nobles so much that he had forgotten not all of the lower nobility married within their station. Whilst merchants had crossed his mind, it had been the wealthier kind who dealt in glass.

"That's what I've sent a few of my people into the guild to find out."

"Here." Darshan tossed Hamish his drawers. "They should be dry enough. Get dressed quickly, I want to get back to the palace. Zah, pole us through the reeds until he's done."

Hamish hastened to don all the clothes he had shed. Fortunately, he wore very few layers and was able to slip into them with some speed. Zahaan waited only until Hamish had tugged down his shirt before returning the pole construct into the ether and propelling them in the same manner by which they had arrived.

They travelled far faster than before. The wind stung Darshan's face and whipped his hair in all directions. He peered through his lashes, trying to make out anything as his eyes watered even with being mostly protected by his glasses. Just how did the elf see at this speed?

"Is that a ship docked at the palace?" Zahaan asked.

Darshan fought to dash the tears blocking his view. He threw up a shield around himself, it increased the force of the wind on him, but he could see.

Sure enough, a massive seafaring ship had docked on the other side of the bridge dividing the eastern docks. Vessels so big rarely settled there. Most were dissuaded by the narrowness of the passage leading to the palace or the monitor boats that guided merchant vessels.

That it had bypassed both of those measures could only mean it carried royalty or an emissary of the throne, but the ship looked neither Niholian nor Stamekian. Darshan recognised the design, though. It was one he never thought to see again. "A Tirglasian merchant ship?"

"Were we expecting anyone?" Zahaan asked.

At Hamish's silence, Darshan clambered his way up the boat to find his husband staring at the ship in horror. "What is it?" Flags flew from the ship's mast. He couldn't decipher all of the emblems, especially not what looked to be a family crest. The only thing he could determine with certainty was that Queen Fiona wasn't on board. The royal clan's crest involved a bear's head. There was something similar, but with what looked to be massive horns.

"That banner," Hamish mumbled in Tirglasian, sounding as though he had woken from a nightmare. "The antlered bear? It belongs to me brother."

Chapter 41

Darshan squirmed in his seat, struggling to find a comfortable spot.

"Sit still already," his father commanded, exasperated. "Anyone would think you'd never sat your backside into a throne before."

He hadn't. Not a living one, at least.

No one had done anything about the massive vine dominating the dais. Unlike the other vines, it hadn't shrivelled back into the ground or died. It shifted beneath him, warping to form a better seat. If anything, the vines had claimed more of the throne room, snugly enclosing several of the closest pillars. Not enough to compromise the structural integrity, but with slight displays of force.

"It won't stop moving," Darshan muttered. The vine adjusted itself at his every shift, trying to match his position. If he could just convince it to—

"Whose fault is that?" his father snapped. "You should've done away with the eyesore." He had made allowances, building a podium atop which the imperial throne rested.

It wouldn't be long before the vines claimed that as well.

Darshan settled deep into his seat. "I like it." The sight certainly gave particular members of the court cause to rethink their words and tone before speaking. And doing away with such a massive plant was easier said. The vine refused all attempts to make it heed him.

Maybe once the hedgewitch arrives. They'd sent for one some time back. Although there were several closer to Minamist, the one he apparently needed was further north. They'd be here within the next few days.

"You would," his father grumbled. "It caters perfectly to your sense of drama."

Rather than react to the snide remark, Darshan waited for his father to allow entry to Hamish's brother. "You should've let 'Mish sit in on this one." Even as he spoke, the vine's base shifted to accommodate another person.

His husband was currently being retained in the council hall's library by Zahaan with a troop of Nulled Ones standing by in case the spymaster needed to keep the man there by force. "He hasn't seen his brother in months." Neither of them thought it would be possible until Queen Fiona was dead.

"And he will," his father replied. "But *after* the crown prince has delivered his message. No matter how much you wish to coddle him, your betrothed's feelings cannot be placed above the safety of the empire. I must know what Tirglas has to say. We need to ensure we are prepared for every eventuality."

"I know." Whatever the message, if it came from their queen, then it would be tempered by Gordon's golden tongue.

His father gestured towards the doors and they swung inwards.

Tirglas' crowned prince stood alone in the doorway. Gordon adjusted his overcoat—the man had to be sweltering under all that leather and heavy cloth—and marched into the room. He said nothing, gave no hint as to his thoughts, didn't even seem to register the people watching his every movement.

Gordon had been amongst the first group of Tirglasians Darshan had met upon arriving at Mullhind. The man shared a lot of similarities with Hamish, especially in their features despite the five years of difference in their ages. The man's beard, a more auburn hue to Hamish's fiery-orange red, was probably bushier. That green gaze never had the same allure as the blue of his brother's eyes, but they did sparkle with a cunningness that was almost Udynean.

If he hadn't been so tall, and dressed in clearly foreign garb, he could've easily been mistaken for a citizen.

Whilst not reaching the height of their father, the man was slightly taller than Hamish. Not as broad in the shoulders either, but every bit as strong. The man favoured the sword and had trained Darshan harder than any captain he'd ever had instruction from.

He was also a Nulled One.

Did the Nulled Ones in the throne room recognise kinship within the man? He knew they could sense the presence of strong magic—as could other spellsters, if they managed to suppress the distortion their own abilities caused—but he had never asked if that knack extended to others of their kind.

Gordon halted at the foot of the stairs and sank to one knee. "*Mhanek*," he said to Darshan's father before offering a slightly shallower bow to Darshan. "*vris Mhanek*. Thank you for seeing me on such short notice."

"Your highness," his father replied, graciously bowing his head. "I hear your family tends to prefer the confines of the royal clan's territory. To what do we owe the honour of your presence?"

"Officially?" Gordon straightened, standing with a casual air and his hands clasped behind him. "I am here to declare war for the death of me brother at the hand of your son. Although, I'm sure you must've heard that by now."

War? Darshan straightened in his seat. He knew Queen Fiona was less than amused about what she saw as the death of her son, but surely not enough to risk the lives of her people. She had been the one to banish Hamish, after all.

"There has been the odd rumbling along the border," Darshan's father confessed. "Nothing serious. Certainly not something to suggest the beginnings of a war."

Gordon nodded. "That'll be me sister's doing."

"Officially," Darshan mused. "That's a rather specific phrase. Do you mean to say you've a reason that is somewhat *less* official?"

"Aye," Gordon replied before clearing his throat. He eyed the Nulled Ones sitting guard along the sides of the room. "A more personal reason that I humbly request privacy for."

"Do you trust him?" Darshan's father whispered.

Darshan nodded.

His father rubbed at his cheek with the back of a finger, then flicked his hand in a twitching gesture to dismiss all others in the room. The muffling bubble of a shield encompassed the three of them as the Nulled Ones filed out.

"I am also—unofficially you understand?—here to see me brother."

"So you *are* aware he is *not* in fact dead." There was no question in his father's words.

Gordon inclined his head. "I am. Me mother, however..." He sighed. "I am afraid she has started to believe her own lie."

Darshan stood and trotted down the stairs. "For what it's worth, I'm sorry." Not for the queen's state—the cold anger over what she had done to her son would never let him forgive her enough to care about what happened to her—but for the pain her children and grandchildren had been put through because of it. "Truly." It shouldn't have been this way. "I never intended this. Not a war." He had known it could've been a possibility, but had expected her to declare it to his face months ago.

Not like this.

"I'd be surprised if you did." Gordon sighed. "I dinnae blame you. Me mum has slipped right into the deep end. There's barely anything left of her now beyond mad ravings. She seemed a little too keen for this war when I started me journey." He stroked his beard. "Makes me wonder if she wasnae looking for an excuse."

Darshan inclined his head, accepting the man's judgement of the queen. They had certainly given her the perfect reason.

That meant he was partially to blame. Fate wouldn't have landed where it did if he hadn't thrown himself at Hamish. *I would've returned home without him.* With a tenuous treaty instead of his flame eternal.

However selfish the senate might declare his decision to be, he had taken the more rewarding path.

"It's a shame," Darshan's father murmured, sagging into his throne. "I was hoping for peace in my time."

"Aye?" Gordon's gaze shifted to Darshan. "Well, maybe we'll all find it in the next ruler?" He extended his hand.

Darshan clasped Gordon's forearm as he'd seen Hamish do so many times with the man's siblings. He had assumed the gesture was for close kin and, by the way Gordon's eyes rose, his guess was close enough. The senate would get their treaty in due time. A stronger one bound by familial ties.

"Of course," his father said. "We will do our best to limit casualties on the border. You, however, have our word that we won't cross into Tirglas."

Darshan fought to keep his expression neutral. If what he heard from Vihaan at the engagement soiree was correct, the troops along the northern border were already stretched thin. They would need to send elite troops to ensure people followed orders. All it would take to inflame the situation was one person.

"If that is the entirety of the message?" At Gordon's nod, Darshan glanced up at his father, smiling as the man inclined his head. "Then let me escort you to the library. Hamish should still be there. He knows you're here and I'm sure he's eager to see you."

Gordon grunted, walking alongside Darshan as they made for the doors. He didn't appear as thrilled with the idea as he first had. "Nae once I tell him why." He took a deep breath, the edges of his moustache stirring as he exhaled. "She tried to reinstate the ancient scriptures when it was clear that you'd taken the southern roads. When the high priests refused, that's when she declared war on Udynea. On *you.*"

"And she sent you to deliver that message." Despite being aware just how that knowledge would affect her younger son. Was that why Gordon had agreed? To soften the blow? "Surely, he doesn't need to know that detail."

The man shook his head. "I dinnae like to keep secrets from him, but there's more." He grimaced. "You see. I wasnae meant to be here. We sort of snuck aboard and took the original messenger's place."

Darshan froze with one hand pressed to the door. "*We?*" Who else would they risk to such a voyage? Not the man's daughter. If it had been Hamish's elder sister, she would've been at Gordon's side. The younger sister? Had they smuggled a spellster out of the cloister? Her knowledge would be welcomed in any Knitting Factory, but she also seemed pretty entrenched where they had left her.

"Ethan's with me. He's waiting on the ship. To that end, I wish to ask a favour of you."

"And that would be?" Darshan replied, uneasiness settling into his stomach.

"Me nephew." Gordon smiled apologetically. "I beg for you to keep him here. The lad's nae safe back home. Nae right now."

He remembered the boy fondly, along with his brothers. If memory served him correctly, Ethan was the one solely interested in his own gender. "Of course." Darshan pushed open the door and led the way through the hallways. "When were you planning on leaving?" It would take time for the boy to adjust and settle. If both uncles were here, Ethan would likely find it easier.

Was the boy not the same age as Darshan's nephew? His height had him looking older, but he was sure of it. Perhaps Ethan would prefer someone his own age showing him around the palace. They might even become friends. The gods knew Tarendra had few people his own age he could securely socialise with.

"I'll be departing with the next tide if I can manage," Gordon replied.

Darshan's thoughts raced. Having the man linger wasn't just for Ethan's sake. "Are you not able to delay leaving? I'm certain Hamish would love to have more family than his nephew at our wedding."

"Your—?" He stared at Darshan. His mouth parted slightly, then briefly disappeared beneath his moustache. "Did I hear right? You're marrying me brother? *When?*"

Darshan swallowed the automatic insistence that they were already married. "In about nine days." He had heavily considered delaying the ceremony until after they had found their hypnotist, but that could bring other dangers out of the shadows. Having Hamish take the title of his husband under Udynean law had always been to keep him safe. For now, the court circled like sharks waiting to scent blood. Any hesitation would see them attack.

Frowning, Gordon rubbed at his neck. "I *should* leave." He chuckled wryly. "I shouldnae have even come in the first place."

He understood that. Even the gods would have a hard time determining what Queen Fiona would do to Gordon once the man returned. Maybe she would spare her eldest child and heir. "It would mean a lot to Hamish to have at least one adult family member present during the ceremony." Especially in the first two days, where the tradition was to have both households share meals, either with each other or as a family unit for the last time.

"Does your whole family immediately pull the emotional blackmail out of their arsenal? Or is it just you?"

"It wasn't my intention to—"

"Aye, it was." He scratched at his chin, his finger disappearing into his beard. "But I'm guessing you also figure what's a few more days?" He gave a sly smile. "I hear that the ship I was to travel home on has been detained until further notice. Something about undeclared cargo."

Darshan chuckled. It sounded like an excuse his twin would think up. "If it would help, I could get you a faster ship afterwards." The pirate hunting ships were swifter than the average merchant vessel. Of course, they wouldn't be able to venture into Tirglasian waters without being accused of invasion, but transferring the man over to another ship beforehand wouldn't be difficult. There were plenty of docks in the northern lands of Cezhory or Dvärghem that welcomed both Tirglasian and Udynean ships.

"Like I said, I wasnae even supposed to stay on that ship. But once me nephew was aboard..." He tugged down the hem of his overcoat. "Well, 'Mish had you the whole way. Ethan would've been travelling alone if I had followed the plan. I didnae want the lad to think we had abandoned him."

"He'll be safe here, I promise." Few would see threatening the boy as worth their trouble. Those who did would be less hassle than their current problem.

Gordon grunted, nodding his head. "I must warn you, he doesnae speak much Udynean beyond a few phrases that I cannae be sure he isnae just mimicking. I tried teaching him more, but you ken how lads can be on their first journey."

"Yes." He grinned, remembering how Hamish had stared at everything as though it would vanish if he dared to blink. "Including the bigger ones."

The man's booming laughter echoed down the hall. "I can imagine 'Mish being all eyeballs. Just look at this palace." He turned on the spot, gesturing to the walls decorated with pictures, the statues crammed into every nook, the endless rows of pillars helping keep the high ceilings aloft. "It's enormous."

Darshan kept his mouth shut on the building being merely the council hall, the man would learn the truth once escorted to the guest palace and he would very much like Hamish to be the one announcing that little revelation.

They walked in silence for a short while before an old thought came to Darshan. "I wonder if you could help me. What are the usual Tirglasian wedding customs? I would like to observe them, if able."

"Have you nae asked me brother?"

"I have. He is being obstinate about the subject." It was all very well for Hamish to claim their exchange of vows in a pokey Tirglas temple was satisfactory when it came to observing his people's traditions, but it didn't feel right having a proper wedding without a nod, at minimum, to the very culture his husband had come from.

"And what makes you think you'll get a straight answer from me?"

That hadn't occurred to him. Gordon was well aware of his brother's interest in men. Did he think it bizarre for Hamish to be marrying a man? "Hopefully, the thought of your brother's disappointment is enough to quell any mischievous ideas." He had never interfered with any of his half-sisters' weddings, even if he didn't like some of the spouses they chose and the idea of Hamish's brother doing so seemed needlessly cruel on the man's part.

"It *is* tempting." Gordon gave a jovial smile before quickly sobering. "But you're right, I dinnae have the heart to ruin his wedding, even good-naturedly." He scratched beneath his beard. "Do you have a coat of arms? Or a family crest?"

"No?" Others in the court had them, and even if they weren't used beyond formal occasions or to denote a noble's personal army in battle. There *was* the royal banner, but it belonged to the throne rather than the family ruling under it.

"Then it might be difficult to observe the custom. When a noble of a clan weds another, they form a new herald."

"Like the antlered bear?" He remembered a little about the man's long-deceased wife. The clan she'd been born into had also refused to send any eligible women to contend for Hamish's hand, claiming the royal line was cursed. It had enabled Darshan to compete under their banner unopposed. He recalled being most amused at the crest being a stag, thinking they were a placid animal, right up until hearing a few hunting stories of men being skewered on their antlers.

"Aye. That's mine and me wife's personal crest." He clapped his hand onto Darshan's shoulder, tugging them closer together. "Seeing as I'm staying for a wee while, how about I explain the rest of them after seeing me brother? And dinner," he swiftly added. "Or both at the same time?"

Darshan chuckled, recalling that the bigger man put away far more food than even his husband. "I believe food could be arranged. I'll have someone escort your nephew, too. However, I better take you to Hamish first or he'll never forgive me." He gestured down a side hall as they reached an intersection. "This way."

~ ~ ~

Hamish had barely believed his eyes when he had spotted Gordon's banner atop the merchant ship. But now the man stood before him, grinning in that stupid slanted fashion that showed off more gum than teeth. He had missed the ridiculous expression, the cockiness behind it, the man's solid presence.

"Brother!" He launched himself at the man, colliding into Gordon and throwing his arms around his brother's shoulders to squeeze with all his might.

"It's good to see you, too," Gordon grunted. He gave Hamish a pat on the back. "Could I have the rest of me arms back?"

"What are you doing?" Hamish demanded, not heeding his brother's request. "You shouldnae be here. Mum—"

"What's she going to do? Disown her heir?" His brother laughed. "If that happens, I'll just move in here." He grinned at Darshan, who stared back like a man struck by a horse. "I'm nae serious, but that was worth it for the look."

Darshan replied with the stiff smile he usually reserved for humouring enemies.

Gordon cleared his throat. "I hear you're getting married." There was a hint of a question lurking in the words. "I see Mum's predictions were wrong again, you didnae become a glorified bed warmer."

Hamish flinched at the memory of his mother's declaration that having somewhere to shove his dick was all Darshan wanted from him. If she had listened to either of them for a second, she would've known their relationship had stopped being solely about sex not long after their first night together.

"We already are married," he replied, grinning upon remembering the intimate ceremony they'd completed before they had left his homeland's borders. "We spoke our original vows under Tirglasian law, but the *Mhanek* willnae consider our marriage official until we take Udynean vows."

His brother stared at him, shocked. "You got a Tirglasian priest to wed you?" He softly stroked his beard. "How? I didnae even ken they'd allow two men."

"They will if you offer them enough," Darshan replied.

Giving a soft exhale of realisation, Gordon bowed his head. The hand that was still wrapped around his beard closed into a fist. "I hate giving you more bad news, but I dinnae ken you're actually married."

More? What other news had his brother given? Was his mother demanding Hamish's return?

Hamish shook his head. It wouldn't be that, she had declared him as dead. He meant nothing to her anymore. "We said our vows." He had been to enough Tirglasian weddings to know they'd spoken the appropriate words. "We even exchanged rings." He held up his left hand, showing the dark garnet and pearl ring that had once belonged to Darshan's mother, resized at the same port they'd married at.

Gordon closed his eyes. He gave his beard a tug, then let his hand drop. "That doesnae mean you're actually married. If you go back to that temple, they'll have nae record of anything except a donation."

Darshan's face had gone carefully neutral, but his eyes flashed with his anger. "When I was in Tirglas, I heard of two women marrying. Is their union not considered just as illegitimate?"

Gordon shrugged. "Maybe? Two women have a better chance of one popping out a bairn in the timeframe than two men."

We're nae married. Not officially. Hamish shook his head. *It doesnae matter.* In a few days, Udynean law would see to that. But he had hoped that having a child as swiftly as they could manage would be enough to satisfy the usual terms of his homeland's marriage agreement, that the news would help mend relations between their lands. But if Darshan wasn't considered his husband under Tirglasian law, then his mother might not even recognise any child as being his.

"It is best if not a soul breathes a word of this," Darshan hissed in Tirglasian. "Not to anyone. If the wrong people find out, Hamish will be in danger."

He meant Onella. Had to. Besides the hypnotist plaguing them, Darshan's half-sister would be the only one daring enough to try.

"I ken how to keep a secret," his brother replied. His voice remained even, but his expression asked a dozen questions.

"Come," Darshan said to Gordon, gesturing down the hall. "I cannot imagine you have had a decent meal throughout your journey. It is close to the evening repast, I can explain everything whilst we eat."

Hamish wrinkled his nose picturing his brother surrounded by all of Darshan's sisters. "I dinnae want to air me family's business in front of your siblings."

"There is a small dining hall not far from here, *mea lux*. I shall have food brought to us. And your nephew."

"Neph—?" He swung to eye Gordon, seeing truth in the way his brother braced himself. "You brought one of Nora's lads with you?"

"Aye. It's nae safe for him at home anymore."

Ethan. His brother could mean no one else. Bruce didn't fancy men and Mac... Well, the lad was young. "Did something happen?" His chest tightened at imagining his mother levelling her disgust at the boy. "Did Mum—?" He swallowed hard, unable to get out the rest. All her little half-truths. The barely visible disdain that had bubbled into raving hatred.

The *death*.

She had given the order to slaughter those he had rutted with in his younger years, if not personally wielded the sword. Blaming them for corrupting his mind, for pulling him away from his rightful path, for tainting his body with their obscene lust.

And when there was no one else left to blame for his actions, she turned on him.

Wrong. Twisted. Unclean. Unforgivable. She had thrown those words, and worse, at him throughout his life. Never before the children—even when she expelled him from the household, her grandchildren had been absent—but they had to know. Ethan had to realise why he was here.

Darshan clasped his hand, the firm pressure of his fingers and the warmth against his skin supporting him more than words ever could.

I tried to spare him. All he had done, everything he had weathered, had been to keep his mother's scrutiny off her grandchildren. But with him gone... "Is Ethan all right?"

Gordon nodded, sombre. "He is. Nora didnae want to wait until Mum turned on the lad. We already ken that protecting him willnae work. Look what happened with *you*."

"That's nae comparable." They had been teenagers trying to defend each other against a threat that should never have been levelled at them.

"He will be safe here," Darshan said, squeezing his hand.

Hamish met his husband's eyes, seeing nothing but confidence. *Just like back in Tirglas.* He had believed it then. It seemed like nothing could overpower a man of Darshan's abilities. Now, he knew the dangers weren't as simple. "That right?" It was one thing to face the threat of his own life, to put his nephew in the same possible danger?

Darshan inclined his head. "I promise, *mea lux*. I do, however, shudder to think how your mother will spin the truth of her missing grandson when she is so eager to seek retribution for her supposedly dead son."

"*What?*" He glanced at his brother only to receive a solemn nod.

His husband groaned, rubbing at his temple. "Forgive me. I intended to tell you with a little more tact." Puffing a steadying breath out his nose, Darshan stood taller and continued, "Tirglas has declared war on Udynea over your death."

"*War?*" Hamish echoed shrilly, once again seeking confirmation from his brother. "What do you mean—?" His jaw clicked shut, held there by an unseen pressure.

"Not so loudly," Darshan warned. He looked around them. The hallway appeared empty to Hamish, but he should've remembered that was often a deception. "I shall explain everything once we are settled. Until then, it would be best if you remain silent." He gestured them to follow.

Hamish did, gnawing on his lip and paying no heed to their direction. *War.* Over *him*. Retribution for *his* death. How could that be? His mother knew he wasn't actually dead.

Was it a ploy to get him back? Did she expect him to come slinking home like a scolded boarhound? She had to know he would do anything to stop more deaths happening in his name.

I cannae do it. Not again. He wasn't strong enough to face her alone. He knew, if he did, he would find himself bending to her will once more.

But could he live knowing the turmoil his disobedience caused? The lives? *It's nae fair.* He just wanted a chance to be with Darshan. To be happy and loved. He hadn't thought it too much to ask of the world.

Clearly, he'd been wrong.

Chapter 42

The scent of pastries and grilled fish tickled Hamish's nose. Normally, it would be enough to set his mouth watering and he'd be several mouthfuls into the pastries, just like how his nephew at the far end of the table was currently doing. But his head was too full of bad news to think of eating a single bite.

"A war," he murmured. How many times had he said those words? He still couldn't wrap his head around it. There hadn't been a war declared in his lifetime. "Are you certain that was her intent?" he asked his brother. "She wasnae just raving?"

Gordon shook his head. "It's true. Nora and meself saw to it that the official proclamation was destroyed just before I left, but Mum can easily draw up another one."

He knew that. Their mother had absolute authority over the land. But she never sent the army anywhere dangerous—all the times Hamish remembered had been to help struggling clans. That didn't mean she couldn't on a whim.

"There is no need to fret, *mea lux*," Darshan assured him. Even though they were alone, and they all spoke Udynean fluently enough, his husband opted to remain chatting in Tirglasian.

The room Darshan had led them to was a dainty space decorated in rugs and tapestries. It housed a single low table and a few pillow piles in the corners that reminded Hamish of the *kofe* houses where men would recline and puff away at long pipes. There was even the same discolouration on the ceiling.

"We do not plan to take any action beyond our usual monitoring of the border," Darshan finished.

"But me mum will press to escalate," Hamish pointed out, his brother nodding in silent agreement. "Those she commands will follow blindly." And they would fight to the last warrior to avenge him.

I'll never be free of her. All this time, he had thought himself finally out from under her eye. Never had he considered she would throw the kingdom into chaos over his choice to follow his heart.

There had to be a way he could stop it all before a single blow was struck.

"What if..." Hamish did his best to wet his lips, the mere thought drying his mouth even before he could voice it. "What if I go back?" His stomach churned at the idea of leaving Darshan behind, of returning to that cage of a castle, of having to live a lie.

Darshan stiffened as if he'd been stabbed. "No! Never. Not for anything. I... I *forbid* it."

His chest tightened at the waver in the man's voice. *I'm sorry.* He couldn't relent. Steeling himself, he faced his husband. "She's starting a war over me."

"Let her!" Darshan snarled, slamming his fists onto the table. "I will ride up there and slit her throat myself if that is what it takes to get her claws out of you."

Hamish jerked back. He knew Darshan had come close to obliterating Hamish's mother during several encounters, but it had always been with her goading him. Never had he suggested killing her. "Dar..."

"*No!*" A thin trail of smoke drifted up from beneath the man's fists. Heartache moulded his face and filled those glorious hazel eyes. "You might have pulled me into the light and warmed my world, *mea lux*, but I would rather be thrown back into darkness for eternity than see you return to her oppressive clutches. I refuse the very notion."

He bowed his head, swallowing to try and free his throat from its current tightness. "I love you, I always will, but I cannae sit here whilst others die in some senseless war because of me."

Darshan's eyes slid shut. A faint trail of tears slipped down his cheek and into his beard. "I understand, *mea lux*," he whispered. "Believe me, I would not relish the thought of fighting my own people, either. But you should not have to pay the price when this is not your fault."

"Even if you *did* return home," Gordon rumbled, visibly uncomfortable as he tried not to look at either of them. "Then what? You'll be coming back from the dead. And even if we're able to clear up *that* misunderstanding... everyone is aware you'll nae lay with a woman. Mum cannae marry you off like she wanted. Most of the clans would refuse the offer."

"*Most*," he echoed. "But not all." The very thought of it made him sick. What sort of woman would willingly marry a man who didn't want her?

"Is that really what we're doing?" his brother persisted, even though he had to know the answer. "Are you nae supposed to be getting married? You want to just up and leave all this?"

Nae. But what was the alternative? Sit on his hands and let people die for nothing? He had done far too much of that throughout his life. He wasn't about to be the reason for more death.

"There has to be another way," Darshan demanded of Gordon. "Something other than having him return to her abuse. He should not have to give up his happiness for your mother's ideals."

Ethan lowered the pastry he'd been attacking like a starved pup. He stared at Darshan, his eyes huge. "You're marrying me uncle?" There was a slight crestfallen note to the boy's voice.

"We *are* married," Hamish growled. He didn't care what some priest's record back in Tirglas said, Darshan was his husband. "So he's off the market."

"*Not,*" Darshan interjected, "if you leave."

The words were like jumping into the winter sea. "You'd find someone else?" The thought carved a hollowness into his chest.

"I cannot rightly say," Darshan replied. "I doubt I would ever find someone who could compare to my beacon."

Hamish closed his eyes, struggling to keep out the image of Darshan living the rest of his life alone.

It wasn't just him anymore, he had to remember that. What he chose, where he went, would affect Darshan and the empire as much as his homeland.

"Going back could stop the war," Hamish whispered. "It could save lives." Putting his own wants aside to serve the people was how a prince was supposed to live. He existed on borrowed time as it was, stolen from the moment the bear first attacked. "It doesnae feel right to sit here whilst other people fight over something like this."

"To be fair," Gordon said. "They'll think they are avenging your death."

"That doesnae make it any better." If Tirglas clashed with the Udynea Empire, they'd be up against spellsters hardened by the ongoing war with Obuzan. Any Tirglasian army would be slaughtered. *All because of me.*

He wasn't worth the death of thousands.

"Of course the reason does not make it better." Darshan reached over the table to clasp Hamish's hands. "And you would not be the man I love if you did not care so deeply."

Gordon cleared his throat. He still refused to look at them and had grown increasingly flustered. Darshan hadn't ever displayed his affection so unashamedly whilst in Tirglas and definitely not before another, Gordon wasn't an exception. His brother must've felt like he had walked in on them rutting.

With his own cheeks heating, Hamish pulled his hands free to fold them neatly before him. "I will nae have anyone going to war over a choice I made."

Darshan's jaw tightened. Then, with one mighty inhale, that emotionless mask he showed the rest of the court fell over his face. "It shall not be *you* they go to war for, but *her* insanity. She shackled you with her ideals and punished you for the crime of being true to yourself. When you did not waver under that abuse, *she* was the one who herded you towards a life you did not want, as well as subsequently abandoning all ties with you when you finally broke free of her will. What happens does because of *her*. There is no one else to blame."

Hamish glanced at his brother.

Gordon immediately held up his hands, denying all accountability. "Dinnae give *me* that look. I agree wholeheartedly with him. I came here to warn you and bring Ethan to safety, nae to lug you back home with me."

"You'd have me continuing to live the life I want and disregard the lives I'll ruin?"

Gordon shook his head. "The only life you'd be responsible for would be your own and if you think I'm going to help you destroy *that*, then you're cracked. As for the rest... Darshan's right, that blame lies on Mum. Dinnae take the responsibility of her failures for yourself. And I've nae even touched on the fact you've nae proof that what you're proposing will work."

It would. He knew that in his bones. "It's what she has always wanted from me."

"Aye, but she could still decide to wage war on Udynea because of *him*." He jerked a thumb at Darshan. "She'd only need to claim that he abducted you and demand recompense."

"Meanwhile," Darshan added, "you could be living a free life here rather than slowly dying back in Tirglas." He shook his head mournfully. "Having you believe any action she took was your fault is the worst blow your mother has ever dealt you."

That wasn't true. There were worse things. She had already taken lives in the name of treason, all because he had rutted with them. *So many deaths*. He didn't want more. He didn't want to return to Tirglas, either, but... "What else can be done?"

His brother fell silent. He stared at the table, his brow furrowed and his lips disappearing beneath his moustache as he pressed them together. "I ken it's nae right for a child to consider it of their own parent, but Mum is nae stable. Give me time. Between Nora and meself, we might be able to have her step down, see her sent to a quiet cloister somewhere in the mountains, take up regency in her absence."

"What if you told your people the truth?" Darshan suggested.

"That their queen lied to them, you mean?" Gordon asked, scratching at his beard. "Aye, you could tell them. But I dinnae ken how they'd react."

"It'll nae mean much anyway," Hamish said. "Nae without me present." No warrior sent by the queen would believe the word of any Udynean.

Darshan toyed with his rings, twisting them one after the other. "Having you near the Tirglasian border could also wind up with you being dragged over it. If not killed."

Gordon grunted his agreement. "Nae to mention they could just as likely accuse you of being an illusion if nae ensorcelled."

After months at Darshan's side, all the travelling through a land where magic was commonplace, he had forgotten how quickly his own could be to lay all the blame on it. "How many clans have swallowed her lie?" He had to know what was at stake. "Has she—?"

"Nae," Gordon's gruff reply cut him off. "We're nae going there. I came here for three reasons, to warn the empire, see you and ensure Ethan was safe. I'll nae discuss anything else about Mum's orders, you hear?" He gave a curt nod before Hamish could argue either way. "In fact, I think we should table the whole discussion, I get the feeling we'll only go round in circles."

"It will be all right, *mea lux*," Darshan insisted.

"You dinnae ken that." None of them could. His brother was right. Going back might give their mother what she wanted, but it didn't mean she would stop. "You cannae see into the future."

"True," his husband agreed. "But I *do* know that an army of any respectable size takes time to amass. We are forewarned, thanks to your brother." He flashed a smile at Gordon, who replied with the bob of his head. "The border guards, along with the relevant nobility, will have the information by sundown."

Gordon's brows rose at that revelation.

"Magic," Hamish supplied. He didn't know if speaking of the Singing Crystals to foreigners was forbidden, but erring on the side of caution was the best course.

His brother wrinkled his nose. "I didnae think they possessed birds with lightning-fast flight." His eyes narrowed, clearly considering if that was also a possibility. "Me main concern right now is what'll happen to the lad." He jerked his head towards Ethan, his voice dropping to a whisper.

"I was thinking of introducing him to my nephew," Darshan said. "The gods know Tarendra could do with a little socialising amongst those his age who aren't also his aunts."

In a bout of coughing, Hamish sprayed his drink across the table. "You're nae suggesting what I think you are, are you?" he managed to say in Udynean, between attempts to clear his throat. "Ethan's bloody ten." Even as the number left his lips, he realised the lad would've completed another year months ago. The first of many family celebrations he would miss. "I mean, he's eleven."

Darshan shot him a perplexed look. "And Ren is twelve. Who better to show the boy around the palace grounds than some strange adult?"

Hamish lowered his head, trying to bury his embarrassment with his drink. "I thought you meant... something else."

"You mean *them*? *Together?*" Darshan scoffed. "What sort of uncle would I be if I started whoring out my nephew? I am not even sure of Ren's preferences to begin suggesting noble houses for his parents to start viable courtships."

Hamish grunted. Tarendra was of an age where his parents would seek out a prospective spouse in suitable households. For a grandson of the *Mhanek*, the boy would be limited to the upper nobility, unless a stronger option presented itself lower down the hierarchy.

No doubt, Darshan would learn in due time whether the union should lean towards women or men. Darshan had already expressed his dread of the day his nephew came to him for relationship advice, as what happened to most who took the role of guide in a *Khutani*.

"He could be entirely uninterested in the whole idea of having a partner," Darshan finished.

And wouldnae that *be a blow to Onella's designs.* What would the woman do if her only child turned out to be uninterested in a relationship? According to Darshan, his twin sister was that way and she had flirted with numerous suitors over the years, taking their gifts before exposing them as being more invested in her closeness to the throne than herself.

His gaze settled on his nephew. He would have to ensure no one sought to use Ethan for their own gain. Difficult when he had only his husband's clout to rely on. *I'll have to start earning some on me own. And convince Daama to teach the boy the same lessons he had leant on managing the court.*

"The language barrier with me nephew might be an issue," Gordon said. "I'd be right in this Ren fellow nae speaking much Tirglasian?"

Darshan frowned. "Come to think of it, I doubt he speaks it at all. It is a pity Ethan could not have expanded his teachings to know more than a little Udynean."

The boy glanced up at the mention of his name, his cheeks darkening. "I ken I'll need to learn the language if I'm to stay," he mumbled before perking up. "But *you* can teach me, right?"

"*Me?*" Darshan froze. His brows pinched together and his eyes, verging on panic, darted from the boy to Hamish.

The expression sharply reminded Hamish how his nephew had suggested the man married him when Ethan came of age if Darshan missed out on winning Hamish's hand. Clearly, the boy wasn't quite over his little crush. "I dinnae think that would be an appropriate use of his time, lad. Me husband has a lot on his plate right now." He forced a grin. "On the other hand, Gordon and meself have all the time in the world."

Ethan sagged onto the table, his unenthusiastic sigh tumbling several flakes of pastry across the glossy wooden surface.

"It's nae the end of the world, lad," Gordon said. Even though he spoke to their nephew, his brother still caught Hamish's eye.

Hamish nodded his understanding that the words were also meant for him. Both Darshan and Gordon were right, worrying over what his mother's actions would only herd him to insanity. Completely shaking it from his mind was impossible, but teaching his nephew how to understand and navigate their new home would be a welcomed distraction.

Chapter 43

Reclining on the plush chaise lounge, Hamish stared up at the ceiling of the bedchamber he shared with Darshan. Once again, he tossed a small cloth ball into the air and tried to use his shield to keep it from landing on him.

The ball fell back onto his stomach, just as it had done every other time. Except for the talent of putting his arrows wherever he wished, nothing about his magic was predictable. Even with the threat of death, the faint shield he usually summoned barely protected him.

Grunting, he threw the ball to one side and laced his fingers beneath his head. *I guess they call us specialists for a reason.* He would've vastly preferred spending as much time as he was able with Gordon instead of practising magic, anyway.

Except both his brother and nephew were currently outside the palace walls. Gordon insisted on purchasing a gift suitable for a prince consort, especially with the wedding being five days away, and Ethan had joined him to take in Minamist. Hamish didn't blame the boy as he longed to do the same. He wouldn't even have minded if his presence spoiled his brother's surprise.

Having people tailing him would've likewise been a minor inconvenience when it meant sharing time with his brother. But with the hypnotist still lurking in the shadows, everyone agreed it was for the best if Hamish stayed under constant guard within the imperial grounds. Always within earshot of a Nulled One.

Gordon found them disturbing. Hamish had informed his brother that the same abilities lingered in his blood, but Gordon either thought Hamish was joking or simply dismissed it as implausible. *Stubborn idiot.* His brother struggled to believe Hamish had magic, refusing to relent even after witnessing Hamish's ability to summon a shield. *If I could do something just a wee bit more impressive.* But with the simplest of magics beyond his abilities, that was proving to be harder than he had originally thought.

The latch on the entrance door clicked.

He tilted his head as the door opened to admit Darshan, still decked in his imperial garb. It was an assault on the eyes, from the heavy embroidery atop gold silk with threads and chains of gold bearing accents of amber. The only relief to the colour was in the deep red scarf draped over the man's shoulders.

Darshan halted briefly in the doorway. "I thought you'd be outside."

"I was." For much of the morning, but there was only so much fuss his mare could take before she grew stroppy.

"And how is your Lass?"

"Being spoilt rotten, from what I can gather." The stable master had returned his mare to her stall, but not before weather a stern conversation from Hamish on the horse's feeding requirements. He hadn't looked after her for so many years, nursing her through several injuries, just for her to founder on rich feed.

Darshan chuckled. "Did I not tell you she would be well cared for?" He unwound the scarf, revealing a small chest tucked under his arm.

Hamish eyed the chest, his curiosity piqued as Darshan attempted to conceal it behind himself. Typically, the palace servants delivered whatever item their *uris Mhanek* requested. What was in it that the man couldn't entrust to someone else? "Aye, but it was good to see her again." He had almost forgotten what it felt like to race across the land with a ton of horseflesh propelling him. He wasn't quite sure if his thighs would ever speak to him again, but it was a small price to pay.

The stable master had also spoken at some length about the prospect of putting her in foal. His brother had mentioned similar in the past, but Hamish had always dismissed it.

Now he wished he hadn't. He had seen the types of horses Udynea had. Some bore the strange trait of a dished forehead, whilst others seemed hardier and bore the quirk of inward-curving ears. All of them were delicate creatures compared to his mare.

He didn't know what mixing their bloodlines would produce, but if he bred her now, the resulting foal could be fully trained by the time their son was old enough to ride. *I could teach him.* There'd be those more suited to tutoring a young prince on politics and magic, but Hamish could make a bloody fine hunter out of the boy.

"I thought you wouldnae be back until later," Hamish said, still idly trying to figure out what was in the chest. "Did the meeting nae go as planned?" The ship carrying the new Stamekian emperor had arrived early in the morning. Hamish knew little about the young man who wore the Stamekian crown, only what Darshan had told him whilst dressing in that appalling outfit.

"It went amicably, I believe." Setting the chest down without a word towards it, he started unbuttoning his sherwani. "It's a shame you weren't there, I think you would've liked him."

"What?" Tearing his gaze from the chest, Hamish twisted in his seat to face the man. He could've gone? "I thought I wasnae to have anything to do with politics until after the wedding?"

Darshan's mouth pursed into a sour pucker. "That edict still stands, but the emperor will still be around for a few days afterwards, I'm sure. And a casual meeting between peers is hardly *political.*"

"Everything's political when it involves the ruler of another realm."

Darshan grimaced. "You're starting to sound like 'Ma." He paused in undoing the last of the sherwani's buttons to waggle a finger in the air. "And I still haven't decided if that's a good thing. Maybe I should've recommended a different teacher."

Hamish rolled his eyes. He knew the reasoning there, Darshan didn't want the very teachings he had learnt as a child echoed back at him from his husband. But Hamish already had enough schooling from Tirglas to know that dealing with foreign rulers was a delicate matter and his mother had made a fine example of the consequences when it went awry. "Why would this emperor want to meet me, anyway?"

"Curiosity, I'd suspect." He shrugged out of his sherwani, tossing it to one side. "I can't imagine the man has ever met a Tirglasian."

Hamish grunted his agreement. "I'd be surprised if he had, we dinnae have much to do with the southern lands." All the empires— Niholia, Stamekia and Udynea—were ruled by spellsters. It wasn't something easily overlooked. That his mother had considered a treaty with Udynea was a miracle.

Merchants traded with them regardless, but guarding caravans over land was taxing. He knew from his short time talking to his elder sister's husband that sailing north past Obuzan shores with cargo from Niholia could be dicey. Travelling around the rocky shoreline of Heimat to any of Udynea's northern ports might've been longer, but it was still a safer passage even with Talfaltan vessels shadowing them and still a shorter distance than for similar goods.

All of that meant very few Stamekians would've had direct contact with a Tirglasian, especially not an imperial prince.

"It's Rami the *Betrayer*, right?" An odd title. Who, or what, had he betrayed?

Darshan hummed a soft agreement as he vanished into the wardrobe to finish changing. "Stamekian people gain an honorific after performing a great deed," he said, his voice muffled. "Emperor Rami was merely considered a forsaken before he gained the throne by overthrowing and executing his father."

"His own kin?" He couldn't have heard that right. Anyone of the Tirglasian crown who overthrew his own parent found themselves facing an assault from other clans, or even their own, quickly enough.

"Believe me," Darshan said, the tone of his voice souring. "The old emperor doesn't deserve your sympathy." His head appeared briefly at the door, tipped to one side with his lips twisted in thought. "Did you see Emperor Rami when he entered the palace grounds?"

"Nae even a wee bit," Hamish admitted. Curiosity had drawn him a little closer to the imperial gates than he should've risked, but the Stamekian emperor had gone no further than the council hall.

"Well, before the man came into power, Stamekia was ruled by Sharik."

Hamish hummed. He had heard that name before. "I think Daama told me this one already. He's the emperor who was cracked enough to believe himself to be a god?" The embodiment of the sun, if he remembered right. Hamish knew of a few men, miners and sailors for the most part, who had become delusional. Some were dangerous, most were only a threat to themselves.

Either way, they never lived long.

"The very one," Darshan replied, the pride in his voice enough to heat Hamish's cheeks. He reappeared from the wardrobe, decked in an ivory sherwani with hints of gold embroidery along the hem. "Thankfully, I never met the man, but I've been told he was a powerful spellster. One who, apparently, kept the rains from his palace and the surrounding countryside for forty years."

"That's nae exactly ideal for crops." Even in Udynea, where the four seasons Hamish was used to became only wet and dry, there had been plenty of rain over the months.

Darshan shook his head. "That it is not and it made Stamekia dependant on outward sources when it came to feeding her people for a long time, worsening over the decades. I doubt his people linked him to the lack of rain, either. He was their god, after all. Responsible for the sunrise every morning."

"Ah." It was worse than what he'd been told. "Daama didnae tell me the people believed his lies. Was that what brought things to a head? The people woke up?"

"No." Having crossed the room to stand before the chest, Darshan ran a finger along the lid. "Sharik lived for a very long time, some say for centuries."

Startled, Hamish sat up. "Spellsters can live that long?" He had guessed those with healing abilities would carry on longer purely due to their good health, but even the healthiest of spellsters had to die of old age.

"It's possible," Darshan whispered, bowing his head. "Not ethically. The ways are forbidden, not even the Knitting Factory knows them anymore. The stories suggest it involves absorbing the life-force of another."

Tirglas had its own tales. His mother would tell them to scare himself and his siblings into obedience as children. In them, people were sacrificed in order to keep others living well past the time they should have. "I thought it was just a myth," he murmured.

"I'm not entirely sure it isn't." Darshan drummed his fingers on the chest lid. "Even when I was a child, the rumours surrounding Sharik were of him being an unsavoury creature obsessed with his Dolls."

"Dolls?" Hamish echoed, a quiet unsettling feeling bubbling in his gut. "As in a child's plaything?"

"*His* playthings, yes. But they weren't toys for children, they *were* children. I hear he had quite the collection. Any pretty child, anyone with a uniqueness about their appearance."

"He kept *children*? As *toys*?" Darshan couldn't be implying what he thought.

"It is exactly as you think," his husband confirmed. "And worse."

Hamish stared at him. How could it be worse?

"He kept his collection... fresh. When there was another, younger, child with prettier features, the old ones simply vanished. That's where the other rumours came from. Many believe he used the lives of the discarded Dolls to lengthen his own."

"And nae a soul challenged him before his son?"

Darshan shrugged, toying with the chest's latch. "Who would challenge the sun? The few who stood against him were always swiftly dispatched." He smiled, the curve of his lips lacking warmth. "He's gone now. Not soon enough for most, but we have their new emperor to thank for that it was at all."

"How did the man manage it?"

"With a sword, I believe. Clean slice to the head. No spellster comes back from that. Not without help."

"I mean, if the bastard was so powerful." And likely paranoid if he had truly lived for so long. "Then how did his son get near him without being burnt to a crisp?"

"Oh, *that*. Like I said, Emperor Rami's a forsaken. That's what the Stamekians call their Nulled Ones. But discussing foreign rulers wasn't why I came back. I have something for you." Darshan presented the chest to him. "Several things, in fact. I planned to gift them to you tonight, but since you're here..."

Hamish flipped open the chest lid. Inside sat a crest Hamish hadn't seen before. "Who does this belong to?"

Mischief flashed to life in Darshan's eyes. "Guess."

Aware that his husband practically hovered, Hamish lifted the crest from atop a nest of silvery silk to trace a finger over the work. A gilded stag's head adorned the centre of the shield. The antlers were more branch-like than those of an actual stag and framed a familiar-looking crown. Flanking the shield was a pair of silver bears standing on their haunches, snarling and ready to defend. Below the shield was the scroll bearing a motto in Ancient Domian.

"Bears," Hamish murmured. As far as he knew, there were none in Udynea. Definitely, not this far south. "A northern household?" One near the Tirglasian border. A new ally? One tied to the throne.

Darshan hung his head. "No, they're meant to represent you and your clan."

"It's *our* crest?" Hamish stared at the man. Darshan clearly waited for something, but what? What could he say? He hadn't even been aware anyone in Udynea knew of the custom. *Except...* "You spoke to me brother."

"Of course. Do you not like it? Gordon assured me that this is—"

"—a custom amongst noble households?" he finished. "Aye, it is." Hamish caressed the plaque, doing his best to ignore the welling emotion in his chest. "I love it." He didn't yet grasp all the symbolism, but to have something that was theirs alone when everything else belonged to the throne... "I just dinnae expect it."

Darshan settled next to him on the chaise lounge. "If things had gone smoothly, we would've had two proper weddings. But you were denied what your siblings had and this ceremony is full of Udynean rituals. I wanted to give you something to reflect your heritage."

He wiped at the corner of his eyes, trying to stop their leaking. If he cried now, he wasn't going to stop anytime soon. "Tell me what it all means. What does the stag represent?"

Redness tinged Darshan's cheeks. "That would be me. The *vris Mhanek* insignia is merely the crown, but I couldn't use that alone." He plucked a little velvet pouch from within the chest, toying with the ties. "I competed for your hand under the same banner that your sister-by-marriage did for her husband, I believe I recalled the right animal."

"Aye." He caressed the antlers. *Branches.* Like the trees Darshan could speak to. All in gold because it was tied to the crown and the light. He would've expected the backdrop to be red, the other colour tied to the royal family, but it was a familiar shade of blue. "Is this supposed to reference me, too?" It was the right hue to match his eyes.

"I hope you'll forgive me for that. It's a gorgeous shade, *mea lux*. How could I resist?"

Wrapping an arm around the man, Hamish squeezed and growled in mock annoyance. He couldn't even muster the energy to be vexed. This was *their* crest. Just looking upon it somehow made their impending wedding more real.

He moved on to the motto, silently mouthing the words, uncertainty sucking his voice. Ancient Domian was still new to his tongue. Daama swore he was improving and, given a few more months of tutoring, was convinced he would be conversing in the language as easily as he now did in Udynean. He wasn't so sure.

His gaze lifted to his husband, one brow rising with it.

Pride twinkled in Darshan's eyes. Did that mean he had at least read the words correctly? "We burn brighter than the flame," his husband translated. "A little dramatic, but no one ever accused me of being subtle."

Hamish grinned. Subtle was definitely the one thing his husband struggled at.

"I also tried to get them to add more points to the stag—even one, so it could be closer to the twenty-pointer you had in your quarters back at Mullhind—but the heraldist claimed more would be garish." He laughed. "Can you imagine? Sadly, the goldsmith agreed. Said it was difficult enough to duplicate in miniature as it stood."

"Why would it need to be smaller?" Most crests were displayed on banners and shields.

"For this." Darshan upended the velvet pouch. A single gold ring tumbled out onto his palm. One side had been flattened into a disc and bore the same emblem as the plaque Hamish held. "I was thinking of starting a new tradition."

"A signet ring?"

"My wedding band," he clarified. "They're in the process of making yours. You'll need to go and have it fitted before the ceremony, though."

Hamish ran his thumb along the underside of the ring Darshan had gifted him in Tirglas. Could it even be counted as a wedding band if the ceremony was ultimately a farce? "How did you get this all done so quickly? Me brother's barely been here four days."

"I'm the *uris Mhanek*, everything I commission is given priority and craftsmen are rewarded for their swiftness. Besides, the goldsmith will gain a fair bit of prestige in being known as the one who'd crafted royal wedding bands." He returned the signet ring to the pouch before setting both it and the plaque aside. "There is something else we need to discuss."

He warily eyed Darshan. He hadn't mistaken the man twisting the ring on his little finger. That was never a good sign. "Such as?"

"When the ceremony is over, when we're officially married under Udynean law, those of the Crystal Court will bring forth their... gifts." He wet his lips. "Most will be small tokens. Frivolous things, jewellery, paintings, statues and the like. But there is likely to be some which are—"

"People," Hamish growled. Like the court often did during the celebration of their *vris Mhanek's* birthday, they would use the opportunity to get rid of the slaves they were displeased with. "You cannae expect me to sit there and let that happen right in front of me."

Darshan held up his hand in surrender. "I know how you feel about it. Even if I was the *Mhanek* doing everything in my power to change things, it wouldn't be instant. And, until the law *is* changed, the court will continue to do as it has always done. I need you to not react, to show no disfavour regardless of the gift's nature."

"I'm nae sure I can do that."

"Please, *mea lux*." He clasped Hamish's hands. "If the court is smart, there'll be nothing to worry about. If not, then it'll be only for a moment. Depending on how many, I could likely free a handful more. They'll be given the same choices. I swear."

Hamish knew that, just as he knew they'd no choice but to go along with it. "There's something else you're nae telling me." It wasn't a question. The man seemed far too jittery for the concerns he'd already voiced.

"There is." Darshan stood and paced the room to eventually halt at the stairs leading up to their bed. "Do you think—after everything you seen, everything I've done—that it'll be a good idea for me to have children?"

"Aye." They had already sent for the Niholian breeders, who were due to arrive sometime within the week. Far sooner than Darshan's first prediction.

Darshan examined his hands as if seeing them for the first time. "This ability... I can't always control it."

"I ken that." But the hedgewitch the dwarven Coven sent had been here for three days. No one could expect the man to work miracles, especially when the dwarf was still getting to grips with the idea of a spellster having anything similar to the powers of the original hedgewitches.

"What if my son inherits this ability? If *I* struggle to keep it contained, can you imagine what a *child* with this sort of power would be like?" He bowed his head. "What if I end up creating a monster?"

Hamish scoffed. "That's nae possible." They couldn't even be sure whatever Darshan had done to himself was possible of being passed on as easily as his spellster bloodline. "He'll be the same as any wee lad." It couldn't be any more dangerous than other young spellsters. And even then, they'd no way of telling how soon the connection would form.

At least they could limit the influence by keeping a moody child high up in the palace where the plants' whispers didn't seem to be capable of reaching Darshan.

Darshan stared owlishly at him for a while, then one side of his mouth hitched upwards. "Such certainty."

"If what you fear is true, that our bairn is born being able to speak to nature, they will have never understood the world any other way. *You* came to it late. They'll grow up thinking that's how it has always been."

"But they'll learn differently."

"That doesnae matter either. You'll be here to guide them. You would've had time to learn control. There'll still be another nine months after the deed is done, after all." More, if complications with the conception arose. "And you'll have me. I ken there's nae much I can teach about magic and whatever this new ability of yours actually is, but I'll be there, supporting you and our bairn whenever needed." And de-escalating if another outburst like what happened with the *Mhanek* reared its head.

"I know you will." Exhaling heavily, he returned to Hamish's side. "I know we've discussed this before but I—" He gave another deep sigh, scrubbing his face and fisting his hair. "I don't even know how to feel about the idea anymore. It sounded so simple *before.*"

"Do you want children?" Once, he knew the man's answer would've been a very passionate negative, but he'd been the one to originally suggest it.

Perhaps, now they would soon be faced with the reality of siring one, the lustre had worn off.

"I want *your* child."

Not quite the response Hamish had expected. He took up the man's hand, clasping it to his chest. "Dinnae you want it to be *ours?*" Any son of theirs needed to have imperial blood for the senate to accept them as Darshan's heir.

"I don't know." He leant against Hamish, burying his face into the shirt. The edges of his glasses dug slightly harder than the rest. "I acted rashly in Tirglas," he mumbled, the words muffled by cloth. "I didn't think. Not when I kissed you. Not when I competed for your hand. Definitely not when I brought you back from the brink of death."

Hamish remained silent, rubbing small circles into Darshan's back as he waited for the man to calmly work through his thoughts. He agreed that certain matters could've been done with more grace, but he'd been just as reckless.

"There hasn't been a day where I've regretted having you at my side, but now…" He lifted his head, staring up at Hamish with glassy eyes. "Your mother has declared war. I'm stuck with a power no one can explain and… and… there's no way to predict if any of my actions will cause any child I help create to suffer. I'm not sure if I want to take that risk."

A valid concern, but there wasn't much they could do about it beyond not involving Darshan. "Anjali has the same parentage as you." He'd vague memories of discussing the option at one point. It wouldn't even require the Niholian breeders. Just good timing.

Darshan shook his head. "I wish that was a viable choice. But I'm afraid I wasn't quite truthful there, having Anjali carry your child wouldn't work how we need it to."

"Is it nae simpler to do it the more natural way?" There'd still be magic involved—he'd about as much interest in sleeping with Darshan's twin sister as the woman had in him—but that sort of conception was the less experimental kind the Udynean healers were adept at.

"Simpler? Yes. But then you would have a child without another parent. Like I said, it would be *yours*. Completely. No one would even consider it as Anjali's let alone mine."

What foolishness was this? He certainly couldn't create a child on his own. "Is it because she's the second twin and doesnae have a soul so she doesnae really exist?" It was the reason Darshan had her as his first choice for a surrogate. Like how her attack on the hypnotised men had been shrugged off as them spontaneously dying, any act she did was considered as coming from the very air.

He didn't realise that included birth.

Darshan nodded.

"That's bullshit." The words slipped out before Hamish could stop them. They were the same ones he'd been saying ever since Darshan first told him of the old belief. And Anjali was one of the fortunate who survived. It made him sick to think how many children had died because of their luck in being born alongside their sibling.

"You don't have to tell *me*. I've lived several decades of having my twin ignored by all bar the servants and those closest to us. If I could strike that belief from people's minds, I would. But the oldest ones are the hardest to be rid of."

"We'll change that." If Tirglas could change people's opinions on how men like himself should be viewed, then this was also possible. It had to be.

Darshan grinned. The corners wavered slightly, but there seemed to be a thread of his original confidence weaving through. "Have I ever told you how much I admire your optimism, *mea lux?*"

"A few times." He held the man close. "It'll all work out fine, me heart. I promise. Our wee bairn will nae come to any harm even if he does inherit your abilities and, if you look on the bright side, he'll always have a heavy defence out and about the palace grounds."

"I hope you're right."

Me too. He hadn't considered any of the worries Darshan had voiced. They were both healthy. There was no reason to suspect something might go wrong.

Squeezing Hamish tighter for a brief moment, Darshan slowly sagged against him. "Do you have much time to spare? I know 'Ma is tutoring you later, but I thought that we could arrange a quiet introduction between you and Emperor Rami. Say... over a light supper?"

"I've enough time for that." If it stopped the man's mind from going round in endless circles, his tutoring could wait for another day.

"Can we stay like this for a while?" Darshan's question drifted up between them, muffled by fabric and the press of the man's cheek to Hamish's chest.

"Aye, we can do that, too." He drew Darshan closer, adjusting the angle they sat at until he was able to lean back on the chaise lounge with his husband half draped over him. "For as long as you want."

~ ~ ~

Darshan didn't know how long he lay against his husband, cradled almost protectively in the man's arms, in a haze of contentment. There was something about having those arms wrapped around him that made him feel surer in himself. There was no judgement, no questioning of his abilities. Hamish's unwavering faith in him made Darshan want to *be* better, to *do* better. To become the kind of man worthy of such devotion.

A knock rattled the suite's entrance.

Grumbling, he burrowed his face into Hamish's chest, immediately regretting the act as his glasses dug into his skin.

"Is that nae the code for a message?" Hamish asked. It had taken no more than a few days for him to notice the difference in knocks, deciphering the common ones had taken him less than a week.

"Close," Darshan mumbled into the layers of linen his husband wore. The code in the knock spoke of a messenger with a package. He didn't want to deal with either right now.

"Should you nae see what they want?"

He should, but he didn't want to leave his husband's embrace. And he must've looked a mess.

Darshan wiped beneath his eyes. Sure enough, his finger came back black from the kohl. There were also imprints on the lenses of his glasses. It appeared to be smeared on Hamish's clothes, too.

His patient husband wouldn't say a word about it, but the messenger would. Such gossip would circulate the palace grounds, reaching ears best left ignorant of his mental state.

Another knock drew a sigh from his lips.

Darshan stood and, hastening to make himself presentable, crossed to the door. *If it's Daama, I swear...* His old nanny always had the worst timing. But she also wasn't one to linger behind closed doors. A truth he had learnt the hard way. "I'll tell them to go away, just—" All ability to speak fled as he turned to his husband.

The way Hamish lay stretched out on the chaise lounge, the sunlight haloing his hair in such a fashion that it appeared to be alight, had him looking divine. The sight set Darshan's heart to pounding and dried his throat.

"Just wait a moment," he finally managed, blindly searching for a door handle. "I shan't be long." He slipped through the door, almost colliding with the messenger waiting on the other side. "What is it?" he snapped, instantly regretting the tone as the woman flinched.

"M-my apologies, *vris Mhanek.*" She held up a moderately sized chest bearing his symbol. "Your scribe? He told me to deliver this?"

He recognised it as the one Maari was steadying filling with deeds from Minamist's Pits, much to the annoyance of Elke, Darshan's accountant. Did that mean Maari had finally bought up every inch of the land? Last Darshan had heard of the endeavour, a handful of landowners were being stubborn about selling their hovels. Clearly, the greed of gold now as opposed to a pittance from the residents later had changed their minds.

Damn. It *was* what he had wanted, but the timing could've been better. He couldn't sneak the chest by Hamish's notice. The man had noticed the smaller box Darshan tried to conceal earlier, this was far bigger.

Darshan took the chest from the woman. It was cumbersome, but not heavy. Dismissing her, he returned to his suite.

Inside, Hamish hadn't moved an inch. He raised an eyebrow as Darshan crossed the room. "What's that? A wee token from some lord?"

He grunted. There *had* been the odd gift since their arrival. "Not quite. It's actually for you. I had intended it as a birthday gift." He set the chest down on the bed and tapped out a quick sequence of magic pulses to open the lock. "And I do apologise for the lack of ceremony behind it, the impromptu arrival has rather caught me off-guard."

Although the rest of his husband's face gave no indication as to his mood, there was a faint creasing of humour around the man's eyes. "*You?* Never." He joined Darshan to open the chest, frowning at the tied bundle of papers. "Paper?" He untied the stack, examining the topmost page with a squint that had Darshan's gut churning.

Did the man not understand what he'd been given? Did they have land deeds in Tirglas? He hadn't considered that. His lessons on the way to his ambassadorial position had focused mostly on trade, but he recalled the clans had certain territorial boundaries. Surely, they had records of where those borders sat.

Did that mean Hamish understood and it was merely the case of Darshan assuming he would react favourably? Darshan hadn't been shy in showering his husband with gifts, but they had largely been necessities. Clothes and the like.

Eventually, Hamish looked up from the page. "Are these contracts?"

"Land deeds," Darshan clarified, settling on the edge of the bed. "I bought up every piece of the Pits under your name." His face heated at the explanation. It wasn't the most romantic of gifts, but Hamish favoured practical over the frivolous. "I thought that, with your unique viewpoint, you could improve conditions for the people living there."

"And your solution was to have me own a piece of Minamist?"

Darshan nodded. Any change was easier done to land they already owned.

"The poorest parts?"

"I want better for my people. I can't count on the senate to not corrupt my word of my orders." He had witnessed it happen to his grandfather during the short time between the fogging of his mind and his death. Only his father's quick thinking had stopped several laws being passed that would've seen the empire spiralling into ruin. "I know the strength of your morals, I trust in them."

"And where do you expect me to get the funds to do that?"

Laying his head on an upraised fist, Darshan fluttered his lashes. "Perhaps your exorbitantly wealthy husband might be of assistance there?"

"You want me to use your money to rebuild the place?"

Darshan shrugged. If that was what Hamish intended. "I'm not doing much else with it. Besides, I figured this would be a better use of your time and skill than arranging soirées and entertaining dignitaries." He had plenty of people capable of fulfilling the former task and he quite enjoyed the latter role.

Hamish pulled out more of the deeds, his lips moving as he

silently counted them, before seemingly giving up. "This is a *lot* of land. Are you sure about this? It'll take *years* to build new housing and upgrade what's already there."

And no doubt many more years ensuring none of it fell apart once his back was turned. "I have every faith in your abilities." He'd only heard of the duties Hamish's mother had put the man to in Tirglas. *A friendly face the people could voice their complaints to.* Darshan couldn't have the same repertoire with the common folk, the people were too scared to speak with their *uris Mhanek*. And, when it came to troubles, the best Darshan had were his spies. Neither helped his people.

Shaking his head, Hamish returned the deeds to the chest. "I cannae believe you." He crawled onto the bed, forcing Darshan to lie back as he was straddled. "You want me to outshine the whole of the Crystal Court by abolishing Minamist's slums, all at nae cost to anyone but yourself?"

"Yes?" Darshan replied, distracted by how his husband hovered over him with one leg on either side of his waist. It was definitely a glorious sight. One he wanted to linger over for as long as possible.

Maybe the man could be convinced to stay here with him rather than meet visiting royalty.

"Are you..." He cleared his throat. As much as Darshan enjoyed being beneath his husband, with the man remaining stationary, all that glorious weight pressing down was making it hard to breathe. "Do you think you could get off me?"

Hamish gave a rakish smile that merrily stoked the fire in Darshan's gut. "I would've thought you'd want me to get you off, nae get off you." He threw his head back and laughed.

Darshan gave the man a hearty push, rocking Hamish backwards a mere hairsbreadth.

Chuckling, his husband made such a display of being wounded that would've fooled any idle spectator.

Darshan, however, knew he had barely shifted the man. He had to weigh half of Hamish's bulk. "I'm serious. You're squashing me."

"*Squash—?*" His indignance had the word spluttering into a garbled mess. "Who was it that has been requesting to put me in this position?"

He had, but with them both naked and moving. Static weight on his waist was a far different feeling.

"And now you object to having me here?" A mischievous spark lit those blue eyes before Hamish's fingers assailed Darshan's sides, slipping beneath his sherwani to tickle him.

"Cut it out," he managed between giggles. "Gods, I—" No matter how he twisted, with his husband's weight pinning him in place, he couldn't evade those hands. Nor could he focus enough to bring his shield up and not hurt the man. "Stop. All right, I yield!"

Laughing almost as breathlessly as Darshan, Hamish ceased his attack. "Victory!" he crowed, swinging his leg back off Darshan. He wobbled slightly as the mattress shifted, almost losing his balance, but swiftly righting himself.

"Cad," Darshan grumbled, giving his husband's thigh a gentle slap. Ever since Hamish had found out how ticklish Darshan was, the man teased him with it.

Hamish's impish smile returned. "Do I hear a request for more?" He lunged at Darshan, his arms outstretched.

Without thinking, Darshan threw up a shield before those fingers made contact.

His husband smacked into the surface, stunned only for a moment. "Cheater!" he gasped, thumping a shoulder against the barrier as though brute force would grant him entry.

"Cut that out." Each whack of his husband's body upon the shimmering surface sent a faint ripple of pressure against Darshan's mind. Annoying but nothing he couldn't tolerate. "You'll break something before my shield gives." He sent a warning pulse through the air to further dissuade the man.

Hamish tipped backwards. He teetered on the edge of the bed for a heartbeat, his arms flung wide in an attempt to regain his balance.

Then he fell, rolling down the stairs to land with a thud.

" 'Mish!" Darshan launched to his feet, instantly rushing to Hamish's side. He hadn't thought the blast was that hard. "Are you hurt?" He cupped the man's face, preparing to heal whatever injuries had occurred. "I didn't mean to—"

Hamish waved him off. "I'm fine," he boomed, still laughing, "I—" He clapped a hand over his mouth, his eyes widening. "That was louder than I intended," he mumbled through his fingers.

"It's all right, *mea lux*. I wouldn't mind if your laughter brought the ceiling down around our ears." He paused, considering the rooms above, and added, "All right, maybe a little. But only because it would bring the furniture with it."

Still sitting on the floor, Hamish craned his head back to stare at the ceiling. "What *is* above us?"

Darshan shrugged. "Nursery? Maybe servant quarters?" That was all he knew about the rooms on the level above. He'd never really given the layout of them much thought. "They're probably empty." The servant's quarters might have one or two people milling around. "The nursery definitely."

His husband's brow furrowed, those gorgeous blue eyes also narrowing. "Why would the nursery be empty? You cannae tell me there's nae bairns in the imperial palace."

"It's a *royal* nursery, made specifically for royal babies. Of which there are none." His siblings might currently be under one roof, but they would opt to keep their children near just as the rest of the Crystal Court did. In terms of weaknesses, children came with a hefty danger of them being used as leverage.

"You mean to say that *our* bairns would be up there?" Hamish pointed at the ceiling. "That's..." His expression became crestfallen. "That's so far away."

Darshan hadn't given any thought to the distance, but he supposed it was.

Hamish tipped his head to one side, clearly lost in his own thoughts. The act shifted the coils of his hair, revealing an abrasion on his temple.

Laying a hand on his husband's cheek, Darshan coaxed his magic into healing the injury. "I'm sorry about pushing you off the bed." He really hadn't thought the pulse would be strong enough to move the man.

Hamish scoffed. "I've had harder falls off me mare. It was a daft accident is all." He laid his hand atop Darshan's, his warmth soaking through the skin. "I ken you would never deliberately hurt me."

"Still..." He needed to be mindful of how he used his magic around Hamish. His husband might be able to handle a little roughhousing, but there were things he couldn't counter. "I shall be more careful."

Releasing Darshan's hand, Hamish got to his feet. "I want our bairns to be closer than—" He rolled his eyes towards the ceiling. "—up there."

"Then they shall." There was a room just across the hall that the Nulled Ones currently used as a place to rest between night shifts. It could easily be repurposed as a nursery.

Or perhaps they could knock out part of the left wall into the room he was certain they used for storage. That seemed a far better option, gifting them access to their child without needing to leave the suite.

Hamish paused in straightening his clothes. "Really? It would be that easy? There's nae some tradition or anything stopping us?"

Darshan shook his head. Not as far as he knew. "Although, I don't know if *easy* is the right word. Remodelling would be needed." And extra guards, but the same could be said if the child remained in the royal nursery. "But for you, *mea lux,* I would bring down the moon if you asked."

A small smile took Hamish's lips. His cheeks darkened. "I think it looks fine right where it is." He drew Darshan into a one-armed embrace. "But keeping our family close is better than any moon."

Family. His heart fluttered at the thought. So did his stomach.

But Hamish was right in that he wouldn't be stepping into fatherhood alone. And he had seen the man around his niece and nephews. He clearly knew more about raising a family than Darshan. *It'll be all right*. He would follow his husband's lead.

And give Hamish everything he desired.

Chapter 44

Darshan rifled through the new reports on the Jhanaar family, squinting under the waning light of a lantern. The entire household had moved into their estate on the border of Nulshar after the birth of their seventh child. Of those children, five were in the age range Hamish described. Of them, the eldest three were women.

Which of the trio had survived their family's slaughter was as much a mystery as everything else. Rumour mentioned only the possibility of the family birthing a child capable of hypnosis, not which one of them had the knack.

He stared at the three papers where he had consolidated information on the women. There wasn't much. None of the academies in Nulshar seemed to have any record of spellsters in the family attending their halls, not even the younger ones. That wasn't uncommon, but it did irk him. If he knew more about them, his people might be able to determine not only the level of her other skills, but predict her next move.

What of the connection to the Kaatha household? Had it been a mere convenient turn of events that enabled the Jhanaar woman to use their name as a cover? There was no evidence in her using it thusly, but she must have to get so far.

There had to be something. If the couple were betrothed, even if it had been annulled, then there'd be some record. But all his searches had been fruitless. Not a one of his people could dredge up anything solid.

It was as though someone had erased every sign.

He leant back in his seat, eyeing the shelves of books and scrolls that made up this section of the imperial library. If this Jhanaar woman was his hypnotist and she had managed to step foot inside the imperial palace, then it wasn't implausible for her to have walked these halls. But to have then destroyed documents?

The scholar in him shuddered at the idea.

Sighing, Darshan set aside the papers to take a sip of his drink. He grimaced as the tepid liquid hit his tongue. When had his tea gained the time to cool? He had only begun digging into the reports a short moment ago.

What time was it? The darkness outside the windows suggested some time in the night. He had arrived during the twilight hour.

Removing his glasses, Darshan scrubbed at his face. His magic buzzed softly through his body, reminding him that he should seek his bed.

Except not being able to find any rest had been what dragged him here in the first place. He couldn't sleep. Not in the stark quiet of his chambers. Not without Hamish. But tradition demanded the man be elsewhere for at least the first day of the wedding ceremony.

Darshan's father insisted it be longer.

How many days had it been? Three? Two? Did the wedding start this coming morning? Or did he have another sleepless night ahead of him?

Maybe he should return to the palace gardens and attempt Hedgewitch Gregor's suggestion of coaxing new growth. That display of Darshan's new abilities had fascinated the dwarf. The man claimed the old hedgewitches could only encourage a plant to grow a certain way.

Darshan could command it.

Even more, he could alter the state, making the plant he desired grow and bloom instead of what should've been in its place. It had only been with seeds, but the dwarf also hadn't been here for long, arriving a scant handful of days before Emperor Rami. Between his usual duties as *vris Mhanek* and the impending wedding, lessons with the man had been haphazard at best.

Darshan wouldn't consider himself practised enough to scale up his attempts and trying the method on an already grown plant. He wasn't sure he wanted to. Seeds had no voice until they took root.

He pushed off from the table, bundling the reports and tucking them back into their leather folder. Whether he chose sleep or practise, his search to understand the Jhanaar woman would go no further tonight.

Maybe he could try the fluke of turning wheat seeds into the deep red, funnel-shaped flowers that grew only in Obuzan's jungles. Zahaan's network would certainly approve of having easy access to one of the world's deadliest poisons. Although, it took a lot out of him to pluck the desired plant from the earth's memory and make it grow from nothing.

Perhaps, if sleep was to evade him, he would be better off meditating. Whilst he had used the Stamekian technique in the past to assist in calming his unsettled magic as a child, it also seemed to help with the connection. It might even soothe his mind enough to let him rest.

Exiting the imperial library, Darshan trotted down the stairs. He brushed his hand along the hedges hemming the path in. The leaves shifted beneath his palm, trembling lazily in greeting. It sent a ripple through the surrounding plants, who all stirred to offer the same welcome.

The original hedgewitches did more than talk to plants. At least, according to Hedgewitch Gregor. The hedgewitches of old had been guardians and caretakers. Emissaries. And, in turn, the plants had protected them. That sat in line with the old Udynean and, even older, Domian stories of dwarven clans vanishing into the forests without a trace.

Had the plants back then responded to threats on their hedgewitches with the same exuberance as they heeded Darshan? Nothing he remembered from the old tales gave any hint of the dwarves fighting back with anything other than stone and bronze weapons. The latter often stolen from Domian supplies.

However, if a Domian spellster had witnessed a dwarf retaliating the way Darshan had inadvertently done with his father, then they might've tried to harness it. *The willow.*

As other plants had done in the past, the bush beneath his fingertips shuddered. Curious how the response was the same wherever he went. All he had to think about was of the twisted tree he had fought and they knew.

It's all connected. Hedgewitch Gregor's words again. Water might've been a barrier for hedgewitches, but it wasn't for the plants. The willow on the *Gilded Cage* had stood alone, yet still reached him. The reeds in the ocean were submerged and still spoke to him, gifting him with the means to see the surrounding wildlife.

The means to see...

To *track.*

Darshan clambered over the hedge, ignoring the muffled objections and faint groans as he sought for bare ground. He settled cross-legged onto the earth, closing his eyes and opening his mind to his surroundings. If he was connected to the world, if he could sense the smallest of creatures scurrying through the undergrowth...

Could he find the person responsible for his strife?

The nearby bushes shivered, confused. They didn't sense the world the same. They could tell the difference between human, dwarf and elf. They even understood the vibrations that meant a being had magic, or the lack thereof indicating they didn't.

But between spellsters? That could be trickier.

He needed this woman found. Needed her here. Needed to tear them from this life. To keep his husband safe. To understand why. Why target Hamish? *Why not come for me?*

The heartbeat of the world throbbed around him, drawing him down into the earth. He hadn't dared do more than skim this consciousness ever since first discovering it. The islet the palace grounds set upon looked strange. *The palaces.* Patches of nothing left huge holes in the network. If she was huddling somewhere inside them, he would never find her.

But if she had been hiding there, the guards' constant sweeps would've brought up something, even if it was only a hint. *She escaped the imperial palace.* Hamish's order had seen the entrances blocked by Nulled Ones long before Darshan made it there. Her absence within the walls led to the conclusion that she had jumped out a low window.

Now he knew the family, the verdict bothered him. Such a fall would've broken bones, which would've required healer training to mend swiftly. Yet the Knitting Factory in Nulshar hadn't heard of any Jhanaar beyond a young boy.

She couldn't have flown. Had she scaled the walls? There weren't many footholds, but he couldn't rule out the possibility. She clearly knew how to evade and let herself into places unseen. Where would be an easy place to rely on nimbleness? The stables? The kitchens?

The palace garden. There weren't any buildings suitable for shelter, but the weather was mild enough at this time of year to not need much. The hedge maze alone would be a warren for the guards to comb through.

Would anyone be there at this time of night? Gardeners didn't actually sleep there. They'd accommodations nearby, though. Currently guarded as heavily as any palace gate.

Darshan slowly turned his attention to the plants slumbering in the shadow of the walls. The various grasses answered first, as eager and brainless as a half-grown puppy. Any order given to them would be abandoned within the next beat of the world. He needed something with more memory, preferably the interwoven network of the hedge maze.

He pushed himself further, searching along the pathways of bushes, slipping past the trees whose slumber ran deeper than most. He skimmed beyond the sway of the pond's little ecosystem, which barely acknowledged his passing along the network.

Something brushed his consciousness, the jolt of a thousand voices.

Darshan teetered on the edge, unable to grasp anything amongst the whispers, before the blast threw him back into his own body. Slowly, he became aware of staring up at the sky.

When had he laid down?

He rubbed his head, but the ache within didn't lessen. Had that been the maze? *It's so jumbled.* Maybe if he was closer?

Pushing himself out of the dirt, he made his way to the palace gardens.

He had always thought the area was like another world in the moonlight. Cold. Mysterious. Lifeless. He strode down the same pathways he had trodden since childhood, taking the meandering route towards the pond.

It was like walking through a dream.

During the day, the wildlife Anjali had collected over the years would fill the place with all manner of honks and chirps. But most had been herded into their yard for the night. The few that hopped or swam around the pond were either asleep or opting to remain silent in his presence.

Finally, his feet took him to the entrance of the hedge maze. *Let's try this again.* Closing his eyes, he opened himself to the noise. *A little gentler this time.*

The whispers returned. Memory and pain, desire for space overlaid with a root-deep dislike for the predators that came with their sharp teeth. The snick of blades echoing with their muffled movements across the land. It was their lot in life to grow and be consumed, but these monsters didn't use. They cut and shred, broke and battered.

Slowly, the image overlaid with his own memories. *Gardeners.*

The whispers turned into the hissing of a million leaves shivering against each other, punctuated by the creak and pop of branches stretching.

Belatedly, he realised his ears picked up the same noise. Was the whole maze doing that? How would it appear to anyone within? Would they mistake it for wind?

He pulled away from the voices, just enough to focus himself without becoming lost within their lamenting. Was there anyone within the maze?

The reply was instant, but not what he wanted. Thorns and weeds. Choking tendrils and parched roots.

All right. He backed away, his hands up in surrender, although the hedges certainly couldn't know that. He would have to find another way. *How?* The trees? They were too slow during the night. The bushes dotted about the hedge? Too sporadic. The same could be said for the flower beds, on top of them having as much memory as—

Grass. There wasn't much here, mostly weeds poking through the gravel than a decent carpet of turf. If he kept constant pressure. Reminded them with every step.

Seek, he commanded. Was someone using the maze as a place to hide? What would they need? A place to sleep. Somewhere out of the elements.

Found. The impression of a person lying in the shadow of a hedge flashed into his mind.

Where?

The image was gone before he could finish the thought, confusion taking its place. He didn't recognise the spot. Unlike his twin, he spent little time in any of the gardens.

Nevertheless, he stalked into the maze, halting at the first junction. Where was the damn woman?

Again, the impression of the spot appeared in his mind. Slightly altered from before. She no longer reclined, but sat up. Alerted.

But what path did he take to reach her?

A soft blue glow on the path to his left caught his eye. It flared to life, then faded with a whimper. *Bioluminescence?* But coming from a plant that wasn't designed for it. *That's new.*

Another burst to life further along the path and Darshan hastened after it.

Darshan wove through the maze, chasing the flares of light in the shadows, ignoring the hissing surrounding him, pausing at every intersection to query the correct path. Every time he did, the image changed. His target was on the move, seeking a way out. Did she know someone was coming after her?

He couldn't lose her.

He soon became aware that he had blown through the centre of the maze and was being led out again. In the distance, peeking over the hedges, sat a guard tower. Was that the woman's goal?

Darshan raced out of the maze, his attention instantly drawn to a figure scuttling along the path. "Stop her!" he yelled, hoping there were guards nearby. She might've escaped the imperial palace, but he was *not* letting her get away now. Not with her so close.

A vine erupted in front of the figure, ensnaring their ankle. They fell to the ground.

Finally. All the concern over when and where she would strike next. It was over.

Darshan had taken no more than a handful of steps towards the figure when a blast of blue flames erupted his way. He closed his eyes as the abrupt presence of light stabbed into his brain, throwing up a shield to deflect the blaze.

Heat kissed his face and seared his skin in the breath between sight and shield. His face tingled as his magic worked to soothe. The mingling scent of singed hair and burning greenery invaded his nostrils, making him gag. He thickened the shield, shutting off everything beyond the sphere.

If only he could block out the screams exploding in his mind so readily. The screech and wail of tortured wood. The wail of charring leaves and grass. It spewed from his mouth and cut his legs from under him, dumping him to the earth. His shield stuttered and failed.

By the time the cries faded into whimpers, she was free and vanishing into the night.

Darshan watched after her disappearing form through lenses clouded by soot, struggling to think beyond the echoes of pain still bouncing around his head. All the other times he'd used the vines, they had ensnared their target without any retaliation. Even his father had struggled and the man was amongst the strongest spellsters alive.

But none of them had expected it. *She knows.* It didn't matter how strong she was, she knew how to deflect the vines. *That slippery—*

He would rely on his own magic when it came to the capture, then. But not in a chase like this. He'd only tire himself out if he went blundering about the place. He needed to corner her first.

He scrubbed at his chin, grimacing as his fingers ran along the singed ends of his beard and renewed the stench of burnt hair.

Darshan dug his fingers into the earth. *Find her!*

The ground churned beneath his hand. From the smallest weed to the mightiest tree... they snapped awake to search along their network.

No trace.

He pushed harder, bending the land to his will. *The tower.* It was the nearest structure. She had to be here. *The little plant-killer.* She had chosen poorly, trapping herself in that cage of stone and metal. This was *his* domain. He controlled the land. He *was* the land. There was nowhere her stunted little roots could take her that he couldn't follow.

He would find her and rend her into compost.

~ ~ ~

The rumble of distant thunder rolled through the sky, answered by a faint shiver from the earth.

Hamish lay still in his bed, staring up at the ceiling as he tried to calculate the distance between them and the storm. He had been through his fair share of wild weather. The castle of his birth was built solidly, but also upon a cliff near the sea. It attracted lightning like a rod.

This storm seemed close enough to be upon them, yet he saw no sign of clouds out his window. Was it coming over the land? Going out onto the balcony could determine the direction, but he wasn't foolish enough to give the storm a target. He'd seen the outcome of that.

With the idea of sleep not easily found again, more mundane matters made themselves known. He tumbled out of bed and half-crawled down the stairs, fighting to be rid of the blankets clinging to his skin. Free, he staggered across the room and into the privy to relieve himself.

A rumbling sound, oddly reminiscent of stampeding cattle, hit his ears a second before the room lurched.

Hamish braced himself against the wall with an outstretched arm as the initial jolt had the room continuing to sway in an increasingly violent manner. He eyed the door. It wasn't far. He could make it there upright if need be and ride out the quake, with or without his smalls around his ankles.

The shaking halted just as abruptly as it began.

He hastened to make himself presentable and exit the privy. He hadn't a lot of familiarity with quakes—Mullhind didn't get many— but he had never experienced one that travelled alone. If the next shake was any stronger, he could wind up trapped.

That wasn't happening with him half-naked.

His gaze swept over the bedchamber upon re-entry, checking for any obvious damage in the moonlight. With him having been moved here only until the wedding was over, there wasn't much in the way of knick-knacks. The plate and mug from his late evening snack had fallen from the table near the windows. One of the chairs was now on its back. Everything else was either part of the walls or sturdy to begin with.

Screams came from outside the door, the shrieks suggesting the sound was of fear rather than pain. Did they not get quakes at all in Minamist?

Gordon... His brother was a few levels below him. Quickly slipping into his trousers, he groped about in the shadows for his shirt. *Eth!* Their nephew would likely be at Gordon's side and safe. Hamish wouldn't typically check on either immediately after a single quake, but this wasn't the usual circumstance. He would feel better knowing no harm had come to the pair.

Dressed, he made his way down the building, surprised at how many people filled the hallways. More people bustled about the further down the tower he went, some in outright terror, others milling in confusion. The majority scuttled about the place like routed mice.

He couldn't hear more than the occasional garbled word to determine a reason for the panic. Should *he* be as concerned?

Abandoning the idea of seeking out his brother and nephew, he carried on down the flights of stairs until he reached the bottom floor. The chaos was thicker here, people pouring through the main entrance like rats off a sinking ship. He peered through the doorway.

Only a hint of black clouds suggested any danger. Was all this panic really because of a little storm? There had to be something more. "Lass." He grabbed the shoulders of a young servant as he neared the entrance. "What's going on?"

She stared up at him, her eyes wide. "The *vris Mhanek*," she wailed. "He has gone mad!"

Dar? That couldn't be right. "What do you mean—?"

The floor rolled as though they were on deck during a squall. The building creaked like an old oak in the wind. Tiles cracked beneath people's feet and fell from the walls. The crash of something heavy echoed from somewhere on the floor above.

"We're all going to die!" someone screamed, setting off a fresh wave of panic.

People threw themselves to the floor, cowering out in the open. Others dove under furniture or into doorways.

Hamish was amongst the latter, keeping one arm wrapped around the servant as she clung to him like a newborn. She trembled more than their surroundings. Her tears already soaked his shirt.

All around them, the hiss of shattering glass or the bang of falling furnishings punctuated the rumble of the earth. But, whilst loud, none of it was the deadliest threat in the room.

He watched the glittering mass of the crystal chandelier swaying above the crowd. Cracks opened around the base, widening and sprinkling dust with every swing upon those cowering below. Shields flickered around some people, keeping those within safe for the moment. But, if the chandelier came down, the ceiling would likely follow along with everything on the floor above.

All he could do was pray it didn't.

Dar... For the first time, he realised he had no clue about the man's full strength or the limit of his abilities. And Darshan outright refused to discuss the matter. How powerful was his husband? *Strong enough.* Or so it would seem.

Was Darshan really responsible for these quakes as the servant claimed? He couldn't imagine the man doing this wilfully. Maybe the thunder Hamish had heard. Had the hypnotist gotten to him?

Slowly, the ground settled.

With his attention fixed on the chandelier, Hamish gently pushed the weeping woman into the arms of another. "Everyone up!" he bellowed, bending to assist one of the servants to his feet. "*Up!*" He pointed at the ceiling. Spidery cracks ran right along the plaster. He had no clue what was holding everything together. "That falls and you're dead." He grabbed another cowering man, hoisting them to their feet and shoving them deeper into the building. At least the hallways had minimal dangers.

Like newborn lambs, others wobbled to their feet. They staggered across the foyer. *Too slow.* He needed help. Where were the Nulled Ones? They were usually ten strong near the entrance. Had they gone to face Darshan?

He picked out a guard's uniform amongst those still tucked beneath a table. Then another. "You there!" Hamish hauled one from her shelter. "Gather your people. I need whatever magic you have at hand to keep that ceiling up, whilst the rest get everyone out."

"*O-out?*" Her gaze darted to the entrance. The remaining colour drained from her already pale face. "But—"

"Dinnae mind what's happening out there. I'll deal with that." How? He didn't know. He would figure something out once he found the true cause. "But it's nae safe in here."

As if proving his point, a section of the plaster dropped to the ground, mere feet from a trembling huddle of children. The group screamed, their high pitch seeming to shake the stupor from the crowd's head.

The guard snapped a salute, then turned to her comrades, shouting the same orders he'd given her. The ceiling swiftly gained the shimmering purple sheen of collective shields. The patchwork wasn't perfect, but it gave people a safe route out.

Hamish aided in guiding the terrified throng into the night, scooping up as many small children as he could manage along the way. The crack of giving plaster prickled his skin. *Goddess, let it hold.*

The shields shuddered and rippled as pieces dropped onto the surface. Each smack drew more shrieks and wails. The press of those around him grew.

"Steady!" he bellowed over their cries. If they all bolted for the door, the crowd would trample the weaker underfoot. "Remain calm." He plucked another small, stationary body from the mass, surprised when his arm tightened around the waist of an elven woman rather than another child. "The shields *will* hold."

He didn't know if his words reached anyone, but the throng did seem to slow enough for him to get an idea of how many there were. *Dozens.* Possibly into the hundreds. How had they packed themselves into the building in the first place?

What was happening to those in the upper floors? People like his brother and nephew. *They'll be fine.* Gordon would know what to do and Ethan was a practical boy who would follow his uncle's orders.

Once he was out of this crowd, Hamish could start rallying whoever was willing to aid in getting everyone else in the building. But he had to get these people to safety first.

They passed beneath the entrance's massive archway. At least that seemed solid, with no cracks or hints of buckling in the wooden frame. The crowd thinned beyond, spreading out across the stairs, with some opting for a more direct route off the sides.

Something heavy smashed to the floor behind him.

Hamish swung to the sight of the chandelier splayed across the vacant tiles.

"I'm sorry," gabbled the elven woman in his grasp. Sweat ran down her forehead, sticking her dark hair to her face. "I know you said to hold, but I couldn't any longer."

"It's all right, lass." At least she had stopped its fall from taking any lives. He lowered her to the ground along with the children who still clung to him like whimpering limpets. "Nae one was hurt and we've you to thank for that." He gave her shoulder a comforting squeeze. Was she a palace servant? Did she serve one of the multitudes of nobles still stuck within the guest palace? There were old marks of where a collar had been around her neck, but no other hints. "Conserve the rest of your strength. Get yourself and these wee ones to safety."

She nodded, smiling wearily, before her attention was drawn over his shoulder.

Hamish followed her gaze. He didn't need to ask what she saw. The massive ink-dark cloud hanging over the palace gardens was enough of an answer. All around them, the star-studded sky remained clear.

The roar of a storm coming to a head echoed through the courtyard. The clouds seemed to culminate around a tower. It was hard to make out in the dark, but the lightning arcing from the thunderhead definitely struck something. Was—?

Hamish peered into the night, struggling to see anything in the gloom.

Was the tower *moving*?

"Your highness!" a guard called, tearing Hamish's attention away. The woman saluted as she halted at attention before him. "Everyone on this level is out. What are your orders?"

"Make this level safe, shore up everything you can. Then escort out those above. If there's any trouble, find me brother. You'll nae miss him," he added as the guard's forehead scrunched in confusion. "He's taller than meself and just as hairy. Tell him he's to get the whole building empty before sunrise even if he has to personally drag some of the bastards out." He didn't know how long the building would stand, or if it would crumble at all, but he didn't fancy having anyone under its roof any longer than could be done.

Again, the guard saluted before racing off to issue the given orders.

Pausing only to ensure the servant woman and the children would be all right, Hamish strode down the stairs towards the dark cloud. If that *was* all Darshan's doing, then the man was definitely pissed.

Why? Hamish had no answer. Hopefully, his husband wasn't beyond reason.

People still fled from that direction. Hamish got as many as he could to steer others away from the buildings. Given that the dark cloud sat only over the tower—now he was closer, he could make out a structure in the gloom—staying in the open was safer than seeking refuge within a crumbling building.

Lightning flashed within the clouds. Forks of it struck the tower, exploding in a spray of molten rock.

His legs froze, then wavered. *Sweet Goddess.* His heart pounded hard enough that he was sure it could leap from his chest at any moment. He'd only seen a glimpse of what was beneath the clouds, but it was enough.

The air echoed with the bang of falling rock. The ground shook, jolting his legs back into action for one stumbling step.

Another burst of lightning lit up the night. This time, it struck the earth and erupted into flame, fully illuminating what remained of the tower and the vines smothering it. They stood as tall as a merchant ship was long, writhing over the tower like a nest of snakes, ripping the walls apart in chunks.

His throat tightened. Every muscle in his body screamed for him to run the other way. This was what his homeland feared, what his mother aimed to shield the kingdom from. Raw magic unleashed indiscriminately.

And his husband was responsible?

Struggling to move upon watery legs, Hamish staggered towards the destruction. If it were true. If Darshan *was* involved, he had to stop him.

A line of people stood not too far from him, backlit by the encroaching flames. He couldn't make out the colours of their uniforms in the sooty light, but guessed they were Nulled Ones. They looked to have formed a circle around the destruction, even as fires raged at their backs and slabs of stone shattered all around them.

Keeping his focus on them alone, he strode closer.

"Your highness," one of them said, breaking the line to stand before Hamish with his hand up. "I must insist that you leave. It's not safe for you to be here."

"But Darshan—" He could see his husband. The man stood calmly before the tower as though it wasn't being violently disassembled at his will.

"*Please.*" There was no mistaking the fear in the Nulled One's voice. Or the way he, and others, flinched at every sound. These were people who remained unaffected by magic, who were trained to protect their *Mhanek* from such power, who could walk through a shield as though it wasn't there.

And, to a one, they were *terrified.*

This isnae magic. Not as they knew it. Not as anyone knew it.

And there was still the raging fire. The Nulled Ones might be immune to magic, but not to the elements. If the flames came any closer, they'd burn the same as any being.

"Let me near him. Let me talk to him." Whatever had driven Darshan to this point, letting him rage on wasn't the answer. He wouldn't burn himself out. The vines reacted to his will, not his power.

A section of stone, larger than a wagon, tumbled across the ground. It bowled right through the line of Nulled Ones, crushing several in its wake.

"Leave him to me," he ordered the man. "You cannae contain this. *I* can stop it." Even as he said it, he wondered if it were true. He *had* stopped Darshan from killing his own father, but his husband had been hurt and frustrated.

This looked as though the man had completely lost his mind. Was reaching him even possible?

Nevertheless, Hamish raced towards his husband, screaming his name without any response.

When he was close enough to grab Darshan, he turned him away from the view, shaking him. "You need to stop! I dinnae ken why you're doing this, but stop it now!"

His husband blinked up at him, then squinted at their surroundings as though waking from a dream. "What?"

"What happened? I'd like to ken that meself." He gestured to the mass of vines. They had stilled in their destruction, but there wasn't much left of the tower beyond rubble.

Darshan grabbed Hamish's shirt, dragging him down with the strength of a madman. "Did you see her?"

He's nae wearing glasses? Only now he had stilled, did Hamish notice the lack. But the man couldn't see beyond the length of his arm without them. What was he doing wandering the palace in such a state? "Have you been attacked?" The man's beard looked less full than when Hamish had last seen it and slightly crisped along the edges.

"The Jhanaar woman!" Darshan snapped. "She went into the tower. I know it. I *saw* her. I'm not letting her get away again!" He clamped a hand onto Hamish's sleeve, towing him towards the tower's remains. "Quickly!"

Hamish held back his husband with a simple hand on the chest. Darshan's heart pounded frantically against his palm. If the woman had been within the tower, she was dead now. *How many others were inside?* All of them couldn't have escaped.

The vines shuddered, resuming their task with a deft single-mindedness. They looked far more sinister now the clouds, no longer fuelled by Darshan's magic, had dissipated.

The crack of breaking stone echoed through the night.

"Dar," Hamish growled. "*Stop.*" He grabbed his husband's jaw and forced the man to look at him, waiting until all movement from the vines halted. "Listen to me and listen hard. You have *killed* people tonight and injured countless others." He didn't know how many. He prayed it was none.

Confusion clouded Darshan's eyes and pinched his face. "I—?" He rubbed at his jaw, slowing over the definitely burnt parts of his beard. "No, I would never." He groped at the sides of his face where the frames of his glasses usually sat. "My glasses. I..." He froze, clarity returning to his gaze with the sharpness of a hawk. "What do you mean *killed?*"

Hamish gestured wordlessly to their surroundings. Where did he start? The vines that stood like a monument? The rubble they'd made? The fire that seemed to be burning out on its own?

What of the earthquakes? Had that been Darshan's doing or a coincidence? More importantly...

How could the man not be aware of doing it? He wasn't drunk, although he did sway like a man several mugs deep. His face stank of singed hair, but that wouldn't mask booze on the breath. He was confused, though. Much like the cousin who had attacked Hamish at Tarendra's *Khutani*.

Was it as he had feared? Had the hypnotist gotten to Darshan?

The cousin hadn't stopped at a simple word, though. It had taken the *Mhanek's* magic to clear the man's mind. Hamish hadn't done anything more than gain Darshan's attention. He had shaken him, but only to elicit some sort of response, not to... *Wake him.* "When did you last sleep?"

"Sleep?" Darshan blinked, shaking his head as though trying to clear it. "Not since yesterday, when you were transferred to the guest palace."

"That wasnae yesterday." He'd been gone from Darshan's bedchamber for two days. They were meant to be getting married the dawn after the one currently brightening the sky. At least, the first of the three-day ceremony was meant to begin.

Hamish stepped back, eyeing his husband at arm's length. He had seen his husband grow weary before, but never to this extent. "You're *exhausted*." What did his healing magic do to Darshan once he was in such a state? Did it remove the effects without fixing the cause? And when that energy was depleted? "I'm getting you to bed." And maybe, once they were high enough that Darshan couldn't hear them, the vines would leave.

Darshan shook his head. "I have to help. If I caused this, I need—"

"—to do nae a thing more," Hamish finished. "Listen. The tower is *rubble*. If she was in there and isnae dead, it'll be a miracle. There are plenty of spellsters capable of mending the injured. Now, I'm going to let you get a few hours of rest, *then* we can trade stories and figure out what happened." In one motion, he bent and swept Darshan into his arms.

His husband flopped against him like a fish cut free of the line the instant his feet left the ground. His eyes closed and his breathing grew shallow.

The ground shook as the vines unwound from the tower remains. They slithered back into the earth, leaving the ground all around the rubble a churned mess.

"Dar?" He tried to rouse the man, but no amount of jostling woke him. "All right, love. Let's get you into bed." How he would get Darshan up all those stairs without fuss was a problem he hadn't yet solved.

Hamish eyed the rubble that had been the tower one last time before turning his back on it and heading for the imperial palace. He would need to start managing this mess once his husband was abed. *How am I going to bloody explain this?* He was going to need Darshan to be coherent before he could begin to understand what had happened here, much less parcel it up in a way the court and servants would grasp.

How many even knew of these new abilities? *I guess everyone's finding out today.*

He really hoped that, after all the terror he had caused, Darshan *had* actually managed to catch the woman who'd been plaguing them all this time.

Chapter 45

Darshan sat in the middle of his bed, his knees tucked under his chin. He clutched the small wooden mouse his husband had carved just for him, running his thumb over the smooth surface. It was meant to be a gift of good luck. It hadn't worked so far.

How he longed to return to that day. Everything had been less complicated.

He stared out through the tatty remains of the gossamer curtains encircling the bed. Strange how he didn't recall their destruction.

But there was much he couldn't remember as of late.

Around him, several of Darshan's most trusted servants tidied the room. Another stood on his periphery, likely fussing with his ceremonial wardrobe. Today was the first of their wedding.

He should've been happy. At the very least, relieved to have made it this far with a killer constantly breathing down their necks.

The first day consisted of leading his family to collect his would-be spouse from their family home. He found it a redundant part of the old tradition, perhaps needed in the time when safety came in numbers and it wasn't uncommon for a groom to find themselves accosted by a rival on the way to their beloved's door. But that was centuries ago. Maybe even several thousand years.

For Darshan, it required a mere walk across the imperial grounds to the princess palace. Nothing he hadn't done in the past. But that'd also been before the incident. This high off the ground, he couldn't hear the plants, couldn't issue commands, couldn't lose himself in them.

He hadn't left his bedchamber since Hamish lugged him up here in the early hours of yesterday morning. He had slept, that much he was certain of and for a great many hours. The fitful slumber of the exhausted.

And in his waking moments?

Hamish had been up to talk. He had looked haggard and visibly perplexed. At first, Darshan's thoughts had swung wildly into the realm of another attack. Then Hamish opened his mouth and spoke of earthquakes, of a storm hovering over a single guard tower, of vines and flames. Chaos and death.

After hearing the account, Darshan was hesitant to leave this sanctuary.

His husband's questions had led their conversation going in circles as the man tried to make sense of it all. He still didn't know what to tell the man.

He'd no memory of the time between being blasted in the face by the woman he had attempted to detain and Hamish's arrival. They had checked him for any signs of hypnosis. That they'd found nothing wasn't a relief.

Never had he lost control of his magic before. The reports of the damage he had done were still coming in. The guard tower was rubble, as Hamish had said. The guest palace would take months to restore. Both the inner and outer walls were compromised.

And the deaths?

There weren't many, thankfully.

He was directly responsible for mutilating a handful of Nulled Ones. Of the normal guard... They'd unearthed three within the tower he had destroyed. Another had tumbled off the outer wall during the quakes. Two more had been struck by lightning.

All because he couldn't control himself.

I'm not safe.

Had he even been right about the woman he chased? He'd no confirmation of anything beyond someone lurking in the hedge maze. They'd found no bodies within the tower that couldn't be accounted for amongst the rosters.

He took a small comfort in there being no outward show of fear from his husband. Not even a glimpse of uncertainty in being close to Darshan after what he had witnessed. Confusion? It had plastered itself across Hamish's face. It was a state they had in common.

Anjali was another matter.

His twin had arrived with the servants, chattering as if to fill the air, always glancing his way with a hint of apprehension that suggested fear wasn't far behind. He'd never seen that look from her before. Not that she hadn't felt uneasy in their youth. They both had, but those concerns were never directed at *him*.

Feared by my own twin. His constant. The welcoming shadow at their nanny's side when they were young and a trustworthy ear as they grew into adults. She had always been there for him every time he stumbled, helping him fix his mistakes, offering support after every heartbreak.

Now she was the one breaking his heart, treating him in that same soft manner in which she handled all delicate things.

He *was* fragile. As much as he hated to admit it. He was chipped and stressed, porcelain put under immense pressure, expected to explode from the smallest touch.

The pad of familiar steps approaching him drew his attention. He tipped his head to one side, his cheek brushing his knee, to watch Anjali approach. For all her talking, she hadn't once addressed him.

She halted at the foot of the stairs leading up to the bed. "You..." She plucked at the neck of her dress, her other hand occupied in toying with the little finger of the first. "You never told me you could shake the earth." There was a faint measure of hurt in her voice. Betrayal.

Darshan couldn't help the gust of amusement that slipped out his lips. With all that had happened, she was concerned he'd been holding back on revealing his full abilities to her? She should've known better. "That wasn't me. The vines... I—"

"Darshi." She climbed a step, then another, slowly as though approaching an agitated serpent camped beneath a bench. "It wasn't the vines that woke me. They certainly didn't disturb the Nulled Ones."

"No," he agreed. They had tested if the Nulled Ones could sense his control over the plants long before the hedgewitch had arrived. They couldn't. It baffled them as much as it had himself.

But magic? A strong enough blast would draw every single Nulled One to the source like sharks to blood.

Was that also how they tracked him around the city? No matter how obscure his destination or how well he evaded them, the Nulled Ones always found him. He hadn't thought of his magic as strong enough to distinguish from the dozens of other spellsters wandering the streets.

He couldn't imagine being stronger than his father. He wasn't. There was no reason to believe otherwise. He couldn't be. He would've known before now.

Or would I?

Ever since he and his twin started to manifest more than sporadic shields, their father insisted they never push themselves beyond what was necessary.

Darshan had followed that rule. He had assumed his limits based on his sparring opponents, had never pushed against his boundaries throughout his years living within Minamist's walls. There was little need. All the threats were accounted for and watched over. Those that tried were vastly outclassed and thwarted before they got close.

And yet, the upper nobility typically bred with the intent of making a stronger generation of spellster. That was how his father had been born. And the man was strong, even though he rarely used that full power. He was a match for many who'd challenged him in his youth.

Darshan's mother hadn't that background. No one had considered her as strong. Not in magic. From what he'd been told—disparagingly at times from his grandfather—she favoured the purist theology of treating their magic as a blessing, of using it sparingly.

Had she been stronger than people realised? Was that why any record Darshan sought of her—be it on paper or via other's recollections—made it seem as though she feared her own self?

"Did you hear me?" Anjali asked, a whisper of frustration whistling through the otherwise soft cadence of her voice.

Where had she learnt that soothing tone? *From Daama.* Where was their old nanny? He had seen no sign of her since the incident. Usually, she was the first to offer comfort. Was she all right? Had—

Had she become one of his victims?

Anjali settled on the side of the bed. "Have you heard a word I've said?"

He shook his head, his thoughts still lost in the possibilities of what he might've done. Daama spent much of her time in the imperial palace and his influence hadn't travelled that far. But there was always a chance she had been elsewhere.

"Should we be concerned that he has reverted to honesty?" Zahaan enquired.

Darshan's gaze flicked to the other side of the room where the spymaster busied himself in laying out the ceremonial wardrobe. The man wouldn't be here if his mother was injured or worse.

Daama was one life he wasn't responsible for taking.

"Shush," Anjali said, motioning the man to return to his duties. "They'll all be waiting, you know," she added to Darshan.

Of course they would be. A wedding couldn't start with one being. They needed both grooms.

She laid a hand on the bed, stretching out for his leg but not quite touching. "Are you sure you're feeling up to this? We can postpone the ceremony if you need more time to recover."

He knew that. The court would rail against it, but ultimately use the delay as a chance to gossip and scheme. They must've all seen what he was capable of by now, be it during his outburst or the aftermath. The senate would be especially interested in using such abilities to further their own designs. *They* would have no issue with the idea of leaving him vulnerable for a little longer.

Except he needed to keep Hamish safe. There were other dangers. Just because they remained silent for the moment didn't mean they weren't out there. But any safety came only with this ceremony.

"I can do it," he whispered.

"Then you need to get up." She shuffled closer and laid a stilling hand on his knee. "You can't go to him like this. You need to bathe—at the very least, comb your hair and see to your beard—and dress in something more appropriate. You look ready for a funeral, not a wedding." She gestured to the linen kaftan and baggy trousers, both in their natural off-white shade, eyeing them with a hint of concern.

It wasn't his usual style, but they were comforting. He needed that right now.

Unfortunately, his sister was right. His clothes might skate by for the first day or two of the wedding, but not with them rumpled and sweat stained.

Darshan slid off the bed and made his way to the bathroom to freshen up.

He took his time making himself presentable. The blast to his face hadn't been more than a few seconds. His skin had healed fine. The hairs were another matter. He had already trimmed off the burnt bits of his beard. What was left was too long to be stubble, but too short to deserve being called anything else. At least it would grow.

His brows were a sorry state, too. Not as bushy as they could've been, but the illusion of fullness was easily remedied with a little kohl.

Mercifully, his hair wasn't terribly damaged, likely due to the low angle of the blast. A few wisps near his hairline had been sacrificed, noticeable only when he ran a brush through it.

Clean and impeccably groomed, he strode into his wardrobe. His outfit had already been chosen for him, a ghastly golden affair heavy with embroidery. Zahaan helped him into it, staying quiet as he smoothed the fabric and assisted with the multitude of tiny buttons.

Darshan glanced at the rack holding Hamish's small selection of clothes. The silver sherwani commissioned for the third day of the wedding was gone, as was the Tirglasian attire he travelled here in. Would the man truly consider wearing the latter in this heat? *Perhaps.* Especially if he wished to show solidarity with his family.

Whilst Darshan was confident that the man would've explained the ceremony to Gordon, how much detail Hamish had given was another matter. Enough that Darshan could utter the traditional words, or would he have to play it by ear?

He ducked his head as his spymaster wound the red scarf around his shoulders. He should've asked Gordon for more insight into Tirglasian customs, then he might've felt a little more prepared.

Fully dressed, he made their way down to the dining hall with his twin at his side. He didn't feel up to eating a single bite, but the rest of his family would be waiting there for him. Half of them, at least.

A familiar figure caught his attention as he entered. Onella sat near the head of the table, calmly sipping tea as if the world hadn't been recently picked up and shaken like a child's toy.

"Sister," he acknowledged through gritted teeth. He hadn't heard of her arrival. How long had she been lurking in Minamist's shadows? "I see you finally made it."

"For your wedding? Yes, I arrived yesterday afternoon. And to such destruction." She had another mouthful of her tea, watching him over the rim.

Darshan took a deep breath. He would not be baited by her. "Why are you here?" He knew the princess palace was overrun by guests that wouldn't normally be there. And that the rest of his married sisters were likely nearby, but none of them were *here*. This portion of the ceremony was reserved for the unmarried.

That she chose this room spoke only of mischief he was in no mood to weather.

"Why?" She lowered the cup, her eyes wide in a display of hurt innocence. "To see my big brother on his way to collect his groom, of course. Although, I thought you already were married. Did Father not accept your barbarian nuptials as you had hoped?"

"No." He brushed it aside with a wave of his hand. Her belief that they had his father's blessing had mattered more than the truth of them being wed. "But we are still considered as engaged and he is no less under protection."

Her lashes lowered. "He will need it."

Darshan launched himself across the room, bowling the table along the floor in a single blast of air. The crash of cups and plates sang sharply for a breath, then stilled.

He thrust his finger under her nose, a wisp dancing on the end of it. "Is that a *threat*?" She dared to push his boundaries now? Had she not heard what he had done in the pursuit of those who meant his husband harm?

She stared at the wisp, one immaculately groomed brow raised. Her cup and the saucer still sat neatly in her hands. "Not at all, brother dear. More an observation."

"Perhaps not the wisest course of action in these times, dear sister," Anjali said. She stood at his side, gently coaxing his hand away and curling his fingers until the wisp snuffed itself out in his palm. "Tempers are already high."

"So I've heard." Onella smiled brightly. "It seems we've our own little Sharik. Not with command over the sky, but of the earth." Her grin gained its usual vulpine edge. "Will we also be seeing *you* referring to yourself as a god? Will it be a formal announcement? Or are we expected to consult the priesthood?"

Usually, he would let her vitriol slide off him. But *this*? The self-stylised God Emperor had become a monster long before falling prey to his appetites. He had lost his mind and scorched the very sky to keep the Stamekian capital clear of cloud cover. "You *dare* to compare me to *him*?" The evil that man had done was without equal. "Father would have your tongue for such slander."

"My mistake." She examined her painted nails as though he wasn't still looming over her. "Not that it matters, you'll come to the conclusion soon enough that you've brought your lover to his death. Parading him about the court has only revealed your weaknesses and set a lovely glowing target over his head."

He kept his hands curled, ignoring the heat radiating from them.

"Although..." she drawled, glancing up. "This new outburst? Destroying your own buildings? Causing the injury and death of dozens? You must admit, it *is* very much like Sharik's early years." Her lips flattened until they were only thin lines. "Hopefully, you don't follow his path in other ways."

Darshan clenched his teeth, his breath huffing out his nose. If she was insinuating what he thought, he was going to blast that smirk off her face, their oath to Father be damned.

"You can, of course, imagine my distress to hear you took Aagney's place in our dear boy's *Khutani*."

"Can I?" Did she think he'd been grooming the boy? She had to know him better than that. "Ren asked it of me before his father arrived in Minamist and he continued to insist even when Aagney *did* get here in time. I wasn't going to refuse my nephew. Not on that."

She took another long drink from her cup. There had to be little tea left. "Seeing how easily you step into the role of father, it's a pity you would not take a similar stance on accepting him as your heir."

"Ren doesn't want to be the *Mhanek*," Anjali interrupted, grasping Darshan's wrist and squeezing even though he made no attempt to move.

Darshan nodded his agreement. Everyone who knew their nephew could see it. Why couldn't his mother?

"And speaking of heirs," Onella said as if their sister hadn't uttered a word. "I wonder what Father thinks of his only son losing his mind like Grandfather did. And at such a young age, too."

"My mind is fine." He might've been weary and confused, but he was still capable of logical thought.

"It's just your *control*, then?" She gestured to a nearby servant. "Another."

The man—one of Onella's slaves, judging by the collar—hastened forward with a steaming teacup. He took the empty one and scuttled back to his original position.

"The court won't weather a *Mhanek* who cannot keep his magic in check," Onella continued before taking a sip. "Perhaps it would be better for the empire if you forsook the throne. Let someone with proper balance handle matters."

"Like *you?*" Although the *Khutani* technically made Tarendra a man, it would be years before the senate would allow him to govern without a regent if their father died within that timeframe. Onella would definitely leverage herself as the best person to guide her son. He didn't even need to factor in that their father wasn't feeling the slightest bit poorly.

Onella's upper lip quivered into a sneer for a flutter of a moment before she smoothed the expression. "I wouldn't dare presume to take the throne in my name."

"Then it's fortunate that none of it is *your* decision to make," replied their father's booming voice. He strode across the room, halting at Darshan's side.

There was a flurry of movement all around them as people rushed to right the table and everything that had been atop it. A lot of broken porcelain and glass littered the floor.

If their father noticed the mess, he gave no indication. All of his attention seemed focused on Onella. "Daughter," he said gruffly.

Delicately placing the cup and saucer upon the table, Onella folded her hands on her lap and lowered her head. "It is good to see you, Father. I hope my darling son has been behaving himself."

Darshan bit his tongue and focused on keeping his features neutral. Onella knew his union with Hamish would end in a child, but when was as nebulous as knowing just what kind of person that child would become. And here she was reminding their father that she already had the perfect heir.

"What are you doing here?" their father enquired in a tone that spoke of locked doors. "No." He held up a hand, forestalling any explanations. "I don't want to waste time with your excuses. You know what today is. Just as you are aware this is not the place to be right now."

Onella lowered her head even further, her chin practically resting on her chest. She glanced up, her gaze flicking to Darshan before returning to flutter at their father.

He had witnessed his sisters get out of a vast array of punishments with similar looks. Not once had it worked when he tried.

"I do *not* expect to see any sign of you until the evening meal," their father said. "And that includes your network. Understood?"

Onella's head snapped up, shock parting her lips. "Yes, Father." Her hands no longer sat placidly in her lap, but gripped her skirts as though she wrung the silk dry.

"Excellent!" Giving a firm nod, their father swung to face Darshan. His gaze swung over the half of the room at Darshan's back. The way those brown eyes paused, he was clearly counting faces.

Are they all here? Darshan twisted to take in the group of four half-sisters and Anjali waiting by the door. The youngest and unwed of his siblings. Apart from his twin, the eldest amongst them was Devak, who was nineteen. Then it was fifteen-year-old Jheel, before Hansika and Aditi, one halfway through her eleventh year and the other on the cusp of it.

Not the most intimidating bunch. If he had met Hamish two years ago, he would've had Vinata at his back. Even in her current gravid state, she was a force to be reckoned with.

"It's time, my son." His father laid a hand on Darshan's shoulder. "Lead the way."

They walked the halls in silence. If it hadn't been for the brightness of their attires, anyone passing by would've assumed they travelled to a funeral.

Whispers caressed his mind. Ghostly at first, but growing louder with every level he descended. The calls were a jumble. Relieved and upset. Questioning and indifferent.

Through it all, a thread of one conscious thought. It wasn't always easy to make out what they were trying to show him and he hadn't the patience to waste time in figuring it all out. The impression was wavering, making it harder to distinguish things. He caught stronger images amongst it all, flashes of himself in Hamish's arms, limp as a wilted flower. Other things, too. A ruin that he assumed had been the tower he destroyed.

Not dead.

Was that what the plants had thought? That he had died? All because they couldn't feel his presence? Had they assumed they'd lost their last connection again?

Zahaan appeared from the shadows to join them as they trotted down the stairs. His spymaster wouldn't be part of the retinue once they were before Hamish's door, but he, like the Nulled One's tailing them, were there to keep them safe.

Strange to think they were in danger within the enclosed area of the imperial grounds. It was hard to see anything out of place. These walls weren't compromised and he couldn't see over them. Not what was left of the tower. Nor the guest palace.

Not dead. The whisper drifted like smoke through his mind even though he walked through the imperial gardens that separate the two palaces, where bushes lined the pond.

Darshan growled under his breath. *He* knew he wasn't dead.

A shimmer of confusion rippled through the bushes. The whispers died to the usual murmur and soft complaints of life.

At least the screaming of the hedge maze was too far for him to hear. It was the last clear thing he recalled before the flames. *I need to fix that.* He wasn't sure where to start, but there had to be a way that didn't leave him dreading entering that section of the palace grounds.

He was halfway across the imperial gardens when he noticed one oddity. Rather than their usual stance of wandering the grounds freely in pairs, the Nulled Ones currently guarded strategic places in groups of eight.

It had to be because of the guests who had been moved into the princess palace. The shift had been done with some reluctance on his father's part. The usual building reserved for noble visitors sat outside the imperial walls for a reason. The throne had plenty of contenders ready to snaffle up the crown the minute the *Mhanek* showed any weakness. Knowing that they schemed was one thing, letting them do so right under his father's nose was practically an invitation for them to make an attempt.

They reached the steps of the princess palace.

Darshan's stomach fluttered. He paused at the bottom of the steps, his mouth slowly drying. *Really now?* he chided himself.

Anjali halted on his left. "Are you still all right?" She laid a hand on his arm, clearly ready to delve with her magic. "Is it your... new abilities?"

Taking a deep breath, he shook his head. "Just nerves," he murmured. Of all the ridiculous things to assail him. What did he have to be worried about? He knew Hamish's heart almost as well as his own. There was no reason for this queasiness.

Even if Hamish had second thoughts after witnessing Darshan's gross display of violence, his husband wouldn't have shirked from informing him face to face.

A low, understanding chuckle drew Darshan's attention to his father. The man stared vacantly out into the courtyard with a soft smile curling his lips as though watching another time. "I remember arriving at your mother's doorstep thinking I was going to vomit up my lungs. Being *vris Mhanek* has never been a guarantee that the parents will accept your proposal." His smile fell. "Sometimes, I wish they hadn't."

Not sure what to say, or if he even should say anything, Darshan glanced at his twin. She didn't seem any the wiser, either.

"But then again…" He cupped Darshan's jaw as though he were a young boy, coaxing his head around until their foreheads touched. "Without her," his father murmured. "I wouldn't have *you*."

Darshan swallowed. It was rare for his father to show anything but anger and disappointment towards him.

"Come on," his father said, seemingly shaking off whatever melancholy had settled on his shoulders. "Your bri—" He frowned whilst biting back the word. "—groom awaits your presence."

Their entry into the princess palace was somewhat less quiet than their journey to its doors. Their presence had been marked and, with the building filled to the brim with noble guests, their every step was watched with hawk-like intensity.

Indistinct chatter filled the halls. No doubt keeping the gossip wheel turning. He hadn't asked what people were saying about his outburst. Onella was probably right, they likely speculated on his lack of control.

They climbed the final set of stairs between him and Hamish's quarters. The entire level had already been cleared by the Nulled Ones. They stood guard at the top of the stairs.

The clang of metal smacking against metal echoed down the hall.

Frowning, Darshan looked for a source to the noise. The Nulled Ones didn't seem bothered. Whatever the cause, it clearly wasn't a danger. Even if that turned out to be untrue, he'd his father and twin at his back. And, if it came to that, his younger sisters, although their skills in battle hadn't been tested.

Leaving those who weren't directly related to him at the stairs, he rounded the corner.

Gordon stood at the other end of the hallway, planted squarely before the doorway in which Hamish leant.

Ethan stood off to the right, clutching a hefty spear to his side.

"Who dares come to claim the hand of my kinsman?" Gordon bellowed, hitting the flat of his sword against his shield.

"What in the world?" Anjali whispered.

"Relax." Darshan hadn't witnessed any Tirglasian wedding rites beyond the union contest for Hamish's hand, but this seemed like the sort of thing that would happen at one.

He took a half-step back around the corner, motioning Zahaan closer and relieving the spymaster of his weapon. The short blade wasn't anywhere near as hefty as Gordon's broadsword, but it would have to do. It wasn't as though either of them intended to wield the weapons in earnest. "I, Darshan *vris Mhanek*, stake such a claim. I come before you to make one of your household a part of mine."

"Then step forth alone. Let the clan test your mettle and judge if you are worthy to wed one of our own."

Looking past the pair in the doorway, Darshan caught Hamish palming his face. The man's shoulder's shook slightly. Was he laughing? *Better be at the ridiculousness of all this.* Darshan had already proven his worthiness as Hamish's husband in Tirglas.

He strode forward to answer Gordon's challenge, his progress halted by a hand gripping his sleeve. "Anje, let go." He glanced over his shoulder when the command wasn't obeyed to find it was actually his father.

"You're not actually thinking of fighting them?" his father hissed. He had been informed of Gordon's status as a Nulled One, as well as how Tirglasians were unaware of their being an antithesis to spellsters. The distrust in his father's wide eyes shone plainly enough.

"Yes? Sort of." He rolled his shoulders. How long did he have to explain things before Gordon got impatient? "It's all for show. He won't hurt me." Hamish would skin his brother alive if the man laid so much as a scratch on Darshan.

His father slowly relinquished his hold of Darshan's sleeve. He stepped back, seemingly ready to summon aid, should it be needed.

Testing out the weight and balance of his borrowed sword, Darshan once more faced Gordon and the man's nephew. He'd never fought two opponents at once with just a sword and never against someone brandishing any sort of poled weapon.

Darshan was halfway down the hall when Gordon let out a bellow akin to an enraged cow and charged at him.

The man's longer strides and speed swiftly closed the remaining distance until they were a few feet apart. Gordon swung his broadsword. The blade gleamed in the lantern light.

Not knowing where the reflex came from, Darshan's own arm came up to redirect the blow with the back of his borrowed weapon.

Gordon tipped forward, his balance thrown. His eyes widened, then a grin slowly split his beard. He righted himself. "I see you still remember our training."

"Barely," Darshan muttered. Keeping the skill honed hadn't been at the forefront of his concerns. But it likely wouldn't hurt to stay limber. Thanks to the Nulled Ones and their constantly armed presence, much of the nobility retained a healthy respect for bladed weapons.

"Let's see how much comes back to you," Gordon hefted his sword onto his shoulder. "Tradition decrees you defeat us to reach your lover's side, but we'll take it easy. Lad!" he yelled over his shoulder, startling Darshan's already jarred nerves. "Advance!"

Ethan was moving before the command was finished. He screamed mightily, his spear jutting before him.

Darshan had a far easier time deflecting the boy's attack. Then Gordon was back to harangue him, forcing him into focusing only on keeping their weapons from his person.

They danced throughout the hallway, Darshan giving ground more than he really wanted. Worse still, he could tell Gordon was holding back, his swings carrying less speed and force.

Ethan was another matter. The boy handled the staff as though it was an extension of himself. He used his smaller size to his advantage, darting in whenever Darshan managed to gain even the most minuscule of upper hands on Gordon, but ultimately leaving the fighting to his uncle.

Darshan had no chance of budging the mountain that was his brother-in-law. Diverting Gordon's attention was the only way. And he would still have Ethan to contend with.

How an ordinary man was expected to get through this unharmed was beyond his comprehension.

He jumped back before the boy could deal a jab to the gut. He couldn't even rid himself of the spear's annoyance. He tried several times, swinging his sword in an attempt to cut the shaft in two. Each time he did, the boy merely pivoted his weapon out of the blade's way, leaving Darshan to fend off both of his opponents.

He needed something to occupy both at once. But what?

The boy closed in again, still aiming low.

Darshan desperately lunged for the spear. His hand closed around the haft. The tip grazed his forearm, his magic healing the wound before the first drop of blood fell.

He redirected the energy, strengthening his muscles, and used the extra power to force Ethan into his uncle's path.

Gordon stepped back, momentarily dropping his guard to right the boy.

Using the distraction to his advantage, Darshan tossed the spear in their direction as he darted around the pair and, with a final burst of strength to his legs, raced for Hamish.

He all but flew into his husband's embrace. Had it always been this firm? He sagged into the man's arms, relishing the strength holding him fast and how tightly that protective circle bound him.

The warmth of Hamish's breath atop Darshan's head preceded the man's kiss. "How are you feeling?" his husband whispered into Darshan's hair.

"Better." He snuggled against Hamish's chest, breathing deeply of the scent permeating the man's clothes. "Definitely better."

Gordon joined them at the doorway, gesturing for his nephew to do the same. He eyed Darshan down the length of his nose, giving a gruff grunt of acceptance before extending his hand. "Me brother will be well protected in your household. It'll be an honour to ken you as kinsman."

Darshan grasped the man's hand.

As soon as their palms met, Gordon tightened his hold. He dragged Darshan out of Hamish's arms and into a hug. "Sorry about that," the man said in Darshan's ear. "After 'Mish said you'd caused the quake, I had to make sure you were still in your right mind."

"It won't happen again." He was aware now. He even understood the rumours of his mother's hesitancy at using magic. He could never become a purist, using it was too deeply engrained to imagine its lack, but limiting himself was doable.

"Good to hear." Gordon released him, exchanging the closeness for a simple hand on Darshan's shoulder. "There was a mention of feasting?"

Darshan nodded. Having the two families share a meal and get acquainted was all the first day required of them.

"Aye there'll be food, you bloody walking stomach," Hamish teased, nudging his brother in the ribs until Gordon stepped back. "But only if you let me husband go so he can carry on with the ceremony."

Grinning, Darshan beckoned his family over as he scrambled to remember the traditional words. Did they even matter anymore? He doubted it.

These next few days were going to be a breeze.

Chapter 46

"**I** thought the feasting was just for yesterday," Gordon exclaimed, already making himself at home on the cushions before the low table. He poked at the array of dishes, suspicious of each and every one although several looked almost akin to the meals served back in Tirglas.

Whether they tasted the same was a different story. Udynean food had a lot of delicate and spicy flavours, with a few Hamish still found sickly sweet. He'd gotten used to most of them, but favoured the less heavily spiced foods.

Their nephew had no such doubts. He sat further down the table, stuffing his face as only a growing boy could.

Hamish settled between the pair, his aching legs objecting to the cross-legged position. "This is how big most meals are." He *had* pictured a small quiet dinner, not this spread that could easily feed twice as many people.

He also thought the night would involve just the three of them with no servants calmly standing off to the side. He recognised neither of the duo's faces. The way they remained silent, clutching jugs and standing like statues as they waited for the order to come forward, prickled Hamish's skin.

Gordon snickered. "Nae wonder you're becoming a little softer around the middle." He patted his own plump stomach, which jiggled.

Unlike how they dined with Darshan's family on the first day of the wedding ceremony, the second day was considered the official final day as part of his old family. He was meant to spend that time readying himself to move into his new home, gathering his possessions, collecting his dowry from his parents and arranging for it all to be packed off. Most of it was either done—like sending the chest of his effects that Gordon had brought from Tirglas to the *vris*

Mhanek's bedchamber—or impossible.

Instead, he had spent the day doing absolutely nothing of consequence with the pair, starting the early morning in the stables, saddling their mounts—Hamish with his own mare, Gordon atop the gelding Darshan had ridden down and Ethan making do upon the biggest horse they could borrow from the imperial guards.

For the first time since his arrival the better part of two months ago, he had ridden out the palace gates and into Minamist.

Darshan had expressed his reservations about travelling the streets in such an exposed fashion, but after the man's loss of control, there'd been no hint of the hypnotist. They'd found no bodies within the tower that couldn't be identified, but there were also several missing who should've been inside. The consensus Hamish had gathered from the guards settled on her being buried under rubble that they were still in the middle of safely excavating.

His journey beyond the palace grounds hadn't been exempt from the dozen guards and Nulled Ones that'd escorted them through the streets. However, after a few minutes of having the solid feel of a horse between his legs, the steady sway of her gait and the creak of her saddle, his ability to care about their presence had melted away.

They hadn't gone far, Minamist as a whole was every bit as sprawling and vast as her palace, but that hadn't mattered either.

Daama had shown him a map of the city during his studies. It encompassed the entirety of the river mouth, scattered across multiple islands that looked so small in ink. Riding through the streets with their towering buildings and glowing signs, he had forgotten about the lack of land.

The sector they travelled had clearly been on the wealthier side, with large windows enabling them to show off their wares without fear of a thief snatching it. Every shop seemed to use the method, from jewellers and tailors to simple bakeries and cobblers.

But it had been a poky place wedged between two brightly lit buildings that managed to catch Hamish's eye. The sign, painted neatly over the door, had declared the place sold eternal flowers.

Inside had been an old man working at a furnace that took up the back of the building. He had greeted them warmly, eagerly showing off his skill of moulding glass into exquisite shapes. The glass smith's speciality was in crafting flowers that looked eerily lifelike.

After watching the man work his craft, he could almost understand how Udyneans believed in the tales of gods falling for mortals.

He had bought a single flower with pearlescent silver-blue petals that shimmered in the light. It currently sat in its velvet-lined box next to his bed. He'd see to it that one of the servants smuggled the gift into their bedchamber during the wedding tomorrow.

In the meantime, he wasn't meant to socialise with his future husband.

Hamish prodded at a platter of rolls set before him. He understood the symbolism behind spending the last day as an unmarried man with his family, but sharing a final meal with them had a sinister undertone that he couldn't shake.

It didn't help that he was keenly aware of the absence of the rest of his family. How he wished they could've been here. Not that he wasn't grateful for the Goddess allowing his brother and nephew to arrive safely, but he hadn't seen the others for so many months. Some he would never see again, like his cloistered younger sister.

"I ken that look," Gordon said as he selected a thick slice of dark brown bread from a nearby board. "You're drifting into those dark thoughts again. How about you take your mind off whatever you're thinking and tell me what the point of all this feasting is again?" He gestured along the table with the bread slice, dropping crumbs onto the red and gold tablecloth. "Besides fattening you up like a winter hen."

"It—" He stopped as his nephew sprawled down the length of the table to pluck a small bun from the pile before Hamish. "Manners, lad. I ken your mum didnae raise you in the bloody woods."

Ethan flashed a sheepish smile before taking a hearty bite out of the bun and groaning. "Sorry," he mumbled around his mouthful, brandishing the bun. "They're like honey cakes, but sweeter!" He snatched up another. Barely swallowing, he bit into that bun as well.

Hamish ruffled the boy's hair. "Dinnae stuff yourself with them. You'll make yourself sick." He turned back to Gordon.

His brother arched a questioning brow as he curiously dipped his bread into a jug of watery brown sauce that Hamish supposed was meant to be some sort of gravy, or possibly soup. "Well?"

"A lot of Udynean ceremonies are symbolic of this or that deity." He had, admittedly, stumbled a little in Daama's tutoring when it came to gods. Udynea had so many, a handful were considered major throughout most of the empire, whilst others were worshipped in one or two villages. Learning them all, and retaining the information, would take more than the short time he'd had. "This final dinner with my family is supposed to symbolise the Potter leaving her mortal life behind to live with Araasi as the Flame Eternal."

Still chewing, his brother's expression took on that politely blank look that spoke of having no clue what Hamish was talking about. Even so, Gordon urged him to continue.

"It's an old tale." One that stretched back for several millennia from what he understood. "Araasi is their queen of the gods—and several other things I cannae remember right now—but she fell for a mortal woman after spending time in disguise at the lass's side. I guess the woman must've fallen for her too."

"That's a nice wee story," Ethan said around a mouthful of food. "Better than the priests' warnings of demons tricking people to their deaths."

Hamish remembered those old tales, although he hadn't set foot in a temple for some years. The demons of legend were always looking to seduce and lure, to drag the unwitting far from a content life at the Goddess' bosom.

Udynea's myths were absent of such monsters. He supposed their own people were dangerous enough that threats from phantoms seemed unnecessary.

"Aye," Gordon agreed with their nephew. "I didnae think they'd have such tales."

Hamish chuckled. "That's only the first part. The queen supposedly has a king, who wasnae exactly thrilled to see his wife in the arms of another. He chased them all over the world until the goddess had nae choice but to let her lover die a gruesome death or turn the woman into a ball of fire to mount her on her godly crown like a trinket." After hearing Darshan first tell the tale, Hamish had barely believed the man's insistence that it was considered a story of love and devotion.

"Now, *that* sounds more like what I expected of Udynean myths," Gordon mumbled. He sopped up some more of the brown sauce with the rest of his bread. "I guess that makes you the mortal woman in this analogy?"

Hamish shrugged. He hadn't thought about it that way. "I guess." That would make Darshan the goddess. The man definitely had enough power to do what some of the old stories back home claimed the original clan leaders were capable of. No wonder Tirglas used to be ruled by them.

Finished with the slice of bread, his brother picked up a few small pastries that looked to be the type typically stuffed with chunks of meat. "Something has been niggling away in the back of me mind since yesterday. Didnae your husband say he'd a dozen sisters?"

"He does. You just met the unmarried ones." He grabbed a few of the same pastries for himself before his brother ate the entire platter. "Most of them are nae a threat."

Gordon shook his head. "I cannae imagine having to watch me back for family stabbing it."

"Onella's really the only one to watch there and she's had most of her claws cut."

His brother froze, squinting off into the distance with his mouth half open for a bite. "I dinnae recall meeting her."

"She's married. You would've seen her during the dinner to honour Emperor Rami's arrival." Most of the court had been in attendance. Just a few from the northernmost estates hadn't arrived. "She occupied the third table to the right before the royal seats—that's where all the people with close familial ties to the *Mhanek* go—along with her husband and son."

"Listen to you." Gordon's mouth stretched into a lopsided smile. "Who would've thought it'd take getting laid for you to learn politics."

Heat crept along his face, his embarrassment bubbling out in a brief chuckle. He glanced down the table, relieved to find his nephew too engrossed in food to be listening. "It's more an act of self-preservation." The night at Onella's soirée had made it clear that deadly games were a popular pursuit. If he didn't learn the rules, he wouldn't live long.

Everything would change tomorrow. Even with them being betrothed, much of the court treated him as just another in a long line of the *vris Mhanek's* lovers. Once they finished their vows, he became a player in their little games. A threat and a target.

He hoped he was ready for it.

"Wait," Gordon mumbled around a mouthful of flaking pastry. "Is she the lass who looks like she chews fish guts for a living? Spent much of the night shadowing that one wee lad as I recall. Thought she was going to put him on a leash near the end."

Hamish nodded, remembering how Onella had all but dragged Tarendra out of the room when the poor boy just wanted to dance. "That's her son. Until we have bairns of our own, the lad's second in line for the throne."

"Oh ho, I see." Gordon laughed loud and long. "She was expecting to have her son swan in after her brother was gone. Now she's all pissy because your presence has swiped the crown off her lad's head before her dad's even feeling poorly."

"I nae want to discuss it."

Still chortling, his brother held up his hands. "Say nae more. We'll stick to neutral topics." He snatched up his mug and beckoned one of the servants to fill it. "Like how piss-weak this beer is. What even is this swill?" He frowned into his mug before taking a swig and grimacing. "You ken what I should've done? I should've kept an untapped keg aboard the ship for you as a wedding present. You cannae get properly drunk on this garbage."

"It's an acquired taste, I'll give you that."

"You could say the same about licking your arsehole, but that's just as unlikely to take off back home." He squinted at Hamish over the top of his mug. "Did you say something about having a bairn? I've seen your husband and I ken he doesnae have the right equipment. He's nae going to—?" He wiggled his fingers at Hamish as if trying to invoke magic.

"*Nae*," Hamish blurted, his cheeks growing hotter. "It's nae what you're thinking."

His brother's face shifted into that of a clearly guilty boy playing at innocence. "I didnae *say* anything. How can you ken what I mean?"

Because it was the same thought Hamish had when Darshan first brought up the idea of them having a child that shared no one's bloodlines but their own. "Dar... he—"

The subtle shuffle of a figure on the edge of his vision drew his eye.

The two servants stood silently enough. As was common when serving a room of men, they were both of the same gender. One was distinctly elven, his long black hair doing little to hide the pink tips of his ears. That man also wore what looked to be an *infitialis* collar.

How loyal could he expect either of them to be?

"It's complicated," Hamish finally mumbled. "Involves magic, aye." The Niholian breeders had already arrived and spoken to Anjali, whose mind hadn't changed since first being asked to carry their child. If things went as predicted, they'd both be expecting fathers come tomorrow night. "Just nae the way you're thinking." He could explain to Gordon in full later, if his brother really wanted to know, but he wasn't sure how much the court knew. Hopefully, his reply was vague enough to be of little use if the servants turned out to be secretly working for another.

Gordon nodded and returned to his meal, deftly stripping the pastry away to eat separately before devouring the small loaf of meat within. He'd eaten them the same way when they were children, despite the heavy reprimanding from their mother.

They ate in silence for a brief while before Gordon turned their conversation to the neutral topics he had promised, drawing Ethan in with questions on how the boy faired in his language studies. Ethan had improved a small bit in the ten days they'd been here, but not enough to wander the palace without a guide.

The reminder of his brother's looming departure tightened Hamish's throat. He knew Gordon would have to return to Tirglas eventually. Maybe it would've hurt less if his brother had stayed a few days and been on his way as Gordon had planned.

Trying to clear his throat, he downed the dregs of his drink and signalled for one of the servants to bring him more.

The elven man stepped forward with the same pitcher the other had used to top up Gordon's drink. He trembled, setting the loose purple rings of his collar to jingling and sloshing some of the beer over Hamish's hand as he poured. "Forgive me, your highness," he babbled, falling to his knees. The pitcher dropped to the floor, hitting the table on the way down. "I am so sorry."

"It's all right, lad," Gordon said as Hamish dried his hand on the tablecloth. "Dinnae worry about the spill. We'll clean it later."

The servant looked aghast. "I would never—"

Hamish took a hearty gulp from his mug. The cool liquid slid down his throat. His brother was right, it had a strange taste. Its passage tingled slightly and left an odd numbing sensation in its wake.

What had he just drunk?

Hamish lunged for the man who had served him, missing catching the loose sleeve as his body convulsed. Pain flared through his every nerve. "You..." he wheezed. "I—" His stomach cramped, rolling like an eel in a sack. Worse than the time he'd eaten that spoilt venison on a dare in his youth.

The servant scuttled back towards the open door that led out to a balcony. "I'm sorry," he mumbled. "I am truly sorry, your highness."

Hamish doubled over, dry heaving all over the table as he desperately tried to vomit up whatever had been in that drink. Saliva dribbled out his mouth, but little else.

"Stop him!" Gordon roared.

Through the growing pain in his gut, Hamish became aware only of the clang of a tray bouncing off the table and a scuffle close to the balcony door. Glancing up, he spied his nephew lying on the floor, the servant pinned under him.

"I'm so sorry," the man continued to ramble.

"You will be," Gordon growled before snapping, "Get a healer!" at the other servant.

Hamish tipped onto his side. His stomach bubbled, twisting and shifting as though it fought to escape. He gritted his teeth, swallowing the scream straining his throat, and dashed the tears blurring his vision.

Gordon grabbed the elf, dragging him out from beneath Ethan's weight. The servant's feet dangled in the air. "What have you done? What did you give him?"

The man shook his head. "What does it matter? He'll be dead soon."

Nae. He was *not* dying here.

Shaking, Hamish pushed onto all fours and forced himself to vomit up everything he could. Bitter liquid and slimy chunks of half-digested food slithered out, the sensation leaving him gasping and gagging.

It didn't stop the pain. His stomach continued to roll. Burning. It felt as though something was eating its way out. Even being left broken and bleeding in the hayloft by the old stable master hadn't felt this bad.

Another heave and a thin stream of blood dribbled onto the rug. His sight slowly grew unfocused, dimming as his body continued to quiver.

The pain continued, biting deeper with every breath.

A hand landed on his shoulder. It squeezed in a familiar act of reassurance. "Hold on, 'Mish," Gordon said. "Help will be here soon. Just hang on."

Chapter 47

*N*o. Darshan galloped along the winding path leading to the infirmary, the hedges on either side shuddering with the echo of his grief. Reaching the stairs, he flung himself off the messenger's horse and bolted for the door, taking the steps two at a time.

It still wasn't fast enough. He knew so little about what had happened with his husband that his mind raced quicker than a bee's wing, conjuring all sorts of horrors that flogged him better than any whip.

The messenger had only minor details. Hamish was in strife. Attacked or poisoned? The man couldn't say. Darshan had reached the steps of the princess palace only to be told the healers had taken Hamish here. Why? A simple attack or poisoning would've required only a little magic.

Was he... dead?

No. He couldn't be. Darshan refused to believe that. *Please, let him be all right.* His husband should've been safe. He was amongst kin. The food had been tested by people his father trusted. This should *not* have been happening. *When I find out who's responsible...*

The ground lurched beneath his feet. Thorny vines sprang from newly formed cracks in the stairs, tangling around him. Seeking.

He stumbled, regaining his footing only because someone grabbed him. Nulled Ones guarded the door with more packing the corridor beyond. A few spoke amongst themselves before peeling off to march along the hallways or peer around corners and into rooms.

None looked to be in the midst of a hunt. Did that mean they had captured whoever was responsible? *Good.* If his husband was injured, those to blame were in for a slow death.

He slid effortlessly through the doorway and down the corridors.

The Nulled Ones weren't here to keep him away.

Darshan halted upon turning a corner and finding the path blocked. The vast majority of Nulled Ones seemed intent on something amongst them. He caught a hint of red hair in the mass. There, then gone.

"Let me pass!" Darshan roared, his voice cracking. He needed to reach Hamish.

The Nulled Ones stood aside, leaving a hulking figure in the middle of the corridor.

"You," Gordon snarled in his native tongue. He stalked towards Darshan with his shoulders bunched and his fists clenched. There was no mistaking the full intent of murder plastered over his face. "You promised you'd keep him safe."

Darshan stood his ground, stifling the urge to waste his magic on a shield. It flickered around him anyway.

A low rumble came from somewhere below them.

Breathing deep, Darshan struggled to remain calm. The shield flared to life around him. Keeping his emotions suppressed was the better option. The only one that would stop the vines from bursting through the building and tearing it apart.

That he wasn't able to reach his husband wasn't helping. Gordon being in his path didn't help. Nothing helped.

The man's progress was halted by a half dozen Nulled Ones. Gordon was tall enough to glare over their heads. "You *swore* that nae harm would come to me brother and now—"

"Do you forget he is my husband?" Darshan snapped back in Tirglasian. "Do you think I *wanted* this? That I would have brought him within sight of this city if I had thought for a second that he would not be safe?" They shouldn't have come to Minamist. He should've aimed for the royal summer home after the attempt in Rolshar. Should've gone directly to a safe house after the poisoning in that tavern and summoned the Nulled Ones.

Damn him. Damn his pride. For thinking everything would be fine once they entered the palace gates, that Hamish would be protected.

"This is my fault," he whispered. "I am aware of that." If his husband was dead, then that would be on him, too. "But right now, I know less about this attack than you do. Is 'Mish still alive?"

Gordon inhaled, his torso seeming to double in size. All the fight had drained from him, leaving only weariness. "He was when they brought him here."

Not dead. But that could be only a matter of time, especially if the healers had chosen to move him.

"He's in the quarantine wing at the end of the hall." Gordon glanced over his shoulder. "They tell me it was poison."

Quarantine? For a poisoning? Had they brought his husband here because they expected him to die?

Darshan's chest tightened as though his own ribs sought to crush him. Did the healers think whatever Hamish had been given was contagious? There were few things that spread with any speed, but none were outside the expertise of a skilled healer. "How is he?"

"In pain." Gordon turned on his heel, following Darshan down the hall alongside a handful of Nulled Ones. "Your healers were working to stabilise him when they brought him here. I havenae been allowed to go near him since."

The constriction on Darshan's chest eased a fraction. He took in the surrounding Nulled Ones, spying Oja amongst those escorting him. "Did any of the healers say if he'll make it?" he asked of the woman. Did the healers even know what was wrong?

Shrugging, Oja shook her head. "They didn't say, *vris Mhanek*."

Reaching the quarantine wing, Darshan strode into the room. He hadn't ever been in this section of the infirmary. There'd never been a reason to. The room looked almost cosy, until his eyes realised the wooden walls were bare and the only light came from globes.

Hamish lay on a bed tucked into a nook, trembling and groaning. Darshan wasn't sure if the light globes were to blame, but his husband looked far more drawn than he would've expected from any mere poisoning.

What had really happened?

Two healers stood near the head of the bed, speaking to each other in hushed tones. No one else occupied the space.

Darshan took a step deeper into the room, the door banging shut at his back and alerting the healers to his entry.

"Poison, *vris Mhanek*," one of them blurted.

"So I've heard." He couldn't take his eyes off his husband as he crossed the room. Settling at Hamish's side, he smoothed back the man's hair. Sweat plastered the coils to his husband's forehead.

Did he even know Darshan was here?

" 'Mish?"

Hamish's eyelids fluttered slightly, then squeezed shut. A whimper bubbled out from between his blood-stained lips, mingling with the dry residues of vomit already caking his beard.

"What sort was it?" he asked the healers. There were a lot of poisons that produced the same symptoms of fever, tremors and nausea. "And why haven't one of you tended to him yet?"

Both healers shuffled their feet, looking between each other for guidance. "He was most adamant that we didn't," one finally said. "Said it would cause more harm than good."

"Who?" Hamish was clearly in no state to give orders.

"The man responsible, *vris Mhanek*."

Darshan pinched the bridge of his nose. "Let me get this straight," he growled. "You are taking advice from the one who poisoned him? Did I hear that correctly?" Of course whoever was responsible for Hamish's current state would prefer a healer to not touch his target.

He laid a hand on his husband's shoulder and closed his eyes. They could be too late as it was.

"No!" both healers shouted in unison.

Like a leaf over a bursting dam, Darshan's magic whisked from his palm into his husband. Unlike other times, it funnelled directly to the man's stomach where—

Hamish shrieked a demonic wail. He arched off the bed, digging his heels into the mattress.

"Stop!" beseeched one of the healers. They hauled Darshan back, and were subsequently thrown off him by a pair of Nulled Ones.

Darshan staggered to his feet. He had already halted the attempt before the contact was lost. Never had he come across a poison that he couldn't heal. "Who was it?" he demanded. "What did they give him?

"This," Oja said, holding out an ordinary-looking mug. "Prince Gordon claims he drank from the same source and has suffered no ill effects."

He snatched the mug from the woman's grasp. Liquid sat in the bottom, silty with small purple granules. Most poisons were undetectable, but this was new. "What is this?" It almost looked like...

Darshan dipped his finger into the silt. His skin barely touched a granule before registering the soft numbing tingle he had come to associate with the magic-nullifying metal. *It can't be. Infitialis* was a beast to mine. It grew in ragged seams, came out in chunks and had to be immediately coated in a special mixture to remain safe. Even then, it was used only as collars on magically-inclined slaves and prisoners.

To get it anywhere near this fine required a grinding that would, more often than not, have the unstable metal exploding long before there was dust.

"Where is the culprit?" he asked of Oja.

"Nearby." She snapped her fingers and two of the Nulled Ones marched back out the door, swiftly returning with an elven man.

He dangled between his captors, held almost on his toes by their steel grip. An *infitialis* collar hung limply from the man's neck.

Darshan sneered. "So, you're responsible for this." He waved the mug under the slave's nose. "Where did you get it?"

The man remained silent. He stared directly ahead, no doubt

already seeing how short his future had become.

With one jerk of Darshan's head, the Nulled Ones dropped the man.

He collapsed to his knees and resumed his dead-eyed stare.

Darshan crouched next to him. "You are aware how much my healers are having trouble determining how to fix what you've done?" He waited for a sign the man heard him.

Nothing.

Sweat gleamed along the elf's forehead, but he continued to stare at some fixed point only he saw. Whoever owned the man had done a thorough job of terrifying him.

Darshan sought along the collar for a hint of an ownership mark. Anyone sending him would be foolish to leave such identifiers, but it didn't hurt to check. There did seem to be a tag tucked into the man's shirt collar. He withdrew it.

Onella's personal symbol stared back at him.

She wouldn't. Under the agreement, Hamish was protected. Was it some sort of trick? *No.* Impersonating a member of the royal family, even one of their slaves, was punishable by death. Not even the assassin guild dared.

This man truly belonged to his half-sister. She had abandoned their agreement, practically killed his husband, and for what? Power she already possessed? Did she really think she would gain more with her son on the throne?

Their father wouldn't let the boy inherit. She had to know that. So... what? This stab at Hamish's life was some petty lashing out? All because she hadn't gotten her way?

I'm going to kill her. There was nothing to stop him now. She had struck the first blow. *She* had broken her word. Their agreement.

The floor creaked, the boards rippling. The scent of freshly broken earth filled his nostrils.

Darshan closed his eyes and, taking a deep breath, sought to suppress his anger alongside all the other emotions fighting to break free. He couldn't let himself be swayed by any of it. Letting his feelings take control now would endanger everyone, including those trying to help Hamish.

And they couldn't do that without knowing what Onella's slave had given him. "If you won't tell us what this is," Darshan grated, "then perhaps a demonstration of its abilities is in order." He shoved the mug under the elf's nose. "Drink it."

The man's mouth moved, speaking beyond the range of Darshan's hearing.

Darshan pressed closer, tipping his head until his ear was almost touching the man's lips. "What was that?"

"I beg you, *vris Mhanek*," the elf whispered. "Please don't."

Rocking back on his heels, Darshan eyed the man incredulously. He dared to ask for mercy whilst his target slowly died in the same room? *The gall.* Darshan twitched his fingers at the two flanking the man, ordering them to restrain the elf.

The Nulled Ones held the elf's torso upright. One tipped his head back, whilst the other forced the man's mouth open.

Darshan lifted the mug high, slowly tipping it as he watched the horror increase on the elf's face. How far would he need to go? Until the dregs dangled on the rim like globs of festering slime?

What would Hamish think? Seeing him torment another like this?

He shook the thought away. If his husband had been in any capacity to see, Darshan wouldn't be trying to pry information out of a slave. He would still be quietly meditating in the palace gardens, not considering his half-sister's murder.

"Wait!" the man cried, wrenching his jaw free of the Nulled One's hand. "It's just *infitialis*! *Infitialis!*"

The healers gasped, jerking Darshan senses back into the room.

He stepped back, his heart feeling as though it hammered at the base of his throat and inside his skull at the same time.

"You *fed* him *infitialis?*" one of the healers screeched at the slave.

He'd been right about that, then. "What'll happen to him?" Darshan demanded of the healers.

"I've only heard rumours of it taking down powerful spellsters," replied the one who had squawked. Now that he spoke with a more even tone, the clip and roll of his accent belied a Stamekian heritage. "It's a poison from my homeland."

Infitialis as poison? He'd never heard of it being used in such a fashion. "How does it kill?" Even before Darshan tried to heal him, Hamish had clearly been in a lot of pain.

The healer shook his head. "I don't know. Those who consume it don't survive this long."

"I didn't want to do it, *vris Mhanek*," the slave blurted. He clutched at his collar, the purple metal gleaming in the low light, and drew forth the tag identifying him as Onella's. "My mistress... You must understand. I have children, *vris Mhanek*. She swore to feed the poison to them if I didn't do it. Please. I failed. She... she'll kill them."

"She won't." Onella might be vindictive and a thorn in his side, but she wouldn't slaughter children. Not over one slave's mistake. "Say that he's a spellster with no healing magic," he said to the healer. "What then?"

The man shook his head. "I don't know."

Sagging into the chair next to Hamish's bed, Darshan rested his forehead on his fingers. "He's in pain." Too much and his husband's heart could give out before anything else took him.

"The magic flows through us," the slave said, absently wrapping his arms around himself. "It hurts to have it severed."

"I am aware," he growled, gesturing to the Nulled Ones to take the man away. Although Darshan didn't remember much pain from the actual nullifying, he had experienced the effects of *infitialis* once during his *Khutani* and even before that, when Onella shot him with an arrow. The metal had entered his body, then. He hadn't wound up like this. "Is there anyone who could know more?" he asked the room.

The two healers looked to each other for an answer and came up with nothing.

The door swung inward, revealing Gordon standing in the doorway, his face drawn. "I heard—" He shook his head. Whatever scraps of explanation had reached his ears, he clearly wasn't ready to believe them. "Is he going to die?"

Darshan clapped a hand over his mouth, quietening the blubbering that threatened to take his senses. If the healers gave an answer, he didn't hear them. He didn't want to think about the outcome. Didn't want to face the idea that he might lose his light.

"We'll be putting him into a coma," said one of the healers. "To ease the pain," he added upon seeing Gordon's confusion.

Gordon's brows only furrowed further. "What's that?"

Darshan thought hard for the Tirglasian equivalent of the word and, coming up short, fell back to his native tongue. "An artificial sleep," he managed to get out, his voice strained. The idea was almost as foreign to him as it clearly was to Gordon. Magical healing didn't require the patient to be in any particular state.

Would it even work? What if the *infitialis* reacted to that? Anything could upset the metal.

"Cannae you just heal him?" Gordon pleaded. "I thought magic could fix anything."

"Not everything," the healer replied. "Certainly not this. Not with magic. Not if what that slave said is true." And they couldn't yet determine *that* without trying again, which ran the risk of killing Hamish.

"What *can* you do?"

"Wait," Darshan said, his voice sounding hollow to his own ears. The healer might think Hamish beyond help, but Darshan refused to believe there wasn't something they could do.

But waiting could also kill his husband.

Which was the kinder death? Fast and painful or slowly slipping away in agony?

Gordon knelt at the bedside. He clasped his brother's hand. "You have to make it through this, you hear me? You've a wedding. It'll be poor of you to kick the bucket before then." He chuckled mirthlessly and quickly sobered. "It's strange," he murmured. "All this time, Nora will have been trying to convince the clan leaders that you're nae dead and I might just be bringing back that very news."

Tears blurred Darshan's vision. He took a steadying breath and tried blinking them away, succeeding only in smearing the tears across the lenses of his glasses.

This wasn't how it was meant to be. He had chased the threat from his domain, left it broken and dead beneath slabs of stone. He—

Not dead.

The whisper hit him like a falling branch. For one moment, the image of the room was replaced with that of the tower ruin. Just a glimpse. Too fast for him to determine any details.

He shook his head. Whatever the blasted plants wanted, this was not the time.

Gordon stood, giving Darshan's shoulder a hearty pat as he faced the healers. "I'd like to bring me nephew in. The lad will want to see his uncle. To say goodbye."

"Of course," one of them replied. "But Prince Hamish will likely be deep in sleep by the time he gets here."

"I understand."

Darshan shot to his feet. "Then I shall inform the Nulled Ones at the door to let him in. They won't permit entry otherwise." He knew that neither Gordon nor Ethan would harm Hamish, but until they determined the truth behind the slave's story, the Nulled Ones would suspect everyone.

He couldn't stay in this room, though. Not whilst people paraded in as though his husband had already passed. He had to leave this place. To go somewhere quiet. To think. *Alone.* It was the last thing he wanted to be. But he needed to expel this fog of battling emotions clouding his mind without harming anyone. He needed answers. Needed the right questions. He needed...

To kill Onella.

Chapter 48

Darshan knew where his half-sister resided. With the guest palace still being repaired and their father declaring the imperial palace off-limits yesterday, Onella would be in her favourite spot at the far end of the imperial grounds where a little garden grew, cultivated by her in their youth. Herbs, for the most part. Nothing dangerous. Not out in the open.

As expected, she lounged beneath an awning, reading and snacking off a small platter. A pair of her slaves played music, one with a flute, the other, an elven lap harp. *Such an innocent tableau.* If Darshan hadn't seen the ownership tag around that man's neck himself, he never would've suspected her involvement.

The musicians faltered as he neared, their gentle melody abruptly turning into an ear-torturing screech. The pair exchanged glances, the one playing the lap harp scrambling to their feet. Both seemed to be elves, or at least had a heavily elven lineage.

Could they hear the rumbling of the vines creeping beneath the earth?

Onella finally looked up, first to frown at her slaves, then at him. "Darshi?" She closed her book and sat upright. "What are you doing here? I heard that someone—"

"Not *someone*," he snarled, levelling a finger at her. "*You.*"

Her frowned deepened. She dismissed her slaves with a flick of the hand and the duo scampered off like a hunting party was after them. "What are you talking about?"

"You..." The ground trembled with his rage. He dug his nails into his palms and fought to steady his emotions. "You sent a slave to poison my husband."

She peered at him as though he'd taken leave of his senses, then scoffed. "I did no such thing."

"Do not *lie* to me!" Vines exploded from the ground, lashing the air. Darshan slammed his half-sister against the wall, keeping her pinned, with his shield. "He is currently *dying* in the infirmary and it was *your* doing!"

She struggled against his magic, her face contorting as she strained with all her might to push herself free.

"You dare to come here?" he growled. "To attack my husband in my own home? To try and take him from me?" The ground at their feet groaned, the call answered by the wall that sectioned off the imperial grounds, fortifications that had survived sieges. "For *what?* Father won't give your son the throne. Not like this."

Onella's face reddened. Her mouth moved with words that hadn't the air to be voiced.

"Are you just seeking to hurt me, now? Is that it? Am I not allowed to be *happy?*"

The wall at her back buckled. Rubble and dust dropped to the ground. Vines crept through the cracks, entwining her legs, clasping her wrists, encircling her neck.

Fear flickered to life in her eyes. That was new. He had seen her contempt in him so often, but never outright terror.

"What's the matter, sister?" he hissed. "Has it finally occurred to you that, just maybe, you've pushed your dear brother too far?" Never before had he noticed how easy it was to restrain her. He hadn't brought the full might of his magic down on her in the past, apprehensive that she'd run to their father with claims of him being the instigator.

Now? What did it matter who she claimed struck the first blow? He could lose his light, his beacon... What did he care that he might lose his inheritance? Udynea meant nothing to him without Hamish at his side.

And it would be so easy to let go, to push his shield that little bit further, to squeeze every last breath from her lungs, to have the vines crush her bones and drag her into the ground. Feed this little garden she had cultivated with her still-beating heart.

Darshan pressed his shield against her. "How many others did you order?"

"None." The word came on a single, frantic intake of air. "I didn't—"

"*Liar!*" He could feel the vines tightening, compressing her chest. "My husband could *die* at any moment." The brightest minds of Udynea swore it wasn't possible for a specialist spellster to spontaneously be capable of healing, but he wasn't prepared to omit that chance. If such magic manifested in Hamish's body with the *infitialis* inside him, what would it do? He didn't know. He wasn't sure he wanted to know. "Don't you dare try telling me you weren't responsible. It was *your* slave who fed him that poison."

She shook her head, frantic. "I gave no order. I wouldn't. Not here. Not under father's nose. You know me better than that."

She spoke a measure of truth. That was always the way with her. The treaty their father had forced between them forbade attacks on any sibling, as well as their spouses, whilst within the imperial palace. She wouldn't ignore that. Not when the punishment was banishment of both herself and her son from the court.

But the evidence spoke differently. "The order came from *you*." Her slave hadn't been hypnotised. That would've been the first thing the healers checked, the first thing Oja—or any other Nulled One— would've informed him of.

"I didn't do it," Onella insisted.

"That's enough!" their father's voice boomed across the grounds. "Put her down!"

Pinning Onella harder against the wall, Darshan spun on his heel. Raw magic seethed through his veins, looking for something to latch onto, to destroy.

Their father marched towards them, flanked by a half-dozen Nulled Ones who looked far more jittery than usual at the prospect of subduing him. "Darshi," their father said, his voice firm and calm as though the man spoke to a toddler. "I gave you an order."

Darshan glanced over his shoulder at his half-sister, taking in how effortlessly she remained in his grasp whilst she struggled to keep enough room to breathe. "Answer me truthfully, Father." Of all the people who could've matched his power, Onella should've been at the top of the list, right alongside his twin. Their mothers might not have been the same, but the bloodline was—her mother being his aunt. "Just how much stronger than you was my mother?"

The weak flicker of a shield briefly shimmered around their father as he came to a halt beyond Darshan's physical reach. "Strong enough." He bowed his head. "And I know she wouldn't have wanted you to—"

"Don't try and use her choice to live the way of a purist on me. If these past few days have taught me anything, it's that I know *nothing* of my mother." He had been taught *stories*. Myths with all the sharp edges smoothed by the passage of time or clouded emotion. "And now my husband..." His voice cracked, words beyond him. He swallowed through a tightening throat, fighting back the tears.

Their father stepped closer, laying a hand on Darshan's shoulder. "I've heard."

Of course he had. Little went on within the palace grounds that the *Mhanek* wasn't privy to. A fair number of conspirators had found out such truths the hard way.

Darshan stepped back, straightening his clothes alongside his spine. Bad news was always best faced whilst on one's feet, or so his father claimed. "I trust you've come with new information."

"Your betrothed is stable. I've set a watch, no less than a dozen Nulled Ones. I've also sent for physicians, which should limit the amount of passive magic he's exposed to."

Stable. A flicker of hope clutched at his chest and had the shield around his sister wavering.

It also roused his suspicions. Never had their father been so helpful. And physicians? Those who practised healing without a spark of magic were a rare sight with the knitting factories so close at hand. He'd never seen one within the palace grounds. His grandfather had considered them as charlatans. There would be talk.

Did the man act out of guilt? "If I discover you were in any way responsible..."

Their father shook his head. "I know you are hurting right now, but see sense, child. If I had given any order that would've endangered your betrothed, he would already be dead."

Darshan bowed his head. How he wished he could've believed that.

"Let your sister go, my son. You're no killer and she didn't do it."

He threw off his father's hand. There it was. *Dancing to the same tune as always.* He refused to roll over this time. He'd too much evidence on her. "Don't you dare take her side! Not on *this.*" He had heard too many tales of wars starting over less.

"I'm not taking sides, I'm thinking rationally." He eyed Darshan up and down, before turning his examination on the wall. "Which you appear unable to do at the moment. You must rein yourself in, seek control and *think.* What would your sister have to gain by doing this now?"

"Nothing." That didn't eliminate the prospect of her lashing out through spite.

"You have other enemies. Ones more capable."

"You're not suggesting the Jhanaar woman had something to do with this. She's gone." Obliterated by the destruction he had wrought on that tower.

An image of the ruin he'd made flashed in his mind's eye. Ghosts of voices murmured something he couldn't quite make out.

He shook his head, quelling the sound as best he could. "Besides, there were no marks on the slave." And the man had confessed to being ordered by Onella. *She threatened him.* Darshan peered at his half-sister. Such an act wasn't merely dubious, it was unthinkable.

What if the slave hadn't been the hypnotist's target?

He released his hold on Onella, the vines dumping her to the ground before slithering into the earth. Their absence revealed a sizable dent in the wall.

The very instant Onella was able to stand under her own power, she hastened to hide behind their father. If she even dared to glance Darshan's way, he didn't notice, his thoughts too busy trying to piece everything together through the haze of anger and grief.

As far as Zahaan and himself could figure, the Jhanaar woman would've been in Nulshar at roughly the same time as they were to target Hamish at the soirée. And again at Rolshar, albeit with less time to plan.

Darshan had assumed the woman followed them down, but if she was able to leave marks within others that held for months, like in the imperial guards, then she could've easily gone ahead of them, taken the most probable path they'd trek and left without anyone the wiser.

He pushed past their father to lay a hand on Onella's forehead, ignoring her sputtering objections.

Scarring on the brain. Not very big, but there all the same. Just as he had begun to suspect. "You were hypnotised."

Scoffing, she batted him away with a single hand. "Don't be ridiculous." She peered at their father out the corner of her eye. "I know how to avoid it."

"Scars don't lie." How long had it been there? Since the soirée she had thrown for him? Older? Was it actually a mark from their father? He could ask the man, but what parent would admit to hypnotising their own child?

Onella harrumphed and folded her arms.

"If you're as innocent as you claim, then you'll help me." With all their networks working as one, nothing could avoid them. They'd scour the whole grounds, flush out anything untoward and deal to them.

Chuckling mirthlessly, his half-sister adjusted her shawl and skirts. "Not a chance." Giving one final tug to her outfit, she turned on her heel and marched in the direction of the princess palace.

"And here I thought," their father called after her. "That you would want to discover just who gave your slave the order. Find out how he got the poison."

Onella halted. Her back stiffened but her head tilted to one side.

How *had* the man gotten his hands on the stuff? No reputable supplier would've sold anything to a slave. Nor would they have been aware that *infitialis* could be used in such a fashion. Darshan pinched the bridge of his nose. *Why didn't I ask?*

"Who knows poisons better than you?" their father added, still trying to convince her to help.

After a long moment of silence, Onella turned back around. "Do the healers not know what kind?"

"It's a Stamekian variant," Darshan replied. She would learn the full truth soon enough, but there was no point shouting it for everyone nearby to hear. If word got out, the usual court games would get messy.

She frowned at the ground, her arms akimbo and one foot tapping a restless beat. "Then that most likely means someone nearer their borders. Or within it." Her head snapped up, a familiar smirk adorning her lips. "I know this is probably a tough question for you, Darshi, but who have you angered that has an estate there? And I mean recently."

Darshan shrugged.

"The Stamekian emperor is already visiting," their father mused. "Perhaps, he would be willing to illuminate us."

Onella peered at him. "Could *he* have been behind it?"

Their father shook his head. "Their lands are still recovering from what their last emperor did. It would be foolish to incite a war."

Darshan grunted his agreement. An attack with such obvious means would place too big a target on the emperor's back.

"But not improbable?" Onella pressed.

"I've met Emperor Rami only a few times," their father admitted. "And briefly at that, but he doesn't seem the type." Once again, he laid a hand on Darshan's shoulder, squeezing slightly. "Get some rest, my son. We'll take it from here."

Rest? Did his father really expect it of him? If Hamish didn't pull through, Darshan doubted he'd ever sleep again. "I'll try."

Giving Darshan's shoulder one final pat, their father strode back the way he had come with Onella and the Nulled One's in tow.

Darshan watched their departure until they were specks in the distance. He wrapped his arms around himself, ignoring the tremors running through his body. His gaze slid to the dent in the imperial wall. *So close.* Any further pressure and the whole section would've crumbled.

He eyed the ramparts. Guards patrolled along its length. Not oblivious to what had transpired—they would've had to be unconscious to not be aware of his outburst—but confident that nothing could cause this wall to break.

Nothing except him.

Darshan fled along the paths leading to the imperial palace. He halted at the steps, craning his neck to take in the building's full height. He knew the real reason why his father wanted him to rest. Up there, in his chambers, he'd no sway over the vines, became no threat to anyone.

But it wouldn't nullify his magic. He had made the guest palace unstable and he hadn't been near it.

If he were to unleash such power *within* a building?

Backing away from the steps, he vacated the imperial grounds altogether. If he was to be alone, then he would find somewhere abandoned. Some place where the only person in danger was himself. He was *not* going to be responsible for any further loss of life.

He wandered aimlessly, his mind flitting from one question to the other. Was this to be his life? Was he doomed to be a danger to everyone around him? How far did he need to be pushed before he decimated everything in his immediate vicinity again?

Why was it only manifesting now? He had been attacked before. More than once, he'd been the target of the *libertas omnium* sect. Never had he retaliated strongly enough to bring down a building or threaten the fall of major fortifications. Was his link with the plants to blame? That didn't require magic. The Nulled Ones wouldn't have been alerted if he had only used the vines to tear the tower apart.

What else had changed?

'Mish. Did having the man around really make that much of a difference? *Yes.* He had pushed himself to the brink, irreversibly altered his very being into something no one fully understood, all to keep the man alive. *Onella was right.* He hated to admit she got anything about him correct, but she had been in this.

Mostly.

She had called Hamish his weakness. The man wasn't that. He was Darshan's shield, his strength, his world.

Without him...

No. Darshan hugged himself tightly, ignoring the strange looks from those he sauntered past. He couldn't think of a life without his light, not even as a possibility. He would use his dying breath to protect Hamish and gladly, even if it meant the world had to burn.

That alone was enough to make him quake.

His feet eventually led him to the destroyed tower. The builders had abandoned it for now, focusing on returning the outer walls to their former strength. They'd cordoned off the rubble with a barrier of stones from the very building.

He climbed over the stones. What other damage could he do beyond shattering the remains to dust?

Wide holes had been dug into the rubble during the search to find survivors. There'd been none, but their efforts still pockmarked the spot. Darshan settled into the middle of one such excavation.

His thoughts continued to tumble, frayed fragments of scattered emotion that quivered through his body. Hugging his knees tightly to his chest, he closed his eyes, ignoring the wetness trickling down his cheeks.

He's stable. Would Hamish remain that way? He didn't know. How long before his husband recovered? No one seemed to know *if*, never mind when. All that could be suggested was to wait. And hope.

He was in short supply of the latter.

This is my fault. If he hadn't whored himself through the court, hadn't used every man who came seeking his aid, then this wouldn't be happening.

And he couldn't fix it. That was the worst part. All throughout his life, he'd been able to mend whatever he screwed up, to wave his hand and have the mistakes just vanish. *Not this.* There was nothing to be done.

"Well now," Daama said. "I assume the *vris Mhanek* dwells within."

Darshan opened his eyes, surprised to find himself the centrepiece in a ball of thorny vines. *So, it's not just anger.* That revelation didn't make him feel better. If anything, it was worse knowing that any emotion could trigger them. He could've handled the idea of reining in his rage. Being completely emotionally detached from everything wasn't feasible.

He peered through the vines, spying Daama standing on the other side of the barrier of stones with his twin at her side.

"Darshi?" his sister called, cupping her mouth. "We're coming over, all right?"

Still tucked into a ball, he propped his chin on his forearm and silently watched the two women pick their way through the rubble. There was so much confidence in their approach. Neither one saw him as something to fear, unlike the muted unease on his father's face.

The vines slowly unfurled, lying upon the earth and leaving him exposed. He scanned their surroundings. No sign of guards either, Nulled or otherwise. It was just the three of them. Alone.

Anjali reached him first, sliding into the hollow with practised ease, whilst their old nanny followed at a more sedate pace. "We've been looking everywhere for you. Father said he had ordered you to rest. What are you doing here?"

He shrugged. It had seemed the more logical place earlier. "I couldn't. Hamish... He—" He fell silent as Daama laid a hand on his head, gently smoothing back his hair.

"We know, my child."

Of course. Everyone within the palace grounds had to be aware by now. Half of them likely already knew about his outburst with Onella. Neither was something his father could easily hide from the court.

Anjali crouched before him, examining with the same clinical eye she gave an injured animal. "You look terrible."

A snort of laughter escaped him. "Thanks."

"How are you holding up?"

"I..." He gave a wet sigh. "I'm a box of birds."

"Oh, Darshi..." His twin had been gifted an actual box full of such creatures. It had been a courting gift from the same man who'd given her the tortoise. But the cargo ship carrying it had been delayed by the weather and the box...

Everything had seemed fine until she opened it.

He still vividly remembered those poor, broken bodies and how she had cried over each feathered corpse, cradling them in turn, desperate to revive even one. But it was several months too late. "I dragged him from one side of the continent to the other just for him to die." He refused to believe Hamish would've been better off if he had stayed in Tirglas, because that simply wasn't true, but the man wouldn't be currently fighting off death if they hadn't met.

"A bit melodramatic." Anjali flopped onto the dirt next to him. "Is there nothing anyone can do?"

"Not with magic. The healers can't do anything for him without killing him. He's in pain, but that'll pass once his body expels the source." If that was even possible. Some poisons could do far worse things than kill. And also providing Hamish's magic didn't turn to healing whilst under the stress. Spontaneous healing was rare and deadly in the best of circumstances. "This is my fault."

"You always think that," his sister chided. "You didn't poison him."

"No." He had done something far worse. "I led him into this shark pool knowing he couldn't even swim let alone defend himself. I let my foolish pride think that no one would touch him, that *I* could protect him from *everything*." Darshan spread his arms wide, taking in the surrounding buildings. He shook his head. He should've known better. "I didn't give him the poison, but I might as well have."

"My poor boy," Daama murmured. She wrapped her arms around his shoulders, pulling him into her embrace as she knelt before him. "My dear, sweet child."

The last fraying hold on his emotions failed. He buried his face into her shoulder, and sobbed like a child with a newly scraped knee as she rocked him from side to side, whispering wordlessly into his ear.

Only once he had cried himself out did Daama withdraw. Even then, it was to fish out a handkerchief and dry his face. The pale cloth came away dark with kohl. "There we are," she said. "Much better."

He didn't feel better. Just more wrung out.

Taking a deep, shaking breath, he turned his gaze to the ruins. It was easier holding himself together if he didn't look at their faces. "The healers put him in a coma."

"That's good, isn't it?" Anjali asked. "He's not suffering."

"But he might never wake up." How long would it take for the poison to work its way through? A day? Two? A week? *Never?* "I'm going to lose him."

"No, the physicians will see him through it." Daama returned him to her embrace, continuing to gently rock him, smoothing his hair. "I know it's hard, my child, but you must not let your emotions drive you in this moment. Now is the time to gather your strength. Those who are to blame shan't be far. They must be punished. *You* must be seen as capable of retaliation no matter how much it hurts inside."

The ones who were responsible? Who did he affix blame to? Onella? The slave? Both had been manipulated by another.

Or had they? How could they determine the age of the scarring on his half-sister? "This is Onella's doing."

Anjali rolled her eyes. "You always say that."

"Because it's true. It's like what 'Ma always says, if it moves and hisses like a snake, you can bet it'll bite like one, too."

Daama gave a curt nod, one side of her mouth lifting.

"Except this time..." He let out a blustery breath, trying to make sense of it all. "She ordered one of her slaves to put *infitialis* in his drink." Had it just been Hamish's? What of Gordon or their nephew? No one said what the effects would be on a Nulled One. He didn't even know if Ethan had any power or followed along with his uncle and grandfather. "But she also shows signs of being hypnotised."

" *Nells?*" Anjali gasped. "Do you think that Jhanaar woman got to her when you were at Nulshar?"

He shrugged. The scar was old. But he had no reference between one given a few months ago or years prior. The idea that hypnosis could linger for so long was an unnerving thought. Anyone could have a trap set within their minds, waiting for the right circumstances for it to spring.

And, if it had been the same woman who had hounded them across half the empire, he couldn't punish her because she was already dead. His husband was going to die and even vengeance was beyond his reach.

The surrounding vines trembled, sprouting leaves. *Not dead.*

He knew Hamish wasn't gone. Not yet. But things could change in an instant.

Images flashed in his head. The same impressions as the first time he'd returned to ground level after his rampage. A building. The tower he had destroyed. He knew it was in ruins. Had the plants not felt it fall? Did they not realise he was in the middle of it?

More flooded his mind. The heat of a fire. The liquid uncertainty of his magic moulding the earth. The sudden compacting of falling debris. The crush of bodies beneath stone. The trickle of escaping blood and the whisper of a final breath.

Bile slid up Darshan's throat. *Enough.* He knew he had taken lives, he didn't need to relive their deaths.

Something smaller flashed through his mind. An echo. A cavern beneath the rubble. A...

Basement? He twisted to eye the other holes that'd been dug. A number of them looked deep. The towers within the imperial grounds had basements that extended beyond the building's circumference, used as a place to store food—and sometimes people—in a siege. He hadn't considered the other towers might possess them or what this one held now.

The plants couldn't tell him more. None of the foliage surrounding the tower had roots running that deep. They only knew of the space beneath through echoes.

He clambered to his feet and, with his twin and old nanny in tow, investigated each of the holes. Most were little more than refilled depressions. A couple had sunk further. He widened those with both shield and vines. They led to small rooms that definitely suggested storage. Beyond the shelves built into the wall, they were all empty. Not that he had expected the find his hypnotist waiting for him.

One room had completely caved in on itself, covering crates and what looked to be racks of something. Weapons? He couldn't be entirely sure.

The gouges in the dirt along one side of the hole the cave-in had caused interested him far more. It was as though something had clawed its way out. The marks looked too widely spaced and too deep to have been done by an animal. He ran his fingers along the grooves. *Definitely a person.* A survivor.

And he was certain of who.

"She's alive," he announced, clambering back out of the hole to brush the dirt from his trousers. "The Jhanaar woman escaped."

"Not possible," Daama said.

"You turned the tower to rubble," Anjali added, gesturing to their surroundings.

In as few words as he could manage, he relayed what the plants had told him whilst also showing them the marks.

"If they can tell you she was here," Daama said once he was finished, "then can they tell you where she is now?"

He turned the question inwards, seeking along the extensive network.

All he got back was a muddled response that he guessed was

confusion.

"They don't know. She could be in one of the buildings." High up where plant senses couldn't reach. "Or aboard a ship. Even be outside of Minamist." It wasn't beyond his reach, he had felt the whole world once, but he had also almost lost himself in it.

He wasn't keen to delve that deep again.

"Fleeing would be the wisest option," Anjali said.

Daama frowned. "Perhaps." She toyed with her bottom lip, pulling and twisting it in that fashion Darshan hated. "I think hiding nearby is more plausible. If she's after vengeance, she'll stick close to ensure her will is done." She turned on her heel and made for the barrier. "We should inform the *Mhanek*. The infirmary isn't the most defensible place."

"Maybe a trap could be laid?" Anjali suggested, following the older woman.

"A trap?" Darshan echoed. "You're not using my husband as bait!" The earth rumbled at his feet. Only for a moment before he tempered his anger, but it was enough to have one of the already disturbed holes crumble further.

His twin frowned at the ground.

Daama eyed him down the length of her nose. "Very well," she said, the tone bringing back memories of punishments lasting well into the night. Of endless magical practice or scientific formulas that didn't stop until he was exhausted. "Ange? Get my son. Darshi? Come with me." She clambered over the little stone barrier and strode off with the confidence of one who knew their words would be followed to the letter.

Darshan found himself trotting behind her like a scolded puppy before he even realised he had moved.

They travelled in silence across the palace grounds and through the imperial gates. His nanny didn't utter a word when they entered the imperial palace and started climbing. Nor when they arrived at the door to his bedchamber.

He lingered in the main room as she carried on to the study, perching himself on the edge of the chaise lounge. Was she after the information Zahaan had collected? There wasn't anything within the notes that she didn't already know.

His leg bounced on the spot, the tap of his heel muffled on the rug. It was quiet without the constant drone of life in the back of his mind. He had noticed the absence the first time he had entered, but it somehow seemed emptier.

Daama re-emerged from the study clutching a cup. "Drink."

A familiar scent tickled his nose and fuzzed his brain. She had given him such concoctions before, in his youth when he couldn't sleep. He had even prepared a weaker version for Hamish after a woman had crept into the man's bed with the intention of violating him.

Darshan put the drought to one side. "I can't waste time with sleeping, 'Ma." How could she even expect him to with his husband's life balanced so precariously? "I need..." He scrubbed at his face and ran his fingers through his hair. "I need to find the woman responsible for this. I need to be by Hamish's side." He wouldn't have the man waking up to strangers. He went to stand, his progress halted by Daama's hand on his chest. "I need—"

"To sleep," she said. "Child, you are in no fit state to do anything. Not now. Rest first."

He shook his head. If he slept, he could wake up to find Hamish was dead.

"The Nulled Ones guard your husband. They will have the infirmary secured top to bottom, something you cannot do alone. Ange shall be alerting Zah as we speak, who will already be doing all you would be able to, including interrogating the slave. They'll get all the answers that man can give. Have faith in your spymaster and your twin. If the Jhanaar woman is still here, she will not escape again."

"But... 'Mish..."

"This is the perfect opportunity. I shall oversee his care whilst you sleep. No harm will come to him. I promise." She picked up the cup. "Now, drink."

He downed the concoction, wrinkling his nose at the bitterness. It might've been years since she had dosed him this way, but age certainly hadn't improved the taste.

"It doesn't warrant that face." There was a soft edge to her scolding he hadn't heard since before his *Khutani*. She fixed his bed, turning down the covers. The faintest hum of a lullaby buzzed in his ear as she worked. "Now come lie down before you fall down."

He obeyed woodenly, clambering onto his bed, sinking into the soft mattress, allowing her to tuck him in without a word of objection.

She brushed the hair back from his face, humming the same song he remembered drifting off to sleep to as a child. It was an elven song that, although the melody was softly cheerful, mourned a home they'd lost. He wasn't sure if Daama actually knew he was aware of that.

He opened his mouth, his tongue seeking some quip that his mind couldn't quite coherently form. Sleep dug its claws into him, dragging him towards a fog he couldn't shake free.

Darshan closed his eyes, drifting off on dreams of ships and nameless shores where his husband waited for him.

Chapter 49

Emperor Rami leant back in his seat, his ice-blue gaze unwavering on the vial. A few specks of the poison floated within, turning the water a sinister purple. The man had recently examined Hamish and his diagnosis was in line with that of the Stamekian-born healer.

Darshan sat across from him, trying to keep his nerves steady with mint tea as per Daama's instruction. It didn't help much. His body was overcome with restlessness. The better part of three days had already passed since the initial poisoning, there had to be something he could do to help Hamish.

Through it all, his husband had made little headway in improving.

The treatment of waiting still gnawed at Darshan. How could his father expect him to stay put? He longed to be out in the search. He could hunt in ways others couldn't. But his father had been insistent on keeping him out of the investigation, and the Nulled Ones trailing him were making sure he adhered to the order. They wouldn't even let him descend enough to make contact with the plants.

He couldn't be content in sitting idly by for days on end, not whilst Hamish still fought for his life with only mundane physicians overseeing his care. Those men usually oversaw people too poor to pay a proper healer. Not a one could've dreamed of ever setting foot in the palace grounds. As it was, they'd been fed little information. *A fever magic cannot heal.*

What if Hamish didn't pull through? He would've brought a good man all this way to die.

Finally, the Stamekian spoke. "I'm not sure what information I can give you that would be of help." Emperor Rami lacked the abrupt, almost tumbling, rhythm to his accent that Darshan associated with people from the neighbouring empire. Had he been raised in the

Independent Isles? Or was a western variant?

Darshan set his teacup on the saucer, balancing both upon an upraised knee. It rattled slightly, halted from tipping completely by his light touch. *If 'Ma saw me being this careless.* It wasn't the first antique set he'd broken. Nor would it be surprising.

He had apparently become quite good at breaking things.

Clearing his throat, Darshan said, "One of our healers is native to your land. They informed us that the usage of *infitialis* in this fashion is popular in Stamekia."

Emperor Rami rolled the vial between his fingers, letting it dangle in his grip briefly before repeating the act. His fingers were long, not as much as an elf's, but slender and perhaps nimble enough to flick the vial as though it were a starblade. "Is that some roundabout Udynean way of saying you're accusing me?"

"Not at all." Neither empire had anything to gain from attacking each other.

The emperor reached for the high collar of his robe before wrinkling his nose and seeking higher for a lock of his lobe-length hair. The silvery-white colour, along with his blue eyes and the bronze shade of his skin, was supposedly a mark of royalty, inherited from the man's unstable father.

Darshan had never seen hair so short on a Stamekian. They cut it only when great violence was to be wrought, some nobles even making a display of gifting it to their adversaries, who responded in kind before both sides attacked. He didn't understand the strategy. Had even considered it a fable, but a man of Emperor Rami's age should've had hair down to his knees. All in that shimmering colour.

It must've been quite the sight before the man usurped his father.

"My people are still recovering from my father's reign," the man said. "War? With Udynea?" He shook his head. "That would be a foolish act."

"My father said as much," Darshan confessed. But no one seemed to know how the poison had it made its way into the palace grounds. Had the Jhanaar woman merely heard of the usage and scraped enough off a bigger chunk of unworked metal?

He shuddered at the thought.

"It *is* true that razor dust is used in my land, but I would hesitate to call it popular. The usage is often political." He set the vial down on the table between them with a clink sharp enough to pluck at Darshan's nerves and took up his wine glass. "It also has a hundred percent fatality rate."

Clearly, that wasn't quite true or Hamish would already be dead. "You don't think he'll live, then?" He tightened his grip on the teacup's handle, preparing himself for the agreement. Stamekians had a habit of being blunt when it came to death.

Emperor Rami lifted his gaze from the vial. "Hard to predict. Like I said, back home, it's considered foolproof against spellsters." His brow twitched. Not quite a frown. Did he consider that Hamish was incapacitated because he was a specialist?

Some of the nobility were aware of Hamish having magic, but few knew the full truth. Darshan wasn't about to let that information run rampant through the court.

"However," the man continued. "If it was going to kill him, it would've done so by now."

Darshan bowed his head in acknowledgement of the possibility. It wasn't enough, though. He needed something more definite. "How does it work? I know the poison is meant to kill, but *how?*"

Those ice-blue eyes surveyed him, narrowing to peer through pure white lashes. "As my husband would say, knowledge does not always grant us freedom."

"Please. I need to know what it'll do to him."

"Nothing," Emperor Rami replied, swilling his wine around. "Not for normal folk. It's mildly uncomfortable, but everything generally passes through in a day. No more harm than a few gold flakes atop one of your fancy dishes."

That couldn't be true. Hamish had been incapacitated for twice as long and showed no sign of improving. Were the herbs that put him in a coma also hampering such bodily functions? "What if the target was a spellster?"

"The body sees the dust as a threat. It tries to nullify as it would any other toxin, except..." The man grimaced. "Razor dust is no less unstable than bigger chunks of *infitialis*. Any magic, be it from himself or to his person, leads to the body tearing itself apart to avoid it. There have even been rumours of the dust exploding in transport."

Darshan swallowed to keep the bile in his gut down. The acidic tang of the tea he had already consumed tainting the back of his throat had him giving an involuntary shudder. Was that what he had felt in his attempt to mend his husband? The pain that had caused Hamish to scream such an unnatural sound? How much damage had he done? Enough to hinder natural healing?

"If he makes it through," Emperor Rami continued. "Then he'll be the first to survive. Everyone will want to know why." There was a question lurking there. Curiosity looking to be sated.

"He's a spellster," Darshan admitted. "But he has scarce magic at hand and little in the way of talent to call upon it beyond one or two tricks."

The man's brows lifted. "A weakling? That makes sense. But I've never heard of razor dust being used on one before."

Darshan gritted his teeth. He understood how weakling was the common term Stamekians used for those with minimal magic, that didn't mean he had to like how flippantly it rolled off the man's tongue. "What of those magic cannot affect?" Gordon had admitted to drinking the same stuff and seemingly suffering no ill effects, but Darshan had to ask.

The emperor took a lengthy swallow from his wine glass. "I have personal experience there. Although, I suffered none of the effects your husband is currently under. That's how I know the razor dust will pass through easily enough. Tahu would be able to tell you more, but..." He rubbed at his temple. "I could send for information. He might know of a cure that doesn't require so much waiting and uncertainty."

"That would be appreciated." The Stamekian capital wasn't far by sea, a few hours given a good breeze. "But would it not be easier to have him come here rather than relaying messages?" It had been strange enough that the emperor chose to travel without his husband when the invitation was for them both.

The man's eyes narrowed. "I'd prefer he wasn't subjected to the imagery of so many collars."

Darshan bowed his head. "My apologies." He'd forgotten the man's husband had once been one of the previous emperor's dolls as well as leashed. "Is there anyone with you who could've supplied this dust?" The Jhanaar woman couldn't have known about the razor dust until recently or she would've used it months ago.

Emperor Rami frowned. He strode across the room to the entrance and spoke with a servant in his native tongue, the words sharp and terse. Stamekian wasn't a language that came easily to Darshan. He knew only a few phrases that didn't help him here.

The emperor returned, sitting stiffly in his seat. "My valet assures me that there was no chance of it being within my luggage. I cannot be as definite about the rest of the ship or of the sailors."

Darshan grunted. He hadn't considered the ship's crew. It made more sense that one of them could've snuck a small vial of *infitialis* dust by anyone inspecting the ship.

"Is there anyone who would seek to eliminate your husband?"

He laughed, earning him a perplexed look from the man. "I would think that list is now longer than my arm."

A hasty knock came from the same entrance Emperor Rami had spoken to his valet at. The door swung open with a bang, admitting one of the *Mhanek's* personal servants.

"My *vris Mhanek!*" She scrambled over to fall to her knees at his feet. "You've been summoned to the throne room. The woman? They've found her."

~ ~ ~

Darshan hastened through the hallways leading to the throne room, his heart pounding as though it would leap ahead without him.

He barely noticed how deserted the place was. No servants hastening off with messages. No spies skulking in the shadows. The air carried a heaviness he hadn't felt in a good long while. *The day Grandfather died.*

This was different. They had her. The woman who was responsible for everything that had gone wrong was actually in their possession.

And she would pay. His father would see to that. Even without the attacks on Hamish and himself, she had endangered several imperial citizens, killed at least a dozen more and assaulted a *vlossina*.

A torturous death was the only outcome.

Being crushed by the tower would've been kinder than an executioner, but a small piece of him had hoped he'd been right in her having survived. Now, he could ask all the questions that had plagued his thoughts since this vendetta started. Including the most important one... *Why me?*

Beyond the young man's plea several months back, his network had found no connection to either the Kaatha household or the Jhanaar family.

His spymaster greeted him at the top of the stairs, along with a Nulled One. The pair swiftly matched his gate as he blew past, although Zahaan had to adopt a little half-skip to stay at Darshan's side.

The man glared at him, but Darshan refused to slow down. "They're waiting for you," he said. "The *Mhanek* thought you might be able to get her to talk before they employed other measures."

"She's still alive, then?" A foolish question, he knew it as soon as the words left his mouth. They wouldn't summon him to examine a corpse unless to identify and he had no idea what she looked like. Rather than wait for Zahaan's response, he pushed on. "How did they catch her?"

"I believe she tried to hypnotise one of the Nulled Ones guarding the infirmary."

Despite himself, Darshan winced. Most of the court was aware of Nulled Ones guarding their *Mhanek*, but they didn't announce their status to the empire. Often, those who attempted an assassination on his father learnt the fatal way. "That must've been quite the shock for her." He was amazed she hadn't encountered one of them before now.

The Nulled One grunted, his shoulders squaring in pride for his kin.

"Did they find out which of the Jhanaar women she is?" Darshan asked his spymaster. There were three possibilities, after all. From what little information he could glean, they'd been close-knit although vastly different.

Zahaan shrugged. "She claims her name is Binita."

That would make her the youngest of the Jhanaar daughters, the one the records claimed as quiet and polite. "You doubt her?" Had she taken the name as some sort of way to pay respects to her dead sister?

"I doubt everything coming out of her mouth. She's..." Zahaan bowed his head. "Well, you'll find out yourself soon enough."

The doors to the throne room were shut, defended by a good two-dozen guards. They really weren't taking chances in her evading them again. *Good.* It seemed he wasn't the only one to underestimate her talents for far too long.

At the wave of his hand, the doors swung open, just long enough for Darshan to enter. He spun at the sound of a grunt, surprised to find his spymaster right behind him.

Zahaan grinned sheepishly and adjusted his shirt. "Shall we?" He gestured to where a small figure stood before the throne with a semi-circle of Nulled Ones flanking them.

She didn't look how Hamish had described her. Not blonde for one. Had she dyed her hair in an effort to throw off the people hunting for her? Or did the golden lantern light somehow make it look darker?

It had to be her, though. Binita. His personal demon.

"I will ask you this one last time," his father's voice boomed through the room. He sat in his new place upon the throne. Without Darshan near, the massive vine base that had destroyed the dais remained unmoving, even the small tendrils wrapped around the nearest pillars showed no sign of stirring. "*Where* did you get the razor dust from?"

If the woman said a word, it was too quiet for Darshan to make out.

Darshan stepped closer, each of his footfalls muffled by the rug. He might've been summoned here, but it was never a good idea to interrupt his father's interrogations. His spymaster continued to walk alongside him, making even less noise.

"You *will* answer me, young lady," his father growled. "Your usual tricks shan't help you today."

"The deep market." Binita's voice softly danced around the room, chased by a wisp of laughter. "You'd be surprised what pops up there."

"And did you hand it to Onella *vlossina Mhanek?*"

The woman laughed. "I'm not sure why you're dancing around the real question you want to ask. Do you not want me to admit I did it?" She leant forward, her movement punctuated by the jingle of chains. "I did. I hypnotised the *vlossina*, allowed her slave to find the razor dust and saw he had easy entry into the prince's room." She twisted, glancing over her shoulder at the Nulled Ones.

Darshan paused as her dark eyes settled on him. A serpent carried less flatness to their gaze. Whoever the old Binita had been, she was long gone.

She smirked. "It was simple."

"How?" Darshan asked, curiosity overcoming him. "Hypnosis doesn't work that way. You need to maintain eye contact, to—"

"Maybe *you* do." She smiled. There was something off about it, a dissonance between the dimpled expression and the predatory gleam in her eyes. "I don't."

He stepped back, stumbling into his spymaster as he focused on keeping the grumble of the earth from reacting to his unease. What Binita claimed matched Hamish's recollection of his encounter with her. *She didn't hold him for long.* But if she was capable of ensnaring a person with a glance...

He spied movement on his periphery. The vine had unwound its tendrils from the pillars. Like hooded snakes, they reared up on either side of his father's throne.

Binita sneered at the display. "Don't waste time in posturing. I am well aware of what'll happen to me if I try it with *you*." She lifted her hands, revealing shackles of infitialis. "Not that I could."

"But you *did* hypnotise my husband."

The woman lowered her eyes, temporarily hooding that feral glint. "He's not your husband yet."

So few knew his Tirglasian marriage was less valid than he had originally thought. Although the idea had unsettled Hamish, Darshan hadn't considered them as any less linked. How had she learnt of it? Or was it an opinion dredged from Onella's mind? "You set people on him when he has done nothing to you." Had she not admitted to feeling sorry about her attempt at using Hamish to kill him? "You've caused dozens of deaths."

"*Dozens* you say?" Her head snapped up. "Only that many?" Binita tilted her head to one side. "How many are you responsible for? How many little edicts has the *uris Mhanek* signed that caused nothing but more ruined lives?"

Darshan wet his lips, once again turning his attention to stilling the writhing beneath the throne room. If they erupted free here, they would not only tear a hole in the floor but also risk bringing down this section of the building.

The vine beneath the throne groaned, shifting to press deeper into the room, forcing his father to abandon his seat or be tossed aside. *Stay.* His command rippled through the ground. There was no need to retaliate. She annoyed him—and made him a little wary— but, with six Nulled One's at her flank and Zahaan at his, he was in no danger.

The vine shuddered back to its original place. The tendrils remaining poised in the air.

Had she gotten to someone within his inner circle? Perhaps Maari, the scribe who handled and translated Hamish's missives. That would explain the old man's sloppiness with the poisoned letter. But hadn't he been cleared of any marks? And Binita's magic definitely left a trail.

Was his scribe like Hamish? It wouldn't take long to see a clean page stuffed into a tainted envelope. And certainly less objectionable than the death she had attempted to command of his husband.

"Although," Binita continued. "I suppose you don't consider the dangers to others, do you? How far in danger did you put the man you supposedly love when you followed the call to the *Gilded Cage*? Did you give any thought to your little specialist's safety when that willow attacked? I don't think so."

"What willow?" his father asked.

Darshan ignored the man's demand for answers. Such knowledge wasn't widely known. She could've got it from interrogating Hamish, but he'd been ensnared only briefly. Was she imprinting on other's memories? That didn't sound like something done through normal hypnosis. "How do you know about that?"

Binita remained silent. She only smiled at him in that slightly detached fashion.

"Take her away," his father ordered. "She clearly needs a little more persuasion before she's ready to give proper answers."

"Wait," Darshan ordered, stepping closer to the woman as two Nulled One's grabbed her. Any interrogation his father ordered could have her losing her very being. "Answer me this question first. Your grudge with me is clear, but why do this?"

"Why?" she hissed, the sound shivering along his neck. "I wanted to show you what you've done. To gift you with the same pain your actions bestowed upon me. I wanted you to feel helpless as the thing you loved was ripped from your grasp. To hurt so much that you'd long for death."

He understood that sort of ache. "Did it warrant taking innocent lives?" All those people she had sent, she had to know what would happen. And the failed poisoning attempts? She must've ordered those poor souls to consume the same poisons to keep the attacks from being traced back to her.

"*Innocent?*" Shrieking, she lunged for him, her momentum halted by the Nulled One's. "*You* didn't care about lives when you took him!"

"Not another step!" Zahaan snapped, inserting himself between them, his sword drawn and levelled at her chest. One thrust through the heart and few healers could bring her back.

If the woman heard him or registered the weapon, she gave no sign. "No one is innocent. I learnt that much after the fallout with Zia's family."

Darshan backed away, getting closer to the second arc of Nulled Ones that had formed from the usual group who guarded his father. "Who?" Did she mean the Kaatha household? He hadn't done much personal research into them once they'd been eliminated from suspicion.

Binita's face contorted. "You don't even remember him, do you? He was *mine*, you know? It was some six months or so." A smile stretched her face as she stared off into better times. "My beautiful, gentle Zia. I was all set to marry him. I would've gained a higher status. My family, joined with his, could've prevented all of us from being torn apart like animals."

It was as Zahaan had said. The Kaatha estate had been set upon by political enemies. "I—"

"And then there was *you*," she snarled. "Everything was planned until *you* came along. Until you were found with *him*. *My* betrothed. My Flame. *You* stole him."

Darshan shook his head. That wasn't how it worked within the Crystal Court. As he explained to Hamish, most marriages were either political or with an eye for magical power. Few involved love. Some didn't find it even after years of being together. Sexual favours were exchanged practically on a daily basis.

"I would've taken him back," Binita continued. "Even after you used him, I would've loved him. But our parents wouldn't listen. Mine wanted nothing to do with a man who would climb into bed with the *vris Mhanek* at a royal whim. And his thought they could do better than me. As if receiving imperial seed up the arse makes a difference."

It didn't. It never had. Those who sought his favour left with no more than they had to begin with, sometimes less. He hadn't even given the court any impression that offering themselves to him sexually would achieve any results beyond an orgasm.

Yet, the men still threw themselves at him on a regular basis.

And he, in turn, had become accustomed to their debauched grasping of power. *Too much so.* Especially to mistake a genuine plea of help for something lesser.

"I don't blame him," Binita said, her voice soft for the first time since he'd entered the room. A flicker of emotion beyond rage sagged her shoulders. "Not for what he did. After all, who could refuse a proposition from the *vris Mhanek?*"

"You think *I* instigated that night?" Whatever had happened between Zia and himself—and he still couldn't single out the memory from a slew of similar nights—Hamish was the only one he had attempted to seduce in a good long while. Before then, he hadn't given a hint towards proposition since his rather disastrous first time.

He would fully admit the likely possibility that he had slept with the man, but it would've been at their suggestion, not his.

Like someone extinguishing a candle, the light in her face was snuffed out. "Of course you did! He wouldn't have done it on his own. He *loved* me and you seduced him. You *used* him. You stole him from me and left him to die like some elven whore! He was my light! *Mine!* He sought your help and now he's dead. You *took* him! You *killed* him!"

Darshan remained silent as Binita raved on. She thrashed against the Nulled Ones restraining her, looking for all the world as though she would tear his throat out with her bare teeth if given the chance.

It had been easy to seek retaliation when their adversary was unknown and the threats to Hamish's life had been no more solid than mist. He had felt nothing but fury in tracking her across the palace grounds.

But seeing the woman responsible for all their strife, watching her fragmented mind shatter further before his eyes, of how her grief solidifying into pure rage.

It was hard to muster anything but sympathy.

"Let me help you." Darshan took a step towards her, halting as his spymaster laid a warning hand on his chest. "I—"

"*Help?*" she echoed, screeching like a parrot. "It's too late for help! It's all gone." Her voice cracked, growing wet and ragged. Her eyes grew glassy. "Him. My parents. They're all dead." Tears fell down her face in the biggest droplets he'd ever seen. "The Kaatha estate has already been swallowed up. My family was slaughtered like pigs months ago. Everyone I ever cared about... gone. All because we lost the alliance, the *protection*, your dalliance denied us."

"I'm sorry." There was nothing he could do about any of it. Maybe track down those responsible for the deaths and see them punished, but it wouldn't mend the wounds festering deep in the woman's heart.

She laughed, a teary and hysterical sound that had the Nulled Ones pressing closer. "Sorry? You're *sorry? You?* The monster who toys with other's emotions, who destroys entire families at a whim and sends hundreds to their demise all because he wanted some dick?"

"That's enough," his father bellowed. "I ordered her out of here. See to it that her execution is swift."

"How many more will die because of your actions?" she screamed as the Nulled Ones obeyed their *Mhanek* and dragged her towards the entrance. "How many families will *suffer* because of you? You might play at being the love-struck boy, but I've seen the real you. You're a disease. A *leech*."

"Wait," Darshan ordered. "I don't want her punished. Not with death." There had already been too much. There didn't need to be any more. She was clearly unwell, lost in the funnel of misery. They should be sending her to the Knitting Factory or a secluded temple.

His father snorted. "Even without the other deaths she's responsible for, she gravely injured a member of the royal household. That's treason."

"And how many have *I* injured in my outbursts?" Darshan countered. He had almost killed Onella. He probably would've completed the act had their father not talked him down. "It was me and my actions, my callous disregard, which took everything from her." He could easily see himself slipping down the same path if he lost Hamish. He'd already risked more than his own life to keep the man alive. "She needs somewhere safe to heal and find peace, not more death."

"You dare play the compassionate fool now?" Binita snarled, her crazed eyes widening further. "I only want one thing from you."

"And that is?" There was much he couldn't change, but if he could soothe her aching...

"You took what was mine. I want you to feel that pain. To watch, helpless, as your chance for happiness slips through your grasp. And then? I want you..." In one mighty eruption of rage, she tore free from her restrainers and rushed at him. "...to die!" Her hands snapped up, wielding her shackles like a bludgeon.

His shield flickered to life as she bore down on him, stuttering under the presence of *infitialis*.

Ropey tendrils lashed all around him, winding around his body, pulling him from immediate danger, shielding him. Other vines lunged for the woman, smacking everyone aside in their eagerness. They squeezed around her torso and limbs, trapping her mid-leap.

Don't crush! The last thing he wanted was to end her life.

He needn't have bothered giving the order.

A single woody vine jutted from the floor. It pinned her in place like a beetle on display. Blood trickled down the shaft, a thin stream at the moment, but only because the vine staunched a greater outpouring.

ALDREA ALIEN

Binita hung there, a soft gurgle escaping her mouth. The same sound he had heard whilst trying to save Hamish's life after the bear attack.

"Be still," Darshan commanded the woman even realising how ridiculous it sounded. With the tendrils of the big vine keeping her in the air, there was little she could do. Being this close to what was essentially a stake, he sensed the barbed tip wedged between her heart and left lung. Any withdrawal would definitely tear either organ. "Let me heal you." He went to lay a hand on her outstretched arm.

Binita twitched away from him. "Don't—" She stilled with a gasp. The colour in her face drained so completely that he almost expected to see it gushing down the vine. "Don't touch me," she finally managed.

"You'll die if I don't." Was she a healer? She couldn't be a specialist, not by the derogatory tone she'd spoken of them. If he had one of the Nulled Ones remove her shackles, her body might heal itself.

A breathless laugh escaped her bloody-tinged lips. "At least I'll go out knowing I took your light with me. My only regret is that he never witnessed your true side."

"He lives, you know," his father said, striding across the room. "You might've poisoned him, but you failed. He will recover."

"No. The poison... It's—" She panted, her head lolling forward. "—foolproof. Kills instantly. No antidote."

"Whoever sold it to you should've told you it only works that way on spellsters who can heal."

She gaped at him. Then her eyes grew unfocused and her head drooped. The rest of her body swiftly followed until the only thing stopping her from collapsing were the vines still holding her.

His father halted at Darshan's side. "And it is done."

Darshan gently supported her body as the woody vine retreated into the bloodstained floor. His father was right. It was over now. All of it.

Should he not feel some measure of freedom? The only uncertainty still left was Hamish's recovery.

Yet, all he felt was hollow.

"Escort my son back to the imperial palace."

"Wait. What did you mean about Hamish?" His husband was going to live? Why was he only finding this out now? "Is it true?"

His father hesitated before nodding. "Somewhat. The physicians believe he passed the crisis point this morning."

Relief shuddered out of Darshan's lungs, shaking his whole body.

His father laid a hand on Darshan's shoulder, gripping tight as if steeling both of them for the bad news. "However..."

"Things are still uncertain." He understood that. Even though his magic mended all but the gravest of injuries, a healer's training wasn't considered complete without basic knowledge of how the body healed without magical intervention. "Can I see him?" He wouldn't dare interfere. He just needed to be at Hamish's side.

"Best not. He is stable and improving, but he's not cured. They suggested a few more days before even attempting to rouse him." His father pulled him close, squeezing Darshan with a might he had never felt from the man before. "The important part is he's not going to die."

Darshan leant against his father, using the man to hold himself up. "I thought I had lost him," he whispered. He could admit that now. He'd been steeling himself for the possibility. Praying, pleading, *begging*, to anything that would listen.

To hear Hamish would live...

"You won't, my boy."

It was just a matter of time—and that simply couldn't go fast enough—but his light would return to him.

He glanced at Binita's body. Already, the Nulled Ones were preparing to remove her. They would take her to the dungeons and keep her there for a few days with the shackles removed to ensure she was truly dead. Providing his father didn't order a beheading. There was no better way to ensure a spellster didn't miraculously revive, but she'd been through enough. "Do we know where Zia Kaatha's body went? She should be laid to rest beside him."

"Their ashes were scattered around the High Mother's temple," Zahaan replied.

"I should—" He fell silent at a firm squeeze on his shoulder from his father.

"You need rest." His father turned to Zahaan. "Take him back to his chambers. I shall send for Daama to take care of him."

"I don't want to be drugged again." It left his mind in a fog for far too long. If Hamish woke up during that time, he wanted to be aware of it.

"Very well. But you are still confined to the upper levels of the imperial palace." He nodded at the Nulled Ones flanking Darshan. "Don't worry, my boy, I'll have this all cleaned up."

Of course he would. That's what his father had done with every mess Darshan made. They just disappeared. The consequences? Minor. The lessons learnt? None. He had wrecked lives. Unknowingly, but still his fault.

And what did he get in return? The love of the most amazingly sweet and gentle man. Someone who didn't deserve all the hardship that had befallen him. A man *he* didn't deserve.

Staying at Darshan's side was Hamish's choice and that glorious man had insisted on remaining, even to his own detriment. All Darshan could do was be worthy of the light his flame eternal shone because Binita was right, he *had* been reckless, relied too much on his magic or others to solve his problems. He had to do better. To *be* better. For the sake of the empire. For the world.

For his husband.

Chapter 50

Hamish's hands shook as he brought the mug to his lips. The broth within was clear and smelt faintly of chicken. He sipped at it, forcing a throat that hadn't eaten properly for days to actually swallow.

"Take it easy," Gordon cautioned, echoing the words of the healers who had left not that long ago. Beyond his brother, there was just Daama in the room. "Your body's been through a lot."

"I ken." Even though he remembered little of the day beyond a searing pain in his gut, wrapping his head around the idea of being poisoned wasn't difficult. That no one had been able to immediately restore him to good health was unexpected.

Only a day had passed since the healers had deemed his recovery as permanent and moved him from the infirmary back into the princess palace. They had also suggested he take time in regaining his strength, but that was just as unlikely. His arms felt as though his bones were made of lead, yet the urge to throw off the sheets and get on with things raced through his veins.

His brother settled on the foot of the bed, eyeing him as though they were both several decades younger and Hamish had just awoken from his first experience with rutting. "How are you feeling?"

"Quite likely exactly the way he looks," Daama replied. "Like shit."

His brother glared at the woman. Hamish didn't remember them having much to do with each other before he'd been poisoned, but that seemed to have changed.

Daama lifted a shoulder. "You can't expect him to feel all that well after a five-day fever and being spoon-fed broth." She gestured to his cup.

"She's nae wrong about that," Hamish said. He took another swig from the mug. This broth was good for when a patient couldn't stomach much. "But I'm nae a feeble old man like you, Gor." And he craved something with more substance. *Maybe a steak.*

His brother chuckled. "If you're cracking jokes, then you must be pulling through all right."

"I'd feel better with some proper food." Even a hearty soup with chunks he could chew would be an improvement. Draining the last of the broth, he pondered on all he had been told over the last few days. "Are they sure it was *infitialis?*"

"Aye," Gordon replied. "And a wee amount to boot." He hung his head. "I'm so sorry. I should've—"

Hamish held up a silencing hand. "You're nae to blame." In all the varieties of poisons and antidotes Darshan mentioned the Crystal Court using over the years, ingesting the magic-nullifying metal hadn't been one of them. The healers who oversaw his conscious recovery during the last two days had also been jittery about the reasons.

All that he could properly determine was that his inability to do more than a weak shield and stick arrows precisely where he wanted was the only reason he hadn't succumbed to the attack. His brother being a Nulled One must've also saved him from even the agony Hamish had suffered. *Lucky bastard.*

"Have they found the one responsible?" he asked.

"Yes." Daama wrinkled her nose as if a dog had just urinated on her feet. "Binita Jhanaar."

The first name wasn't one he recognised, but the latter was more familiar than he ever wanted it to be. *The hypnotist.* "I thought she died." He remembered the rubble Darshan's berserk outburst had caused. How could anyone have survived that?

Or had the attack on Hamish been set in the slave's mind long beforehand? *A last desperate attempt from beyond the grave.*

"We all thought her gone, child," Daama said.

Hamish listened in silence as the woman briefed him on everything that had transpired throughout the days he'd been unconscious. The woman had survived by hiding herself in the tower's storerooms beneath the ground only to claw her way out sometime between him carrying an exhausted Darshan to bed and the search party. From there, it had been a matter of her skulking in the background until the opportunity to target him again presented itself.

Gordon let out a low whistle once Daama was finished. Had his brother not heard the full story before now? "Lass was determined, I'll give her that."

The memory of the hypnotist's eyes flashed before him. The cold anger. The burning madness. "What of—" He fell silent as the door swung open.

Darshan stood in the entrance, transfixed as though he saw a ghost.

"Me heart!" Beaming, Hamish set his mug aside and beckoned the man closer. He longed to leap from the bed and greet Darshan halfway, but he wasn't sure if his legs would hold him. Falling on his face when he was still recovering wouldn't be a good look.

His husband crossed the room slowly, stopping before the bed with his hands clasped primly before him. "I apologise for not coming sooner, *mea lux.*" He didn't look quite like the same confident man Hamish had first met. His clothes weren't anywhere near as brash, either. The tunic and baggy trousers, both in an undyed off-white, looked like something Hamish had seen when travelling through the temple quarter. "My father wouldn't allow it until the healers declared you as safe for me to be near."

"I ken." Darshan's whereabouts had been one of the first things he asked after waking. Although, the idea that Hamish wouldn't be safe in the man's presence was new. What else had happened whilst he was unconscious? "When you said it would be me last meal with me family, I didnae think you meant that literally." He grinned, surprised when Darshan's answering smile remained small and restrained.

It could've been a trick of the light, but the man looked close to tears.

"I suppose the attack also mucked up the wedding." Hamish hadn't given too much thought towards the ceremony since waking, focusing more on getting better, but the final day when they spoke their vows should've been days ago. They both should've been mired up to their necks in all the details and celebrations that came after.

Darshan shook his head. "I... I don't know." He delicately dabbed at the corner of his eye. They definitely looked slightly on the glassy side and oddly absent of the customary kohl. "It hasn't really seemed that important."

"I believe the *Mhanek's* retinue is dealing with much of the mess," Daama replied. "There have been quite a number of messages sent your way," she added to Darshan. "Most are requests for your presence or dinner invitations, that sort of thing."

Hamish grunted. Of course the court took this time to reach out to their *vris Mhanek.* Anything to cosy up to the man. Better yet to take advantage of his distracted mind. "Nae doubt there were some marriage proposals in the mix."

"Naturally."

"Are you serious?" Gordon blurted. " 'Mish wasnae even declared dead and they were trying to steal his husband?"

Hamish chuckled, wincing at how dreadfully weak it sounded to his own ears. "Well, they can bugger off. I'm nae going anywhere soon." Smiling up at Darshan, he entwined their fingers together. "And I'd come back from a thousand deaths to stay with you."

Darshan closed his eyes as he squeezed Hamish's hand. He settled on the mattress, first merely perching on the side of the bed, then settling back further until he was curled next to Hamish with his head on Hamish's shoulder. A tearful sigh escaped his lips, then another, turning more and more into sobs with each exhalation.

"Dar?" He rarely saw his husband this emotional and never in front of others. He wrapped an arm around the man's shoulder, trying to rub his back despite the awkward angle.

Daama looked from her master to Hamish and back. She patted Gordon on the shoulder. "That would be our cue to leave."

"Aye," his brother replied, swiftly getting to his feet and making for the exit. "I'll see you another time, 'Mish."

"Don't break him," Daama said as she followed Gordon out the door. "And see that you drink the rest of that tonic the healers gave you."

Hamish wrinkled his nose at the thought of downing another mouthful of the bitter liquid that was meant to fortify him. His husband looked as though he needed the concoction more.

He waited for a while after the door shut, listening to Darshan's near-silent weeping, holding his husband tight as the man trembled with each tearful breath.

Only once Darshan had stilled, did Hamish dare to speak.

"Love?" he whispered as he gently smoothed back the man's hair. "It's all right, me heart. *I* am all right. The healers have declared me free of *infitialis*." Not that he felt cured. A week of bed rest with little to nourish him had made his limbs weak. His body still spoke of a deep-set tiredness that he couldn't shake. *Of all the things to feel.* He'd been unconscious for days, how could fatigue still gnaw at his bones?

"I thought I'd lost you," Darshan replied, his voice still thick with unshed tears. He lifted his head, his eyes obscured behind the fog that had taken his glasses. Little streaks ran through the mist where his eyelashes brushed the lenses clean.

"You honestly think I'd leave you to face the dark again?"

"I feared it for a while."

"When I've a life involving a loving husband and children waiting for me?" He squeezed Darshan, pulling him close again to plant a kiss on the man's forehead. "Never, me heart."

Sniffing, Darshan sat back and cleaned his glasses on the edge of the sheets before drying his face. "I've missed that bravado. But, in all honesty, you would've died had your magic learnt to heal before the razor dust passed through."

Razor dust? He hadn't heard anyone call it that. Had the woman responsible for poisoning him told them? Was that why he was still alive?

He went to ask and caught Darshan grimacing.

"*I* would've killed you had I continued trying to heal you."

"You dinnae ken." He clasped Darshan's free hand. "And you dinnae cause any harm. See?" He patted his stomach. Even after a mere week, there was a little less padding. "I'm all in one piece."

Smiling slightly, Darshan returned his glasses to their usual place. "I apologise. I didn't mean to—" He pressed his lips together and exhaled out his nose in one drawn-out blast. "I must look a mess." He scrubbed at his face, drying his cheeks on his sleeves.

"You think I care about that?" Hamish cupped his husband's jaw. Darshan's beard was still damp, although less scruffy from its brief charring. "I'm just sorry I wasnae there for you." He couldn't imagine being in Darshan's place, watching his love suffer, helpless to fix it, not knowing if he'd pull through. And all without the person he needed the most being in a position to reassure him.

Darshan leant into the touch, turning his head slightly to press his lips against the heel of Hamish's palm. The act seemed to give him strength. "I'll be fine now you've recovered, *mea lux.* I just need you to get better."

Hamish's gaze ran over his husband, once again taking in the starkness of his attire. "You're looking a wee bit more sombre than usual." He'd never seen Darshan wear anything plain beyond the heavy outfit Gordon bought the man during their journey to the cloister.

"You mean this?" He plucked at the tunic. "I'm in mourning."

"Who died?" Had they gotten at one of Darshan's siblings? His twin? His nephew?

"Binita Jhanaar."

Was that not the same name Daama had said? Their stalking hypnotist? "The woman responsible for poisoning me?" He knew Udyneans viewed death a little differently from the usual Tirglasian mindset. They didn't all reside at the Goddess' bosom for one. Their afterlife was far more varied, consisting of fields and oceans much like the real world. But he'd never seen Darshan grieve for someone who had attacked him. "You're mourning her death because…?"

Darshan hung his head. "I failed her."

"How?" He held up a hand as his husband went to answer and pointed to a bottle sitting on the table where he had last eaten a solid meal. "Fetch me that first, will you?" As much as he hated the tonic, he needed to regain his strength. "Might as well get it down me, *then* you can explain."

Darshan obeyed, dragging himself off the bed and down the steps to gather both the bottle and the glass sitting next to it. Handing over the last of the tonic, he resumed his perch on the side of the bed. "There's not really much else to say. I failed my duty as *vris Mhanek*. I should've listened more when aid was requested."

Hamish cradled the glass, not relishing the idea of swallowing the liquid within. "I dinnae follow."

"Drink and I'll be brief."

Darshan's explanation held a lot of facts Hamish had already heard from others. But the man was far from brief. His sentences wandered, the blame he took upon himself thick in every word.

Hamish set his glass to one side, the tonic within well and truly gone even though he had drained it in shuddering sips. "Her attacks were an act of revenge. A one-sided feud. How is blaming yourself as much as she did the answer?"

"Because I *am* to blame. I'm the root of everything bad that happened to those families. The very act that led me to you also sealed their demise."

"You slept with a man who propositioned you." They'd both done similar more times than either of them could count in the years before they had met, the difference being that Hamish had often been very deep in his drink. "Was this Zia fellow direct about what he really wanted?"

"I don't know. And I've tried to think about that day. To see his face. Remember anything. But with all the favours the court has tried to get out of me, all the men I've slept with..." He hung his head. "He's just another meaningless blur."

"She said her parents learnt of you being with him? Did anyone catch you two together?"

Darshan shook his head. "If we did, it clearly wasn't memorable. Not like the last one."

He'd told Hamish the full story there, of the dalliance that had seen him sent to Tirglas. Having objects lobbed at him whilst naked would be enough to make anyone remember. "I hope you're nae still blaming yourself for *that* one. He shouldnae have come on to you in the first place."

"And *I* knew he was engaged."

Hamish shrugged. "So you're both to blame there. But if Zia didnae tell you the reason behind him seeking your audience, then how could you have had a say in anything that came after?"

"You're forgetting that, before I arrived in Tirglas, I simply didn't care about anything beyond my next source of pleasure."

"I dinnae believe that." Darshan might get it up quicker than himself, and be ready for more than Hamish could handle, but if he was solely interested in pleasure, he would've grown bored with Hamish by now.

Darshan scoffed. "You didn't know me back then."

"I've heard enough to get a good idea." His husband had become stuck in an endless cycle where the slightest sign of affection was pounced upon by his father or used by the court. He'd been cheated on as well as witnessed men willing to cheat for power and had others chased off at a word from the *Mhanek*, including friends.

In the face of that, how could he care about anyone beyond what brief joy they could offer?

The *Mhanek* opting to send Darshan to Tirglas had been the best thing the man could've done for his son. The time at sea would've given Darshan space to centre himself.

"The way I see it," Hamish continued. "Things would've ended differently if Binita's parents had listened to her, if they had chosen to unite their families rather than seeking to forge other connections." No doubt, they had sought some sort of compensation from the *Mhanek*, if not an attempt to set their son up as Darshan's consort. "Then they would still be here. And when trouble finally reared its head? They also could've petitioned your father for aid."

"They did. He turned them down. Even answering a simple plea could've been twisted into the *Mhanek* granting favouritism towards one of his son's flings."

"Dar..."

"Two families died through my actions. And what did I learn? Restraint? We both know I displayed none of that in Tirglas. Humility?" He laughed as though the thought was absurd. "No, I'll tell you what I learnt. That I can screw up—I can cause literal lives to be lost—and receive the love of the most amazingly sweet and gentle man in return. *I* get my chance at happiness. *They* don't even get a grave. *That's* why I'm in mourning for the woman who poisoned you."

Hamish's thoughts sunk into the memory of when he first learnt about the lives his mother had taken. That had been several decades ago and it still haunted him. For his husband, this was a fresh wound. Further proof that his actions had far-reaching consequences, as well as a dint in his pride.

He knew from experience that neither revelation was pleasant to swallow.

Darshan stood. "You know the worst thing?" he mumbled, walking along the top step until he was at the far end of the bed. He swung back to face Hamish, not waiting for an answer. "I could see myself going down that same path. If you hadn't pulled through. I—" His voice cracked. He rubbed at his beard. "I don't know what I would've done."

Hamish closed his eyes, taking a deep breath as he shut out the thought of leaving Darshan to continue on in the world alone. Would he have returned to the man he had been? Growing increasingly cold and distant until nothing could've lit up those hazel eyes again? "Me heart..."

"Look at me." Darshan spread his arms wide. "Do you still want this? Knowing how dangerous it can be at my side? Knowing what chaos I've caused, the lives my carelessness has taken?"

"Now you're just being daft," he gently chided. Where would he go? What would he do? Everything he had ever wanted was right here. "I—"

"Don't think I wouldn't give you every provision you could possibly desire. You are my light, I only want for your safety and your health wherever you choose to be."

"Love, where else would I want to be than at your side? You made a mistake, one that spiralled beyond your control, but so did they."

"*I'm* the *vris Mhanek*." He clutched at his chest as though he planned to rip his heart out. "I should've known better. I should've *been* better."

"You're nae the only one of status who has made a mess of things. Or have you forgotten that me mum is trying to start a war?" At least Darshan was willing to admit his faults. To improve.

Groaning, Darshan buried his face in his hands. "I had."

"I understand what you're feeling." His husband believed himself the seed of chaos and death? They were well-matched there with Hamish having also inadvertently sown his own crop of loss in his youth. "But you're also nae that man any more."

Darshan chuckled dryly. "He was hale and hearty when I first kissed you."

"I dinnae think so. He was a mask you'd forgotten how to doff." And had lost somewhere deep in Tirglas. "If you had been here, if they had laid out all the facts straight, you would've stopped it. But just because you couldnae do it doesnae make what happened your fault."

His husband stared out into the distance, toying with his rings in silence. He didn't look convinced, but he also didn't argue.

Hamish spread his arms, reaching out to him. "Come on, I think we both need another hug."

A soft snort of laughter escaped Darshan before he muffled it. Even so, he crawled onto the bed and back into Hamish's arms. This time, rather than curl up like a child in need of comfort, his husband opted to straddle Hamish's legs and drape his whole body atop him.

Hamish relished the extra weight. He had missed having Darshan near whilst he slept. He linked his fingers at the small of Darshan's back and, resting his chin atop the man's head, closed his eyes. Maybe like this, he would finally be able to get some decent rest and shake the lethargy clinging to his soul.

He couldn't have been lying there for more than a short moment before a familiar restlessness took his limbs. *Bloody tonic.* He couldn't fault it. The healers had said it was meant to energise him and it did. But with his lack of movement, it was his thoughts that raced instead.

"Dar?"

A drowsy, slightly querying, hum was the man's only reply. At least one of them was getting some rest.

"About the wedding."

"We've already spoken about that. Everyone has already been waiting several days. I'm certain they can linger for a few more until you feel strong enough. Don't worry about it."

"Aye," he murmured. It wasn't quite the wedding his thoughts had settled on. "But since we're speaking of people waiting on us... Are the Niholian spellsters still around?"

Darshan nodded. "Of course. They understand you've yet to recover your full strength, but they'll be ready when we are."

"Then let's nae delay them any further. What do we need to magically create this bairn?" Was it done with blood? A strand of hair? Darshan had given him no specifics, although he must've known after speaking with the Niholians.

His husband sat up, keeping himself from falling back onto Hamish's chest by bracing himself against it. "*Excuse me?*"

"I dinnae see any reason to wait for our vows to be said." He had agreed on the conception happening after the ceremony in the beginning because he saw little point in arguing over the timing. But if he hadn't pulled through in this last attempt, he wouldn't even have had the chance of a child. "Why cannae we do it before? Me brother's wife was halfway through her first pregnancy by the time he married her."

His husband leant further back in Hamish's grasp. "That was different. I doubt a child had been your brother's intention at the time."

Probably nae. He knew natural conception was haphazard. A couple conceiving that way could spend years or a day before the act became a successful one, if it happened at all. And where Darshan and Hamish might not be able to claim their own child as accidental, did that mean they couldn't just change their minds about when?

"We should be married under Udynean law by now," Hamish pointed out. It was *one* day. He clasped Darshan's shoulders. "Dinnae you think making this bairn is already clinical enough? We dinnae have to be so precise with the timing." How could either of them perform knowing people would expect them to trot out with the ingredients for new life on their wedding night?

Right now, no one would be waiting for them. The only expectations were of their own making.

His husband eyed him in the same fashion Hamish had gotten from the healers the last few days. "Now? Are you certain? The razor dust…" He shook his head. "Maybe it would be best if we waited until you've recovered all your strength."

"I'm strong enough to do this."

Uncertainty flickered across Darshan's face. He gnawed at his lip with such determination that Hamish was a surprise the man didn't bite a chunk off.

Hamish caressed his husband's cheek, running the pad of his thumb along the lay of his beard. "Dinnae think about why we're doing this. Or of what'll come after. It's just us." He grabbed Darshan's collar and dragged him closer. "Now, how about you show me how two men can make a bairn?"

That hazel gaze dropped. "Same way you grow anything." His lips curved, a hint of the Darshan he had first met lingering in the cocky tilt. His hands slid down Hamish's torso, stopping to untie the knot holding his smalls fast. "Start with the seed."

Chapter 51

Hamish stretched, groaning as he savoured the silken glide of the sheets against his skin. His whole body buzzed, satisfied beyond measure. Typically, when he reached the climax, he would float for a short moment, bask for a while longer, then return to the present.

This was definitely different.

Was it the way Darshan had worked him like their lives depended on it? Never had he been milked to the last drop quite so vigorously, not even on the rare occasions his husband sucked him dry.

Maybe it had to do with the revelation he had survived an attack that had been fatal to every other spellster. The high of just being alive. He hadn't felt it the first time Darshan brought him back from the brink of death in Tirglas, or after the poisoning with the miner's wax. But his mind had been preoccupied with other matters then, he'd had the space to think this time.

Beside him, Darshan gave a considering hum. As usual, it had taken the man a little longer to reach his end, but he had done so in a blaze of light and sparks. He dangled the wide-mouthed bottle containing his seed before his nose, critically examining the contents. "When I think of all the times before arriving at Tirglas where I had spilt such essence. Before forging this connection to the earth..." He lowered the bottle. "What a waste."

Hamish rolled onto his side. "But if you'd made a bairn back then, it wouldnae have been ours." The man's seed wouldn't have lasted long enough for Darshan to reach Tirglas, much less make the return trip. Not unless they managed had gotten one of those Ancient Domian preservation domes working.

Any time before now would've meant having a child with someone else.

Hamish wasn't sure how to feel about that. He had helped raise his nieces and nephews, but those children didn't doubt he was their uncle rather than a parent. How different would raising another person's child be if they saw him as their father? He wanted to believe it wouldn't have mattered. Certainly not for the child.

"I suppose that is true." Darshan bit his lip, his gaze drifting off to stare blankly at the ceiling.

"Love?" Hamish waited until his husband's head turned and those hazel eyes were focused on him. "What's wrong?" Had Darshan decided that now wasn't the right time after all?

"Nothing? Everything?" He clasped Hamish's hand, lifting it to his lips. "I know you want children, but I feel I'm entirely unprepared to be a father."

He'd heard that line before. Both from his brother and his sister's husband, not long before their wives were due to give birth. "It's nae as though you dinnae ken this was coming." The man had spoken of it numerous times since first confessing his love to Hamish.

Darshan returned to gazing up at the ceiling, his brow furrowed. "But shouldn't I *feel* ready?"

That was a familiar sentiment, too. One he knew how to deal with after talking his sister's husband down from his first-child panic. "Nae one is completely prepared. And it's nae as if the bairn will come immediately." If it worked at all. That was a possibility the Niholian breeders suggested they prepare themselves for.

Darshan nodded, a slight smile plumping his cheek. "I am aware of how children grow. And after that time is up? I become a father, even if I still don't know what I'm doing by then."

"You're never going to shake that feeling, Dar. From what I've witnessed from me siblings, nae parent does. Every wee bairn is a new experience. Even me sister couldnae predict what each one of her four children was going to be like." The unpredictability of it was the beauty of life.

"What if we wait?"

Hamish swallowed, relieved that the man's focus was on the ceiling rather than his face. "If we hold off until you feel ready, it'll never happen." He had already waited long enough for the chance. If someone bundled his child into his arms tomorrow, he wouldn't flinch.

Darshan scoffed. "I'm not talking about for long. Just another year. Give us time to settle."

Maybe it was because he was still recovering from his recent brush with death, but Hamish was very aware of his own mortality. They'd no guarantee that he would still be around in a year.

He was under no delusion that time would eventually run out for him. He was thirty-eight now. Waiting a year would mean the child was born when he was pushing forty. When they were ten, he'd be close to half a century old. His siblings would be grandparents by then.

And when his child was old enough to have children of their own?

Would he be around to enjoy watching his grandchildren grow for long? The average life expectancy in Tirglas wasn't in his favour. A man was lucky if he made seventy and blessed by the Goddess if he reached beyond eighty.

He doubted any of that had occurred to his husband, even if Darshan was only four years his junior. *Spellsters live longer*. Hamish had suspected that for some time. It stood to reason magic that healed a person instantly would also slow the ravages of age. Hamish could never have that ability.

Now could be all they had. He didn't want to waste it. But how could he begin to explain any of it to Darshan? "I dinnae want to wait any longer."

"I know. I just—" He trailed off with a blustery sigh.

Propping himself up on one elbow, Hamish gently coaxed his husband to continue. He'd clearly been holding back reservations the last time they spoke on this. It would be better for the both of them to get everything out in the open now.

"I'm making excuses, aren't I?" Darshan's self-mocking laugh bounced the bed. He released Hamish's hand to fist his own hair, tugging it hard enough that Hamish thought he might tear a clump out. "This is so foreign to me. I never considered children before you—not in any good light, at least—there's so much that could go wrong and what if, in the end, I become like my father? Or, may the gods protect me, some jaded bastard version of my grandfather?"

That last concern was similar to one Hamish had heard from his sister, which turned out to be bollocks. "You're nae going to turn into your father, me heart. *I* will be there to make sure of that. I assume I get to have a say raising our bairn, being their other parent and all."

"Gods," Darshan mumbled, rubbing at his temples. "I'm not even considering *that*, am I?"

"Like I've been saying, me heart. Everything will be fine. We'll figure it all out."

Darshan's shoulders shook in soundless laughter. "Always there to ground me with the truth." He smiled up at Hamish. "I love you, *mea lux*. And I promise I'll strive to be a man worthy of your affections."

"You already are." He brushed Darshan's cheek with the back of his finger. "And you... you were strong enough to face me mum, to battle for me hand. To face off against everything your own lands has tried to throw at us. This? This'll be nae obstacle."

Raw adoration shone in his husband's eyes. "You're definitely going to be the better father."

"I've had more practice guiding mood-swinging young men," he teased.

Darshan laid a hand upon his chest, his eyes widening in shocked offence. The whole effect was ruined by the sudden appearance of a broad and cocky grin. "I suppose you have. And that will likely serve you well in the court."

"Aye, I've seen how petty they can be."

Still grinning, and with his face once more flushed with his usual confidence, Darshan wriggled off the bed. He hopped to his feet with enviable ease to trot down the stairs and set both bottles on the table before beginning to dress. "Do you feel well enough to walk? I assume you wish to be there at the conception."

Hamish chuckled. "Well, traditionally, the father is there for at least *that*." He swung his feet over the side of the bed, testing how well his legs held his weight. The Niholian breeders were situated a few floors down. "I think I can manage stairs."

Nodding, Darshan slipped into his tunic and opened the door.

Several men stood outside, all wearing the red garb of the Nulled Ones.

Hamish snatched the blanket, swiftly covering himself, but the Nulled Ones seemed more interested in Darshan's presence than his own. They bowed to the man, fanning out in anticipation of his exit.

"Alert the Niholian breeders we are ready for them," Darshan commanded. "And see that Anjali joins us," he added before pushing the door shut.

Sealed away from any idly roaming eyes, Hamish released his hold on the blanket and slowly descended the stairs. "There were guards outside me door?" He hadn't noticed any standing there when his husband entered or when his previous visitors left. "How long have they been there?"

"Always. Father insisted."

"I just thought..." His cheeks grew hotter with each word. "You're nae exactly quiet." They must've heard Darshan.

"They're Nulled Ones," his husband said as if Hamish hadn't been able to tell from the uniform. "They would've heard worse." His husband eyed him, no doubt taking in the careful way Hamish walked. "Are you certain you're up to the journey?"

"It's just down a few stairs," Hamish muttered as he tugged on his smalls. If he couldn't manage that, then it was time to strap him into one of those floating chairs he'd witnessed whilst helping the court evacuate the guest palace.

"The Niholians will want to do their task in a sterile environment, which means the infirmary." Darshan plucked at his bottom lip. "Shall I see to it that your horse is made ready? Or maybe one a little closer to the ground?"

"I'm nae an invalid, Dar," he growled, hauling up his trousers with more force than he needed. "I can walk." After a week of bed rest, it would do him a world of good to get his body back into the idea of moving under its own power.

Darshan stopped him as he went to don his undershirt. His husband placed a hand on Hamish's chest. The slight coolness of the man's rings was fast replaced by the warmth of magic flooding Hamish's body, gently shaking the tiredness from his bones. "You certainly seem fit enough. No ill effects from the razor dust." His voice grew smaller the more he spoke.

"I told you, love." Hamish laid his hand atop Darshan's, curling his other beneath the man's chin and tipping it upward. There was no mistaking the faint sheen of tears being held back. "I'm fine. You dinnae have to worry about me so much. We Tirglasians build our people sturdy."

One side of Darshan's mouth lifted in a smile, the whisper of his grief lingering in the corner. "That they do." He closed the small space between them, squeezing Hamish's torso, his cheek pressed to Hamish's chest. "And for that, I am grateful."

Wrapping his arms around Darshan's shoulders, Hamish breathed deeply of the scent that emanated from his husband. The usual sweet aroma of perfume was nonexistent, leaving only the freshness of grass after the rain that was purely Darshan. *Home.*

He hadn't realised how much he missed it.

As they stood in silence, his gaze alighted on the box sitting next to the bottles, the one that held the glass flower. No one had moved it since he had put it there on the day of his poisoning. He had expected to awake and find someone had already gifted it to Darshan as some manner of mollification over Hamish's state. Had everyone assumed the flower had been for himself? Did it even still hold the flower? He would be pissed if they had taken it.

Wordlessly slipping out of Darshan's grip, Hamish staggered over to the table. He picked up the bottles to move them.

A muffled exclamation of protest reached Hamish's ears. "Don't you think you should finish getting dressed before we descend?"

Hamish nodded absently. He might not be cold standing in this closed off room, but he didn't plan to cross the courtyards without a shirt. "I'm nae going to be long." He dragged the box across the tabletop, the wood giving a slight screech.

A peek confirmed its contents. The flower twinkled in the lantern light as if winking secretly.

Certain that nerves would see his legs give if stood for long, he settled on the chair and gestured for Darshan to join him. The box sat between them like a shield. His stomach bubbled with a hectic mix of boyish eagerness and sudden uncertainty. He'd never courted anyone, much less given them a romantic gift. There'd only been the ornaments he would whittle for his family.

Like the mouse. He had been caught off guard at the closeness of Darshan's birthday and, even though Darshan owned hundreds of fancy trinkets, Hamish had wanted to give him something. He hadn't expected how pleased the man had been with the simple gift. He treated the wooden mouse reverently, giving it pride of place in his study.

Knowing that this flower would likely receive similar adoration was the only thing keeping the tightness from his throat.

Nevertheless, he felt his smile waver slightly as he slid the box closer to his husband. "For you."

Darshan took it, murmuring his perplexed gratitude. "You got me a gift?" Sudden alarm took his face and lifted his voice. "Is that a standard Tirglasian practice amongst newly-weds? Gordon didn't mention anything beyond a crest."

Chuckling, Hamish shook his head. "It's nae that. Just open it."

Darshan obeyed, gasping as he flipped back the lid. "*Mea lux,*" he breathed. "You got me an everlasting bloom?" He tenderly took hold of the vibrantly green stem, lifting it from its velvet bed. The blueness of the petals gleamed in the light. Away from the haze of the furnaces and brash sunlight, it looked far more fragile than those of an actual flower.

Hamish rubbed at the back of his neck. "You said it's customary for men to gift each other flowers. I thought, since you couldnae—" He fell silent as Darshan laid a hand on his shoulder.

"It's beautiful. I—" Darshan's voice cracked slightly. He looked on the verge of tears. "I love it."

Hamish beamed. Warmth returned to his core, the same fuzzy kind as when he had gifted the wooden mouse. It washed away the foolish uncertainty and reinvigorated his body. Was this how Darshan felt every time? No wonder he was always giving Hamish things.

Darshan traced the minute details on the petals, seemingly lost to the world. "No one has ever given me a flower before." Even his voice sounded distant. "Gold. Jewels." He gave a soft self-mocking laugh. "*People.* Never a simple flower." His gaze lifted. "Just when I'm sure I know everything about you, you go and surprise me."

More heat surged to his face. "I'm nae that complicated, me heart." Wrapping an arm around Darshan's waist, he drew the man closer.

"And you deserve soft things."

A faint redness kissed his husband's cheeks. "When did you have the time to buy this? From memory, the man who makes these doesn't do palace visits."

Hamish nodded, even though he didn't understand why the glass smith wouldn't oblige the crown. But he had ventured into the city on the only day where it had been allowed. "The second day of our marriage ceremony, before..." Hamish's throat tightened on the memory, how the pain had danced like knives through his body. He coughed, trying to shrug the feeling before Darshan caught on. "Before the meal with me family."

"I see." Darshan rolled the glass stem between his fingers. The glow from the lanterns glittered off the petals. "Since we are in a giving mood." He set the flower reverently back into its box. "How about I show my appreciation?"

Before Hamish could think of an answer, his husband flung his arms around Hamish's neck and pressed their lips firmly together.

Hamish lost track of how long they remained there, him seated and half-clothed, his husband draped over him, clinging as though he feared Hamish might yet disappear. It didn't matter. He would linger all day if it helped.

Eventually, Darshan disentangled them and let Hamish finish dressing so they could deliver the bottles to the two Niholian women waiting for them in the infirmary.

His stomach bubbled at the thought. He had prayed to the Goddess for a way to have children of his own for so long, it was finally on the way towards happening. *Please, let this work.* He would ask for nothing else for the rest of his life if she granted him this. He'd *want* for nothing else.

Chapter 52

They descended the stairs, slowly so as to not agitate the bottles' contents. Darshan kept a close eye on his husband, ready to catch the man should his legs give. They hadn't for the last three flights of stairs, but the fourth could be what did him in. Or even the trek out through the imperial gates and across the palace grounds to the infirmary.

What had he been thinking, doing this now with the man still recovering from the razor dust?

But Hamish had given him the soft look that never failed to turn Darshan's will to water. *And here we are.* Other men would've sought to abuse such an obvious weak spot.

Darshan wasn't even certain if his husband knew the power he had over him.

They turned the corner and Darshan spied the familiar figure of his eldest half-sister at the far end of the hallway. *Wonderful.* He hadn't seen her since his grief-riddled attempt on her life. The last thing he needed right now was another confrontation.

Darshan ushered his husband along, trying to hurry the man without appearing flustered. His half-sister didn't appear to have noticed them and he'd rather not linger for her to get the chance.

They were almost to the next set of stairs when Onella called his name.

He whirled about to face her. *Of all the cheek.* A shield shimmered around him at the mere thought. He kept himself between her and his husband as he forced his expression to remain civil. "Was there something you required, sister dear?"

Onella regarded the display with amusement. "No. I just wasn't expecting either of you to be out and about." She looked Hamish over. "I see your toy is recovering well."

Even though Hamish stood at his back, Darshan felt the man tense. He could picture those bushy brows lowering into a scowl and the annoyance flashing in that blue gaze.

"You—" Darshan froze as he went to take a step closer only to have his husband's hand alight on his shoulder. He took a deep breath and clenched his teeth. "You really don't know when to keep your mouth shut, do you?" he growled.

Humming, Onella examined her nails. Her fingertips were stained with dark dye. "At least *I* can contain my emotions enough to not threaten the lives of everyone around me in a tantrum. By the way..." She glanced up, her expression turning sombre. "Vinata had her child this morning. A *son*." She smiled slightly, the corners of her eyes looking pinched. "Just as the priests predicted."

"That's—" Hamish fell silent as Darshan tapped the back of his hand on the man's chest.

"*Had?*" he queried, peering at his half-sister. He'd heard that phrase used too many times when it came to fallen nephews and it wouldn't be the first time Onella orchestrated infanticide. Nothing was ever traced back to her, of course, but it was awfully convenient that Tarendra was the only surviving grandson out of all the *Mhanek's* children.

Onella sneered. "You can't pin this one on me. I had nothing to do with it. The cord was around his neck."

Darshan closed his eyes. *Oh, Vin.* Snatched away in the end by some twist of fate. The same end that could come to any of them.

"Can they nae save the wee lad?"

Yes. If the child wasn't gone for too long and the midwives were quick. Would they have tried? That was the actual question.

"I don't know what fables my brother has fed you," Onella replied. "But magic is not some cure-all. And death is not something lightly reversed."

Except, hadn't *he* done just that with Hamish? And the pest of a horse he had ridden all the way from Tirglas. Were bear attacks and poisonings that different to this? *Maybe.* But maybe not.

If he could get to Vinata's son before they disposed of the body...

Darshan opened his eyes, pinning his half-sister to the spot with a glare. "Where's Vin right now?"

She shrugged. "The infirmary?"

He nodded. Of course she was there. The healers would want to look over Vinata and possibly the baby.

Shoving the bottle he held into Hamish's hand, he turned on his heel to stride down the hall. Every step had him a mere hop away from breaking into a run.

"Dar?" Hamish called. He tried to match Darshan's pace, but was quickly left behind. "What's the rush?"

"Don't you dare do what I think you're up to!" Onella screamed after him. "Vin won't thank you for it!"

She would if his efforts bore fruit. And what was bad about trying? His sisters had already lost too many children over the years. He wasn't going to let another slip away.

His descent through the princess palace became a blur. People scrambled to get out of his path. He took the stairs two—three—at a time, uncaring that he risked his neck with every leap. Too much time had already been wasted.

Outside, the horse he had ordered for his husband waited. He vaulted aboard, barely settling into the saddle before urging the beast into a gallop. *The gates.* Why did they always have to be closed? He flung a sky spark into the air above the imperial gatehouse.

The gates opened sluggishly.

Rather than wait for the guards to declare it safe, Darshan bolted through as soon as the gap was big enough. He aimed the horse for the other gate between them and Vinata's son. Those manning the second gatehouse, perhaps seeing him streaking across the courtyard like a madman, were quicker to respond to his demand of entry.

He tore through the entrance.

The flash of a person walking the path ahead was all the warning he had before his mount reared and threw him to the paved ground. Pain flared down his side, the sting of abrasions and the deeper ache of a broken rib. The buzz of healing nipped at their heels.

Darshan rolled to his feet, gritting his teeth against the persistent throbbing in his shoulder. Looking for his mount, he caught the animal's flank disappearing around the side of a building. *Damn beast.* He didn't have time to chase it down.

The infirmary wasn't that far. *On foot it is.*

He limped on as his magic continued to mend his injuries, running as soon as he stopped feeling as though his footfalls would shatter his bones.

Unlike the last time he had ventured near the infirmary, there was only the usual handful of guards outside. They saluted as he trotted up, granting him entrance without a word. He must've looked a state. Sweaty and dirty from the fall.

A brief query to a passing servant led him to Vinata. He burst into the room, barely taking the time to register who was within before stalking over to the bedside where Vinata sat clutching her son. She watched his approach with fearful confusion. Never had he seen her pale face so blotchy or her eyes so red.

He would make it better. It was his duty as elder brother and *uris Mhanek.*

"I'm so sorry, Vin. I just heard." He held out his hands. "May I?"

Panic widened her eyes and dropped her still trembling chin. She glanced over his shoulder, seeking guidance.

A figure moved on his periphery. Little more than a blur.

Yaatin. He didn't much like Vinata's husband. Yaatin wasn't a bad man. A bit reclusive, often nose-deep in his botany studies, and he treated his sister well. Still, something about him always rubbed Darshan the wrong way.

Darshan brushed the man aside, pinning him into a chair with a blast of wind, ignoring his spluttering objections.

"I wish there was time to explain more," he said, turning back to his sister. "But I think I can bring your son back."

Pity crumpled her face. "Darshi..." She tightened her hold around the bundle. Fresh tears flowed down her cheeks. "It's too late. He's—" She bowed over her son, keening.

He gently lifted the bundle from her grasp. "I promise, Vin, I shall do my best." The child was still warm thanks to the blankets and his mother's heat. This was still going to take a lot of power. More than he alone had to give. *Help me,* he beseeched the earth. He'd already used himself as a conduit once, what harm was there in doing it again?

A vine erupted through the floorboards to a chorus of screams.

He glanced over his shoulder to find several healers crammed in the doorway. *Fools.* Darshan wrapped the tendril around his wrist and let his magic slip into the little body. A shudder slunk up his spine and settled in his shoulder. Delving into the dead, even the recently departed, was never pleasant.

Unlike with a living being, there was no natural flow to the power he poured into the baby. It settled everywhere like water into a dam. The picture it gave was too much to make out anything clearly. There didn't seem to be any abnormalities that would drag him back to the other side. Just an ill-fated act.

Well, he had already held fate in his hands and moulded it to his will.

Heart first. If he got it beating again, got the blood flowing, that would be half the battle. He knew how, he hadn't ever attempted it on anyone so small, but what else could be done?

He placed two fingers on the baby's chest, concentrating on sending the smallest of sparks from them to the heart. The body in his grasp twitched. Another second shock had the limbs stiffening. He tried a third.

"What are you doing?" Yaatin demanded. "Stop it this instant!"

Darshan held up his hand, silently commanding the man to wait. The third shock had the heart give a sluggish thump. *Please.* He coaxed his magic to go deeper. *Just a little more.* He gave the tiny heart another shock.

Something tugged at his magic, a flailing force that sought to drain him. He dropped to his knees, halted from falling further by his hold on the vine. Fire danced through his veins, robbing him of his voice. He had felt this pull just the once.

When he brought Hamish back from the clutches of death.

His magic flowed from him, rushing to replace what had already started to decay, to set organs to work, to get the blood pumping. The baby's heart pounded a frantic tempo, Darshan's own close to bursting as it fought to match. The will to live was strong, but the body attached to it was too weak to act on its own, to get what it needed the most.

Air.

Like steering a water-laden boat through a storm, he guided his magic to the task at hand. He needed to get the lungs working, but every time he tried to direct the course, his magic slipped from his grasp.

He bent over the small body in his arms until the tip of their noses touched. Focusing for one brief burst, he let his own breath slip out of his mouth, guiding the air up his nephew's tiny, flat nose and down. It left Darshan dizzy, but he could think of no other way to fill those lungs.

Darshan sat there, waiting. Hoping. Praying. The drain on his magic didn't lessen. He gave over another breath, his head spinning on the point of collapse. *Be enough.* Any more and he would pass out. He couldn't risk that.

A thin wail pierced his senses.

Tears welled in his eyes at the sound, blurring everything. He didn't need to see.

His nephew wriggled in his arms, tiny limbs thrashing haphazardly as they sought for something to cling to.

Darshan rocked back, almost falling to the ground. As it was, he swayed on the spot. He didn't care. He'd done it! He had brought the baby back. His nephew! Vinata's son would live.

He could reverse *death* itself!

Someone took the baby from him. The murmur of too many voices filled his ears. *The healers.* He wiped beneath his glasses, trying to clear his sight. Only once he relented and cleaned the lenses did the world come back into focus.

Sure enough, healers crowded around the child. They muttered amongst themselves, occasionally looking his way.

From her place still in the bed, Vinata strained to see over them.

Anger clamped around Darshan's chest. He had saved the boy and the first thing the healers did was poke and prod at the child as though it was some hitherto unseen creature. "Give him to her," he croaked.

The healers paused in their examination. They eyed him with a wariness that only further ignited his blood.

"I said," he snarled. "Give my sister back her baby!"

They scrambled to obey, bundling the child into his blankets and slipping him into Vinata's arms. His sister stared at her son with a smile that wavered as though she would burst into tears again.

"Leave!" Darshan commanded the healers, wobbling to his feet with the aid of the vine. The last thing either parent needed was a bunch of people observing their child like an experiment. He glowered at the healers as they hastened out the door, their exit hindered only by the bulk of his husband in the doorway.

Hamish stood like a statue, his mouth hanging open. He barely moved as the healers slipped by. The bottles they had filled, in a time that seemed an age ago, still dangled in his hand.

Darshan joined his husband in the doorway, collecting the bottles lest they slipped from Hamish's fingers. Which was whose? He didn't know anymore. Hopefully, that detail wouldn't matter.

Hamish continued staring ahead, barely blinking. "You—"

"Yes, me." Darshan gently ushered the man out into the hall, gesturing down it in the direction of where the Niholian breeders would've set up their equipment. Did the duo still wait for them? "Shall we leave the parents to their bonding?"

His husband followed, no less bemused. "You brought him back."

"I did." He laid a hand on his chest as they strolled down the empty hall. His heart still pounded something fierce, but it was slowing.

"Are you all right?" They both knew how much it had taken out of Darshan when he healed the mauling Hamish received from that bear. Without the man recovering well enough to practically carry Darshan out of the forest, he wouldn't have made it back to the Tirglasian capital alive.

But this had been different. He hadn't used himself to the point of exhaustion. The familiar weariness of overuse was still there, manageable but jiggling in the back of his head like a half-forgotten tune. "Given rest and food, I shall be fine. I'm just glad it worked."

They turned a corner, then another, heading down a different, but no less vacant, hall. Where was everyone? Had the healers and servants been evacuated from the building? He wasn't a danger.

Hamish laid a hand on his shoulder, squeezing almost to the point of it being painful. "Dinnae make a habit of it, all right? I dinnae want to lose you."

"I promise, I'm not about to go gallivanting off trying to bring back every fallen soul." He knew what he had done—even in his elation of bringing the child back, he had known. *Used forbidden magic.* The laws were stringent on what could and should be done. The dead were meant to stay dead. Bringing them back perverted the natural way of life.

It's just a baby. His nephew hadn't even taken his first breath. *Father'll smooth things over.* He would claim the child wasn't completely dead, that the healers had made a mistake.

The alternative was to return Vinata's son to his original state and not a soul in the senate would demand that.

They finally reached the room. By the murmurs on the other side, the Niholian breeders definitely waited. Darshan's stomach fluttered. If things went smoothly, their own child would be conceived today.

Hamish halted him outside the door. "Before we go in to do this. Those other options you mentioned? How many of them are doable that didnae require either of us to be adulterous?"

"Realistically? A couple." He had hoped there'd be more choices, but after speaking with the Niholians and his twin, they'd the option of a different surrogate or him artificially impregnating a suitable woman.

He had hoped the idea of Hamish doing something similar with Anjali, but she had sharply reminded him that it wouldn't work. Even if he officially claimed the child as his heir, or if they lied about the Niholian breeders having a hand in it, someone would find out the truth. It would only take a smidgen of doubt and their son would spend the rest of his life defending his parentage. He refused to risk that all for ease.

Darshan strode into the room.

The Niholian breeders barely paused in setting out instruments, several he'd never seen before. One involved a tube set on a spindly frame that the woman kept peering down and adjusting.

Was it one of the fabled magnifiers? He'd heard about them during his days in the healing academy when the instructors spoke of advanced healing techniques. Always in that same coveting tone.

If one was needed for this conception technique to work, then no wonder the Niholians kept it secret. Magnifiers weren't a thing easily made. They required the most exquisite lenses and expert handling. Both skills the neighbouring empire guarded well. Even sketches didn't make it to curious eyes.

"Where's your sister?" Hamish asked, breaking the fascinated hold the magnifier had on Darshan.

He tore his gaze from the instrument to take in the rest of the room. A high-set bed sat near the table where the Niholians worked, ready for its patient. There was a screen placed by the door, shielding the modesty of anyone in the room from casual entry. No places for a person to be hiding.

No Anjali.

Had she changed her mind? She'd given no indication. Or had that been mere politeness in the face of Hamish's condition?

They had no backup and it would take time to find someone suitable. Too many would eagerly accept, if only to use the child as leverage later on. *Or abscond with them.* His twin would never, but someone else...

He hadn't even considered anyone would kidnap a newborn until Daama brought it up. The idea of people making off with a baby that wasn't theirs shouldn't have surprised him, slavers did it all the time, despite the laws his grandfather had put in place.

"Maybe she's still on her way?" Darshan suggested. Anjali could be anywhere within the palace grounds. If she was in her usual spot within the palace gardens, then she had quite the trek to here.

"You speak of your surrogate?" asked one of the breeders, waving away their concerns. "Her presence? It matters not for the moment. Is that our raw material?" She took the bottles from Darshan, holding each one close as she peered into the cloudy glass. "Who has the stronger magic?"

"Him," Hamish said, indicating Darshan. "Nae contest. But—"

The woman chuckled. "Let me guess, you cannot remember whose is whose?" Grunting, she returned to stand before the magnifier, upending the bottles' contents into two smaller vessels.

Curious, Darshan slunk up beside the woman. He watched as she placed a droplet onto a sliver of glass and slid it beneath the tube. "How does this work? If you're allowed to tell me," he swiftly added. Niholians were a prickly lot when it came to their methods, even those that weren't jealously guarded.

"We are all made of two halves in the beginning." She cupped her hands, bringing them together with a crack. "At conception, those halves fuse to make one when—"

"Yes, I know all that." His father had sired a daughter practically every year since Darshan's birth and into his twenties. Whilst only a dozen lived now, his sisters ranged from his thirty-four years to eleven. He was very aware of how natural reproduction worked. "I mean, how does it work with two men. They don't naturally fuse."

The woman pursed her lips. "Have you ever tried using magic to transform a person? To change their appearance?"

Darshan shook his head. "That's impossible." Healers had tried for centuries. All they had managed to cause was unbearable pain.

"Quite. But this is similar to such altering. Both halves are susceptible. And why not?" She peered down the tube. "They are designed to rapidly change. Coaxing one into a receiving form is simple. Nature takes it from there."

"Then why do so many fail?" If it was as easy as she claimed, it wouldn't still be considered experimental.

She looked up from the magnifier. "The problem lies within the surrogate. It's easier with women because we deal with their own material. The body will always prefer its own. Now hush." She flapped her hand at him. "I must concentrate."

He sheepishly backed away to stand next to Hamish. Maybe he should've specified the servant take a horse to hasten his sister along.

The door banged open, causing everyone to jump.

Anjali hastened around the end of the screen, her hair plastered to her forehead and her clothes in shambles. Judging by the dirt on her skirts, his summons had pulled her away from tending to her menagerie.

She casually made her way to his side, before grasping Darshan's arm and dragging him off into the far corner of the room. "What happened to waiting until after the wedding?" she whispered in Ancient Domian, eyeing the Niholian breeders with a heavy degree of suspicion the entire time. "Have they forced a time limit on you?"

"Of course not." With their services originally planned several days ago, he had expected it, but the Niholians took the obstacle in stride.

"Then what's going on? The man you sent seemed to think it was urgent."

Shrugging, Darshan indicated his husband with the tilt of his head. "Someone decided we've waited long enough."

Her lips rounded in a silent exclamation. She twisted the mass of her hair upon itself, knotting it with a deftness that he had never managed even when the strands fell to his waist as hers did now. "Never thought *you* would be responsible for conception outside of wedlock," she quipped, returning to Udynean.

Laughter bubbled out of Darshan's lips, the sound mostly nerves. Unlike one or two of his half-sisters, he hadn't ever been placed in a position where such was possible.

"Oh aye," Hamish teased. "He's a right rebel making it halfway through a wedding first."

"We are almost ready," announced the woman standing by the magnifier without so much as a glance up from her task.

Anjali's eyes lit up at the sight of the instrument. "Is that what I think it is?"

"Yes," Darshan said. "But let's not get distracted. You can ogle later."

The second Niholian, the one who hadn't spoken a word since their arrival, came over with a small bundle of cloth. "I'll be sure to talk Irina into letting you look through it afterwards. But first, come with me." She guided Anjali behind a second screen.

The rustle of fabric spoke of clothes being discarded. When his sister reappeared, she was garbed in a plain robe. She trotted over to the high bed, clambering onto it.

"Remember," the woman said as she assisted Anjali in lying down. "No magic. Not from you or any others upon your person."

Anjali nodded as though she'd heard the warning before. It was possible. She had spent a great deal of time with the pair since their arrival.

No one had uttered a word of it to Darshan. "What's this?" he demanded. *No magic?* How was she supposed to defend herself if someone attacked? *Father's going to be livid.* He would confine Anjali to the imperial palace at the very least.

"We are creating life through unnatural means," the woman replied patiently, clearly having had this conversation with other men. "Magic interferes and attempts to correct our changes. You risk losing the child if it is used on them, or your sister, before six months."

"Although, we recommend until after birth," Irina added. She strode over with a small bowl and funnel.

Uncertainty bubbled in Darshan's gut at the sight. The end of the funnel was quite long and narrow, as well as slightly curved. He didn't need to ask what they planned on doing with the instruments. But, after witnessing the delicate way Irina had utilised the magnifier, he had expected the rest of the procedure to have the same finesse.

"I would suggest you take this opportunity to leave," said the other woman. "And don't worry, we make our patients unconscious for the next part. Your sister won't feel a thing."

Darshan clasped Anjali's hand, loosening his grip when she winced. "Allow me to stress that you can still back out of this. I'm certain we can find someone else willing to take up a surrogate position."

Scowling, Anjali batted his concerns aside with an imperious flick of her wrist. "Nonsense. If anyone is carrying the miracle combination of my brother and his husband's child to term, it's going to be *me*. Frankly, I'm appalled you would even *consider* anyone else as suitable."

"But—"

She once again flapped her hands at him as if shooing one of her unruly animals out of the garden. "Hamish, dear?" she called out to his husband who was already on the other side of the screen. "Could you please take my worrywart of brother back to your room? I think he needs more rest than you do."

Gently cupping Darshan's elbow, Hamish turned him from the bed and towards the door.

Rest. Darshan didn't think he could, not knowing that they were close to becoming expecting parents.

He glanced over his shoulder at the trio before the view disappeared behind the screen, catching the Niholian woman rendering his sister unconscious with a delicate tap to the forehead. *No going back.* This either worked or it didn't. How long until they knew? Days? Weeks?

He turned back to Hamish. His husband was oddly quiet. "Do you think you're well enough to proceed with our wedding?"

"Aye," Hamish replied. "I think I can manage that."

Darshan lengthened his pace, towing Hamish. It would take a few days to wrangle the court, but the faster they spoke their vows, the sooner the nobles would disperse, limiting the danger to his sister and their baby.

Chapter 53

arshan paced up and down the room, eyeing the door leading to the temple's main hall. The priestess had seen him shuffled into here almost as soon as he had arrived at the temple, instructing him to remain whilst the court settled. It was strange, waiting for everyone else to be seated before he presented himself. Usually, he was the one already ensconced on his throne.

He wished he wasn't waiting alone, wished he had something to occupy his mind other than the nervous dread worming through his thoughts. *Anjali.* She would've nattered off his ears with news amongst her animals, gotten him lost in which one she spoke of until he needed her to start over.

But he couldn't call on her. Although she would be nearby, seated in the front row and surrounded by Nulled Ones alongside their father, the Niholian breeders had impregnated her with Hamish and Darshan's child only two days ago. This was the uncertain stage where even the Niholians couldn't predict whether what they had done would take root and grow.

His stomach bubbled at the new thought. Was he going to vomit? That wouldn't be the best sign to start the day on. *Deep breaths.* He tried. It did little to soothe his nerves.

Why was seating everyone taking so long? Surely it was time for him to stand before the altar. Where was the bell signalling for him to enter? After so many wasted days, he wanted this ceremony over with, to get on with his life without anyone able to question the legality of his marriage.

How was Hamish holding up with all this hanging around? *Most likely better than myself.* The sheer patience of that man.

Darshan settled on the bench, the sole seating in the room. He leant back against the wall and closed his eyes. The stone's coolness soaked through his wedding attire. It didn't slow his buzzing mind, but it did halt the descent of him turning into a sweaty mess. He toyed with the old signet ring. He'd had it for years. Hanging around his neck as a child, then resized several times as he grew from lanky teen into a man. But it was time to lay it aside and take up a new crest, one that included his husband.

He wished Hamish was back at his side. The man would be in the foyer by now, being tended to by his brother and Zahaan, waiting to walk up the aisle.

Darshan had chafed at that. The role was typically reserved for those lesser in power and, being a prince, Hamish was definitely his equal. But the high priestess refused to have them walk to the altar together and Hamish seemed unconcerned with the idea. As far as Darshan had been able to gather, that was what the men in Tirglas typically did during their weddings.

The door creaked open, jolting Darshan upright in his seat. Was it time? Had he somehow dozed off and missed the bell?

His father's head appeared through the gap. "Darshi?" He fully entered the room, joining Darshan on the bench.

Dread clutched at Darshan's chest as he took in his father's stiff posture. Had something gone wrong? Was Hamish all right? Was it Anjali? It didn't sound chaotic enough outside for any attack.

"Son?" His father cleared his throat with a blustery cough. "There comes a time in a man's life when he—"

Nervous laughter barked out Darshan's mouth. "I think you're a little late for the sex talk." By at least a few decades.

Not that his father had been there to give it when the time came. As Daama had done with most things, she'd schooled himself—alongside his twin and her son—on all she knew of the subject. When he and Zahaan had disclosed they were interested in men, she took it in stride by roping in a Nulled One with similar preferences to tutor them on the rest.

Pursing his lips disapprovingly, his father continued, "I want to apologise. I know I'm not the perfect parent. Gods, sometimes I forget just how old you actually are." He ran a hand over his head, removing the crown that sat atop his greying hair. "My only defence is in wanting you to have—"

"A child?" Darshan finished, smiling brightly in a manner that he knew would annoy the man. This was meant to be his and Hamish's day, no one was going to ruin it. "Well, you get your wish."

His father stared down at the crown dangling in his grasp. "What I've always wanted," he said, his voice strangely soft. "Above all, was for you to have the same happiness I had with your mother. Seeing you intent on travelling the self-destructive path has pained me for a great many years. There were times I wondered if you would even live long enough to inherit your birthright."

Darshan remained quiet. Whilst it was true he had long since thrown away the idea of living with restraint for a life of drunken debauchery, he'd never knowingly done anything that would've endangered his wellbeing. He hadn't been aware his father held such concerns for him, especially with his nephew right there, still young enough to be moulded into the perfect *Mhanek*.

His father smiled. "But you found your way back without my meddling."

"Not completely," he admitted, his thoughts turning to the giant of a man with fiery-red hair and stunning sapphiric eyes. Of the soft brogue when Hamish spoke and the timbre of his laugh. The way the man's smile made the world shine brighter. "I never would've set foot in Tirglas without you sending me there." To think he might have missed it all if he had lived a proper life.

"If he is your flame eternal as you claim, the gods would've found a way. They always do."

No. Any other way would've been too late. If the countess his father originally picked as the ambassador had actually gone, the union contest for Hamish's hand would've advanced as normal. And Hamish would've taken his life to avoid a feud amongst the clans over his refusal, just as he had attempted by goading the bear that mauled him. It had almost succeeded with Darshan there. If it had happened *without* him?

He couldn't tolerate the thought for long without his chest aching.

His father knew nothing of it beyond the odd rumour. Nor was it Darshan's place to tell him.

"I admit," his father continued, clapping an arm around Darshan's shoulders. "When I first heard your announcement through the singing crystal, I was certain the messenger had misheard. All those years I struggled to instil a sense of responsibility, of ownership, to your heritage. The times I had despaired you would ever find someone you deemed worthy of settling down with. And *children?*" Chuckling, his father shook his head. "I had completely given up on you ever having an interest in producing an heir. Then he comes into our lives."

Darshan squirmed, waiting for the barbed comments on Hamish's nature. Frustration collected in the corners of his eyes. Was his father really choosing *now* to criticise Darshan's choice?

"He's good for you. Any fool can see that." His father bowed his head, the corners of his mouth curving into an embarrassed smile. "*I* should've seen it sooner."

All the usual snide comments and sarcastic retorts caught in

Darshan's throat.

"And, Darshi?" He tightened his grip around Darshan's shoulders, shaking them slightly. "I'm proud of you."

He stared at his father, unable to believe what he had heard. *Proud?* His father hadn't shown pride in him since the first time he learnt how to summon his shield at will.

"I know don't say it often enough, but..." He rubbed at his nose, sniffing and giving a small cough. "You might not have grown the way I expected, but I'm proud of the man you've become and I think—" His brow creased slightly, then he smiled, his brown eyes red around the edges. "I *know* your mother would've been, too."

The world turned blurry. Darshan blinked madly, fighting to keep his vision clear as well as to stop the kohl from smudging. He could've weathered the derision of standing before the court looking as though he had been wandering in the rain for hours, but to present himself to *Hamish* in such a state? *Unthinkable.* Of course, his glorious light wouldn't care about such details, but the man deserved Darshan's best.

Only once he was certain the waterworks were under control did he face his father again. He swallowed, forcing his throat to work, seeking the words he wanted to say. "Father, I—"

The temple bells rang their dull, almost mournful, knell. Not exactly the cheery beginning to a wedding.

"Sounds like it's time for you to get married." His father patted him on the back as he stood.

A soft chuckle bubbled up his throat. He stilled the urge to retort how he already was, no matter the true legalities, and followed his father out the door.

~ ~ ~

"Hold still," Zahaan growled. The man had fussed over Hamish's attire from the moment they arrived at the temple, straightening the seams and smoothing out any wrinkle that dared show itself. He currently stitched a poorly sewn button back onto Hamish's collar, muttering under his breath.

The man probably would've been done if Hamish was able to remain kneeling in place without his leg bouncing like a boarhound new to the hunt.

"Sorry," Hamish mumbled for what felt like the umpteenth time. He had managed to restrain himself from wandering all over the temple foyer, but that didn't mean his body was content with being at rest.

Finally, Zahaan cut the thread and stood back to critically eye his handiwork. "Are you all right? You're shaking something fierce."

"I'd wager it's nerves," Gordon replied as the elf gave Hamish's collar one final adjustment. "I got me insides so knotted during me wedding that I almost threw up at the altar."

Hamish laughed. "I remember." His brother had looked so unwell, that everyone, even his newly-wedded wife, had expected Gordon to vomit as soon as he tried to speak his vows. "But I dinnae feel sick." A little anxious about why they were still waiting, maybe, and definitely ready to get on with the ceremony, but not ill. "What's taking them so long?" Everyone had to be seated by now.

His brother smiled. "What's the rush? I doubt Darshan's planning to skip out on you."

"I ken that." He stood, absently smoothing his sherwani to the sound of Zahaan's irritated hiss. Throughout all the doubts Darshan had expressed over the months, marrying Hamish had never been one of them.

A bell rang from somewhere deep within the temple. That was his betrothed's cue to take up position by the burning brazier of the Eternal Flame.

Hamish swallowed the lump welling in his throat and, with a final tug at his sherwani, stepped towards the closed doors, waiting for the second bell.

At his back, he caught his brother's low snicker. "Look a little happier, 'Mish. You're getting *married*, nae going to the gallows."

He tried to muster a glare, but found himself unable. Did he really look that terrified?

Gordon clasped Hamish's shoulders, squeezing firmly. "I ken exactly how you feel. You'll do fine. Just—"

The doors swung open, permitting Hamish's entrance with a flurry of fanfare. Rows upon rows of eyes seemed to bore into him. He had met most of the Crystal Court, had even been the focus of several banquets, but that attention had never been without Darshan at his side. Alone, he felt extremely exposed.

His stomach cramped. Maybe he *was* going to be sick.

"Remember to breathe," Gordon whispered in a rush before scuttling through the doorway and off along by the wall. The otherwise stark stone was decorated with huge garlands of flowers and leaves, even the massive statue of the Goddess Queen, Araasi, was draped in them. All dry as far as he could determine from a casual glance. His brother came to a halt by their nephew, who was already seated near the burning brazier.

Hamish's gaze slid from his family to the figure at the far end of the aisle. *Dar.* His breath caught in his throat. Everything else in the temple seemed to fall away.

His betrothed stood before the brazier, illuminated by at least a dozen globes. Decked all in gold and backlit by the flickering fire, he shone brighter than any jewel.

Hamish's own silver attire wasn't anywhere near as gleaming.

Taking a steadying breath, Hamish walked down the aisle in a daze, his every step seemingly a foot off the ground. The crowd on either side of him was a blur of faces with few familiar ones.

The light notes of an elven lap harp sang throughout his approach. The melody vibrated through the temple, accompanied by the gentle flutter of flutes and the hum of a choir. The tune was almost familiar, an echo of home. Had his brother taught them a Tirglasian song? *Nae*. Gordon hadn't the ear for music.

The choir's singing swelled as his feet carried him past the halfway point, they didn't appear to be speaking any actual words. Nevertheless, the tune still had his stomach fizzing.

Each step didn't seem to be getting him there fast enough. He itched to take the rest of the aisle at a run and hope his nerves would settle once he was at Darshan's side. *I cannae do that*. Race up to the altar like a child excited for his first day on the hunt? Even his brother wouldn't approve of that display.

After what seemed like hours, he finally halted before his betrothed, barely able to breathe past the raw mix of emotions sticking in his throat.

The crown of the *vris Mhanek* sat squarely on Darshan's head. Hamish hadn't ever seen it before. It was more intricate than he expected from its depiction on the *vris Mhanek* signet ring. The gem-studded band swept up into a network of golden spikes that looked much like the spires of the imperial palace. It looked heavy and a far cry from the simple coronet of the Tirglasian throne.

It also wasn't the only thing that glittered. Beyond the usual sparkle of gems woven into his royal attire, Darshan wore a hint of eyeshadow much like he'd done at their engagement feast, matching his clothes by being in shades of gold and red.

He peered at the man. Darshan's eyes seemed misty behind the glasses. "Are you about to cry?" he whispered. He hadn't picked his betrothed as someone who'd get emotional over a ceremony—Darshan had been verging on flippant throughout their wedding in Tirglas—but he looked ready to burst into tears.

Darshan shook his head. "I'll explain later, *mea lux*." He looked Hamish over, a faint smile tugging at his lips. "You look good."

The high priestess stepped between them before Hamish could respond. She spoke, not to them, but to the crowd, "We are gathered on this splendid day to witness our *vris Mhanek*, the jewel of the empire, her future might and heart—"

Looking around the woman at his very-soon-to-be-permanent husband, Hamish caught the man rolling his eyes. He didn't blame Darshan, the high priestess sounded as though she spoke about one of their deities.

When she was finished with her praise of the future *Mhanek*, she spread her arms wide. "As Araasi has the Flame Eternal, so do we illuminate our paths with a flickering light, for love is not a constant glow, but a living being that must be nurtured and protected or else be doomed to sputter and die."

Two small children left the choir to scamper up to the woman. They each handed her a single unlit candle before returning to their spots.

The high priestess held the candles aloft, almost taking out Hamish's eye as she swung to face the statue of the goddess. If the woman noticed, she didn't let it stop her. She presented the candles to the statue as though they were more than mere tubes of beeswax.

With them standing almost at the statue's feet, the marble figure towered over them. Hamish couldn't see the crown from this angle, but a cool blue light glowed upon the statue's forehead.

"Hear us, Araasi, and bless this pure union with your good grace. May the Flame never die." She lowered her hands as the choir repeated her final statement, turning to hand over the candles. "Have you both committed your vows to memory?"

Hamish nodded along with Darshan, immensely relieved that he *did* still recall them. It would've been difficult to forget, his head still echoed with the high priestess' booming voice as she taught him. He couldn't remember how long he had stood before her, mimicking her every word into the early morning air until she was satisfied—even then, only barely.

Even if, through all the mishaps, he *had* forgotten, all it would take was to listen to Darshan and repeat the phrases when it came to his turn.

Darshan looked less than prepared, but he clasped Hamish's free hand nevertheless. "Under Araasi herself, in the light of the Flame Eternal, I pledge myself to you, both in this life and through all that comes after. My breath is yours. My tongue knows only your name. My gaze seeks no other." He raised their clasped hands high. "I shall uplift you from sorrow and pain. The shield of my magic will always accept your passage. Your desires shall be as my own and you will want for nothing."

In the haze that surrounded Hamish, he barely heard the words over the velvety tone of the man's voice. *I accept you as me husband.* That was all he wanted to say, all he really needed to. *All these rehearsed promises...* Were they necessary? He already had Darshan's love. What more could any man offer?

"I swear, as this flame burns—" The candle in Hamish's grasp ignited with barely a pop. The flame danced joyously on the wick. "— my guiding light will be no less steady and the path we walk together will never darken. You are the light inside me, the beacon ahead and the sun above." He wet his lips. "Without you, my world would wither."

Hamish wasn't one for extravagant words and the Udynean vows had seemed unnecessarily floral from the first moment he heard them, but there was something about hearing it from Darshan that turned the words into the finest poetry.

The high priestess cleared her throat, her lips firmly pressed together in disapproval. That last sentence wasn't part of the traditional vows. She nodded for Hamish to reply, fixing him with a stern look.

Choked up as he was, he almost couldn't speak. *Breathe.* Hamish bowed his head, gathering his voice. "I, Prince Hamish of the Mathan clan, accept your vow and add to them a pledge of loyalty of me body and me heart to you, Darshan *vris Mhanek.*"

The light of Darshan's answering smile all but seared the remainder of the words from Hamish's thoughts.

"I pledge meself to—" He faltered, biting his lip. *Nae yet.* That line came later.

Darshan squeezed his hand, still clasping it high between them. He twisted his grip, miming lifting.

Right!

"Under Araasi..." Nudged free, and aided by the lengthy reciting the high priestess had insisted on, his vows flowed from his lips. Right up until he reached the part he had fumbled on during their rehearsal, the crucial bit of the ceremony.

The one piece he couldn't do.

Hamish stared at the candle in Darshan's hand. "I swear, as this flame—" Everyone expected him to ignite the wick with minimal fuss. Except...

"Go on, child," the high priestess urged. She had insisted he make the attempt during the rehearsal, too. Despite being told he hadn't ever managed more than a crude shield.

He couldn't, not with magic the way Darshan had. He'd tried so many times, working himself up to the point where he had foolishly queried his betrothed's feelings about his lack of strong magic, only to be faced with loving reassurance that Darshan truly wasn't concerned. The man likely wouldn't care if the candle in his hand remained unlit.

But there was more than two of them here and, as Hamish slowly became aware of the crowd's disapproving murmurs, he realised he must've been standing silent for some time.

Darshan wordlessly stepped closer. He entwined his arm around Hamish's, tilting his hand enough to bring the candles together. The flame kissed the other's wick and caught.

With his cheeks burning, Hamish completed the rest of his vows, without Darshan's final addition.

"Under the watch of Araasi, these two men do declare themselves as one," the high priestess said. She raised her hands imploringly to the statue. "We put the threads of their union in your hands so that none may seek to break them. From the light of dawn to the end of night, so be your will."

A string of polite claps resonated from his right, reminding Hamish that they stood before the entirety of the Crystal Court.

How did they feel seeing their future ruler finally married? *Mixed.* If he listened to Zahaan, then some were definitely thinking of ways to use this to their advantage whilst a handful would be put out that their avenue to a quick rise through the ranks was effectively sealed off.

The high priestess turned back to them as her final words were echoed by the choir. "In keeping with Tirglasian custom." Her displeasure was thick on every word, but she persisted. "They will now exchange rings." She gestured imperiously for Zahaan to come forward.

The man hastened to join them. He didn't stay long, all but throwing the rings at them before returning to his seat between his mother and Anjali.

Although it was far too early for anyone to tell, Anjali cradled her stomach as though her hands were enough to shield it from the world. She leant over, whispering something to the spymaster which had the man bowing his head and fussing with his hair.

Hamish jerked his head back around as Darshan took up his right hand.

"I love you," his husband murmured in Tirglasian, slipping the ring onto the third finger of Hamish's hand. The proper one to symbolise a Udynean marriage. He already had a ring on it, the one with the aquamarine stone Darshan had purchased back in Tirglas.

"And *you...*" Hamish replied as he slid the matching ring onto Darshan's finger, letting it join the wooden band he had placed there so many months ago. "...are me light." Rather than release his hold on his husband's hand, he drew them closer together, bending down to be at Darshan's height in preparation for the sealing kiss.

A grin parted his husband's lips, his breath puffing through his teeth. A familiar spark took his eyes. He stretched up, roughly claiming Hamish's mouth.

Hamish's stomach bubbled anew, this time with the knowledge that everyone watched them. They had shared little more than a friendly handshake in front of more people whilst in Tirglas and, barring a few drunken snogs during their travels, each public kiss had been short and chaste.

This was anything but.

Darshan's lips parted, seeking entry with his tongue and, once found, delving deep.

A soft moan tightened Hamish's throat only to be swallowed by his husband. Everything, beyond the man in his arms, melted away. His heart demanded more. He pulled Darshan closer, delighting in how effortlessly they melded.

Someone cleared their throat, snapping Hamish back into the reality of where they stood.

He broke the kiss to find the *Mhanek* standing beside the high priestess.

The woman wordlessly held out a cushion to the man. A simple golden band sat atop the red velvet, the front engraved with the same crowned deer and twin bears Darshan had commissioned for their marriage crest.

Hamish stared at it, unsure what he was meant to do. He hadn't expected this. No one had mentioned a crown. Back home only the rulers wore them. The heir might get a braided leather thong whilst their parent lived, but never the consort.

"Kneel," the *Mhanek* ordered.

Hamish lowered to one knee. He couldn't remember his mother's crowning, if there'd been much ceremony beyond calling the clans to witness, and he'd only vague memories that'd been the formal announcement of his brother as the heir. Was he expected to say something?

Darshan's hand fell on his shoulder, lightly squeezing in reassurance. His husband wouldn't let him make a fool of himself.

The *Mhanek* held the coronet high above Hamish. He remained that way whilst rattling out a speech in Ancient Domian. Hamish barely caught every other word, but it sounded as though the man sang Hamish's praises. Or maybe Darshan's in his choice of spouse. It was hard to be certain.

At last, the *Mhanek* fell silent and the coronet settled on Hamish's head. It fitted neatly, but not enough to be tight. When had they gotten the right measurements for his head? He didn't recall it amongst the flurry of tailors fitting him for his formal attire.

Darshan's father stepped back. "Arise, Prince Hamish, consort of the *vris Mhanek*, and greet your court."

Hamish obeyed, getting back to his feet and clasping his husband's hand when it was offered.

As one, they turned to face their audience.

The entirety of the Crystal Court was on their knees, bowing as low as each was physically able. His mouth went dry at the sight. He knew the court would recognise him fully once they were married, but he hadn't expected this reaction. Would they always do this?

He definitely wasn't prepared for that.

Chapter 54

The ballroom glittered. Candles cast soft, yellow light from every corner, bouncing off the gold-vein marble floor and absorbed by the blackness of the ceiling. Music already flooded the ballroom. It wasn't the lively little jig Darshan had commissioned, but close to it.

Darshan had eyes only for his husband. He watched Hamish take in the glittering splendour, saving every minuscule twitch of awe upon the man's face. The candlelight gleamed against Hamish's silvery-blue attire and shone radiantly off the coronet. Coupled with his stature, he looked like a god.

"Dance with me?" Before his husband could answer, he drew Hamish out onto the dance floor. The rest of the court, having filed in one by one after presenting their gifts, stood along the edge of the room. They waited for Darshan and Hamish to begin the first dance of the night.

Hamish grimaced. "Right now?" His gaze seemed to settle on something over Darshan's shoulder. One of the tables laden with little delicacies? Darshan wouldn't be surprised. But how could the man think of food?

The music increased in volume as they reached the middle of the room. The notes bounced through the air, urging Darshan's body to keep up. He squared himself, getting ready to lead.

His husband paused, tilting his head. "Interesting choice."

"I hope you like it. I had it commissioned just for this occasion." And he rather expected the composer would grow quite rich on other such offers, just as the musicians would be invited to play at quite a number of parties for some months. Although, if the man had stolen it directly from Tirglas... "Do you know it?"

"Nae, but it sounds almost familiar." His husband's hand settled on the small of Darshan's back, turning him slightly. "I think I might even be able to lead."

Darshan wordlessly switched his grip, clasping Hamish's hand in anticipation. Whilst he did prefer to lead, dancing with such a tall partner did make certain moves difficult, if not outright impossible. He stared up at his husband, waiting for the man to choose the dance.

His husband guided Darshan in a small two-man circle, setting a gentler pace than expected. They followed each other in silence, the music slowly swelling.

Then, as the tune at last picked up pace, Hamish led them through a quick four-step that Darshan was all too familiar with, having been subjected to the same dance many times during his short ambassadorship in Tirglas. At least he could be certain the dreadful, screeching torture device they insisted was an instrument wouldn't rear its head.

A low tattoo of drums joined the lighter notes. It vibrated through the room, all but drowning out the flutes and lap harp.

Hamish hooked his arm into the crook of Darshan's elbow, swinging them about, their feet stomping to the drumbeat. Darshan remembered being flung around the Tirglasian hall with such steps. It played havoc with his balance, but the thrill of the air rushing across his face only urged him faster.

His husband paused halfway through a rotation, sending Darshan colliding into that broad chest. Grimacing in apology, Hamish continued to direct their passage across the dance floor in a flurry of intricate moves that Darshan struggled to match.

He caught a glimpse of the surrounding crowd. Other couples also danced. A few seemed to attempt Hamish's movements, failing even more so than himself. But then, none of them had spent several extravagant nights in Tirglas, dancing until they were exhausted.

Nor did they have a partner as sure-footed as his husband.

Hamish, seemingly noticing Darshan's predicament, slowed his steps. Unbidden, Darshan's heart beat a little faster. *Fool.* He knew enough about the man to know him as thoughtful. This gesture shouldn't have him feeling giddy. Maybe the dancing was more at fault there.

Or perhaps it was the music. His heart pounded along to the beat of the drums, his blood sang to the strum of the lap harps. His head floated somewhere near the ceiling.

The rest of the ballroom fell away until he could've sworn it was just them dancing out in the heavens. His gaze slid upwards. The dark marble captured all light, concealing her secrets.

The music slowed to fluttering trills of various woodwind instruments. The notes shivered along his skin.

Darshan pressed close. Without all the stresses of the ceremony and the uncertainty behind the attacks hanging over them, he was finally able to relax, to enjoy just being in his husband's arms.

The candlelight dimmed. Night hadn't yet fallen outside, but the fading twilight wasn't strong enough to dull the blue light shining from the ceiling as dozens of luminescent globes made themselves known in the black marble, the pattern reminiscent of the constellations.

"Wow," Hamish breathed, his face tilted upwards.

At this angle, Darshan couldn't see his husband's expression. He didn't need to. The awe in the man's voice was enough and it swelled his heart. "Could you really have given this up?" he found himself asking. "Gone back to Tirglas, to that wretched life?" The idea was everything he feared. That Hamish agreed it wasn't the best course of action had done little to still the uncertainty gnawing on his heart.

Rather than give an answer, his husband stared silently up at the ceiling for longer than was really necessary to take in every detail. Their dancing halted, leaving them lightly swaying on the spot to the tune.

"To stop a war before it started?" Hamish softly mused. "Aye. A kingdom's wellbeing is more important than the whims of one man."

Darshan grunted. It was a very *him* thing to say. Sacrificing his desires was how the man's mother had raised all her children. Whereas Darshan knew he'd a selfish streak wide enough to accommodate the both of them.

Hamish tore his gaze from the ceiling to finally lock eyes with Darshan. He caressed Darshan's cheek as though this could be the last time they saw each other. "Leaving wouldnae have helped matters, would it?"

"No," Darshan agreed. He nuzzled his husband's hand, relishing in the coolness of those calloused fingers against his skin.

"Just promise me one thing. When the reports up north start rolling in. The causalities. The attacks. Dinnae tell me."

He drew back a half-step, squinting against the light haloing Hamish's head. "You wish to be kept in the dark?" Had he heard that correctly?

"Aye."

"I promise, the reports shan't grace your eyes nor breathe a word into your ears." Defending their border was another matter. And there was the slight issue with the Tirglasian border also being shared by Obuzan, Udynea's ancient enemy. Having their forces split in keeping one country from massacring itself on their borders whilst maintaining their impasse with another was just begging for trouble.

"But my father doesn't plan on attacking anyone."

"I ken that. But if I ken what's happening, how many lives she's throwing away, I'll want to do something about it. And I'm nae sure if I can trust meself to do the right thing."

Darshan flung his arms around the man's torso, squeezing them together. "You *always* choose the right thing, *mea lux*. That's what I adore about you." His own moral compass had been tarnished by years of navigating the Crystal Court, but he knew Hamish's was made of sturdier stuff. "I have every faith in you."

With his ear pressed to his husband's chest, the rumble of the man's low chuckle rolled through Darshan's head.

"You give me too much credit," Hamish murmured, tilting Darshan's head to plant a gentle kiss on his brow. He wrapped his arms around Darshan's shoulders. "And *I* promise, I'm nae going anywhere."

Darshan knew that. Still, he burrowed deeper into Hamish's embrace, his fingertips digging into the rich silk. Breathing deep of his husband's scent, he forced himself to take a step back before Hamish's hold on him wasn't the only firm thing. "Since we've rather forsaken dancing, perhaps we should leave the floor to those who still are?" They were in no danger of anyone colliding into them, but it didn't negate accidents.

Nodding, Hamish eyed the crowd around the table. "Hungry?"

"Ravenous," he breathed, pressing them together. Apart from the almost clinical spilling of their seed two days ago, there'd been little time for intimacy with his husband. It was long overdue. "Just not for food." How he longed to drag the man into some dark corner and have his way. If it wasn't for the mingling people expected of them, he would've forgone this entire debacle.

Hamish gave a brief chuckle. "That too," he murmured, the corners of his eyes wrinkling further. "But I havenae eaten a thing all day."

Darshan grunted. With his stomach bubbling away, he hadn't managed to consume more than a few lightly spiced pears for breakfast. Eating was a good idea. They would need something to maintain his energy. "Are you also looking to mingle?" As much as Darshan wanted to, he couldn't keep Hamish out on the dance floor all night.

Hamish shook his head. "Ask me again when I've eaten, but *you* probably should."

"Steering me back onto the proper course again, *mea lux*," he teased, shooing his husband in the direction of food. "If you insist, I'll go play socialite whilst you eat. Don't scoff down too much, though. It's no fun when you're bloated."

Hamish grinned. "Aye, I've learnt me lesson there." He bent, hesitating slightly before planting the faintest of kisses on Darshan's lips. Then, he was off across the dance floor, taking a direct route to the food-laden table.

Bereft of his husband's attention, Darshan strolled through the crowd. He plucked various snacks and drinks from trays as servants passed by. His people would see that a proper meal was sent to his chambers later, but he couldn't resist the sweet treats on offer.

People hastened to gift him their well-wishes as they sauntered along. Most of it was the usual lip-service he expected, although he'd enough genuine congratulations from his extended family and closest allies, to make the rest palatable.

At least he could be sure no other gifts would appear. *And without a single slave.* Mercifully. He had dreaded every moment when one of the houses came forward. Perhaps word had come that such offerings wouldn't be seen as favourable. *Good.* It was about time the court understood what he tolerated.

One particular man in the crowd caught his eye. He stood off to the side, wine glass in hand, and a dark green shawl draped over what appeared to be the attire of a border captain. He didn't appear to be here to make some announcement and quite a number of the nobility would send their younger children into the military, if only to get them out from under their feet.

"Captain," Darshan called, drawing the man's attention. He didn't know the man's precise rank, but few nobles gained a higher distinction than the one their aristocratic ties gave.

The man jerked his head up, his eyes widening that split-second before he bowed and gave the customary greeting Darshan had heard far too many times this evening. He'd a soft accent reminiscent of those from the north.

"Formal uniform at a wedding?" Darshan jested, halting before the man. "Are you anticipating a return to duty so swiftly?"

The captain's cheeks darkened slightly. He fussed with his shawl. "I would have come in something more appropriate, but I—" Laughter escaped his lips in a nervous gasp. "It would seem I have been in the empire's service for so long that I've outgrown my civilian clothes."

Darshan casually raised his brows, feigning a slight interest in the man's personal dilemma as he sipped at his current glass of wine. "Well, the empire certainly appreciates your diligence in patrolling her border. Where are you stationed?"

"Up north. Not far from where the Cezhory and Tirglas borders meet." He fiddled with the stem of his glass, the pale wine within sloshing about.

"And how goes it on the northern border?" Quietly, he hoped. "Are you experiencing much trouble?"

The man shook his head. "The Tirglasians are massing more than usual near the base of the mountain range, but they're a fair distance from the border and are sticking to the spot." He scratched at his jaw, his fingernails scraping over the short beard. "I hear the order is to not engage, but that hasn't stopped the refugees pouring in."

Again, Darshan's brows rose, somewhat involuntarily this time. He hadn't expected people might opt to pack up their lives and vacate the area *into* Udynea. "Are we getting many?"

"There were a lot when I left, but I expect more have piled in since then. Nobody knows what to do with them. We've been escorting them to a camp not far from the city, but—" His gaze darted over Darshan's shoulder and the harried expression of badgered youth crossed his face. "I do apologise, *vris Mhanek.*"

Darshan tensed. "Whatever for?" Had he been drawn into some elaborate ruse to put him in a prime position for an attack?

"Gaalen!" a woman called, waving her fan at them. "*Sweetie!* There you are." Huffing and red-faced, she tottered over to stand between them. "I've been up and down this entire ballroom looking for you. You simply must meet—"

"*Mother,*" Captain Gaalen hissed, his face slowly draining of colour. "This is *his* reception." He jerked his head towards Darshan.

The woman tapped her son on the shoulder with the tip of her fan. "Don't interrupt me. I'm certain your friend can—" She gave Darshan a cursory glance, then froze, her head whipping back around. Her face grew redder. "Oh, *vris Mhanek!*" She curtsied low. "I didn't realise he was talking to *you.*"

"Evidently not," Darshan murmured into his wineglass.

Clearing his throat, Captain Gaalen drew his mother back upright. "May I introduce Viscountess Shavita?"

The woman bowed her head, halted from sinking back to the floor by her son's grip. "My most humble of apologies, I shan't interrupt your conversation further." She threw a sharp glare her son's way as if he was somehow to blame. "I will wait for you in the garden." Offering Darshan another low curtsy, she snapped open her fan and strode off into the crowd, fast vanishing from sight.

Captain Gaalen sighed. "Forgive me, *vris Mhanek*, but I must be off." He downed the last of his wine and straightened his uniform.

"If you don't mind me saying, you don't look dressed for courting." Nor did he look that enthusiastic about it. Darshan hadn't been subjected to such practices, but he had witnessed many of his sisters go through the act. Barring a few duds, they'd always been giddy about meeting a prospective spouse. Or perhaps his father was merely proficient in weeding out the dross.

The man gave a weak smile. "To be frank, I wasn't expecting to be."

Darshan sipped at his wine, trying to maintain a neutral expression. "I see. Not enjoying the matchmaking, I take it?" He hadn't been all that fond of the idea either.

"It amuses you."

"A little," he admitted. "I've been there."

The captain cocked one brow but clearly knew his court manners better than his mother to keep himself from enquiring further.

"Parents do like to insert themselves where they're not wanted." Never had his father been as crass as to attempt matchmaking during a wedding reception, but there were other functions where the entirety of the court had attended. "Mothers especially, or so I hear."

The man's poor attempt at a smile stretched into a genuine one. He glanced around them in an almost conspiratorial manner. "I couldn't transfer to the palace, could I? Perhaps as a personal guard? Or some remote outpost somewhere?"

"Avoiding someone?"

"How about every eligible nobleman in the empire?"

Darshan chuckled. "Which delightful man is she currently trying to steer you towards?"

"Lord Kaami, I believe."

"Ah." Darshan took a long sip at his wine. He hadn't realised Lord Kaami was looking to settle down. Memory told him the man wasn't at all interested in anything involving intimacy. "Watch out for his father. Lots of repressed self-loathing there. Gets a bit handsy when he's drunk."

Captain Gaalen's lips pressed together as his brows lowered into a worried frown. "Duly noted." Visibly steeling himself, he bowed his farewell to Darshan and strode off in the direction his mother had taken.

Darshan watched the man leave, a faint knot of pity tightening in his stomach. Could he find a place for a border captain in the palace's ranks? *Probably not.* Any suggestion Darshan made would always be taken under heavy consideration, but the captain was still a noble and his father preferred they didn't hold positions within the palace. Captain Gaalen's skills would no doubt be of more use serving at an outpost.

A familiar face appeared through a gap in the crowd. A person he didn't expect to see attending. His half-sister, Vinata. She sat with her back against the wall, cradling a small bundle whilst her husband stood at her side.

"Vin!" Setting his empty glass on the tray of a passing servant, Darshan hastened to her side. "What are you doing here? And with your son?"

She beamed up at him, bouncing her son as the boy sleepily

burbled away. "You've already done so much, but I came to seek a blessing."

"Oh!" How could he have forgotten the old tradition of newly-weds blessing newborns? "Of course." He cradled the small bundle. The baby was warm in his grasp.

Huge steely-grey eyes stared up at him in the eternal expression of amazement he had seen from so many small babies.

To have that much awe for the world. He had spent a great many years without such wonder in his life, regaining it only after meeting his husband. "How has he been?" A few days had passed, but he knew how easily it was for things to go wrong when they were this young. "Have you given him a name yet?" He knew tradition decreed waiting until the naming ceremony that came after the first month, but most didn't.

"He'd well," Yaatin replied, beaming with all the pride a father could have for his son. "You'd never know he came into this world cold."

"We decided to call him Nishaan," Vinata added.

"A fine name," Darshan murmured. He brought a globe of light to life, balancing it on his fingertips, smiling as the boy's gaze shifted from Darshan's face to the magic. He gently brushed the globe over Nishaan's forehead, chin and heart. "May the gods treat you kindly, little one."

"I also wanted to ask you," Vinata said as he handed the boy back to his mother. She cradled the baby to her chest with one hand and clasped her husband's fingers with the other, holding the man's hand to her shoulder. "*We* wanted to know if you would consider being his guide."

"His *Khutani* is a very long way off." At least twelve years, if not longer. All manner of things could happen in that time.

"I know, but I figured if he's looking to you for guidance, he's less likely to be a threat."

"Not that we'd ever consider vying for the throne," Yaatin added, looking as though he might faint at the thought. Their marriage might've garnered a fair bit of prestige for the man's household, but they were still very much small fish swimming alongside sharks.

"I've never once considered that you would." Darshan ran a hand over the downy hair covering the boy's head, his thoughts drifting to his own child. "And I would be honoured." If anything, he could teach the boy how to navigate the court, a skill both of his parents severely lacked.

~ ~ ~

"Slow down, lad," Hamish said, ruffling his nephew's hair and interrupting the boy scarfing down another mouthful. The boy had planted himself at the end of the table and looked prepared to work his way down it. "You're going to clean the whole lot before midnight."

Ethan wrinkled his nose. His nephew was too occupied in stuffing his face to pay much mind.

"I've tried to tell him the same thing," Anjali said. She sat next to his nephew, an arc of Nulled Ones keeping almost everyone else back.

"He's a growing lad. Who should be eating hearty meals, nae these treats." Hamish snatched a jam-filled bun from the boy's plate, savouring the sweetness that assailed his mouth. "Where's Gordon?"

As if speaking his brother's name had been a summons, the man appeared through the crowd, his arms spread wide. "There's the groom of the night! One of them, at least." Gordon gave him a hearty clap on the shoulder, before draping himself over the back of Ethan's chair. "I thought your husband would've dragged you off by now."

"A newly-wed couple mingling with those who stood witness to the union is customary," Anjali said.

Gordon held up a hand in surrender. "I'm nae disputing that. But your brother looked ready to get on with the nuptial bedding right at the altar."

Hamish gagged on his current mouthful of bread. He choked down the lump, chasing it with a gulp of wine someone thrust under his nose. He stared at his brother, aghast and still trying to catch his breath.

At her place seated by the wall, Anjali's whole face scrunched. "Could we not mention that? Ever?"

"I'm with her," Hamish managed between clearing his throat and trying to will away the heat taking over his face.

"And look at this." Grinning, Gordon tapped the side of Hamish's coronet. "A high and mighty consort now?"

Hamish grimaced. The band didn't weigh much, but he was still getting used to its presence. Thank the Goddess there were few functions where he'd be required to wear it. He sidled down the table, filling a plate—and, occasionally, his mouth—with whatever morsel caught his eye. Sometimes, several times, like with the candied dates.

His brother tailed him, plucking smaller portions to chew on. "I hear you and your husband are expecting?" His brows lowered along with his voice, even though he spoke entirely in their native tongue. "And that his sister is carrying it?"

"Aye. Early days though." He wouldn't dare hope anything would come of it until the first six months had passed. Even then, a lot could go wrong in the three that followed.

Gordon hummed thoughtfully around a mouthful of what had

looked to be a ball of rice coated in some sort of yellow paste. He seemed to be enjoying it and went in for seconds. "I'm nae going to ask."

"Good." He grabbed a couple of the rice balls out from beneath his brother's greedy hands, popping one into his mouth before Gordon started nicking them off his plate. The paste was sweet and tangy, but also spicier than he had anticipated, enough to make his eyes water and stole his voice for a few breaths. "I dinnae think I can explain it beyond they magically fused me and him together, then put it in her." He gestured to Anjali, who was now conversing with Zahaan.

"And where has he gone?" He gestured to the whole ballroom with one sweep of his arm. "I'm surprised he's nae tied to your hip."

"He's around." He spotted Darshan talking with what looked like a guard, although he didn't recognise the uniform. *Nae one of the palace's men.* A noble's personal protector? They seemed a little too confident talking to Darshan to be of low rank. Was he one of the imperial army? Every noble was required to serve amongst them at some point. Did he have news on the Tirglasian border?

Nae. He had asked Darshan not to tell him of anything pertaining to the border, he couldn't go about specifically requesting information.

"You eating those?" Gordon asked, swiping the rice balls off Hamish's plate before he'd an answer.

Hamish conceded the whole plate to his brother. He had satisfied his stomach enough with pickings, if hunger bothered him later, then he could send for food. Maybe even convince Darshan to feed him like in one of those raunchy poetry books he had plucked from his husband's personal library.

He glanced back to where Darshan had been talking to the guard, finding both men gone.

A quick skim over the heads of the crowd was all it took to relocate his husband. Darshan stood near the wall not too far from them, cradling a baby as he talked to a couple who were presumably the parents.

Hamish's heart fluttered at the sight. For all his husband's protests and fears of becoming an inadequate father, he held the child with the same confidence as he faced the world.

"Your highness!" a woman called, drawing Hamish's attention to a servant hastening through the crowd in their direction. She carried a baby wrapped in a dark cloth. She halted before him, curtsying as best as she was able whilst clutching the small bundle. "I know he's of common origins, but I..." The woman bowed her head and, seeming to gather her strength, lifted her baby higher. "I humbly request your blessing."

"Blessing?" Hamish echoed, glancing at his brother for help as if Gordon knew any more than himself. "I'm nae a priest."

Bewilderment took the woman's face. "I did not suggest—" Panic lit her eyes. "If I have offended his highness…"

He held up his hands, attempting to still any alarm before it took hold. "Nae at all. I just—"

Someone cleared their throat, the sound familiar.

Darshan neatly inserted himself between Hamish and the woman. "I believe what my husband is trying to say is the custom you seek is not one observed in Tirglas." He turned to smile back at Hamish. "You don't have to be a priest, *mea lux*, just touch the three centres. May I?" he asked of the woman.

Even as she nodded, she looked ready to keel over. "Of course, *vris Mhanek*. I would be honoured beyond measure."

Darshan took the child from the woman, holding it close as Hamish had seen him do just a short moment ago. He closed his eyes and, with the tips of his fingers glowing, lightly touched the baby's forehead, chin and chest. "May the gods smile upon your child," he murmured, returning the baby to their mother.

The woman bowed low, babbling her appreciation, before scuttling off.

"What was that?" Gordon asked. He leant against the table, gnawing on a strip of what looked to be dried meat, although Hamish didn't recall seeing anything like it on the table.

"It's an old tradition," Darshan replied. "One of our oldest. Newly-weds are considered to be favoured by the gods. We supposedly become vessels of their power. For the rest of the night, at least. Babies who are blessed by either of the couple are likewise favoured for prosperity."

"All you did was touch his head and chest," Hamish pointed out. There'd been no anointing or prayers such as when the priests back home blessed people.

"The three centres of self." Hamish's confusion must've shown, for Darshan gestured to his own forehead. "Thought." His hand dropped slightly to his throat. "Voice." Again, his hand fell. This time to rest upon his chest where his heart was. "Soul. The three things that make our identity."

"You think your soul is in your heart?"

"Where else would it be?"

Hamish shrugged. He'd never really sat down and thought about it, but he had envisioned it taking up all of his body, not just a piece. The priests back home had always been vague on the subject. "Everywhere?" He chuckled.

"What is so amusing?" Darshan dragged him closer, leaning on

619

Hamish's arm as his stare grew intense. "*Share.*"

"Just that, with magic being so common here, I'm surprised Udyneans still have all these superstitious beliefs."

"Magic breeds superstition, *mea lux*, be it through fear or wonder. Just because we understand how the world works, doesn't mean we stop believing in gods." He smiled, running a forefinger down Hamish's chest. "Or fate."

Before Hamish could think of a response, the haze of his thoughts was broken by his brother's coarse snort.

"Would you two bloody bugger off already?" Gordon smirked around his jerky. "Honestly, it's getting embarrassing watching you."

"Nae more so than it was watching you trying to get up in your wife's skirt on your wedding day," Hamish retorted. At least they weren't trying to undress each other in public.

"Nevertheless," Darshan interjected. "It *is* an enchanting suggestion." His hand alighted on Hamish's arm. The desire that danced in his husband's eyes was hot enough to scorch a man where he stood. "Come, *mea lux*. I think it's time we left the court to its own devices."

Wetting his lips and nodding, Hamish followed his husband towards the exit, staunchly ignoring his brother's crude suggestions that trailed their departure.

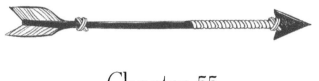

Chapter 55

Taking their leave, they made for their chambers whilst the reception revelry continued without them. Hamish was acutely aware of Darshan's silent presence at his side as they left the council hall. They strolled through the imperial gates, the cool night air caressing his skin. With their fingers firmly linked—the heat of his husband's skin hot in his palm—it felt like Darshan was the only thing real in the entire world.

The usual Nulled One presence was absent outside the *vris Mhanek's* suite. Hamish wasn't under the delusion that they were alone, but it was nice for the guards to give them that illusion.

Darshan tugged at Hamish's hand, drawing him around to grab a fistful of collar. *"Finally,"* the man growled, the tone a primal rumble that prickled Hamish's skin. He dragged Hamish down to his level.

Before Hamish could collect himself to think, his husband's mouth was on him, obliterating any lingering questions with a kiss that threatened to turn his bones to water. He wobbled a step back to brace himself against the door, his legs planted either side of the man.

His husband took full advantage of the pose, rubbing himself against Hamish's groin, no doubt acutely aware of the growing interest forming there. The moans that escaped Darshan's mouth were sinful, further feeding Hamish's desire.

Darshan's hand slid along Hamish's waist, briefly seeking entry beneath the waistband before falling to caressing through the layers of silk. His touch alternated between delicately tracing the shape of Hamish's steadily hardening length and long, firm strokes that had Hamish moaning and thrusting against the flat of Darshan's palm.

Hamish's own hand wandered, patting across the door in search of the handle. If he didn't get his husband into their suite soon, he was certain Darshan would finish him right where they stood.

The latched clicked and the door swung inwards, dumping them onto the ground and pushing much of the air from his lungs.

Hamish lay still, regaining his breath, as his husband lifted himself onto his hands and knees.

"Well now," Darshan purred, drawing his mussed hair away from his face. His crown had fallen off, rolling across the bare floor and stopping out of arm's reach. "Aren't we a little eager to be horizontal?"

"You're the one bloody feeling me up in the corridor," he countered. "The bed is right there." Hamish jerked his thumb in the direction of the curtain-shrouded mattress. He couldn't see it in the gloom, but he knew the approximate placing.

There were other shapes in the room. The light leaking through the doorway gleamed upon metal and jewels. The wedding gifts.

His grinning husband righted himself.

Hamish got to his feet, eagerly following Darshan as the man guided them across the floor. Their chambers were lit only by the moonlight, gracing one half of the room. It was that half which Darshan towed him towards with the single-mindedness of a frustrated teenager.

The chaise lounge had been moved, its dark shape a mere outline in the pale light. Hamish relaxed into it, unable to restrain a grin as Darshan fell upon him, barely able to answer the fervent kiss before his lips stretched tight again.

Over and over their mouths met in teasing brushes, the slow strokes stealing Hamish's breath. He cupped Darshan's head, trying to slow his husband's advances, to gather enough space to regain his composure, to *last*. But he couldn't resist the sweet glide of those lips, the lingering taste of wine on Darshan's tongue, the warmth of the breaths they shared.

Soon, he found himself answering heat for heat.

Darshan's breath hitched at the sweep of Hamish's tongue. His fingers danced up Hamish's neck, lightly playing with the nape before sliding deeper into the hair to finally close around the coronet. How it had stayed on through everything, Hamish didn't know. "As much as I love seeing this on you," Darshan purred, his voice husky. "It's going to get in the way."

"You didnae seem to care a moment ago."

"Such cheek." Darshan pushed him back, causing Hamish to fully recline upon the chaise lounge. "Perhaps your mouth requires a different outlet."

He mumbled an agreement, although little in the way of actual words escaped him. The bed wasn't far, its shadowy bulk looming on the edge of his vision. He eyeballed the distance. The comfort the mattress offered didn't seem worth the trouble of moving.

Movement amongst the curtains caught his attention, pulling him out of the fog of pleasure and setting his heart to pounding. An assassin? *Nae*, he groaned. Not here. Hadn't they been through enough? Could they not have this night without something going wrong?

A hand alighted on his cheek, turning his head. "*Mea lux?*"

Hamish stared into his husband's eyes, seeing only concern. The sight further tightened his chest. He pointed towards the bed and whispered, "Something moved."

Before Hamish finished speaking, Darshan flung a spark towards the spot. It exploded into a globe over the bed, illuminating the entire room in a bright white light.

Squinting, Hamish peered at the bed. A network of leafy vines hung over the sturdy curtain rails. "What's all that?"

"Isn't it a part of Tirglasian custom to spend the first night of marriage beneath a bower?"

"Aye." They hadn't much opportunity to observe that tradition whilst leaving Tirglas given the lack of trees on the ocean. Had his husband been talking to Gordon again? "But they're naewhere near *that* fancy." And Darshan would've known that if Hamish's brother had spoken to him.

"Oh." All at once, his husband looked crestfallen. "I can—"

Hamish clasped Darshan's shoulders, pulling the man on top of him. "Dinnae change a thing." He hadn't been concerned about the tradition, but seeing his husband go to the trouble, especially when the man could hear plants, infused him with a warmth that threatened to steal his voice and welled in his eyes.

His husband delicately cupped his cheek, caressing his skin and smoothing back the edges of his beard. "Are you all right?"

Nodding as much as Darshan's hold on him would allow, Hamish wrapped his arms around the man's waist. "I'm grand. It's perfect. I love you."

Darshan beamed and Hamish's heart fell for him all over again.

He tipped the man back. A surge of questions bubbled along his tongue, demanding to be answered. "How are they growing?" His husband wasn't bothered by dried plants, but these were green. Were they still alive? Hamish failed to spy any sign of a pot or trough of dirt around the base of the bed. Was Darshan currently being barraged by their screams? "How did you get them in here?" They were high enough that Darshan had to descend several levels before he started to hear whispers.

"Through the balcony door." Darshan gestured to the section of glass taking up much of the wall at their back.

Twisting in his seat, Hamish easily spotted the thick trunk of vine creeping along the floor and down. How had he missed that earlier? Or the faint breeze that nipped at him? "That's some security hazard." A direct route to the *vris Mhanek's* room? The Nulled Ones must be having pups.

"The base is guarded, worry not."

Absently nodding, Hamish returned to staring at the bower. White flowers dotted the foliage, almost glowing in the light. They looked similar to the one he had caught Darshan growing one night, before the man showed him how he could summon a poisonous bloom from a different kingdom. He doubted they were the same, but they did remind him of—

The glass flower. The one he had bought for Darshan before the second day of their wedding turned sour. It wasn't the same colour, but the conical shape was close enough. It currently sat on a shelf near the bathing room, nestled in the neck of a glass vase. It gleamed in the light.

A soft whistle drew his gaze back to Darshan. "You looked a world away."

"Aye, it just got me thinking on how real it all is." He settled his hands either side of Darshan's waist. "You're really mine." *Forever.* Not like in Tirglas. They weren't on a two-year deadline to have children to still be considered as married. They could take their time.

Live how they wanted.

"Yours?" Darshan breathed. With his husband backlit by the globe, much of his face remained in shadow. He laughed softly, the grin stretching the man's lips all too obvious. "*Mea lux*, I belonged to you well before tonight." He softly swept his lips across Hamish's.

Hamish cupped the back of his husband's head, keeping him from leaving, and deepened the kiss.

Darshan bent his head, burrowing beneath Hamish's beard to leave messy, wet kisses along his neck. With his new position, Darshan rocked atop him, the friction of each maddeningly slow sweep inching Hamish ever closer to bliss.

He grabbed the man's arse, squeezing to the sound of Darshan's encouraging moan, intensifying the pressure.

Darshan reclaimed Hamish's mouth, exploring with his tongue before drawing back to bite Hamish's lip. Their breaths mingled, tangling so much that it was hard to distinguish one breathless groan from the other. The globe stuttered and died, its creator suitably distracted from keeping it alight.

His husband's movements slowed, becoming faint shifts between their panting.

Hamish stared up at him, dazed and bewildered, his eyes slow to readjust to the sudden gloom. He was too close to the edge. Sparks of pleasure danced through his body, demanding satisfaction. Could Darshan not feel it?

Darshan ran a finger down the side of Hamish's face, pausing upon reaching the jaw to run his thumb over Hamish's swollen lips.

The tingle of healing whispered across Hamish's skin. He licked his lips, briefly tasting blood. Had Darshan bitten a little too hard? He hadn't even noticed.

His tongue also grazed Darshan's thumb. Hamish took the opportunity to suck on the tip. With one leg, he coaxed his husband forward onto him.

Darshan obliged, pressing his whole body against Hamish. But rather than continue their mutual slide towards the edge, he gave a single kiss, then slid to the floor.

Kneeling before the chaise lounge, his husband undid the ties to Hamish's trousers with practised ease. He tugged them down, halting his efforts to untie the smalls only to suck on the tip of Hamish's length through the damp linen.

Hamish bit his lip, his husband's name slipping out on the breath of a groan. "Slow down, me heart." With one hand, he cupped Darshan's jaw, stilling those kissable lips with the press of his thumb. "This is *our* night. We have time. There's nae a thing to concern ourselves with."

"Nothing," Darshan agreed, placing a kiss on the pad of Hamish's thumb.

In one jerk of tearing cloth, Hamish's smalls parted in the man's grasp, allowing his length to spring free. The expression that took Darshan's face bordered on feral. He wet and bit his lip as if planning on devouring Hamish whole.

The heat of his husband's heavy breath bathed Hamish's skin, rendering him incapable of sound.

Darshan's gaze lifted. Even the pale moonlight couldn't hide the lust burning in those hazel eyes.

Faced with such desire, Hamish almost came undone on the spot. *Goddess, let me at least last until he touches me.* He'd already gone off early on Darshan enough times to know the man would take it in stride, but he really didn't want tonight to be one of them.

"I should've dragged you aside sooner," Darshan growled, wrapping his hand around Hamish's length and stroking with aching slowness. "Taken you within the council hall."

Hamish let his head fall back, half-lost to the warmth radiating off Darshan's palm. His head swam with the image of being bent over a desk or on his knees in some tiny room whilst his husband had his way. Would they have returned to the ballroom after? Chatted away to the court with each other's scent—the taste—still lingering on their skin, their breath? Masked only by the wine? "Wouldnae that be considered scandalous?"

Darshan's wicked chuckle shimmied along Hamish's length, causing it to twitch. His husband had to have noticed, yet he continued with his languid touch. "Very," he replied, his voice gravelly.

"So, you're just going to tease me?" The question hissed out through the grinding of his teeth. If his husband wanted him to last, he was going the wrong way about it.

"No," Darshan purred. The heat of his breath enveloped Hamish. "I most definitely am not." His head dropped beyond Hamish's immediate sight as he placed fluttering kisses down the entirety of Hamish's length.

Hamish bit his lip to keep any further protests at bay, a gasp escaping as the kisses were replaced by the warmth of his husband's tongue sliding back up. His head lolled back onto the arm of the chaise lounge. He grabbed hold of anything and everything, searching for a way to root himself to reality as his body trembled, his thighs parting as far as they were able with his trousers binding him at the knees.

Still, Darshan kept the slow pace, each curl of that wicked tongue or his wet kiss designed to tease despite his words. In the space between, barely giving Hamish time to breathe, he stroked Hamish's length with deft fingers.

Hamish's hips fast followed in time until he was thrusting into his husband's fist, his bare backside caressed by the furniture's rich fabric.

Darshan paused briefly after one particularly final-feeling upward drag of his tongue along Hamish's length. Before Hamish could gather the breath for words, his husband sucked on the tip. He slid further down with each suck and bob of his head, abandoning his kneeling position to shuffle into a different angle, one better designed to accommodate Hamish.

It threw a curtain of hair over Hamish's view. Hamish drew it back, holding Darshan's hair at the nape, to carry on watching his beautiful husband.

If Darshan noticed, he gave no sign. He seemed lost in his own actions, moaning in a needy manner that, even with his husband's mouth tight around Hamish's length, still managed to set his ears to burning.

Heat continued to pool in his groin. His breath rasped out a mouth gone slack as his mind slowly succumbed to pleasure. Darshan's hair slipped from his fingers as he grasped Darshan's shoulders, clenching rhythmically to each downward stroke.

Then, he was over the edge. His back arched off the chaise lounge, thrusting him further down Darshan's throat. His own tightened on a cry, strangling it before more than a breath could escape.

Hamish's legs finally gave. He collapsed back onto the chaise lounge. With his heart hammering and his head spinning, he stared blindly at the ceiling, waiting for his body to stop buzzing, for his chest to finish feeling as though it would explode.

"Are you all right?" The question that finally pierced Hamish's consciousness carried a roughness that had his body shivering with the very recent memory of why.

Hamish rolled his head, tilting it to eye his husband.

Darshan had settled back at his feet, an arm draped over Hamish's left knee. His bejewelled fingers idly circled the kneecap of Hamish's right leg. Even through the wrinkled layers of bunched fabric, it sent a faint, tingling warmth through his body. "*Mea lux,*" he purred. "Have I truly rendered you speechless so early in the night?"

Still concentrating on regaining his breath, Hamish shook his head. "Just surprised me is all. I wasnae expecting you to do it here." He patted the chaise lounge. "Or for you to be this insistent." He should have. The times when his husband wasn't easily stirred could be counted on one hand.

Darshan ducked his head, but not before Hamish caught him grinning like a boarhound who had swiped a roast. A soft chuckle graced the silence. "I admit, I let my desires run unchecked. I simply cannot help myself when it comes to you. Especially when you look this delectable." Even in the shadows, Hamish felt the man's hungry gaze upon him.

Hamish doubted he looked anything other than a completely undone mess. He was still sprawled on the chaise lounge, naked at the waist, drenched in moonlight and sweat.

He reached for Darshan, prepared to give the man as good as he had gotten, only to have his husband rock back onto his heels and out of reach.

Bouncing to his feet, Darshan wordlessly strolled across the room, illuminated only by the moonlight. He slipped into the shadows. There was the faint impression of his movements, punctuated by the rustle of cloth being discarded.

Hamish tracked the sound, unsure where his husband was headed. Definitely not their bed.

A tongue of flame appeared in the darkness, balancing on Darshan's hand. He touched it to the lantern hanging near the doorway leading to the bathing chamber. The resulting glow didn't light up the whole room, but it was enough to make out the disarray of Darshan's clothes scattered over the floor.

Clad in only his smalls, his husband paused in the doorway with one hand curled around the frame, twisting to look over his shoulder. "Are you coming?"

If his body hadn't already just been drained of every drop it could offer at this moment, Hamish bloody well might have at the sight. "Aye," he managed.

"Bring the box with you as well. I've a feeling it shall be necessary." Without another word of explanation, he disappeared into the room. The faint squeak of taps and the rush of water swiftly filled the silence.

Hamish slowly sat up. *Box?* What box? Did his husband mean the one the glass flower had arrived in? That didn't sound right. Clearly, Darshan meant something else. But what?

He went to pull up his trousers, halting as he grabbed the waistband. Darshan was always perfectly content to strut about the suite naked, even if Hamish preferred not to. But there was no reason he couldn't. If there was any time when no interruptions would be a given, it was tonight.

Gathering himself, he staggered to his feet and, toeing off his footwear, finished his husband's effort in undressing him.

He turned to the pile of presents from the court. Was Darshan after some insignificant piece he hadn't noticed? There were a few chests, none of them easily portable. Did any of them hold the box he was after? There were a handful of them around the right size scattered amongst the pile. A few rattled as he picked them up. One was heavier than the rest, holding what looked to be a figurine made of solid gold. He investigated one of the chests. Most of the gifts within were good for nothing beyond looking pretty.

His gaze fell on a familiar container. The wooden surface was about as long as his forearm. And within? He opened the lid.

As expected, a length of moulded leather lay nestled in its velvet bed. The toy they'd lost somewhere on the way across the lake to Rolshar. Or a decent replica. *Necessary?* Not exactly. But no less enjoyable.

Clutching the box to his chest, Hamish hastened to join his husband in the bathing chamber.

The bath was ready by the time he entered. Steam filled the room, smelling faintly of incense. It flattened Hamish's hair and beaded on his beard.

Like most of the tubs in the palace, this one was recessed into the floor and surrounded by gleaming tiles. Small shelves sat on the far side, holding various bottles and an array of candles that illuminated the space with their soft ruddy light.

Darshan glanced over his shoulder, swiftly turning to fully take Hamish in. "Well, if this isn't a sight from my deepest dreams. I think..." He slowly untied his smalls. The light linen had no chance of masking the fullness of his husband's arousal. "Considering how long the day has been and how much dancing we did, a bath is in order."

"Says the man who has already sucked me off."

Darshan paused, his thumbs hooked into his waistband. "You'll have to forgive my eagerness." He hauled down his smalls, letting his length spring free.

Hamish wet his lips and tightened his grip on the box. *Get a hold of yourself,* he chided. This wasn't his first time.

"Are you planning on joining me?" One side of Darshan's mouth hitched upwards. He slipped into the water, much of his body obscured by suds. "Or are we just watching?"

Setting the box aside, he almost vaulted across the room in his eagerness.

He slipped into the water, a sigh slipping out as he leant back against the tub and let the heat soak into his skin. There was a subtle brininess to the steam that he couldn't quite place. Some sort of salts added to the water?

Hamish grabbed a dark clay bottle from amongst the vast selection scattered about the nearby tiles. He'd grown fond of the woodsy smell this mixture gave off.

He washed himself, the decades of being forced to bathe under the watchful eye of his mother's guards making him quick and efficient.

Catching movement on the edge of his vision, he lifted his attention from himself to his bathing companion. Darshan sat at the opposite end of the bath. The man stood up in the water, his erect length on full display as he cleansed himself.

Hamish leant back to watch, sure his husband was making a show of it. There was no way anyone washed themselves so slowly, or with so much soap.

He slid closer as Darshan turned to pluck another bottle from the shelf, dragging the cloth from his husband's grasp. Hamish made an attempt at bathing the man. His hands wandered south a little more than necessary, toying with Darshan's length, revelling in the shuddering gasps and soft moans such touches garnered.

Huffing, Darshan collapsed into the water, straddling Hamish's thighs. The man's bare fingers entangled in Hamish's hair, his mouth slanting over Hamish's as their tongues occupied with each other. They parted only to gulp down a breath before colliding together again.

Time seemed to stretch out into forever. Each kiss was an eternity. Hamish's heart throbbed madly in his chest, answered by the same beat coming from his husband's.

Slowly, Darshan's kisses shifted from mouth to neck, sucking hard enough to mark skin. "When we are done here, I plan to make long and passionate love to you." His words, coarse and slightly muffled by the attention given to Hamish's neck, were still clear enough to make Hamish's breath rasp.

Hamish mumbled something that he hoped had him sounding agreeable.

"However..." Darshan finally surfaced enough for Hamish to see more than his own beard. "If we don't do something now about this—" He gestured to his still-erect member as if Hamish hadn't felt it straining against his abdomen. "—then any further passion is going to be wasted rather quickly."

Wrapping a hand around his husband's length, Hamish started stroking in firm movements.

Darshan's breath hitched and, biting his lip, he rocked in time. But it wasn't long before he began that impatient squirming Hamish knew all too well. This wouldn't be enough. "Where's the box?"

Hamish rolled his eyes, searching for the little wooden container and spying it atop a cabinet on the other side of the room. Right where he must've put it in his haste to join Darshan in the water. "Out of reach. I could just go down on you?"

"Tempting," his husband breathed. Darshan followed his gaze before returning to nuzzling Hamish's neck. "But as much as I love your magical mouth..."

"Magical?" Hamish echoed. He'd never heard Darshan refer to his mouth as that before.

"Quite." Darshan raised his hand.

The box rattled atop the cabinet, leaping up to fly across the room and into his husband's grasp.

Darshan slapped the box against the ledge, scattering bottles as he fumbled one-handed with the latch. "I've a particular desire to be filled and you're momentarily out of commission."

"We could wait until I'm ready." He was already halfway there, it wouldn't take much. Of course, being ridden wasn't his favourite position, but if that's what Darshan craved...

The latch released and Darshan flipped open the box. "I have plans for you once we're in bed, but I wish to have this in me now." He slapped the toy into Hamish's hand.

Hamish gripped the toy's shaft, well aware his face had grown hotter than the steam could account for. "You are definitely nae beating around the bush tonight." He properly examined the toy. It wasn't the same one they'd lost, the shaft of leather lacking the exposed metal disc on the bottom that Darshan used his magic on to make it vibrate.

"Where's the fun in making you guess my desires? It's far more entertaining seeing how flustered you get when I tell you them." Darshan rifled through the bottles, coming away with a small jar of thick lubricant.

Hamish slicked up the toy as Darshan set about preparing himself. Although the man didn't linger on his task, he clearly wasn't quick enough.

By the time Hamish was satisfied enough with the new toy to slip it into Darshan, the man looked halfway to completion.

"Gods," Darshan moaned, his head lolling forward.

"Nae any gods," Hamish purred, noting the ragged intake of Darshan's breath against his skin. "Just me." He had become quite skilled in the toy's usage during the months between Darshan first gifting him with the original and Nulshar. All the little tricks. The angle that his husband preferred, the force, the speed.

He would occasionally wish he had enough magic to further drive the man crazed with pleasure, but Darshan swore it wasn't necessary.

Like now.

His husband sagged against him, wrapping his arms around Hamish's torso, pillowing his head upon a shoulder. His already heavy breathing grew more so with each thrust until a low moan started up. It vibrated their chests. Pressed as close together as they were, it ran along Hamish's whole torso and straight to his groin.

Hamish loved that sound. It was raw, inelegant and wild. All the things his husband wasn't in so many other moments. A shame that he rarely uttered anything close to it unless something, be it Hamish or a toy, was buried deep inside him.

And if Hamish didn't finish this soon, his husband could likely easily sway him to the idea of swapping the toy out for himself.

"Come on, me stag," Hamish purred into his husband's ear. He altered the toy's indulgently deep strokes, matching how he worked the man's length, quickening Darshan's journey to the edge. "It's time you roared for me."

There was the faintest hitch in his husband's breath. His body shuddered.

Darshan threw back his head, announcing his arrival to the ceiling. The sound bounced off the tiles until anyone listening would be mistaken for thinking a herd of deer had taken over the room.

Hamish leant against the edge of the bath, watching his husband come back from his bliss. The way his shaky panting evened out. How the glazed look in his eyes slowly returned to focus on Hamish, the cause of his pleasure. The pure, slightly embarrassed, grin that took a decade off his face.

They'd years for Hamish to etch the sight into his mind. He soaked in every second as though the man might die tomorrow.

Darshan laid his hand upon Hamish's chest. In the haze of pleasure clouding his husband's eyes, a fragile softness shone through that Hamish doubted many others had seen. "*Mea lux*," he purred. "My light in the dark." He walked his fingers up Hamish's chest, pausing to caress his neck before cradling his head. "You are my world."

"Quoting your vows so soon? Is the toy that good?"

His husband gave a wicked chuckle as his free hand slid between them. "I can think of something better." Slim fingers curled around Hamish's erect length.

"Nae tonight." He had obliged Darshan's desires for the man to ride him during what they'd thought had been their first wedding night, but he'd his own cravings and they didn't involve the man on his dick.

Darshan froze, his expression suddenly blank. Then he blinked and, smiling softly, removed his hand. "If that's what you'd prefer. It's not as though we don't have the rest of our lives together to enjoy each other."

Hamish shook his head. "That's nae what I meant, me heart." Chuckling, he pulled Darshan against him. "I still want sex," he said, following his husband's brash honesty in speaking his desires. "I'm just nae in the mood to have you riding me."

Relief gusted out his husband's mouth and rolled his eyes back. "Thank the gods."

Hamish laughed. "I'd have to be dead to nae want you."

Squeezing his eyes shut, Darshan pushed off from him.

Cursing himself under his breath, he grabbed his husband's wrist, keeping him from exiting the bath. "Sorry. I didnae—"

"No. You needn't apologise." He caressed Hamish's forearm as though it might shatter. "But I must remember not to push you until you've fully recovered."

"It's been four days."

"And I'm perfectly fine not doing any more tonight, *mea lux*." He cupped Hamish's head in both hands and kissed him. "Contrary to the stories I'm certain you've heard about me—"

"You mean like how your twin says you're all about size?" Hamish teased.

Darshan shot him a warning look. "—neither your dick nor that mouth is the reason I fell for you. I was far more interested in your gentleness, your compassion. Such a sweet soul subjected to so much pain." He rested his forehead against Hamish's. "I love you, *mea lux*.

This you." He pressed one palm firmly on Hamish's chest. "The one inside. Your sharp mind, your gentle and sweet soul. Your enormous heart. Everything else is a bonus. I wasn't just waxing lyrical when I said you are my world. I don't know what I'd do if I lost you."

He pulled Darshan back into his arms. "I'm nae going anywhere, me heart."

"Well, I do hope you plan on getting out of this bath." With a mischievous smile that danced in his eyes and wrinkled his nose, Darshan slithered out of Hamish's grasp. He lifted himself out onto the now-sodden tiles, suds clinging to his backside.

Hamish followed, slipping slightly in his attempts to right himself. He grabbed a towel, rubbing vigorously at his skin with the soft fabric. No matter how many times he ran the cloth over his skin, he never felt completely dry. Not like back home, where the coarse fabric would scour off a layer along with the water.

He'd barely gotten to his waist when an extra pair of hands appeared to assist him. Whilst the radiating heat evaporated the remaining water dripping from his legs, the hands took particular care to ensure his length was dry.

"Dar..." Hamish turned in the space between his husband's arms.

A softly questioning hum came from Darshan as he delicately laid his chin upon Hamish's chest.

Sweet Goddess. With the angle the man stood at, Hamish's length rubbed against his husband's stomach. Coupled with the way Darshan stared up at him... *Bastard.* The man had to know the effect this was having on him. "Bed?"

Darshan smiled and even that simple, warm expression had Hamish's heart beating faster. "I thought you'd never ask." Stepping back, he laced their fingers together and led the way.

Chapter 56

They made it as far as the door before Hamish could no longer deny the desire stirring through his blood. He tugged Darshan to him, moulding them together.

Darshan made the most gorgeous little squeak as his back met the door frame. His eyes, dark in the flickering shadows, examined Hamish with lidded lust, daring him on.

Hamish eagerly answered the challenge, bending to claim his husband's mouth. Their lips met, the supple glide of them over each other quickly turning insistent with need.

As much as Hamish wished it wasn't true right now, the difference in height was too great for their lengths to meet whilst they stood. Grinding against the dark trail of hair gracing Darshan's stomach carried a whole other realm of pleasure.

Breathless laughter further parted Darshan's lips, the sound greedily consumed by Hamish. His hand slid from where he braced himself against Hamish's chest, slipping between them to ghost across the tip of Hamish's length.

Moaning, Hamish thrust up harder, hoping to encourage his husband to increase the pressure.

The fingers of Darshan's other hand dug into the nape of Hamish's hair, pulling them apart. The lust in the man's eyes had gone feral. "Bed," he commanded, the huskiness in his voice tingling along Hamish's skin.

"Aye," Hamish replied, drawing his husband back to him.

Darshan slithered out of his grip. He crossed the room, not stopping even when Hamish caught up. "You ought to be ashamed of yourself," he mumbled in that same rough tone. "Getting me this worked up so quickly." He gestured to his length, as if Hamish hadn't felt it hardening against his thigh as they kissed.

Grinning, Hamish settled on the edge of the bed, his arms wide in a plea for Darshan to join him.

"Just look at you." With one hand splayed on Hamish's chest, Darshan pushed him flat onto the mattress. "Absolutely shameless." There was a teasing quirk to his lips as his fingers danced across Hamish's skin in little brushes. The touch slid lower, gliding along Hamish's shaft, its trailing absence having his hips lift off the bed.

Hamish wasted no time with such games. He fisted his husband's length in response, pumping hard until Darshan's ragged breath spoke of being in a similar state.

In a jolt of movement, Darshan latched onto the hollow of Hamish's throat, leaving Hamish gasping and unsure which one of them had moaned.

His husband licked and sucked with enough force that Hamish was glad for his beard's length. He'd definitely need to cover the marks the man had just left.

Darshan resurfaced, fervently crushing their lips together and gasping when they finally parted.

Before his husband could take full control of the situation, Hamish shifted his hips, deliberately bringing their erect lengths together. He continued to thrust against his husband, relishing a sensation he had never known before the man showed him.

Darshan's lips parted in silent bliss. Those hazel eyes rolled back, his lids fluttering.

It was enough in the way of encouragement for Hamish to continue. All this playing, the teasing, the revelling of just having each other in their arms... There was so much he'd never been aware of before Darshan. Every other encounter had always gone straight for penetration.

He couldn't have asked the Goddess for a more loving man.

Eventually, Darshan stilled their movement with a single hand to Hamish's hip. "One moment," he breathed, offering a quick peck to the tip of Hamish's nose before crawling further up the bed to retrieve the oil sitting on the shelf tucked behind the headboard.

Hamish wordlessly positioned himself on his back in the middle of the bed. His stomach fluttered in eager anticipation, no less than it had the first time they'd made love. He tried to steady his breath, to slow the frantic beating in his chest lest he went off before they'd the chance to do all they wanted with each other tonight.

The bedding beneath him had just started to warm with his body heat when his gaze drifted to the bower above, the white petals ruddy in the lantern light. A fresh warmth burrowed into his heart. He hadn't asked, hadn't even expected, and his husband willingly absorbed Tirglasian traditions into his own.

With an exclamation of triumph, his husband resurfaced from behind the headboard, brandishing the bottle of oil. He settled between Hamish's already spread legs to pour some of the liquid onto his fingers as well as on Hamish.

The cool oil trickled between Hamish's butt cheeks, drawing an unsteady gasp from his lips. "I see we're nae wasting time."

"You aren't the only one eager for more, *mea lux*," Darshan purred, working the oil into Hamish's skin with aching slowness.

Just when Hamish thought his husband might be waiting until he begged, a finger slipped in.

Hamish tipped his head back, sucking and biting his lip as he ground against Darshan's hand, feeling himself grow more pliable under the man's ministrations. A familiar warmth suffused him, eking a contented murmur from his lips. From their very first time, Darshan seemed to know Hamish's body thoroughly.

There was something oddly intimate about this bit that Hamish couldn't place. Maybe it was the fact he'd never even heard of preparation before Darshan and, as such, hadn't done it with anyone else. Or perhaps it was the meticulous attention the man paid to the act, never moving on to the next step until he was satisfied Hamish was ready.

Although, sometimes, his husband was a little too thorough. How many fingers were in him now? Two? Heat continued to burn through him with every stroke, pooling in his groin.

Biting back an impatient whine, Hamish pressed harder against Darshan's hand, seeking to hasten each inward thrust. He needed more, needed to feel something deeper within him than those fingers could go. *Now.* "Dar," he pleaded, his voice ragged. He caressed one side of his husband's jaw.

Darshan lifted his gaze, immediately locking with Hamish's. He nuzzled Hamish's palm, his shorter beard prickling slightly, before leaving fluttering kisses that tingled along Hamish's skin. "Ready, then?"

"Aye."

Giving a soft grin, he withdrew his hand and finally took off his glasses, placing them on the same ledge he'd taken the oil from.

Hamish took the opportunity to draw his husband close. He cradled the man's head, just staring into those eyes, taking in every detail, the separate rings of green and brown, how wide his pupils had become.

Darshan looked back in puzzlement, his brow furrowing slightly.

"I love you," Hamish whispered.

The change in his husband's face was instant, the smoothing of his brow, the slight skew of his lips and the extra lines gathering at the corners of his eyes. He tipped forward, their foreheads touching. "My beacon," he breathed against Hamish's lips.

Which one of them started the kiss, Hamish didn't know, but they swiftly returned to rubbing and grinding against each other, panting into the other's mouth, grasping at whatever flesh they could to maintain the closeness.

Darshan shifted, slipping beyond the reach of kisses to kneel between Hamish's legs.

With his arms still resting on his husband's shoulders, Hamish felt the man's back shift, twisting slightly as he lined himself up. His heart skipped an excited beat.

Then there was just pressure and fullness. It stole his breath. Pebbled his skin.

Darshan continued his inward press, not stopping until they were joined as much as possible. He held them close, his fingers digging into Hamish's thighs. With the angle of the lanterns, his face had been thrown into the shadows.

Hamish reached out, tilting his husband's head up with a brush of his finger upon that stubbly chin.

Darshan's gaze, half-hooded and hot with lust, blazed up Hamish's body. With a languid roll of his hips, Darshan withdrew a ways, drawing out a mutual groan. Flashes of light briefly haloed the man, magic barely contained. "Gods," Darshan growled. He trembled, his breath shaky. He tipped his head back, fisting his hair. "Do you have any idea of the things I want to do with you?"

Some. And he was probably agreeable to most. "I'm nae going to break if you're a wee bit rough, me heart."

A savage possessiveness gleamed in his husband's eyes. "That so?" Darshan thrust home again in one stroke that saw the both of them inch up the bed.

Gasping, Hamish wrapped his calves behind his husband, holding them together. "Aye," he grunted back, casting the dare.

All semblance of civility fled his husband. Darshan hoisted him higher, shoving a few pillows beneath Hamish's back to keep him in place. His hips started moving in earnest, each thrust quick and hard, leaving Hamish light-headed and breathless, his senses overwhelmed.

Hamish wasn't certain he could do more than lay there. He clutched the bedding, trying to give himself something in the way of leverage and attempt to match the rhythm. He'd enough experience in this to succeed in usual circumstances.

This wasn't one of them. But each of Darshan's thrusts left his legs jellified and his body arching. His movements remained ungainly, hindering his path towards pleasure.

After a while, he gave up and concentrated on bracing himself to keep from hitting the headboard.

His husband's movements grew more forceful as the pleasure continued to swell, thrusting harder and harder. His head sagged, loose hair obscuring much of his face. His mouth hung open, his every laborious rasp further warmed Hamish and filled the silence between Hamish's own pants. Sweat covered his forehead and dripped from his nose, but he maintained the pace.

Hamish had grown accustomed to reaching the end around the same time as his husband. This time, by the erratic way Darshan's hips moved, the man would clearly arrive before Hamish.

Sure enough, Darshan grabbed his hips, holding them tight together as he came undone with a snarl.

The primal sound prickled Hamish's skin and flooded his senses. Unable to move any other way, his body arched, his hips grinding against Darshan's as his husband continued emptying into him. His eyes rolled back. A soft groan coiled its way out his mouth.

Soon, he was following Darshan's lead, spilling his seed into the night with a strangled grunt.

His legs chose that moment to buckle, dumping his full weight onto the pillows that propped his rear up. He lay there, not bothering to attempt moving whilst his heart pounded like a bolting horse. But that small measure of support was stripped from beneath him as Darshan methodically removed each pillow before collapsing onto Hamish.

With his husband nestled securely in his embrace, Hamish closed his eyes, focusing on the beat of his heart and the press of Darshan's stomach against his own with each heaving breath.

"I needed that," Darshan murmured, the words distorted with his cheek pressed to Hamish's chest.

"Aye," Hamish managed. It had been a long time since anyone had taken him so vigorously. "What did you say about going slow?" That'd been Darshan's promise on the way over. Take it easy tonight until they were both certain Hamish could handle it after the poisoning.

Darshan harrumphed, the blast of it pebbling Hamish's right nipple. "Who urged me on?"

With his laughter whispering on a breath, Hamish went to caress his husband's hair.

Something tugged at his wrist, pulling him back. He jerked his arm away. Or tried to. The vine tangled around the limb only tightened its hold.

Uncertainty, tinged with a thread of fear, creaked up Hamish's throat as he realised both his arms were equally bound. None of the other vines had seemed so clingy. "Uh... love? Little help?" He was not about to spend the rest of the night being tied to the bed like some of the men he had read in Darshan's erotic books.

~ ~ ~

Darshan sat up, squinting at the problem before fumbling to don his glasses and get a better look. Even with clearer sight, he wasn't certain he saw correctly. Bemused, he watched his husband struggle with freeing himself of the vines. Not that the vision of his husband bound wrist and ankle to the bed wasn't a dream straight from his darker desires. If he hadn't already sated his body, he definitely would've been tempted to make the best of the current situation.

"Dinnae just *stare.*" Hamish tugged at the vine binding his right arm. The flicker of a shield appeared around the limb for a heartbeat, then was gone. The presence of a barrier didn't seem to have any effect on the plant.

Darshan carefully unwound the tendril from Hamish's wrist, growling, "*Mine.*" He moved on to the other arm, freeing it as he uttered the same admonition.

By the time he reached Hamish's ankles, the vines had already abandoned their hold.

"That outcome was... unexpected." They'd had sex plenty of times closer to the ground—sometimes, directly on the soil—but the plants hadn't ever bound Hamish before.

"Aye," Hamish mumbled. "Maybe you should send it away?"

And be rid of the bower before the next sunrise? That would completely negate the whole purpose of growing the thing in the first place. "There's no need for anything so drastic." Darshan peered at the vines. The sensation tingling off them felt close to being ashamed. *You should be.* They knew their presence was to look pretty for tonight and be transferred to the imperial garden in the morning.

The leaves curled tighter on themselves, the tendrils coiling shut like ferns. Even the flowers closed their conical petals.

"Is that going to happen every time now?" Hamish asked.

"No, I believe we've—" He glanced over and froze at the sight of his husband reclining on his side in the middle of the bed.

Hamish looked ethereal in the lantern light. The leather thong that usually kept the man's hair in place had slipped loose sometime during their lovemaking, leaving the thick coils to tumble over his shoulders and halfway down his torso.

Darshan had seen such friezes gracing temple walls and the vision of it before him set off a flutter deep in his gut. He longed to sink his fingers into the coils, to draw his husband close and claim that mouth.

He crawled across the bedding to do just that, softly at first, then with greater hunger as Hamish responded in kind. His hand slid from his husband's head to his chest, slipping even lower as he luxuriated in the dense hair carpeting the man he so desired.

Chuckling, Hamish rolled onto his stomach, pinning Darshan to the bed. "You're a bloody sneaky bastard," Hamish murmured, his usual soft brogue rough around the edges. "Trying for a second time."

Swallowing thickly, Darshan tried to ignore how the fluttering sensation shifted downward at the heavy press of Hamish's bulk. "If we are keeping score, then I believe this would be the *third*." His husband hadn't yet said a word about the stirring happening in Darshan's groin, but the man had to have noticed the hardening length nestled against the cleft of his buttocks.

Sure enough, Hamish's back stiffened. He reached behind him, grinning. "Damn your appetite. This—" He caressed Darshan's length, rocking slightly to rub it between his butt cheeks. "—is going to be the death of me."

Scoffing, Darshan rolled his eyes. "Hardly." He knew restraint. He didn't exercise it nearly enough, but it wasn't an entirely foreign concept.

"I can just see it now," Hamish continued, most definitely lining himself up to accept Darshan's length again. "The *vris Mhanek's* consort, screwed to death on his wedding night." He pressed back and Darshan slipped inside. With the delicious weight of his husband bearing down on Darshan's hips, there wasn't a single pause of hesitation.

It tore a groan from him. He clung to Hamish's thighs, sensing the minute trembles running through the muscles. His husband's legs continued to quiver even once he had fully taken Darshan.

Unable to move, Darshan waited to see what the man had planned.

Hamish lazily rocked on top of him, his abdomen undulating slightly like a veil dancer and those gorgeous sapphiric eyes becoming half-lidded.

Darshan released his hold on his husband's thighs to run a hand up Hamish's chest. With the smallest amount of focus, he ghosted a thin layer of cool air to his fingertips.

Hamish shivered, his skin pebbling. But he didn't ask Darshan to stop. His eyes, startlingly vivid in the dim light, twinkled encouragement.

He played with the intensity, skimming it up the middle of his husband's torso, then back down in a weaving pattern. Upon reaching the base of Hamish's semi-hard length, he increased the force of his magic.

A coarse and ragged moan tore free from his husband, echoing in the chamber.

All at once, Hamish froze. He clapped a hand over his mouth, mumbling through his fingers, "I didnae mean to—"

"It's all right, *mea lux.*" Slowly, he drew Hamish's hand away from the man's face, running a thumb over the knuckles. For so many years, his husband had been forced to seek pleasure silently or risk causing death, to the point where Darshan rarely heard a sound louder than a hushed groan or soft keen. "There's no one around to hear. Just me. And I would very much like to hear *you* roar for once."

Grinning, Hamish ran a splayed hand down Darshan's torso, sending fresh murmurs of interest to his groin that he was pretty damn sure the man could sense. "You ken, I cannae move as fast as you like this way." His body bounced as he gave a small, derisive snort. "And I'll nae have the endurance even with your healing helping me."

With some effort, Darshan was able to lift himself up to cradle Hamish's head in both hands. "We don't have to go at some breakneck pace." Whilst he favoured hot and heavy, it wasn't needed. "I enjoy going slow just as much." Like this, he was free to drink in the sight of his husband atop him, of the weight pressing him into the mattress, the soft murmurs of pleasure running through his body as the fires of bliss were steadily stoked. "I promise," he purred. "You could never leave me wanting."

Hamish returned to rocking, changing from a purely front and back motion to a circular one. He arched backwards, bracing himself with his hands on the bedding, his fingers clenching each time Darshan reached the right spot.

Keeping a firm grip on his husband's waist, Darshan aided the rhythm. He couldn't move much, but he thrust his hips as much as he was able in time to Hamish's downward rolls all the same, burying him deeper.

Soft curses tumbled from his lips. Through their panting, his ears caught the utter nonsense of multiple languages blurring together.

How? *How* was *this* more intense than the frantic pace he'd set earlier?

No longer capable of restraining the desire to have his husband closer, he stretched out his arms, pleading. "Come to me, *mea lux.*"

Hamish settled atop him, resting on his elbows. Great curtains of fiery orange-red hair draped either side of their heads, further blocking off the outside world. Light peeked through the gaps, barely enough to see by.

Unable to resist, Darshan dug his fingers into the coils, pulling

Hamish's mouth to his. With the full weight no longer pinning him down, he thrust into his husband, greedily swallowing the man's moans.

His husband shifted. His arm dropped, moving furiously as he stroked himself, hastening his completion.

When Hamish finally reached it with a muffled groan, Darshan wasn't far behind. He threw his head back, disengaging in the act of being with his husband in anticipation of reining in his magic.

But there was no hurtling of his senses out into the abyss, leaving him drunk on his own pleasure. This burrowed into his core, grounding him in his surroundings. The heat of Hamish's skin and the whisper of his breath, the answering growl that hissed out Darshan's lips, the buzz of his magic coiling through the air...

All of it was, for a brief moment, one.

Darshan stared up at his husband as the world slowly returned to its separate elements. His beacon. His flame eternal. He caressed Hamish's jaw, luxuriating in the softness of the man's beard. "I am the luckiest man in the world."

Hamish laughed softly, bouncing them and sending ripples of pleasure through Darshan's body. "Oh, aye? And why's that?"

"I got to marry the man of my dreams." So few in the court were fortunate to share their union with someone they loved.

He held perfection in his hands.

His husband's mirth escaped in a gasp. "Me sentimental stag."

Darshan rolled his eyes at the moniker. "You are never going to let that go, are you?"

"*Me?* You're the one who put it on the marriage crest. Besides..." One corner of his mouth lifted. "I like it. You're elegant in so many ways. It's nice to see the other side of you."

"Such insolence," Darshan breathed.

Hamish shook his head, his laughter less restrained. A soft blue glow haloed the man's hair.

Tipping his head, Darshan peered beyond to the bower above. The flowers had changed. He hadn't asked them to, but they'd done it all the same. The conical petals, no longer a chalky white, were a luminescent blue with a centre that glittered like sky sparks. They looked almost familiar.

Hamish twisted, staring over his shoulder at the flowers in a daze. "I didnae realise the glass smith had modelled me gift on an actual flower."

"I don't think these flowers existed before now." The flower *did* almost look like the one Hamish had gifted him. *The everlasting glass bloom.* It sat not too far away and did look awfully like the ones above them. The same shape and colour. Although, the glass version lacked

642

the glow. *Life echoing art.*

Was that what he had done? Spontaneously created something new? Whilst in the midst of an orgasm?

Laughing to himself, Darshan settled deeper into the bedding. He raised a hand towards the vines. One slithered down to let him caress the glowing petals. A familiar perfume drifted up from within. He inhaled deeply, sighing. He knew that scent. It was them, the musk of their lovemaking.

Hamish drew the flower closer, cautiously sniffing before breathing deep. He coarsely exhaled with a shudder.

"Exquisite, aren't they?" Darshan murmured. Amazing how they had become an exact replica of the glass flower sitting not terribly far from them. Even the glittering centres gave of the impression of reflecting light rather than making their own. "I think they'll be a wonderful addition to the imperial garden." They would need studying, too. Who knew what properties they might have beyond their glittery appearance?

Spluttering incoherently, Hamish surfaced from within the depths of the flower. "You cannae plant these out in public, they reek of—"

"—us?"

"Well, aye," Hamish conceded. "But of *us* having *sex.*"

There was that. Although, he doubted anyone beyond them would make the connection. "I've a personal garden outside the eastern wing." It wasn't much, it never had been. Recently, he'd been using it as training with Hedgewitch Gregor. With it hemmed in a high stone fence, access would be limited. The alternative was to leave them bound in pots upon his balcony.

The vines trembled, the hiss of leaves rubbing against each other loud.

"All right," Hamish said, winding his arms around Darshan's shoulders. "I give in. Put them in your wee garden. At least then I'll ken where to find you in this sprawl of a palace."

"I'm not *that* difficult to locate." Still, he conceded to Hamish's embrace, burrowing himself against the man's chest. He tucked his head beneath his husband's chin as they rolled onto their sides, growing increasingly relaxed as Hamish caressed his upper arm. He toyed with the luxurious carpet of red chest hair, enjoying the glide of it beneath his fingers. "I think a nap is in order." With the snap of his fingers, he extinguished the lanterns.

The light of the flowers lent a soft glow to the room, barely outlining his husband.

"Aye." Hamish's grasp pulled Darshan closer. "Sleep sounds grand."

"Then, perhaps, you could show me a little of your Tirglasian marriage customs? I'm most interested in how you intend to exercise your rights towards not allowing your spouse to leave the marital bed until midday." He hadn't heard of such a tradition until the man's brother blurted it out as they were leaving the ballroom.

A blast of his husband's mirth warmed his head. "You insatiable bastard," he muttered, still laughing. "Aye, I'll show you tomorrow." Cupping Darshan's chin, Hamish coaxed his head back to gently slip Darshan's glasses off and stow them safely on the ledge. "But I think we both need more than a wee nap. Any more tonight and I think you might actually break me."

Maybe it was the fatigue leeching into his mind, but he found the idea mildly ridiculous. "You're nowhere near that fragile."

"Finally ready to admit it, then?"

He hummed his agreement, well aware that Hamish had professed his resilience a great many times. "That doesn't mean I've any desire to test your limits." With a little wrangling, Darshan managed to capture his husband's hand and bring it to his lips. "I think we both deserve a gentler life from here on out, *mea lux.*" A lot of people wouldn't agree, but he intended to ensure nothing ever endangered this bliss.

Hamish murmured something that sounded like an affirmation. A low snore hissed out soon after, the sound curving Darshan's lips.

Rest well, my light. Pressing a kiss to the back of Hamish's fingers, he snuggled against the warm bulk. Lying in the dark, his weariness had him drifting on a haze of hot skin, a beating blue glow and the residue of pleasure.

After tomorrow, they'd be off on a month-long stint at the imperial country estate where there'd be no concerns beyond each other's pleasure to worry about. Once they returned, it would be as though Hamish had always been a part of the Crystal Court.

Strange to think that he longed for such normality to begin. *Become domestic.* A self-mocking snort rattled his nostrils. When he thought of all the times he had run from the very idea...

Tipping his head back, he watched his husband sleep. The rise and fall of Hamish's chest, the gentle sawing of each inhalation and the soft sigh that followed. Rhythmic. Soothing and solid.

Darshan lazily ran a hand along the side of Hamish's face, gliding over skin and hair in equal measure, smiling at the twitch of his husband's nose, a barely perceptible movement in the gloom.

He is good for you. His father's voice whispered through his thoughts, bearing a pride so fresh and foreign to Darshan. But true. Life before his impromptu trip to Tirglas had stagnated. He had grown jaded. Indifferent to his own people. It had cost lives.

And in the time since he'd known Hamish?

Marriage changes a man. The old echo of his grandfather returned to bounce around his drowsy mind.

He had thought it a warning. Once. Never had it occurred to him that *he* would be the one to change so drastically. That he would welcome it. This life had been worth the wait, worth every struggle. He might've wished for less strife, but they'd overcome so much. Whatever else fate threw at them, they'd face it the same way.

Together.

Epilogue

Hamish sat upon his mare, watching the builders across the street as they tore down yet another derelict Pit building. No matter how many times he saw the process, he could never get over the ease. What would've taken a dozen Tirglasians months to dismantle was done in days with half the manpower.

Most of the builders were spellsters. They levitated huge sections of wall to the ground from several stories up to be further dismantled by those less magical. The once towering building was already down to its last levels. It would be completely demolished by sunset. The rubble would take longer to deal with, especially when he was insistent on using as much of the old materials as they could, but the area would be clear to rebuild on and getting these dangerous buildings replaced with stable housing was his priority.

Satisfied progress was running smoothly, he turned his mare from the site and directed her down the street with a gentle click of his tongue. People worked along the road, too. They filled potholes and laid down new cobblestone.

On the edge of his vision, he spied the Nulled Ones who shadowed him collectively regroup, a couple darting ahead to scout out any dangers. Not that there were many found on the edges of the city. Not when it came to him. Most of the Pit's inhabitants knew who he was and what he was doing.

And there was a lot still left to be done. He'd thrown himself into this project upon their return from a month-long retreat out in the country. It had taken a fortnight to sort out all the deeds, then another seven months to get things to this point. So much demanded his attention.

Even after counting all the deeds, Hamish hadn't realised how big the Pits were until he had taken a walk through it. *Bigger than*

Mullhind. Maybe even bigger than two of his old home city. How many people had become lost in these shadows?

He wasn't sure if he could fix it all, but he was definitely improving lives that would've otherwise perished. That had to count for something.

He frowned at the sight of a bunch of children scuttling up and down a cart filled with materials used to fix a chunk missing from the road. A lot of them were quite young, even younger than those Hamish had seen working on the sheep farms in Tirglas.

A word was clearly needed with the people he had put in charge. They already grumbled over his command that none of these projects were to be done with slave labour. That didn't mean children were a viable substitute. And ones this young should've been out playing or learning, not doing the job of adults.

The sight disappeared around the corner as his mare plodded on. It was time he checked on the progress of the school. It shouldn't be much longer before the building was complete.

Finding teachers to fill the classes had been a struggle. The idea of knowledge being free to those with little was something that had confused even Darshan in the beginning. If they were to eradicate slavery in their lifetime, they had to give people a way up that didn't involve selling themselves or others.

His passage took him past the communal bathhouse and nearby latrine. He wrinkled his nose, trying to ignore the stench of the latter. The Pits didn't have access to the same drainage system as the rest of the city. He was steadily changing that, but people still needed somewhere to go in the meantime and those places needed to be excavated every so often.

The people currently dealing with it had been plucked from the nearby jail. All petty thieves or conmen with a few dealers, working to pay back the community they'd wronged. It wasn't the Udynean way—most of them had been scheduled for sale to the mines—but this was the system Hamish preferred.

A breeze wove its way between the buildings, greasy with the hint of cooking, but infinitely better than the alternative. He crossed the bridge, one of many that bore ramshackle houses on its sides.

The school building sat in the middle of an island like a frog on a rock. Builders crawled on it like ants, some securing roofing to finished sections whilst others worked to erect walls on the rest.

A group of children squatted just beyond the construction. A few chased each other amongst their peers, playing the same games he'd witnessed in every village. The majority listened to an elven woman gesturing to the building as she explained the process.

Such groups had been trouble not that long ago, the gangs making use of little fingers by turning them into thieves or distractions. There were still pockets of disorder, but they were weakening. Around here, desperate people were responsible for crime. Without those shackles, they were free to explore, to expand. Some chose not to, but there wasn't much he could do about that except hope they'd change.

"Prince Hamish!" cried out someone from behind, the sound urgent but not frantic.

He twisted in the saddle, easily spying the young man hurtling towards him on horseback. Swinging his mare around, Hamish waited until the man had slid to a halt before him. He eyed the man's outfit. *A royal messenger.* Who had sent him? The *Mhanek?* Darshan? "Catch your breath first, lad."

Nodding, the man took several deep breaths. "The *vlos Mhanek*," he said, still slightly winded. "She's in labour."

"*Really?*" He knew babies sometimes came early, but there were still two more weeks before the full nine months.

The man bobbed his head. "Yes, your highness. The treasured one requested your presence."

Treasured one. Daama's official title. That meant Darshan was still in his meeting with the senate and the northern viscounts.

He urged his mare forward, galloping along the roads with the messenger on his heels. With the winding roads and crowds, it would take hours to reach the imperial palace. There were the boats, but that would mean leaving his mare behind with the messenger until the Nulled Ones caught up. The message had already taken just as long to reach him, and that wasn't including the time spent trying to find him.

Growling under his breath, he steered Lass towards the nearest dock. He would have to chance it if he wanted to be there when his child was born. How small a risk could it be anyway? The Nulled Ones couldn't match their speed, but they had ways of tracking his route that reminded him of the old Tirglasian tales of soul thieves.

At the docks, Hamish vaulted off his mare and threw the messenger his reins. "Dinnae lose her, you hear?"

The man snapped a salute. "I'll protect her with my life, your highness."

"See that you do!" he bellowed over his shoulder whilst running for the nearest row of boats. This far from the palace grounds, none bore the imperial symbol and most were already laden with cargo.

Still, if there was any lesson he had learnt well from Darshan, it was the art of using his title to convince unsure people to do as he wished. Adding a generous donation, procured from the messenger's coin pouch, didn't hurt.

In little time, he was speeding under bridges and through channels, the salty air combing through his hair and stinging his eyes. They wove around slower boats, the woman powering the plume of water propelling them somehow managing to turn her craft with barely a shift of her hand. Maybe it was the elven ancestry. He wasn't a perfect judge, but her ears had enough of a point for it to be a possibility.

They passed beneath yet another massive bridge to the sight of the palace walls. "That way!" he commanded before realising that she might not hear him over the roar of the wind. He pointed in the direction of a platform at the base of the bridge connecting the palace island to the temple quarter. Without some sign of ownership to the imperial household, they'd never reach the palace's private docks.

The boat kissed the platform with the faintest tap.

Thanking the woman, he leapt ashore and raced up the incline towards the palace gates. They stood open, the customary guards at attention on either side. The group saluted his passing.

He halted a few steps into the palace grounds, his legs close to dumping him where he stood. "*Horse,*" he managed to order between his lungs persistent demand for air. Even though he could see the entrance to the imperial palace—shut as always—he'd fall flat of his face if he tried running the distance.

After a little scurrying, a guard presented Hamish with one of the sleek messenger horses. Usually, he wouldn't subject such fine-boned creatures to his bulk, no matter how strong the stable master claimed them to be.

This time, he'd no such compunctions.

Clambering into the saddle, he urged the horse into a dead run. The beast took off, heeding his command with barely a flick of an ear.

He stared at the council hall as they galloped by. Darshan would've been in there when the message came. Was he already at Anjali's side? He had to be. Or would the senate be so cruel as to demand their meeting came first?

The imperial gates opened as he neared. Word of his arrival must've reached those on duty. The path to the palace steps was likewise clear, enabling him to race all the way to the entrance. Abandoning the horse before anyone could grab the reins, he headed inside.

He scaled the stairways, barely pausing to steady his breath before racing for the next flight. Why they wanted Anjali birthing the children in the royal nursery was beyond him. The infirmary made more sense, and lacked all these internal stairs to reach, but the midwives kept insisting. Tradition seemed the only logical answer. He hated how much it bound people here.

Their baby wasn't going to wind up in the royal nursery. Darshan had been of the same mind in keeping their child close and a new room now led off the *vris Mhanek's* suite, the disused storage area renovated whilst they were away.

Hamish was almost on his hands and knees by the time he reached the right floor. He staggered down the corridor, listening for the screams of a woman in labour, or even the wail of a baby. The silence that greeted him didn't give him much hope. There was a chance—there was *always* a chance—that the baby hadn't made it.

He halted outside the door, not sure if he had the strength to face that truth on his own.

Maybe it wasn't time after all. His sister had mistaken other pangs for labour several times, twice with his youngest nephew before giving birth to the boy. That would explain the silence.

Goddess, please. Let all be well. He slid open the door, peeking around the wooden panel.

His sister-by-marriage lay in the bed, calm and quiet. The midwives bustled around the room. Not a single one of them seemed concerned about her. He searched for a hint of Daama's presence. The old nanny would definitely want to be here. Was she in the adjacent room? That was where the babies traditionally slept.

Anjali smiled at him as he fully entered the room. It was the same euphoric smile his sister had given with every new baby. Her belly definitely didn't look as rotund as it had been yesterday. "Didn't expect you to arrive first."

"Dar's nae here?" His husband should've definitely reached the imperial palace before Hamish. He knew there had been orders to not disturb those in the meeting, but he thought news of a future ruler being born would've been an acceptable reason.

Had the messenger gotten it wrong? Or had he been sent with old news?

"Your highness!" one of the midwives blurted, announcing his presence to everyone else. "How unexpected. Please, sit." She gestured to a nearby chair. "Your sons were very eager to enter the world."

"I missed it, then?" He had raced all this way, risked losing his mare, only to be late. "Hold a minute," he said before the woman could answer. "*Sons?*" He hadn't misheard, had he? "Plural?" Even though the Niholian breeders insisted magic wouldn't disrupt the growing process past six months, no one had dared to check the gender let alone how many there might be.

"Yes." Smiling, the woman nodded. "Two very healthy boys."

He swung to Anjali as if the midwife could've miscounted. "I—"

"Go." His sister-by-marriage gestured towards the doorway. "Greet your sons before my father catches word. You'll never get another chance to see them in peace."

The *Mhanek* was currently tied up in the same meeting that delayed Darshan, but he had grown more erratic in the past few months. His interest in Anjali's pregnancy bordered on obsession. Even the midwives didn't pry into the woman's health as much as her father did. Who knew how he would react once he learnt his grandsons were born?

Smiling his farewells to Anjali, he slipped into the other room.

The space didn't hold much. The warm light was quite dim and shone via a single lantern bearing a globe. There were a few chairs— one big enough to be for nursing—along with a little table. And the cradle sitting right in the middle.

Daama stood over it like a ewe with newborn lambs. He almost expected her to stomp a foot in warning at his approach. Instead, she smiled in that motherly fashion he'd only seen her direct towards Anjali and Darshan. "Come on, then. Bit late to hang back now."

He halted at the foot of the cradle. Inside, two small bundles lay. Both perfectly swaddled. *Me sons.* He'd have to get used to that. He sniffed back a tear. All the years he'd thought it impossible and here it was. Here they were.

He gently peeled back the blankets of one, then the other. It was difficult to tell in the dim light, but their skin seemed to have the same faint coppery shade that lingered somewhere between his husband's lighter, olive-brown and his own darker tone. "There's nae a blemish on them," he whispered.

Daama silently smiled up at him.

"Do you think they're spellsters?" He didn't know how they checked, only that there was a test. Would they be as strong as Darshan? Had they inherited other traits as the man had feared? How were they going to test for *that*?

"I'm certain at least one will be. It's very rare for two Nulled Ones to be born to a couple, never mind as twins. But worry about it later." She gave him a few firm pats on his arm. "I'll be back."

Consumed in just watching his sons, he barely acknowledged the woman's final words let alone her leaving.

He re-swaddled each baby before lifting one out of the cradle. They were so small. Smaller than his sibling's newborns. Did that mean they wouldn't grow as tall? "You lads are going to need to get big and strong, you hear? Cannae have your da and cousin being the only giants around here."

Of course, there was no reply beyond those pale brown eyes peering up at him. He knew enough about newborns to not get his hopes up that they wouldn't inherit his eye colour. Every single one of his nephews had the same steely grey at birth and they now sported green or brown.

"I don't care what my father said," Darshan's voice echoed from down the hall. "I specifically requested that I be informed the *minute* my twin went into labour." The door opened, admitting him and the servant he was berating. "I demanded that—" He froze, staring at the bundle in Hamish's arms. " 'Mish?"

"Would've thought you'd beat me here," Hamish said, trying to sound jovial despite the lump forming in his throat and the tears in his eyes. Even though he cradled one of their children, it was seeing the overwhelming awe on Darshan's face that suddenly had everything feeling real.

His husband took a hesitant step closer, as if fearful this was an illusion fit to burst with any sudden movement. "Is that...?"

Hamish nodded. "One of them."

Darshan mouthed the words back at him. "*Twins?*"

"Aye. And both boys."

His eyes widened. Darshan clapped his hands over his mouth, his shoulders trembling. A noise that sounded suspiciously like a sob escaped him.

"Dar?" Dread bubbled in his gut. He knew there was a deep-seated belief when it came to multiple births that those born after the first were without souls—that very belief was how they were able to claim their children had no mother. But it usually meant ill for those children.

The shaking of his husband shoulders increased, the tearful squeaking melting into laughter. "*Two boys?*" He raced to Hamish's side, throwing his arms around them. "My father couldn't even produce more than myself, no matter how many times he tried. And we get *two* at once." He grinned down at their other son. "Just look at them." Darshan lifted the baby out of the cradle. "*Perfect.*" The ghost of a frown twitched his husband's brows and his head tilted slightly to eye Hamish. "How did *you* get here so fast? I thought you were overseeing your projects in the Pits?"

"Boat."

Humour further creased his face. "It has only taken you—How long? A year?—to fully grasp their usage?"

Hamish scoffed. "I'm nae riding Lass everywhere because I dinnae ken how the boats work, I take her because I want to."

This revelation seemed to do nothing towards diminishing Darshan's mirth. He rocked the baby slightly. "You know, Jheel is getting married soon. She could bless them."

"Jheel?" Hamish echoed. He hadn't heard anything about the young woman since her courting with the glass merchant's son had become official.

Darshan shrugged. "Father gave his blessing. They'll be wed by the end of the month. Did you not know?"

Hamish shook his head. He hadn't heard a thing about any weddings. "Guess I'm spending a little too much time in the Pits." That would have to stop, especially now their sons were in the world. He would still need to check on things, but maybe not on a daily basis.

"Here we are!" Daama said as she walked into the room. She bore a pair of clay nursing cups. "I finally managed to sterilise them to my liking, but I insist we do this no more than once." She shot Hamish a meaningful look. "Only the gods know how your people manage to stay alive long enough to build an immunity to anything whilst pumping gods knows what into your babies."

"What's this?" Darshan peered into the top of the cup, dipping his little finger into the liquid and tasting. "Milk? Have wet nurses gone out of fashion?"

"Every Tirglasian bairn's first meal is of the land," Hamish explained. For most that was cow's milk. For a few in the plains, it was mare's milk. When it came to Hamish's family, it had been sheep. "Although, I used to help Nora when she was busy by feeding me nephews this way."

Hamish settled into the massive nursing chair, the wicker creaking alarmingly under the padding. He gently tipped the cup's spout to the baby's mouth, letting a few small droplets trickle out at a time.

After a while of watching him, his husband perched himself on the end of the other chair and mimicked the act with their other son. "I must confess, I haven't even begun to think of names."

Nor had Hamish. He hadn't dared for fear that it wouldn't be. "There's time." They'd a whole month before the naming ceremony to try out several and decide which was a better fit.

With the baby he held having drunk their fill, Hamish set the rest aside. He leant back into the chair with the child draped on his chest.

Rather than immediately fall asleep as his nephews had done, those big eyes continued to stare up at him.

"Hello, wee lad," he whispered in Tirglasian.

"What are you doing?" Darshan hovered over the cradle, their other son already within.

"It's called—" He squinted at the far wall, trying to think of an easy way to phrase it. "Well, bonding is the closest thing. Newborns cannae see far, you ken? Only from the breast to the face." That was what his sister told him when he'd asked why his nephews always stared so intensely at anything within range.

"Farther than I can without my glasses, then?" his husband chuckled. "But why are you still holding him?"

"To let him ken me face and me voice. Me heartbeat." He had lost track of how many times his father had comforted him in his youth, but he still recalled the steady beat that always calmed him. He held out his free arm. "Come here. Bring his brother, too."

Darshan obeyed, snuggling against Hamish's side. The wicker squeaked and squawked at the extra weight. "Are you sure the chair will hold all of us?"

"Hush," he whispered. "Just be still, me heart."

With their heads pillowed on Darshan or Hamish's chest, the babies stared up at them.

"Gods," Darshan breathed once they'd fallen asleep. "It's like falling into an abyss." Not taking his eyes from either of the babies, he snuggled closer. "I can't believe we made these."

Hamish stroked the down gracing their heads. It was too soon to determine what colour their hair would be. Hopefully not his brashly orange-red shade. "Nor can I." He hummed an old tune that had the boys' eyes suddenly agog at first as it shook their bodies. Then, their little lids slowly slid shut until they were asleep again.

Still feeling watching, Hamish fell silent.

Darshan stared up at him, those gorgeous every-colour eyes wide. "What was that? You've never sung anything like *that* before."

Heat took his face. He didn't sing at all. Not much. Definitely not in company, be it in Tirglas or here. "It's just a wee lullaby me dad used to sing." He didn't recall most of the words, but the tune? That was etched into his bones.

"It was beautiful. In a vaguely haunting fashion." His gaze dropped back to their sons. "Definitely did the job."

"Always does." He reckoned it might even still work on his nephew, despite Ethan nearing his twelfth year.

His husband laid his head back on Hamish's shoulder. "I'm glad it's twins. I'm not sure we'll have another chance."

"I hope we do." They both came from big families. He definitely had room in his heart for more. "Dinnae you want your own horde?" That was how Darshan had always spoken about children in the past.

Darshan gave a considering hum. "Maybe try for a daughter?" He grinned. "I suppose that means risking siring a firebrand like your niece?"

Chuckling, Hamish wrapped an arm around his husband's shoulder. "Aye." His fierce little niece was a handful all on her own. "We breed our lasses stubborn."

Darshan wrinkled his nose in mock disgust. "I've noticed. Although..." He grinned down at their sons, laying his head on

Hamish's shoulder. "If these boys are anything like your nephews or my sisters, they're going to be a handful to deal with."

"We'll cope." They weren't alone. Darshan had literally dozens of assistance at his beck and call.

"We'd need Anje's blessing and..." He clicked his tongue with a wet, drawn-out pop. "She would've understood if they were girls—as ridiculous as you see it, altering inheritance from being solely through the male lineage to anyone is less important than other matters—but I can't ask her to carry more for us purely because I want them."

"You *could*. She could refuse, but asking isnae a problem." It didn't even have to be straight away.

Darshan remained silent for a while.

At first, Hamish thought his husband had joined the twins in slumber, then the man gave another thoughtful murmur.

"I'll think on it, *mea lux*. Closely. Two is more than enough, for now." He wriggled deeper into the chair, positioning himself at an angle that would keep the baby he cradled from slipping. "I don't suppose you'd hum that lullaby again? I've had a trying day with the senate and I do believe our sons have the right idea."

Chuckling under his breath, Hamish drew his husband closer, tucking both babies against his chest in the process. "For you, me heart? Anything." He returned to humming the lullaby, stopping only to press a kiss upon his dozing husband's forehead.

Eventually, the outside world would encroach on this little bit of peace, but right now, reclining here with his newborn family nestled against him, there was no more a magnificent place. This feeling, the peace of completeness, had to be what it felt like to rest at the Goddess' bosom.

For the first time since Darshan brought him back from the brink of death, Hamish didn't feel as though he was living on someone else's borrowed moments. He was right where he was meant to be.

"Thank you," he whispered to the heavens. "For sending him to me." Darshan had led the way to his freedom, had given him a life he'd never dared to dream, had shown him he was worthy of all the things he had longed for.

They had lit their own path, just as Darshan had promised. And now they'd two sons to look after? They'd only more light to show the way.

Now, it was his turn to lead them down the path he knew better. Their sons would grow never knowing the abuse of Hamish's mother or the bigotry of Darshan's grandfather. They would grow to be better, to understand one certainty above all others.

That, no matter what came to pass, they were loved.

THE END

ABOUT THE AUTHOR

Aldrea Alien is an award-winning, bisexual New Zealand author of speculative fiction romance of varying heat levels.

She grew up on a small farm out the back blocks of a place known as Wainuiomata alongside a menagerie of animals, who are all convinced they're just as human as the next person (especially the cats). She spent a great deal of her childhood riding horses, whilst the rest of her time was consumed with reading every fantasy book she could get her hands on and concocting ideas about a little planet known as Thardrandia. This would prove to be the start of The Rogue King Saga as, come her twelfth year, she discovered there was a book inside her.

Aldrea now lives in Upper Hutt, on yet another small farm with a less hectic, but still egotistical, group of animals (cats will be cats), and published the first of The Rogue King Saga in 2014. One thing she hasn't yet found is an off switch to give her an ounce of peace from the characters plaguing her mind, a list that grows bigger every year with all of them clamouring for her to tell their story first. It's a lot of people for one head.

aldreaalien.com